REST for the WICKED

REST for the WICKED

A History Novel

Naida West

BRIDGE HOUSE
BOOKS

Rancho Murieta, California

Pierce-Arrow hood ornament courtesy The Buffalo Transportation/Pierce Arrow Museum, www.pierce-arrow.com

LCCN: 2009943811
ISBN 978-0-9653487-0-6

Interior design by Pete Masterson, Æonix Publishing Group, www.aeonix.com
Cover by Megan K. Welsh, Spring Creative, www.springcreative.biz

Published by Bridge House Books
P.O. Box 809
Rancho Murieta, California 95683
www.bridgehousebooks.com

Printed in the United States of America

Fact, Fiction and Acknowledgments

This novel includes many real people, names unchanged. It is also representative of people who arrived in California in the 1890s, or were already here. They all witnessed the end of the Gold Rush, the end of the Old West, and the first deep depression of the modern period, which took the shine off the California dream.

The major characters are fictional, and obviously, the more they interact with real people, the more the real people become fictionalized. So this is a spectrum from documented or remembered fact at one end to representational fiction and pure fantasy at the other. See endnotes for a list of the real and the fictional, and what's true and what's not.

I am grateful to many people for sharing the stories of their families: first Ellen Cothrin Rosa, who has been an invaluable source throughout this long process. She also shared photos, genealogies and maps (including the one two pages up), and drove me to good hiding places for Billy. She and her cousins Jessie Grimshaw Saner and Anita Granlees Macklin provided more than facts. They shared the wisdom and humor that only intelligent, long-lived people can as they look back. Other local people who opened windows to the past are: Dwight Dutschke, Hilda Granlees, "Johnny" Granlees, Clair Arditto, Jake Schneider, Gordon Van Vleck, Avis Cothrin Navarette, Frankie Engel, Karen De Jong, Lou Blodgett, Margaret Rose, George Signorotti, "Aunt Mig" Waegell, and Blanche Spencer Lawson. Every one of you helped, and sadly some of you have left us. I am aware of handling precious goods, and beg your apology and indulgence if I have tarnished them in any way.

Thanks to all the people who shared research, including: Dixie Lester, Ken McKeon (for erasing any possible link between McKeon and McCoon), and Harold Ethington for going that extra mile. Also to Ruth Younger, Pete Masterson, Jacqueline Hansen, Elizabeth Pinkerton, Elsworth Rose, Everett and Jackie Fox, William Scheiber, Wilma Menke Welden, Dennis McCown, Rhonda Morningstar Pope, Charles Wollenberg, and Mike Eaton of the Cosumnes River Preserve, for providing Karen Bennett's "The River that Got Away"; and the helpful staffs of the Sacramento Archives and Museum Collection, Sacramento City Library's history collection, the History Room of the California State Library, and the Oakland Museum.

Special thanks to the Musers for perceptive comments throughout.

Rancho Murieta, California
October, 2009

Dedicated to Bill Geyer for his ten years of support, listening, historical conversation, deferred jaunts, and comments on the seemingly endless drafts.

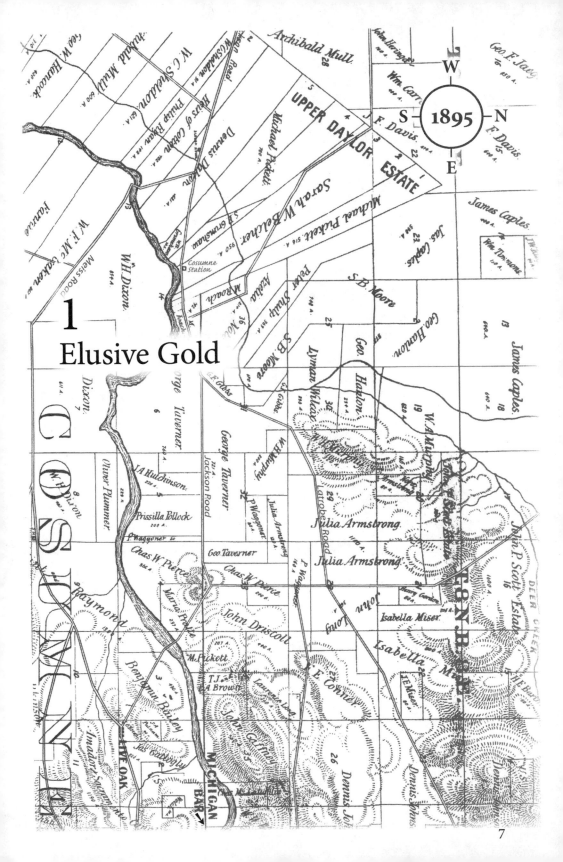

1
Elusive Gold

1

HOWCHIA SPEAKS

A rosy-breasted bluebird stretches her wing on one of my branches as the first light of day cracks the darkness. In the tall cottonwood across the river, vultures still sleep like old men with hunched shoulders. Not long ago this oak in which my spirit dwells stood taller and I could see much farther. My big arms shaded the home place where my people and I once lived.

As Eagle Woman I pounded acorns, cared for my son, and sang to locate illness for our doctor, always believing that my people's way of life would continue forever, as I assumed it had in the past. When I died I should have walked the pathway of ghosts to the happy land, but I looked back and my spirit entered this oak.

About twenty dry seasons have passed since men in yellow hats cut off my heaviest branch and sawed my trunk most of the way through. With a sound like the crack of lightning I split apart. My upper portion toppled and peeled a wide swath of bark down to the earth. Men came in their motor-trucks to haul most of me away. Only my weak lower branch remained. But I am still here, nourished by this fertile mound made from the ashes of my people and the leavings of our lives—robes of feather and hide, rabbit-skin blankets, broken bows and baskets fashioned from dream spirit. Earth took it all back into herself.

A frenzy of shoots sprouted from the joint of my branch. They raced each other up to where my upper trunk had been, and now four or five of them have bark and limbs of their own. The one in the middle is the tallest, and from a distance I look like a tree again. But I am not well.

Rain rotted much of my severed trunk, and floods washed earth from my crown roots. Fungus grows at my base. Where my bark is missing the beetles and borers tunnel freely, so I am dying even as part of me strives to be young again.

An arrow of sunlight shoots through the oak forest, suddenly brightening the boards of a weathered old cabin abandoned a human lifetime ago. The old man who once lived there trained wild horses to the saddle, before horses became pets. High above me two silver needles silently pull threads of white cloud while, inside the massive houses built on my people's hunting grounds, the newest people step into golf or tennis clothes, or put coffee cups in the holders of their motorcars for the drive to Sacramento.

Over the river's rustle I hear a strained whisper: "Howchia, can you hear me?"

It is Rock Man. In my long time on earth he has rarely spoken. "I hear you."
"I am weary of boredom," he says.

The rock muffles his voice and makes him sound more distant than he is. Since the time of the Ancients his spirit has dwelled in an upright boulder on the far side of the chaw'se, mortar rocks for pounding acorns. The first time he spoke to me I was a girl, feeling his black skin made smooth by the river. Now he is wrapped in a prickly blanket of berry canes. When he was human he hunted gigantic hairy animals with frightful tusks, and he protected his family from wolves with bigger jaws and teeth than the ones I saw in my lifetime, wolves that could crush the bones of the giant buffalo now gone from the world.

"I liked it better underwater," he groans. "The fish told me of their travels."

Long ago Rock Man explained to me that the river ran much wider back then, as the earth warmed and the icy fastness of the mountains melted in torrents.

"Is it day or night?"

"Morning," I tell him. "The robins have arrived from the north, and the men from the big houses are driving to their offices. Some of them want to move boulders and clear the earth. They dream of deep crevasses in which to put steel pipes twice my height when I was human, and of mammoth grading machines that break tree trunks like sticks and turn the earth upside-down. They want those giant wheels to pack the clay so the new roads and pads for houses cannot shift and crack."

He-lé-jah pushes through the bushes, fixing me with his golden eyes.

"Where are you going?" I greet him in the way of the People.

"Doing my morning rounds," he replies. "May I rest on your limb?"

"You are always welcome." Sunlight has made that limb stronger.

Haunches rippling as he measures the distance, the big cat levels his gaze and then springs, flying upward to a perfect landing. I enjoy the feel of his weight settling along my branch, tail ticking, big paws kneading.

"I was thinking about the changes around here," I say to him, and Rock Man.

Coyote soft-trots up to my mound, already ruffling my leaves. "You mean the speed with which your people died out?"

"We are stronger than ever, Old Man. Just a little camouflaged."

"My people are back too," says He-lé-jah.

"It was a way of life that died," I clarify. "First my people and then the white farmers and ranchers. But End Time will come for all."

"Any basket will break when the load is too heavy," Coyote agrees.

He has that teasing slant in his amber eyes. "Tell us how your people fared in the time of farms and first railroads."

We see Billy again, my granddaughter's son.

❧❀

It was the season of longer days and second grass. You could almost see it growing on the hills, in the river bottom, along the road, everywhere. It left the short grass of winter limp and yellow in its shade.

Billy McCoon stood up and rubbed his sore behind. He'd sat too long on a block of sandstone swishing grass roots in his coffeepot, always keeping an eye on the cows. After cleaning the roots, he'd push them back in the mud. Grass must not be wasted. So much life depended upon it. The winter rains had made the river overflow this small pasture, and now the new grass sprouted ever closer to the receding shoreline. He had learned that the roots sometimes gripped balls of earth containing bits of gold that had been stirred up and carried downstream in the floods. Later he would pan out the mud and add any new gold to his stash. He kept it in an eggshell-half inside the tiny gift basket his mother had made for him when she said he'd become a man. But now he needed a rest.

Inhaling the fresh energy of the earth, he ached to dig in his toes and run as fast as he could just for the joy of feeling his muscles work. But he could not leave the cows. He needed this employment and was proud to be earning a dollar a week caring for Mr. Swain's six-cow dairy. Instead, he trotted over to the big oak and swung himself up to the low branch.

He walked in his balanced way along the limb and sat down against the trunk, which was about the width of his room in the back of the barn. The leaf buds above him admitted the power-giving sun, and he looked over the area where the umne, the People, had gathered acorns and hunted from the time of the Ancients. Before the gold frenzy, the related peoples had lived on both sides of the Cosumnes River. Now he watched it curve toward him from the northeast and flow away toward the vast wetland where four rivers came apart and re-braided themselves as they meandered into the San Francisco Bay.

He wished he could talk to somebody. But that was a daydream. Since the last of the Cosumne people had left, the only person who ever came here was Mr. Swain, driving up on Saturdays to check on things. He'd been here just two days ago, stayed long enough to give Billy his money and say, "How you doin? Good! See ya next week."

From the time he was eight years old, when not working with the Cosumne men, Billy had found solace in this oak, at first waiting for his stepfather to return. He still missed Pedro. But when the two old widowers Antonio and Efren let him sleep in their hut and treated him like a son, he gradually came to think of them as family. They knew a little Spanish and a little English, but at home they spoke the tongue of the People. They told him the exciting story of how the remnant of the once-large Cosumne tribe had come to live here, in the place called Old Sheep Corral. From them, Billy honed the skills that Pedro had taught him, for they had all worked in Mission San Jose and for many years at Sutter's Fort. But after the headman and others died of disease, the remaining members of that tribe, once again shunning a place where many had died, tied their belongings and their babies on their backs and walked over forty miles to Auburn—all but the young brothers who worked on the Jaimeson place.

Billy had stayed on at Sheep Corral to help Mr. Swain tear down the old huts and sweathouse and build the big dairy barn over the top. He needed to be near the home place of his own umne. He and his mother and sister were the last of the Sacayakumne, earlier called the Lopotsumne.

Billy had also made friends with the white sons of the neighboring ranchers. He worked in the fields with them, and then romped and fished with them when the work was done. That lively bunch of boys lived for fun and didn't seem to care that he was a half-breed.

He missed them, and the times when he used to wait outside the schoolhouse when his work was finished. The bell would ring and Wallace and Johnny would burst out the door, grinning when they saw him, and the three would race each other to their houses to fetch fishing poles. Billy taught them fishing secrets. Sometimes they went with Roland, Ted, Gumper, and others. They had the most fun on long summer days, when they'd climb the ropey grapevines to thrilling heights in the oaks and cottonwoods. There they'd swing from tree to tree. Billy would often be the first to drop twenty or thirty feet down into the river—howling with fear and glee. He loved the wind in his hair and his stomach in his throat. At the mossy bottom he'd push up and explode through the surface. His friends would be cheering in the trees.

Sometimes girls swung on the vines too, and those who dared would drop to the river with petticoats flying. Most of them were gone by now, married or boarding at ranches where they worked as hired girls. A few had gone to Sacramento to board with relatives or family friends, and like the boys, the girls went to the high school that changed them all.

Wallace, a year younger than Billy, had begun to change even before he left for Sacramento. He worked last summer in the wheat harvest, not beside Billy but with the high-school boys, and when Billy tried to edge in they said there wasn't room for him. All summer his friends went to barn dances and community picnics. At first Billy went too, expecting to meet the girls from Sacramento. An exchange was going on. The city boys and girls in whose homes the country relatives had boarded most of the year came in the summer to stay in the homes of their country relations. So the tribe of young people expanded. But all they talked about was life in the city—ball games, horse races, and bands in the park on Sunday afternoons. They had nothing to say to Billy, though some of the girls looked at him from the corners of their eyes. He could tell that the boys didn't want him around those girls. He was different.

But that didn't matter, he told himself. Having all the responsibility for Mr. Swain's cows left no time for picnics and dances. He was a man now, saving money to build a better house for his mother. Indian men twice his age rode freight cars from distant places to work in the fields around Slough House for less than he earned. They took their money back home to wives and children.

The rushing river didn't cover the fluting meadowlarks and piping red-wings in the cattails, or the cheeping of yellow finches as they swooped from branch to branch. Each to its own kind. Those birds were getting ready to do the same thing that boys constantly talked about doing. But Billy was of another feather. People knew he had lived at Sheep Corral with full-blooded Indians. And they knew that he'd had calf eyes for Iris Flower even as a very young boy. She had been much older than Billy and didn't know how it hurt him when she returned sick and sorry that the white boy who promised to marry her left her for a white girl. Her baby was born dead, and she died soon after during the sickness that drove the Cosumne to Auburn. Now she lay in the ground at the side of Mr. Swain's barn. *If only that hadn't happened—*

But it did happen, Old Efren used to tell Billy in those last days before he and his people left. From that wise old man Billy learned the hard lesson of not looking back when trouble struck, but to ask himself, What can I do now?

To his surprise, the ears of the two cows drinking at the iron trough were down below the rim. Dairy cows were always thirsty, but the sun wasn't high yet and he'd filled the trough this morning. He leaped from the tree and ran to look. Almost empty! He primed the pump, and soon water came gushing out the pipe from the cool depths of the river. The cows sucked around it. He kept the trough full so they wouldn't wade into the bog on their way to the river for a drink, so this was puzzling.

As he pushed the steel tongue up and down, he noticed a trickle of water running down the slope. He looked on the uphill side of the trough. Sure enough, a small arc of water spurted from the welded seam. Billy pulled off a willow twig about the right diameter and poked the small end into the hole. The wood would swell and stop the leak for a while. He'd keep it plugged until Saturday, and Mr. Swain would fix it with solder.

No sooner had he resumed pumping than the bellow of a cow startled him. Though the willows he glimpsed the tan hide of a thrashing cow. Stuck in the bog!

He ran up the hill, threw the door open in the back of the barn, passed through his room and into the main barn where the tools hung on pegs. He grabbed two coils of rope, the hammer, the short length of pipe that he used as a cinch, and the long pipe.

Back down the slope he found Half-Ear screaming in the way of cows. The whites of her eyes showed mortal fear. If he didn't get her out fast she'd drown in the mud. Usually they stayed out of the bog when the trough was full, though once in a while they wandered into it for no good reason. This time, however, it was his fault.

His mind flew through the steps of making a windlass, as always going back to the early memory of his stepfather Pedro Valdez pulling cows out of the mud. By the time he was eleven, with Pedro long gone, Billy was praised by Antonio and Efren for being able to do it by himself, though his arms were weak turning the cinch. Now that he had a man's arms, that part was easier.

He selected a spot near the cow and between two sturdy willow trees. Feet planted uphill from where he wanted the long pipe, he jammed it down into various places until it sank in the mud at an angle inclining toward the slope. He felt it scrape past rocks into solid ground. Stepping back to get more height on it, he hammered the flattened pipe-end until it was less than shoulder high.

Then he threw rope around the base of the willows on either side of the pipe, making slipknots, pulling them tight, securing the rope to the bottom of the pipe. The extensive roots of willow trees anchored them against the worst floods and hence had the strength to stop a windlass from being pulled out by a thousand pounds of cow.

Now to lasso her. He walked the other rope down to the frantic animal— Half-Ear, named for the ear accidentally torn off where the Swain earmark had been notched. This cow had never been helped out of the mud by Billy, so he must show his calm. By now she had sunk another hand. Ignoring her bellows, he watched how she tossed her head. He needed to understand that. Then he made his loop and whirled it slowly, talking low and steady.

"It's me, girl, your friend. I'll get you out."

The lasso fell where he wanted it, and he pulled it tight under the bony ridge at the base of the horns. Then he took the other end up to his windlass pole. Placing the pipe cinch against the pole, he wound the rope around both pipes as Pedro had done, and pulled it taut between cow and pipe.

Now as he turned the cinch, walking round and round the pole, each turn inched the cow up a bit more from the mud. He felt the limpness of her legs as she bellowed and tossed her head. This always took time, but as Billy steadily turned his winch, the cow rose ever higher and toward him.

The most dangerous part was releasing the terrified animal. The horns of these cows were short compared to the Spanish cows, but short horns could be dangerous too. He didn't want her to feel too much ground under her or she could trample him before he got the rope off. And even if he didn't get hurt, the loose rope would snag in the rocks and bushes. He had no horse to help, so he had to do it right.

The moment came when he felt the muddy cow rise a little on her own power. He slackened the rope and strode quickly to Half-Ear, speaking in his soft way for cows. She was tiring, not tossing her head so much. She'd just made a mighty push and was saving her energy for the next. He guessed that one hoof was on solid ground.

"Good girl," he said, stroking her neck with his free hand like when he was about to milk her.

The rope was tight; he had to work his fingers under it, against her bony head.

She yanked back. He'd been quick, jerked his hand away before his fingers got pinched off. This could take several tries. The good thing was, he'd judged the moment right. She was not sinking. On the fourth try he flung the loosened rope up over her horns and yanked it away as the cow lowered her head to resume her violent struggle.

Billy stood ready to lasso her again if she started to sink. But she lurched forward a good amount, and he knew she was all right. By the time she bolted free of the bog, he was back at the windlass untying the ropes.

"My heavens! That sure were somethin' special, the way you did that," said a female voice some distance behind him.

Billy looked up the slope and saw Lizzyanne, a white girl. He hadn't seen her for a year. She hadn't gone to school either. Neither had her brothers. Like Billy, those boys had labored on local ranches for many years. People said their father drank like an Indian, meaning he drank until he was almost dead. Billy felt shy before Lizzyanne, recalling that she'd swung on the grapevines once or twice. Gumper, in the know about such things, had said she'd done it to show her bloomers.

Now, pink and ripe, she came swinging down the hill with a shoe leather flapping. The sight of her in that threadbare dress with her big breasts swaying from side to side tightened his chest so he could hardly breathe, much less talk. With unintended force he muscled the pipe around in circles to loosen its hold on the earth.

"Vernon says it takes guts to do that," she said. "You're brave, Billy McCoon."

His ears and cheeks burned as he gathered the parts of his windlass.

Lizzyanne stood before him with her hands behind her, still swaying a little. Her fine brown hair covered half of her freckled moon face. "I'll hep you carry them things back to the barn." She sang the last word up and down.

Wordless, tingling up through his core, he handed a coiled rope to her.

2

Billy existed in a thrall of longing. All he could think about was Lizzyanne. She came to visit for a half hour on Mondays after getting Miss Pollock's clothes on the line, and she came again on Thursdays when she had the dough in the bread pans and Miss Pollock went to Walsh Station to visit her sister. But she had to hurry away to tend the stove and get the loaves in the oven before the dough became too light.

When she was there with him, Billy felt a wildfire burning inside him.

As the days grew warmer and the grass browned on the hills, each of Lizzyanne's visits took him one step closer to what the boys talked about but which Billy had never done. She taught him how to kiss with his tongue moving. She taught him to touch her where she liked, but so far she hadn't let him do what every beetle, bird and coyote was doing. Never had he counted the days of the week so carefully.

Today was Monday, and he thought it would finally happen. He forgot the cows. She was in his room removing his shirt and standing against him with nothing between them but the thin fabric of her worn-out dress, her nipples grazing the quivering muscles of his chest. It embarrassed him that he quaked everywhere from his knees to his teeth. Surely experienced men didn't do that.

She put an arm around his neck and reached up with her other hand, running her fingers through his hair. "You got a thick Indian mane," she said, pressing into him. He couldn't believe how good it felt. He was about to explode.

"Open your eyes, Billy. I wanna see thet green color, like moss under water."

He opened his eyes in time to see her look down and shove him away.

Her upper lip curled. "Eeeyuck! What's that?" With her fingertip she touched the wet spot on his trousers.

That did it. He turned away nearly yelling in frustration, but instead put a shaky hand on the pile of blankets on the bed and said, "Let's lie down and rest."

"I ain't gittin' no baby like my sister did, with no husband. Ever'body treats her like crap. Pa beats her. He'd kill you for sure, you bein' Injun."

"Marry me then." He'd never given that a thought before.

"You're stupid, Billy. I just said, Pa'd kill you."

He was trying to reassemble his mind and needed a good fast run so he could think. "I gotta go to... to, ah, down to the store." That's it. He kept a couple of nickels in the bandana around his calf. He'd buy her some candy and maybe she'd be nice again.

Lizzyanne's brown eyes seemed to soften. "How long you be gone?"

He opened the door. "I run fast. A few minutes." Then maybe he'd be able to kiss her good-bye without shaking.

When he returned with the candy, she was gone, and so was the tiny gift basket from Ma. Immediately he noticed its absent zigzag pattern against wood of his crate cupboard, and yet even that special basket was nothing compared to the fear that he'd lost Lizzyanne.

For two days he moved around like a chicken with its head cut off, forgetting how to make hotcake batter or how to bank the hot coals of his fire. He couldn't sleep at night, and he would have forgotten to milk the cows if they hadn't mooed at him. In the morning starlight when Mr. Driscoll came, Billy loaded the first milk can on the wagon bound for Sacramento, but stood there forgetting the other can until the man laughed at him and said, "You're still asleep, Billy."

He had lost his power. By Thursday his head hurt from wanting her. He wouldn't know until the sun was straight overhead whether she would come to him again, this being her day. The sun crept so slowly upward in its arc that he wondered if he'd gone into a spirit world where it would stand still for-ever and cows would never move from where they were. But then he noticed sunlight on the outer rim of a cow pie that had been entirely in the shade, and he sighed with weak hope, turning again and again to look up the hill.

There she was! At the door to his room.

He tried not to run, not to squeeze her too tight as he put his shaky arms around her, afraid she was a figment of his imagination.

But she hugged him back like nothing had happened! Her lips moved against his neck. "I 'sposed you had plenty 'a baskets being Injun an' all, and wouldn't miss that itty-bitty one. It's a dear thing fer buttons and such as that."

He'd all but forgotten the basket. "What did you do with the gold?"

She pulled back and nearly shouted, "Gold?"

"In the eggshell."

Her expression changed from confusion to dismay, and then to a child about to weep. "I threw it in Miss Pollock's trash pile. 'Sposed it were jes' a dirty ole eggshell. Oh thunderation!"

"Don't worry about that, I can always find more. It buys a few things, is all. My mother gave the basket to me and I am giving it to you."

He kissed her on the mouth the way she liked, but she squirmed away and begged him to show her how to find gold. He explained that grass sometimes grabbed particles of gold before it sank down in the mud, and that he used a coffeepot to wash the roots.

She left in a hurry, calling over her shoulder. "I'll bring the basket on Monday."

∽

On Monday she forgot the basket. She did bring one of Miss Pollock's bowls so they could "wash roots together." Billy wasn't even faintly interested in teaching her how to wash gold. He did it to make her happy. He hoped she'd grow weary of that tedious chore. But she did not.

∽

As usual, Mr. Swain came on Saturday to pay Billy his dollar and give him some garden truck, this time carrots and chard. "I'm going to stay and work on the house 'til about dark," he said. "Thought you'd like to take some time off while I'm here. Go visit your people or something."

"I sure would like that, Mr. Swain. And thanks for the pay." He handed back the pie tin from last Saturday. "Tell Mrs. Swain thet there apple pie were the best I ever ate." He wasn't one to exaggerate. He'd savored every crumb of it and shared some with Lizzyanne.

"I'll tell the missus." Mr. Swain looked toward the river. "Even this place is dryin' up after all that wind. And now comes the heat."

"Yup," Billy agreed. New grass was sprouting on ground that had recently been two feet under water. Even the bog was firm and greening. "Don't worry," he said, "I'll keep the cows outa that clay in the river." They ignored the trough now and followed the grass to the river's edge, wading out to drink.

There was a dangerous vein of adobe in the middle of the stream. "I laid out some willow switches down along the shore to drive the cows out with, if they get in that adobe."

"You're a good hand, Billy McCoon. You earn your pay."

That was high praise. Pleased, but awkward and wordless, Billy looked down and changed the subject. "How long 'fore I gotta be back?"

"Oh, get back by the evening milking. I'm gonna rent the house out, so there's a lot to fix up, and a lot to take out. I might just spend the night here."

Who would rent the house? Billy didn't ask for fear of being nosey. But he knew things would change and that worried him. He went to his room in the barn and took a handful of money from under the loose floorboard and tied it in a fold of his calf bandana to buy food for supper. It occurred to him that he shouldn't mention that hiding place to Lizzyanne, though that thought in no way dampened his longing for her.

Billy ran past wagons laden with heavy equipment for the mines and men from China with baskets dangling from shoulder-poles. Free as a bird, he flew past the Roache and Waggoner places. It was about three miles to his mother's house. He turned up the trail to the little cabin. It had washed off its rocks in the big flood a couple years back, but with the help of Mr. Swain, Wallace, and Mr. Driscoll, they had retrieved the cabin from the grasp of the big oak and levered it onto new piles of rock. Still it tipped some.

He opened the door and breathed the familiar smells of dried herbs in the rafters and his mother, life. The two small windows gave little light, and when his eyes adjusted and skimmed over the three cots along the walls and the table and chairs in the middle of the room, he assumed that Ma and Isabella were at the river.

He went down to the river. On both sides of the trail, the sage scent of wormwood brought to mind his mother's stomachache medicine. A big branch of a cottonwood lay across the path—fallen from the same old tree he'd sat in so many times. Ma and Isabella wouldn't be able to move such a heavy limb, so he wrested it out of the way and left it alongside the path.

The bushes and small trees at the river's edge were draped with shirts, dresses, sheets and towels, and trousers—some steaming in the afternoon sun. Empty washtubs with long grass knotted through their handles stood near the different batches of clothing with matching numbers of grass knots in buttonholes. Ma's way of remembering which things belonged in which tubs.

Isabella wasn't there.

Ma was on her knees scrubbing cloth on a flat stone. She then scooted onto the rock with her legs in the water from the knees down, dipping the soapy cloth in the moving stream in front of her. He realized he wasn't ready to speak to her about Lizzyanne, but that was all right because he'd been gone several months and she wouldn't acknowledge his presence, much less talk to him, until the time-of-pretending was over. So he watched her wring out clothes and whack them on the boulder brought downstream in the big flood.

He considered the time-of-pretending to be a silly tradition, and he walked around so she'd know he was there. Finally he said, "Ma, I've come for the day."

Her back and arms stiffened briefly, but she continued working.

Once, a long time ago, he'd brought Wallace home to get a remedy for Wallace's grandmother's arthritis, and Ma at first acted like Billy wasn't there. Wallace tried to get Billy to explain why Indians did that, but Billy didn't know why; and then Wallace told the rest of the boys and they all snickered about it. Superstition, they called it, a word always applied to Indians.

Isabella didn't observe that tradition either, and would talk to him. "Where's Isabella?" he said to his mother's back.

After a while, like she was taking a rest from her work, Ma slowly turned her head in the direction of the downstream path.

Billy smiled sadly as he walked down the trail, having made his mother acknowledge him. Rounding a corner, he saw his little sister with her back to him. She wore a faded dress, probably a cast-off from a white woman, and was collecting early blackberries, putting them into one of Ma's baskets. The sun glinted reddish highlights in her shoulder-length hair. When he'd last seen her, he'd told her how his own father, Perry McCoon, had died riding a bucking horse in competition with her father, Pedro Valdez. Isabella had been hungry to hear about her father. Ma never spoke of her dead for fear of the ghosts, so Isabella knew nothing about Pedro. She'd been a baby when he left.

"Howdy, sister," he said in English, as usual.

She whirled around. "Big brother! You here?"

He smiled. "I'll get the high ones." He reached over her head, picked the darkest berries and placed them carefully in the basket.

Bees droned all around, visiting the many flowers still on the canes. That, and the mossy smell of the river took Billy into more of his childhood memories.

"You 'member my father?" Isabella asked, obviously thinking about their last conversation too.

He saw no reason why he shouldn't tell her about her father. "Yup. Pedro Valdez. He was good to me, and I wanted to be just like him."

She stared into the tangle of thorny canes. Then, resuming her picking, she spoke in a small breaking voice that sounded like pride. "Now I have a last name. Isabella Valdez."

Another thing the People weren't supposed to do was speak their own names.

"Mrs. Pratt said my father was Joaquin Murieta," Isabella said. "Was that bad bandit my father?"

Billy chuckled. "Hell no. People say that doan know their ass from a rock."

She let that settle, then asked, "Was my father nice to Ma?"

"Ho!" That emphatic Indian word felt more right than the English yes.

People had different stories about Pedro, and because he'd ridden with the famous bandit, they repeated that cockeyed story about his head being brandied in the big pickle-jar instead of the real Joaquin Murieta's, but Billy couldn't believe that. However, he did think it was likely true, as some people said, that the rangers had paid people to say the head was Joaquin Murieta's, to get the rich rewards. The hand of Three-Fingered Jack had also been preserved in brandy and displayed alongside the head. Billy supposed that up until now all Isabella knew about her father was what Ma had said one day when she was little, that she had hair like her father, with a reddish tint and some wave.

Billy had no idea what happened to Pedro, but he felt certain that so fine a man would not rob the unarmed Chinese miners and then kill them, as Joaquin Murieta was supposed to have done.

"Mebbe my father's alive," Isabella said, "and you could find him and bring him back to live in our house."

"No, he's dead," Billy assured her.

"How do you know?"

"He loved our Ma. He'd be livin' here if he 'as alive." As far as Billy knew, his mother never had a man after Pedro. Pedro had loved her, and now that Billy loved Lizzyanne, he thought he understood all there was to know about love.

Isabella moved to a new place and found more blackberries without red on them. "I'm glad he loved her," she said when he followed. She turned to him with her head tilted so that her hair fell away from her face. "Does a ghost stay where its person died? Or does it fly to that person's home place?"

"That's just superstition. Don't be skeered'a ghosts, 'an they won't come after you."

"Tell me everything about my father."

Billy knew very little about his stepfather's activities when he was gone from home, which had been frequent. He'd also become suddenly uneasy, like it was disrespectful to talk about the man he'd so admired. The little basket was full now, and in the back of his mind he was beginning to shape what he'd say to Ma about Lizzyanne.

"Naw," he said, "I doan know much about him. Let's go back." He started walking.

"You really are Indian," Isabella said from behind with a tease in her voice.

Ma was stretching a towel over a low bush upstream.

Billy stopped and called, "Ma, you ready to talk?"

She made no acknowledgement. It would take a while longer.

Back in the cabin, Isabella sat on the edge of her bed, picked up a high-top shoe and began blacking it with a coal. She liked to wear shoes. Ma never did. She said shoes made you blind when you walked, they blocked the power of the earth. With that one superstition Billy agreed. Besides, shoes hurt. He'd once borrowed a pair from Wallace but couldn't bear the pain. He gave them back, wondering how white boys could run in those foot traps.

"Big brother," Isabella said, "people call me Indian Mary, same as Ma."

Sitting in his old chair at the table, he raised a shoulder. "People call us what they like."

"They gave me a last name too, but not the right one."

"Not Valdez?"

"No." Isabella picked up a rag and began polishing the shoe. "I was cleanin' for Mrs. Long when a man in a suit come in and wanted everybody's name an' where their folks was from. Mrs. Long told him all the names of the people in the house and the men in the barn. He dipped his quill in the ink and wrote those names in a book. Byembye he points to me." Isabella gruffed her voice to sound like a man. "'What about that girl? What's her name?'

"Mrs. Long says, 'Oh, that's Mary, daughter of Mary Lambut. Indian mother. Spanish father. About twelve years old.' He asked if I'as a housekeeper. Mrs. Long said yes and he wrote that in the book."

Ma came through the open door, allowing a glimmer of recognition to cross her soft brown face. Billy politely ignored her.

"That same man talked to Mr. Swain," he told his sister. "Pro'bly wrote me down as Billy Swain. So are you Mary Lambut now?"

"No. Mary Lambut Long. Mrs. Long told me so."

Ma gave Billy a shy smile, which meant she fully acknowledged his presence and he could talk with her.

What he wanted to say would be awkward with Isabella in the house, so he pulled the leg of his trousers up, untied the bandana from his calf, and handed his sister the bundle of quarters. "I'm stayin' for supper," he said. "Go buy what you need from the store." It made him feel good to provide for his family. In a few years he'd have enough money to buy the lumber, nails, and roofing for a second room on the house.

After Isabella left, Billy sat at the table and spoke to Ma in the language of the People. He told her all about Lizzyanne. Ma listened well.

"She makes me weak with love," he said. "I forget what I'm doing. She won't couple with me. I want to marry her. What should I do?"

"Does she want to marry you?"

"No. She said I'm Indian and her father would kill me."

Ma looked out the small window. "You need to dance," she said. "You need to go to a big time."

"But Lizzyanne wouldn't be there. How would that help?"

"Son, dancing gives power. And maybe you would meet an Indian girl."

"Indian girls love white men," he said, tempted to remind her that she'd married two of them when she was young, if Pedro counted as white, but he restrained himself. "And white women don't like Indian men."

"Lizzyanne likes you."

"Not to marry. Not to put a baby in her blood."

"You need to dance. It's time you found your spirit."

Maybe Ma was right. Lizzyanne had driven him crazy. "Where will the next big time be held?"

"Up near Clear Lake. A place called Tu-le-yo-me."

"Never heard of it."

"Three day's travel north."

"I can't go. I have to stay with the cows."

Ma lowered her head and spoke almost in trance talk. "In old times other peoples came to our big times. We went to their big times. Young people had fun and loved each other. No trouble. If a man wanted to marry a girl, he gave a gift to her parents. No trouble. Now we have no hy-apo to plan. No men know how to build a roundhouse. No land to build it on. No dance doctor."

Suddenly alarmed, she looked up at him. "Son, don't let that man kill you. Stay away from that girl."

But Billy knew that was impossible as long as she came to him.

3

Running back to the Swain place, Billy made up his mind to attend any big time within running distance. He would meet other young women and maybe dance away his jumpiness. Just being around other people might dislodge Lizzyanne from his mind. He shouldn't scoff at Indian ways just because white boys did. They didn't know everything.

Come to think of it, the evening gatherings at the wheat and hops harvests were like Indian big times. Most of the men worked from farm to farm and camped on the open ground. Summer nights were warm. There'd be campfires with singing and storytelling. Wives and daughters and girlfriends camped with their men. People of all skin colors danced and, yes, went into the bushes together. He could ask Lizzyanne to meet him there. He'd need permission from Mr. Swain to leave the cows locked in the barn at night, and maybe that wouldn't be good, but the problem disappeared behind the vision of dallying with Lizzyanne when she wasn't in a hurry. When she had the whole night.

Ahead, he saw the big barn set back from the road and the house perpendicular to the road, the two buildings defining the turnaround area. Mr. Swain's wagon stood in front of the barn where he'd parked it, in the exact place where Mr. Driscoll stopped each morning by starlight with his wagon half filled with butter casks and milk cans. Billy would load his cans and casks with red S's on them—the only thing he could read, the hiss on the Swain name. He liked to stand a minute or two watching Mr. Driscoll turn the team around and drive west toward Sacramento with the swaying lanterns lighting the rutted road. Then he would pick out three warm eggs and take his breakfast makings out to the fire pit.

Now it was dusk. A lantern glowed somewhere in the empty house. Billy went to the stoop and spoke loudly through the open door. "Sir, can I help you?"

"Billy? Good. As a matter of fact, you can." Mr. Swain's voice grew louder as his silhouette appeared. "Come in. You can help with the kitchen counter. The cows are waiting to be milked, but this won't take long."

Billy followed him through the vacant front room and around a corner.

The lantern in the kitchen stood on an iron range—the kind Billy intended to buy Ma someday. Mr. Swain went to a long, thick redwood plank on the floor and bent to lift one end.

Billy picked up the other end and held the plank on its thick edge as he maneuvered himself to its center so he could hold it up while Mr. Swain nailed on the sturdy legs. He was fast and sure with the hammer and soon had three nailed on. Billy helped him turn the board over and held it while the man nailed on the other three legs. When they got the counter right side up on its six legs and pushed it against the wall, Mr. Swain sounded happy. "There now. They can put cupboards under there." He pointed beneath the counter.

They. A dreamy part of Billy had wondered if Mr. Swain would let *his* family live in the old house some day, but he knew that was unrealistic.

"Just one more thing." Mr. Swain picked up a roll of thick tin.

Seeing it was heavy, Billy helped. They unrolled the tin on the counter, which had obviously been measured for a perfect fit, including the overlap at the front and side edges. The tin kept trying to roll up again, so Billy held it down and kept it straight while Mr. Swain pounded small nails along the front edge, dimpling the tin in regular intervals. He made a triangular fold at the corner, hammered it hard and nailed it on both sides of the leg. The smooth hard surface, Billy realized, would be perfect for butchering venison, pounding and tenderizing tough meat, chopping greens or whacking the heads off fish—many uses. And there'd be no wood splinters in the food. As Mr. Swain hammered, a thought that had been niggling in the back of Billy's mind came to the fore. He might be asked to leave.

Mr. Swain worked fast—three raps with the hammer per nail, one to get through the tin, one to drive into the wood, and one for good measure.

Billy knew the question could be seen as rude and prying, but he couldn't help but ask. "Who's gonna live here?"

The answer came muffled through the two nails in Mr. Swain's lips. "Renters. Man, wife, younguns." Rap rap rap. He measured a thumb's length, removed the next nail from his mouth and continued talking with the last nail jerking around. "Been meaning to have us a talk." He took out the last nail, set it in place, and looked at Billy, not hammering.

"These people might want to keep you on here, but then again they might not. They'll be responsible for the dairy. It happened fast. Sorry about that. But I meant what I said before. You're a good hand. If they don't want you, I'll take you down at my Elder Creek place. There's room for you in the barn. I got a man there now, but I could use you to train horses and help with the calving. Fifty cents a week plus supper. What do you say?" Pounding the last nail in, he grabbed another handful from his pocket.

Billy was accustomed to disappointment and sudden changes, but now he felt too confused to answer.

"Think it over," Mr. Swain said. "I'll see the man tonight and we'll talk again tomorrow. Go do the milking now. The tin's behaving. I'll do the rest. Thanks for the help."

Billy went out as Mr. Swain loaded his lips with nails. The hammering resumed when he entered the barn, redolent with the scent of earth, cow-dung, grain, and chickens. He also smelled the nests of rats, the thieves that raided his flour sack at night and left droppings for him to pick out of his hotcake batter every morning.

The cows shifted and lowed. He lit the lantern and tied the four cows to be milked to the feeder bin. The calves of the two non-milkers lay on the straw beside their mothers, unaware that they would soon be sold for meat. Then there'd be six to milk—until Mr. Swain took Half-Ear and Margie back to his new place to be mounted by a bull.

At the rain barrel outside he washed the teat-rag, and then returned to put the stool under the first cow. He stroked her, wiped her udder, placed the pail under her, all the while thinking: What will I do if the renter doesn't want me? Should I go to Elder Creek?

After some dry pulls—udders had to be primed too—the milk began to sing in the bucket. He didn't want to leave his home place, an area much larger than what Ma called home, because he'd worked from the time he was seven years old on ranches from Michigan Bar to Slough House, and all those places were part of his personal place—all the men he'd worked for or helped with troublesome horses and the many places where he'd fished and played as a child. And now Lizzyanne. He needed to be near her. Ma and Isabella too. He liked knowing that he could be at Ma's place in a few minutes if she needed help. Also, as the last man of the umne, he felt he should stay near the burial place of the People. Isabella was right. He really was Indian. So, moving the stool to the third cow, he knew that he must hope the renter would keep him here, and pay him. He didn't want to work for food any more, like most Indian boys did. He was a man, and he had plans for the money.

By the time he set the stool beneath the fourth cow, he knew that he would gladly accept fifty cents a week to work at this dairy, half what he earned now. The renter would be in the house while he went to the wheat harvest big times, and that would allow him to be with Lizzyanne at night, if she agreed. So the problem of the new renter could be a solution to his other problem.

Soon he was on his straw mattress, and he could almost feel Lizzyanne in his arms. They would lie beneath an overhanging elderberry tree, quiet and private, with the soft sand beneath them and the river murmuring in baby voices. The coyotes would be howling as they were doing now, and he satisfied himself that the consummation of their love would feel just as breathtaking as his urgent imagining.

❧

In the morning Mr. Swain came by when Billy was turning his hotcakes on the saggy old washtub. He was dressed in a suit, having gone to church in Live Oak.

"Billy," he said, "I'm sorry to say, the renter doesn't want you to continue here, even for food. You have to be gone by tomorrow morning."

Tomorrow was Monday! He wouldn't see Lizzyanne.

"His wife's a hard worker," Mr. Swain was adding. "Between the two of 'em they can handle everything. They've got a horse and wagon." He looked kindly at Billy from the shade of his wide hat. "You wanna come work on my new place?"

"No thanks. I'll find work around here."

4

The bright rim of the orange moon crested through the trees as Billy treaded the cool water and let the river massage his tired legs and feet. The moon would be full tonight. That such a massive object could sneak up on the world and float upward—silent and powerful, hovering, an obvious danger to the earth—but never do injury was a profound mystery. Mother Moon, the People called her. She raised her giant head and shoulders above the shadow trees in the June twilight—a presence as big and strong as Billy's hopes. Lizzyanne had said she would meet him at the campfire.

It had been a long day of sweating with the wheat-harvest crew, driving and caring for the Percherons that pulled the thresher combine, sixteen horses at a time. He substituted fresh horses from the corral when needed. Billy no longer itched with the chaff that had swirled around him since dawn. He'd come upstream, away from the other workers, to swim naked against the cleansing river. With every passing minute Mother Moon awed him more, just as she must have amazed the People and the Ancients.

On shore again, he whisked most of the water away and pulled on his clean trousers and shirt, which smelled of the sunshine and the willows upon which they'd been drying since morning. He had been a pieceworker since he'd lost his employment on the Swain place, and he was the only local man working on the Dixon harvest this year, although several of the crew he'd seen at past harvests. About twenty in all, they were every shade of tan, brown and black. At least two Indians: Tom Virgin and a man from Colorado called Chief, who had a face like a corroded hatchet. A Mexican who spoke little English, two Portagees with their wives and children, and a tall, lanky black man who had come from the South as a slave but now was free.

Fortunately, girlfriends, wives and children were camping on Dixon's land too. Lizzyanne wouldn't feel out of place. Earlier, after Mr. Dixon announced the end of the day, Billy had gone into the shed attached to the horse corral and cut his hair with the shears. Now, he could tell by the touch that his wet hair looked better. He'd been born with the heavy straight hair of a pure-blood Indian. Cutting it short made that less obvious.

He took the willow switch he'd sharpened for cooking, and with the butt end of it dug up the three, gutted brown perch wrapped in his bandana. Sniffing them, he knew they'd stayed cool in the deep sand. Everything was going well. He picked a bunch of miner's lettuce that grew in a shady nook in the riverbank, tucked it into the two shirt pockets, and then walked across the stubble toward the fire. From a distance the people all looked black with the fire in their midst and the wine-red sunset in the west. More had arrived— children and some local boys not on the crew, looking for some fun.

As he drew closer, Billy's heart quickened to see Lizzyanne. She was laughing with the others as a Portagee told a story in his funny accent. She hadn't left a space for Billy. An Indian from New Mexico who'd come on the freight train with Tom Virgin took a gulp of wine from a big bottle and passed it on.

"This hyar's General Sherman's land," the black man said. "William Tecumseh Sherman. He done laid the Carolinas flat, an' this very night he be leadin' three armies cross Georgia. Won't be long now 'fore the war's over 'n done with."

A white man said, "I been around here fer five years and ain't never heared of thet Sherman fella."

Billy didn't care about the war talk that excited so many people. He just wanted to sit beside Lizzyanne.

"Sherman owns it, all right," another man stated. "Dixon's got a lease."

"General Sherman," the black man corrected. "Whole lot of people is seein' a new Moses in dat man. He's endin' slavery. Sure as anythin' the North'll win now."

Billy found a spot at the fire as close to Lizzyanne as he could get, two men and a child away from her. He caught her eye in the firelight and said to her mind-to-mind, *Come sit by me.*

As the talk continued about how General Sherman got title to this land on which they'd all been working, the bottle passed to Lizzyanne. She took a long drink and passed it on. She looked happy, hugging her knees through her worn dress. The men between Billy and her took swallows from the bottle and it passed to him. He passed it on to the woman, all the time looking steadily at Lizzyanne.

He kept his eyes on her because he couldn't do anything else. Her laughter reached inside him. Never had he wanted anything this much. He ached to feel her against him, if only her arm.

At last she rose to her feet and came to him, waiting for the little boy to scoot over and make room. The bottom rim of the moon broke free of the trees, and the night turned on like Billy's heart. She was his! Everyone could see that. He would live the dream that had haunted him day and night. He took her hand, which she'd left idle between them, and as their palms met, lightning sizzled through every part of him.

Her eyes glistened in the firelight, and her face was a kiss. He rubbed the back of her hand with a thumb, hardly aware of the people munching cobs of roasted corn. A guitar rippled a series of strums, and the player started to sing. Everyone joined in the singing as they roasted meat on willow switches.

Once I had a home, boys, and a good one you all know,
Though I have not seen it since long long years ago.
I'm going back to Dixie once more to see 'em all;
Yes, I'm going going home, boys, when the work's all done this fall.

"I brought us some fish," he said into Lizzyanne's sweet ear, "and some greens to eat while the fish cooks."

She looked interested, so he pulled the juicy round salad leaves from his shirt pocket and put it in her willing mouth.

"Mmm, thet's good," she purred.

He unwrapped the fish and skewered them on his willow switch, pushing the butt end in the ground near the fire. Then he picked up Lizzyanne's hand again and closed his eyes to savor the magic of it, as silent and powerful as the upward floating moon. He and Lizzyanne existed in their own world, apart from the others who talked and laughed beyond the range of his heart. He fed her more miner's lettuce. The tip of her tongue made a circle around her lips. He wanted to kiss those lips. He wanted her all over.

The skin of the perch crinkled and steamed over the fire.

The wine bottle returned. "Those two are busy," said the mother of the boy as she crawled behind Billy to give it to the next man. He hardly noticed for looking into Lizzyanne's eyes.

The skin of the fish split open. "I don't like it cooked too much," he said, surprised by his low and gravelly voice. He moved the switch back from the fire and whispered into her pretty ear, "Lettin' it cool some."

When he picked off a tender flake of fish and put it to Lizzyanne's mouth, her lips reached for it. She put a flake of fish to his mouth, and he pulled it in with his tongue. They both smiled. They picked off pieces of fish, and this slow eating was a painful joy as he sat on the volcano within him, all the time seeing and feeling her willingness.

"I have a place over there," he whispered into her ear, inclining his head toward the love nest he'd prepared so carefully. "We could finish our supper there with no people lookin'."

The moon, now rising fast, would light their way like a lantern.

Lizzyanne took another gulp of wine, which had just arrived. Billy passed it on. "Let's go," she whispered.

Yes! With galloping heart Billy wrapped the remaining fish in his bandana and took her hand, helping her to her feet.

He led her away from the fire, through the stubble, away from the people as, behind them, the guitar rippled a Spanish chord, a reminder of the way Pedro had played his guitar during those long-ago nights. "It's over yonder by the river," he said, "Just past the horse corral."

A few people started singing in Spanish.

Ay, ay, ay ay.
Canta y no llores
Porque cantando se alegran
Celito lindo los corazones.
...
Antes que venga tu madre, Cielito lindo, dame un abrazo.

Time had coiled around itself, weaving a happy piece of his boyhood with the start of manhood.

Abrazo meant a love embrace.

They passed the corral, half of the thirty horses droopy in sleep after their long day of work and a big grass supper gathered by Billy. Sixteen fresh horses were ready to start tomorrow. Beyond the corral, Billy led Lizzyanne into the dense vegetation of the river bottomland, making sure the little branches didn't whip back on her.

Almost there. They were on the faint pathway that his feet had tamped, her hand still transmitting eagerness.

Suddenly a rustle in the bushes. Billy turned to look. Perhaps a deer.

Soft whispers, men conspiring. He dropped her hand.

Men stepped out of the willows, their muscular torsos and arms naked in the now blue moonlight. Dark hair swathed their chests like bear fur. They wore trousers and boots, the hair on their heads bushy or falling over their noses. Young men. Six, he counted, moving apart to surround the two of them.

His heart, already loud from love, stuttered into the rhythm of fear. He recognized an Indian hater among them. In soft jeers they took turns saying things:

"Well, whatdawe got here. A white girl an' a Injun nigger."

"You wanna fuck, girl? We'll show you how."

"Yeah, alla us."

They moved their hips at Lizzyanne. He saw her terror as they circled like wolves. He couldn't fight them all.

"Nigger lover girl."

"Us is Injun haters."

"Gonna kill us a Injun tonight."

"Yeah."

"Yeah."

Whispers. Their smiles rounded in the moonlight and then faded as they slowly circled and stepped out of the light. They were older and most of them bigger than Billy. Trying to keep them all within his sight, he turned slowly with them, then whirled to see the ones at his back. Should he pull the knife from his calf thong now? He could kill one for sure, but then he'd be in the grasp of the others and they'd have Lizzyanne, and if they didn't kill him he'd die with a rope around his neck. Indians didn't get a fair shake. And if they killed him they'd have to kill Lizzyanne too, after they got through with her, so she wouldn't contradict their lies. His short life was ending.

They tightened the circle, each bent forward with hands outstretched, ready to grab him. No knives that he could see. They planned to beat him to death.

One rushed at him. Others too. He dove to the ground between two of them, catching a glimpse of three men grabbing Lizzyanne.

He hit the ground rolling, leg up, hand on knife, when a body landed on him. His arm was pinned down. A boot toe rammed his ribs from the side, delivering sharp pain.

Lizzyanne cried out in a muffled way.

With a wild twist he wiggled partly out from under the man on top, pushing at the hands trying to strangle him, and felt the sole of his foot meet Earth. Power came up from her and he sprang on that leg, burdened by the lopsided weight of the man sliding off him.

He flopped on the ground—his hand free, the grip of his enemy loose. Billy shoved, somersaulting backwards to confuse them, when two more men dove at him. He kicked a head as he tumbled.

The nickering of nervous horses guided him.

A boot banged into his back. The others were on their feet again, after him. He made a violent twist, a boot just grazing his head, and scrambled into the brush, elderberry by the scent, a helper.

The woody stems parted for him as he pushed and pulled himself toward the corral. Grunts and oaths followed close behind. Grasping hands slipped from his kicking feet as he plowed into the berry briars, uncaring of the thorns. The briars slowed them, and he wriggled under the barbed wire that ran through the berries. Now he was among friends with powerful weapons.

Jumping to his feet he made his way into the milling workhorses, some half-rearing or whinnying, all stepping around on hooves twice the size of normal horses. "It's me," he softly told them, stroking their high withers. "I need your help." They knew him, but had been startled to see him now.

"Outta my way!" shouted a pursuer in the corral, maybe all three of them.

Breathing the exhales of the Percherons, Billy rapidly patted his way through them, working toward the clever wooden mechanism on the gate, as familiar as his own hand.

Throwing the elbow bar, he shoved the gate open.

The horses flowed through it like water, frightened by the men at their rears but perhaps not as frightened as the men facing those rears.

With a well-aimed leap, Billy grabbed a mane and pulled himself up, kicking the animal's wide sides to get out the gate with the others.

He reined with heels and mane, wheeling and thundering back through the briars and elderberries where he could still hear Lizzyanne trying to scream.

In the moonlit clearing he saw her on the ground, a man on top. He couldn't trample that man, but, roaring with anger, ran the Percheron at the one holding her legs.

The man dropped her legs and dove into the willows. Billy lunged after him, the Percheron unhampered by the dense brace of young trees. He urged the animal on until a scream told him a hoof had made good contact.

Wheeling back to Lizzyanne, he saw one man running. He went after the one trying to pull up his trousers, hopping toward cover.

Aflame with hatred, Billy kicked the somewhat resisting horse to overrun the man, and felt intense pleasure when the man tripped and fell. The scream told him that a hoof had landed, but not on the man's back. That would have cut off the wind.

As the fear and horror of the night caught up with him, Billy heard the cries of the two injured men as well as other men yelling "Ho! Ho!" at the loose horses. In the blue moonlight he could see them standing in lines with their arms out like fences. He also heard Lizzyanne sobbing.

She was alone in the tiny clearing. He leaned down for her hand, but she ran away, shaking her head and bawling.

⌐◡

Lizzyanne never spoke to Billy again.

The injured men had broken legs. No one seemed to care that Billy had been trying to protect Lizzyanne. Those who apprehended and took him to the steel jail in Cosumne didn't care about her, and now she didn't care about him.

Two days later the Justice of the Peace, William Robinson Grimshaw, allowed Mr. Swain to become Billy's guardian. And that's why Billy began working on the Swain ranch in Elder Creek after all.

He felt lucky not to have been hung.

growing up we
s, just like you
t. I wanted to

place and

e pretty
vender

and
ape
ed
y
d

...nters away, perhaps to
...lt Billy's growing up was,
...ng. It pleases me to see the gri...
...er the faint tracks of the road. As a...
...ms his arrow. No car-roof blocks my v...
...most of Mae's dark curly hair, and her fac...
...she died. Now she always looks like she did in
...he stops the car at a tilt on my mound, and the
...dances as she turns the key to silence the motor.
...ls in her cheerful way, "How are you?"
...eting of her people. They expect a short happy answer
...ead.
...ply, asking in the way of my people, "Where are you com-
...o expect a short happy answer.
...ne," she chuckles. "Never thought I'd be in limbo this long."
...e you going?"
...ly knows, and that's the truth!" She slaps the wheel and throws
...back in a hearty laugh. Then she wipes the tears with her sleeve and
...ne with her twinkly blue eyes. "Where are you going?"
...e laugh together until I scold her in a joking way, "I won't always be
...k in this mud, you know. Some day I'll dance around a fire with my people.
...ur songs will carry to the ends of the world."

She catches my impatience. "Oh, I'd so like to dance again too."

"Your people don't dance much anymore."

"Not like we used to. Say, when you get to your happy land, could I come and dance with you? Is that possible? Would I be admitted?"

"Ho, just tell them you're an old friend of mine."

"That's nice," she says. "My people won't let outsiders in heaven. Or so I was told."

We listen to the river surging with mountain snowmelt.

"It was hard for Billy when he was growing up," I say. "I had it easier. We lived with our own people and danced with the neighboring peoples. We knew what to expect."

Coyote butts in with, "It's more fun to run into strangers and see what you can get away with. I would have tricked Lizzyanne into doing it with me." He yodels a happy howl.

Behind the wheel of her motorcar Mae says, "One thing I loved about Billy, he wasn't tricky at all. He was kind."

. what it got him," Coyote shoots back.

ahead of the story, Old Man," I say.

houghtful. "Coyote has a point. When I was

r own people and danced at the neighbors' place

nia. I knew what to expect all right, but I didn't like

life was more exciting."

ear that?" Coyote gloats.

Yes. That's the same reason my granddaughter left the hom

ent to Sutter's Fort."

***

IOWA, 1884

Six-year-old Mae kneeled on the sofa and gazed out the window at th spring morning. Lilacs in bloom next to the house made a lush la frame for the straight rows of young corn in the field across the road.

Two plodding horses and a flat-bed wagon briefly interrupted her view as it passed by she saw in the wagon a large wooden crate of a size and sh she hadn't seen before. Beside it a lady in Sunday clothes wept and dab her face with a handkerchief. Just behind the wagon came a two-seater bug crowded with people. Recognizing Myrtle on a grown-up's lap, Mae jumpe off the sofa and ran out the door. She liked this friend and didn't see enough of her on account of the farms being so far apart.

The driver kept the horses walking slowly past the yard, and Mae stepped alongside, smiling and waving at Myrtle, and wondering where little Sarah was. Not long ago Myrtle's family had invited all the neighbors for miles around for a picnic at their place, and Mae and Nora had played with Myrtle and Sarah all day long. Now, Myrtle looked at Mae with sad eyes and flapped her hand once.

Puzzling over that, Mae stood watching the two rigs roll down the road.

Suddenly another buggy came hurtling up the road. The sweating, blow-ing horse turned into the yard and stopped. A man in a dark suit stepped out with a black bag and left his horse in its harness. He nodded at Mae as he quickly strode to the door and knocked.

Then to her surprise Hank arrived in the farm wagon pulled by the fam-ily's old swaybacked horses. They had been running too. She hadn't realized that Hank had been gone.

The man at the door was talking to Mommy, and Hank drove straight into the barn, so Mae ran after him.

"Why is that man here?" she asked as he unhitched the horses.

"He's the doctor. I fetched him. He'll see to Nora."

"Oh."

Four-year-old Nora, who slept with Mae, had cried in the night with a stomachache. "Is the doctor going to give her some bad medicine?" She wrinkled her nose at the thought of it.

"Doan know." With the horses in their places, Hank started pushing the wagon back to the wall. "Go find out, why doncha."

Mae ran back to the house and started to mount the stairs to the bedroom when George, her twelve-year-old brother, stopped her.

"Mom said we should all stay downstairs," he said.

Emmett and Farley came down the stairs dressed and combed. Emmett, the eight-year-old brother Mae liked the most, said, "I'm hungry" and ran to the kitchen with red-haired Farley just behind.

Mae followed them, but Mom had not cooked breakfast so they all looked around, not knowing what to do.

Daddy and Gramps came into the kitchen. Gramps sat at the table while Daddy told George to go to the chicken house and get plenty of eggs. Mae sat in her chair across from Gramps.

It was strange seeing Daddy make coffee, and stranger yet when he broke the eggs, so very slowly, into Mommy's mixing bowl. He was whipping the eggs when Mae heard footsteps coming down the stairs. She jumped up, nearly knocking her chair over, and ran to see Mommy and the doctor. They were talking. Being polite, she waited until they said good-bye at the door, but before she could ask what he did to Nora, Mommy took Mae by the hand and led her upstairs.

"It'd be a shame to expose the boys and all," she was saying. "You're exposed already so, Mae dear, stay with your little sister and do what you can to help her."

By now they were at the bedroom door. Mommy opened it and nudged Mae inside the room and shut the door in her face. The key clicked in the lock and was removed. A key-shaped piece of light remained, from the window at the end of the hall.

"But I'm hungry," Mae yelled through the door."

"I'll bring your breakfasts," Mommy's voice said.

～

Mae desperately wanted out of that room where Nora whined and moaned. It felt like she was there for years. Every morning she would comb her hair while standing in her nightshirt on a hot rectangle of sunlight from the window. Hearing the kitchen door downstairs, she would rap, hoping to get someone's attention. But they wouldn't look up, so she'd watch the hats of her brothers—Hank, George, Farley and Emmett—and then Daddy, as they stepped off the stoop on their way to the barn or the fields. Soon afterwards bursts of grain would fly from the porch to Mommy's cries, "Chi-icky, chick-chick-chick. Chi-icky, chick, chick, chick." The chickens would come running and peck each other until they found places where all could eat peaceably. Mae would try to comb the snarls out of her long curly hair, but it was always tangled. As the days went by, her head developed thicker and thicker mats. Before this confinement with Nora, hair-combing had been the worst part of every day, when Mommy trapped her in the swale of her frock and held her between her big strong thighs. The comb tore into her snarls and Mae couldn't help but shriek with the pain that never seemed to end. Nora would watch with big eyes. When it was Nora's turn, Mae would smile to hear *her* scream. Now Mae realized how bad she had been, and she wanted to promise Mommy that she would never smile like that again, if Mommy would only let her out of that room.

After the chickens were fed, footsteps would clump up the bare wood of the stairs, and Mae would stand like a lost waif before the door, hoping to melt Mommy's heart when she unlocked it. But Emma would set the tray on the floor—most mornings two bowls of mush, a pitcher of cream, and a clean thunder mug—and wave Mae aside so she could see Nora on the bed. Sometimes her eyes were red and she would say, "How're you feeling, Baby?" Nora would moan as she did all the time. Mommy would pick up the tray of yesterday's dishes and the stinky mug, and lock the door. Three times a day she brought their meals, and it was the only thing that happened.

Sometimes Mae sat on the floor in the corner and pressed her hands on her ears so she couldn't hear Nora whimper. Or she would play a little with her raggedy doll, trying to pretend Nora wasn't there, but mostly she yearned to be outside racing through the plum trees or up the corn rows chased by Emmett, or playing pirates with him and Farley on Daddy's old stagecoach. One day she heard a rap at the door. She went to the door and asked, "Who's there?"

"It's me," Emmett said in a quiet voice. "Ain't nuthin' to do around here."

"Unlock the door and let me out."

"Mom's got the key."

Nora moaned loudly.

"Is Nora gettin' better?"

"Maybe. She don't cry so much now. Doan eat much either. Not even a bite today."

"Mom and Dad think you'll get sick too."

"I ain't sick."

Mommy's voice called from downstairs, "Emmett, where are you?"

"Gotta go," he force-whispered.

Mae discovered a way to pass the time. She would sit against the headboard with Nora and tell stories. Nora would lean her damp mass of crinkly red hair on Mae's shoulder—she sweated all the time. Mae soon ran out of the old stories so she made up new ones.

One afternoon Mae told about the golden streets of heaven and all the angels gathered there. Nora smiled to hear that she would be given wings. An actual smile! "Then you can fly over our heads," Mae kept on. "The boys will look up and see you swooping around. They'll wish they could fly too!" Mae felt Nora relax.

Locked in this room where their folks couldn't see Nora do the things that they called cute and dear, she seemed sweet. Mae thought maybe she did love Nora after all, like she was supposed to. She sang her favorite song, "Old Man Tucker," as many verses as she could remember. She sang "Oh Susanna" and the song about Sweet Betsy from Pike, who showed her bare arse to the whole wagon train. She even acted out the stories. Sometimes she told about Gramps leaving Ireland on that sailing ship where people vomited and died and were tossed overboard. She figured this would make Nora feel better by comparison.

One morning Mae woke up looking at the pale light in the window. There was a stench, and yet she knew the thunder mug contained only pee. She pushed her toes over to Nora. Through something slimy! Nora's leg felt like cool clay. Mae sat up. Nora's nightshirt lay open on the dry washboard of her chest, but her eyes were shut.

Mae threw the sheet aside and saw a terrible green mess with a streak of red through it. Nora was lying in it! She knew better. Mae punched her in the ribs. She didn't move. Mae punched again, but the yellow eyelashes lay still on Nora's white cheeks, the freckles over her nose and cheeks all but faded away.

Mae grasped the lashes of one eye and looked under the lid. A white expanse shocked her, like a boiled egg. The same under the other eyelid. Frightened, she scrambled out of bed and ran to the door screaming, "Mommy, Mommy!" She pummeled hard on the door that was always locked.

Emma came at last. So did Gramps. The boys inched into the room in various states of dress. Mommy went to the bed and kneeled down, taking Nora's wrist. After a minute she let out a whine like a hurt dog and then said in a scary voice, "She's gone."

Gone? Nora was right there as plain as anything.

"Help me, Ed," Emma said. Mommy and Daddy rolled Nora in the reeking sheet and carried the twisted bundle out the door. Gramps followed with George and Farley. Emmett looked scared too, just like Mae felt.

Mae could hardly hear herself ask, "Can I go too?"

Mommy turned all of a sudden like she'd forgotten Mae was there. "Come down to the kitchen," she said with tears shining on her face, "I'll wash you of contamination. I'm so glad you didn't get the typhoid."

⤳

After Nora's funeral Mae was the baby of the family again, and the only girl. When the family rode to town she sat on the buckboard in Nora's old place, not in the wagon bed with the boys. She loved it that they bought her ribbons of different colors, and at home let her load her biscuit with jam. They let her cry for a longer time when she was hurt, as they comforted her. But though Mae liked to be babied, in her heart she was no baby. She knew she had benefited from Nora's death.

⤳

Mae started calling her mother Mom, like the boys did, and Mom didn't watch the children as closely as before Nora's death. She spent more time in her room. This left Mae free to roam with Emmett and his friends from the neighboring farms. On the Fourth of July they stole coins from the secret jar in the kitchen and jumped the train to the circus in Orange City. Mae traveled to other towns this way too, sometimes alone. The engineer would slow down so she could catch up and fling herself at the caboose stairs, holding on for dear life to the steel railing.

When she was about ten, her girlfriends in school complained about the housework they were made to do, but Mom never asked Mae to beat rugs, wash clothes, or scrub floors.

One day when they were in the kitchen Mom mentioned that Mae favored the Hamiltons. "You're so like your Aunt Phoebe," she said, kneading bread in a washtub. The sleeves of her dress were rolled up to her shoulders, and beads of perspiration stood on her forehead. The muscles of her big arms swelled as she punched down the ball. "Did you know? Phoebe was quite the actress in New York City."

"Oh, that's what I want to be, Mom, an actress! Is Aunt Phoebe older than you?"

"She's my baby sister. You have her looks."

"Oh, I want to see her! When will she come visit?" Mae realized that she couldn't remember anyone from her mother's family coming to visit.

Hands stringy with dough, Emma picked up the heavy ball and in a single motion slammed it down on the countertop. The force flattened the ball. "She'll never come," she said.

That puzzled Mae, as did the ferocity with which her mother worked the dough. Teeth bared and clamped over her lower lip, she folded one side of it over the other and whumped it down with the heels of her hands, big bubbles snapping, turned it around, folded it the other way, and repeated those moves. Then she attacked it with the rolling pin, making a long strip of it.

"Let's invite her," Mae suggested.

Emma scooped brown sugar from the sack and poured it on the dough, saying only, "She wouldn't come." She threw on a pan of raisins, put pieces of cinnamon bark in the stone mortar, and pounded hard with the pestle.

Mae had to yell. "Why won't she come?" She could feel the frown in her forehead. This made no sense. Everyone loved to visit the Duffys.

Mom flung the ground cinnamon over the sugared dough. "She just won't."

"But *why* won't she come?"

Mom floured her hands again. She picked up one side of the heavy sheet of dough and tucked the edge over, rolling it lengthwise with her hands into a long snake.

"Because I've been disowned, that's why."

Mae didn't understand, and Mom's upset tone told her she was onto something big. Fast and furious, Emma rolled the giant snake back and forth with the flats of her hands to make it uniform in width, the tail thrashing. Finally it lay inert along the entire length of the countertop.

"What does disown mean?"

The butcher knife gleamed as Mom whacked the snake with force that would surely dent the already dimpled tin countertop. Clack, clack, clack, she segmented the thing from head to tail. Then she turned away to fetch the larded pans from the table.

Puzzled more than ever, Mae stole a pinch of dough and popped it in her mouth—yeasty, delicious. Mom wiped her arm across her eyes, leaving a streak of moisture in the flour dust. Her voice quaked. "It means they won't even answer my letters."

"But why?" More than one lady at a dance or in a market had pulled Mae aside to say that her mother was the most wonderful woman they had ever known.

Slowly turning her head from side to side, Mom loaded the big flat pans with the spiral rolls. Her voice squeaked, "I can't talk about it now. Ask your dad."

Mom carried the pans to the shelves above the range where they'd rise again before baking, and as she stood there her broad back moved in spasms. Mae digested the disturbing fact that her strong and able mother was weeping. Sorry to witness this reversal—she was always the one who cried—Mae left the kitchen.

That night Gramps came to Mae's room to say good night. To her question, he explained that disowned meant parents didn't like what their daughter or son was doing and the punishment was never to see that child again, never to write, and never again to help them or send money.

This surprised Mae in two ways. First, that parents told grown-up children what to do, and second that Mom had done something very, very bad. Yet she had been a teacher and everyone loved her. When tramps came knocking, she always gave them something to eat, and she kept butter on the table in case somebody came in for coffee and a slice of her good bread.

"What did she do, Gramps?"

"Married me boy."

"What was wrong with that?"

"He was born Irish." Beneath the smear of white hair, his watery blue eyes seemed to be all that was left of his narrow face, and the beard covering his chin fell like a length of white silk down past his belt, a slim beard on a skinny old man.

Born Irish. "You mean because you and Grandma came from Ireland?" A year ago the family had buried Grandma Duffy on a small hill in the middle of the front field.

The white beard inched up and down as Gramps nodded.

"But that's not fair! Daddy couldn't help where he was born or where you were born."

"They told her not to marry him and she did."

"But *why* didn't they want her to marry an Irishman?" All day long she'd been digging for the answer.

"Ye'll learn that for yourself one day, I'm sorry to say." He patted her shoulder. "Good night."

6

1888

I'm getting on in years," Mr. Swain told Billy as they drove up Elder Creek Road. A number of farmers along this stretch had switched from wheat to fruit. Billy recognized plums, apricots, peaches, and grapes; but the fruit was sparse, the winter having been cold and long. Mr. Swain flicked the reins to pass by Diggory Hobbs on his one-horse potato seeder.

Raising a hand to Diggory, Mr. Swain added, "The renters got in a financial muddle and I decided the place isn't worth the bother to me any more. Got me a buyer, cows included."

Billy realized this would be his last ride to Cosumne on this wagon. About twice a year he'd been hitching rides to visit his mother and sister.

"I'll be sortin' through the barn," Mr. Swain continued. "Hope to leave around noon tomorrow. You want a ride back?"

Billy nodded. "If I'm not there by noon, go ahead. I'll walk." It was only about twelve to fifteen miles, and he enjoyed long walks.

He had worked so long on the Elder Creek place that the bad night of the wheat harvest had receded to a dark corner of his mind. Over the years it had generally stayed there except on rare occasions when a woman made him think she could bring him peace instead of disaster. Lizzyanne had taught him to stay away from white women. Then came two Indian women. He'd been so hungry for love that he told Mona it was all right when she confessed to stealing the stashed money for Ma's house. Mona spent it on a drinking spree and returned to him sick and sorry. But then she ran off with the few coins saved from his next week's pay. When he heard that the Indian she'd been drinking with beat her to death, all Billy could do was lie in bed and stare at the can lids nailed over the knotholes on the wall. Mr. Swain and the other hands finally got him on his feet again. Two or three years later came Teresa. Men made fun of her clubfoot, but Billy loved her and took care of her when she was drunk—until she disappeared with the money he'd saved after Mona. That's when a door shut inside him. He lost his hunger for love. He had the strength of a boy, but like an old man resigned himself to being alone.

Now he waited while Ma pretended he wasn't in her house. She was pack-ing her chomuch, as Indians called travel sacks, now removing dried herbs from the rafters. Isabella had said they were going to a big time at the place of Jesús Oliver in the Buena Vista rancheria. It had been so long since the last big time that his sister couldn't even remember going. Trying to decide whether to go, Billy turned to the kitchen range—the one nice thing he'd been able to buy Ma—and fingered up a dollop of nu-pah. He'd been eating salted and peppered food for so long that the acorn pudding, the mainstay of the People, tasted bland and thick. It stuck to the roof of his mouth and he worked it away from his teeth.

Isabella looked up from tying her shoes. The morning light slanting through the little window made her look tired and old, with wrinkles on her forehead and around her eyes. Every time he visited her, he felt a jolt to see how much she had aged. Maybe the three dead babies, each from different men, had something to do with it.

She said, "Goin' someplace is better'n settin' around. Come to Buena Vista with us. People're comin' from all over."

This was the first time in all these years that Billy felt he had the time to attend a big time. "All right," he agreed. He wanted to be with Ma and this was the only way to do it. He was also curious how the big time would go. The few elders left who supposedly knew the old ceremonies had kept their knowledge bottled up a long time, and younger people had no idea what to do.

Ma acknowledged Billy's presence as they left the house, her eyes twinkling as she spoke the old tongue. "*Cudja*. Good, you dance. You find your spirit."

They crossed the bridge and passed the Bridge House Store, where a man on a wagon was paying toll, and continued east on Jackson Road. Second grass thrived all around them and a flock of yellow-heads flitted along the barbed wire fence ahead of them. From the Brown place they would catch a ride on the Howdy wagon.

Something white came jerking toward them in the roadside ditch. Walk-ing toward it, Billy was surprised to see the cropped head of a white-haired person pulling with one hand and an elbow while pushing with twisted legs. One leg bent outward at the knee, the other stuck straight out at the hip. The knee of the hip-out leg bent sharply inward with a foot dragging under the belly. Swaddling rags muddy from the ditch protected the limbs and extremi-ties, and he couldn't tell the sex of this person, who was constantly looking down, no doubt watching for rocks and broken glass in the ditch.

Ma said. "Something for you." She stepped over a rut-puddle at the side of the road and dug down in her chomuch.

As the person looked up, a toothless grin transformed the face into some-one much younger, a woman. She leaned on her good hand and jerked her foot beneath her as a sort of chair. In that awkward position she opened the filthy old flour sack she'd been dragging and Ma dropped in a big chunk of bread. The little woman looked at Billy with eyes flattened in a squint that he seemed to recognize.

Strangely, Ma didn't ask the polite question about where she was going, and the woman scrabbled away without a word.

Ma and Isabella walked on. Billy caught up and asked, "What happened to her?"

"No one knows for sure," Ma said. "She doesn't talk. Some say she jumped off the bridge at Lamb's Crossing because a man left her. But that's just a story." Ma's shoulders bumped up. "Lily moved away while you were living at Sheep Corral. She came back to heal, but her bones were all wrong. I could have helped if I had known."

"Lily?" He remembered that squint. "Is she my friend?" The one he'd run and played with as a young child.

"Ho, she's the one."

Dumbfounded, Billy walked in silence.

Then Ma said, "White boys throw rocks at her."

Instantly, rage flamed in Billy's stomach. It clenched his fists and teeth, and he knew he would have killed at least one of those boys if he'd seen that. He calmed himself before saying, "I could carry her to the Howdy place. She's not heavy. Maybe she'd like to go to the big time."

Isabella spoke in English. "Better leave her alone. She gets skeered an' screamin' if people touch her. She doan understand nuthin'."

Billy looked back at Lily scuttling down the ditch. "Where is she going?"

"To the store," Ma said as she continued up the road. "Mister Allen gives her meat and milk that's starting to turn… broken crackers, things like that."

Billy recalled the rocky gorge at Lamb's Crossing and the immense yellow pines felled to serve as the bridge bed—a good place to jump if you wanted to die. There were times he could have jumped from that bridge, had it been handy. "Does she live with somebody?"

"Ho, a blind auntie."

Billy ignored a four-horse bus with four benches filled with staring white people. As they rolled by, he was thinking about the power of love to bring harm. Soon a man about Billy's age came down a path and joined them on the road. The man acknowledged them with a slight nod. His clothing, brown skin, soft features and black spiky hair told Billy he was Indian, probably in mourning about a year. He walked swiftly despite the curvature of his legs, the opening in his baggy trousers gaping with each step. Obviously he had no woman to make buttons from the buttonwillow tree and to sew them on. Mrs. Swain had taught Billy to do that, and had given him a needle.

Ma didn't much like the man or she would have spoken to him. Isabella adjusted her stride to walk beside him, and Billy walked behind them with Ma.

Isabella asked the polite question. "Where are you going?"

"The big time," the stranger said as he swung his bowlegs in front of him at a rapid pace, propelled it seemed by his muscular shoulders and arms. His elbows poked out of holes and he wore a bearskin vest, hair side in. Billy recognized bear from the texture of the leather and the look of the dark fur spilling out the armholes and neck.

Ma spoke to the man in the old tongue. "Are your people coming?"

He answered in English. "Mebbeso."

"People call you Cowboy," she said.

"They think that's funny," he replied, this time in the old tongue with the accent of Nisenan people from the American River and its tributaries.

Ranch hands joked about cowboys with bowlegs, but Billy knew this man's deformity had been present from early childhood. He had seen it before in children who survived starvation.

In silence the four turned right onto Ione Road and soon passed the tall headstones of the Michigan Bar Cemetery. From there it wasn't far to Pony Brown's place.

Pony's son Sam was a so-called squaw man, a white man with an Indian wife. She was from the Howdy family, who lived and worked on the Brown place. Today Pony was loaning his hay wagon to the Howdys so they could give their friends a ride to the big time. People were already sitting around a bricked-in spring, joking and laughing in high spirits. Many of them, like Billy, probably hadn't been to a big time in years. Welcoming the four of them, a woman handed Ma the long-handled dipper. This deference to her as an elder pleased Billy. When the dipper came to him he drank deeply of cool water that tasted of the underground rocks.

Billy and others looked around the new barn while more people arrived. Then Sam Howdy drove the wagon out of the barn pulled by a span of mules. Everyone climbed in and they were on their way to Buena Vista.

Little children squealed and laughed as they bounced over holes and ruts in the road, and when Sam turned south onto Ione Road, they leaned hard against each other, exaggerating the natural pull until they lay in a giggling heap. Some were obviously half-white, and that always meant Indian mothers.

The sun warmed Billy as the wagon lumbered up the road that stretched before them like two gray ribbons in an expanse of green. Older girls whispered among themselves, some of them looking at Billy. But his door was shut. The old man beside him dozed as the wagon rolled up and down the gentle hills dotted by oaks. Billy was facing east where the hills mounded into bluish mountains, behind which floated the white Sierra range as far north and south as the eye could see. To the west, glistening streams threaded through the vast Valley of the Sun under a blue blue sky.

The children played tag, jumping over the outstretched legs. They staggered and laughed as they dodged each other and dove across their mother's laps. An elder began to sing. Billy vaguely recalled that old walking song. Ma and the other elders joined in. Billy learned the repeated chorus. He sang and then listened as the elders belted out the verses. The pleasure in his mother's face made him glad to have come, if only to see that.

As the miles passed he felt lighter of heart. Something good was happening. He had been isolated from the People, who had seemed to disappear. Now as he looked around, he realized that the Indian half of him wasn't just an old mother and emptiness. The People were not dead, nor were they defeated. This was a lively bunch with memories as old as the world. The song teased him with reminders of old stories he hadn't thought about for most of his life.

The singing stopped. They were passing nice houses and a brewery with big kegs showing through the windows. Girls whispered as the wagon rattled over a bridge and turned left up the main street of Ione, the tall redbrick steeple of a church soaring behind the stores. The elders sat like statues. Along both sides of the busy street, white people put their heads together pointing and talking about the wagonload of Indians in their town. Maybe they too had thought all the Indians were dead. Others stared from upstairs windows. Billy sensed fear in the wagon, and he remembered reports of murders, beatings, and hangings of Indians. Fixing his gaze on the steeple, he wished Sam would hurry the mules through the town.

"Hey squaws," a male voice called, "wanna fuck? I got a penny."

Billy quickly located the white boys grinning from the boardwalk, one pointing at himself and jerking his hips. "I got a nickel," another yelled. White women covered their mouths beneath wide eyes and raised brows, to hear such a thing, but they stared at the People as though they had caused it.

The children stared back, but the elders pretended not to notice. The old man next to Billy got a tic in his eyelid. Billy breathed easier when the wagon rolled beyond the town, past the marble gravestones and up a hill. They passed a racetrack, probably the one Mr. Swain had talked about, where spectators came from far and wide to see the horse races. Maybe the immense field in the center of the track was where Mr. Swain's relative coached Indian boys to play baseball. Billy didn't know how to play that game, but he liked the idea of Indian boys competing against white boys. It was brave of them, because the white boys wouldn't want to be defeated. He wondered how this other Mr. Swain made it safe for the Indian players.

The land soon became ugly with strip mines dug into a dead-white earth. Here and there unpainted shacks peeked out of the high chaparral. Pathways led to the road, and people came down them to join the migration to Buena Vista. Sam Howdy spoke to the walkers, inviting them to ride, but they waved him on. "Your wagon is full," they replied, or "It's not far. We like to walk." Everyone smiled.

Billy loved seeing this friendship among Indians. Like a snake shedding its skin, he felt his guard against being Indian sloughing away, replaced by a feeling of sensitivity to others in the wagon and on the road, people who had suffered in many ways. It became easy to imagine living in bygone times. He glanced around at the older girls who had been looking at him. Maybe his inner door would open.

The wagon turned left, and farther up that road the land became lush and green. At the Buena Vista Saloon, a rock building with open doors and men drinking inside, Sam reined the mules to the right up a tree-shaded wagon trace. Billy had never been to this rancheria, but he'd heard that Indians around here hoped to be given ownership of their land some day, to farm it. Jackson Creek dried up in the hot season, so some of the Buena Vista people migrated to Slough House every summer to harvest Mr. Sheldon's corn. They built temporary houses from the spent stalks—teepees, the white hands called them. They told Billy that most of their men also worked in the local coal and limestone mines while the women raised onions and squash near their houses in this beautiful valley. No doubt their ancestors inhabited many of the ancient oaks

The road climbed a little way up the hills forming the southern side of the valley. A whoop went up as they stopped in a grove of huge oaks. Squealing children leaped to the ground and raced away. Billy felt the joy of hard-working people looking forward to a little fun with no white people around. Maybe there would be competitions and storytelling, in addition to the spirit dances.

A roundhouse had been dug into the base of a small hill, the dirt raw at the entrance and the wood of the roof new. Above the roundhouse, on a somewhat level hilltop, he could see goalposts and the dark mops of children's heads as they darted around.

Cowboy helped Isabella jump down. Billy helped Ma.

"I'm glad this is no Cry," Ma said. "I'm tired of death."

"They are going to dance the Ghost Dance," Isabella said.

That was a new dance taught by a man who'd recently come from east of the Sierra mountains. Not long ago, in Billy's hearing, a couple of white men had talked about a new dance that made Indians bloodthirsty. They said it was outlawed in some states.

Cowboy shook his head and said, "That's bullshit."

"You mean ghosts comin' outta the ground to kill the white people?" Isabella asked.

"Ho! Bullshit." Cowboy walked up a path toward the playing field, and Isabella walked with him. Clearly she liked the man. Billy wondered if he would meet a woman who would follow him around like that. Maybe in the dancehouse tonight. He didn't plan to dance, not knowing how and not wanting to look foolish, but he would watch.

Ma went down to the roundhouse entrance, which burrowed into the hill like a coyote den, and joined a group of elders greeting each another. One of them was Captain Jesús Oliver, who had seen to the building of the dance-house. Some people didn't know the Spanish way of saying Jesús, and they called him Casús. Near the dancehouse, a number of mighty oaks touched hands. Like people, oak trees bleached with age and their bark became more deeply furrowed. He sensed the spirits in those old trees. Maybe later he'd feel something during the dances when the pounding feet were supposed to call the spirits of the dead up from the ground.

He looked out over the valley he'd just driven through, and turned around to see people building shade ramadas for the visitors. Nearby stood a handful of cabins and two old-style conical houses made from vertical slabs of cedar bark—all new. He walked up to the playing field full of children frisking with a hide-covered ball. Men were converging on the field, all of them younger than Billy. Across the field, Isabella and Cowboy were talking to some people, but then they all walked down to the other side of the little hill and sat down in a circle beneath an oak. Not knowing anyone else, Billy was about to follow them when he saw Cowboy reach inside his vest and pull out a flask of whisky.

Cowboy bit down on the cork and twisted it off, handing the bottle to Isabella. She drank from it. People old and young started joining their circle, and Cowboy took another flask from the other side of his vest. A cheer went up as he handed it along for all to drink.

With an aching sadness and a bad feeling in his stomach, Billy now understood why Isabella knew this man and why Ma didn't like him. Cowboy knew where to get liquor, though many stores refused to sell it to Indians. This explained why Isabella looked so old. Liquor did that to women. She was walking down the path Mona had gone. Some of the young people from the wagon were joining the drinking circle, including a girl who had looked at him. She looked up to him now, beckoning a little with her head. He turned his head from side to side and knew his door would stay shut.

He slumped down against the trunk of a tree, a kind he didn't recognize, too far from the drinking circle to see the eyes of the people, but he knew they would soon be vacant and hollow. He'd known a drinking Indian who had lain down before an oncoming train. Mona and Teresa and Indian workmen he'd known had tried to explain that liquor gave them the power to go outside the bad world for a little while. At every opportunity they risked a lot for that bit of joy. Liquor, Billy knew, was a trickster, though he didn't judge people for being fooled by it.

Young and old in that circle hugged their knees or nodded and smiled as various people told stories. Isabella leaned into Cowboy's shoulder like she was dreaming. Billy was an outsider, but he knew he would be welcome to join them. They were good people with injured hearts. But he could not drink with them.

He looked at the children romping on the field along with some of their big brothers and a few men his age. If he'd known the rules of the game he would have joined them.

A cheer from the drinkers drew his attention back o them. A man had just come from a temporary house of pine bark with a large jug of red wine. The drinking would go on for a long time, Billy knew, and sorrow ran through him like tainted water. He closed his eyes, absorbing the power of the sun. A while later he opened them and saw Ma walking down the hill to the drinkers. She approached from behind and touched Isabella's shoulder.

Isabella twisted around and spoke to her. He was too far away to hear through the noise and laughter of the game, but by the way Ma shrank back he knew his sister was loud and rude. Normally Isabella was respectful to her. Liquor was talking, as it had talked many times to him. Ma turned away and came up the hill as though her feet had become much heavier. When she got to Billy, her eyes were pools of pain.

"Son," she said in a weak voice, "Please make your sister leave those people. She can help us ready the dancehouse."

"She won't listen to me." He knew, having failed with Mona and Teresa. It only made them angry.

But the look on his mother's soft old face made him get up and try, though his stomach wasn't in it.

"Go away," Isabella yelled at him when he asked her to come with him.

He returned to the dark figure of his mother on the hill, her long black skirt blowing to one side. Putting a hand on her shoulder, he said, "I'm going back to work."

"Son, you have not met everyone here, and the dancing has not started."

"That is true," he said. Many people he didn't know were visiting under the willow-shade structure or playing the ball game, and he had not met Jesús Oliver or his son. "Maybe another day. This is not a good time for me to find spirit."

I understand, her nod said.

7

When Mae began to change into a young lady, as Daddy put it, she spent hours at the bathroom mirror studying her face and holding up her hair in various styles, though her brothers pounded on the door and ordered her to come out so they could use the flush toilet and not have to go to the outhouse. If it was Farley, she felt no remorse and let him go outside, even in a blizzard. She was thankful not to have a greasy nose and pimples like some of her friends.

A seventh-grade pupil now, she noticed that the eighth-grade boys were looking at her in a new way. Some of them were practically grown men, having skipped so much school when they were needed on their farms. They looked at her like men in novels gazed at beautiful ladies. This gave her a secret thrill.

When school let out for the summer, boys appeared at the door. "Make yourself to home," Mom would say, gesturing toward the parlor. "Would you fancy a cinnamon roll?"

They gobbled up the sweet rolls. Sometimes Mae strolled down by the creek with a boy, and they'd see Daddy in the shade of the willows sharing a jar of john barleycorn with a neighbor. Mae would lift a hand in greeting, graceful as a young lovely in a novel.

This new life came to full bloom at the dance at the Henderson place just after school let out for the summer. She'd always loved to dance, atop Daddy's shoes when she was little, but now something new was happening. The boys and even some of the men looked at her when she straightened her back and walked through the crowded room pretending not to notice them. Young men would follow her with their eyes when she danced with another. And her dance partner would laugh when she laughed, like a puppet on a string.

She went outside to catch her breath. The mown hay smelled sweet in the night air, while through the open doors and windows the music of fiddles, piano, and washtub bass kept up the toe-tapping beat. The Henderson furniture stood around the yard, the guests having carried it out to clear the room for dancing, and high above everything a blanket of stars sparkled over the Iowa landscape. A boy was looking at her from the shadows and she acted the lovely lady, pretending not to notice. She knew him of course. Filling her lungs, she exclaimed to no one in particular, "Ah, the night is so languorous!" A word from a book.

"Ah, but it is!" the boy replied in a voice as high as a girl's. She smiled to herself, doubtful that he knew the meaning of the word.

Then one summer day Jules stood on the doorstep selling farm equipment. Mae drifted by the door as Mom told him they didn't need any, and saw him notice her. He said he roomed with his aunt and uncle, people known to the Duffys. Mom asked him if he'd like a slice of buttered bread fresh from the oven. He did, and he sat in the parlor exchanging a few words with Mom and Mae. Later, Mae and Jules strolled along the creek and she realized that this grown man was no puppet on a string. He returned two days in a row to tell her about his hometown in a different part of Iowa and the baseball games he'd played there.

Turning to her he said, "Say, you got your folks wrapped around your little finger, doncha?"

She smiled demurely, noticing an odd glimmer in his brown eyes.

"I'd let you wrap me around that pretty little finger of yours anytime." With that, he drew her into the willows and kissed her on the mouth for a long time and hugged her so tight she could barely breathe. Blood surged in her ears. She nearly fainted with the intensity of the new sensation inside her. Something about that kiss scared her. She pulled back and ran home. She peeked around the front room curtain and watched him leave on his trap, but then immediately felt sorry to have been so childish. Perhaps he'd never return.

The next day, to her happy surprise, Jules knocked on the door and she agreed to walk with him again, this time determined to be more mature. She studied him closely, wondering why an adult man would be interested in a girl just thirteen. He was, she realized, short and somewhat awkward, not what a lady in a novel would want. Still, it awed her that she seemed to be conquering a grown man. As he'd put it, she felt like she might be able to wrap him around her little finger.

Near the willow-lined creek again, and out of view of everyone on the farm, he stopped and pulled a blue velvet box from his pocket. Looking a little fierce, he put it in her hand. She opened it.

On a white satin cushion lay a sizeable gold watch etched with twining vines and leaves. It had a bow of gold with a pin to affix to the breast of a frock. She picked it up and felt its weight. Real gold! She could hardly believe this was happening. Other boys had brought wildflowers, but this!

"Well, aren't you going to open it?" Jules said, almost angrily.

She couldn't immediately see how to do it.

He snatched it away. Inserting a thumbnail into a tiny groove, he popped it open and handed it back.

It took her breath away. This watch had no numbers, but three wands of filigree gold, including a second-hand, that pointed around a scene carved in white coral. A tableau of Greek ladies stood in front of a rosy background that glowed like a sunset through the minutely cutout vegetation. The women shocked her. With hair like the Statue of Liberty, they lounged in a leafy glen, two of them on the ground and one standing, all apparently unaware that their wispy veils didn't begin to cover their private parts. Their breasts were entirely bare. Out of doors! And yet something about the flush of pink through the white limbs, arboreal and human, conveyed religion, though they were obviously wicked. Who would dare fashion such a thing? Her face burned as though she were spying on those ladies right alongside Jules, as though he were looking at her bare breasts instead of theirs, and at the joining of their legs.

She handed it back, "I hadn't ought—"

"No, look!" He opened his arms to the world and gave what sounded like a memorized speech. "The beauty of nature abounds just like in this here watch. But my dear sweet Mae, you're beautifuler than those Greek maidens. You honor me with the gift of your company. Please wear this gift and make me happy."

"Jules, it must have cost a fortune!"

"I made a good sale this week. Take it and think of me."

"You're going away?"

His brown eyes had that glimmer. "No."

He jerked her to him and whispered, "Not yet." His large, warm lips pressed hers and his body felt oddly lumpy, but he kept on kissing her. She became aware of an intense heat on her chest and neck, as though she had the ague and had been plastered with mustard. Uneasy, she pulled away, out of breath.

"I'm going back," she said. This time she let him walk her to the house as a lady in a novel would. That night she did something no Christian girl ought, though she'd done it many times since Nora's death.

The next morning the bathroom mirror revealed that her chest and neck were red! She looked more closely. It was mottled red. Alarmed, she returned to her room. Hours later she could still see the bottom edge of the red when she pressed her chin down as far as it would go. She must be coming down with something. Fearing that, she finally called Mom and timidly opened her frock to her.

"A rash," Emma declared with a worried look. "I'll send George for the doctor."

The doctor was puzzled too. Mae had no fever, and since she felt well he couldn't explain it. "Maybe a sensitivity to the washing soap," he concluded.

But they'd used the same Fels Naptha as always. Mom didn't say that, nor did Mae, because she'd begun to believe it was no coincidence that the rash covered the same area that had felt scorched the previous day. God was punishing her. Alone in her room she feared the scales would fall from the eyes of others and they would see her rash for what it was, a stigma of sin. Maybe Gramps, in his long life, or Hank, who had friends that consorted with unchaste women, understood things like this. She didn't dare set foot outside her room lest she be found out.

Days passed and the stigma remained. Mom brought plates of food and told everyone, including Jules, that Mae was under the weather. Five days later, to her great joy, the rash faded. And on the sixth morning it was gone. Quickly she forgot about God and wanted to see Jules again, reasoning that she'd been rude after he gave her a valuable gift and she should make it up to him.

She knew he'd be at the Strockmorton's dance on the Saturday before school started, in two days. She would go to the dance wearing the watch so her friends could see it. She also wanted them to see her dancing with a grown man who was clearly smitten with her. Thus Mom must see the watch ahead of time and get used to the idea.

At the sight of it in its velvet box, Mom sucked in her breath and her face was the picture of horror. Without even popping the lid to see the scene inside, she said, "No, young lady! This is far too dear. And from a grown man! Give it back." She turned to Daddy. "Ed, tell her!"

Daddy lowered the Sears Catalog. Gramps creaked out of his chair and climbed the stairs, heading for his room. He liked peace and quiet.

Frowning at Daddy and then at Mae, Mom spoke in her teacher voice: "Young girls never accept expensive gifts. And to think, at your age! You should accept no gift of any kind whatsoever from a grown man. You must give it back!"

Mae couldn't believe that this same mother who'd let her ride the trains and pretended not to notice when she stole money and hid in the loft to avoid helping with supper, would speak to her with such lack of understanding. How was Mae to grow up if her mother made decisions for her? This was terribly wrong.

"He gave it to me," she said, "and I can take it if I want." The next came out as a sudden inspiration. "That's a human right in this country. As self-evident as the right to happiness!" She hadn't memorized the Preamble to the Constitution for nothing.

Emma turned to Daddy again. "Talk to her, Edward Duffy!"

The boys came in from the barn. Mae heard them washing up at the sink by the back door. Daddy picked up the catalog and resumed reading.

"This is your fault," Mom told him, voice rising. "Fathers are supposed to be the disciplinarians."

Emmett and Hank slunk into the front room and watched from the davenport.

Daddy threw the catalog aside and stood up. "You, telling me it's my fault? You, who spoiled that girl rotten?"

The other two boys came in and plopped in easy chairs, Farley snickering as he looked at them. All his life Farley had been saying Mae was spoiled rotten. She felt like strangling him.

Instead she went to her room and tried to compose a verse to add to her cigar box, but couldn't. She didn't like her parents arguing about her and hoped it would stop, but their muffled voices could be heard long into the night. Meanwhile the boys' footsteps sounded in the hallway, and Mae heard them talking and joking before their two doors shut. None of them understood her determination to be a lady on her own.

The next morning no one spoke during breakfast. Then to Mae's horror, Daddy told Hank to handle the corn harvest while he and Mom drove Mae to the Catholic school in Alton. He went out to hitch the horses. Mom went upstairs and packed Gramps' old steamer trunk with Mae's belongings without looking at Mae, even when she grabbed her clothes and returned them to the drawer. Silently, Mom put them back in the trunk. Mae felt like her life was ending. They were taking her to the Catholic girls' school! Such extreme punishment she did not deserve.

Back outside, Daddy was on the buckboard and Mae tried to run to Myrtle's house up the road, but Mom grabbed her before she could start, and with Hank's help forced her onto the buckboard to sit in the middle where she was trapped. Daddy snapped the ribbons and they were off.

As the miles dragged by, she could hardly breathe for the hot burn of betrayal in her heart. They didn't love her. It had only been a pretense. They were getting rid of her. She hated them both.

Expertly manipulating the reins, Daddy turned to Mae and said in his quiet way, "The nuns will be good for you."

"I will never be a Catholic!" she cried. "You can't make me be Irish and Catholic both!" She tried to leap from the wagon but Mom's muscular arms held her—Emma Duffy, who'd been a Presbyterian in New York! It was so unfair!

She fought and wept and stared at them with hot eyes.

"B'gory," Daddy said to the horses, "you best step lively." He flicked his oiled whip above their rumps and they leapt into a run.

Inside the two-story brick convent building Mae watched her father sign a paper and hand over an envelope of money to the Mother Superior. Never having seen Daddy with money of his own, she concluded Gramps was a party to this, and she hated him too.

"You," Mom said to Mae when they were ready to abandon her, "will receive the best schooling to be had in Iowa. Make the most of it."

It took several months before she stopped practicing hateful things to say to her parents next time she saw them, with God hearing every word of it. More months passed before she began to work in earnest on her school assignments. Under the gentle tutelage of Sister Delphine, the music teacher with a twinkling Galway accent, she began to believe that she could become an accomplished pianist and violinist. Music made the school bearable, that and her secret correspondence with Jules. But soon she forgot to write him back and was glad when his letters and postal cards stopped coming. She had met other boys, the brothers and cousins of the girls at St. Mary's.

She attended baseball games and picnics with groups of young people. Sometimes she allowed a ballplayer to steal a few minutes with her behind a bush. The pitcher of a local team declared he was "morbidly attracted" to her, adding that the dark blue line around the paler blue of her eyes "mesmerized" him. Back in her room, when the other girls were out, she studied her eyes in the mirror but couldn't see such an outline.

Three years passed at St. Mary's, with peaceful summers on the farm. The nuns loved and trusted her, especially Sister Delphine, whom she loved back. But their trust was misplaced, because Mae continued to find new ways to slip out and be with boys.

8

During Christmas break in 1892, Mae was home from school and in the front room with her parents, the boys out on the sleigh. Mom waved a piece of paper, "Ed, you can't ignore this dunner. They are family."

He looked at her. "Aye, and family should oonderstand I've a weakness in me lungs." When he got agitated, Daddy reverted to the Irish accent of his childhood.

"Weakness in the head, I'd say! You hadn't ought to'ov bought those fancy horses. It cost the whole harvest and we can't pay a dime on the rent!" Her fists dented her thick waist under her apron. Never had she talked to Daddy in that tone.

"Em, you fail to mention our daughter's fancy schoolin'. And that fiddle."

Mae didn't feel one speck guilty about St. Mary's, having been forced into it.

The volume and pitch of his voice increased as Daddy pushed out of the chair. "What kind of people talk to kin on paper? Lawyer talk! Goddam order of the Joostice of the Peace! And don't you forget, I need Pal and Belle. No man can farm with sick old horses!"

"Edward Duffy, your own kin don't trust you any more."

"Well, I can't say as I trust them either, and that's a fact! Makin' a federal case over that broken-down old wagon! And slip shovel. That were plain mean." He drilled her with the blue flint of his eyes. "Who's side you on, anyhow?"

Emma dropped the hand with the paper and turned her graying bun to him. Her thick shoulders jerked with silent weeping, her neck creased from years of working in the sun. Gramps was supposed to get his share of the farm income, with Daddy and the boys doing the work. Last year Gramps had gone to live with Uncle Ephraim and Aunt Susanna.

"May I see it?" Mae pointed. Emma handed over the document with an embossed seal at the top. In fancy script it referred to Daddy's promises and said if he didn't pay twenty-five hundred dollars ($2500) by the end of three months, the family would be evicted from the property. A cold piece of writing indeed. Would deputies yank Mom, a descendant of Alexander Hamilton, out of her house? Impossible!

Daddy sank into the faded green chair, the spark gone out of him.

A week later he hitched the team to the sleigh and returned Mae to St. Mary's for her spring term. Luckily no blizzard overcame them, but the snow and underlying ice made it hard going for Pal and Belle even in their snowshoes.

The wintry weather dragged on.

In mid-April Mae sat at the small secretary by the dormitory window writing a letter while snow blew across the grounds. "Mom, I have been asked to play the piano for the graduating class." She dipped the pen in the ink. "I do so want a new gown, white and lacy and nipped in at the waist in the modern mode. Sister Delphine wants me to play Chopin, and I simply must have a proper gown!"

"I'm coming," Emma responded by postal card. "We'll find a gown in Orange City."

Mae pressed the card to her bosom, thrilled that her mother saw this as the important event it was.

In Orange City, which was considerably larger than Alton, they selected a stunning gown, and in the afternoon Mom put up Mae's hair. "You've become a lovely young lady," she said. "Did you know you can have any man you want?"

"You mean to marry?"

"Yes, so don't waste yourself on salesmen and such. Marry a man with land. Always remember, value is in the land."

⌒

Back home in May, having just turned sixteen, Mae loved the spacious farmhouse, so very grand after the tiny room she'd shared with three other girls. She spent most of her time in the hayloft re-reading her California Joe novels and then going a mile up the road to visit Myrtle, and Ruby who lived on the next farm. They weren't married, unlike some of Mae's old school chums. Ruby and Myrtle listened with obvious admiration to Mae's stories about Alton and St. Mary's. They hadn't gone beyond the eighth grade, but Mae enjoyed giggling with them about the things that had happened since they'd last seen each other, what kind of a man they would marry, and how grand it would be to live in a city. She showed them her collection of postal cards from young men looking smart beside their bicycles or with baseball bats over their shoulders, but none of them came close to what she had in mind for a husband—a strong, handsome hero who would die for her. The problem was meeting such a man. No California Joes lived around here. On that, all the girls agreed.

In her own home, Mae worried about the family troubles. Daddy appeared to be on the brink of losing the farm. All because of Uncle Ephraim, who with his wife and five children lived on the adjoining section. Ephraim terrified his children, all much younger than Mae, and made them afraid to eat for fear of being thumped behind the ear for bad table manners. Emmett had worked for Uncle one summer and eaten at that table. He told Mae that Uncle would watch for mistakes, then jump up and give them a thwack. Fearing a slip-up, their little hands would shake as they transported food to their mouths, trying not to spill. At almost every meal, one of them would flee from the table in tears and Uncle would haul the culprit back by a twisted ear, sit him down, and make him eat properly. Knowing they would later get a thrashing in the woodshed, they could barely eat for sobbing, though he ordered them to sit up straight and be quiet. Emmett declared that if he'd been born in Ephraim's house he would have starved to death by now. Considering the way he wolfed his food down, Mae agreed.

Uncle Ephraim kept pressing his case against Daddy about the farm rent owed to Gramps. By the end of May, when the planting was normally done, the field was still wet due to the overflowing creek, the heavy spring rains and the snowmelt. Some people along the Floyd River had lost livestock. Houses had sailed away. Farmers couldn't plant because the seed moldered in the ground, so now, with the season shortened, most of them planted only what their own families could eat or their wives could put in jars. Mae had learned that her friends' fathers secured bank loans to tide them over to next year's harvest. But Mom said there'd be no loan for Ed Duffy, with this record of default.

Today Daddy was meeting again with Uncle in the office of the Justice of the Peace to work out a settlement. Mom paced around the kitchen staring out the windows at the useless fields. Worried, Mae took Emmett outside on the porch.

"I don't understand why Gramps won't speak up for Daddy."

"Gramps ain't long for this world," Emmett said, shaking his dark curly head. "He don't hardly know what's going on from day to day."

Mae held her tongue about Emmett's grammar. She hadn't been over to Uncle's place to visit Gramps, but Mom said he'd been coughing all winter and spring.

"Well, the floods sure weren't Daddy's fault!" she said.

Emmett shrugged. "Dad ain't about to pay what he don't have."

"Doesn't have," she said quietly. Emmett took correction better than the older boys, but he had a wrinkle between his eyes.

She feared that Gramps judged Daddy as lacking initiative, that greatest of American virtues, and that Ephraim saying those things all the time was influencing Gramps unduly. Daddy had been the best stagecoach driver in South Dakota, skilled and dangerous work. Maybe he didn't do well in the business of farming, but they ought to have mercy, as the sisters would say.

A half hour later Daddy burst into the house singing, "We're going to Californy with a gold pan on our knees! In a Pullman car! And Ephraim's buying the train tickets!"

California!

The instant that word sounded in her head, all Mae's dreams fell into line.

Mom began to smile again. Neighbors came to say farewell. Daddy arranged to rent a freight car. In a fit of remorse, Ephraim gave him the old farm wagon. With the help of the two older boys, George and Hank, Daddy loaded the wagon and drove the furniture and household goods to Alton, where his reserved car waited on a sidetrack. Inside the car, they built stalls for Pal and Belle, and tied down all the furniture and boxes. The agent had warned that riding in a freight car was like living in a continual earthquake. Unsecured items would fly around. This would spook the horses, and they could thrash and break their restraints, and their legs. So during the ten-day trip to California—often the car would be sidetracked—Daddy and one of the two older boys would live and sleep inside the dark car where they could soothe the horses.

Daddy wanted to take his stagecoach to California; but Mom, the practical one, pointed out that with so many children playing in it "all these years," it was ruined beyond repair. "Just take the bare necessities," she repeated. "We don't know where we'll be living."

So the Ed Duffy family left the old stagecoach slouching beside the barn.

They also left the piano that Mae played so well and much of the furniture. Ephraim's family would move into the house, which was the bigger of Gramps' two houses, and Cousin Sally would play the piano.

For the last time Mae crossed the field with Farley and Emmett, and this time Mom. They waved the train engineer to a stop and boarded for the first leg of the trip to California—two weeks behind Daddy and the two older boys. None of them looked back, least of all Mae. California was the land of gold and dashing men.

9

Farms flashed by the dining-car window as Mae, Mom, Farley and Emmett topped off their suppers with peach cobbler. Mae saw the same excitement in her brothers that she felt in her heart. Red-haired Farley had the expression of a prisoner who'd just made a jailbreak. Not since leaving home had he nettled Mae with his usual sarcastic comments. He was too happy.

Mom, who had seemed dispirited before the announcement about California, looked almost girlish. With a smile, she pushed the dishes aside, unfolded her map, and pointed to a circled dot. "That's Dry Town," she said. "See? In this stripe called the Mother Lode." She ran her finger up and down the map, north to south. "This is where all the gold is found."

Mae put her head close to Mom's to see the foothills of the Sierra range. "Those mountains go on a long ways," she noticed.

"From the scale, I figure about four hundred miles." Mom turned the map around and gave it to the eager boys.

They leaned over it, red and black curls pressed together, Farley pointing at the Bay of San Francisco. "Oregon," murmured Emmett, "and Mexico down there." The exotic names heralded adventures to come.

The boys, Mae realized, could make their fortunes directly from what nature put in the earth. In addition, one or more of them would inherit the farm in Iowa. Her chance, however, depended entirely on finding the right man. Women were scarce in California, according to the novels, and this augured well for her. There wouldn't be too much competition, and she had the advantage of her looks. Still she would complete her last year of high school. In today's world a diploma made a lady more desirable, and she planned to get every advantage she could. The important thing was to settle in a place with plenty of men. Dry Town perhaps.

"Mom," Farley asked, "you sure Mr. Henderson wasn't talkin' through his hat when he told us to go to Dry Town?"

Emma shrugged. "Mr. Strockmorton's uncle made a fortune there back in forty-nine, and he maintains that area is still the highest producer of gold in all the world. Look there." She pointed to the dot on the map. "Dry Town is on the Forty-Niner Trail. That speaks for itself."

The white-coated porter picked up the dishes and disappeared through the metal swinging doors. "It's been a long time since I didn't clear the supper table," Mom said quietly.

"You know," Mae said, "I think Gramps must have felt like we do now, when he left on that sailing ship for America."

Farley responded without a jot of sarcasm, "We's goin' to a new world like he was, 'cept we'll git there in seven days."

"Instead of forty-two," Mom supplied.

"An' not gettin' sick as dogs," Emmett piled on.

∽

Back in the Pullman car Mae climbed into the upper bunk and slid the curtain closed. She undressed on her knees, folding her frock so it wouldn't be wrinkled the next day. In her nightshirt, she lay on the sweet-smelling sheets and pillow as the transcontinental train sped toward the gold fields.

Entirely awake, she realized that this train was a palace compared with the steerage area below decks on that sailing ship from Ireland. Gramps had left a stone cabin overflowing with parents and nine children, all fed from a meager patch of rotting potatoes, and now, near the end of his life, he owned two 160-acre farms and two nice houses. Little wonder that he felt the move to the United States had made him equal to the European upper classes. Sometimes in a joking mood he called himself Squire Duffy, and the light in his eye belied the joke.

Mae saw it differently. With the train rocking and the bright stars reeling by the tiny window, she knew that this next step westward would complete the transformation of the Duffy family. Iowa farmers were common folk, not like the grandees of California with their vast holdings. She imagined a day in the future when she would hire a private car on the railroad and go to New York. She would shop on Fifth Avenue and, in a cab drawn by elegant horses, would visit Aunt Phoebe and the Hamilton relations, if she deigned to pay them a call. She would speak of pressing matters in California. The Hamiltons would accompany her back to the station and help her stow her purchases in the private car, admiring the gold trimmings and velvet chair seats said to furnish such cars. Then she'd bid them farewell.

Oh how sorry they would be for disowning Emma!

∽

The next day the open stares of a carload of soldiers heading west reminded Mae of what Mom had said about getting any man she wanted. Quickly she made the acquaintance of some young soldiers on the train. They boosted her out a window while others pulled her by the hands to the roof of the car. There she kneeled beside them, the wind blowing her hair and robbing her of breath. With care, she imitated the soldiers and stood up, feet braced against the rocking of the train. Exhilarated, she threw her arms wide to embrace the wind, laughing, every part of her alive.

"Where are you headed?" asked Miles, who stood with an arm around her, though that wasn't necessary. The train lurched, throwing her against him.

"The California gold fields." She demurely separated herself from him by pressing her hat to her head. "Where are you headed?"

"Indian reservation here in Wyoming," he shouted over the wind.

"Is there a war?"

"Naw, not now, but you never know when there'll be another escape, like the one Geronimo pulled off. Egad, jes' a year or so back, the Seventh Cavalry lost twenty-five men in a scuffle to get the Sioux into Wounded Knee Reservation. Killed more'n three-hundred Injuns afore it was over. You never know when them bastards'll get loose." He gave her a look. "Say, wanna see me shoot?" He pulled out his revolver and pointed it at the small brown critters that popped out of the ground and stood on their hind legs.

"Sure!" She was already in the Wild West!

Miles kneeled, got a bead on an animal and squeezed. The gun cracked. He handed the gun to Mae. "Go ahead and try it. It's Army issue—Colt revolver." Like a girl in a wild tale, she copied his moves and, with him showing her how to clasp her wrist and prevent injury from the kick, got off a shot. "Missed by a mile," she laughed, returning the Colt. Just then her hat blew off, and she laughed to see it sailing away with the smoke from the engine.

She stayed on the roof for over an hour, unconcerned about blowing hair and the sun on her face. She even liked the smell of the smoke.

The soldiers were looking for buffalo. "They're hunted out," said one of them.

"Naw," Miles contradicted. "There's millions of them critters. Mere mortals can't kill off so many as that."

⤶

Only two incidents on the journey gave pause to Mae's constant euphoria.

The first occurred in the middle of a barren desert, a day after the soldiers' car was detached. The train had stopped for the engineer to examine a washout in the rail bed, and the passengers went outside for some air. Neither Mae nor Emma noticed that the boys failed to get back inside when the train started up again. They thought they'd be elsewhere in the train as they often were. The day had turned very warm, the windows all pushed up. The passengers sat in silence, none of the usual joking and chatter as they crawled along the tracks. Mae feared the train would jump the tracks as one did yesterday; they'd waited three hours for that wreck to be cleared. And whenever the train picked up a little speed, Mae feared it would tip over.

After about half an hour, during which the sagebrush desert never changed, they creaked to a stop at a giant barrel on tall legs. Again all passengers filed outside. The only signs of civilization were the telegraph poles beside the tracks, disappearing in the distance.

"The boys! Where are the boys?" Emma cried.

So began a half hour of terror as they ran among the passengers for the second and third time. Mom wrung her hands waiting to talk to the engineer, but the trainmen stood in a huddle talking about the rail bed and the couplings. The train seemed small as a toy in a bleak landscape—pale mountains just visible in the distance. Mae thought about Nora passing in her sleep, and now Farley and Emmett could die gruesome deaths in this desert. Sick at the thought, she squinted eastward at what appeared to be the glare of a shimmering lake, and yet the train had passed no lake there. Her eyes were playing tricks on her. Maybe this was a desert mirage like the ones she'd read about that cruelly misled dying prospectors.

She didn't know if the boys could survive until the next train came along, or whether they could be taken aboard another train without tickets.

A tiny dark spot hovered above the mirage of a lake. As she stared at the wavering dot it seemed to be getting a little wider. Then, slowly, it broke apart into two tiny points. She shaded her eyes, expecting them to disappear, but they did not. They grew larger. Excited, she pulled her skirt above the tops of her shoes and trotted to Emma, now beseeching the railroad men to wait.

"Mom. Look!"

The men turned and looked. Mom's lips quivered as she said, "Lordy, it's the boys!"

The conductor fixed her with a hard stare. "Mrs. Duffy," he gruffed, "you best keep your family in your sights after this. We don't never go back for those that lack the sense to git aboard after a stop. Understand?"

Mae and Emma waited outside the train while steam shot from under the cars. The boys caught up just as the train jerked forward again. Their shirts were dark with sweat, their chests heaving, their faces red with sun and exertion.

Mom shooed them in, saying under her breath, "Like to scared me half to death!"

The entire last day on the train was memorable. Early in the morning they stopped in a small town named Reno. Out the window Mae saw men walking around in denim trousers tucked into laced boots, just like Western miners were said to wear. The conductor announced: "Two hours stop. Get out, shake a leg. Eatin' house and four-holer just up the road." He eyed Farley and Emmett in their seat. "We leave in two hours, so git yerselves back on this here train. Hear?"

Snickers hissed up and down the car, and the boys blushed.

Stepping off the train, Mae inhaled the fragrance of sage. A cool breeze rattled the cottonwoods and whipped the rags of Indians standing along the rails with outstretched palms. Emma, Mae and the boys looked past them, as the passengers were advised to do. Tufts of green prairie grass between the freshly painted buildings were a welcome sight after so much barrenness. Best of all, Mae could see the California mountains, high as the ramparts of heaven and pink in the early sun.

When the passengers reclaimed their places, including Emmett and Farley, the train began whistling and rolling. At first, the incline was gradual, but it rapidly steepened. Three more engines had been added in Reno for the climb ahead. As the train crept higher and higher, the conductor drew the passengers' attention to the long wooden sluices that carried logs down the mountain to a lumber mill in Reno. The mountains acquired the dark upholstery of evergreens.

Clouds covered the sun and Mae began to feel chilly in the car, strange after the heat of the last few days. People were shutting windows and singing old favorites like "Oh Susanna" and "Battle Hymn of the Republic." A family in the back sang "Dixie" to a great deal of grumbling up and down the car. Then "I've Been Working on the Railroad" united the passengers once more. Snowflakes began to fall.

"Approaching Truckee and Donner Lake," announced the conductor in a practiced singsong. "The Donner Party camped on its shore that fearful winter. Ate each other when the food gave out. Plumb out of their heads with hunger. They turned vicious. Murdered to git fresh meat, human flesh. But they all starved to death anyhow. The worst disaster of all the pioneer emigrations. Only a few miles from here."

Gasps came from all parts of the car, everyone staring out the windows. "Ya'll ready for your noon dinner?" said the jokester in the back.

A female voice asked, "Which way is that lake?"

"You'll see it out the windows after we leave Truckee."

The train slowed to a stop. "Truckee!" The conductor called. "Eat your noon meal at the station if you've a mind, but don't go looking for no lake. We roll out of here in thirty minutes." He lit the oil sconce near the doorway, for heavy clouds had darkened the car.

The Duffys stayed in their seats and ate the sandwiches they'd purchased in Reno. "Look at that!" Mom declared, staring out the window, "It's snowing like the dickens! Can you imagine! In June. Why, back home my roses are blooming."

In the seat in front of them, two ladies in black picked up their things to leave the train. They pulled hats over their old-fashioned twisted-back hair, buttoned their black coats, and made their way up the car. They stopped to speak to the conductor, which took quite some time, and then continued out the door. A man and woman entered the car in snowy coats and hats; but the conductor, who normally punched the tickets of new passengers, appeared not to notice them. He stood staring at nothing.

Mae was puzzling over that when the conductor cleared his throat and made another announcement: "I just heard that half the Donner Party survived. And some never ate human flesh."

"Where you hear that?" a man called.

"Those two ladies just got off this car." The conductor pointed. "Claimed they was Donner sisters and they was trapped in the snow along with the rest. They'll catch another train to Sacramento."

Stunned, Mae reached over and put her hand on Mom's knee. "And to think we were sitting behind them all that time!"

"They never said a thing," Mom added, "Not as I recall."

They had not joined the joking, singing, and storytelling that enlivened the car every evening, and they'd sat quietly through the announcement about the Donner Party.

"They did say one word," Mae recalled. "Remember? I asked one lady if she knew what all that white stuff was back there in the desert. She said it was salt. Now I know how she knew that. She walked through it! My teacher told us they had to walk to lighten the loads, or the wagons would sink through the salt crust."

Mae got up and went to the open door and peered into the blowing snow. A diffuse gray light penetrated the clouds and the snowfall, and the Donner sisters were gone. Mae went to the ladies' toilet, but a sign on the door said, "No admittance. Wait until train is out of town."

She returned to her seat and stared out at the wintry scene. Likely those women had eaten human flesh too, she thought, despite what they'd said. Now she really did feel like she was in California—where everything was astonishing.

With all the passengers in their seats, the train commenced its climb up the mountain. Mae tried to concentrate on the conductor's oration about sixty feet of elevation to the mile but her mind kept returning to those women.

She was looking out the window at Donner Lake far below when, with a sudden whooshing noise, the mountain scenery vanished into darkness as though someone had blown out a lamp. The invisible conductor explained they were in a snowshed, one of the tunnels that had been built to keep snow off the tracks. The train burst into the light again. Ahead stood the granite peak that the Donner Party had tried to scale before snow forced them to return to the lake camp.

Suddenly a violent jerk threw Mae into the seatback. Her head went light in the wrong-way gravity. Screams ripped through the car. The train was careening backwards down the steep grade! Her heart was in her throat.

"We've broke off the train!" a man yelled.

Mae's arms tingled with fear and she felt sure the car would leap from the rails and hurtle down the abyss. A whoosh, then sudden blackness. A snowshed, iron wheels going too fast. *Please God, let me die instantly.*

A piercing squeal overwhelmed the screams. A male voice called over the noise, "The Westinghouse appliance!" Mae knew that to be the air brake. The squeal of iron on iron continued, and the car did indeed seem to be slowing down.

Squeezing Emma's hand in the dark, Mae said a rapid Hail Mary though her mother wasn't Catholic. The conductor must have been in a forward car. His comforting voice was nowhere to be heard. Amazingly, the car came to a stop inside the tunnel. Weak from fright, Mae realized the tunnel was long and level. This had helped them stop. People all over the car whimpered with relief. What would happen now? Did the engineer realize they had broken off the train? Would they sit here and freeze to death?

People whispered in the dark. After what seemed a very long time, a violent jolt stopped her heart again. Screams, one of them Mae's, reverberated in the car, and then the conductor's voice was saying: "All is well. We're back on the train. All is well."

Mae recalled the brakemen and engineer examining the coupling on this very car. Perhaps, they had known it was defective.

Again the train lurched forward, and after a time came into the light and started up the steepest grade again. Mom squeezed Mae's hand, terror on her face. But this time the train leveled out and entered a long tunnel that the conductor said took them beneath the highest peak, beneath Donner Summit.

"Thank God for the brakes," Mae told Emma.

"Thank God, period," Emma returned in the darkness.

"Sorry about that trouble, folks," the conductor called. "This is Summit Tunnel. Normally by now I would'ov finished with the story of how Chinamen in hanging baskets drilled this tunnel—"

"Chinamen in baskets?" somebody exclaimed.

"To speed the work," the conductor said in the dark. "You heard about the race of the two railroads to lay track? One going east, the other west?"

He told how the workers had taken a locomotive engine apart and hauled the pieces to the top of the mountain above where the train now moved through the tunnel. They reassembled the engine and used its power to drill shafts down into solid rock through which they lowered the baskets, each with two workers. "One Chinaman drilled west, the other east. That made the work go faster. I heard tell they learned that in the China mountains. The railroad company learned it from them."

Not until the train emerged from Summit Tunnel and went down some long easy slopes on the other side of the mountain did Mae fully release her breath and regain her joy to be on the threshold of California.

In Sacramento they stepped off the train inside the cavernous station where several other trains steamed in temporary repose. The place reminded Mae of an oversized barn with people scurrying about like a huge flock of chickens. Everything echoed, the thumps of dropped bags, the squeak of handcarts, people chattering and calling to one another, iron doors slamming, and an occasional tenor cutting through with "All aboard!" After seven days on the railroad, Mae had become friends with some of the passengers, as had Mom and the boys. Now everyone said their farewells.

Collecting their luggage, the Duffys went outside. Amid a maze of tracks and all manner of buggies and rigs, they boarded an electric streetcar headed for the R Street Terminal. The trolley jerked and wobbled along a track parallel to a road lined with warehouses before which ten- to sixteen-horse teams drowsed in their harnesses while men packed the wagons with goods from the unseen river behind the buildings. Smokestacks and an occasional rim of an enormous paddle wheel was all Mae could see of the ships on the river. But she could feel the vitality of this port city.

They got off at the small terminal where they would wait over an hour to board the No. 9 to Folsom. To pass the time, the four of them went outside to see the wide Sacramento River and all the seagoing vessels, some coming, others departing for San Francisco. On a gangplank below them, a line of men passed gunnysacks hand-to-hand from a barge up the levee to a warehouse. "Wheat," Mom surmised.

The two-car train looked quaint after the transcontinental with its giant engines. This one chugged past the houses of Sacramento into open country as the conductor informed the passengers that this twenty-two-mile stretch had been California's very first railroad, "built by the Sacramento Valley Railroad Company back in fifty-six to accommodate the Gold Rush traffic."

"That there sign back there said it were the Southern Pacific," said the ever-curious Emmett with his persistent bad grammar.

"That's right, young fella. The SP bought this line and 'bout every other railroad in the state."

They passed farms and were suddenly dwarfed beside green vines atop a dizzying number of poles two stories high on both sides of the track. The giant plants draped over a netting of rope looked for all the world like Jack and the Beanstalk vines. "Just look at those beans!" Mom exclaimed.

A woman turned halfway around in her seat. "Them's hops."

Mae had never heard of hops. A cigar-like odor poured through the open windows and wagons came toward the train on the parallel road, each one piled high with crates stenciled MENKE HOPS. She leaned forward and asked the lady, "Do people eat hops?"

Turning, the lady wrinkled her nose. "I'll say not! They put it in beer. Sacramento's got breweries galore. Why, you could float a barge on the beer drunk there of a night. That's why we're moving back to Folsom." She turned forward, a child on either side of her.

Briefly the train stopped at Mills Station, then sped toward Folsom—total travel time under an hour. Waiting at the station for the spur line to Latrobe, Mae and Emmett stretched their legs on Sutter Street, the muddy main road through the town. Passing a saloon window they saw ladies in frilly frocks, no doubt ladies of the night. She grabbed Emmett by the arm and hurried him away. He laughed good-naturedly at her.

Back at the station, they boarded a little engine-car with a fat red smoke-stack. Emma, Farley, Emmett and Mae sat on a bench along one side of the car facing several people on the opposite bench. Very soon the houses of Folsom gave way to green hills stippled with what appeared to be enormous apple trees.

"I wonder what kind of trees those are," Mom said. Mae recalled those same trees when they were coming into Sacramento.

A gentleman opposite them said, "You must be new to California."

About Daddy's age, the man wore a waxed mustache, a high-collared white shirt and a brown pinstriped suit. One of his legs crossed over the other with the toe of a shiny brown shoe occupying the space between the benches. "Those are oak trees," he said. "You'll see them everywhere in the state, except the highest mountains and deserts."

"You have deserts in California?" Mom asked.

"Why yes, down in the southern part."

"Well thank you," Emma said with a gracious smile. "I appreciate knowing a little about our new home."

"Moving to Latrobe, are you?"

"We heard Dry Town was a good place. My husband, Mr. Duffy, arrived a week ahead of us. He's been securing employment and finding us a place to live. He'll be at the station to meet us."

"I see. Well, let me be the first to welcome you to Latrobe, the most up and coming town in the state if I do say so myself." He tipped his bowler hat. "The name's Miller. James Harrison Miller. Introduce Mr. Duffy to me and maybe I can help him in his search for employment."

"Why that's very considerate of you," Mom said. "Do you mean in Latrobe?"

"Yes, I own the hotel that houses the station." Passengers on both sides stifled smiles.

"How far is it to the gold fields," Emmett inquired of Mr. Miller.

As all the smiles blossomed with teeth, Mr. Miller said, "You're there."

The train whistled and wheezed into a town nestled in low hills, and Mae stepped down on a platform. Everyone headed across the tracks to where a sign proclaimed: MILLER HOTEL. The white two-storied building had an upstairs deck with a railing that wrapped all the way around it. People in rocking chairs were fanning themselves on the deck. In but a few hours California had gone from cold to hot, and Mae thought she finally understood the miner's song: *Sun so hot I froze to death; Susanna don't you cry.*

Daddy wasn't waiting in the lobby, nor was he outside with the other rigs. Mr. Miller disappeared into an office, and a round clock on the wall said five o'clock. Mom left Mae and the boys with the luggage while she talked to the hotel clerk.

Farley joked, "Don't see no gold yet."

"You don't see any gold," Mae corrected.

He gave her a stare that could have withered a horse, but she was used to it.

Mom returned. "Your dad won't be meeting us, so I bought us a ticket to Michigan Bar. He's staying there." She didn't seem perturbed, so Mae figured Daddy had an important appointment. Still, she felt sorry. She had missed him.

Mom led them outside to a high wagon with springs shaped like giant Indian bows placed belly to belly. This would be a smooth ride. The three-seater had a striped green canvas roof supported by tall poles. White lettering on the green omnibus read: LATROBE, MICHIGAN BAR, BRIDGE HOUSE, SLOUGH HOUSE, WALSH, PERKINS, SACRAMENTO. MR. ZUMWALT, PROPRIETOR.

The heavyset man helped them stow satchels and boxes under the seats, and then flicked the ribbons to start the team on the last leg of the long journey.

Farley inquired of him, "Where's the best gold mine?"

The man chuckled softly. "Alla yung men ask after golt."

Mom shushed the boys with a look, but Mae saw the gleam in her eye as she sat erect on the seat with the wagon floating over ruts and holes past the busy commercial establishments and the Simas Hotel.

10

Coyote stretches, hips high until his spine cracks. With a grunt he turns around and lies down. "People sure do love to travel," he says with a sniff.

"It stirs their blood," I tell him.

"They love to couple too," he says, "Mae was looking for it."

Mae speaks sternly from her motorcar, "My people don't think like that."

He unleashes a warbling howl.

I try to help. "She wanted a man to make her proud and provide a good home for her babies."

"Just what I said. All females are the same."

Mae gets in the last word. "I suffered from aspirations, is all."

❊❊

Mom paid for another room in the Ruman Hotel, across the hall from the one shared by Daddy, Hank and George. With a sweet smile she asked Mrs. Ruman, who was giving them a key, "Would you happen to know whether my husband is in?"

The slender gray-haired lady shrugged. "Try down the street at the saloon."

The furrows deepened between Mom's eyes. She thanked the woman, picked up her valise and struggled after Emmett, who followed Farley up the narrow staircase.

"Guess he wasn't very anxious to see us," Mae said in the echoing chamber of the stairs. She lugged her crate upward, securing her violin case on top with her chin.

Farley, arriving at the top with the heaviest crate, turned and said down to the others, "You're quick t'judge 'im. He could be meetin' someone at the saloon."

Mae recalled that Daddy liked his john barleycorn.

She and Emma set their luggage in the room overlooking the river while Farley and Emmett took their bags to the room across the hall. Mae quickly joined them.

George, sitting up from where he'd been resting on the bed, took his hands from behind his head. "Well, well. Look who's here!" A big smile stretched across his narrow Duffy face—small nose, high forehead, a hint of freckles.

"I expected you'd be out panning for gold," said Farley.

"Naw, I go at it with a pick. In the New Chicago Mine."

"Is that the name of your claim?" Mae asked.

George laughed. "It's the claim of a bunch of fancy pants in San Francisco. I work a hundred and sixty feet down under. Never seen nuthin' like it."

"Hank and Daddy work there too?"

"No, Hank—"

Mom opened the door and stuck her head. "Don't say anything. I mean to hear it all, but right now where's the privvy?"

George pointed. "All the way down the hall."

Mae needed to go too. She followed her mother to a small room with a flush toilet. Back in the hallway Mom put a finger on a window. "Mae, look. Can you fathom that?"

In a field of row crops below, ten or twelve people in bare feet and trousers cut off at the calf were stooped over, pulling weeds. Their round straw hats clung to their heads and she couldn't see their faces. She'd never seen unshod people of any kind working in a field.

Back in George's room, Farley and Emmett were telling about the journey. Mom stretched out on the bed, exhaled a long sigh, and said, "I can still feel the rails beneath me."

"Mom, I'm going to get Daddy," Mae said opening the door. Over her shoulder she flashed a grin at Farley. "Be sure to tell George how you two got stranded in the desert."

Mae changed into her purple striped frock with lace around the collar, returned to the boys' room, and got Emma to tighten her corset and fasten the buttons down the back. She glanced in the mirror, poked loose strands of hair into her updo, and skipped downstairs to the main street of Michigan Bar feeling like a lady of the Wild West.

The Ruman Hotel stood at the butt end of the town's main road, where it turned sharply to cross the Cosumnes River bridge, over which Mr. Zumwalt had just driven them. A person in the same kind of loose trousers and wide straw hat that Mae had seen in the field came trotting across the bridge toward her. This one held a long pole across his shoulders, from the ends of which swung two large baskets. His feet made soft thumps and the bridge bounced slightly with each step. The closer he came, the clearer she saw his thin mustache. By the eyes she knew he was Chinese. Only in a schoolbook had she seen those exotic people. Not to be caught staring, she walked up the boardwalk ahead of the little man. A loaded wagon rumbled toward them and turned onto the bridge. The crates were marked "Michigan Bar Pottery Works." Sections of clay pipe lay stacked in the wagon, secured by ropes.

This town looked much older than Reno. Most of the storefront establishments needed another coat of paint. All the men on the street looked at her, and she knew that she looked good. As she passed in front of HEATH & CO STORE, she heard Daddy singing "The Galway Piper" in the distance. She followed his voice to a saloon on the river side of the main street, the stores so close together she couldn't see the water.

With a hand on the swinging doors, she stood on her toes looking for Daddy as he sang in the smoke-filled interior. A sudden thought struck. She couldn't recall whether decent women in western novels went into saloons. And something else kept her from going in.

Daddy finished, "pi-i-ping Ti-im of Gal-waaay." As he sustained the last note, the clapping and whistling drowned him out, and she was thinking that he hadn't put himself out to meet her and Mom and the boys at the station. He was enjoying his barleycorn while she'd been looking for a warm hug and a big smile from him.

An unkempt fellow with a horse-face staggered out of his chair and lurched toward her. That did it; she decided to return to the hotel. She hurried across the street, up the boardwalk and ducked into Heath's Store where the shelves were loaded with goods all the way to the ceiling. A corner of the store, she noticed, was the U.S. Post Office, with a grid of decorative brass boxes and a Western Union Telegraph counter. No one else was in the store except a friendly middle-aged man.

Mr. Heath introduced himself, and Mae explained that she was new in town. She told how the family had come in two bunches. He said he'd met Mr. Duffy, and she gave back that she'd met Mr. Miller on the train.

"A fine family," said Mr. Heath. "Children about your age, or a mite older."

"Girls or boys?"

"Both." He smiled in a proprietary way. "Elizabeth's the oldest. Did he point out his house when the train went by?"

"No."

"A fine place. The best around here. but I understand the family moved out."

"You have a fine store," she said. Obviously she had evaded the ugly man. "I'll be back to see you soon."

Out on the boardwalk, somebody whistling a Stephen Foster tune came up from behind. The whistling stopped and the man clapped her on the shoulder.

With a start, she arranged her face in a frigid stare, then slowly turned, expecting to wither Horse-face. But it was a different man, smiling blue-eyed through a blackened face, the outlines of which were oddly familiar.

"Hank? Could that be you?"

He slapped his thigh laughing.

She laughed with him as they strolled to the hotel. He explained that he was returning from his work at Knight Foundry in Sutter Creek, and was covered with soot. Other men also seemed to be returning from work, one tying goods to his saddle at the rail in front of a butcher shop.

"Where're the horses?" she asked.

"Boarded at the livery stable, other end of town. Sorry we couldn't meet you at the station, but George works just this side of Dry Town and I work in Sutter's Creek. We need the horses to get back and forth."

"Oh." She had misjudged Daddy. That's why he hadn't been able to drive to the station. "What's a foundry?" she asked.

He gave her a look intended as ironic, but in blackface it was hilarious. She giggled as he delivered a comical speech.

"So you don't know what a foundry is? Mae of the books and fine school. Well, a foundry is a place where iron is melted and poured into sand moulds to make heavy equipment for the mines. You'd oughta see this one, Lady Duffy. Big as all git out, high ceiling of corrugated sheet iron." The humor left his voice, and he continued as though in awe of the place. "A crick runs through it, but that's not what turns the big wooden wheel with a wide belt and, by turns, all the others; it's the water comin' down from the high hill in wood troughs. Used for hydraulickin' in the sixties, but now it keeps the wheels of the foundry all a-turnin' to beat the band. Brings to mind the workins of a giant watch. You'd have to see it."

When they got upstairs in the hotel, Hank, in his exuberance to see Mom, just about picked her off the floor heavy as she was. She looked startled but happy.

Hank pulled out a pocketful of silver coins and spread them on the dressing table. "See that? My first pay! Supper's on me. There's an eatin' house down the road. But first, I gotta go scrub in the river."

∿

On the way to supper, the four boys fetched Daddy from the saloon, and they all walked to the opposite end of town.

George opened the door for the others, saying in a whisper, "Keep in mind, the proprietress here lost her mister in a horse accident several days ago."

In respect, everyone quieted down. Mrs. Clark, the owner and cook, seated them at a plank table and informed them that supper today was mutton stew with dumplings. She brought each of the males a mug of beer. Mae realized that something queer was happening. This was no longer a family of parents with five children, but a bunch of equal people. It felt good, like California was supposed to feel.

They exchanged news. Gramps poorly in Iowa, gold scarce in the river or covered up by hydraulic slickens. The only kind of panning men did any more was in the creeks, where they could find "flour gold," fine as milled flour, but only the Chinese had the patience to stick with that, being as how it paid so little. The big vegetable field behind the hotel was indeed worked by China-men, and many of them also worked for the hydraulic mining company. In fact, they made up the bulk of the workers. This led to a discussion of a Chi-natown across the river and the fact that the Duffy furniture and boxes were being stored over there for twenty-five cents a week, a figure that Mom said was too high, considering everything was out in the weather.

Mrs. Clark brought an iron pot of stew and a ladle. As they took turns helping themselves, others made admiring sounds at the tasty vegetables and the light dumplings.

"You got work yet?" Mom asked Daddy.

He finished chewing his mouthful. "Nothin' yet."

She launched into a spirited description of Mr. Miller and his offer to help. Mae contributed what she'd heard from Mr. Heath, concluding "the Millers are a very well-to-do family."

Daddy took it all in like it was mildly interesting.

Hank took a swig of beer, wiped his mouth on his sleeve, and said, "Dad, I think you'd oughta go on over there and see Mr. Miller. Why, they got stagecoaches and mule-trains acoming into Latrobe from ever which way. Mr. Miller knows all about the drivers and owners of the lines. He's friends with the railroad too, I heard. People around here say there wouldn't be no Latrobe atall without Mr. Miller. I b'lieve he's got a hand in every concern in these here parts."

"Hmmm. Mebbeso," Daddy said. "Doan know."

"What do you mean you don't know?" Mom demanded.

"Just that. Doan know."

"Don't know what? If you'll go see him?"

"I'm thinking on it."

Chewing a hunk of gristle, George weighed in. "Maybe we'd oughta men-tion the money situation."

Emma's brows came together. "Go ahead."

George exchanged a glance with Hank.

Hank, the eldest, seemed to grant him permission to talk. George leaned hard on his fork to separate mutton from gristle. "Well, the hotel's too dear and the horses is eatin' up a bundle at the livery stables, here and in Sutter Creek and New Chicago where me and Hank are workin'. We've about used up all we started with and, well, I don't think we oughta live so damned high on the hog, in a hotel. Anyhow the Rumans is about to throw us out." He popped the meat in his mouth and chewed like it was leather.

"Whatever's got into you?" Mom countered. "That woman would have told us such at thing when we checked in."

With George's mouth occupied, Hank filled in, "She ain't likely to do the hard talkin'. Ask Mr. Ruman. But Dad, Mom, here's the thing. My butt's wore out ridin' back and forth to work fifteen miles. I found a place over there, and I'm moving in tomorra. Just wanted to see you got here all right." He cleared his throat. "You see, well, I'm twenty-four now and it's about time I was saving up for a life of my own."

George gave him a pained look.

The two boys stared at each other for quite some time, and then Hank grinned in a giving-up way.

"Aw, all right. I met a girl." He put his fork down and rubbed his palms on his thighs—a sure sign he was nervous—but a smile cracked his freckled face, not a joking smile but a happy one. Hank was serious about this girl.

"That's awful sudden, isn't it?" Mom asked with a frown.

In a burst of laughter that he could no longer contain George sang out, "It were love at first sight!" He made disgusting kissing sounds at Hank.

Hank turned red, but smiled nonetheless.

∽

By the time they got back to the hotel the sun was down and Mr. Ruman stood at the counter. Daddy and the boys went upstairs. Mr. Ruman said a number of investors were coming to town tomorrow with reservations for the entire second floor. He added that he knew of some unused cabins in the area, and if the Duffys made friends with the owners, in exchange for a little work they might be able to occupy a place for free. He turned over an envelope and started to draw a map.

"Free houses? Are they decent?" Emma asked. "Big enough for all of us?"

"You'll have to go see for yourselves." Mr. Ruman continued drawing.

"I mean," Emma insisted, "we've got five, well at least four, employable men here, including my husband who is about the best stagecoach driver in the country, and I'd think we could pay enough rent for a decent house." She smiled nicely. "Don't mean to be ungrateful though, for the suggestion."

Handing Mom the envelope, Mr. Ruman said, "The stage lines I know of around here already have drivers. And there are men that drive their own stagecoaches. Some drive their own freight wagons. Your husband could haul ore and gravel from the mines to the railroad, but he'd be competing with Indians who work for next to nothing. It's none of my business, but your mister told me he wasn't likely to do that kind of work."

Mae understood why Daddy had gone upstairs. She also thought about the land in Iowa that would be split between Daddy and Ephraim someday soon. Daddy could sell his share to his brother for cash or payments to hold them over.

This had never been a talkative family, but in the hotel room that night they talked. George preferred to move to New Chicago near the stamp mill where he worked, even though "That there noise day and night'd drive a man loony, or deaf." Mae wanted to live in Latrobe, a bigger and better looking town than Michigan Bar. Daddy thought the best prospects for Farley and Emmett were in Michigan Bar. So they compromised and agreed to move into one of the free cabins and stay there only until they saved a little money and decided where the new house should be.

The next morning was Sunday, and they all looked at a cabin about half a mile downstream of the hydraulic operations. The owner, a friend of Mr. Ruman's, walked with them, telling them how a prospector had built the cabin of the prevalent shale, stacking it without mortar. On top, beams had been placed side by side, and heavy slate laid on top.

This one-room, one-window place, Mae realized as they looked at it, was surely more disreputable than the stone cabin Gramps had left in Ireland. It stood back from the river in the midst of what had once been hills. If hills could cry out, these would be screaming. They'd been cut down with water cannons into unearthly shapes and angles, the muddy slurry washed down the river. One positive aspect of the cabin, however, was that the landowner said they could picket the horses on the grassy bottomland downstream. In exchange the boys would cut wood for the owner.

Inside, the spider-infested cabin made her skin crawl, but she told herself this was temporary. Daddy rode Pal, with Belle in tow, over the bridge to Chinatown to recover the wagon and some of the furniture. When he returned with the loaded wagon, the boys filled up the cabin with two narrow beds and two kitchen chairs placed back to back between the beds. The kitchen table, sundry chairs, and the many crates with the family's belongings they set up outside. There wasn't even a nail on which to hang the old washtub. The boys would sleep in an old tent that Mae hadn't seen before—Ed and Emma had camped in it before Hank.was born, when Daddy was still driving stage.

"We might as well put up a sign that says, Welcome to Poverty," Mae remarked to no one in particular. No California Joe would court her while she lived in such a place, so her dream would have to wait.

That evening before sundown Emmett took the frying pan to the river to "wash gold." He later told Mae that he was stopped by an old-timer who told him that gold couldn't be panned in a frying pan. "Grease gets in the pores," he'd said, "so the flour gold can't stick. And Hank and George were right. The slickens buries the gold so's it's too hard to find."

At dawn the next morning the boys hitched up the wagon. The four brothers and Mae rode through rolling oak grasslands, brown from the heat, to the place called the New Chicago Mine—an industrial site surrounded by a clutter of tin shacks and a couple of actual houses. Full of smiles, Hank yelled good-bye and commenced walking the last three miles to Sutter's Creek. Mae wondered when she'd see him again. He would go to his ladylove. It was romantic.

Farley landed work right then and there on the doorstep of the mine manager's office. George vouching for him was all it took. Emmett could have signed up too, but he shook his head and plugged his ears against the intense racket of steel stamping through rock. So Mae and Emmett drove the wagon back to Michigan Bar.

Two days later the family received a postal card from George. He and Farley had rented an abandoned shack made of pine back when pine trees had been plentiful. With picks in hand and carbide lanterns on their hats they were working deep down in the earth.

Four days later Farley showed up at the cabin, having walked. He told Mae and the folks that it was the worst job he ever saw, and he wasn't about to spend his summer daylight hours shivering down in cold and damp. "It ain't natural," he declared. He looked into the two large enterprises in Michigan Bar, the High Hill Mining Company and the Michigan Bar Pottery Works, the latter making use of the clay unearthed by the former. High Hill hired Farley to help direct the water in the heavy hoses. He was lucky to get the work, because most of the workers were Chinese.

Perhaps Daddy was also looking for work, asking the men he met in saloons if they'd heard about something, but he kept putting off his trip to Latrobe. "Might as well finish looking around here first," he said.

Every day Mae rode Pal to Heath's Store to check for mail at the Post Office counter. On the seventh day Mr. Heath handed her a large envelope addressed to Mr. Edward Duffy. The return address said: Justice of the Peace, Alton, Iowa. With an uneasy feeling she carried it to the cabin.

Daddy was ready to go to town, but he sat on an outside chair and read the first page. He looked up over the heads of Emma, Mae and Emmett, his eyes bluer than ever, and said, "My dad died."

He turned the oversized page slowly. Minutes passed in which he seemed to stare at the writing rather than read. Meanwhile Mae's mind wavered between the sad fact that Gramps was gone and the realization that with the inheritance, the family would soon move to a decent house. Daddy pointed to the page and handed the document to Emma.

Reading a minute, Mom looked up and said in a monotone, "He left everything to Ephraim."

Everything.

"Ed," she said, "we've both been disowned."

11

Daddy lost his temper every time Mom hinted he should look for work. By day he sat in a chair that Mr. Heath kept on the boardwalk outside his store, visiting with anyone who happened by and reading the newspapers left by others. At night when he could get money from the boys, he drank whisky in one of Michigan Bar's saloons, and when he had no money he went anyway. Other men bought him beer so he'd entertain them. He sang the Irish songs and told the spellbinding tales of his stagecoach days, complete with holdups and close shaves with Indians. His days in the Black Hills, Mae came to realize, had become his life's monument, to which he often returned with a faraway look in his eye and a special tone in his voice. As for employment, he had a ready excuse. My health, he would say with the palm of his hand on his chest. One time Mae heard him tell Mom, "The boys are grown. They can support me for a change."

Emmett left the cabin with his bedroll slung over his shoulder. He said he would work on the Misers' sheep ranch a few miles away. "Not even a man with a sluice box can pan enough gold to feed hisself," he grumbled. "The independent miner can't compete with the big companies."

Mae walked with him through Michigan Bar, stopping halfway across the bridge. She had a panicky feeling that she wouldn't see much of him again. The way it came out was, "Farley's the only one left to home now." Emmett knew that she and Farley didn't get along.

"Whatcha gonna do?" He kicked a pebble and she heard the faint splash below.

"I don't know. I can't just head out like you're doing, being female and all. But when I'm around the folks in that place, I feel like I can't breathe. I know girls are supposed to stay and take care of parents." *In a comfortable house paid for by the parents.* Thinking how far the family had fallen in such a short time, she felt tears welling.

Emmett twisted his face like it was a puzzle he couldn't solve. He patted her on the shoulder and then walked away. She watched him cross the rest of the bridge and trudge up the hill and disappear around a bend.

That afternoon Daddy came to the cabin and told Mae he'd learned that the Driscolls needed a hired girl. "Go on over there," he said, "and they'll take you in."

Hired girl! "But Daddy, I want to graduate from high school."

He sat on a kitchen chair outside the cabin. "There ent no high school around here. Besides, it's summer. Get some money ahead, then go to Sacramento High School." He pulled off his shoes, "That's how it's done hereabouts."

She looked to Mom in the shade of the cabin. She had always seen to Mae's interests. Now she pushed the rocker with her bare toes, up and down, her half-gray hair streaming past her elbows. She had fallen into melancholy. "Promise it'll be temporary," Mae begged. "My being a hired girl."

Mom's face was blank. Gone was the mother who'd made a fifty-mile round-trip to Orange City to buy her a special gown and fix her hair.

Daddy leaned back on the hind legs of his chair until it stopped at the uneven shale of the cabin wall. Mae wished him out of that chair and on his way to work someplace. Any place.

⁓

The next morning Mae pulled on an old frock, now uncomfortably tight across her chest and short of her high-topped shoes. "It's folly to wear good clothes to do dirty work," Daddy had said. She threw some things into her quilt, slung it over her shoulder, managed a civil nod his direction, and left with resentment pinching her heart. Fathers were supposed to work.

A couple of Chinese, hydraulickers by their hip-high rubber boots, met her on the trail as she walked to the little town of Bridge House. The Driscoll place was on the north side of the river, so she had to cross the bridge and then go upstream a piece. The fresh air felt like any June morning in Iowa, but doubt and humiliation slowed her steps. She'd done enough housework to know she hated it, and she worried about minding a newborn baby and other little children, which she'd never done before.

The path led to a cluster of buildings on Jackson Road. She passed a store with a so-called California porch across the entire front. The false front above the porch bore the painted words: BRIDGE HOUSE: MERCANTILE, DANCE HALL, SALOON, STAGE & TOLL STATION. The man on the porch would be the toll taker; however, pedestrians crossed free of charge.

The little town had a few houses, and people were watching. Embarrassed by her old frock and bare head—only poor girls went about hatless in June— Mae hurried onto the AUSTIN WIRE BRIDGE, as the small sign called it, and looked down at the water about thirty feet below.

The bridge perched on high rocky outcroppings on both sides of the little river, which had obviously carved out this stony gorge, though the flow was weak now and full of brown slickens. People said no rain had fallen since mid-March. To Mae, this seemed a dangerous drought, but Californians considered a six-month stretch without rain to be normal. Just after she stepped off the bridge at the other end, she came to a fork in the road.

A stagecoach clattered toward her, raising a cloud of dust. As the hooves thundered by and drummed across the bridge, she leaned over and wiped dirt from her eyes with the hem of her skirt. When she looked up, a farm wagon was stopping beside her. Apparently, it had come across the bridge behind her. Her eyes met the brown eyes of the young driver, nice eyes.

"Y'all goin' fur?" he asked, not waiting for an answer. "I'd be 'bliged t'give you a ride. Name's John Dunaway." He lifted his damaged straw hat.

Something about him put her at ease, like she was talking to Emmett. "No, thank you. I'm almost there."

"Where?"

That was a nosey question, but his expression was friendly. By the tattered clothing and his grammar, she knew he was poor. She didn't want to encourage his attentions. "Up there on that little hill," she lied, flicking a hand in front of her.

"Oh, the Pratts. Have a good day." He lifted his hat again and clicked his team onward.

She passed two small houses before she came to the top of the hill where a whitewashed farmhouse stood half surrounded by a wraparound porch and several outbuildings. A slim, older woman kneeled in a garden at the side of the house, weeding vegetables.

"I wonder if you would be so kind as to direct me to the Driscoll place."

The woman straightened up and eyed her. "I don't say this to everyone comin' down the road, but you can cut through our place, out there past that Chinaman by the sheepcamp." She pointed a long bony finger. "Go past that there eucalyptus tree and you'll see another place off to the right a little. That's the Driscolls an' Granlees. You'll see their big barn by the dry crick to the left."

"Much obliged," Mae said, thinking she'd rather be going anywhere else. The ubiquitous oaks she recognized, so she figured that the more upright tree had to be the eucalyptus.

On a floor without walls stood a tiny covered wagon with a chimney poking through the canvas. A Chinese man sat on a chair before the little vehicle scraping what appeared to be lambskin. She nodded to him and hurried past.

With the reticence of a dunce sent to the corner, she arrived at her destination—the back wall of a single-story house made of planed wood of a pinkish hue. She followed a beaten path between the end of the house and what appeared to be a wall of yellow sandstone with a door, a dugout built into a small hill. On top of that hill stood a colossal oak with huge branches shading the redwood house as well as the dugout. She walked around to the front of the house, its California porch awash in morning sunshine. A hand pump stood beside the stairs of the porch. At least she wouldn't be hauling water from the river.

"You Mae Duffy?" a female voice called.

Mae couldn't tell where the voice came from. The sun was glancing off the front windows, blinding her, "Yes."

"C'mon in. I'm changing the baby."

The door was ajar. Mae pushed it open and stepped into a dark room bisected by a parallelogram of sunlight on the floor. As her eyes adjusted she made out several chairs of various kinds and three boys in overalls, the largest of them school-age, the youngest maybe three. Their blond heads all needed combing.

Presently a small woman clumped into the living room on one normal shoe and the other built up four or five inches on a wooden sole. She had a newborn baby in her arms. "I'm Mary Granlees," she said without a smile. "Been expecting you." She tossed her head to get the fine brown hair out of her eyes. "These here're m'kids." She nodded at the boys and slightly lifted the baby. "This is Agnes Hilda Granlees. Follow me."

Mae followed the limping woman through a door to the kitchen, where a washtub of clothing boiled on the stove and steam went out the open window. A short, dark-skinned young woman stood looking at Mae while stirring the contents of the washtub with a heavy stick. She wore an antiquated black dress with a full skirt. Her dark auburn hair was cut off at the shoulders and trimmed across her brows, and her black eyes looked tired above her slightly aquiline nose.

"Indian Mary," Mrs. Granlees said with a nod at the young woman. "Mae, I want you to take over here in the kitchen. Finish the wash, help with the youngsters. That all right with you?" Her blue eyes looked out of a face that quite possibly had never smiled. The baby started to cry.

"Uh, all right," Mae stammered. This didn't seem the right time to press her for the pay arrangements. She would wait for a quiet time.

"Good." Mary Granlees flicked her hand at Indian Mary. "Go along now."

Murmuring something about being Isabella, the young Indian wiped her damp face on her skirt and left.

When the screen door slammed shut at the front of the house, Mary Granlees confided, "You'll be a better influence on the boys. That half-breed comes in with liquor on her breath. Leaves her own baby with her mother. Old Indian Mary's a better sort. Full-blooded."

Thus began two weeks of the hardest work Mae had ever done. She slept with the boys in their room, got up in the night to help five-year-old Georgie to the outhouse, or to change his sheet if she was too late. She rarely got enough sleep, and dragged through the days going from drudgery to crisis and back again by turns. Georgie ran away every chance he got. He nearly drowned in the river. He cut his face trying to shave with his dad's straight razor. He came close to falling down the Pratt's well. Mae found him screaming and hanging onto the windlass that rolled up the bucket. He drank himself into a stupor on old man Driscoll's snake oil medicine, which had an odor like tar and licorice—the old man being Mary Granlees' pioneer father.

When Mary Granlees was exasperated with Georgie, she took off her shoe with its layers of wood and smacked his behind with it. She then pled with Mae to get the bawling child out of her hair. "No rest for the wicked," Mary often lamented.

Besides running after Georgie, every day Mae was to wash the diaper rags, the sheets with urine stains, grimy towels, and the stinking overalls and shirts of the two men in the house. She was also assigned the churning of butter in little barrels, not only for family use, but for sale in Sacramento. Mr. Driscoll, Mary's father, drove the butter and milk to Sacramento each morning before dawn. In addition, Mae was to make the beds, keep the floors clean, and see that there was wood beside the kitchen stove at all times. That involved keeping the local woodcutter, Mr. Peevey, informed of the exact height of the wood stack—measured with a yardstick. As if that wasn't enough, Mr. Driscoll asked her to soap the tack of the workhorses in the barn.

This she did while trying to watch Georgie in a barn full of hazards for little children—loft ladders, pitchforks, and a crotchety old horse. Additionally, three men had opened the side wall of the barn and were in the process of building an extension. They had piled a bunch of boards with protruding nails, and Mae was having a hard time keeping the little boy from climbing on it. No wonder Mary Granlees never smiled!

Mae shook her finger at Georgie and said, "Now you stay where I can see you, hear? And don't go near those boards."

In the sunlight coming from the open barn, one of the men, who appeared to be in his late thirties or early forties, turned and looked at her with green eyes. He had straight black hair to his shoulders, which made him look Indian, as did his callused bare feet; but she liked his face. When he spoke, his voice was quiet and rich. "I used the soap this mornin' so that tin's not enough. I'll go get the other one."

He turned and went to a dark corner of the barn. When he returned with another tin of saddle soap he kept his eyes down as he handed it to her.

"I'm Mae," she said, surprising herself. "What's your name?"

"Billy."

She turned away wondering what had gotten into her to speak to him like that.

Later, she pounded mashed potatoes in chicken broth until the mixture was like milk.

"I don't have enough milk," Mary explained. "I'm not a good mother. Buried my first baby. On Jack, I learned to give 'em chicken broth and mashed potatoes. They don't like it. They're sickly 'til they can eat other food. So I try to get 'em to take a little milk too."

Mary Granlees couldn't do much work because of trying to nurse or force-feed that crying baby. The skinny little thing screamed all the time, turning red, kicking her stick-like legs, and waving her arms as though she was being tortured.

At the end of the first week Mae forced herself to ask Mrs. Granlees how much she would be paid.

"You mean actual money?" The tough little woman looked surprised.

"I was hoping to save money to go to Sacramento High School."

"Wasn't my understanding you was to get money too, besides bed and board. I spoke to the man who talked to yer daddy."

"Oh," was all Mae could muster, fingering her sore, reddened hands.

That evening she heard Mary Granlees tell her father, "A body's 'bliged t'follow that girl around to see she don't leave dirt in the corners. And what's more, she can't cook a meal worth eatin' if her life depended on it. Old man, get youself to bed."

"Don't send that girl packing without another to take her place," the old man said in his Irish accent.

Small and crippled though she was, Mary Granlees had steel in her. It showed in her eyes, and Mae didn't dare cross her, though it brought tears to her eyes to be talked about like that—and within hearing range. One benefit of being a hired girl, she had imagined, was to live in a happier place than her own sad cabin. Not so here. Father and daughter got on all right, but not daughter and husband.

Mae learned that old man Driscoll, the Irish settler, had built the dugout when he first came to California and prospected for gold in the river. Then he got married and built this larger redwood house. Nearly twenty years ago his wife had died. A sandy-gray shock of hair stood straight up from his head, and he had a bald spot in back. Little Georgie said at the table one day, "Grandpa's hair fell off backwards," which brought a ghost of a smile to Mary's lips, the first smile Mae had seen on an adult in more than a week. The old man's beard didn't quite reach his belt buckle, but unlike Gramps, this rail-thin Irishman had a sour twist to his puss. Mae was glad when he came in for supper too tired to upset people with accusations about things not getting done right. Every evening he finished shoveling food through the hairy hole of his mouth, pushed the plate away, crossed his arms on the table, and laid his head down to sleep, always with a few strands of mustache or head-hair in the gravy or butter. Mae would remove the dirty plate and leave him like that until Mary and her husband got under his arms and walked him to the back bedroom. If the husband were gone, as he frequently was, Mae would act as one of the crutches.

Robert Granlees, Mary's husband, didn't work as hard as his father-in-law. Plenty of times he'd be on the porch taking his ease with a harmonica before supper. Once when the family was at the table and Mae was dishing out seconds from the stove, he leaned back in his chair, balancing on the chair's hind legs and the toes of his shoes, and said, "I'm going over to see June about that money they owe me."

Mary narrowed an eye at him. "What'll you do with the money?"

"It's my money and I'll do with it as I damn well please."

By now the old man was snoring at the table.

"I'll not have you wakin' the boys when you get in," Mary warned with a steely glare.

"Oh no?" He rocked his chair forward, stood up, and strode out, pulling his hat from the peg on the wall.

ᔌ

That night when everyone was in bed, Mae was awakened by a loud female voice, "Don't you raise your hand to me!"

"BULLSHIT!" Answered a male voice so loud it reverberated in the house.

The three boys sat up, Georgie whimpering. Mae got up and went to his cot to comfort the little boy. Bert whispered to his older brother Jack, "What's he gunna do to her?"

"Dunno," said Jack.

A big thump shook the near wall, accompanied by a female moan. Another thump on a more distant wall quickly followed.

"Now get up and gitcher sorry self to bed," Mr. Granlees roared.

Mary must have done it, because the house went quiet.

The next day Mary Granlees clumped around a little slower. She sent Jack to the Pratt place to fetch Old Indian Mary, the mother of the one who wasn't a good influence on the children. A wrinkled, dark-skinned woman arrived shortly.

Mary Granlees accompanied Mae to the cheese house, as the dugout was called, and picked out potatoes for the noon dinner. She put them in the swale of Mae's frock. It was cool within the stone walls and pleasantly scented from the curdling cheese—some called it cottage cheese. The earthern floor with piles of potatoes and onions yielded a rich aroma. For light, they'd left the door open. At the roofline on either side of this single room, two small windows let in more light, though they were too dirty to do much good. As for a stove, Mr. Driscoll must have cooked outside when he lived here. A bed, a chair, and a trunk would have filled the room.

"Old Indian Mary will work here each morning, "Mary Granlees said. "She'll leave when Georgie goes down for his nap. The extra pair of hands will help." She selected eggs that the boys collected each morning, put them in her apron, and left.

Indians worked for food, as everyone knew. Mae still had hurt feelings over what was said about dirt in the corners and her bad cooking; and now, clutching the potatoes in her skirt and shutting the door behind her, she followed Mary Granlees back to the house, realizing that the old Indian woman would do the same work she had been doing, supposedly doing it better, and get less money than Mae wanted to earn. This didn't augur well. She found the nerve to catch up to Mrs. Granlees and say, "I was hoping to get some pay for working here."

"You been eatin' good and sleepin' on a decent bed. Most girls don't expect pay. They meet a man and get married. Why didn't you say somethin' about that the first day? We would'ov got another girl."

"It never seemed the right time to say anything."

"Well, I'll ask my dad. Meantime, wipe up the floor before you put Georgie down. He peed all over it. And then beat the front room rugs."

Mae tasted grit as she beat the sand and dust out of the rugs. Mom's words came back to her: *Marry a man with land.* These people had land, but it was a poor life for the woman.

Late the next morning Mary Granlees told her to scrub the kitchen floor. "Work around her at the stove." She tilted her head toward old Indian Mary, who was peeling potatoes into a pan of water.

With resentment rising like a fist in her throat, Mae scrubbed around wide bare feet so thick with callus that people called it horn. Some referred to such feet as hooves. Old Indian Mary stepped aside for her. To think that she would be on her hands and knees while a barefoot squaw did the easy work! *She's here because I'm a failure and maybe it's true.* Mae realized she hadn't been trained to do housework, nor did she want that training. Quite the contrary, she wanted to play the piano and be a lady. She needed to quit this torture. Money or not, tubs of boiling water, lye soap that peeled her hands, and a crying baby with messy diapers, were about to make her lose her mind. How did women stand this all of their lives? And nothing more to vary the days than snot-nosed children running you ragged. This was not the life for her.

"The water's filthy," Mary Granlees said, having returned to the kitchen. "Change the water." That meant more work at the hand pump.

Straightening her aching knees, she got to her feet and looked directly into Mary's blue eyes.

"Well then, I guess you can change it yourself. I'm done here, and if you can find a couple of dollars to pay me for this last two weeks, I'd be obliged." She dropped the brush in the dirty water, splashing on both of them, and found herself looking not only into Mary Granlees' eyes, but also Indian Mary's. The latter seemed to be telling Mae something without moving her lips.

When Mary Granlees clumped angrily out of the kitchen, the old Indian woman spoke so quietly that only Mae could have heard. "When Georgie sleep, you, me go talk." She pointed out the window.

12

Mae followed old Indian Mary through Pratt land. Ah Chung, whittling on the step of his sheepcamp, raised a hand to Mary as she passed. A small cabin she hadn't noticed before stood off to the right before they went down the incline through scrub oaks and rocks and clumpy bunchgrass into the river bottomland. Mae followed those brown feet with a full inch of callus. Mary sat on a rock situated in the damp sand bordering the river and motioned to the adjacent rocks.

Curious about what would follow, Mae chose a block of brown stone with orange stripes and sat on it. Grass had sprouted along the lapping shoreline. About a hundred yards downstream, the iron truss bridge spanned the river.

Mary seemed content within herself, not uttering a word even though she'd done the inviting.

"You must live around here," Mae offered by way of small talk.

Now that the work was over, she felt a thrill of release and something more—danger, impropriety, or both. Mom had told her about how Indian men in loincloths used to take the wash off her line in Dakota Territory. When Emma rushed outside yelling, "No, no, no. Mine!" they laid the clothing in her arms and left. Not long afterwards those same Indians and hundreds more attacked General Custer and killed every last one of his troops. Relations between the races had never been the same again, but Emma always vouched for the basic good nature of those Indians. She said they had grown up taking whatever they wanted from the countryside, and the wash on a clothesline seemed no different to them than the wild plums in the trees. Now, sitting beside Mae, was a very different kind of Indian.

Indian Mary nodded. Yes. She lived nearby. Her eyes followed the river as it flowed under the bridge. Her dark face was broad with a small flat nose tucked neatly between her wide soft cheeks. Mae recalled the daughter's skin being lighter, her face narrower, and her hair dark auburn. "Your daughter doesn't look like you," Mae said.

Mary Granlees had called the daughter a half-breed.

The old woman continued to watch the sun-spangled river.

Mae repeated what she'd said, thinking that perhaps she understood only pidgin English, which Mary Granlees used with her.

"You daughter name Isabella?" Mae said it with embarrassment, knowing she couldn't speak pidgin like those who'd always lived around here.

"Yes. Isabella," the old woman said.

"But they call her Mary?"

"Many white ladies name Mary. Inyuns name Mary too." The smile made her look jolly.

"Maybe they don't know her name is Isabella."

The old woman shrugged again, the universal gesture.

"Your house, where?"

Mary pointed with her head. "Yonder."

Mae pointed toward Bridge House, which couldn't be seen beyond the high rocks. "By the town?"

"This side the river."

Mae let the silence come between them while birds whistled and the river rushed around the boulders.

"You wanna work at Driscoll place long time?" Old Mary asked.

So that was it. "No. Not another minute. I wanna teach piano."

"Umm," Mary said, "Miss Miser have piano."

"My brother works for Isabella Miser."

Indian Mary nodded. "Isabella Miser."

"Does she have children?"

"You betcha. Children from her children too."

Grandchildren. "Where is the Miser place?"

With a finger Mary drew a quick map in the damp sand, showing the trail east from the Driscolls, which led to a stream emptying into the river. She added a handful of sand, showing an elevated ridge along the stream. "Big house," Mary said, denting the sand with her brown finger.

Given the major points on this map, Mae realized the cabin in which her parents lived was probably as near to the Misers as to the Driscoll-Granlees place.

"You mother, father live by here?" The old woman asked.

"In a cabin upriver. Bad house!"

The old woman looked at Mae with obvious compassion. "Doan live in bad house. Sometime bad house make people sick."

"Yes!" Mae agreed. "That house is not healthy. Do you live in a good house?"

"Ho. Good house. *Cudja.* Good. Big tree. Spirit good."

Mae looked at the woman, who continued to look at the river. "My mother is sick." She placed her hand over her head, and then her heart. "She sick here, and here." It felt good to talk to someone about Mom, someone outside the white world.

Indian Mary nodded knowingly. Several minutes passed, the river gurgling. "Bad house," Indian Mary pronounced. "You mother and father no oughtta live dere no more.

"We have no money for a better house," Mae said, realizing she had no need to speak pidgin. This woman understood everything. She'd just been slow to start talking. Far from her earlier feelings of insult and denigration, Mae now felt an easy sense of being part of the day, sitting here in the shade of a cottonwood tree with the cotton floating around them, gathering like dust bunnies in the rocks and behind deadfall branches. It planted seeds without effort. Time had seemingly come to a stop—this river, this sunlight, this gentle breeze, two women whose age and race didn't seem to matter.

"Where bad house?" Indian Mary asked.

Mae pointed up the river on the opposite bank. "Not far from Michigan Bar. Made of shale rock. Full of spiders. It's got a dirt floor and one window."

"Door on west side?"

"Hmm. I'm not sure."

"West side where sun he go down."

"Yes. The door's on this side. That's the house."

"Baad house," old Mary agreed, nodding vigorously. "Man build house with fren. Kill fren in house. Bad spirit in house. Mebbe bad spirit get you mother, father. Bad house."

Mae had opened this subject with a completely different meaning of a bad house, but now this other meaning seized her. Everyone knew that some houses were haunted. Daddy wouldn't want to live in a haunted house —Gramps had told of an Irish banshee spirit that screamed and chased the living until they died of fright. But where would the folks move?

As though hearing her question, Old Indian Mary pushed off her rock and said, "You come. See good house."

"You mean your house?"

She shook her gray-streaked shoulder-length hair. "No. Mebbe house for you. Come see."

"But we have no money to rent a house," Mae said, rising.

"Mebbe house cost no money."

"Do you pay for your house?"

"No. You come." She set off at a fast pace, her horned feet treading over rock and prickle without a flinch, and the frayed hem of her frock swishing past the bunch grasses as they ascended the bank to the level of the bridge. Mae realized that this woman's California roots went back to time immemorial. Of course she knew all the cabins and what happened to the people in them.

Quickly they crossed the bridge. Indian Mary turned right and followed a footpath behind the dancehall side of the store. The path led between several small cabins. The nicer houses had been built along the road. She stopped before an abandoned shack with a crooked smokestack jutting askew from a flat roof. A broken crate lay before the door, and thick spider webs draped the unglazed windows.

Indian Mary stepped over the crate to the threshold and pushed the door. It creaked and swung wide, showing a dirt floor. She turned to Mae, smiled a mouthful of good white teeth, and said, "Good house."

If that's a good house, Mae thought, we should stay where we are.

"Come look inside," Indian Mary was saying.

"No," Mae said shaking her head.

"Good man lived here."

"What about that one?" Mae pointed to a frame cabin about twenty yards away. Also vacant, that one was built off the ground and stood plumb. Thick webs draped across the broken windows, but the door looked squared and tightly shut.

Mary appeared to be in deep thought. By now Mae knew she would speak when she had something she wanted to say.

"Doan know," Mary finally said of the better house. "Mebbe no dollah. Mebbe bad spirit. Doan know."

"I'm going to look in." Mae walked over to it, picked up a stone from a decorative line of similar white stones, possibly making the edge of an old flowerbed, and with it parted the spider webs, allowing her to see inside. There was a plank floor thick with dust, and good plank walls. No holes in the walls. This house would be well worth the move.

Indian Mary continued to stand near the first cabin.

"What's wrong with this place?" Mae called. "Why isn't anyone living here?"

"Blood," Mary said. "Big blood." With the index fingers she traced a circle in front of her as far as her arms would reach. "On floor. Blood from man. Got shot."

"Oh my, a man murdered here too?"

"No. He was shot in river."

"Where?"

She pointed up the river. "Byem bad house. Friends take him home on horse. Put him down on floor." She pointed to the house Mae was inspecting. "Blood on floor. He die good, with his wife, his children, his friends. Good peoples. They bury him good."

Indian Mary seemed lost in thought, staring past Mae's shoulder.

"Did you know that man, the one that was killed?"

The old woman dipped her head. *Yes.* "Good man. His fren good. His fren my man. Now I go my house." She turned and walked swiftly up the path without saying good-bye.

Following her long enough to see her crossing the bridge, Mae went into Bridge House Store. Just as she'd hoped, the proprietor was alone. The small man with a pale complexion answered her questions. She learned the name of the murdered man, Jared Sheldon. He had built the cabin to give his wife and babies a place to stay while he was building a dam about a mile upstream. His main house was in Slough House. He died in a gunfight over the dam. When the shooting started, a ball entered one side of Sheldon's chest, under his arm, and went out under the other arm.

"Took a while before he give up the ghost," the store proprietor said. "His friends brought him back to that cabin and stretched him out on the floor. He bled to death before the eyes of his little wife and three youngins. His lifeblood spread out and soaked the floorboards. The stain's still there. Folks doan wanna live there on account of it, being superstitious and all. That were in fifty-one."

"Sounds like you were here then."

He shook his head. "No, but that's the story folks told when I got here."

"Where can I find the owner of that cabin?"

He scratched his head, patted the few hairs back in place, and said, "Ask down in Slough House. Anybody can point the way to William Chauncey Sheldon's place. That's the dead man's son. He's built himself a mansion. Well, that's all I know about it."

∽

Mae returned to the Driscoll-Granlees house. Careful not to wake Georgie, she tied her things in her blanket. Mary Granlees followed her to the door with baby Agnes on her hip. The built-up shoe was holding that side of her weight as she stood in the threshold.

Mae said, "You got any money for me?"

"Nope. Sorry."

"Well, I'm sorry to be leaving you," she lied. "Just wanted to get my things and say good-bye." *And I hope your husband doesn't kill you.*

Mary Granlees' flipped the long straight hair off her face and said nothing.

"If you need me for emergencies, I suppose I might be able to come back for a day or two." It took all Mae's strength to utter those words.

Mary lowered her chin and raised it in a slow nod. "Some girls can't do this kind of work. Heaven help them when they get married."

~

Heaven help them when they get married dogged Mae's footsteps on the mile or so back to the shale cabin. Sweating the whole time and headachy from lack of sleep, she did not look forward to telling the family she had failed as a hired girl.

The washtub lay upside down on the bare earth beside the cold fire, dented all the more for having been used as a stool. Two broken demijohn barrels that Daddy thought he could restore and sell if he ever got around to it lay in the yard, along with Farley's frayed trousers and a disorderly pile of gear—old tack, a broken thunder mug, a bent cooking pot, mismatched straps for hitching the horses to a wagon, a couple of switches. All sorts of clothing hung from the tie ropes of the tent, some having fallen to the ground.

Farley was not in the tent. She pushed open the door, which had been ajar. The cabin smelled salty-sour. Did Mom smell this way now? Sure enough, she lay in her sackcloth nightshirt on the unmade bed, arms at her sides, staring at the open beams of the ceiling. The big soft lumps that were her breasts had slid off the mound of her stomach, and all of it moved ever so slightly with her breathing.

"Mom," Mae said, "you all right?"

Emma didn't even look at her.

"I've come back. Just couldn't abide the work in that house. In the morning I'm going to the Miser place to see about giving piano lessons." She waited. "Well, talk to me, Mom. Everything all right here?"

"Uh-huh." Barely audible.

"You got anything to eat?"

Emma's shoulder moved. A faint shrug. She didn't know.

"You want me to make a pot of coffee?" Maybe that would wake her up.

Emma kept watching the ceiling, maybe a fight between spiders.

"Well, I'll make some anyhow." She put her blanket of belongings on her cot and went outside to start the fire.

When the coffee was ready, Emma didn't want any. She wouldn't get off the bed. Mae sat outside on a kitchen chair and sipped her coffee. Mom's melancholy was worse. If it hadn't been so late in the afternoon Mae would have ridden to the Misers rather than sit around here, where she could do nothing to help Mom, and where she felt the weight of that melancholy stalking her. But it wouldn't be polite to drop in on the Misers at suppertime.

Covered with mud, Farley returned from shoveling hydraulic runoff into an industrial-sized long-tom all day. Listening to Mae's story about her hard work, he made a show of being not the least bit surprised she'd quit. As he left to wash in the river he said over his shoulder, "You been spoiled all your life."

Damn. It was so like him to walk away while making her mad instead of facing the music. She felt like running after him to deliver a swift kick. Instead she dug under the folks' bed for supplies and started potatoes boiling over the fire. She had bacon sizzling in the frying pan by the time Farley came back from the river and was stirring in flour and water from the settling keg to make gravy.

Farley hung up his "washed" clothing—the wet long johns a light shade of brown instead of their original white. By now the sun was down and the mosquitoes sang around Mae when she went into the cabin to check on Mom. Emma hadn't moved. The trees on the riverbank looked black in the twilight when she returned to the fire and sat on a chair.

"What's wrong with her?" She lifted her plate toward the cabin.

Farley was sitting opposite her with the little fire between them. "Aw, she's like that all the time now." He leaned forward and ladled gravy over his potatoes. "I'm 'fraid she won't live long if she don't get up and move about."

"Has something happened here?"

He looked up at her, the firelight exaggerating the shadows on his face, which looked part disgusted and part resigned. "Dad isn't trying to find work and George is in jail."

"Jail! What for?" Appalled, Mae put her fork down.

"High-grading."

"What on earth is that?"

"They caught him leavin' the mine with high-grade ore under his hat and in his pockets, pure gold. Charged 'im with grand theft. He had a trial. Now he's blacklisted in the California mines and has to pay a $500 fine. Course they went through his place and took back all the gold he pocketed. He'll sit in jail 'til the judge gets the five-hundred simoleons."

Mae couldn't imagine George doing anything illegal. "We've got to do something. How much can you come up with?"

"Well, most of my pay goes to Mr. Heath for supplies. The rest I hang on to. Got about twenty-five dollars."

"What about Hank and Emmett?"

"Emmett don't get paid 'til summer's end when they bring the sheep down from the range. Hank talked his father-in-law into giving a hundred dollars. But that's all he can do. Him and Sophie just bought theirselves a house, with her daddy's help, and they're buyin' furnishings. Hank's in pretty big debt."

There hadn't been a wedding party, neither Hank nor Sophia wanting to cause her parents to go to that expense.

Mae said, "So we've got a hundred and twenty-five dollars."

"Yup. Looks like poor old George'll be in that cell a good long time."

"Why'd he do it?"

Farley gave a sarcastic hoot. "I'd wager thet fine woulda been lighter if'n he'd kept his damned mouth shut. 'Stead, he stood up there and told the judge all the miners do it. That was his *entire* defense. Impressed the judge like a turd in the buttermilk. He asked an impertinent question too. Said, 'How you think so many men 'round here bought theirselves them fancy big ranches and stocked 'em with cattle, making fifty-cents a week in the mines?' I told him when it was over he shouldn't oughta said that. He says to me it's a tradition in California, a miner's right to take what he can if it fits in his pocket." Farley shook his head in the waning firelight. "You shoulda heared the mine manager say his piece. Whew! They shore do aim to stop that tradition in its tracks."

Sick about this turn of affairs, and to think of George in jail knowing his family had no money to back him up, Mae nibbled a little, then tossed the remains of her supper at the landscape where the wild dogs would clean it up. Farley was still eating. She let the silence separate them. She also let the smoke protect her from the mosquitoes.

Hoofbeats. A walking horse approached.

"Dad?" Farley called. "That you?"

The white blaze on Belle's nose and her white socks were all Mae could make out. Then a pale shirt and Daddy's light hair. Belle stopped short of the mostly spent fire, where random coals flared. Impatient to get to the grazing ground, she pumped her head and munched noisily on the bit. Daddy slid off, standing a minute with his shoulder leaning on her before letting go of the horn. Then he staggered toward them. Ten feet away, Mae could smell liquor on his breath.

"Farley, gimme a dollar," Daddy slurred.

"I'm done helpin' you drink up every cent of my pay. We need it for George."

In the red light from the coals, Daddy's belligerent face looked like the Devil. "I said, gimme two bits!" He picked up a switch and stumbled after Farley, who, on his feet and still holding his plate, dodged Daddy's misdirected blows. Snickering in the twilight he brought to mind a circus performer Mae had seen in Iowa. Daddy lurched after him like a hog going to war, sideways, swiping with the switch.

Farley looked ridiculous as he leaped around the coals avoiding the slashing weapon. Giggling, he finally conceded. "All right, all right. You can have two bits, but that's all."

Mae could hardly believe what she had seen and heard. Daddy was a fool! He snatched what Farley took from his pocket, pulled himself up on Belle and vanished into the dark.

"What's happened to this family?" Mae said when he was out of sight.

"Well, I don't know about the rest of you," Farley said with practiced scorn, "but everything I eat I earn."

Unlike the rest of you, he meant.

13

Mae slept by fits and starts. Dilemmas tangled her brains and mosquitoes kept her busy. She recalled the high spirits of the Duffys when they left Iowa, and her expectation that Daddy and the boys would be making good money by now. But the boys were scattering to make their own livings, and Mom had slid away in spirit. Farley said George would leave for the silver mines of Nevada as soon as he got out of jail, and would never set foot in California again. Mae didn't imagine Farley would stay around for long either. How would she come by the money to care for the folks and herself? Everything had gone wrong. There wasn't any more free gold in California, and no man would look twice at her in this horrible cabin.

Outside the door, wild dogs growled at each other. They could smell the salt pork under the bed, and the other supplies. They scratched on the door. Those starved animals ran in packs. Out in the tent Farley kept a knife under his pillow to fend them off, if he had to, but he kept no food in his tent so they'd left him alone until now. The Duffys didn't own a gun, possibly the only people in the entire West who didn't, outside the poorest of the Chinese. Finally the dogs went away and the night grew still. In the larger scale of things, living in this cabin was just a short step from the way those dogs lived.

She wished she had a wise advisor. The little frame St. Joseph's Catholic Church on Jackson Road didn't have a resident priest. Mary Granlees had said that a priest rode in on horseback every other Sunday after finishing mass in Sutter's Creek. Maybe she should go next Sunday and see if it was the right Sunday. If so, she'd ask the priest to hear her confession. If, if, if. She flopped over for the hundredth time.

More than confession. I need a friend.

In the morning Daddy lay snoring in their bed and Mom was coming back inside after relieving herself somewhere in the bushes. Mom lay down and stared at the ceiling. Mae's heart wrenched to see that.

She dressed in her good day frock, dipped half a raw potato into the cold gravy and ate it while fetching Pal from the downstream pasture. She packed her music in the saddlebags, mounted the tall horse, pulled up her skirts, and crossed the river without getting her skirts wet. Her spirits lifted a little as she put distance between herself and that infested shale cabin. It occurred to her that she needed to stay away from Mom or she might catch the melancholy too. *Bad house.*

Indian Mary's map was accurate. From the Driscoll-Granlees place, a path led to a dry stream. She followed it about two miles to a ridge where another dry stream went down past a busy mining claim. There, a mule plodded round and around a post—surely a form of earthly hell for an animal—dragging a "stone boat," a wagon without wheels, tin-lined on the bottom and filled with heavy rock. It was crushing quartz rock. A very bowlegged Indian was sledge-hammering the quartz and shoveling it in the path of the boat. Another man shoveled the finely crushed rock into a long-tom, a long sluice box with ridges, and then rinsed the leavings with buckets of water from a man-made pond where the dry creek had been dammed. Farley had described this simple method for extracting gold, used by Mexicans and other poor miners. Still, what Emmett had said was true. No one could compete with the hydraulic company or the underground mines that had stamp mills for crushing the quartz and sluice runs as long as corn rows for separating the gold.

A white man squatted beside the pond, carefully pouring quicksilver from a two-foot-tall can into a long-tom. Gold stuck to mercury and helped greatly in extracting it from pans and sluice boxes, Farley had said. Mae had seen those big lead canisters in Heath's Store and in Bridge House Store.

Deciding to verify her directions, she turned Pal toward the man using the mercury. But at that moment he set his pan down, jumped up and shooed away some cows that had come to drink from the pond. He yelled, threw rocks, waved his arms and followed them a long distance. Rather than wait for him to return, she rode to the bowlegged Indian.

Pal acted skittish on account of the racket of the tin-lined "boat" and the Indian sledge-hammering quartz.

"Excuse me," Mae said, "Where is the Miser house?"

The bowlegged Indian looked up, his dark face lumpy and purplish. His shoulders looked huge, no doubt from work with shovels and sledge hammers.

"Miser house, where?" she repeated.

He turned and pointed. "Bymbye you come to the Miser house."

"Cowboy," yelled the white man from the distance. "What's she want?"

The Indian pushed his shoulders and palms skyward, the universal sign for bewilderment.

Mae hurried along. Good old Pal picked his way through rocks, high grass and ground squirrel holes. He never stumbled. She loved his deep reddish brown coat with shiny black mane, tail and socks.

A short distance away she came to a tiny cemetery shaded by large oaks and surrounded by a wrought iron fence. At the four corners stood red sandstone pillars narrowing to pointed tops. She dismounted, left the reins over the fence and walked around the enclosure to read the inscriptions:

> EDWARD A. HUGHES
> WHO DEPARTED HIS LIFE APRIL 24, 1862

On a very small white marble stone:

> RUTH AND WILLIE
> CHILDREN OF
> WILLIAM AND LAURA
> RUSSEL

On the largest stone:

> SOLOMON MISER
> 1823 – 1876
> I SHALL SLEEP BUT NOT FOREVER
> THERE SHALL BE A GLORIOUS DAWN
> WE SHALL MEET TO PART NO NEVER
> ON THE RESURRECTION MORN

She had found a dead Miser, but where were the living? She walked Pal to an old shack that was falling into the hole that had been its cellar or, as they said in California, cheese house. An oak tree spread its branches over this former dwelling, around which she saw bits and pieces of broken pottery. Near to what had been the door was a pile of blue-green stones, not rounded but crudely quarried. She led Pal onward to a wall made of the same cut stone in much larger blocks, and then rode him down the steep little hill.

There it was, a whitewashed farmhouse facing Latrobe Road. On the return trip she would stay on the road and cross the Michigan Bar Bridge instead of traveling through difficult country.

Beneath several black walnut trees, the house and rail stood back a gracious distance from the road. A roofed well with a windlass to reel up the bucket reminded her of a pussy-in-the-well picture from a McGuffey's Reader. A stately barn kept the house company. This looked like a prosperous place, with oak-dotted hills mounding on the other side of the road.

She knocked on the front door. The door opened, releasing the smell of oatmeal cookies. A tall slender lady older than Emma smiled a welcome like she was overjoyed to meet someone new. Her hair was gray, but she had about her an aura of unusual vitality—the opposite of what Mom's had become. Behind her, four curious little children, no doubt grandchildren, peeked out of another room like a clutch of chicks.

Introducing herself, Mae added, "I've been a hired girl and I give piano lessons. Was hoping you could use a piano teacher."

"Well now, it's not every day a piano teacher comes knocking on my door. Won't you come in and have a cup of coffee?" Every syllable of that spoken with a smile.

Mae smiled too as she entered the large parlor. Mrs. Miser stuck her head outside for a moment, looking at Pal at the rail. She closed the door behind her, remarking, "Good horse flesh you got there."

Identical chairs with tan and white-striped fabric on deep cushions stood opposite a settee of matching fabric and construction, which some people called "matchstick" on account of the narrow dowels supporting the back and armrests. Under the furniture a richly patterned Persian carpet covered most of the floor. A carved mahogany mantel topped the stone fireplace. This room would be cozy on a winter's night. And just as Indian Mary had said, the Misers owned an upright piano. Shelving on both sides of the piano contained many books. How Emma would have loved this room! Before her melancholy.

"Can't say as I need a hired girl," Mrs. Miser was saying. "I got Agnes and Lillian. Agnes? You in there? Fix us some coffee and bring out some of those good hot cookies. We got a visitor." A woman with gray hair plastered back from her plain face peered out the kitchen door.

Mae seated herself in a bouncy chair—deep horsehair and springs—pillows behind and beneath her.

Sitting down opposite her, Mrs. Miser explained. "Agnes came across with me and Mr. Miser back in fifty-three. Lillian's my daughter. She and her mister live here too. Agnes thought she'd find her fiancé in California. He'd come across in forty-nine, before us, but when we got settled here, we tried every which way we could think of but couldn't locate her gentleman. Never heard hide nor hair of him, though we wrote to more newspapers than you could shake a stick at. Agnes has helped me with my kids since the day I met her back in St. Louis."

"You mean she stayed when she didn't find her fiancé?"

"That's right. She never wanted to leave for fear she'd miss her man if he answered our advertisements. The mister and I thought that was quite the bargain, to have her watch over the babies. Never in our wildest dreams did we imagine she'd be with us all these years. Six babies later! Eight in all. Let's see," she looked at the ceiling and moved her fingers. "Nigh onto forty years now, it's been, and she never did tell us her family name."

"Why not?"

Mrs. Miser raised her salt and pepper brows. "She planned to change it when she got married." She lowered her voice. "I'm afraid she'll go to her grave without a family name." A delightful arpeggio of happy laughter poured from her. "Now, tell me. When did you come to California?"

"First of the month, with my folks and my brothers. We came from Iowa."

"This month?"

Mae nodded. "We expected to find gold."

Mrs. Miser slapped her knee to another explosion of laughter. Recovering, she wiped tears with the hem of her apron and said, "You know, it never ceases to amaze me that folks're still traipsing out here believin' they'll strike it rich. Where are your folks living?"

"Michigan Bar for now." It hurt that Californians considered the Duffys to have been fools for their misguided hopes. By this time six children had come through various doors, the eldest girl about twelve. They watched and listened from around the walls.

"My grandchildren. Some are Laura's. She brought 'em up for a couple of days from Walsh Station. The rest are Lillian's."

"Is Laura the one whose children are in the little cemetery?"

"Ruth and Willie. Bless their baby hearts. Well, no need to look back. I knew your folks weren't settlers or I would'ov known you. There was a time when I could name every living soul in Michigan Bar. Guess we've been so busy around here, what with the school and all. Just haven't been out and about. We teach our children here in the house along with the neighbors' kids."

"I think you've met my brother Emmett."

"Emmett Duffy is your brother?"

Mae nodded. "Hope he's been good help to you."

"I assume so. My son Joe runs the sheep now. He's got a family and a house of his own up the road a piece."

The plain woman with the severe bun entered the room carrying a tray with cookies and a tea set, which she put on a table between the settee and the chairs. Seating herself beside Mrs. Miser on the settee, she started pouring coffee into the cups.

"Agnes," Mrs. Miser said, "this is Mae Duffy. I told her how long you've been with me, and I still don't know your last name." The two women laughed together, sharing a look born of long and close association. Mae bit into a cookie—cinnamon, brown sugar and black walnuts—tasting even better than it smelled.

Mae swallowed and pushed toward her goal. "My folks are under the weather just now, and I need to make some money to help with the family. I'd also like to save enough to go to Sacramento and finish high school, my last year."

Mrs. Miser nodded eagerly. "Agnes, let's put our heads together and figure out if we can be of any help to Mae, and t'other way 'round."

Before the coffee cups were drained and a good many of the cookies consumed, mostly by the children, Mae knew she had met a resourceful woman in Mrs. Miser. Her husband had been killed almost twenty years ago when his loaded freight wagon slipped off its block while he was making a repair underneath. Left with eight children, Mrs. Miser and her eldest son Joe were now buying properties and expanding their holdings. Her daughter Lillian, with her husband and their four children, also lived here, and there were frequent visits by Laura and her children. Agnes obviously helped a great deal in this household and always had.

Mrs. Miser squeezed an eye half shut, scrutinizing Mae. "What would a pretty girl like you most like to do with her life? I don't mean to hear about schooling, but the end to which schooling is a means."

Unaccustomed to adults asking penetrating questions, Mae had to think a minute. She decided there was nothing to lose in being truthful, so she described her family situation, except for the bad news about George, concluding, "I believe having a high school diploma would make me more eligible to marry a good man with land and stock. That's what I'd like to do. We'd settle down and have children. I'd like to have a house this big, so I could have a hired girl."

"Well, now we're getting someplace. Notice, Agnes? She don't limit her search to one single man."

Agnes took the joke in good humor, laughing along with Isabella Miser.

Mrs. Miser returned to Mae. "You been to Dixon's Grove?"

"No, ma'm."

"Well, if you go there of a Sunday, you'll meet eligible men. In fact, the Fourth of July is next Tuesday. Just about every man in the whole territory, young and old, will be there. "You'd ought to go and bat those pretty blue eyes at all of them, the loose ones that is. Why the Grimshaws got several grown boys, never married. And if you like 'em a little younger, the Sheldons got three boys—well two that'd be about right in age." She laughed with Agnes, slapping her knee. "Have I got that right?"

"I'll say," said Agnes.

Mae liked everything she was hearing. "Sheldon? You mean the Sheldon family of Slough House?"

"Sure do. Aristocracy around here, owners of a lot of land around Slough House."

"I heard about a Sheldon killed by miners. Bled to death in a cabin in Bridge House."

"That's the one. His son, W. C., is quite the interesting gentleman. He is tinkering with corn, making new kinds by crossing pollen. A few years ago the Sheldons finished their grand new house in the Queen Anne style. They have three girls and three boys."

Silently rejoicing, Mae listened carefully to Mrs. Miser.

"So you get yourself on over to that picnic on the Fourth. Then when September rolls around, I could use you to help me with my school. I could use some help with the beginning readers. Agnes here has her hands full with my grandchildren, the ones too young for school. Would you be interested in that?"

"I sure would! But I've got to find some way to earn money right now, maybe piano lessons, if any of your family could use them." She made a gesture toward the little people around the walls.

Mrs. Miser squinted an eye at her and said, "Come to Dixon's Grove on the Fourth. We'll talk there. Meanwhile I'll talk to Lillian."

14

On the buckboard beside Daddy, Mae rode to Dixon's Grove like a barbarian going to Rome. Not to sack it, which Sister Delphine had said was the common misinterpretation, but to partake of a more privileged world. She had a plan. Having returned to the Misers to see about borrowing a summer hat, she'd found in Mrs. Miser a willing conspirator. The lady not only lent her a straw hat that nestled at a fetching angle in Mae's updo, but also a floral-patterned parasol, the stem of which now rested on Mae's shoulder as she and Daddy drove down Meiss Road south of the river.

This morning she had looked at herself in the still water near where Pal and Belle grazed, and smiled. In her lacy, cream-colored gown, most recently worn at the St. Mary's graduation, she looked like one of the "young lovelies" mentioned on the social pages of the Sacramento newspapers. No other girl with as ample a chest could have a narrower waist, with the possible exception of the wealthy few who'd had their lower ribs removed. A feral ringlet dangled beside her ear. The effect was more than all right. Giving the parasol a twirl, she had felt like her old self for the first time in weeks—like she'd felt on the roof of the train.

A dark snout had poked out of the river, spreading watery rings. A long furry back crested—an otter! How they survived in this muddy water she didn't know. She froze, not wanting to give alarm. More otters broke the surface, diving under and popping up again, long black bodies. They were playing! One of them came to the shore. The dripping animal waddled on short legs over the sand about ten yards from Mae. Careful not to move, she turned only her eyes to watch. The otter lay down, rolling and squirming as though scratching its back in the warm sand. One by one, four smaller otters pulled up on shore and rolled like their mother. To Mae's delight they began to chase each other and frolic in the sand, mother as well as pups.

After quite a long time, Mae's neck grew sore, and she had to move her head.

For an instant the otters resembled an architectural frieze in their varied poses. Then, swift as a bullet, the big one streaked into the water and vanished. The pups followed in a blur of flashes. Only the disturbed water gave them away. Laughing quietly, Mae wished she could dive sinuously in the water and play without the restraint of clothing. She wished Mom could too. But then she turned her attention to the day ahead. It was important to meet the Sheldon boys and charm them, but she would also play a little.

For days she had quashed any outward sign of excitement or anticipation, lest she inadvertently interest Farley in attending the picnic. Having him or Mom with her could have upset her plan. On the other hand, Daddy, whose easygoing nature and fine singing voice always attracted people, would be an asset. But Mae wanted more family around her, so she had secretly posted a note to Hank, giving vent to her enthusiasm and hoping to become better acquainted with Sophia, her new sister-in-law.

"But Mom needs her rest," she had written, "so I think it best if you two could meet us at Dixon's Grove. I do hope you will come!" At the bottom of the page she had drawn a map, showing how to go on Meiss Road and thus avoid the bridge toll.

To her great joy, Sophia had responded by return post that Mae shouldn't bother over the food. Sophia would pack an Italian picnic. Perfect! Sophia's family had been in Sutter Creek since the Gold Rush, now owning land and a grocery store. The family picnic would be respectable.

Even the weather cooperated. A pleasant little zephyr had blown in from the southwest, cooling down the intense heat. Pal set a fast walking pace, and Belle fell in step with him. Daddy had trained them to the harness together. Both held their heads up. Transported by such a fine team, Mae floated above the unhappy mess of her family. Handsome as he handled the oiled reins, Daddy was a naturally slender man, now combed and trimmed and dressed in his white shirt and dark suit. No one could have guessed they lived in a hovel. Others on the road called cheerful greetings, everyone obviously on their way to the picnic. Daddy lifted his bowler hat with finesse. Prepared for conquest, Mae smiled and dipped her head beneath the pretty parasol.

A mile or two short of the grove, a rider on a drab cayuse pony overtook them. Mae found herself looking into the wide smile of the same young man she'd met on her way to the Granlees' place that first morning. She'd seen him now and again, mostly on the road. Mary Granlees had told her he lived in the back of the Grimshaw barn, just like an Indian. Nonetheless, in her mood of gaiety and high expectations Mae couldn't help but practice her allure on him. "Good morning," she sang out. "Going to Dixon's Grove?"

"Shore am." He walked his jug-head horse beside her at the pace set by Pal and Belle. No one was coming the other way—everyone going to Dixon's—so he didn't block any traffic. He wore a brown high hat like Emmett's, the one his friends in Iowa had given him as a farewell gift. It was indeed a popular hat in the West. His worn but clean brown shirt had a wavy, almost swirly pattern like the hair on some dogs. And the mustache he was obviously trying to grow had a ways to go before it filled out to manly proportions. He kept looking at her.

"You shore are a sight for sore eyes," he finally said.

She laughed and tossed her head. "I'm not always dressed like a hired girl."

"I'll say not!" He lifted his high hat to Daddy. "Sir, my name's John Dunaway."

"Pleased to meet you, young fella. I'm Ed Duffy. Looks like you've met my daughter."

"Yup. And that's a mighty fine team you got there."

"Tis indeed," Daddy crowed, "if I do say so myself."

Coming toward them was an old gray nag pulling a buggy. John dropped back, but took his place beside Mae as soon as the rig passed. "Ole Doc Walker, headin' home to Michigan Bar," John said. "Thet poor old fella sure don't have much time fer play."

"All work and no play makes a dull boy," Daddy said lightly.

John gave him a friendly grin but returned his attention to Mae, his head at an angle. His shoulders drooped as his expression softened, and his rein hand dropped. She knew he couldn't think of more to say, but couldn't stop looking at her. This went on for too long.

"Is that the road to the Grove?" she asked, pointing to where wagons and riders were turning in toward the river.

"Oh, ah, yup, right ahead," John answered. On the last, his voice cracked. He put his chin down and made his voice unnaturally low. "Yup, to the right." He cleared his throat. "I'd sure be proud to show you folks around."

Mae began to wish she had never invited him to talk. If she didn't get rid of him he would foil her plans. Proper young men like Jared Sheldon would think she was taken. And most men of any standing would be turned away by seeing her with a poorly mounted man with bad grammar. Judging by the goods he hauled, John worked for wages just a notch above the Indians. She looked straight ahead at the parade of rigs and riders, and wished him away.

John, however, rode beside them as though tethered to the wagon. He stayed with them as they drove toward the river marked by the dense oak grove ahead, and he tried to keep her talking. She answered with a terse yes or no.

"No need to stick with us," she finally said. "We're looking for my brother and his wife. Good to see you again." She looked sternly at the enormous oaks at the end of the road. Still, he continued to ride beside her.

Turning to Daddy, with the parasol between her and John, she said in a quiet voice. "Ooh, I wish he'd take a wrong turn."

Daddy showed no comprehension.

"I plan to race this pony today," John said. "They's always a good race at Dixon's on the Fourth of July."

"How long is the track?" Daddy inquired.

"A half-mile," John provided.

"Well, maybe Mae will ride Pal in the race," Daddy said lightly. "She's as good on horseback as any man."

Mae couldn't hide her annoyance. "Daddy I'm not about to race a horse in this gown." Turning to John, "I doubt you'd beat a donkey on that sorry animal." Buzzard bait, she was thinking.

"Whoa now, don't sell this here little gal short. She's a goer." John didn't sound the least bit put off. In fact, he was still smiling.

Mae momentarily shut her eyes. She must simply ignore him. They were approaching a grassy field where wagons and buggies were being parked near a number of hitching rails. Beyond that was the grove shading the still-green grass up and down the river. On that grass in the shade of the magnificent oaks, a colorful array of blankets had been spread. Most of the horses had been ground-tied in their traces, others tied to the rails and young trees. Daddy pulled up to a rail. John, already dismounted, asked if could help in any way.

"Well, maybe you could—"

"No, we'll do fine by ourselves," Mae interrupted. "Now if you would please excuse us, we've got people to find." She started to climb down, but John hurried over and put his hands on her waist.

She shook her head at him. "I'll get down on my own, thank you."

He stepped back and watched her step on the wheel and jump to the ground. A silly smile spread across the lower half of his face. "I shore do admire a filly with spirit."

Please leave, she silently wished.

Other people were pulling up in various rigs, many on horseback. "Halloo," called a familiar voice from a distance. Mae turned to see Hank and Sophia in a buggy pulled by a trotting sorrel. They were running through a fallow field to pass the slower traffic. Holding onto her wide straw hat, Sophia's merry laughter could be heard over the noise of the hooves.

Hank's pale Duffy complexion was flushed with pleasure as he pulled up beside Daddy. "We seen you on the road and was hell-bent to catch up." A good-sized man of middle height and sandy hair, he jumped to the ground and strode to John with his hand out. "I'm Mae's brother, Hank Duffy."

"John Dunaway," John said, pumping his hand, obviously delighted to ally himself with more of the Duffy family.

Hank helped Sophia—a plump, vivacious girl with laughing eyes and a rosy flush on her olive complexion—down from the buggy. He introduced her to John as "Sophie." Mae decided to call her that too.

Hank took from their buggy a bulging cloth-covered hamper. "Sophie packed enough to bloat Napoleon's army," he announced with pride.

Several young men and boys were gathering around Pal and Belle. They petted the horses, patted their hind quarters and scratched between their ears, which that pair always loved, but they also stole looks at Mae. Sophie made a point of flashing her shiny new ring in the sun. Discreetly, Mae looked the men over, keeping as far away from John Dunaway as possible. Meanwhile

Daddy loved the spotlight, puffing up his chest as he answered questions and talked about the breeding of his team—mostly Morgan, some Thoroughbred, some American Saddle Horse.

"Flashy," somebody said.

"You going to race 'em?" asked another. "I see you brought saddles."

Smiling good-naturedly, Daddy gave a little shrug. Lacking shed or barn, they always kept the saddles in the wagon. "Hank you want to race?" Daddy threw out.

Hank was looking at Belle like a lost sweetheart. He ran the backs of his fingers down her velvet nose. "Maybe. Is there a purse?" He pulled apple slices from his pocket and fed them to her, and to Pal.

"Yup. Betting too," a stranger hobbling his horse replied.

"How big a purse?" Hank asked, pricking up his ears like a bloodhound.

"Hundred bucks, last year."

With a shock, Mae realized they needed that money for George.

Daddy seemed to be thinking that too. "When do they race?" he asked.

"Mid-afternoon," one of the men said.

Another chimed in, "But not so late we can't help the winners drink their earnings up." Laughter and backslapping crackled through the little crowd, and murmurs about previous races. Meanwhile John Dunaway inched too close to Mae.

She linked arms with her sister-in-law, pulled her under the parasol and steered for the main part of the grove of ancient oaks. "Let's us girls go scout while the men get acquainted," she said. The other men watched them go, but John followed like a puppy dog.

Shielded by the parasol, Mae turned to Sophie, jerked her head toward him, and rolled her eyes.

A twinkle enlivened Sophie's eyes. She was in the game, and Mae saw why Hank loved her. It was best to keep moving when you had a puppy at your heels, but speed didn't stop John. All but panting, he followed, first at their heels then at Mae's side.

The tinkling sound of a calliope drew their attention. With Sophie suddenly in the lead, Mae found herself in the crowd around a carousel with painted horses plunging up and down. A red banner fluttered from the peak of the blue canvas top, a wisp of steam trailing upward from the steam engine that moved the thing. It seemed to Mae that this wonder could have resided in a magical oak forest in an Irish fairytale. Sophie steered toward the densest part of the crowd, weaving through family groups and children that were watching people ride wooden horses to the merry strains of the calliope, a tune Mae didn't know.

Mae glanced around. "I think we lost him."

Still on the move, Sophie said, "There, let's hide in those big hats." She pulled Mae along. Moments later they stood in front of two young ladies in nice gowns of muted colors topped by plumed hats. Mae faced the revolving platform that held the shiny brass poles that pulled the horses up and down in random synchrony. The riders were people of all ages, and the speed of the forward motion was such that Mae couldn't make out anything on the other side. She knew she was hidden.

"Do you mind?" Mae asked the girl behind her. "I hope we're not blocking your view."

"Heavens no." Pretty blue eyes studied Mae for a moment. "I don't think I've seen you around here."

"I've recently moved to this area, with my family. My name's Mae Duffy. This is my sister-in-law from Sutter Creek, Sophie Duffy."

"How do you do? I'm Polly Sheldon."

"Sheldon?" Mae turned all the way around to see a young woman about her age or a little older, with blond-streaked light brown hair curling around her shoulders beneath a wide plumed hat. "If you're from Slough House, I've heard of your family," Mae said, "and was hoping to meet you."

"Well, you've got the right people. This is Katy Irene, my cousin, and my baby sister Kittie—Tooty, I call her." Polly gave the freckle-faced girl about five years old a fond squeeze of the shoulders. "My other little sister and my silly brothers are in a race they can't win. See, there they are." Polly smiled and waved at the riders. "Those three boys with jackets and the girl with the braids. That's Jessie." Sitting staight on her wooden steed, Jessie appeared to be about twelve years old. She waved back.

Little Kittie looked up at Polly and said, "I wanna ride again."

"You've been on that thing twice, and that's enough for now."

Just then the music changed, and Katy Irene and Polly started to sing along with the calliope. They put their heads together and harmonized—black-eyed Katy Irene, blue-eyed Polly, and gray-eyed Kittie trying to catch up with the words. Mae couldn't help but join in singing the popular Stephen Foster song that she had learned in grade school. All around, people sang.

> *Many were the wild notes her merry voice would pour,*
> *Many were the blithe birds that warbled them o'er;*
> *Ahhhhhh!* (voices crescendoed up the scale)
> *I dream of Jeannie with the light brown hair,*
> *Floating liiiike* (holding the note much longer than the calliope did)
> *a vapor on the soft summer air.*

At this satisfying end, Mae, Katy Irene and Polly broke out laughing like they'd known each other for years. Sophie hadn't known the words, but she laughed along with the rest. What fun it would be to have them all for sisters! A stray thought of Nora intruded into Mae's mind—what would she be like now?

The carousel slowed and people jumped off the horses. A moment or two later, the three Sheldon boys and sister Jessie, a tall bony girl, stood in the circle with Mae and Sophie.

Polly introduced her brothers Jared, George, and Lauren, a boy about ten. Mae noticed that three fingers from Lauren's right hand had been sliced off just below the knuckles. Jared, a tall dark-eyed young man probably several years her senior, intrigued her. His dark mustache was full and trimmed. George was about the same height, and she couldn't decide whether Jared or George cut the better figure of a man. Both could have been pictured in fashionable magazines. They had an aristocratic appearance and manners—each nodding at Mae and Sophie with just the right tilt to their heads at the introductions. When Jared shook her hand, he seemed to give it a little extra squeeze. A hint of things to come? Excited, she realized that this was not only a handsome young man, but one who stood to inherit a great deal of land. He could be her California Joe!

George had a blue-eyed Anglo-Saxon look and a dignity rarely seen on one so young—about her age, she guessed. Neither brother said anything. Their white shirts, open a little at the neck under dark coats, suggested a mix of propriety with youthful flair. They both looked wonderful. If nothing else happened today, she had won the first battle. She had met them. Both Jared and George were somewhat shy, according to the Misers. Well, that was a problem Mae welcomed as a challenge. She was accustomed to boys being tongue-tied at the sight of her.

"Come," Katy Irene said, beckoning as they left, "Meet the rest of the family." Sheldons and Duffys trailed behind. Mae and Sophie walked behind George and Jared. Mae gave Sophie's arm a squeeze meant to thank her for all the help she'd been in ditching John Dunaway.

And then, as they left the carousel, there he was, scanning the crowd for her. In his culry shirt he looked all the more like a lost dog. His brown high hat could have been long pointed ears meeting over his head. In a moment they would pass right by him.

She raised her brows at Sophie, rolled her eyes in John's direction, and turned to walk backwards while striking up a conversation with Polly who walked behind with "Tooty." This turned her back to John Dunaway while Sophie steered.

"What a delightful place this is! Who owns it?" Mae asked, gesturing around the Grove.

"Mr. Dixon," Polly said. "He uses this part for the benefit of the people. We just love coming here." They were passing beside John.

"How long has Mr. Dixon held these picnics?" Mae kept it up.

Polly frowned a little, thinking. "Can't rightly remember. I sure hope he keeps doing it. The Fourth of July is my favorite picnic of the year."

"I hope he keeps doing it too," Mae said, then whispered to Sophie, "Safe?"

Sophie nodded in the affirmative.

Mae walked forward again. They all stopped at a big red and white checked cloth upon which an older couple took their ease, the man resting his arms on his knees, his polished high-toppers anchoring him. A small, trim lady, somewhat younger than Mom—no doubt the wife—sat demurely with her knees to the side. She wore an old-fashioned, high-necked chintz gown. On a kitchen chair sat a plump older lady with white hair and a kindly smile. She watched the arrivals with obvious pleasure.

Stealing all their thunder, an excited horse stepped around as far as his lead rope would allow—tied to a sturdy oak limb. The sleek dark horse snorted and jerked, reaching about ten feet short of the edge of the cloth. For a moment he stilled himself, long necked and high tailed, looking at the busy grounds. He laid his ears back and whinnied. Compared with the big-barreled horses Mae had grown up with—saddle horses that could pull loads as well—this animal had a narrow chest. His long legs appeared too delicate for his weight, which would have been less than Pal or Belle, though this horse was taller.

On the picnic cloth stood a large basket of fresh peaches. The other baskets remained covered. A barrel for making ice cream, with its steel insert and crank, stood at the ready, a bucket of coarse salt beside it. Squatting in pink cloth slippers, a Chinese man was distributing plates on the picnic cloth, each with a folded napkin. Never had Mae seen a more exotic being. He wore a dark blue silken tunic, his head covered by a brimless cap of the same fabric with a band of scarlet and gold appliquéd around it. A black braid hung down from the nape of his neck past where his waist would be. Long slits in the sides of his tunic revealed blousy trousers underneath, and his decorated cloth shoes appeared untouched by dirt.

Polly introduced Mae and Sophie to her parents and grandmother. Mr. Sheldon nodded a formal "Pleased to meet you," but did not stand, which was entirely to be expected. He wore a starched collar and a brown handle-bar mustache waxed in the style of Germany's Emperor Bismarck, with the fine points turned up in rigid hooks. Anna Sheldon, on the other hand, appeared to be a humble pioneer woman. That both were handsome came as no surprise. The younger generation had by now seated themselves, obviously eager for their dinners.

Removing a linen cloth from a huge hamper, Mrs. Sheldon unveiled a colossal mound of fried chicken. The boys reached, grabbed chicken pieces, and filled their mouths. It made Mae happy to see that they were no different than boys anywhere. "Won't you eat with us?" Mrs. Sheldon sweetly inquired of Mae and Sophie.

"We can't," Sophie said. "I see our people over there." She pointed across a crazy quilt of cloths and grass—probably more than a hundred people breaking into their hampers. "If I don't get over there pronto, Mae's dad won't know what he's eating." She gave a bouncy laugh. "I fixed an Italian picnic."

"Are you are Italian?" Mr. Sheldon asked.

"Second generation," Sophie responded.

"Mmmm," said young Lauren with his mouth full, "Mom, you've d-d-done it again."

Mae would like to have stayed—she hadn't yet engaged Jared or George in conversation. But it was time to leave. She looked around the Sheldon family, giving Jared and George the full brunt of her sparkling smile that had so mesmerized the baseball team in Alton, and asked, "Maybe I'll see you at the horse race?"

With a twisted smile, Jared pointed to his ballooned cheek—his mouth too full to speak—and resumed chewing.

"W-w-we're racing our n-n-n-n-n-new horse," George said, stuck on the "new" so long Mae feared he'd never get past it. What a shame, she thought, that he was afflicted with an embarrassing speech problem. Come to think of it, Lauren had stuttered too, but he was too young anyway. So of the three Sheldon boys, only Jared remained of interest to her.

"George," Papa Sheldon was saying, "Enunciate that clearly." It was a command.

George's face reddened and he looked down—this fine specimen of Anglo-Saxon manhood! His family appeared to have frozen, bringing to mind the terrified otters this morning before they dove in the river.

Lauren broke the silence, asking of Mae. "Are you r-racing your horses t-t-today?" A brave stutterer with missing fingers.

Before Mae could say, I don't know, Mr. Sheldon hammered, "George, I told you to repeat clearly what you said before, and I expect to be obeyed. Now what did you want to tell these young ladies?" His chin was up as he waited, looking into the trees.

Never had Mae been so uncomfortable.

Hearing nothing, Mr. Sheldon unfolded himself and straightened to his considerable height, staring down at George like Zeus from Mount Olympus.

George started "W-w-w-w-w-w-w—"

Sophie interjected, "We've got to get going."

"Yes," Mae jumped in, "we're needed at our picnic."

That diverted Mr. Sheldon. "Young ladies, what my son is trying to say is that we'll be racing Shamrock's Wind here." He gestured toward the horse. "Many of our neighbors are placing bets on him. You might consider that. I sent for him from Ireland, where he was bred for racing, and this will be his first race on American soil."

"Thank you for the tip," Mae said. "Where does one make a bet?"

"Do you know the Grimshaws?"

"Don't believe I've met them."

"Right over there." Mr. Sheldon pointed toward a large family gathered around several blankets. "Ask for Mr. Frederick Grimshaw. He manages the money and keeps the bets."

"That's our cousin," Jessie said, flipping a braid to her back as she examined the gnawed chicken leg in her hand.

"Thank you again!" Mae gave a hint of a curtsy and hurried away with Sophie. "Can you fathom that?" she said into Sophie's ear.

Sophie responded into her ear. "He was cruel to his son."

"Poor George," Mae said. "He looks for all the world like a young… ah…"

"Nobleman," Sophie filled in.

"Yes. That's it exactly. Well, sorry to say he's out of the running for me." They were skirting a cluster of kitchen chairs filled with sandwich-munching occupants.

"There's still Jared," Sophie reminded her when they were past that group.

"He's as handsome as George." Mae liked his looks a bit better.

With a giggle, Sophie tossed over at her, "I'd say George wins that contest." They had practically arrived at the Duffy blanket where the men had broken into the food. "Maybe I just like blond men better. You know, Mae, I've never met a man in my entire life who holds a candle to Hank in looks."

Hank, hearing this as intended, turned red.

"Oops." Sophie covered her mouth in feigned embarrassment.

Mae joined the fun. "Well I guess that's to be expected. Brides are known to lose every shred of good sense."

She looked at Hank, whom Sophie now kneeled beside. He was too heavy to ride against Shamrock's Wind. But somebody had to do it, and Mae was wishing she'd brought her riding britches.

15

Mae picked at Sophie's antipasto—pickled carrot, cauliflower, peppers, and preserved meat, strange to her Iowa palate—and voiced her thought. "We might not take the purse, but I think we should enter the race and give it a try."

"Ah-ah," Daddy warned, putting oil-and-vinegar–soaked tomatoes on a slice of sourdough bread, "Don't quit before you start. If we're in it, we're in it to win."

Near the Duffy picnic blanket was the beer vendor's booth, where a lot of men were joshing and laughing, mugs in hand.

Hank said, "Well then Dad, you ride 'im. I'm too heavy."

"Nope, not me. It takes a wilder heart, a gambler's heart. Guess I'm gettin' old. Mae's our best chance."

"Sophie's a good rider too," Hank said.

"I didn't bring my riding britches," Sophie countered. "Besides that, Pal and I don't know each other." After a couple of minutes eating her bread and meat slices she said, "Why don't we enter Pal now, and then find someone to ride him?"

Everyone agreed that the noon dinner could wait. Mae and Sophie covered the food, and they all went over to the Grimshaw picnic.

The three-generation family sat around two blankets loaded with corn on the cob, loaves of fresh-baked bread, a bowl of whipped butter with a knife sticking in it, a pan of cooked sausages, baskets of ripe plums, three choco- late cakes, sliced tomatoes and much more. A slim lady with white hair in a bun and two younger women sat on kitchen chairs. The older one wore the shadows of many hardships in her wrinkles, but the set of her mouth indi- cated that she had triumphed over them. The Grimshaw men and children lounged on the grass around the blankets.

A roguish-looking young man with wavy blond hair lay on his side hold- ing a buttered ear of corn. His big blue eyes gave Mae an appraising once-over. She could tell he was accustomed to winning his way with the ladies.

Fred Grimshaw was probably a bit older than the other one but younger than Mae had expected the race money-handler to be. Sitting upright on the grass with his ear of corn, he wore a white shirt with a standing collar and rolled up sleeves. His light brown hair was short, and it mounded higher on the unparted side. His mustache filled the space between his straight nose and his upper lip—a man of definite style, showing none of the lady-slayer attitude of the reclining man. He put down his corn, wiped his hands on a napkin, and removed a gold watch from the pocket of his shirt.

Flipping the cover open, he said to Daddy, "Five more minutes and I would have closed the race. He smiled cordially at the Duffy group and picked up a pencil and a small ledger book. He wrote down Daddy's answers: Pal, gelding; rider: unknown; owner: Edward Duffy; Michigan Bar. He held the pencil as though expecting something more.

After a few moments, he said in a somewhat embarrassed manner, "That'll be two dollars, Mr. Duffy."

Daddy looked confused. "You mean to enter the race?"

"Yes. Helps pay Bill Dixon for the use of the grounds, and the boys who cut the weeds and fill the holes on the track."

Daddy gave him two quarters. Hank dug in his pockets and emptied them of change. Counting it," Mr. Grimshaw said, "that's thirteen cents over." He started to hand the change back to Daddy.

"Aw, lay it on my horse," Daddy said.

Fred Grimshaw looked up in a quizzical manner and spoke quietly. "The minimum bet is five dollars. You could make a side bet with somebody. I'm only handling the winner. We don't figure odds."

"I see," muttered Daddy, handing the change to Hank.

Somehow in the presence of Fred Grimshaw and the man with the roving eyes, Mae needed to explain. "We're new here, and we didn't know there'd be a horse race. We didn't know there'd be a merry-go-round either. Next year we'll bring more money."

John Dunaway stepped out from behind the Duffys and said, "Fred, I'd be 'bliged if you'd let me to borrow five dollars on my pay to put on Mr. Duffy's horse, in his name."

Mae was too surprised to say anything.

"You aren't betting on your own horse, John?"

"No, take her out of the race. She's on her monthlies."

"Thanks for reminding me, John. With my cousin's fancy stallion in the race, I'd better talk to the owners of the mares." He picked up the ledger, turned a page, and noted $5 for the Duffy's bet.

Mr. Grimshaw confided to Daddy, "We'd trust John Dunaway with our lives."

"That's mighty friendly of you," said Daddy to John.

"We're grateful to you," Hank added, shaking John Dunaway's hand so hard it looked like he might take his arm off.

Recovering herself, Mae said, "Thank you very much, John. And I'm sorry you can't race your horse." She was also sorry she'd called that horse a sorry animal.

He turned to leave, touching his hat.

A thought struck her and she hurried after him. He was walking fast.

"John," she said when she got two steps behind. "I'd like a word with you."

He turned around, obviously surprised.

"Let's talk in private." She glanced at the picnic spreads around them. "Maybe over there"—pointing to the south side of the grounds, which looked unoccupied.

As they walked together at the edge of the shade, the band struck up a march and Mae couldn't help but step along to the music. John kept his eyes to himself, no longer a puppy dog. She felt sorry for acting the way she had.

"I wasn't very nice to you today. Please forgive me."

"You bring me here to say that?"

"Well, yes, and there's more."

"I'm listening."

"It was kind of you to help us lay down a bet. I wanted you to know that we really do need to win. You see, there's family trouble, and if we don't get some money in a hurry, my brother, well, he's... I don't know how to repay you."

"No need to pay me back or tell me about troubles. I seen enough. Jes' hope you win." He put his hands in his back pockets and looked over at her. "You got some'm more under your hat?"

She blurted it out. "Yes. I've got to ride Pal in the race. I'm the only one light enough and he and I are, well, pals. But I can't do it in this gown. I was thinking, since you work for Mr. Grimshaw, and he lives nearby, well, I was wondering if you had an extra shirt and trousers I could put on, and maybe an old hat to keep the sun outa my eyes. Being as how we live so far away and all."

A tiny smile turned up the corners of John's clean-shaven mouth—a rather shapely mouth for a man. "Sure I got some clothes, if you don't mind holes and such. I 'speck they could use a good washin' though. That all right with you?"

"Oh, yes!"

He shifted his weight to his other hip. "Where you gunna change?"

That was a problem. She looked around. The ladies' outhouse upriver would be natural, but she was getting a wild hare of an idea.

"It'd be fun to make people think I'm a boy. She laughed and enjoyed the look coming into John's face, recalling what he'd said about admiring a filly with spirit. Twirling the parasol, she gave him playful look. "Maybe people'll think the mysterious rider is my brother Emmett. He'd do it, too, but for being in the mountains."

"With the Misers' sheep."

"How did you know that?"

He looked across the picnic grounds. "Well, I been aware of your family 'round these parts for some time now."

⌒

Mae took a deep breath to still her trembling heart, and then, behind the big oak, in broad daylight, pulled off her dress and laid it on the ground, then undid her front-laced corset while craning her neck around the tree. People were still ambling toward the racetrack. John had dropped the pile of clothes at her feet and then left for the track. She looked behind her. Nobody. *Daddy sure was right about my wild heart.*

John's shirt was huge in the shoulders and so threadbare she feared her breasts would show through. And it stank to high heaven. "Whew!" She buttoned it, two or three missing at the bottom. She overlapped the tails and jammed the shirt down the trousers all around, pulling the narrow rope through the belt loops. Reeling in a lot of slack, she tied the rope so it hung down the side. The soft old Levis were big and way too long. She turned around—still no one there thank heaven—and rolled up the pant legs so she could walk. The stained felt hat belonged to the Grimshaws—left on a nail in the barn for anyone to use. Her pinned-up hair filled the space and made the hat snug. The brim flopped over her eyes. She exhaled and grinned. Nobody would know her. She was on a lark!

She hurried to stow her gown, straw hat and parasol on the buckboard. Pal's saddle was gone from the wagon bed. No doubt Hank had already saddled him. She then strode like a man toward the racetrack. It was out in the open, no trees to dodge. All the people were there, even the band. By now

Daddy would have recorded Pal's rider as "Duffy boy." Waiting for the clothes had made her late.

Breaking into a trot, she pulled the shirt out in front, hoping to hide her jiggling breasts. Her pointy shoes looked funny under those wide, rolled-up Levis.

The horses were lined up at the starting line, barefoot Indians in clothing about as bad as hers holding a few of them. Daddy, holding Pal, gave her a hidden smile. In a riding skirt sewn into culottes, Polly Sheldon swung a leg over Shamrock's Wind.

Mae wished she'd had a chance to run Pal around the track a couple of times to get him used to it. But Daddy had walked him around it and reported back through Sophie that they'd done a good job removing branches blown down by recent winds. He also told her that somebody said the track had been used for so many years that the rocks had all been removed.

She didn't look at anyone, but stroked Pal's neck, telling him, "I know you'll do your best, boy." She mounted. From the saddle she couldn't see the red handkerchief a quarter-mile away, nailed to the post. That's where they'd turn back, to finish at the start.

Shamrock's Wind was jumping around, Polly trying to control him. It took Mr. Sheldon and his two boys, Jared and George, to hold him. He was literally rearing to go. Pal, of course, waited calmly.

Daddy handed up a small switch. "Just a little on the rump now and again to remind him. Run 'im full out. He can take it." Daddy was excited.

A man on a platform began to orate. People quieted to hear. "This year, I'm offering a one-hundred-dollar purse in gold coin. Winner take all." A hurrah went up, then hushed as he continued. "Fred Grimshaw collected four-hundred and eighty dollars in bets. Winner take all. Any side bet for placement etcetera is your own affair."

The crowd roared its approval. Hats flew into the air. Five hundred and eighty dollars in all! Two hundred more than needed to get George out of jail!

She counted fifteen restless horses, including a big bay ridden by the flirtatious Rhoads Grimshaw—a cousin of Fred's according to John. Pal hadn't been on a racetrack since Daddy bought him three years ago. The former owner had raced him regularly when he'd been a three- and four-year-old. At seven, he was still in his prime. Mae had run him up and down the road in Iowa plenty of times, and always felt a sense of flying like Aladdin on a magic carpet.

A bugle blew the musical phrase that started all horse races. Leaning forward, poised with the switch, Mae tensed for the last note. With it, a gun fired and she whacked and kicked Pal into action.

"Go, boy!" she said over his neck. He was listening. She applied the switch lightly. People stood along both sides of the track, screaming and waving their arms like a giant centipede struggling to turn over. She saw rather than heard them. Already in a trancelike state she became part of the rocking gallop, the rhythm of Pal's heart, the mutual will to win. They were catching up to four horses in the lead. Rhoads Grimshaw on the bay. The Irish horse not in sight.

At the turnaround, dust blinded her as the bay and two other horses scrambled ahead. Pal's strong Morgan blood helped him dig in hard and turn with an exhilarating lunge that headed them toward the finish. She flew on her magic carpet, past the others, past Rhoads Grimshaw. Then, with the brim of her hat standing up against the wind, she was riding alone! Yet she urged Pal faster.

Dark nostrils flared alongside. Polly Sheldon glanced over from the saddle. The head of the Irish horse beat up and down like a piston. Shamrock's Wind was gaining.

Mae lowered herself to lessen the drag of the wind. "Go!" She switched and willed Pal more speed as she breathed with him and felt his slippery sweat through the trousers. He stretched, ticked the ground, stretched, ticked.

Something streaked out from the crowd—a sausage with legs, a little dog. A child with outstretched arms toddled out next. A small woman dashed after the child. Shamrock reared.

Not breaking stride, Pal leapt over dog and child.

A thump. The crowd shrieking. The horse must have fallen! Polly could be hurt.

No one cheered as Mae and Pal crossed the finish line. Everyone stared at the downed horse and rider, and perhaps an injured woman and child.

Mae turned and trotted Pal back beside the track as other horses raced to the finish. Shamrock was on his feet, shaking, and, to her relief, the entire Sheldon family surrounded Polly, who stood off the track. The horse had not fallen on her, and no child or woman lay injured, not even the dog.

Now people began to clap for Mae, some pointing and yelling, "Who's that rider?"

Mr. Dixon stood with the purse held high while Daddy, Hank and Sophie hopped for joy and hugged each other. John Dunaway stood back, smiling. Mae, grinning, raised a hand at him.

Pal's calm disposition had given her the victory. He knew that hazards existed on any roadway. Daddy would accept the purse, and soon George would be out of jail. Laughing out loud, she trotted Pal to the wagon—not wanting people to smell her. This time she would change in the lady's outhouse.

16

B y now everybody knew Mae was a girl. And a local celebrity!
"Congratulations," the Sheldon girls said more or less in unison as
Mae stepped outside in her lacy white frock, John's old clothes in her extended
arms so as not to contaminate her any further. They had been waiting for her.

"Thank you, thank you!" Mae said. "But I got help from that dog, sorry
to say."

Polly, with an abrasion on her otherwise fine-looking straight nose, added
with a pained smile, "And the baby boy."

"And his mother," Mae completed. "Sure you're not hurt?"

"Naw, just some bruises."

"She's our t-tomboy," said Katy Irene under the aqua plume of her hat.
"We came over to invite you and your f-family to come over to our b-blanket
for some p-peach ice cream. My grandmother has a s-secret recipe. You never
tasted b-better." *Three stuterers in that family.*

"Ice cream, ice cream," chanted little Tooty as she gripped Polly's hand.

"I'd love that, and I'm sure my family would, too. Thank you. I'll go ask
them. But first, did I get this hat on right?"

Polly and Katy Irene went to work rearranging the hat, poking at stray
locks and inserting hat pins while Jessie and Tooty looked on with fascination.
"You should go down to the river and wash that dust off your face," Polly advised when she finished. "I already did."

They seemed anxious for her to look good, like they wanted Jared to like
her. Sisters helping a shy young man. Well, she would take all the help she
could get. And her heart was still flying, having rescued her brother George
from that jail cell.

At the water's edge, with the Sheldon girls gone to their picnic, Mae
bunched up her skirts so as not to soil the hems in the mud. She was bent over,
applying water from a cupped hand to her face when a man's voice surprised her.

"Mae?"

She turned to see John Dunaway. "Oh! Excuse me, but I'd like a little
privacy. Your things are there on the bank."

"I see them. That's not why I'm here. I'm turning my back."

Patting her face dry with her underskirt, she made her way up to dry land
and shook out her skirts. "Do I look all right?" she asked him.

He turned around, eyes smiling. "I'll say you do!"

"No dirt on my face?"

"None."

"Good. As you can see, your clothes are all there."

"Thanks, but I was wonderin' if you'd… ah…" He removed his high hat and turned the brim in his hands. "Well, if you'd see fit to let me take you to the… barn dance on Saturday at the Gaffney place."

"A dance?"

"Yup. The Gaffneys have a dance 'bout once a month, in summertime anyhow. An' I'd sure be proud if you'd go with me."

"Well, sure. I could do that." She owed him that much. She couldn't have won the race worrying about her legs showing. Anyway, it might be foolish to think Jared would be less interested if he saw her with John Dunaway. Maybe it'd get his blood up a little. "I've heard of a family named Gaffney. Where do they live?"

"Up the trail from where you used to work, 'bout three-quarters of a mile up east of the Granlees." He looked down suddenly, perhaps recalling that she'd told him she worked for the Pratts.

What a silly goose she'd been to fib like that! She'd done it so he wouldn't insist on giving her a ride, and now she was going to a dance with him. *Oh, what tangled webs we weave,* as sister Delphine used to quote.

Pink showed through John's tanned face. "I'll shore be right proud taking you to the dance. If it's all right, I'll pick you up at five at your place."

"You know where I live?"

"Uh-huh. Is it all right, at five I mean? They have eats at the dances. The dancin' goes on purtineer all night. Sometimes there's scrambled eggs in the mornin'."

"Sure, pick me up at five. Oh, and John," it occurred to her to say, "come over to our picnic and get your five dollars back. Daddy's got the purse."

A furrow appeared between his brows and his blue eyes narrowed, annoyed. "I told you, I don't need it back. I'm headed outta here now. Got a chore to do for Miz Waggoner."

❧

Back at the Duffy blanket, Sophie and Hank sat exchanging quiet words, Hank working on mug of beer. Nearby, Daddy held forth at the beer vendor's table. She went to him first, whispering the Sheldon's invitation into his ear, then to Hank and Sophie. It didn't seem polite to announce it in the hearing of those who were not invited. But after standing and waiting, she finally said, "Come on, let's go." She hooked an arm toward Daddy.

Hank pushed the palm of a hand at her in a wait signal.

"But they're—"

"We need to talk about the winnings," he said quietly. "Dad," he called, beckoning him.

Daddy came over, signaling his drinking friends to wait for him.

Mae was in a hurry, not sitting down, so Hank stood up and spoke to the three of them.

"I think Mae should get a hundred dollars. She did the riding. I'll take the money to pay the court and pay my own debt to my father-in-law."

A man came up roaring his congratulations. He and Daddy broke into laughter, and then Daddy slapped his back and steered him toward the beer vendor. Drinking pals.

Hank shrugged and finished his speech to Mae and Sophie. That leaves eighty dollars for Dad. Farley wrote me that Dad's wastin' a pile on drink."

Mae nodded, but also realized that Daddy was enjoying himself. If she got the hundred dollars—a thrilling thought considering she'd never had any money of her own—he would have eighty to have some fun with.

Hank straightened his shoulders and walked over to Daddy, saying in a voice loud enough for Mae to hear, "Dad, give me the winnings."

"Son," Daddy said turning around with palms up and a smile on his face, "we've got money to spare! I've a few dunners of my own to clear, you know." He turned back to his friends and paid for another round.

"Well," Mae said. "Are we going to stand here or should I go by myself to have some good ice cream?"

Hank took Daddy by the arm. "Come on, Dad, you'll want to talk horses with Mr. Sheldon."

"All right," Daddy said, gulping what remained in his mug—a mug lent by the vendor. "But let's take some to the Sheldons and show we're sportin' winners. How 'bout a gallon jug?" he called to the obliging vendor.

17

The band was playing an odd little waltz as Mae crossed the shady picnic grounds with Daddy, Hank, and Sophie. It put her in mind of circus music for flying trapeze performers. Adding to the unearthliness, into the small pauses of the score intruded the discordant tinkle of the distant calliope playing another melody in a different key. Mae was grounding herself for perhaps the most important visit of her life.

Just ahead lounged the unsuspecting local aristocracy, Mr. William Chauncey Sheldon, now on a chair beside his mother, the white-haired lady in a black lace frock with a watch pinned to her ample breast. Legs crossed, W. C. smoked a cigar, while around him the young people dug into the ice cream dished out by their Chinese servant.

Daddy set the jug of beer on the Sheldons' checkered cloth and waited while Mae introduced him. She could tell he made a good impression, and continued to do so when he sat down on the grass and exclaimed over his bowl of ice cream that it was ambrosia from heaven. He stayed for a short visit and then lifted his hat, thanked Mr. and Mrs. Sheldon, and headed back to his drinking friends. This left Hank to answer Mr. Sheldon's questions about Pal, something Hank did with enthusiasm.

As the horse talk prevailed, Mae finished a bowl of the most delicious ice cream she'd ever tasted. The peach chunks made her mouth water, they were so full of flavor and sweetness. Seeing a few peaches still in the basket, she asked Mrs. Sheldon if she might take one home to her mother, who was ill. With a kindly smile Mrs. Sheldon shoved the whole basket at her while speaking in a low voice so as not to interfere with her husband's monologue.

"Take them to her," she said, "We have plenty."

Thanking her, Mae hoped she hadn't been presumptuous.

Mr. Sheldon was presenting the lineage and training of Shamrock's Wind, the horse himself adding a flatulent cloud that wafted slowly through the warm afternoon. Moments later the band commenced a new piece.

Polly said to Mae, "I'm going to ride Shamrock at the Valensins' Saturday after next."

"Valensins?" Mae knew nothing about them.

"Oh, you'll have to go to their track sometime. Dad, do they have a half-miler?"

"I doubt it. They cater more to Thoroughbreds, now that more of them are being imported, and this breed does better in a longer race. Maybe there's still time to check with Mr. Valensin about entering a grade horse. You certainly did well on him today, Miss Duffy."

He continued, "The track's a mile circuit, groomed, people fenced off. No dogs. Betting for show and placement and so forth." He revealed his teeth in a smile that barely moved the waxed curls at the ends of his mustache.

"I love the Valensin races," Jessie chimed in. "They're a Duke and Dutchess!"

The white-haired grandmother chuckled. "The Duchess of Hicksville."

Everyone laughed.

"Seriously," Katy Irene said, "Count Valensin is from Italy, but he lives in Hicksville, just fifteen miles or so down the road. A grand place with a beautiful racetrack. He owns the best horses and breeds them on his stock farm in Pleasanton. They've got so much money! Uncle's a friend of his, aren't you?" She looked at Mr. Sheldon.

Mr. Sheldon added, "The whole world got an inkling of the Count's worth last year when *The New York Times* reported that his last will and testament bequeathes to his son Pio exactly one dollar." He paused while that sank in. "The article went on to say that the Count recently refused an offer of $100,000 for Sydney. That's one of his stallions."

Obviously the Sheldon children knew all about the disinherited Pio. The boys were smiling among themselves.

"News like that keeps the younger generation in line," Mr. Sheldon added with a jovial smile.

Everyone took that in the good humor in which it was clearly intended, and Polly said, "The Governor and senators go to the Valensin races."

Through all of this, Jared Sheldon had not uttered a syllable.

"Do you ever ride your horses in races?" Mae asked him directly.

He shook his head, mouth closed like a cat that swallowed a canary.

"He leaves that to me," Polly said with a laugh.

"Where do you live?" Jessie asked Mae, looking up from her ice cream.

"Yes, where?" the dowager wanted to know.

All eyes turned to Mae, and she knew she must not tell them about the awful shale cabin. "A little this side of Michigan Bar."

"This side of the river?"

"Yes."

She didn't want to get specific. "Actually we're moving out of there," she improvised. "You see, we're just now looking at another place. In fact I think we'll move there in a day or two." *What a liar I am!*

Thankfully, Katy Irene changed the subject. "Mrs. Miser said you give p-p-piano lessons."

"That's right. I teach violin too." Mae had never given a lesson of any kind, but every one of the younger people visibly perked up at that, including Jared, who raised his brows above his warm brown eyes, a sort of dark hazel color. That look went right to her heart.

"Do your s-students come to your place?" Katy Irene asked.

"No, we left our piano in Iowa. I go to their places." *The Misers if I'm lucky.*

Katy Irene smiled and Mae realized she'd rarely seen a more attractive girl—big dark eyes and coloring like the peaches, with loose dark curls around her face and shoulders. It was unfortunate that she had that little stammer.

"Grandma, we've been looking for a t-teacher," Katy Irene said. "And I w-wwant to improve my t-technique before I start at the college."

Mr. Sheldon said with a wryly raised brow, "You might want to leave a little something for the music teachers at Mills to impart."

"I hope you know he's joshing," the grandmother chided. She then looked steadily at Mae "Could you start right away?"

Mae was nodding "yes" when Mrs. Sheldon said in a quiet voice, "Maybe you young folks oughta have one of your musical afternoons. That way you can get acquainted with each other's music. Do you two play too?" she asked Sophie and Hank.

Laughing, Sophie shook her head in time to, "No, no, no, no."

Hank said, "Not 'less you count whistlin'." With a grin at Sophie, "I think we'd better go back and keep an eye on your hamper. Thank you for the tasty ice cream. Good to meet you all. No need for you to come, Mae."

Grateful to him, Mae sat with her legs to the side and watched them go. Looking around her, she steered back to the one thing this family seemed most interested in. "Do all of you play instruments?"

"All us younger generation," said Polly, "except Lauren. Katy Irene plays guitar, banjo and piano. I play piano and Jessie's learning that too. George plays trumpet, and Jared plays the violin. He's our singer too."

Jared played the violin! "Do you all play together?" Mae directed to Jared, hoping he'd say something.

He smiled and nodded.

"Jared's good on the violin," Mr. Sheldon said with an approving look at his son.

Pure joy pumped through Mae at the thought of playing duets with a sweetheart, and perhaps a husband.

Katy Irene said, "I don't play piano like Polly can. She's a whiz."

Mae wanted to ask why none of them were playing in the band today, but she needed to return to the target. "I'd just love to join you in a musical afternoon. What day would be best?"

"How about Saturday?" Mrs. Sheldon said.

"Hold your horses," said her husband. We'll have to see how far the boys get with the plum harvest by Friday; and you, Jared, plowing the new bottomland."

Just then the band music stopped and a drum roll quieted the picnic grounds. Mr. Dixon was standing on the bandstand as the musicians carried their instruments away. He beckoned to Mr. Sheldon.

Not about to lose her opening, Mae said to Katy Irene, "I could come by on Friday afternoon and hear you play. To get us started."

Mr. Sheldon was helping his mother get up—a lady hardly any taller on her feet than in her chair. She walked proudly, arm in arm with her son, while Jared and the other boys passed them on the way to the bandstand.

"That'd be grand—Friday afternoon," Katy Irene said to Mae. "Is that all right, Auntie?"

"Fine with me," Mrs. Sheldon said. "Let's all go see."

"See what?" Mae wondered aloud, having miraculously won round two. She was invited to their house!

Mrs. Sheldon shook crumbs from the skirt of her summery print dress. "Dad's going to fire the cannon," meaning her husband.

Mae left the basket of peaches on the Sheldon blanket and walked with Katy Irene and Polly, who held Tooty's little hand.

"Mae, Mae!" called a distant child.

She turned to see Georgie Granlees waving at her. His family was also headed to the bandstand. Mary Granlees raised a hand in greeting—the familiar grave visage and long straight hair. The two Indian Marys, mother and daughter, were there, no doubt helping with the baby and keeping Georgie in tow. With so many ladies in light calico and white day dresses, they looked out of place in their black, old-fashioned skirts and blouses.

Mae squeezed into the crowd in front of the bandstand. Down beyond it, on the opposite shore of the lazy little river, cascades of grapevines covered a high green wall of trees.

Two familiar faces came smiling toward Mae through the crowd, Mrs. Miser and Agnes.

"That's a purty hat you got there," Isabella Miser teased, "on a girl who rides like the wind."

Mae laughed and twirled the parasol. "Why, thank you kindly. I do rather fancy it. I believe you know the Sheldons?"

"Of course," said Mrs. Miser, nodding toward them. "How do you do?"

At that moment Mr. Dixon began orating and all looked up at him.

"For those new to these parts, I'd like to introduce the widows of the first pioneers of the Cosumnes River Valley—sisters who came in the second wagon train ever to cross the Sierra Mountains into California. These girls, and they were girls then, traversed the untamed continent with their family and settled here before gold was discovered." He cupped his hands in a loud stage whisper to one side and then the other, "We won't mention the gold their family found all through forty-seven." Chuckles rumbled through the crowd.

"Well, these two ladies lost no time in marrying the owners of the Spanish Land Grant of this area, Jared Sheldon and William Daylor—stalwarts already settled here in beautiful Rancho Omochumne. They took one look at these comely little ladies and got themselves partnered up in a hurry." Friendly laughter.

"Then the sisters embarked upon a new journey, one fraught with different hardships and sorrows. Their men often had to be away or out working the large ranch, and the sisters' houses were at least two miles apart—the only houses in the entire area—so they faced isolation, wilderness, Indians, morbid disease, and lawless gangs of miners when the gold fever started. They did backbreaking work, carried water, and gave birth time and again. As the years passed, they buried infants and husbands, and yet they endured.

"They mothered two clans of outstanding citizens to whom they bequeathed their courageous spirits. These sisters are as fine a pair of pioneers as could be found anywhere in California. Now, if you would please come forward, Mrs. Sarah Rhoads Daylor Grimshaw."

A drum purred as the queenly matriarch of the Grimshaw clan mounted the platform and stood beside him, crowned by her bun of snow-white hair. Mae clapped with everyone else. Mr. Dixon consulted his paper before announcing:

"Please come forward, Mrs. Catherine Rhoads Sheldon Mahone Dalton."

The straight-backed mother of W. C. Sheldon stepped up on the bandstand and stood proudly beside her sister. Everyone clapped again.

Mr. Dixon quieted the crowd with the flats of his hands "Now, each of them will say a few words."

The sisters looked at each other and came to a wordless decision.

The Sheldon matriarch spoke first, and Mae listened with every fiber of her being to the woman into whose family she hoped to marry. The stout little lady spoke with confidence, meeting Mae's eyes and, it seemed, the eyes of everyone in the audience.

"We usually fire the cannon at home on the Fourth of July," the lady began. "That's been our custom, but we thought you might like to see this relic of a bygone era shoot its wad."

Jared, George, and Fred and Rhoads Grimshaw were pushing and pulling a small cannon out from under the bandstand, and the lady continued.

"I don't know if you newcomers know the story of my first husband's death. He was shot and killed by gold miners over at Cook's Bar—Bridge House they call it now, or Live Oak. He'd bought three hundred acres there and planted corn, squash and beans, but he needed to dam the river to irrigate his crops. He made a bargain with the miners, duly set down on paper and signed by the parties. It said the dam would have a sluice and he was to let the water flow through it every day except Saturday night and Sunday. That's when the miners did their drinking so it wouldn't bother them. My husband also agreed to pay each man for the loss of a day's work. But the first time the water flooded their claims, they went back on their deal. Pulled the guard off the cannon, spiked it and—"

A female voice called, "What do you mean, spiked it?"

Pointing to the weathered field piece, the lady explained: "They pounded a metal spike in where the powder's supposed to go. See, in there." Mr. Sheldon had opened a little hatch and was pouring in black powder from a small leather bag. People behind Mae jumped like popcorn to see it, children lifted to shoulders.

"Time ran out for my husband. The shootin' started."

A man in the crowd yelled, "Where'd he git a cannon?"

"Oh yes, well, he took it from Sutter's Fort—by then the place was emptied out, cannons free for the taking. He set it on the high bank of the river with a twenty-four–hour guard, just in case. He had a dozen loyal ranchers on his side. Told the miners they'd get blasted if they so much as touched that dam with their axes. But they started chopping it, and the cannon couldn't be fired. It woulda saved his life. That was July 12, 1851. We always remember him on the Fourth of July by firing the cannon that he couldn't fire that day. I like to think he hears it. He'd sure be proud to see all of you here—Americans, good farmers, good ranchers, so many good people. Thank you."

People clapped. Then Mr. Dixon asked Mrs. Grimshaw if she'd like to say something.

The Grimshaw matriarch looked at the hushed audience, cleared her throat and said, "There's more pioneers here than the two of us. I see some forty-niners." She pointed her finger with each name: "Plummer, Bailey, Meiss, Sanders, Priscilla Pollock, Mrs. Pratt, Mr. Driscoll." She looked around, searching. "Browns, Misers, More of us're passing each year, but I see the children: Ingersolls, Hauskins, Granlees, Gaffneys. Taylors, Wilsons. Well, that's a few anyhow. I guess that's all I got to say. But my son Fred wants to say something, if that's all right." She looked at Mr. Dixon and he nodded.

Sandy-haired Fred Grimshaw, the bet-taker for the race, jumped up to the platform and spoke plainly. "Neighbors, we've heard about our past and I'd like to mention the future. Some of you might know, the Southern Pacific Railroad is thinking about putting a line up through here, right along Jackson Road, connecting Sacramento with the mines and ranches of Amador County. That's just the kind of progress we need, to get our produce to Sacramento, and we've got to get behind it. A thing like that would increase the value of this land around here a hundredfold. And it'd likely be followed by a telephone line, too, someday. This area was populated to a greater extent thirty years ago. We don't want to see it decline any more. We all need to stand up for progress. Some of us are going to meet to talk about what we can do to help. So keep your ears and eyes open."

Clapping resumed as Fred Grimshaw jumped down, and it continued as the grandmothers left the band stand. Meanwhile, Jared, grandson of the murdered pioneer, rolled a ball about as big as an undersized cantaloupe down the throat of the cannon, which by now was aimed across the river.

Mr. Sheldon lit the fuse hanging outside the hatch, and those around it stepped back with plugged ears. The whole crowd put fingers in their ears. Mae, however, wanted to hear it.

A deep-throated ka-boom moved the ground under her feet, and she felt like her chest and ears had been punched. Kittie-Tooty screamed and then wailed. Polly picked her up and hugged her as, across the river, the leaves of a cottonwood showered to the ground while birds flushed upward. People were cheering.

"Oh my!" Mae exclaimed to Polly, "Can you imagine what it must have been like in the War Between the States with all those cannons firing?"

"Terrible. Tooty dear, hush now. It's all right. That's just for fun on the Fourth of July. Shhh. Quiet, baby." Other young children and babies were howling too. Polly petted Kittie's towhead as the child sobbed on her shoulder.

"Let's take her to the merry-go-round," Polly said. Tooty looked up from Polly's shoulder, suddenly smiling though her tears.

"I'm coming too," said Katy Irene. The Sheldon boys were busy pulling the cannon toward the wagons, and men and boys started to play horseshoes not far away.

Glad to be alone with Polly and Katy Irene, Mae walked with them in the dappled shade of the grove. "Now I know more about the man your brother Jared was named for," she said to both of them. "How old is Jared?"

"He'll be twenty at the end of the month."

Perfect—unless he's mute. To appear impartial, she asked, "And George? How old is he?"

"Sixteen come December."

Just a little younger than Mae, but possessing the worst stutter she had ever encountered.

They arrived at a line of people who'd just come from the bandstand. Polly took three nickels from her skirt pocket and handed them to the man at the little red gate. Not having a nickel, Mae said, "I've done enough riding for one day. I'll watch."

As though an afterthought, she added as Polly and Kittie were about to step up on the platform, "Jared doesn't say much, does he?"

"Oh, he gets going pretty good at times. After you get to know him." Polly smiled encouragingly. Tooty climbed aboard a blue and red steed.

Relieved, Mae felt her spirit soar. The gates of Rome had opened. True, he was shy, but also a musician, a person of finer sensibilities. And she could still feel the warmth of his brown eyes.

18

Brimming over with success, Mae went to the Miser place to return the hat and parasol. She blurted it out the moment Mrs. Miser opened the door, ending with, "I'm certain they'll invite me to one of their musical afternoons after I see them on Friday. Did you know Jared Sheldon plays the violin? We could play duets together."

Mrs. Miser lifted a knee and gave it a slap. "Well, I'll be! I should'ov thought of that when you said you'as a violinist."

Escorting Mae inside, she yelled into the house, "Agnes! Mae's here with news!"

Agnes seemed equally pleased. Mae walked over to the piano. "I hope I haven't lost my touch."

"Touch? Well, you just set yourself down there and limber up."

Mae floated through a couple of pieces like she'd been born playing them. Joy, she realized, directed her fingers to land on the right keys.

"Could I come back tomorrow with my music? I would so like to practice before I go to the Sheldons."

"You bet. Bring your music over here any old time you've a hankering. We love hearing you play, don't we, Agnes?" Agnes nodded, and so did all the children who had materialized while Mae was playing. All stood looking at her like she was Lillie Langtry.

She felt like hugging every one in the house. Here, she had found real friends.

It had been a long hot day, but Mae felt a lightness of spirit after being in the Miser family. Stirring the nine eggs into the sizzling salt pork, she noticed the slope of Daddy's shoulders as he sat looking down, far from the fire so as not to feel its heat. Something bothered him. As well it ought, yet she felt only sorrow for him.

Farley tenderfooted back from the river in his dripping longjohns and sat down too hard. She didn't correct him. The lifespan of that washtub seemed less her problem now.

"Mom," she called. "Supper's about ready."

Daddy fetched Emma from the cabin and helped settle her in her rocker next to his chair.

"I need ten dollars to pay my debts," he told Mae as she handed him a full plate.

She didn't hesitate. "Sure." With ninety dollars she still felt rich. But she was a little alarmed that he had gone through his eighty dollars so fast.

The next afternoon, Mae practiced her Czerny exercises and her favorite Chopin Nocturne. Afterward, two of the Miser grandchildren wanted a lesson.

She gave a beginner lesson to five-year-old Annie and a semblance of a lesson to pretty little Alice, just two and a half. Grateful to be invited to supper, she refused money that first day, but agreed to teach the three grandchildren who lived in the house full time, at twenty-five cents apiece, once a week. So now she was less of a liar. And in her stockings she carried the tiny wafer-thin gold pieces, forty-five dollars per shoe.

After an ebullient supper at the full Miser table, the quince pie tasted heavenly with the clotted cream. As the last bites were licked up, Laura's husband excused himself and went out to the barn. Children short and tall went out to play with the water they reeled up from the well. Mrs. Miser declared the front room too hot, so the women hauled the kitchen chairs out the back door and sat in the shade of a honey locust tree. They smiled at the children's antics—the younger ones already naked and muddy, the older ones down to their bloomers and throwing buckets of water, all screaming and laughing. Crevice Creek at the back of the house was barely damp in places.

Agnes brought out the coffee tray, and Mae confided to Mrs. Miser how much she wished her parents could live in a better place. She explained that after paying "certain debts," they had only ninety dollars of race winnings left. She told about Farley's difficulties finding work and Daddy's trouble with his weak lungs—that's how he was explaining it nowadays. She concluded, "So we can't pay rent. Where we are now Farley cuts wood for the owner. I was wondering if you might know of a better house where his woodcutting might pay the rent. The one we're in now is filthy and horrible."

"Well I declare, this is providential," said the lady. Putting cup and saucer down, she picked up a fan from the tray, snapped it open, and fanned herself as she spoke. "I just heard tell of a place today. Couple miles down the road." Tilting the fan, "Agnes, don't we have more of these?"

Agnes got up and went inside.

"Is the house on your road?" Mae asked.

"Yup. Down Latrobe Road just before you get to Stone House Road. In fact, Stone House is named for the very house I'm talking about."

Another crude stone cabin, Mae presumed. She'd seen them sprinkled around the countryside, nothing more than small walled rooms. The Duffys already had one. John Driscoll had told Mae that gold miners from Ireland had built most of those little places in haste.

Mrs. Miser was saying, "The builder of the stone house abandoned it years ago when the gold panned out. John Long owns the place now and about three hundred grazing acres. I hear the people living there cut wood for him. That widow has what… Agnes, is it five youngsters?"

Back with a fan for Mae and folded newspapers for Lillian and Laura, Agnes said, "Seven. Name's Mrs. Smith."

Mrs. Miser went on. "Yes, that's it. She's about to move out. That's what her boy Shadrack said the other day. Eleven years old, delivers our wood in return for milk and eggs."

"He's a right good boy," Lillian added.

Mae's Japanese fan moved the air, cooling her damp face. "Is it nice?" she asked, "I mean better than the other rock cabins around here?"

Mrs. Miser, pinching the delicate ear of her porcelain cup, fanned that question away. "This one's much better." She took a sip and put the cup down. "Rocks would be the wrong word. Those stones were quarried by skilled workmen, fitted perfectly without any mortar. What, Agnes, three or four rooms?"

"Three. Folks say it's the nicest of the gold-miner houses."

"To be had for delivering firewood?" Mae clarified.

"That's what I hear. Git yerself on down there and take a gander. Place like that won't be empty for long," Mrs. Miser warned.

🙾

With a couple hours of daylight left, Mae decided to look. Waving good-bye, she galloped and trotted down Latrobe Road as the blazing sun sat on top of the low hills. Every living thing except Mae and Pal was hiding from the heat.

Crevice Creek trickled here and there on her right in a fairy-tale landscape. While the road went up and down steep rocky hills, the creek bed fell steadily into a deepening slate gorge. Sometimes the water dripped over thin gray sheets of shale like pages of a stone book. On the left, dark boulders rose like natural cathedrals surrounded by oak groves. Cathedral Rocks, she named the place in her mind.

The Duffys had no sidesaddle, so she rode like a man with her full skirt over Pal's rump. The soles of her feet were a little sore from the coins pressed into the stirrups. The dampish creek bed veered to the right and meandered into a flat valley while the road continued to hug the side of a hill. Rounding a corner, she saw the house made of large yellow blocks. This was the same sandstone that lined the cheese house at the Granlees-Driscoll place, surely from the same quarry.

The dry grassland on her right borrowed red from the sunset, as did the house—one-story, decent looking, solid, with a flat slate roof. Children were playing around a large oak tree that would shade the house in the morning and half the afternoon. She heard the muffled sound of an axe. A low wall of the same stones ran about thirty yards along the road in either direction from a curved entrance into the earthen yard. Just a few steps down the road from the house, a door framed by the same sandstone blocks poked out of a hillside, and she knew enough about California to recognize a cheese house, to keep food cool in summer and unfrozen in winter.

With growing excitement she rode into the yard and saw the depth of the house, much larger than the shale cabin. Here each stone was a uniform size, about two feet long and half as wide and thick, tightly fitted in a brickwork pattern. No spider holes. The ends of square beams jutted through the top stones, notched to make the beams fit. Matching the blue-gray roof, the slate windowsills on either side of the door would support flowerpots.

The children came around the back of the house to look at her, and the axe blows were suddenly louder as Pal stepped to where the house no longer blocked sound. A slender boy, naked above the waist, was chopping wood and throwing it into a crude cart. Every one of his ribs showed, and he was shiny with perspiration. Shadrack.

A gaunt woman came outside with a load of something in her apron.

"Howdy," Mae said, walking Pal toward her.

The skin on the widow's bony face looked taut and thin surrounded by strands of brown hair that had come loose from her bun, and the two vertical wrinkles above her long nose made her look cross. Her tunic of a dress had been scrubbed of color. "Kin I hep ya, miss?"

"I just came from the Mrs. Misers' place. She said you were leaving, and I'm looking for a place for my family to live."

A tired voice, "Where they livin' now?"

"Near Michigan Bar. An awful place. My folks are both poorly and need a better place, but it takes all our money to buy food." Seeing the woman's head tilt in thought, she hastened to add, "I was hoping to look inside."

"You're ridin' good horseflesh there," Mrs. Smith said in a skeptical tone.

Mae had to think a minute. "Pal isn't for sale."

Looking toward the sunset the woman continued to squint at Mae. "Lemme get shed of this here and I'll show you the house." She took her load to the cheese house.

Meanwhile, Mae tied Pal to an iron stave with a hole in it, the other end pounded into the oak tree. "We gotta horse too," said a girl about four years old. She pointed up the hill at a swaybacked nag. The rabbity animal was nosing around a boulder for dry grass too short to be seen. All the children watched Mae.

Mrs. Smith returned and showed Mae inside. The house was surprisingly cool. By evening, wooden structures in this part of the country felt like ovens, but this thick-walled house with north facing windows had been wisely built. Four crude cots stood side by side in the main room. Soiled dishes had been left on the table at the window. A fireplace of the same yellow sandstone provided cooking in the west wall, fitted with two iron swivel arms, each supporting a hanging pot. On the back wall, doors opened into two smaller rooms, one with a double-sized bed and the other with two small beds with straw poking out of the mattresses. Farley could sleep in the main room, no longer outside in the tent, and Mae and the folks would have private rooms. This place looked too good to be true.

The sandstone glowed a soft gold in the light from the front window, giving the place a friendly feel despite the confusion of beds and odd things that children throw around. Children's shouts outside could hardly be heard through the stone. "You're leaving then? Did I hear right?" Mae queried.

Frowning at the slate floor, the women shook her head as though denying that, but nonetheless said, "We can't make it no more. The mister died a while back"—she gestured with her head toward the back of the house—"an' my boy's cuttin' wood and sellin' it for next to nuthin'. I can git work in Sacramento. It's a big city. I heared a woman can make a living for her kids there. My boy could work in the train factory and not be killing hisself."

"When you leaving?'

"Soon's I git our belongings down to Sacramento an' find work. Meantime, the kids gotta eat." She exhaled like she doubted she could accomplish all of that.

"You think the owner of this house would mind having a new family move in?"

"That ain't none a' my business. All I know is, nobody's comin' in here 'til we're out, whenever that is, and I'd 'preciate it if ya don't tell Mr. Long I'm thinkin' on leavin.' He lives up this road."

"I passed a house about three bends back."

"That's the one."

The landlord didn't know. Good, he wouldn't have anybody else lined up. "Did I hear right? You don't pay rent money? Just deliver his firewood?"

"That ain't none a' yer business."

Mae plowed on. "Well, my folks'll want to see this place. But Mrs. Miser's right. It won't stay vacant for long after you move out. When do you think that will be?"

"Like I said. When I find a way to git to Sacramento." She was looking Mae straight in the eyes.

"There's a wagon in back," Mae said.

"That old pony cart's all we got. Ain't big enough to haul us and our belongings too. When the mister died I'as 'bliged to trade the wagon to the undertaker for a decent buryin'."

"We have a wagon," Mae said, suddenly seeing a way out. "My brother could move you."

In the light from the windows, the woman's eyes shone like dark beacons. "You tellin' me he'd drive me and my kids and all our goods twenty-five miles down to Sacramento?"

"If you let us move in here and don't tell anybody else about it."

The door flew open and a very young boy with a dirty face came in yelling, "Ma, I needs me a drink!"

"Well then, quitcher chasin' around like a wild Injun. You won't parch yerself so. Come mornin' we'll go to the river."

"I needs a drink NOW!"

"We don't have none."

"But I seen water in here." He looked around the room.

"Shad needed it. He's working like a horse."

The little boy's lower lip pushed out, and his shoulders sloped downward as he left, shutting the door behind him.

Water would be a problem, Mae realized on her ride back to the folks. But that could be Daddy's job. He might even enjoy it, kind of like his stagecoach days, only he'd be delivering water from the river, maybe to people up and down Latrobe Road in exchange for little services, or money. That's how many people lived when they had no work. Mrs. Miser's son-in-law had called this the Panic of '93.

19

Mae arrived at the shale cabin singing Stephen Foster songs. The whole ride she'd been excited about living three or four miles closer to the Sheldons. She would pot flowers for the windowsills and invite people to visit. Mom would break out of her melancholy and sew curtains for the windows. They could get the rest of their furniture out of storage and under a roof. Jared Sheldon would court her. She would charm him. All her experience told her she could do that.

Walking Pal past the open door that spilled lamplight across the dark yard, she waved at the folks—Daddy on the chair reading a newspaper under the lamp hanging from the rafters, Mom on the bed as usual. No sign of Farley. She hung the bridle on a point of jutting shale, removed the saddle and blanket and laid them in the wagon bed. Then she led Pal down the bank to the bottomland. He sucked a long drink, folded his legs, rolled, hooves in the air, and then stood up shaking water.

Leaping out of the way and laughing in the dark, Mae waited for him to drink again and before leading him back to the wagon. She removed her outer clothes, waistcoat and skirt, and hung them over the side of the wagon. With her special stick she went to work on Pal. "Oh, you're such a good boy," she crooned as she scraped the dirty, sweaty, hairy water off him, much of it streaming down her elbow. "We'll make you pretty, yes we will." The night air was soft on her bare skin and cool through her camisole and knee-length bloomers. She felt good all over. The cosmos had taken a mysterious turn in her direction.

It was too dark for anybody to see her in her bloomers, so Pal led her along the path to the place where the bank sloped down, and she hobbled him in the green bottomland.

A cow mooed.

Mr. Thompsons's cows weren't supposed to be there. He lived a long way back from the river and was supposed to get his four dairy cows out of there in the morning. The landlord, Mr. Parker, insisted on that. Water was one thing, coming down the river all the time, but grass was another. Just last week the two men had a row on account of Mr. Thompson leaving the cows longer every day and not staying with them. Now, here they were at night! The Duffys had grazing rights for the two horses because Farley kept Mr. Parker supplied with wood. Well, this had to be reported.

Back at the cabin Farley still wasn't home. Mae found Mom's rocking chair in the dark and brought it to the light of the open door, telling them she had something important to say. She helped Mom up from the bed and into the chair. Mae sat on her cot, which was flush against the rough shale where spiders hid in a thousand crevices. Maybe they suppressed the bugs and lice and mosquitoes, so Mae tried not to disturb the webs though she shuddered to think of those hairy-legged things creeping around at night. Often she woke up with painful bites. She would have made her bed outside on the ground but for the bats and snakes and packs of starving dogs. But now she had found a new house! Daddy looked at her expectantly.

Briefly mentioning supper and piano lessons at the Miser place, Mae could hardly contain her excitement as she described the stone house and its benefits. "You see Daddy, Mom, I'm so happy about going to the Sheldons on Friday. You know I've got my sights on Jared Sheldon, but I'm not about to ask a man of any standing to this place. I could in that house. We could ask him in, and Mom you could serve him your good cinnamon buns, baked in a cooking box in that big fireplace. You see, that house would change my life—our lives. You might become in-laws of the Sheldons." She mentioned the cheese house and the wall along the road with the grand curved entrance. "And it's ours, if only Farley cuts wood for the owner—which he already does for Mr. Parker, so I don't see that stopping us."

"Well I'll be jiggered!" Daddy said with a big smile.

"Oh, I want so much for us to move there. Don't you, Mom?"

Mom's shoulders twitched, and her toes continued nudging the earth just outside the open door, propelling the rocker imperceptibly.

"We could move in there tomorrow. I just know Jared's mother will invite me to a musical afternoon, and Jared could drive me home. He's the oldest son, twenty years old, and I've never laid eyes on a finer young man. He doesn't have a sweetheart either. His sister Polly told me."

Unable to restrain herself, she jumped up and whirled around in her bloomers and camisole, and made foot and hand gestures like a vaudeville dancer in a finishing flourish.

Daddy's eyes gleamed.

"Think about it. I'm getting to know Jared socially!" She clasped her hands and let the word sink in. "They grow specialty fruit and ship it all over the country. Jared's father is a gentleman farmer. He travels far and wide, imports Chinese pheasants, and invites senators and such to his place to hunt. Jared's the oldest son; someday he'll inherit. They have maybe a thousand acres along the river." This was a guess; for all she knew they had twice that. She watched to see if that registered on Emma. Did her eyebrows elevate slightly? "Land, Mom, they've got valuable river land!" Seeing no response from her mother, she went on.

"Besides fruit, they raise corn, alfalfa, and I don't know what all. They have hired men! Oh, I just know Jared is the man for me! This is my destiny. To be a Sheldon!"

With Mom's hips bulging through the slats of the rocking chair, she resembled a sack of flour, but her mouth straightened in a ghost of a smile as she spoke.

"Mae, you sparkle so when you're happy! That young man won't find another like you."

Nowadays Mom rarely put that many words together.

"Your mother's right on that score," Daddy agreed. "Just give him one of your smiles and he'll be putty in your hand."

Mae sighed and sat on the bed. "You understand why I can't have him see this horrible place, don't you? So we've got to move down there right away."

"That place have an outhouse?" Daddy asked.

"I don't remember seeing one, but there's a cheese house. So they must have a simple old outhouse. If not, one could be dug."

"I couldn't do it," Daddy said, "with the misery in my back."

"Farley could," Mae said. "Mom, Daddy, I'm not saying that place is perfect, but it's a dandy house to get for nothing. And this place doesn't have an outhouse either."

Daddy asked, "What about water?"

"Well, a creek runs by the house. It's dry this time of year, but—"

"No water in the summer!" Daddy interrupted. "Why even a coyote would perish. Men would kill for the water we've got right where we are. Didn't I hear right at the picnic? That lady saying that Sheldon fella got himself killed in a fight over water?"

"But Daddy, you could fetch water at the river, maybe go on a regular run with the wagon and a couple of barrels. I saw other houses along Latrobe Road. They all need water. Or maybe Farley could dig a well—"

"How far from that house to the river?"

She thought about the hill between that house and Jackson Road, and the distance from the road to the river. "Surely not over three miles, maybe two and a—"

"Three miles from water! Where would the horses graze? And the milch cow?"

"What milch cow?"

A horse was approaching and Daddy put up a hand to quiet her. After a few seconds, he relaxed into his chair. "It's Farley." He could tell one horse from another by the sound of its hooves.

Belle's big black head poked through the door, looming over Mom in the rocking chair, with Farley still mounted. Mae laughed at the funny sight, but Farley wasn't smiling. He had lost his employment at the High Hill Company.

"We was wondering what happened to you," Daddy said. "Go ahead and picket Belle and come tell us what kind of luck you had today."

"Don't get your hopes up," Farley warned, reining the horse around.

Farley sat on the folk's bed, gobbling leftover beans from the pot on the floor. He then recited a litany of financial difficulties told to him today by ranchers and businessmen. Once again, he had canvassed a wide area but failed to find paying employment. With her eyes closed, Emma kept the chair in slight motion with her thick bare toes.

When Farley had nothing more to say, Mae told him about the house. "We should go over first thing in the morning and finish the deal."

Daddy raised his brows. "Is there more to it than Farley's woodcutting?"

"Well, the widow is hard up and can't get out of there 'til she gets a ride to Sacramento with her kids and all, and gets a new place to live."

Farley's face was taking on the stubborn look of a boy being led to a bathtub.

"But the house is free," Mae repeated.

"The hell it is!" Farley bellowed. "There's the woodcutting. And how many kids does this female have anyhow?"

"Seven."

"And I 'spose she wants all the beds an' such moved?"

This was not turning out well.

"Tell me, little sister, you wouldn't a' had the gall to tell her I'd move 'em, would' ja?"

"Well, she'll expect that, as part of the—"

"You did!" Now he shouted at the top of his lungs. "You told her I'd load up all that stuff and drive her to Sacramento?"

"Well, I thought you could—"

"Course you did!" He hooked his thumbs in his back pockets, leaned over to her with the narrows of his eyes. "And cool my heels in Sacramento 'til she's got all her affairs lined up?"

"Well, just a place to live and—" Stopped by Farley's exaggerated expression of disbelief, she said, "I guess I shouldn't have let—"

"Would' ja listen to that!" With great energy, Farley removed his hat and threw it down in the corner. Turning back, he glared at her, two inches from her nose, like a bull about to gore her. "Stop promising which way I'll jump, girl. I got news for you. I ain't your henpecked husband!"

I'm not, Mae corrected in her mind. Farley had grown touchy of late, maybe because he couldn't find work. Maybe he was jealous of the other boys for being free to move away. George had refused to return, even after the five hundred dollars bailed him out of jail. He'd gone over the mountain to the silver mines of Nevada. Mae thought she understood how Farley must feel, because if he left home, she couldn't leave, maybe not even to marry Jared Sheldon. Somebody had to stay and take care of the folks. She and Farley were staring at each other.

Mae started, "Why don't we just drive on over there in the morn—"

"Why don't you just—"

"Hold your horses," she yelled back. "I'm not done!"

He made a heroic shrug and sat down on the side of the folks' bed.

She continued, "No promises were made. Let's just go look at the place. It'd be an outing." She turned her palms up. "What is there to lose?"

"We might as well go at that," Daddy agreed amicably.

Emma kept rocking, eyes closed, perhaps not wanting to relocate any more than she wanted to join the conversation. She had sunk to a place where she wasn't actually living, like she was pulling some invisible blanket over her head. Was it the fast descent into poverty? In a place famed for its riches? Or Daddy being disowned? She'd worked hard on that farm in Iowa and hoped it would be theirs to pass on to the boys. Maybe she was thinking that if she hadn't married Daddy, she'd be living in a mansion in New York. That sure could bring on a melancholy. Still, a better house would help.

Mae thought it best to change the subject. "Daddy, where did you get the money for a milch cow?" All the remaining money was in her shoes.

"It couldn't be helped," he said, looking down. He glanced up at her with a painfully twisted face. "We need milk more than we need that violin."

"My violin!" Dropping to her hands and knees, she pushed things around under the bed. The violin box was gone.

She turned to the three of them. "You did that without even asking?"

"Well," Daddy said in a low tone, "Nobody thought it'd do any good to ask."

"So you just took it!" She jumped to her feet, outrage burning like thorns aflame in her heart. Her parents had argued about the violin in Iowa, Daddy calling it too expensive. Mom had defended the purchase, asking what else was money for but to help the children get ahead. Sister Delphine had wanted Mae to learn the violin in addition to piano.

Now Mom did nothing but rock in that chair.

Standing up, Daddy seemed to be filling out at the seams like somebody was blowing air into him. "This is just the way it is, young lady," he said, "and you'll have to get used to it. The family paid for that violin and now the family needs the money back."

Farley piled on. "That's right, Mae. You sure don't need no fiddle."

"How dare you say that! I was planning to take it to the Sheldons when they ask me to a musical afternoon." Rising to her feet she glared at her father. "Jared Sheldon and I were going to play a violin duet together!" *And we'll play duets after we get married.* She nailed each of them with a look.

"Music is my living. I could have given lessons on that instrument!" With her heart burning, she couldn't begin to find the words, and something inside was starting to break. "Music is my *main chance.* And you did this for milk!"

"But Mae, you weren't giving violin lessons," Daddy pointed out.

"You made sure I never will!" Instead, she'd been out there finding them a better place to live, which should have been his job. Tears stung the backs of her eyes but the heat of her rage dried them before they got all the way out.

Daddy muttered, "Maybe we're living just fine right where we are."

"Maybe you are living just fine in this filthy den with spiders sucking your blood all night, but I'm not!"

"You admitted that place don't even have an outhouse."

"I said Farley could dig one."

"There you go again!" Farley bellowed.

"You're twisting things. We were talking about my violin. Daddy, please go get it in the morning before they bring that cow over."

"I can't. My word is my bond. We shook hands on it." His unctuous tone enraged her all the more.

She was about to inform him that he had also pledged to God and man to care for his wife and family, and did a lot more than shake hands on it, but Farley was roaring: "I don't have the first notion what house you're talking about, but I'll say this. I ain't about to dig no outhouse when the folks is satisfied right here. So you can stick that in yer fancy bonnet."

She sputtered with fury. "Oh, you're so, so... ignorant! You don't know what you're talking about!"

"Oh now you've stepped into dangerous territory, little sister. Well, let me tell you. You're the snootiest, nose-in-the-air filly I ever had the misfortune to share tight quarters with, and I've had it up to here." He slashed a finger across his throat and glared at her with round eyes made redder by the smoky lamplight so near to his frizzy red head.

She sneered back, "What's eating you? Nobody'll hire you? I'm the one whose property's been stolen. I'm the one who's trying to get us to a better place—"

Farley made a fist and pulled back for a punch.

Daddy grabbed his arm.

Mae's feelings came undone. "I'm so ashamed of the way we live! I'm ashamed of all of you."

Silence.

She disliked including Mom, but at that moment a flour sack in a rocker was all she could see. The gracious lady from the New York Hamilton family was gone. She'd become one of them—no decency, no fairness, no concern about grammar. They were all strangers. And they outnumbered her.

"I can't stand it here one more day. I'm going to Sacramento. Tomorrow!"

"Good riddance," Farley hurled back. "Maybe you'll learn how hard it is out there when you don't have other people to feed off of, QUEEN MAE."

She gave him a shove, pushing him back on the bed. If she'd had a knife, she might have stabbed him. "Maybe you're too ignorant to recall that I planned to give half my piano money to the folks."

With a sarcastic bark of a laugh, he pulled himself back to sitting, and then to standing. "You took a hundred dollars to Dad's eighty."

"I won that fair and square!"

Emma spoke. "I thought you were going to the Sheldon's tomorrow."

That stopped her. She had a piano lesson to give and a young man to charm. She couldn't leave tomorrow. She had to be invited to a musical afternoon. But as reason arrived, the tears piled up and spilled down her face. Daddy and Farley, who rarely agreed on anything, were standing before her puffed up like turkeys and looking at her like she was an idiot. She couldn't abide another minute.

She sat on the bed, removed her shoes, pulled her stockings off and poured the gold coins into Daddy's hands, spilling them on the dirt floor when he couldn't grasp them fast enough. "There, that's to buy my violin back. Use it for the dumb cow, too, if you have to. I don't care."

Grabbing the quilt Grandma Duffy had made her, she plumped it up to fit in her arms—piled so high she couldn't see. She kicked the crate with her clothes and valise before her, struggling past Mom to get outside, determined to sleep near Pal and Belle. Then she remembered those stupid cows.

She made her bed under an oak tree halfway between the cabin and the horses. The pressure in her heart burst wide open and she fell weeping upon the quilt. What next? Would they sell her clothes out from under her? The parents who had treated her well had changed. And Emmett was gone when she needed him. She didn't blame him for leaving. She bawled into the quilt and pillow, the same pillow she had shared with Nora long ago when they'd been locked away from the family, the quilt made with thousands of tiny stitches and meant for her trousseau, the one that always gave off a subtle aroma of... what?

Love and belonging, that's what. Grandma had loved her.

20

Three bird tones woke her, a snippet of a melody, C-A-B whistled twice. Rosy morning light filtered through the oak branches, and the dawn air smelled fresh. No dog had attacked her. Carefully she checked around her legs. No rattlesnake in the covers, where Mary Granlees claimed they liked to sleep for the warmth. She could see the shale cabin, Farley's slouching tent, the wagon with its tongue down, scattered furniture, pots, pans, washtub, shirts, shoes, and rubbish. Remembering the anger and hurt of the night before, she closed her eyes and listened to the river's rustle and the sad downward song of a mourning dove. In a few hours it would be blistering hot.

She dug through her crate for her everyday dress and pulled it over her camisole and bloomers, then tender-footed down to the willows to relieve herself. After that, she bent over the river to splash water on her face. Her eyelids felt hot and puffy to the touch. She had cried for a long time. She stared into the river, searching to see her reflection, but the murky water gave nothing back.

She was about to leave when a snout poked up in the middle of the river. An otter, then another, sinuous backs cresting. It was the same family she'd seen the day of the horse race. This was their place, early morning their time of day.

The crash of a rifle knocked her off balance. Turning toward the sound, she crouched low, nerves buzzing up her arms and hands. Maybe a hunter. Hank had said otter skins brought fifty cents apiece in Jackson. But no hunter stepped up to look into the water.

Several minutes later, still crouched and hiding, she saw the willows thrash. Farley's red head and Daddy's sandy-gray one pushed through the leaves. They were in their long johns, stepping gingerly on bare feet.

"What was that?" Daddy asked in a loud whisper. "We heard a gunshot."

She shrugged, even in danger unable to forget what they'd said to her last night. "Maybe a hunter." She headed back to her tree.

Daddy followed, telling Farley to scout around.

A minute or so later, as she folded her blankets, Daddy sat down under the oak. "Yep, musta been a hunter all right." He scratched his stubbled chin. "I been thinking, maybe it was wrong, not mentioning the violin. Prob'ly shoulda told you."

"Wouldn't 'ov done any good. You were right about that."

"I shoulda mentioned it."

Fighting tears, Mae set the bedclothes on top of her loaded crate and mashed the pile down to keep it from spilling out. He murmured with his head down and she had to pay close attention to hear.

"Guess I'm not much of a provider. The kind a girl wants." He looked up with his pale blue eyes. "You know, I was thinking in the night. Maybe we oughta go on down this mornin' and look that house over."

An array of feelings collided in her. He was sorry, bargaining for her favor. He had all the money, and she couldn't buy a frock to wear to the Sheldons. He wasn't working for his family like a real man would. He was weak. She needed to get free of him before she said something more to regret. Even unsaid, such thoughts were a sin. *Honor thy father and mother.*

"We'll have a good time. Drive down as a family. Whatdaya say?" He gave her a wide-eyed smile of anticipation like she was a young child and he was asking her to guess which hand held the candy.

She couldn't smile.

Farley came running through the bushes, gasping in a hoarse whisper. "Dad, there's been a shooting. Mr. Thompson looks to be dead."

Daddy jumped to his feet and looked all around. "Step lively!" he said running toward the cabin. "There's a killer hereabouts."

Abandoning her crate, Mae tried to outrun the bullet she imagined aimed at her back. She made it to the door at the same moment as Farley. Daddy was already inside, nothing wrong with his legs.

Barring the door, Farley rasped, "Dad, we gotta git ourselves a rifle. Nobody in this territory goes around without one. Why there's shootings 'round here all the time."

Daddy looked at Mom on the bed. "Em," he said, "There's a killer on the loose."

Slowly Mom turned her eyes to him, but then continued staring at the ceiling, the blanket in disarray. Only her eyes and the slight rise and fall of the old dress that she slept in night and day hinted of life.

Farley and Daddy yanked their trousers and boots on. Daddy dug an old-fashioned pistol from the folks' trunk, and pocketed a box of bullets. This surprised Mae. She hadn't known he owned one. Possibly from his stagecoach driving days. "C'mon, Farley," he said, "let's go look around. You girls stay here and keep the door barred,"

Daddy grabbed his hat and left.

⌒

Locked inside with Mom, Mae thought somebody must have gone crazy. From what she'd heard, that wasn't unusual in California. She watched a daddy longlegs in the window catch a fly, wrap it up, and take its time getting into position to suck the life-blood out of its kill. No sound came from outside, and she hoped Daddy wasn't behaving rashly to go after a killer with nothing but a pistol.

"I sure hope they know what they're doing out there," she said to Mom.

The large lump on the bed had not stirred. Was she thinking about what Mae had said last night? Did she think nowadays? In the silence, Mae found herself reliving that awful quarrel. The words she had spoken wouldn't go away.

Mae handed Mom a piece of a biscuit dipped in cold gravy. "I doubt we've got anything to worry about, you and me. If they'd wanted to kill us they'd'ov done it before now."

Mom got up on an elbow, chewed in slow motion, and then slumped back down on the bed again. She smelled worse all the time.

Daddy and Farley were gone too long, Mae began to realize. She passed the time thinking what she'd say to the man with the cow, if he came to deliver it while Daddy was gone. *Sir, it was all a mistake.*

Finally a sound. A trotting horse grew louder until it stopped just outside the door. A man with the cow wouldn't be trotting. Then a knock at the door. Mom still didn't move on the bed.

Quietly, Mae lowered herself to the hard-packed floor, down on her belly so she could look under the door. Inches away, a pair of scuffed brown boots pointed at her. Behind that, two big hooves.

"Sheriff's deputy," a male voice boomed.

In a fright to get to her feet, Mae bumped her nose on the latch. She peered around the corner of the tiny window, the spider jumping in its web. The hind end of a sorrel horse came into view, then the whole horse and a man standing at its head with the reins. He had almost no chin. There was a tin star on his brown-checkered shirt. He had a gun in his holster, and a rifle in the boot of his saddle.

"It's a deputy all right," Mae told Mom over her shoulder as she unbarred and opened the door a crack.

"Howdy ma'am," the man said, touching his hat. His eyes were in shadow, but she could see them searching the cabin's interior. "You the Duffy women?"

"Yes," Mae said. "My brother saw Mr. Thompson shot dead. What happened?"

"Edward and Farley Duffy are in custody for questioning. They wanted you to know." He pushed past Mae and started throwing blankets aside and looking under the mattress of Mae's bed.

Stunned by the news, she almost couldn't speak, but got out the fact that she'd slept outside and heard the shot.

The deputy ordered Mom to get up so he could look under that mattress. Mom didn't respond. He told her again. She looked at him with vacant eyes, and Mae stepped forward to help her to her feet. Under the mattress, the deputy found the black stocking with the ninety dollars in gold coin. He pocketed it.

Studying Mom, he asked, "Are you sick, ma'am?"

"No." Almost inaudible.

He helped her back into bed and dipped his head at Mae. "You come on outside with me." Maybe he realized that Mom could no more sneak out and shoot a man first thing in the morning than she could jump over the moon.

He searched Mae's blankets and crate under the tree, probably looking for a gun, then told her to ride to town with him. They rode together in the saddle, the short distance to Michigan Bar. Dismounting in front of a small, unpainted house, Mae read the sign above the door: JUSTICE OF THE PEACE. By now she realized that the family could be in serious trouble.

The deputy escorted her inside to a hallway with the bench. Told to wait, Mae sat on one end of a bench. On its other end slouched none other than Mr. Parker, the landlord. He glanced up at the deputy, and a look passed between them. Then, folding his arms, the chinless deputy stood against the wall and stared at nothing.

Mr. Parker looked down at the floor, his palms on his Levi-clad thighs. He seemed unfriendly, which was unusual.

Mae broke the ice. "I heard a shot first thing this morning. Daddy and Farley got there a minute later. Then Farley said he found Mr. Thompson, dead."

Mr. Parker's vacant expression never changed. His hat stood between them on the bench.

The deputy shifted his weight. With his checkered shirt tucked into tight trousers and a belt cinched around his waist, the bulge of the gold-filled stocking in his hip pocket was plain to see.

"You know," she said to Mr. Parker, "I was meaning to talk to you this morning so I might as well do it now. Mr. Thompson's cows were on your property last night when I hobbled Pal out there."

The man dropped his head into the palm of his hand, elbow on the armrest, twisting away from her. She lacked the heart to continue.

Just then a bareheaded lawman, also wearing a tin star, came out of the next room and asked Mr. Parker to come in. The chinless guard stayed with Mae. More quiet time passed, during which Mae heard only the faint drone of talking men behind the closed door.

Then the door cracked open and a man said, "Bring her in."

Mae sat on a chair to the right of Mr. Parker, Daddy and Farley to her left. The deputy poured out the gold on the desk in front of the older lawman, and dropped the stocking next to it.

"Where'ja git this?" the interrogator asked Daddy, closing his hand around the gold coins and then letting them leak through his fingers.

"Sir," he responded, "That's what's left over from the purse we won at the race in Dixon's Grove on the Fourth of July."

Mae and Farley both nodded. Mr. Parker didn't look up. The man at the table began to pick up the individual coins and reinsert them in the stocking.

"Miss Duffy," he said as he did this, "I understand you heard a row between Mr. Parker here and Lon Thompson. Why don't you tell us about that in your own words. Don't leave anything out."

As he repacked the stocking, Mae told how upset Mr. Parker had been over the cows being left in the river bottomland, and how he said he wouldn't put up with it one more time. Trying to tell it word for word, to the best of her ability, she couldn't bring herself to look at Mr. Parker. "It got kinda loud, the yelling I mean. Not Mr. Thompson. He wasn't yelling. I'd say he was trying to get Mr. Parker to calm down."

The lawman lifted the stocking, now filled, and handed it to the deputy as he pointed his head at the door. The chinless deputy escorted the three Duffys back out to the waiting room, closed the door and stood waiting beside it, the stocking bulging in his pocket. It was quiet in the hallway for about ten minutes. Then the older lawman opened the door a crack and whispered to his partner.

As the door shut again, the deputy cleared his throat. "Looks like you're all free to go home now. Parker confessed to the shooting." He held out the stocking, giving it to Daddy, who took it with a gracious lift of his hat and a nice, "Thank you, sir."

Relieved that they had the gold back but greatly unnerved by the morning events, Mae walked away from the building with Daddy and Farley. They stopped at Heath's Store for bacon, eggs, and fresh bread, saying nary a word about what had happened.

∽

Back at the cabin, Mae realized it wasn't possible to remain angry as the four Duffys ate from plates balanced on their laps. They were sitting on chairs outside the shale house, Mom in her rocker. Every once in a while Farley hurled a rock to keep the starving dogs at bay.

"We should all be thankin' our lucky stars," Daddy said as he swabbed his plate with a hunk of bread. "It's not every day a man of the landowner class admits to a murder of the hangin' sort when he's got poor folk handy to pin the blame on. The two of us runnin' with a gun…" He shook his head as though to erase the image. "I'm grateful to Mr. Parker, and the rest of you should be too." He popped the bread in his mouth.

Farley's forkful of scrambled eggs hung suspended between plate and lips.

"But Dad, they find the bullet in a dead man and check to see what gun fired it. Your gun was no match. They woulda checked. It's the law." He forked the eggs into his mouth.

Daddy widened his pale eyes at Farley. "Not if a money-strapped lawman is friendly with a landowner. There's two kinds of law, son, one with the niceties you're talking about and the other that's been around since the first king signed a law and winked an eye."

Daddy now looked at Mae. "You going to the Sheldons to give that piano lesson?"

"Oh, for the love of Mike! What time is it?" Not expecting an answer from people without watches, she ran to her crate, found her watch and flipped it open. A little past ten. "I've got to get ready," she called as she hauled her crate back in the cabin. "I'll ride Pal."

"As I told Farley," Daddy called back, "Mr. Parker's headed for a rope in San Quentin, so he won't own this place for long. No tellin' what's to be done with it. I say we drive over to that stone house and take a gander. Mae, you can dress and go to the Sheldon place from there, being as how that's on your way."

Farley did not object.

The cosmos had come back into alignment.

21

Daddy approved of the house. Farley did too. However, Mom just sat in a chair and stared out the front room window. Apparently it took more than a better house to dislodge a melancholy that deep.

After about twenty minutes of hot discussion, the gaunt widow Smith came to terms with Farley. He would drive her and her brood to Sacramento, and help them find a place to live and unload the wagon. But if by six o'clock they hadn't found a place, he would unload the wagon at the cathedral, where surely someone would help them. To compensate Farley, Mrs. Smith gave him her old horse and wood cart. In any case, she couldn't afford to feed a horse in the city.

Mae rapped the bust of a brass angel with the well-wrought little wings, its rounded breast making contact with the brass plate. Corseted into her black gabardine suit with the whalebone point of the waistcoat tight over her belly, she felt stiff as a knight in heavy armor and slick with perspiration from the ride on the swaybacked horse. Katy Irene opened the door with exuberance, obviously glad to see Mae. She wore a shift of light cotton with loose elbow-length sleeves, and Mae felt foolish for overdressing.

Mentioning that most of the family was out and about, Katy showed Mae where to put the nag in the barn, where she'd have hay and water. Briefly Mae explained that the good horses were needed to help the family move. Back in the house, Katy laid Mae's music down in the parlor and took her on a quick tour of the house, obviously the pride and joy of the family. With a wave at Mrs. Sheldon working at the stove in the spacious kitchen, Katy Irene led the way up the staircase, the temperature rising noticeably, to a high second floor where each Sheldon child had a separate room. Between bedrooms, Katy moved a ladder from where it stood against the wall and placed it into an opening above. Climbing the sturdy rungs, she led the way to the "tower room."

Mae stepped into a stifling hot room with six sides, each side with a large window. She turned slowly around, getting an eagle's view of the Cosumnes River Valley.

"Snow!" she exclaimed to Katy, seeing the long line of white-peaked mountains to the east. She wanted to transport herself there by some magic and roll in it. Close to the house a thick stripe of jungle green defined the course of the river and Deer Creek, which ran parallel to each other not a quarter-mile apart. The Sheldon house stood closer to Deer Creek than to the river.

Mae helped Katy Irene open the windows. With the early afternoon sun pouring in she felt lightheaded in the heat and knew that the perspiration would soon show as unsightly wet spots.

"We c-call that The Thicket," Katy said, with a gesture toward the heavy vegetation. "Uncle is strict about trespassers. S-Sometimes he chases them out at the p-point of a gun."

"Just where does your property run?"

"You m-mean Uncle's property?" Katy giggled. "D-don't worry. Everyone gets mixed up about that. I was m-mostly raised here with my cousins. We're close in age, and I spend most of my time here, so that's a natural m-mistake. I'm supposed to be living w-with my grandmother, Uncle's mother, up the river a bit. But Uncle and Auntie are like parents to m-me."

"What happened to your parents?"

"I'll tell you on the way down. I'm about c-cooked and you must be too. L-leave the windows open. It'll vent some of the heat, so the bedrooms w-w-won't be so hot."

Starting down the ladder, Katy explained that her mother died giving birth to a younger brother because her father hadn't ridden fast enough to get the doctor. He'd drunk a few toasts with his friends at the Slough House Inn, not realizing how much his wife was bleeding, and by the time he got back from Sacramento with the doctor, Katy's mother had bled to death.

"Wasn't there a doctor in Michigan Bar?"

"Not back then. He blamed himself for her d-death."

Katy looked back over her shoulder as Mae followed her down the hall-way. "My father couldn't take c-care of me and a new b-b-baby by himself.

That's why he married that other lady so fast. At that time m-my father was r-running the Saunders Inn at the other end of M-Meiss Bridge, collecting toll and tending b-bar."

Katy was now descending the staircase and talked as she went down. "M-My father k-kept a portrait of m-my mother above the bar, and he looked at it all the t-time. H-he missed her something awful. I c-can remember that. I was s-seven when he put a g-g-un in his mouth and k-killed himself."

"Oh my gracious! I hope you didn't see that."

"No, but I heard it and came r-running. His w-wife had put a cloth over his h-head and held me back so I couldn't look."

By now they were in the hallway near the front door. Turning into the parlor, Katy continued. "I'll never forget that day. I l-loved my dad."

Disturbed by this story from a pretty girl with a cheerful disposition, Mae took her music books off a sundries table and followed Katy Irene across the oriental carpet to an upright piano. The tall wooden shutters on the high windows and the glass doors leading out to the lawn and flower garden were the height of fashion, as were the swag draperies and ferns.

"I think his w-wife was jealous of me. He used to take me for l-long walks, holding my h-hand. He s-said I reminded him of my mother. Her name was Catherine too, Katy for short. That's why I added Irene to my name, so people d-don't get mixed up."

"Do you remember your mother?"

"A little. I was young."

"Where's your brother, the baby? Or did he die, too?"

By now they stood before a Chickering piano, the finest of the uprights.

"Yes, he lived. Grandma took us both in at first, b-but she didn't have time for a new b-baby. She owned and managed the Slough House Inn. She'd just had a b-baby of her own by Mr. Dalton, her third h-husband." With a giggle she said, "She'd lay the b-baby to sleep in a box under the bar and go right on serving drinks. She kept me, but g-gave my brother up for adoption to old friends in Placerville who c-couldn't have children of their own. They loved him. I saw him now and again when I was growing up, but we weren't close. I was c-closer to Ed, the baby under the b-bar."

"So your grandmother had a baby the same age as her own grandson? Did I get that right?" This was confusing.

"Almost the same age. Ed's a year older than m-my brother." A big grin lit up her face. "You can do that when you s-start having babies at fourteen. Grandma had s-six children by three d-d-different husbands. Remember? You heard all her names at the Fourth of July picnic."

"Yes, but I must've forgotten some of it." She needed to pay closer attention if she was to marry into this family. "So you have a step-grandfather. Did Mr. Dalton help raise you?"

Katy waved that away like a gnat. "Oh no. Grandma got rid of D-Dennis after Ed was born. He was s-s-seventeen years younger and she found out he m-married her for her money—you know, the Inn, the business, the ranch, all the p-property. She overheard him t-talking to his friends one night, and that was the end of him."

On that interesting note, Mae sat on the swivel stool, put the clothbound music books on the music stand of the Chickering, and played the piece she'd practiced on Mrs. Miser's piano. It went well, and Katy was enthusiastic about wanting lessons from her.

"Why don't you play something for me now," Mae said, "and I'll get a notion of where you are in music."

While Katy's fingers pranced through Schumann's "Happy Farmer," Mae was digesting the fact that Katy's grandmother owned the Sheldon property, just as Gramps had owned the Iowa farm. But unlike Gramps, the Sheldon matriarch had been married three times and had six children. Mr.Sheldon was only one of them, on an equal footing with Ed Dalton, who was younger than Mae. So Jared might not inherit anything in Mae's lifetime! He was hardly the heir apparent. On the other hand, he lived in a magnificent house and was a handsome young man who enjoyed music. And you never knew about inheritance. Dying people often surprised people with their wills.

Next, Mae asked Katy to sight-read a more advanced piece, a fugue by Bach. As Katy stumbled through a run, Mae stopped her and explained what Sister Delphine had said about runs being like strings of pearls, each note given equal space and emphasis. Unless it was a diminuendo, in which case the pearls gradually got smaller, softer. Or gradually louder in the case of a crescendo.

Katy nodded with smiling comprehension.

"Try it," Mae said.

As Katy was trying various kinds of runs, Mae glanced up and found herself looking straight into Jared Sheldon's brown eyes. Her breath seized up and she felt out of air. He was standing in the hallway with a bucket in hand, every inch as handsome as she remembered him, but now wearing coveralls tucked inside high black boots. Caught watching, he walked onward, his boot-falls muffled by the woven mat in the hall, and then ringing on the tiles of the kitchen floor. A back door opened and closed.

Katy Irene grinned in her irresistible way. "Well, how'd I do?"

"Oh, ah, good."

"You think I've got enough t-talent to study piano at Mills College?"

"Sure you do. And I'll ask, do you think I have anything to teach you?"

"Oh, yes. I'll tell Grandma."

The one whose purse would pay for the lessons. "I couldn't help but notice your brother just now—I mean your cousin, Jared. What's he working on today—cattle?"

"No. We don't have cattle any more, just a couple of cows. I think he's working on the p-peach orchard." She glanced at the clock ticking loudly on the white marble fireplace mantel. "Why don't we go and t-take a look?"

Mae restrained her enthusiasm. "I'd like that." The clock bonged five times.

Grateful, Mae accepted a parasol from a bouquet of them in a closet under the staircase. Then she followed Katy Irene into the kitchen for a drink of water. Little Mrs. Sheldon was bent over a large cookstove, streams of perspiration bracketing her rosy face. Her sleeves were rolled up; but unlike Emma's thick biceps, this woman's arms were thin and wiry as she plunged a potato masher into a pot of simmering plums.

"It's hot as H-Hades in here," Katy Irene observed.

"Well, dear, go along then," Mrs. Sheldon told her sweetly.

Katy Irene went over and kissed her aunt's temple. "I worry about you, Auntie, w-working so hard all the time. You should go rest and cool off in the cellar."

"You're a sweetheart," Mrs. Sheldon said, adding as she looked at Mae. "Isn't she?"

"Sure is."

Outside, they followed a path down a gentle slope toward the river. The back of Mae's hand, the one holding the parasol, felt like it was frying in the sun. They passed by a field of harvested corn, stalks broken and bleached brittle in the July heat. Oddly there were teepees made of corn stalks around the sides of the field, five or six of them.

"What are those teepees for?" Mae asked.

"Indians from Jackson Creek come each year to harvest the corn. That's pretty far away, so they build shelters they can use for several nights."

They were crossing the dry bottom of Deer Creek. The peach orchard was on the other side looking healthy and green. Directing a high-handled plow and a team of shiny black horses, Jared gave a nod to Mae and Katy Irene but said nothing as he continued his work.

Mae loved seeing him wrestle the hand-plow over uneven ground and guide it with the big shoulder-high handles. The leather of the harnesses and his high black boots were oiled and shining. The horses, as black as his boots, were obviously well cared for. Instead of a plow, a row of closely spaced steel discs cut through the soil at a tilt as Jared guided the harrow. The scene emblazoned itself on Mae's mind—horses, tack, weeds removed beneath the surface so as not to rob the trees of water—all in the strong, competent hands of the namesake of the original pioneer of this property.

"George and Lauren are picking the French p-plums," Katy Irene was saying. "Let's go over there and get some."

Mae followed reluctantly on a narrow path as Katy explained about The Thicket, an undisturbed area of native vegetation left the way it had looked to the first Sheldon.

"Are those grapevines on those trees wild?" Mae asked.

"Yes. The grapes are little, like C-C-Concord grapes. Tasty though." A few steps farther she added, "Deer and b-birds are safe in The Thicket, except when Uncle hunts, b-but that's rare. P-Polly practically l-lives out here. She's a n-n-nature lover."

They came to another orchard where George and Lauren Sheldon were picking plums in company with two Chinese men in peaked hats. Shallow boxes of plums lay in soldierly lines between the rows of trees. One Chinaman was kneeling over a box, quickly filling it with fruit from a bucket. All worked together, the sons of the owner beside his Chinese laborers. George Sheldon was picking a tree nearer to the girls.

"We just came down to g-get some fresh plums," Katy Irene told him.

"G-g-g-g-go a-a-a-a-a-head," George finally got out.

"They're all so perfect in their b-boxes," Katy said to Mae. She went to one of the Chinese men, who looked up from the box of fruit into which he was placing plums one layer deep. "We'd like some good ones to eat," she told him.

Standing up, the man smiled broadly and bowed, showing the peak of his hat. This looked like the one who had been at the picnic, but now he wore an ordinary work shirt and trousers. He selected the biggest, juiciest plums for Mae and Katy Irene and laid them in their open palms, two each.

"Do they speak English?" Mae asked on the way back to the house.

"Pidgin."

Mae bit into a delicious plum, leaning forward to keep the juice off her clothes. "Do they have families here?"

"Shin Sin does. He lives with his wife in a c-cabin along the l-levee. All the Chinese live there. When Uncle n-n-needs more help, Shin p-passes the word and someone shows up. He gets good w-workers."

"I thought Indians did the farm work in California."

"We use Indians for c-corn and hay. But these Chinese m-men are specialists with f-fruit. They learned it in China. They know h-how to prune and p-p-plant. They know when to pick. They wrap the f-fruit in tissue paper and pack it just so. Uncle is p-particular about getting the ripe fruit to m-market in good condition."

"Does Jared have a lady friend?"

Katy Irene raised her brows. "That was a change of subject!" She smiled. "I doubt he's ever had one."

Surprised, Mae considered that his extreme shyness might have saved him for her. They were back at the house, and Katy Irene invited her to cool off in the cellar. They pumped two glasses of water at the sink.

Mrs. Sheldon stood at the range dipping plum preserves into jars, her face redder and wetter than before. On the stove, a large pot of potatoes launched more steam into the overheated air. Mae followed Katy Irene to a door in the inner wall of the kitchen.

"T-Take a rest, Auntie," Katy Irene said opening the cellar door.

"I'm getting dinner now, but might join you down there."

"She's working herself to d-death," Katy said to Mae in a voice Mrs. Sheldon would overhear. "We've all t-told her to serve us bread and c-cold meat in summer, but she won't listen."

"Working men need better fare than that," Mrs. Sheldon called after them.

Katy took a kerosene lamp from a peg and lit it with a match from her pocket.She led Mae down the stairs into air that cooled the perspiration on Mae's face. With every step the temperature dropped a little more. At the bottom it was almost chilly, and the lantern cast parabolas of light across the dark walls. Narrow shelves from floor to ceiling held enough jars of preserved food to keep Napoleon's army marching for a year.

Katy motioned Mae to follow her past an old davenport to a far corner of the room, to what appeared to be an indoor haystack. She hung the lantern on a hook screwed into a rafter, pushed the hay aside, and lifted the handle of a thick-walled metal box standing on end, larger than two armoires put together. It contained blocks of ice, much of it chipped away. Katy handed Mae one of two ice picks left there, and together they stabbed out chips of ice and put them in their water glasses. After the box was shut and the straw pulled back over the front, they returned to the davenport. Katy set the lantern on a small table and sat down.

Mae couldn't restrain her enthusiasm. "This is grand, to have ice! Where do you get it?"

"Every spring the m-men go up to the Rubicon River to c-cut ice."

"I'll bet Jared would like some iced water about now. George and Lauren, too. I don't see how men can work all day in heat like this."

"They get used to it. I don't m-mind the heat like some do." Katy turned herself sideways on the end of the davenport and tucked a shoe under a leg, facing Mae. In this position, they talked and drank their water, Mae telling bout the farm in Iowa, exaggerating a bit about how nice the house was.

After a while, more footsteps of a female lightness tapped back and forth upstairs—no doubt Jessie, Polly and Kittie back from the store.

"I'd best be going now," Mae said, getting to her feet.

Katy Irene looked up at her. "For a minute there, I thought you were interested in Jared."

That she would say this inviting thing with such a friendly expression gave Mae a blast of hope. "Actually, I am, and was hoping you could give me an idea on how best to, to, ah…"

Katy swung her foot to the floor and stood up with a sly expression on her pretty face. "Do c-come over for our musical afternoon tomorrow. That's your b-best chance with him, through music." She grinned.

"Oh Katy, I'm so obliged! Truly I am. What time?"

"Come at four-thirty."

22

Saturday was a day of high hopes for Mae as she anticipated the musical afternoon. It was also moving day. Yesterday, Farley left Mrs. Smith and her brood at the Sacramento Cathedral and drove the farm wagon back in the long summer twilight.

After breakfast, Mae, Daddy and Farley put everything from the shale house in the wagon. They folded a narrow mattress and stuffed it into the wood cart, Mae accidentally tearing her old dress on a broken slat, and helped Mom onto the mattress so she could rest for the seven-mile ride. Mae rode on the buckboard with Daddy, the milch cow plodding behind on a rope. Farley rode the bony nag that pulled the cart in which Mom lay on her back looking at the blue sky.

Mae imagined that they resembled the ragged Indians the folks used to see dragging their belongings from place to place in Dakota Territory. A spectacle for curious bystanders. Farley's red hair and whiskers frizzed out in all directions. She finger-combed dirt and cobwebs from her own hair and tried not to make eye contact as heads turned on the main street of Michigan Bar. At Heath's store she went in, too, so she wouldn't have to talk to people while waiting outside for Daddy to buy noon dinner supplies. Then they continued to roll down the main street of town.

Some of Daddy's friends waved. "Come back and sing for us," one of them called.

Daddy doffed his hat. "You'll have your hands full keepin' me away."

They crossed the bridge to the Chinese side of town and stopped for their furniture and goods. It took longer than Mae planned for the three of them to unload and rearrange their possessions, piling them high and tying everything down for a bumpy ride.

As they rattled up the shale ribs of Michigan Bar Road, Mae urged Daddy to drive faster.

"Not with your mother's good china back there," he said.

It was one-thirty by the time they got to the Miser place. Mae stood up and called before the horses came to a stop, "Anybody home?"

Daddy got down and helped Mom to the outhouse while Mae and Farley took the three horses to drink at the water trough kept filled for travelers, a legacy of the days when Solomon Miser had been a freighter. Mr. Heath had said the Misers once charged toll for traveling this road constructed by Chinese labor in Mr. Miser's pay.

Quickly the Miser clan was at the wagon. Daddy, in his gracious way, mentioned how he'd heard so many nice things about them and looked forward to being a closer neighbor. He introduced Farley and tactfully implied that Emma was under the weather. The Misers showed equal tact by not letting on that they knew her actual condition.

"We're having noon dinner," Mrs. Miser said. "C'mon in and join us."

Mae could see that Daddy was about to accept, so she interjected, "Thanks, but we're in a hurry. I've got to be at the Sheldons at four-thirty and I want to help get the furniture arranged first." She flipped her watch open and saw that it was already 1:45.

Luckily, Mrs. Miser understood the urgency.

Half an hour later they arrived at the stone house. Mae helped Mom into the house and took the rocking chair to her. Farley and Daddy stepped through the door carrying the kitchen table between them.

"Stop. Before you bring that in," Mae said, "I've got to clean the floor. Help me get all this trash out of here first."

Not even slowing down with the front end, Farley blared at her, "First! Little sister, first I'm gonna eat."

"Well, you can do it outside. Take the table to the shade of that big tree."

Like she wasn't there, they placed the table before the front room window, the Italian sausage and bread wobbling on it. Next they brought chairs. Daddy got out his knife and cut fat slices of both items, his good cheer grating on Mae's nerves.

Upset and worried about the time, Mae downed a few bites before she swept around table legs and boots, trying not to act grumpy. The slate floor needed a good mopping too. It would have been so easy to clean an empty house! But it was already after three o'clock and she needed the furniture and boxes to be out of the yard and in the house when Jared Sheldon drove her back. So the mop would have to wait.

Finished eating, Daddy dragged two ruined Smith mattresses out of a bedroom while Mae helped Farley carry a large crate out of the house. It contained baby things and men's clothes—a crude cradle stuffed with moth-eaten knit goods, stained diaper rags, and clothes and boots of a size too large for Duffy men—doubtless once worn by deceased Mr. Smith. Also in the crate were books about farming and other subjects of no interest to the Duffys. Even empty, that crate would have been heavy. She was biting her tongue so as not to beg to put it down for a rest, when Farley yelled, "Faster. Lift it higher. You're breakin' my back!"

Practically running in a down position, she got the crate through the door before she dropped her end. Her fingers were red, stuck in a curl. Farley was the picture of disgust. She bit back all the things she wanted to say about what an oafish, selfish lout he was, and refrained from kicking him in the shins.

After more frantic sweeping around beds and chairs brought in too soon,

Mae gave in to the ticking watch, which told her it was already 3:20, and appropriated a bedroom. She pulled off her torn dress, looked at the white lacy frock she was about to put on, the one she'd worn on the Fourth of July, and realized that she was covered from head to toe with sweat and grime. And they had forgotten to bring the settling keg. After the bumpy ride the water would have been brown, but it was water. She wanted to scream.

Instead, she kept her head and marched in her bloomers and camisole to the wagon. She found the box with the Fels Naptha soap, opened the big jar of drinking water they'd dipped from the Miser trough, went to the other side of the wagon and poured a quarter of the water over her head, making suds with the bar of soap. She rubbed her face and arms with leftover suds, and cupped it under her arms. She was pouring the remainder of the water all over herself when Farley spied her.

He let out a howl and lit out after her with a raised fist. She beat him to the bedroom, shoved the corner of the bed against the door to keep him out. He was pounding and pushing.

"Spoiled rotten-apple queen of the May," he shouted. "I'll give you a thrashing you won't forget."

"Go jump in a lake," she shouted. Over her shoulder toward the open window, she yelled, "Help Daddy! Farley's gone crazy. I need you."

Soon on the other side of the door she heard Daddy trying to calm Farley down. In a pause she shouted back, "Daddy, I've gotta talk to you. Alone."

By the time the shouting ebbed and she had her dress on, and watch pinned to it, she pulled the bed away from the door and went out. Daddy was feeding Mom bread and sausage, Farley nowhere in sight.

"Please, Daddy, I need you to drive me to the Sheldons right now."

"You could ride Pal."

"No, I'll need a ride back when it's over. I'll say you're busy moving and need the horses."

Comprehension spread across his face. "You want that Sheldon fella to drive you back."

She could have hugged him.

With her damp hair combed out and pinned up, she almost felt normal as she rode down the road, driven by the best horse handler in the world. The four or so miles soothed her heart, and the music books in her lap told her who she was. All the trouble with cows and a murderer and moving to the new house with a crazy brother and melancholy mother, all of that belonged to some other girl, one destined to become another beleaguered Mrs. Smith. Mae's hopes were pinned on Jared Sheldon and civilization.

⌒

On the shady porch, Mae knocked with the breast of the brass angel.

Mrs. Anna Sheldon opened the door and welcomed her with smiling blue eyes beneath her center-parted hair done up in a bun. In the parlor, Polly and Jessie and Kittie, little Tooty, greeted Mae in a way that made her feel entirely respectable. Tooty, remembering Mae, came up to her and smiled shyly. Mae smiled back and shook the little girl's hand.

George entered the parlor with his trumpet, Lauren empty-handed and nearly fingerless on one hand. Jared came in with his violin case, his father just behind him, both of them tall, square-shouldered, dark-headed men. Again something sizzled through Mae at the sight of Jared. His name alone had that effect on her.

He gave her a shy smile.

"Play that Chopin Nocturne," Katy Irene insisted of Mae, explaining to the others, "She's very g-good on the piano."

Not quite herself yet, Mae was relieved that Mr. Sheldon intervened. "No wait" he said, "we're expecting more guests. I just saw them from the tower room, driving down the road."

Mae joined the girls in the kitchen, all giggling as they stirred more sugar into the big crock of diluted lemon juice, everyone with a tasting spoon. They all chipped a bucket of ice from the cellar and laughed back up the stairs to rustle up the trays and glasses. More happy talk and giggles accompanied the dipping of the lemonade, three ladles going, into the glasses, others adding ice. In a line of girls, Mae delivered lemonade to the orderly parlor walled on two sides with windows, a room where ferns cascaded in green fountains from their very own high tables, and well dressed men and boys smiled as they reached for the clinking, sweating glasses. Mae heart relaxed downward another notch from the anger of the morning.

Smacking his lips, Mr. Sheldon was saying something about Whitney lemons from Rocklin when an aged female voice sang out from the front door, "We're here!"

Mrs. Sheldon jumped to her feet and rushed to the hallway. "Mother," she exclaimed, escorting the Sheldon matriarch and two other ladies into the room, but not before Katy Irene bounced in ahead of them, wiggling her fingers in a hello to Mae. One of the visiting ladies looked familiar, the one with the gray hair twisted in sections back from her face. The younger lady had something of the same look about her.

"I've said it before," said the one that seemed familiar, "but I'll say it again. Your son has a lovely house, Catherine."

"You remember my grandmother," Katy Irene said to Mae, touching the shoulder of the stout lady who had given a speech at the Fourth of July picnic. "Her name's Catherine, too."

"Of course I do," Mae made a slight curtsy to the lady. She'd seen pictures of Queen Victoria and thought Grandmother Catherine resembled her.

Now the grandmother took over the introductions. "Elitha Wilder," she said, nodding at the tall older woman first. "Elitha is my oldest friend in California. We came across the prairie together back in forty-six. This pretty young lady is Olive, Elitha's daughter."

"You came across on a wagon train?" Mae blurted out, instantly realizing that was stupid. Of course there had been no railroad.

The Sheldon grandmother responded for her friend. "Yes, ours was the second wagon train to cross the California mountains." An unnatural twinkle remained in her eye, as though she expected Mae to catch on to something.

Katy Irene spilled it. "Grandma crossed the plains with the Donner Party. Mrs. Wilder's maiden name is Donner."

Astonished, Mae now understood where she had seen that lady before. "You sat just ahead of me on the train when my family came to California. The conductor told us who you were, after you and the other lady got off at Truckee."

Mrs. Wilder turned her black eyes to Mae. "Why yes, now I think I remember you. You were in our car." She smiled. "My sister Leanna was with me, now Mrs. App from Jamestown. We were on our way back from visiting relatives in Illinois."

Mae felt dumfounded to be talking to one of the very ladies she had tried to get another glimpse of on the train.

Turning to Mrs. Sheldon, Elitha Wilder asked, "Can I help with anything?"

"No, you just sit yourselves down and have some of that lemonade."

"Son," Grandma Catherine said, addressing Mr. Sheldon, "I think it might be nice to go outside and finish our lemonade on the porch. It's so very nice in the shade of your giant bamboo trees." She gave him a fond smile.

"That's a splendid idea," he said with a grin that made the wire-thin curls at the ends of his mustache quiver.

Without one word from Jared, Mae realzed, the tall shuttered doors were pulled back and the glass doors behind them opened to a veranda overlooking the shady lawn. Chairs and a whatnot table were carried outside, and everyone quieted as Mae sat on the piano stool.

She had dreamed of playing for Jared Sheldon, a lover of music. In her dreams she played perfectly, but now as she placed her hands on the keys, doubt overwhelmed her. Her hands felt shaky, and she knew she would stumble.

With her heart gone wild she stood up to face them. "I can't do this. I haven't practiced it."

"You played it for me yesterday," Katy Irene objected.

"Not all the way through." She hadn't told them that her family had no piano and that's why she couldn't practice.

"Oh please," Polly, Jessie, and Katy Irene pleaded almost in unison, with Tooty a beat behind.

"No, I'm sorry. I'd so much rather hear you Sheldons play first."

"Miss Duffy," Mr. Sheldon said in a firm tone, "We are not harsh critics. Please turn around and do your best."

It was an order! "But I don't think—"

Now Jared spoke for the very first time in Mae's hearing. "If s-s-she d-don't w-w-want t-t-to—"

"Jared, for heaven's sake," Mr. Sheldon interrupted, "think through what you're saying first. Now, start over and enunciate each word."

Flushing dark red, Jared stood up and was about to step down to the lawn and leave, when Mr. Sheldon pointed at the chair he was abandoning.

"Sit down."

After a brief hesitation, Jared returned, sat down and looked at his shoes.

"Now, speak clearly to Miss Duffy."

Jared struggled valiantly, and Mae felt terrible for him. She also felt terrible that he, too, was afflicted by stuttering. Many people considered that to be an indication of a simpleton, and schools often refused to admit such students. It also pained her to see him—a twenty-year-old man—with his tail between his legs when his father bossed him around. The hero of her girlish dreams, her California Joe, melted away before her eyes, and a sorry-faced boy took his place.

"Please, William, not now," Mrs. Sheldon was saying to her husband in a quiet, tense tone.

Mr. Sheldon directed himself to Jared, "I'm waiting, son. Have you thought through what you want to say?"

Looking down, Jared nodded.

"Then say it clearly without that infernal stammering."

George, who stuttered worse than Jared, was examining the high leaves of the giant bamboo imported from China. Lauren, with his maimed hand on his thigh, flashed Jared a sympathetic glance. Three flawed brothers.

Mae realized that Jared had tried, at his peril, to defend her decision not to play, and now she felt it was her responsibility to rescue him from torment.

"Mr. Sheldon," she announced, "I will play the Chopin Nocturne, and I know you'll forgive the mistakes I will surely make."

She swiveled the stool back around to her music and played from her heart as Sister Delphine had taught her to do. It flowed easily now that mistakes no longer mattered, and she made next to none. Everyone clapped and she swiveled around to face her audience with a smile, her mind running over the possibility that Jared was only tongue-tied in her presence, as a few boys in Iowa had been, and normally spoke smoothly. But before the clapping ended, she knew in her heart that he would always stutter, and always obey his father.

"She plays the violin, too," Katy Irene was saying. "Sh- Sh- Show us, Mae!"

"I didn't bring my violin. Anyway, I'd so much rather hear Jared. Why don't Polly and Jared come in here and play something together?"

That suited everyone. At the piano Polly played the challenging accompaniment of "None but the Lonely," a German lied normally sung by a vocalist. Jared played the melody as though the strings of his violin vibrated from his very soul. Goose bumps rippled up Mae's arms. He understood loneliness. True musicians, Polly and Jared played beautifully together. Next, Polly lifted her guitar from its case, an exotic California instrument Mae had not seen before. She played a piece with a Spanish rolling bass while Jared played harmonic inversion on his violin to George's trumpeted melody, rife with trills and long sustained tones. The trio took the whole room to an exotic place.

And so the afternoon progressed, the musicians loosening up more as time went on. At one point Mae borrowed Jared's violin and fiddled in the old-fashioned style to Polly's lively piano, playing "I've Been Working on the Railroad." Mae made the train whistle like the men in Iowa used to. After one go-through, Jared sang the words without a jot of stuttering. He laughed at Mae's whistle. For Mae, music had wiped the audience away.

Little Kittie piped up, "Sing the one 'bout the grizzly bear."

Jared grinned, standing to sing, and Polly accompanied him on the piano.

The song had several verses and a chorus. Each verse moved the story along. When a preacher went hunting, supposedly against his religion, he encountered a grizzly bear and scrambled up a 'simmon tree. The bear sat on the ground looking up at him. Jared emoted as he sang, enacting with body and face the humor of the words:

> And the man climbed out on a limb.
> He cast his eyes to the Lord in the skies
> And this much said to him:
> Oh Lord, you delivered Daniel from the lion's den;
> You delivered Jonah from the belly of the whale;
> And the Hebrew children from the fiery furnace;
> And now I do declare,
> Oh Lord, if you help me for goodness sake,
> Don't you help that bear!

Mae clapped and laughed along with everyone else, including Mr. Sheldon, whose expression she thought conveyed genuine pride in his son.

When the railroad clock bonged five times, Polly, Jared, George, Katy and Mae played on, but the Wilder ladies and Mrs. Sheldon went to the kitchen to bring out more refreshments. They brought cake, frosted cookies, coffee and cream. The aromas passing by weakened the resolve of the musicians, and all followed to the verandah.

Mrs. Wilder and her daughter Olive, who was an unmarried schoolteacher, had said little, though they smiled often. Most of the sociable chatter came from the Sheldon girls talking about the harvest gatherings at neighboring ranches. It sounded like fun. Grandma Catherine partook of the cake as though evaluating each ingredient. Meanwhile, Mae wondered how she would get back to the stone house.

She was sinking her teeth into an interesting cookie spread with dog-wood jelly, which Polly said was made from the flower buds of a tree in the yard, brought from Yosemite Park, when Mr. Sheldon spoke in his stentorian manner. "Miss Duffy, that's an Irish name, isn't it?"

Caught off guard—everyone knew Duffy was Irish—she inhaled a bit of cookie, which stuck in her windpipe. Before she could cover her mouth, the first cough sprayed bits of wet cookie. She couldn't stop coughing. As every-one waited for her to recover, Mr. Sheldon, who sat two seats away, wiped the outer corner of his eye with a napkin.

When she managed to subdue her coughs, Mr. Sheldon asked, "You told us you were moving. Where do you live now, Miss Duffy?"

Giving full rein to the tickle in her throat, Mae bent forward in another coughing fit. Though less embarrassed about the new house than the shale cabin, nonetheless here in the Sheldon mansion the facts of her family situ-ation loomed grotesque in her mind. She lived in a rent-free house formerly occupied by no-accounts. At last, wiping tears with her linen napkin, she accepted a drink of water from Mrs. Sheldon, who had run to the kitchen to fetch it and was leaning over Mae with a kindly look.

The water helped. Mae smiled her thanks through blurry eyes, reminding herself that it didn't matter any more where she lived, now that Jared, nice as he was, wasn't the man she wanted. Mr. Sheldon was waiting.

"Latrobe Road," Mae said in a cough-roughed voice.

Taking a long draw on his cigar, Mr. Sheldon said, "I am acquainted with all the landowners along that road. Are you renters perhaps?"

Not even renters. She gave it to him with precision. "Just today we moved into the stone house near where Stone House Road meets Latrobe Road."

Stiff as a poker in his straight-backed chair, Mr. Sheldon appraised her. Everyone was looking at her except Jared, George, and Lauren, who quietly nibbled their cake. She felt like a medical curiosity, and it occurred to her that she really should go to Sacramento.

Lauren asked, "That house on the Long place?"

Mae nodded, noticing that he didn't stutter at all this time, though he had done so previously.

Katy Irene said, "That's a nice little house. Those stones are n-n-nice."

Silence prevailed as forks pinged on dessert plates and cups clacked in saucers. From habit, Mae glanced at Jared to see if the revelation of Duffy poverty had changed him—not as far as she could tell. But it didn't matter.

"Yes. The stones in that house were well cut," Mr. Sheldon allowed. "A professional stone cutter must have quarried them. The Irish come from a rocky island. They know how to work with stone, and they help each other. Isn't that the case, Miss Duffy?"

Her fighting spirit returned. "I wouldn't know about that. My father never worked with stone. My mother's a Hamilton, related to Alexander Hamilton."

Unproven. In the silence, she heard the echo of her defensiveness.

Polly spoke up. "Dad, the Irish are all different."

"Of course they are. Not all are intemperate, not even all Catholic. What work does your father do, Miss Duffy?"

"He was a farmer in Iowa, but he's at his best with horses," she said, "training and handling."

"Ah yes. The horse that won the race. Send your father over here sometime. I might be able to use him."

Her stomach tightened as she felt herself assigned to the lower classes. But it didn't matter any more.

Kindly, Mrs. Sheldon turned to Mrs. Wilder, the former Miss Donner, and sweetly asked, "How are George and Jim doing?"

Mrs. Wilder explained that they were harvesting wheat. "Good boys. Men actually. I shouldn't keep calling them boys."

"George is married now, isn't he?" Mr. Sheldon asked, apparently having given up with Mae.

"Engaged."

Grandma Catherine explained to Mae, "Elitha's husband, Ben Wilder, is a respected spokesman for the ranchers in the county. He's a staunch Republican and a pillar of the Grand Old Party."

Lauren piped up, "And he shot Grandfather Sheldon."

Mae could hardly believe her ears.

Drilling Lauren with a hard look, Grandma Catherine said, "There was shooting on both sides, Lauren, and no law to moderate. It was a different time, and nothing's to be gained by dredging it up again."

Once more the parlor fell quiet, except that Olive squirmed.

Then Olive said "My father didn't kill him, and no evidence was brought forward to say he did. He wanted to be tried, to clear his name, but—"

"Leave it be," Elitha Wilder told her daughter. "That was a long time ago and the world has changed. Catherine's right about that."

In the silence Mae stood up and gathered dishes. "I'd best be heading back to home." She started toward the kitchen with a stack of plates.

"Who drove you here?" Mrs. Sheldon came after her to ask.

"My dad. He had to get back to the house and set up furniture. I didn't know when I'd be finished."

Back in the kitchen with the girls, all cleaning up the dishes, Polly whispered to Mae, "Auntie Anna asked Jared to drive you home." *Trying to put me together with him, like Katy Irene's been doing.*

The afternoon had been fun but also discomfiting. She had wanted a man with a spirit more daring than her own.

When she returned to the parlor, all were saying their good-byes. The Sheldon matriarch offered to drive Mae, but Mrs. Sheldon objected, noting it was miles out of her way. George was on his way upstairs two steps at a time.

"Jared, you drive her," Mr. Sheldon said. "Use the buggy. Hitch Christmas."

Silently Jared escorted Mae to the barn.

23

The heat had been building up all day, and now with the low sun in their faces at the start of the drive, the horse lathered fast although walking.

Mae thought about the different subjects that might be sociable, but with Jared conversation was difficult. She went straight to the important thing.

"I had a grand time today. I especially loved 'None but the Lonely.' It gave me goose bumps."

Seeing him struggle to respond, she continued, "You have a wonderful family. I just love your sisters, and Katy Irene. If I could pick out a girl to be my sister, I'd pick her or Polly."

"Everyone l-l-loves P-P-P-P-Polly."

Mae decided it was an imposition upon him to initiate conversation.

But he did it on his own. "M-my d-d-dad is a g-g-g-g-g good a-and int-t-t-telligent m-m-man."

That brought her up short. Mr. Sheldon had seemed callous to Jared, and now Jared was praising him—the father who, she suspected, contributed to his stammer. The father who had ordered him to drive her.

As they overtook a slow buggy, Mae heard the snoring and saw Doctor Walker's long legs protruding through the bows of his buggy, one crossed over the other, the shoe leathers worn most of the way through. He lay peacefully asleep on the seat with his hands stacked on his chest. Maybe up all night with a sick person. His loyal horse knew to keep to the right of the road and to return the man home at a slow pace.

They were about to pass the roof of the Cosumnes Store and stage stop when Mae found herself looking straight at John Dunaway—on the porch, all dressed up and leaning forward on a chair as though about to pounce. He jumped to his feet and gave Jared the flats of his hands.

Jared reined the horse to a stop under the roof.

Horrors! This was Saturday. She had forgotten her date with John. They were to have gone to a dance at the Gaffney place. He was to have picked her up at—when was it? Five o'clock. She flipped her watch open. Two hours ago! And here she was in Jared's buggy! John would think she'd left him in the lurch on purpose. She'd been preoccupied with too many things. Yes, including the effort to reel in a more socially prominent man. *I am guilty. Caught in the act, no matter what excuses I try to make.*

John's steely eyes, now inches from Jared but focused on her, made her feel like a mouse under a diving hawk. She looked up the road like he wasn't there.

"Well, we goin' to the dance?" he demanded. Not a question.

Maybe she could pretend that Jared intended to deliver her to him and she could go to the dance with John and soothe his feathers, somehow. In her meekest voice she said, "I'm sorry, John. I meant to get word to you. Something came up and made me late. Hope it didn't cause you any trouble."

"Oh, not at all!" The sarcasm fractured his voice. "Just lost work s'all. And the good will of Mr. Grimshaw. He had to drive his own prunes to Sacramento, and here I stand near his house making a liar of myself. I borrowed a nice rig and drove to your place, like you an' me agreed. But your place was all cleared out! With nary a word to me." Again his voice broke. "Rode all that way!"

"You shouldn't have invited me if you needed to work this afternoon." The instant that left her mouth, she knew it sounded mean.

His lips trembled and she expected him to yell, but he spoke in a tone that broke her heart. "Guess I were sacrificin' for somethin' that meant a great deal to me." He turned and walked away toward the field behind the store.

Deeply ashamed to have been so thoughtless, Mae noticed Jared staring up the road. No doubt also embarrassed. Watching John's back recede into the ripe corn, she reflected on how hard he worked to get ahead. He prided himself on keeping his word, especially to Mr. Grimshaw, a relation of the Sheldons and a farmer with one of the largest spreads in this area. John depended on Mr. Grimshaw for his chance.

A headache stabbed her temple as Jared flicked the reins, and it seemed an eternity before Christmas pulled around a bend and out of view of a curious lady and a child who had come out of the store in time to hear the row. For about a mile, until they turned on Latrobe Road, she silently scolded herself for forgetting the man who had helped her get clothes so she could ride and win the race. He was the one who sprang George out of jail

They were passing a farmhouse when a dog bolted from the porch barking like a fiend from hell.

Christmas shied and then lunged into a full-out run. Fear tingled in Mae's hands. Many people were maimed and killed when runaway horses bolted through wire fences and rigs overturned because of dog attacks.

Fighting to keep the horse on the road Jared yelled, "G-get t-the r-r-r-rock. B-by m-my shoe."

She grabbed two good-sized rocks from the little pile.

It wasn't for nothing she'd learned to aim rocks—competing against Emmett and Farley to knock cans off of the old stagecoach. Now, the barking dog ran along her side of the buggy, gaining on the horse. She let fly, hitting it on side of its head. The barking stopped. In the wind of the speeding buggy she stuck her head out to look behind. The dog was heading back to the house with an unsteady walk.

"I got him," Mae said, returning the other rock to Jared's pile.

"Th-th-thanks." By now he had slowed Christmas to a trot, but he maintained that gait for a while to allow the horse to release his fear.

Somehow it didn't surprise her that the yard of the house was still littered with trash, boxes and ruined mattresses. Farley's tent and snarled ropes lay in a jumble. Despite what she'd told Daddy about wanting the place to look nice, nothing had been done since she left. Mom hadn't cared enough to shake off her lethargy and help clean. But it didn't matter any more.

"Now you see how the Irish live," she said as Jared pulled to a stop. How she could have imagined being proud of this place was beyond her now. "I'm going to Sacramento," she added.

"N-n-ow?"

For some reason that struck her funny bone, like she could spread her wings and fly the twenty-five miles. Her teasing impulse returned. "Would you drive me there if I asked you to?" She flashed him a sidelong look.

He broke into a slow smile. "D-d-d-depends."

"On what?"

He raised his brows up and down twice, and she knew he was teasing her back. She recalled Farley telling her what men around here said, *Do your praying in Ione and your whoring in Sacramento.* For the love of Mike, a sense of humor lurked behind all that stammering!

She continued in a mock-prissy voice. "I don't know what kind of girls you're used to, but I assure you, I'm not one of them." She lifted her chin and gazed across the slate roof of the house. "So you can keep your eyebrows under control."

He threw back his head and guffawed, normal as any man.

Then he tried to say, "Wh-why're y-y-you going t-t-to S-s-s-s-s—"

"Sacramento," she helped.

He nodded.

"Ohhh," the air fell out of her. "I don't know. So many things. I want to start over. My family was happy when we were coming to California. But everything went wrong. Mom's uh, well, something's wrong in her head I think. She won't even talk. And Daddy gave up looking for employment. I'll just say it: He drinks too much. It seems like they're both dying in their own way and there's nothing I can do about it. My brothers have scattered, except the one I can't abide. Farley's in there." She dipped her head toward the house.

Jared looked over at her. "A-a-are y-y-you all r-r-r-right?"

Seeing sympathy in those brown eyes, she said. "Sure, I'm fine, thank you."

He was quiet.

"Actually the last several days have been awful," she decided to explain. "I had a fight with Daddy about his selling my violin. He didn't tell me 'til it was too late. That's why I didn't have it today. Then the sheriff questioned us about a murder. Did you know? Mr. Parker shot and killed Mr. Thompson, in Michigan Bar, right outside the house we were in before. And we were hauled in and questioned. Anyway, yesterday we moved the Smith woman out of here—a bunch of this trash is hers—and today got ourselves moved in. I barely made it to your house on time on account of that. I thought the folks'd be better off here, but now I think I was just fooling myself." *And put too much store in being closer to you.*

She wiped a tear. "I sooo wanted to do music with all of you today! And with all that going on I just flat forgot about the dance, and John. I've hurt his feelings."

She felt a hand on her shoulder, the fingers lightly patting. It withdrew. Tentative, unsure, unpersuasive.

She closed her eyes and put her head back, inhaling deeply and blowing it out. "You see, I need to find my own chance. It's not going to happen here. At least don't believe it is."

"Y-Y-Y-You have t-t-t-talent, on a h-horse and on th-th-the p-p-p-pian-no."

"Around here, horse races and piano lessons don't do much for a girl." *The right man would, but there'd have to be a strong attraction.* "I'm leaving because I'll have a better chance in a city."

She gathered her skirts. "I loved the musical afternoon. Thanks for the ride, and for everything." She stepped down.

Nodding, he clicked Christmas into motion.

Already packing in her mind, she almost forgot. As Jared turned the buggy around in the road, she called, "Please tell Katy Irene I'm sorry I can't give piano lessons. I'm leaving on the first stage in the morning."

He smiled and saluted. "G-g-good l-luck to y-y-you." He drove away.

Sacramento Streetcar Routes

The first trolley cars, built in the 1870's, were very small with a bumpy ride. Many of them started out as horse-cars and were converted to electric operation.

II
Descent to the Underworld

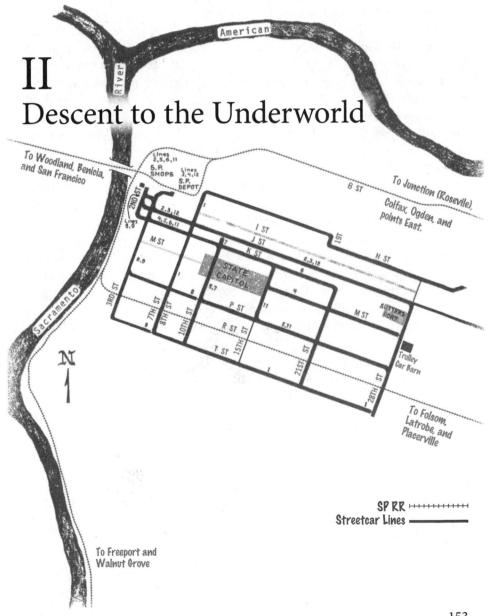

American River

To Woodland, Benicia, and San Francico

Lines 2,5,6,11
S.P. SHOPS
Lines 3,4,12
S.P. DEPOT.

2ND ST.

Sacramento

To Junction (Roseville), Colfax, Ogden, and points East.

B ST

Lines 8,9
2,3,12
4,5,6,11

I ST
J ST
K ST

19T

H ST

M ST

8,9

STATE CAPITOL

2,3,12

3RD ST

7TH ST
8TH ST
10TH ST

5,7

P ST

11

4

R ST
15TH ST

5,11

M ST

SUTTERS FORT

T ST

21ST ST

Trolley Car Barn

28TH ST

To Folsom, Latrobe, and Placerville

N

To Freeport and Walnut Grove

SP RR +++++++++++
Streetcar Lines ———————

24

Coyote's nose twitches as the stench of intestinal secrets ripped open floats our way. Not far from where I am rooted, Condor is feeding on the carcass of a buck. He steps around on it, testing his footing, and then yanks at the putrid meat with his hooked bill, pulling up as he grips with his talons, first one foot and then the other in a slow dance through the slime. The sinew snaps. His head jerks back and forward, easing the lump down his gullet. The pink gizzard-bag shivers in the black ruff at the base of his naked neck.

He swallows the maggots along with the deer's final meal. Molok, we call him, is not disturbed by rot. He eats the frights and horrors that the dead have endured along with their joys—the romp of young legs, the caring of a mother's tongue, the abandon of coupling, the pride of gaining esteem among one's kind—all that this buck has achieved and lost and felt now churns in the belly of Condor.

With a great whumping of wings the giant bird climbs the air and settles on the branch of a cottonwood tree. Here he dozes while his meal is transformed, soon to rise again as dreams.

Dreams flow from him like bats at twilight abandoning their roosts. He dreamed the trails I once walked, my son fighting the Españoles, gold seekers killing my people, ghost dancers beseeching the spirits to kill the intruders. He dreams the big houses rising from our hunting grounds, the new gambling halls of my people—all that happens in the world.

"Dream well, Molok," I tell him, "for when you die our stories will cease."

"So it's all a vulture dream," Mae murmurs from her Pierce-Arrow. "The turns of chance that put us where we are in the march of time, that turn our hopes upside down and kill good people while the wicked find rest."

"Yes. He digests the past and dreams the present. Since the time of the Ancients people have tried to foretell how their stories will end. I do it too. But no one can predict the strange twists a dream will take."

"Does this mean people will cease to exist if Condor dies?"

"Of course."

"Isn't he too powerful to die, a bird that can do all that?"

"Many of the Animal People are dead and gone forever. He is no different"

"Any basket will break when the load is too heavy," Coyote says again, then adds with an amber twinkle in his eye, "I like his dreams."

✱✿

The morning was still and hot when Mae mounted the steps of the stagecoach. Smiling a greeting at the two ladies on the seat opposite, she sat on the padded bench as far as she could get from a grim-faced old man. The horses lurched forward and accelerated to a gallop down the bumpy road. With forty-five dollars in her stockings, Daddy having given that much back, and a few coins in her valise, Mae thrilled to be leaving a backwater and heading into life's mainstream.

Times had changed. Nowadays, young ladies traveled by themselves. Amée Crocker, for example, the daughter of Judge Crocker, recently sailed to Spain and had a love affair with a bullfighter. The newspapers reported the scandalous details, calling her not a sinner but a famous "young lovely" from Sacramento.

And surely the most famous young woman of all was Nellie Bly, the daredevil reporter who recently traveled around the world in just seventy-two days, all the while sending missives that were printed in newspapers worldwide. In awe, Mae had read those reports with the girls at St. Mary's. Nellie had been detained in exotic situations that would scare the pants off most men, and yet she set the world record for speed. Now there was a new kind of woman!

And Lillie Langtry! "The world's first independent woman," the San Francisco newspaper brayed. "Tough as any man." But beautiful, and rich. Lillie owned gold mines in Nevada, stables of race horses in various locales, and a grape ranch north of Sacramento that she called Paradise. The article made sly references to Mr. Langtry, who tolerated her adoring men. Princes and commoners alike gathered in hopes of catching a glimpse of her. What was that sentence? After the part about Lillie writing a series of novels and having them published in English and American periodicals—dedicated, with his permission, to the Prince of Wales? *Everything is possible to a woman with beauty and force of will.* Lillie taught them that.

Silently Mae repeated those words to herself

Oh, and not to forget Annie Oakley! That feisty five-footer beat every man alive in shooting contests. Recently she performed for Queen Victoria in England. Mae was no newspaper reporter or actress, and she could barely fire a gun, but she knew she was a beauty with plenty of spunk; and if those women could travel around the world by themselves, Mae Duffy could certainly go to Sacramento.

Everything is possible to a woman with beauty and force of will. It stayed in her mind as the coach stopped to pick up two men at Perkins Station. It continued to beat with the cadence of the rocking coach as they passed through a gigantic hops field. At the bottom of the narrow hallway of towering green vines, she breathed in the strong scent to fortify her for the grand experience of life on her own.

One of the men from Perkins was staring at her. She pretended not to notice. At a sign announcing Leaving Horst Hops Farms, the horses lunged again into a lope and the stage burst into sunlight. "Mr. Horst don't like dust on his crop," one of the middle-aged ladies said to her friend as their bosoms bounced and they held their hats.

A peach orchard flashed by, also a thriving cornfield and recumbent dairy cattle in green pastures chewing their cuds. This was the fertile bottomland of the American River. She caught shiny glimpses of the river flowing west-ward into Sacramento.

The road acquired a new name, J Street, which they followed for a while, before turning left on 28th Street, where the horses slowed to a stately walk. The young man inquired of no one in particular, "I wonder why this road is called a street."

The woman with the sharp beak said, "This was a road in Spanish times, and someday new houses will fill in every speck of open country around here. That's why they put the streetcar station way out here."

The coach was passing a waste area overgrown with weeds. A ruined two-story building stood in the middle of it, but no stairs led to the gaping doorway. "Was this place here in Spanish times?" Mae asked.

"Yes. That there used to be Sutter's Fort," the same lady asserted, leaning over Mae so she could wiggle a gloved hand out the open window. "At one time that building there was the home of General Sutter. They're commencin' to rebuild the fort for the sake of history. There, see? That crew of men?"

"How long ago did General Sutter live here?" Mae thought to ask.

"Well, let me see now. that was in forty-two or –three…" Whispering to her-self, she counted the fingers of her glove, "It's nigh onto fifty years ago, I'd say."

"A fort with no wall," said the young man who was always looking at Mae.

"Used to be a high wall around it," the woman informed him. "They'll rebuild it."

"They musta built it poorly," he said. "Back East there's many a building still standing after mor'n a hunderd years."

"Pooh!" The lady waved the thought away, "that there fort was strong as any in the country. After Sutter left, men come with wagons and carried the adobes away for their own places. Broke the walls down with sledgehammers. My own dad did, when I was a girl. Saw it with my own eyes."

The stage turned into the N Street Station, the transfer point to the street-cars of Sacramento City. A sign on the large car barn announced: Sacra-mento Electric, Power And Light Company, 1893. A brand new building.

Seated beside the door, Mae stepped out of coach. Mr. Winger was al-ready trotting with the lead horses of the six-bit team, still in their harness-es, to the horse barn. He would hitch up a fresh team for the return trip. A rolled-up door in the back side of the new car barn allowed her to see inside the enormous structure, where a swarm of men hammered on the metal skin of a sleek car with rounded corners. She'd never seen such a thing.

"I seen streetcars like that back east," the young man from the stagecoach said. "I lived there with my uncle last year and we was always going to—"

"I'm sorry," Mae interrupted, not about to allow this silly fellow to latch onto her, "I'd rather be alone if you don't mind." She turned and walked toward the front of the car barn, where two sets of tracks curved though portals from two different directions, each with electric wires strung over the tracks.

Following her, he muttered, "Just thought to tell you them there's to be the streetcar of the future." She watched him amble to a bench outside the station and, with difficulty, remove a smashed sandwich from the pocket of his blue jeans.

Smoke and steam rose from the back of the building, no doubt coming from the generating equipment, which somehow created the electrical current that fed into the wires above the tracks. Sophie had said that on a shopping trip to Sacramento the generator had been broken down and the Electric Company hitched the trolley to a horse, like in times past.

Here, Mae realized, were three stages of progress right before her eyes—horse trolley, electric trolley, and the sleek car of the future. That was to be expected in Sacramento, where everything was up-to-date and constantly improving.

Buying a sandwich inside the station, she seated herself at the end of a small counter where she could spread out the newspapers attached to dowels. She browsed through the *Sacramento Union* and *The Sacramento Bee,* her eye going first to the fashion advertisements, but then to the notices for employment for young ladies. Most positions paid twenty-five cents a week after room and board was deducted. But then she saw a position that paid twice as much, the Pacific Water Cure and Health Institute on 7th and L Street.

The man behind the counter said it didn't matter which line she took, M or J, to get to that address. The M-line trolley was pulling in just now, bell dinging, the Sacramento Electric, Power and Light Company banner along its flank. She picked up her valise and hurried outside as several people got off. The trolley reminded her of a rectangular wooden insect with long feelers that felt their way along the wires. She stepped on and gave the conductor five cents, holding a pole instead of sitting down. She'd been cooped up long enough.

By all appearances, Sacramento hadn't been touched by the economic hard times. Great new houses were under construction around 22nd and 23rd Streets, workmen applying fish-scale shingles to the upper story of one such house. In the peak of the roof they had installed a pretty sunburst of spindles. Looking down the cross streets, she caught glimpses of mansions that could have been mistaken for European palaces. On the corner of 18th sprawled a gabled mansion with at least three stories and a round tower with a pointed turret. Between the mansions stood modest whitewashed houses, all with neat picket fences and well-kept yards.

At 15th Street, the car stopped at an important-looking building. The conductor called out, "Agricultural Pavilion." Several people got off. The trolley turned down L Street. This gave her a close view of the State House, a structure right out of the pages of her old schoolbook, the section on ancient Greece. Men were planting sapling trees between it and the Pavilion.

She got off at 7th Street near the Pacific Water Cure and Health Institute. It looked like a three-story house, but for a brass placard next to the door listing various kinds of baths—Electric, Turkish, Russian, Medicated Water, and Vapor—none of which Mae had ever heard of. But she loved the advanced sound of it all.

She tapped with the doorknocker. A girl somewhat younger than Mae opened the door clad in a plain black frock with white starched apron and cap. Mae explained about the newspaper advertisement. The girl escorted her to an office where a lady, probably over fifty, sat at a desk writing in a ledger. Behind her a bank of windows opened to similar mansions along L Street.

"So you've come about employment," the lady said. "Please sit down. Thank you, Patsy."

The girl curtsied and left. Mae sat in a straight-backed chair with padded gold velvet cushions on the seat and armrests. So far, she liked everything about the place.

To her surprise Mrs. Clayton introduced herself as the owner and hydropathic physician. Thrilled to hear that females in Sacramento could achieve such heights, she answered Mrs. Clayton's questions about why she wanted a position.

"You're hired," the lady said. "You'll be paid fifty cents at the end of each week, and of course you'll receive your meals and sleep in the dormitory with the other girls."

"Oh I'm so obliged to you!"

As the lady wrote in her book, Mae glanced at a gilt-framed certificate on the wall naming Sarah Babcock as a Commissioner of the Sanitary Commission. The signature caught her eye: President Abraham Lincoln, in Washington D.C., dated in 1862.

Mrs. Clayton was smiling at her. "My maiden name was Babcock."

"That was you?" Seeing the nod, "You were famous before you had a husband!"

Smiling through her frown lines, Mrs. Clayton folded her hands on the desk. "A long way from famous, my dear. My duties during the War Between the States were, and I quote that document, 'as constant and arduous as that of a soldier on the battlefield.' I'm sure that was a bit exaggerated."

"Did you meet President Lincoln?"

"Sometimes, at the White House. I'll take you through the Institute and explain your duties."

What privilege to work for such a lady! Mae could hardly believe a woman would be appointed to a position high enough to meet with the President of the United States. And Lincoln at that! Furthermore she'd thought that only men would be physicians and owners of medical establishments. Amazement interfered with concentration, and she had to force herself to pay attention to the details of the various water treatments, the electric baths, and special baths in rooms painted an array of different colors.

The first floor served the all-female clientele of the Institute, with several small bedrooms for ladies whose treatments lasted more than a day. To assist these ladies, sometimes Mae would need to get up in the night or before dawn. A big table and elegant sideboard stood in the dining room. "This is for our guests," Mrs. Clayton said. She opened a door to the kitchen, nodding for Mae to enter, "You will eat here with the other girls."

A Chinese cook in a black smock and brimless black cap turned from the steaming pots on the range. He had a long gray braid down to his waist. "We call him Cooky," the lady said. He grinned so big his cheeks all but eclipsed his eyes.

Mrs. Clayton showed Mae the door through which the help entered. She then led the way to the second floor, which she occupied herself. The hired girls cleaned it by turns. Up another flight of stairs was the room where Mae would sleep with the other girls. Also on the third floor was a storage room filled with kettles, buckets, bed linen, white aprons and caps, and strange implements.

Lastly, they descended to the basement. Lighting a kerosene lantern, the lady explained, "My husband had this place built in 1870. The first floor flooded too often. Most buildings in town did. So the City raised the streets and sidewalks ten feet, a little more or less in some places. Second floors became first floors. Buildings from here to the river have basements that once were finished rooms on first floors."

Walking by, Mae glimpsed a dim bedroom with a poster on the wall—a Chinese woman in a tight tunic slit up the leg to mid thigh. Hemp slippers lay beneath a narrow bed. Cooky's room. The next rooms had been kitchen, dining room and parlor, now full of boxes and upside-down furniture. At the back wall, Mrs. Clayton pointed to a coal bucket beside a small hill of coal mounded under a chute from the alley. "You'll keep Cooky in coal."

Mae nodded.

A uniformed girl was squatting at the base of one of several large settling barrels and kegs that stood beneath a pipeline with faucets. Obviously the city water was full of mud like the silted Cosumnes River.

"This is Peg Monaghan, Mrs. Clayton said, "This is Mae Duffy. She'll take over this duty from now on."

"Where do you put the mud?" Mae asked.

"You clean out one barrel each day and take the sludge up to the alley in time for the mud wagon. Before three in the afternoon."

As they left the basement, Mae said to Mrs. Clayton, "You must have a lot of laundry to do, with so many bathrooms."

"Yes, we do. All the girls help with that. And Mae," she added as they arrived at the first floor, "it will be your duty to see that all the windows in the Institute are shut in the mornings and the draperies drawn before the sun strikes the glass. That keeps the lower floors tolerable in summer. In the evenings, when it gets cooler outside than in, open the draperies and windows to let the Delta breeze come through the place."

One of the girls approached on her way to the basement, face hidden behind a pile of sheets.

Mae and Mrs. Clayton stood aside to let her pass. "Patsy," Mrs. Clayton said, "This is Mae Duffy, our new girl. Please find her a uniform."

Pale fish-eyes appraised Mae from behind the pile of laundry. "Yes'm."

ᔐ

The first two weeks taxed Mae's strength. It seemed she was constantly running up and down four flights of stairs with various burdens. She boiled and washed sheets and often lugged tubs of wet sheets up the stairs, for wrapping the patients, something Mrs. Clayton attended to. Every day she dragged two or three sludge buckets up the stairs to meet the boy with the mud handcart; and, of course, she took coal up to Cooky. To keep pests away, she and Peg daily scrubbed every inch of the metal webbing and metal posts of the beds upon which the guests slept—sanitary couches Mrs. Clayton called them—and refitted the mattresses with linen. On her hands and knees, she scrubbed the floors of the bathrooms and water closets, as did the other girls.

"Girl," a customer would yell from a tub. "Come wash my back."

But the worst was the flushing of colons. Mrs. Clayton explained that autointoxication was the cause of most illness, particularly among females, and that flushing out the intestines once a week would keep toxic agents from seeping back up toward the heart and lungs where they caused illness and possible death. To receive this flushing outside their own homes, a number of women came to the Institute on a regular basis. Afterward they often stayed for a special herbal bath prescribed by Mrs. Clayton. Hence they maintained their health and beauty. Mae, however, felt sure that inserting the enema tube into the bungholes of women lying on their stomachs and then holding the rubber bag high above them until it was drained adversely affected her beauty by causing frown lines. And the constant washing up after these treatments, particularly when accidents occurred as those women failed to hold it until they got to the flush toilets—a great luxury—was detrimental to her peace of mind, if not her health. The whole thing disgusted her. She lost every drop of interest in the water cure business. She needed to get free of the place.

The constant scrubbing and washing with strong soap reddened and cracked her hands, and each day the pain worsened. Once, right in front of her, one of the clients said to another as they donned their hats to leave the Institute, "Irish girls can be trained to make good maids. Their knees are already toughened and they don't care if their hands get red." Whereupon Mae learned that people in Sacramento also disdained the Irish. A serious disappointment.

"Be that as it may," said the lady, "I wouldn't want *that* girl in my home." She tilted her plumed hat toward Mae, who was passing by with a bucket of cleaning rags and soap. "I don't like her attitude."

Smarting from such remarks Mae yearned for better company. Besides Cooky, the only male she'd met since starting to work here was Paul the mud boy in the alley—his arms slathered with mud, his face and hair and clothing speckled with it. He spoke with an Italian accent she could barely understand.

Mae didn't fit in with the Irish maids. Even at night when Peg talked about her days in the Catholic girls' school on 10th and G, Mae didn't feel like sharing her experiences at St. Mary's. On two Sunday mornings she attended the grand Cathedral of the Blessed Sacrament, but even there she hadn't met any men. She'd felt shunned as she walked the two and a half blocks with Peg and Patsy, who all but shouted at each other in their howling Irish brogue.

At night she lay tossing in the hot and steamy third-floor room, thinking about how best to steal time off from work to find another position.

25

After a long day of colonics, Mae picked at her noodles and vegetables. At six-thirty, the kitchen sweltered like the steam-bath room. The three other girls at the table looked wilted, too. Cooky sat like a statue against the wall, arms folded on his belly, staring at nothing—a man with an unnatural tolerance for heat.

"Peg," she said quietly to the girl on her right, now sucking a noodle up from her bowl, "I'm going out for a walk. Would you please open the windows and draperies for me when it cools off?"

Peg's green eyes rotated to Mae as the end of a noodle whipped into her mouth. "An' what'll you be givin' me fer it?"

"Five cents."

Peg agreed and Mae went out the kitchen door to freedom.

The shade in the alley gave no respite from the heat, and the stench about knocked her over. The brick walls between the buildings served as an oven, slow-cooking the rotten scraps in the open rubbish bins. Two ragged men were rummaging through them.

In front of the Institute the white-hot disk of the sun struck her face. The city was broiling. It would be an hour or two before the sun sank below the horizon. The birds were in hiding. Likewise the people. She walked up L Street to the grass and trees of the Capitol Building, as the State House was called in Sacramento. Capitol Park was open to the public, but as she looked up the diagonal walkway to the Grecian building the place appeared to be deserted. Everyone had gone home.

She ambled along the sidewalk that skirted the Capitol, a row of stubby palm trees with enormous pleated leaves on her right, and brushed her hand over the stone pillars that supported a heavy chain threaded through them. Turning up a walkway to the Capitol's main doors, she climbed the wide granite steps and turned around to look toward the river. In the glare of the low sun, she shaded her eyes to admire the magnificent houses across 10th Street. They resembled a row of tall wedding cakes with cupolas, a term she'd picked up from the Institute's clientele.

A few traps and shays rolled up and down the street with horse hooves ringing on the new macadam surface. A lady and gentleman cycled past, each on a gigantic wheel with a tiny wheel in the back—a fashionable way to take exercise in the city. Mae wondered how they climbed on such unstable contraptions.

Squinting down M Street, which bisected 10th, she knew the city tank wagon had just been by. Puddles glistened on the unpaved road. The few people walking the paths up and down M looked like black stick figures. It would be an unpleasant walk with the sun in her eyes, but she wanted to see the Sacramento River again. Maybe ocean vessels and riverboats would be sailing and docking at this hour. Nothing soothed the eye on a hot day more than a large body of water. She headed down M Street.

About a block from the Capitol, she found herself overtaking a young girl with a bucket of beer, not the small size. The poor little thing had to use both hands, and as the bucket struck her knees, the beer splashed her worn dress.

Coming alongside, Mae asked, "Would you like me to carry that?"

The child set the bucket down and squinted up at her. The pinched expression on her little face turned into a smile with missing teeth. "Oh, yes, ma'am!" The last word rose and fell in a high-pitched glissando. A pottery worker in Michigan Bar talked like that, a man from Texas.

"You just point the way," Mae said picking up the bucket. Children commonly carried beer to their fathers in Michigan Bar, but generally they were boys and older than the little person who now marched smartly at her side, gazing up with starry eyes.

"What's your name?"

"Eugenia," came the bright response. She was thin. Her dress hung too high above her scuffed high-top shoes and skinny shins with no stockings. As she walked, her damp brown hair flopped around her face.

"My name's Mae."

Under Eugenia's guidance, Mae continued into the sun past ever more derelict buildings, including a saloon, now about five blocks from the Capitol. Why, she wondered, was this little girl obliged to walk so far for beer when it had been available closer at hand?

Mae never imagined that this up-to-date city had such an area, where too many little wooden houses, some slouching to one side, crowded together without space for gardens. Trash lay everywhere and the odor of outhouses competed with the stench of garbage. They turned right on 5th Street, into the shade of a building, and then left into an alley. A gang of dirty children, half in shade and half in sun, glanced up from their game of kick the can.

Eugenia opened a door and entered a shed attached to the back of a house. Gaslight glowed from the open door, a place with no window. Mae stood wondering whether she should follow with the beer.

A loud thump, like furniture being overturned, stopped her.

"Darlin', ya'll back so quick!" sang a female voice with a giggle and a Texas drawl. "Where's the beer a-at?"

From around the doorframe, Eugenia's little arm appeared, finger beckoning.

Mae took a step toward it, but a man burst through the door and rushed past her, bumping the bucket and sloshing beer down the side of her dress. He went by so fast she barely had time to notice that his half-buttoned trousers and the coat under an arm were of quality fabric. The collar, which had come unsnapped from his white shirt, stood haywire over his cheek. At full tilt, he ran up the alley, jumped into a fine black buggy, and whipped the bay to a lope.

At the door stood a young woman tying the sash of a white kimono. Backlit with gaslight that circled her head like a halo, she resembled an angel with pale blonde curls. The kimono with watermark clouds all over the silk had to be dear.

"Way-ill," this apparition drawled, looking from Mae to Eugenia, now standing beside her in the doorway, "who'd you bring home this ta'am?" A smile curled the corners of the woman's lips like a generous piping trim on a gown, a smile of love for Eugenia.

Eugenia grinned, gap-toothed, "Her name's Mae. She carried the bucket."

Stepping out and taking the beer, the blonde woman said, "Ma name's Helen Rose. Won'cha come on in an' hep' me drink this? What's left of it?"

Mae hesitated. She was curious about Eugenia's home life, but could Helen be a lady of the night? Of whom people spoke in hushed tones? "Who was that—" man, she started to ask before realizing it would be rude.

The woman waved the episode away with a smile. "Oh, he's ma brother. Stopped baa to talk. You caught him comin' outta the water closet. C'mon in. Have a drink." With that irresistible smile, she ushered Mae into the small room.

Helen set the bucket down by the bed and motioned Mae to sit in a frayed, overstuffed chair while Helen set the rumpled bedclothes to right. In addition to the double bed and the chair, the furniture included a battered wooden trunk against one wall, and a narrow table against another wall. Upon the table stood a tin pitcher and washbowl, comb and brush, and some small jars—all reflected in a cracked, unframed mirror. A rug of nondescript color covered the rough wooden floor between the bed and Mae's chair.

Mae wondered why a chamber pot was under the bed when a water closet was to be had. She decided not to ask. She would visit for a few minutes and then leave.

Helen dipped out a cup of beer and handed it to Mae. "Y'all got family in Sacramento?" She settled at the head of the bed, leaning against the wall with her cup of beer, a bare leg dangling over the side.

Mae explained where her family lived. Drawn by Helen's interest, she told about her father's inability to find work, and how George, Hank, Farley and Emmett were working in various enterprises in these hard times.

As they talked, Eugenia went outside.

"You got a sweetheart?" Helen asked with a flirtatious smile.

Feeling free to talk to this stranger, Mae said she might have been sweethearts with John Dunaway if she hadn't accidentally stood him up. Why she said a thing like that she didn't know—maybe just to talk. She wanted to learn about Helen. "What brought you here to Sacramento?"

Helen said she'd ridden up California's long central valley on a horse with Eugenia, searching for a place to live. They arrived in Sacramento a week ago. She did indeed hail from Texas and was a widow. Eugenia's brother and sister had both died of illness. Mae waited to hear about Helen's brother who'd upset the beer, but no mention came.

She let that rest, expressing sorrow to hear of such bad luck. "How did your husband die?"

Helen fondled her cup, took a swallow from it, and with a glance veiled by long lashes, said, "Murdered."

"Oh, my! Is that when you left Texas?"

"Ah sure did. Glo-ry howdy! Set Eugenia in the saddle with me and rode 'crost Texas, New Mexico, Arizona, the Mohave Desert, Tehachapi Mountains, and down into Fresno. You been there?"

"Fresno, no. But I heard of it." One of the Miller girls from Latrobe had married a man with a farm around there. "I heard about trouble with the railroad down there."

"You got that ra'at. Many a ta'am ah got me an earful 'bout the dirty dealin' of the railroad. Why, men there don't hardly talk 'bout nothin' else." Helen kept a little smile on her face no matter what she was saying. She smiled shyly into her beer. "Sacramento's a ra'at pretty place—if'n a body kin get outa this neighborhood."

Mae realized that both of them needed someone to talk to, and each found in the other a listener without high and mighty judgments. Mae's qualms dissolved, and she was curious about Helen's long ride with Eugenia. Helen obliged her with a rousing description of the cold nights and wild animals and other hardships. This was another brave young woman who set out to make her own way in the world, but Mae doubted anything would be written about her.

Unaccustomed to drinking beer, Mae's tongue loosened all the more. She told how she hated the Water Cure Institute and couldn't figure out what to do next.

"Way-ell, if John's the man you say he is, why'n'cha stay where you was an' marry him?"

"Maybe I left for fear I'd do just that. He's got no money to speak of. Did I mention that?"

Helen raised her cup in a happy toast, "Ah always say, better a rich man's darlin' than a poor man's slave."

Mae threw back her head and laughed, the first good laugh she could remember since coming to California. Then she spoke the truth. "I didn't want to settle down to babies and a hard life on a farm without seeing what Sacramento has to offer."

"Way-ell then," Helen declared, rising from the bed as she untied her kimono and let it drop to the floor, "let's us go see 'bout that." Her curvy white body with its blond bush was stark naked. Without a trace of modesty she turned to the trunk, stooped over it, and pulled out a pile of garments and laid them on the bed. She stretched a corset around herself, showed her plump backside, and said, "Would'ja hep' with the stri-ings?"

"I couldn't go out in public looking like I do." Mae said threading strings over hooks and pulling them tight. I've been on my hands and knees in this old thing and now it's got beer on it. So I'll go on back to the Institute. You still want me to put this on you?"

"Yep. I'm a'goin' anyhow." After a pause, "Why'ncha go on back to where you live 'n get in somethin' na'ace. Then meet me at The Old Corner. Oh, hayll, jes' borrow one'a ma'an. You look the same sa'az."

Mae didn't know where The Old Corner was. "What about Eugenia?"

"She comes with her momma. I don't never leave her alone at na'at."

The chance to go out in Sacramento, risky as it might be, excited Mae. She hadn't been anywhere interesting since she got to the city. But she didn't want to walk all the way back to the Institute and answer questions, only to walk alone through dark streets to a place she mightn't find, in a downtown she'd never seen before.

"Maybe I'll try on one of yours," Mae allowed, "if you truly don't mind." Clearly Helen Rose's wardrobe reflected an affluence she must have had prior to her husband's murder, not the poverty of this shed and alley. "There, finished," she patted the taut strings of Helen's corset.

Helen whirled around with a big smile on her face. "This'll be fu-un!" The corset nipped her waist to almost nothing and pushed up her bosom. The bottom V of it didn't quite cover her privates. She seemed like a child, yet also the sister Mae had missed ever since Nora died.

Helen handed Mae a crinoline petticoat and corset, and then held a ruffled red satin gown under Mae's chin. "Yup, this is the ra'at one for you, with all that black curly hair and them pretty blue a'az."

Mae quickly undressed, fastened the front-hooking corset, and wiggled into the red gown. Meanwhile Helen put on a gown of royal blue velvet. It set off the blond hair curling about her face and shoulders. But when Mae looked down at herself, she was disappointed.

"It's too long," she said, seeing the satin on the floor.

"Lil thang, aint'cha? Jes hold them skirts up." Helen was behind her, fastening the buttons.

"But the back'll drag and get dirty."

"Oh poof! Don't worry 'bout tha-at."

"Well, I'll hold it up all the way around when I walk."

Helen leaned over the table toward the cracked mirror and started painting her lips. Eugenia burst in.

"Ah played kick the can with 'em, Ma! Ah played with 'em!"

"Oh didja, darlin! That's mighty fa'an!" Helen laid down her compact and hugged Eugenia, picking her up off the floor.

"Now let's wash up," she said, setting the smiling girl on her feet.

"Them rascals wouldn't let her play with them before," she said to Mae while dipping a cloth in the pitcher of water and dabbing dust and perspiration off Eugenia's face. Then she sat on the chair with the girl standing between her velvet-clad legs and gently, section by section, combed her daughter's tangled hair.

Eugenia never whimpered, never even frowned. It ran through Mae's mind that her own mother hadn't loved her this well.

"I'm hungry, Momma," Eugenia said.

"'Course you are. Where ya thank we're goin'? Huh?" Helen gave her that flirty smile. "Why ra'at down to The Old Corner! We'll get your supper there."

Mae didn't mention that Eugenia's frock was soiled, frayed, too short, and now torn beneath one arm.

26

Eugenia skipped swiftly down the alley and around the corner up 5th Street. Clearly, Helen trusted her to know the way to The Old Corner.

The hard heat had lifted from the summer twilight, and a pleasant warmth bathed Mae's bare arms and neck. The rustle of the red gown added to the feeling of exhilaration and mild danger as she gathered an armful of satin to keep it off the ground. Some people would shame her for going out like this, but she wouldn't do anything wrong. Helen might, however, which added excitement to this somewhat naughty adventure.

As they walked up 5th Street toward the heart of the city, Helen's blue velvet gown, tight around her much-exposed bosom, moved with her like a live thing, skimming along the path at the side of the road. The slinky fringe of her bag danced with each step.

"I'm curious," Mae said. "Did they catch your husband's murderer?"

"Yep, they shore di-id."

Mae was about to ask for more detail when Helen added, "Both of 'em."

"You mean… two men murdered him?"

"No. They caught the ones 'at murdered my husbands, both ta'ams. The other'n warn't murdered."

Struck dumb, Mae studied her companion's perfect profile, wondering just how many husbands she'd had.

"Wouldja ma'and," Helen added after a silence, "if we don't talk about this ra'at now? It hurts my heart." She flashed Mae a sad little smile. "Maybe some other ta'am."

"Oh, I'm sorry. I didn't realize—"

"Ah've never been the same since that first murder."

"Eugenia's father?"

"No. That one's ala'av and kickin'. Truth be told, he's on my tail."

Another husband. Mae let it rest. Every question brought yet another revelation. Mae's exhilaration cooled as she began to wonder if danger might lurk in the company of Helen Rose. But she wasn't going back now. She'd watch herself tonight and tell everyone she had to be in by eleven o'clock, which was the truth. Mrs. Clayton was very strict about that.

Ahead, Eugenia arrived at J Street, the busy heart of the downtown. She jumped on the boardwalk and skipped around the corner. Turning the corner herself a few seconds later, Mae saw the city before her. Conflicting piano music floated into the street from open doorways, and groups of men smoked cigarettes on the boardwalk, turning their heads as she and Helen walked by—two young lovelies out for the evening air, in gowns such as famous actresses would wear.

"They sure got bushels of saloons in Sacramento," Mae remarked as they passed another open doorway.

"Shore 'nough," Helen smiled sidelong at her. "A hundred and eleven of 'em."

"Oh my! Did somebody go up and down the streets counting?"

Helen giggled. "A man Ah know did jes' that. He's head'a the Saloon-keepers League. Owns the plaice we're going to now. Truth be told, he's a friend of ma'an."

Eugenia was waiting on the corner of 6th and J for buggies and wagons to go by.

On the other side of the street stood a one-story saloon in the midst of taller buildings. A four-story hotel snuggled against it on one side. Under the roof of the saloon ran two black banners, one on the 6th Street side, the other facing J Street. They met at the corner like a black hatband on a square head. White lettering on both sides spelled out: THE OLD CORNER! Each side depicted a white buffalo charging toward the corner. A lively piano beckoned from inside.

"Look," the little girl exclaimed, pointing up. "Them buffalos is gonna butt hayeds."

Mae laughed with her. "They can't see each other, can they?"

All giggling, the three crossed the street in a break of the traffic, Mae holding her gown out of the puddles left by the tank sprinkler. Suddenly, galloping horses and a hurtling coach careened toward them. Mae hiked her gown and ran laughing, as did Helen and Eugenia, all jumping on the boardwalk just in time.

Twin potted cypress trees flanking the open door gave the place a high-toned look. To the left of the door, a half-barrel tacked to the wall served as a sign: BUFFALO BEER, SHARP—COOL 5¢. To the right of the door, lettered on a painted-over window: POOL AND BILLIARDS, WINE AND LIQUOR.

Inside, Mae immediately spied the piano player beyond the far end of the bar. Like a traveling wave on a lake, men's heads turned to look at her and Helen, men at the bar and at the many tables of the large establishment. Smoke haloes crowned the hanging gas lamps, and somewhere wooden balls were knocking against each other. Obviously, this was a popular gathering place, but Mae didn't see any other ladies.

"Let's go sit by the piano," she suggested.

Suddenly very much in charge, Helen responded, "In good ta'am, but first we gotta git this li'l darlin' some supper. The middle of the bar's the best." She moved to an open space between men and slowly turned toward the crowded room, most of the men staring at her. Mae squeezed in beside Helen, who now wore a demure smile as she surveyed the room—as though looking for someone—chin down, eyes up in the innocent manner of a girl not quite certain where she was, but hoping she'd be welcome.

Coming full circle, Helen picked up Eugenia and sat her on the bar with her worn and muddy shoes swinging in the air. Men crowded around, asking if they could buy Mae and Helen a drink. In about two minutes the bartender had a plate of food for Eugenia, fetched by one of the men from someplace next door. He plunked her on a barstool and put the plate before her. By now Mae and Helen were both drinking whisky, Helen flirting with eight or ten men at the same time.

"I'd be honored if you'd sit with me at my table," said a male voice.

Mae turned to see a man not much younger than Daddy holding his hat on his chest. Mae, not Helen, was the object of his attention. "First tell me where it is," she bantered.

"Over there by the piano."

"Well now, that's a horse of a different color." Carrying her drink, she told him to lead the way. Despite this bravado, something in her felt like a kitten in a roomful of big dogs.

"But I can't stay long," she added. "I've got to be back where I live by eleven." This way he wouldn't get the wrong idea.

She put her whisky on a table with a chair tipped forward. The next table was full of men playing cards. In the middle of their table, gleaming in the light from the overhead lamp, stood a sizeable heap of gold coins. Only one card player looked up when she passed—about Hank's age, sandy hair spilling out from under a bowler hat. The other players studied their hands in deep concentration.

Settled at the table, Mae asked her escort, "You live around here?"

He replied in a rapid mumble. "Not exactly, name's Smith."

She took another swallow of whisky. They talked a little, and she felt emboldened, giving him her real name and where she worked, and even telling him she hated it there and intended to quit tomorrow.

The piano man changed to a type of music she had never heard before, a marching bass with the treble playing lively counterpoint. He was bouncing on the stool, fingers flying over the keys. The beat made Mae happy all over. She couldn't help but tap her toe and sway from side to side. Mr. Smith watched her with interest.

Parting the crowd of men, Helen suddenly appeared on the arm of a prosperous-looking gentleman. She leaned down to Mae's ear and said. "We're going next door. Wouldja ma'and keepin' an eye on Eugenia? She's settin' over there behind the bar watching Misha pour drinks." Helen's smile was innocence itself. "She does so love to watch him do tha'at."

Disturbed by this turn of events, Mae said, "I've got to leave by ten-thirty."

"Doncha fret over tha'at." She patted the top of Mae's updo. "Ah'll be back by na'an-thirty." She and the man went out the side door into the night.

Mr. Smith pointed with his head in the same direction. "The Belvedere's got a pretty view from the top floor." He gave her an odd smile.

Recalling the word Belvedere on the tall brick hotel that shared a wall with The Old Corner, "she said, "I think it's time I—"

"You two want another drink?" inquired Misha, the barkeeper, suddenly showing up with a big white cloth tied around his rotund middle and a tray of full glasses balanced on the fingertips of one hand. He was setting drinks before the card players at the next table.

"No, thank you," Mr. Smith said. He opened a small purse brimming with gold coins. "But I'd like to interest you in minding that little girl while we step out."

We! Bristling like a porcupine, Mae told Misha, "I'd be obliged if you'd inform Helen when she gets back that I'm taking Eugenia home." She stood up and took a step.

"Just a minute!" Mr. Smith clamped a hand around her upper arm.

She leveled an icy stare at him.

Undaunted, he held her fast and gave her arm a little jerk while maintaining a sickly smile. "Name your price, you little vixen."

By now Misha had vanished through the crowd.

"Let go of me," Mae growled through her teeth.

"Look, missy," he squeezed her arm harder, "I don't know what game you're playing, coming in dressed like this with that other whore, acting hard to get." He shook her. "Stop playing with me."

"Unhand me!" she demanded. He was hurting her. All the card players looked up.

His jaw was set. "If you don—"

"Excuse me," said a man rising from the next table. The sandy-haired card player added, "The lady said let go of her. We all heard it. Now I'd be obliged if you take your hand off her."

He narrowed his blue eyes at Mr. Smith, his hands hanging in a relaxed manner, though they somehow looked menacing beside the tan of his checkered suit jacket.

Mr. Smith released her arm, whisked his hat off the table, and made his way through the men to the front door. "Damned if I'll come back here again," he yelled at Misha so all could hear.

The barkeeper watched him go, then turned and stared at Mae with a dark furrow between his eyes.

Rubbing the red fingerprints on her arm and feeling shaky, she thanked the card player.

The other players were waiting for him to rejoin them, but he looked at Mae and said to them. "I'm out." He turned his cards over. "Anything more I can do?" he said, smiling just a little at Mae. "Buy you a drink? Walk you home?"

His blue eyes were friendly, but she didn't know what to do. If they took Eugenia home and found the door locked, she'd be left waiting in an unsavory alley until Helen got there.

"I sure did mean to leave," she told him, "but if you'd like to stay a while and listen to the piano man with me, I'll wait here for Helen. Or you could go back to your card game." *Please sit with me.* "I'm grateful for what you did, and I don't want to trouble you more."

He toed the floor with his shoe, then shifted his weight and looked at her. In that caramel-colored checkered suit with the high-buttoned vest fitting tightly over the waist of his trousers, he looked very modern.

"Okay," he said waving a hand toward the bar. "Bring us a drink. Misha!"

At that moment the piano player ran a fingernail up the keyboard and announced as he stood up: "Taking a break."

Mae shrugged at her rescuer. "Sorry, all my plans seem to be changing."

"You leaving?"

She flashed him a mischievous smile. "Maybe I'll just—" She sat on the piano stool, whirled all the way around, and placed her hands over the keys. Oh, how she missed playing the piano! "That is, if you'll protect me from the dragons." She looked up at him in a teasing manner.

He laughed and took the seat Mr. Smith had vacated.

She began with some chords, playing around to find the right key. "You like to sing?"

"I've been known to." His smile broadened—square jaw, white teeth, a face more interesting by the minute.

With the slow bass of a waltz going, she launched into the melody.

> *After the ball is over, after the break of morn,*
> *After the dancers' leaving, after the stars are gone,*
> *Many a heart is aching, if you could read them all—*
> *Many the hopes that have vanished after the ball.*

Men gathered around the piano, all singing the well-known song, tenors and a basso profundo harmonizing with the melody carriers, including her sandy-haired friend. They sang with gusto. More singers pushed from the back, and soon Mae could barely see her friend, but thought she heard his voice among the others as she went through the verses. At the end, while men were clapping, a tap on her thigh made Mae look down. Eugenia was grinning up at her.

"You can play the piano!" Eugenia squealed with delight.

Mae picked her up and sat her on top of the upright. All the men smiled because Eugenia looked like a little pauper princess with her gap-toothed grin.

"Hold your hands like a bowl," said one of the men.

Eugenia cupped her hands on her lap. The man dropped in a coin. Others did, too—all in a merry mood.

Mae went into a new song, one that Patsy had taught the girls a few nights earlier. The chords were simple, the beat a waltz; but when she started the song, no one knew it, so Mae sang out the funny words by herself:

Daisy, Daisy give me your answer do.
I'm half crazy all for the love of you.
It won't be a stylish marriage
For I can't afford a carriage,
But you look sweet
Upon the seat
Of a bicycle built for two.

Everyone clapped and laughed.

"Play it again!" Eugenia yelled.

"Yes, play it again!" men chorused.

The next time brought more singing as the men learned the words. Unable to think of another popular song that she could play without music, Mae launched into the Chopin Nocturne she had played at the Sheldons.

A hush fell over The Old Corner. Loosened by the whisky and energized by the happy atmosphere, Mae lost herself in the lush, sad chords, which always brought to mind a moonlit garden with fragrant roses and a fountain tinkling in a dark corner where lovers met. Without conscious thought, she let her fingers run through the romantic sequences, and then finished with a flourish of her own.

Applause and huzzahs resounded in the room.

"A round of drinks on me," shouted a man.

Havoc reigned, men pushing toward the bar, all trying to get a free drink.

Knowing she couldn't top that piece, Mae was relieved to see the piano man return.

"Go ahead," he invited, smiling at her and nodding at the keys.

Rising, Mae shook her head. She lifted Eugenia down from the piano and set her on the floor, guiding her through the crowd. The card player's eyes met hers in an asking way. She nodded, and he walked toward the door.

An unspoken understanding caused her to reach for his elbow at the exact moment he raised it to her, and they made their way past the busy bar.

Waving to catch Misha's attention, Mae called. "We're taking Eugenia home. Please tell Helen."

27

Leaving the smoky saloon behind, Mae entered a heavenly August night—quite warm, but enlivened by the little night breeze that Sacramentans talked about with such pride. It cooled Mae's damp brow.

"I'll walk you back to wherever you live," the man said. "You never know what you might run into, in that gown."

"I do feel better with you," she admitted.

He was smiling at her in an admiring way, a smile illuminated by a stunningly bright light that buzzed and gave off smoke at the top of a very tall pole—an arc of a current besieged by huge beetles and a cloud of millers, the dead insects crunching underfoot on the boardwalk. The other lights on J Street were soft gas lamps on much shorter poles.

"In that case," he was saying, "let me introduce myself. Name's LeRoy Parker. Friends call me Butch."

"Mae Duffy," she returned. "And this is Eugenia."

He raised his hat and bowed in an exaggerated manner, first at Mae then Eugenia. "Howdy ma'am. Howdy ma'am."

Eugenia rewarded him with a grin minus two front teeth. Mae smiled too, pleased that he didn't see her as a lady of the night. But as they ambled along J Street, none of them in a hurry, he began to snicker through his teeth.

It felt like stabs of a needle. "What are you laughing at?"

He snickered again, kicking a rock along the boardwalk. Then he tilted his head with bowler at her, his face a happy smile. "Unhand me. Where'd you get that?" His mouth hung open in anticipation.

Embarrassed to be made sport of, she continued walking. "I read books."

He came alongside. "Is that how they talk in books?"

She took offense. "Some do." Lifting her chin she asked, "Don't you read books?"

"A few about the Wild West." The quiet way he said that told her he knew she had more schooling than he did.

She felt fine again. "That's my favorite kind of book," she said. "I like the California Joe novels."

Turning on 5th, they walked away from the gaslights and the traffic of J Street. Now they were on the trodden path along the now dark road. Eugenia looked sleepy and was having trouble keeping up, so they walked ever more slowly.

"You from around here?" Mae inquired.

"Nope, passing through."

"Where do you hail from?"

Face obscured by the dark he said, "Was in Wyoming a spell."

"I mean where were you raised up? Where are your folks?"

"Dead. It doan matter."

"If they're dead, it does matter."

"People always ask each other where they're from, but it doan matter."

"But—"

"People like to go on about their rich folks and big houses and how they're always sailing to Europe, but mostly it ain't true, and those lies stand in the way of real friendship. Where we come from oughtn't to be important."

"I never thought about it that way. But probably people are just trying to find something in common, and they start with where they grew up."

"Okay," he said in a giving-up tone. "Where are you from?"

She provided a frank summary of why the Duffy family had come to California.

"See what I mean? I'm not from Iowa so it don't give us any more to talk about. Only makes you wish your daddy did better. You happier now?"

He had a point. Mae had never met anybody like him. "All right. I'll ask an important question. What are you looking for in life?"

A buggy rolled by. He let the hoof clatter fade up the road. His own footsteps became audible again, the slow stride of a careful man. "Haven't made my mind up yet, but sure been thinking on it of late."

"You like farming?" She reached back and took Eugenia's hand to help her keep up.

"Mebbe. Thought I'd look for some ground in Round Valley."

"Where's that?"

"A long piece north of here. But now I'm seeing what's to be had in Sacramento."

"Same reason I'm in Sacramento."

"See, now we have something in common."

She explained how unhappy she was at the Institute and how she hoped to find another position tomorrow. She also told him how she'd met Helen and come to be at The Old Corner in Helen's gown.

He took it all in, not asking for more detail.

She went to something that had been on her mind. "Back there, I had the notion you were carrying a gun."

"Keeps me safe travelin' through these dens of iniquity in Californy." He chuckled. "You been to San Francisco?"

"No, but I'd sure like to go."

"Why?"

"Why not? I hear it's ten times bigger than Sacramento—the biggest city west of the Mississippi. I hear everything a person can dream of is there. They even have baskets that people ride in, hanging from giant balloons that float around in the air."

"I wouldn't mind seeing that. Hey, this your house, Eugenia?"

Part of the light from the gas lamp on the corner of M came over the low side of the house to the shed in back. It gave hazy form to the sleepy little girl hanging on the doorknob. Mae turned the knob and the door opened.

"Butch," Mae said, hoping he didn't mind her calling him by the name his friends used, "I'll put her to bed and change my—"

"Take your time. I'll wait out here." From his vest pocket, he snagged a cigarette paper and leaned on the building with one foot on the wall—a gentleman with the charm of a little boy.

Inside, Mae found the matches on the table under the mirror, lit the lamp, and took off Eugenia's shoes. She laid the limp child in bed rather than struggle to find nightclothes.

"Kiss," the little girl murmured, reaching up.

Mae gave her a hug and a heartfelt kiss on the cheek.

That seemed to revive her. "Next time willya put me on the piano, when we go there? Willya?"

"Maybe," she lied. She didn't want a next time in that place.

Eugenia pushed up on her elbows. "Willya teach me to play the piano? Willya?"

"I'd like to but—" Quickly pulling the gown over her head and undoing the corset she explained, "I don't see how I can teach you. Misha wouldn't want lessons going on while he's doing business."

She pulled her own loose frock over her head and petted Eugenia's hair back from her face. "Good night. Sleep tight. I'll blow out the lamp."

"No!"

"But your mother'll come soon."

"I'm skeered in the dark!"

"Oh, then I'll leave it on. Butch and I will wait just outside until your mother comes."

Butch understood.

It was pleasant leaning against the building in a place so dark he couldn't see her dirty dress and her lack of a corset. They talked in low tones about Sacramento. Some time later Helen arrived in a buggy and waved good-bye to the man driving. She seemed pleased that Eugenia was in bed. It was too dark for her to see that Mae no longer felt a sisterly bond. She had come to Sacramento to improve herself, not to sink to the depths of perdition. "Good night," Mae told her, leaving with Butch.

"G'na'at. Y'all come back and see us someta'am."

⤴

Butch accompanied Mae to 7th and L and into the alley. The cooler air had somewhat dulled the reek of garbage. At the back door of the Institute, he gingerly kissed the top of her upswept hair. The alley was deathly quiet, dim light spilling from two buildings across the back way.

He nearly whispered, "You said you might not be here tomorrow. Where can I find you?"

"Maybe I'll still be working here, I don't know; but please don't call on me here." She needed the freedom to do what seemed best, and didn't want any complications.

"You could meet me at The Old Corner."

"No. People mistook me for something I'm not. I don't want that again."

"Mae, we are what we are, no matter what other people think. You are a beautiful, spirited, talented, classy young lady. Don't worry about what other people think. Don't let them tell you where you can and can't go."

She liked his words, but remained troubled. "You say we are what we are. Well, you know who I am. I told you all about me. But I don't know the first thing about you. Not even how you earn your keep. So I don't know what you are."

He ran a finger down her cheek. "I was too busy being mesmerized by you. See, I do read books. Now, how 'bout meetin' me at eight o'clock at The Old Corner tomorrow. I'll be there for a number of hours."

"Playing cards?"

"Yup. If I'm not done by eight, you could play the piano. Misha would like that. The piano man doan get there 'til nine. Want me to tell him you're comin'?"

"No. You see, I do care what people think about me. I can't help it. I just can't go to a saloon by myself looking for a man I don't know."

He let out a quantity of air. "Okay, here it is. I'm not perfect, but I'm a basically decent fella tryin' to get on his feet after a setback in Wyoming. Tryin' to build up a little nest egg while I figgger out where I'm headed in life."

"I notice you dress like a gentleman and bet on cards, so you must have some way of making money."

"If a man knows what he's doing, there's money in cards."

"I've always thought of cards as a way for men to have fun while they're losing money."

In the half-light she saw his grin. "I thought you said you favored western novels."

She thought for a second. "You a professional gambler?"

"You might say that, but it's temporary. Now it's late. Let's talk tomorrow night. But for Pete's sake, get yourself a place to live that's not in a roomful of washerwomen. Mae, I need to see you again. This is an unusual situation. It calls for unusual action. Do come by at eight tomorrow night. Otherwise I'll call on you here. Sorry, but I wouldn't be able to help myself."

He pulled her gently into his arms and kissed her, long and passionately. Her lips were raw with sensitivity and her body burned with the desire to keep pressing against him. Other boys, and Jules, had kissed her, but their kisses had never gone to the center of her like this.

He turned and left with a salute.

She watched him go, knowing it would be difficult to stay away from the The Old Corner tomorrow evening.

28

The next morning Mae told Mrs. Clayton she needed to visit her ailing aunt in Oak Park, and begged to have the day off. Mrs. Clayton hesitated, but then agreed. "That's a nice new area," she said of what the newspaper advertisement had called California's next real estate boomtown. "I hope she's been seen by a doctor." Mae mumbled something about how she surely would recover with a little help today.

"Take the horse trolley at 28th," Mrs. Clayton said. "The electric doesn't go to Oak Park yet."

Thanking her, Mae hurried to the Capitol Building, where in about ten minutes she learned that to be eligible for a position she would need a certificate of type writing and short hand. No exceptions. The man in the employment office reached beneath the counter and handed her a sheet of paper imprinted along the top with a likeness of a large three-story building. "This is the best school for young ladies," he said tapping it with his index finger.

Under the building she read: STOCKTON BUSINESS COLLEGE AND NORMAL SCHOOL—SBC. Her eye went to the bottom line: Tuition $18.75 per month, board and room included. Five-month course.

"I heard about a school in Sacramento," she said.

"Atkinson's Business School. Men only." The dark bags beneath his eyes gave him a tragic look. "Here in the Capitol, male applicants are preferred over ladies," he said, "so even if you had a certificate, you'd stand little chance of being hired." He turned his back and entered a room behind him, shutting the door.

Back outside on the Capitol grounds, Mae contemplated her situation as the cathedral bells chimed the unchanging little tune and then bonged nine times. She sat on a bench, wondering if she should spend all her money on the school in Stockton, and not have enough for a certificate, by a long shot. Or should she use her force of will and her looks to snag a Capitol position despite what the man had said. No. Something about his face told her he was understating the problem. Only males were employed in this important building.

A squirrel bounded across the freshly mowed grass and raced up a young tree with a brass plaque on it—many of the young trees bore plaques that gave their Latin and English names. She marveled that with so many poor people and penniless immigrants in town, the squirrels hadn't all been eaten. She thought of Shadrack Smith, whose mother might send him here with a snare and a few peanuts. The same perky squirrel ran down the sapling and up the next one as though certain that God would keep him safe. She, on the other hand, needed a different kind of work and wanted to see Butch Parker again, but neither seemed likely to warrant God's assistance. Stockton was about fifty miles away, and Butch was in Sacramento. That ended it for Stockton.

Still, she needed another source of income and a place to live. Mrs. Clayton wouldn't pay her until Friday, and Mae's frugal nature made her want to save all her money as insurance against unforeseen trouble.

An aching loneliness seized her right in the midst of this busy city—streetcar squealing around the corner, horse-drawn conveyances rattling over the macadamized street, and people talking in animated voices as they hurried along the walkways. Everyone else had someone to see and somewhere to go.

Except for positions in private homes for half as much money as she earned at the Water Institute, she couldn't think of what kind of work a young and inexperienced lady could get. One night Patsy had told her frightful story about how she'd been treated in private homes. To keep body and soul together, she had endured the slobbering attentions of a demented son in her first house until she couldn't stand it any more. With difficulty she found a new position in another house, but very soon the master of that house began entering her room at night and compelling her, on threats of having her name blackened for any other home, to do nasty things with him. She gave in and crept around quietly after that; but somehow the mistress found out, and from that moment on, the lady made Patsy's life unbearable. Mrs. Clayton had taken a chance employing her over the uproar of that woman. But even without that kind of trouble, Mae knew she wasn't cut out to be a maid. God had put her on earth for something better. But how could she find her *chance*? Was Butch the answer? She could still feel his lips on her mouth. If only he were here and she could talk to him.

Three men in dark suits approached, coming from the State House. Engrossed in conversation they strode by without giving her a glance. She watched two pairs of women with parasols walking on the L Street sidewalk, sometimes in sunshine, sometimes in the shade of the many young trees. These women looked happy. They too had somewhere to go. The very nature of life, she realized, meant going somewhere.

On the bench lay an abandoned section of *The Sacramento Bee*. She picked it up and glanced at the advertisements. A wasp-waisted woman stood beside the urgent words: ELIMINATE BODY FAT! LIVE TAPE WORM HEADS IN CANDY-COATED PILLS PROVE TO BE A SIMPLE REMEDY.

She'd heard of that. The heads attached themselves to a person's guts and grew into long worms that ate a person's intake, thus reducing the flesh. How one got rid of the growing snakes remained a mystery to Mae. Wouldn't they bloat the stomach? But many fashionable women used this slenderizing remedy, so there must be a way to eliminate the parasites. Perhaps she should buy a vial for Mom as a birthday gift. Shedding flesh might help her overcome the melancholy. The vials cost ten cents apiece in the advertised pharmacy.

Glad to be blessed with a naturally slim figure, Mae scanned a full-page advertisement with four boxes across the page and six down, twenty-four boxes in all, each containing a sketch of a female wearing a different type of corset. Such daring, Mae thought, for the store to advertise undergarments visually in a newspaper! The last box showed a girl maybe two years old. "No child is too young for a corset," the caption stated.

Weinstock, Lubin & Co. also advertised ladies' afternoon attire, haughty women in frocks that hung straight on their figures. The ladies strolling on

L Street dressed like that. The next page listed upcoming weddings. At sixteen, Mae was the age of many brides. She laid the paper on the bench, asking herself what she did best.

Play the piano. She could teach. Music might lead to something. Someone at the cathedral might know the whereabouts of a music store, a good place to start.

She headed for the cathedral, just half a block away. Beneath the raised sanctuary, Mae entered a room filled with books, rosaries and other religious items for sale. She rang a little bell on the counter. A smiling lady came to help, one who indeed knew about Sacramento's music store: A. J. Pommer. She said Mr. Pommer would know of anyone who wanted piano lessons.

Mae headed to 9th and J, hoping no one from the Institute would see her. From the outside, Pommer's store looked very plain, but a note on the window caught her attention. The public was invited to a Saturday Club musical afternoon at 3 P.M. in the home of Mrs. McCreary on 10th and L—one of those wedding-cake houses Mae had admired yesterday. And she was invited!

Inside, the store was crowded with shiny pianos reflecting light from the front windows and the overhead gaslight—uprights, square and concert pianos. Violins, drums and a variety of tin whistles and flutes lined one wall. Glassed cabinets brimmed with music books and sheet music.

She waited for a customer to leave before placing her dilemma before Mr. Pommer—a tall, somewhat stooped man with thinning hair. "I want to teach piano," she told him. "Are there enough people in Sacramento who want lessons that I could support myself that way? Paying for room and board somewhere?"

He wrapped his long fingers around his mouth and peered at her through round spectacles. "Depends. A fair number of people are giving lessons in town, so you'd have to find your customers. If you're real good, you might pick out a living with the chickens. You'd need a low-priced room and a good board arrangement. You see, most teachers are married ladies giving lessons in their own homes. In their spare time. They don't depend on the income, and don't need to charge much. Some teach the children of their friends, just for the enjoyment. That's your competition."

"Do you know of anyone looking for a teacher who'll go to their house?"

"Well, that puts a new wrinkle on it." He exhaled slowly. "Let me see, maybe one or two. I could give you the names."

"Oh, if you could, please." She smiled and gave a little half-curtsy.

"But first, go over there and play something." He pointed at a new concert piano, a mahogany Steinway with a propped-up lid. Starkly elegant, the piano had virtually no decorative carving. How would her playing sound on a piano this fine and modern? She felt young and awkward sitting before an instrument designed for the likes of Johannes Brahms or Edvard Grieg. Lacking the whisky that had loosened her last night, she put her hands on the keys and played the Chopin Nocturne again, but couldn't conjure up the right feeling, and she stumbled again and again.

From the corner of her eye she saw Mr. Pommer grab his mouth. She couldn't turn her mind away from the displeasure on his face. When at last she finished, she looked up at him. "I've never played a piano with such stiff action. I'm used to a loose touch. It made me skip notes… gave me a case of nerves." Like a child making excuses.

He picked up a book of music, opened it to a random page, and placed it on the piano before her. "Sight-read that." He stood looking over her shoulder, which always distracted her.

But good fortune had smiled upon her. It was the same Scriabin Etude the nuns had made her practice. She didn't like it but knew it well. Playing somewhat slowly like a good musician reading it for the first time, she got through it without error.

"You'll do as a teacher for intermediates," he pronounced.

Soon she was knocking on the door of Congressman and Mrs. Grove Johnson at 720 H Street, a house that seemed modest for a such a man, and modest compared with the ornate mansions she'd just passed getting there. The wide porch, tall windows, and decorative woodwork looked cozy, and a flowering vine entwining the porch arbor smelled sweet.

A short, barrel-shaped woman with a gray bun on her head opened the door. Beneath the lady's tight day dress, Mae could make out the ridges of the style of corset—large pointed brassiere cups and a solid front halfway to her knees. It erased any variation in body width below the bust. She had a thick neck, and her large blue eyes registered surprise. "Yes?" she said.

Startled by the lady's force, Mae explained, "Mr. Pommer at the music store heard me play the piano and thought someone here might be interested in lessons."

"When could you start?"

Mae swallowed her surprise. "Today?"

Mrs. Johnson invited her into the parlor for a cup of coffee, and went to fetch it herself, apparently lacking a hired girl. The square piano against the wall was a popular model that had a weakness in the upper register. At Pommer's store, such pianos sold for $50. The uprights cost more like $200, and a price tag of $450 hung on the mahogany grand she had played.

Mrs. Johnson returned with a tray of coffee and cookies. As they partook of this pre-noon repast, the lady inquired about Mae's musical training. She quizzed her on other matters too. Clearly she possessed definite ideas, and she gazed so directly into her listener's eyes that Mae felt like a child losing a game of stare.

"If my children were horses," Mrs. Johnson declared, "I would give them their heads. Teach the basics, but don't kill them with scales. An interested student makes an interesting person and a better performer."

By the time they shook hands, it was decided. Mae would return at four-thirty this very afternoon with suitable music in hand. Two girls in the family would take a half-hour lesson each, back to back. The two, who were about Mae's age, were presently decorating the Agricultural Pavilion for the start of the annual California Exposition.

Back at the music store, Mr. Pommer smiled to hear of Mae's success. He beckoned her into his cluttered office and called up Mrs. Johnson on his telephone. That she agreed to pay for music on credit was clear from the one-sided conversation. After he hung up the speaking tube, he looked through a leather book and copied numbers on a scrap of paper.

"Here you go." He handed Mae the paper. "Call up those ladies and arrange to meet them. You might rustle up more lessons. When you're done calling, come out on the floor and we'll find some music books for the Johnson girls." He left the office.

She stood there a moment, realizing that he actually wanted her to use his telephone—the wooden box on the wall with the tubular listening piece on a cord and a jutting black speaking funnel. She had never used one before. No telephone lines had been strung in her part of Iowa, nor had they come to Michigan Bar or Slough House. Not even the Sheldons had a telephone.

She picked up the listening tube and turned the crank, as Mr. Pommer had done. "Central," a man's voice announced. Mae snuggled close to the box and felt foolish talking to a man she couldn't see. She read the first number.

"Speak louder," the voice ordered.

Mae squared her shoulders and spoke up. "Do I give you the other numbers now or later?"

"What other numbers?"

"The ones I want to call next."

"No, hang up, then pick it up again for your next call. And lady, you don't need to yell."

Gripping the tube against her ear, she was startled by a series of loud, short rings, and a woman's voice singing out, "Hel-lo-o."

Nonetheless, the conversations went well and Mae arranged two more lessons next week, both on H Street. Now she loved Sacramento again. She could feel herself stepping into a whirl of grand houses and respectable ladies, but never again becoming familiar with their bungholes and bare bottoms.

By five o'clock she'd finished her first lessons at 720 H. The Johnson girls turned out to be interesting young ladies, and Mae pocketed twenty-five cents—half as much money as she made in an entire week at the Institute. But she had no idea where to find a room that wouldn't cost more per week than she could make, not to mention board. By now her stomach was growling. She couldn't stop thinking about Cooky's tasty meals. All she'd had since breakfast was a small cookie.

She decided to wait a few days before telling Mrs. Clayton she planned to quit. Having lessons scheduled next Tuesday and Wednesday evenings, she might as well stay at the Institute until she found a suitable room. By then she might have secured another position through her new friends.

The pressing problem was that if she failed to show up at The Old Corner tonight, Butch might go to the Institute, and that was against the rules. So despite serious qualms, she would go meet him there just once. She tried to banish her fear by reminding herself that she'd made progress today. Force of will was working. She was now a friend of Congressman Johnson's family, and the wives of an attorney and a merchant with a store on H Street. Mr. Pommer was something of a friend, too. Things were looking up in Sacramento.

And yet, after a delicious supper at the Institute, and after donning her purple-striped frock and pinning her watch on her breast, and making sure her money was well hidden in the crate beneath the bed, her heart whispered caution as she walked to The Old Corner.

29

"There she is," called a man as Mae stepped through the open doorway.

She looked behind her. No one was there. Everyone in the place was staring at her—men at the bar, card players, and the piano man. Butch alone kept his head down.

Two men grabbed her arms close to the shoulders. "You're coming with us," the shorter one said, shoving her toward the door. They were lawmen in knee-length coats with brass buttons running up the front, and round stiff hats with short brims. This was some awful mistake. Scared out of her wits she called, "Butch!"

Just as that left her mouth, they pulled her, stumbling, out the door and around the corner to a wagon with black sides and roof. Yellow letters on the side spelled: Police Patrol. She wasn't resisting, but couldn't seem to keep up with them. Why didn't Butch come to help her? Last night he had helped her.

Choked by fright, she finally blurted out. "What'd I do?"

They lifted her off the boardwalk and set her inside the wagon. The tall officer with shoulder-length hair stood on the iron step at the back of the wagon, watching to be sure she stayed there while the other one climbed the high seat in front to drive the span of black horses. She looked down to evade the stares of the lawman and the curiosity seekers, Butch not among them. Humiliated beyond anything in her experience, and praying none of her new acquaintances or Mrs. Clayton would see her, she sat on the floor like a captured animal as the wagon jerked forward and rolled down J Street. They had gone about one block when an excited boy called out.

"Look, they got a whore in the Black Mariah!" Two more boys emerging from a saloon hurried to stand next to the first one so they could see her. The three grinned as they joked and watched until Mae could no longer see them.

Tears of rage welled in her eyes. She had done nothing wrong! And why didn't Butch help? It was his fault she'd gone to that place. The clatter of hooves on the macadam street didn't last long. Very soon the wagon was in the earthen courtyard of a large whitewashed brick building with tall arched windows spaced evenly along the two floors. The blast of a nearby riverboat made her jump. They were near the water.

The wagon stopped, and the tall lawman signaled her to come with him. The driver joined them, and they walked her through a door marked: CITY JUSTICE COURT. Her head buzzed and she couldn't catch her breath. "What's going on?" she asked

By then she was standing before a high counter with a young man looking down at her. "Name and address," he said, quill in hand.

"What am I here for?"

"Name and address," he repeated.

"Mae Duffy." She couldn't bear to have him write Mrs. Clayton's address in his book, which his nib was poised to do. A lady who had known Abraham Lincoln shouldn't be implicated in whatever this was. "There is some mistake," she said. "What's this about?"

The tall officer with the long hair said, "Answer the question. Then we've got a few questions for you. Just brought you in for questioning."

"What about?"

"In due time. Now tell the man where you live."

Mortified, she gave the address on L Street. "I work there, at the Pacific Water—"

"We know that address," snarled the shorter policeman, still gripping her upper arm. "Come with me." He yanked her up a hallway.

"Mrs. Clayton is a pillar of this town," said the tall lawman from behind. "She'll be interested to know where you go at night."

"Please, there's no need to tell her," Mae said, twisting around to plead with her eyes.

"I beg to differ," he said.

They arrived at a door. Inside the little square room was a round oak table with three chairs. The short lawman shut the door and gestured for her to sit.

"Now," said the tall lawman, putting his hat on the table and running his fingers through the dark wavy hair that rested on his shoulders, "tell us where Grace Berry lives." Settling in his chair, he leaned back a little on the hind legs and surveyed her with flat, dark eyes.

The shock and confusion seemed to have no end. "I don't know a Grace Berry."

The shorter man rattled words at her so fast, it took a moment to under-stand. "So you're not going to cooperate?"

"I don't know anyone named Grace Berry," she repeated.

"I'll refresh your memory," the little man said, then shouted. "The female you was with last night."

"Oh, I thought her name was Helen Rose."

"Helen, then. Where does she live?"

In her mind, Mae saw Eugenia in that bed lifting her arms for a kiss. Would the child be hurt if Mae answered that question? "She has a daughter," she said.

"We know. We know! Where does she live?"

"I just met her and I don't want to get her into trouble, for the child's sake."

The spunk of that little girl had sprung loose the buried memory of Nora, who had died in Mae's care, and something fierce in Mae wanted to keep the child safe.

"Listen, missy," said the tough little officer with dark eyes and black brows joined together, "she's already in trouble. So are you, if you don't cooperate." He leaned forward and tapped out the words with a forefinger on the table. "You was wearing her gown last night. We know your kind, so don't play in-nocent. Tell us where she lives and you walk free."

How did they know she'd worn Helen's gown? Had Helen told them? Had she implicated Mae in some crime? Or did Butch tell them? The words barely squeaked out of her mouth, "What did she do?" As far as she knew, there was no law against being a lady of the night.

"Stole a hundred and fifty dollars off a gentleman last night."

"Oh." So Helen was also a thief.

The tall officer joined in. "She shoulda took the measure of her mark. That man's got friends in high places. One way or t'other he'll get his money back. You can be obstinate, but then you'll be an accessory to the crime. We'd book you. You'd go to jail."

"If you put Helen in jail, would the little girl go with her?"

The beetle-browed lawman seemed about to pop with fury. His mouth opened to speak, but the tall one held up a hand.

He said calmly, "Mrs. Clayton would find the child a place to live. She started an orphanage in town. Nobody has done more for abandoned children."

"But Eugenia isn't an orphan," Mae objected. "And she won't be abandoned unless you take her mother away." No stranger, Mae felt certain, could love Eugenia like Helen did.

Still, Helen ought to have thought about Eugenia before stealing a gentle-man's money. Or was Eugenia the reason she stole it? To buy her clothes and food. Times were bad—"National Panic," as *The Sacramento Bee* termed it. Maybe the only way Helen could get by after her husband's murder was by selling her virtue and stealing from men. But that didn't make it right. The tall officer motioned the other one to leave the room, which he did without hesitation, shutting the door behind him.

The big lawman tossed back his dark locks, leaned forward and said, "I'm Inspector Oberon Jones. Tell me about yourself. How you came to be with Grace Berry last night, or Helen Rose or whatever her name is. Don't leave anything out. And first, how old are you?"

"Sixteen." Deciding she had nothing to lose, Mae told the whole story. Maybe if she told it well enough, the man would take pity on Eugenia and not send her to live with a stranger. As she talked, the high cheekbones of the man's face remained placid, the dark eyes neutral. His wavy hair would be the envy of most women, but this was a man's man, perhaps a man recently from the wilder places of the West. By the light in his eyes, she knew he enjoyed looking at her. Did he notice that she spoke without the common errors of grammar? That she was no typical Irish housemaid? She mentioned the piano lessons. Surely that set her apart. When she told him that a man named LeRoy Parker had saved her from the man in the saloon, a flicker of recognition crossed his eyes.

Inspector Jones stood up, a tall lean man with plenty of muscle. "I need you to show me where that woman lives." He gestured for her to walk with him.

He seemed like a gentleman. On the way down the hall, she said, "I'll show you where they live, but please don't tell Mrs. Clayton about this. I did wrong in going to The Old Corner with Helen, but I won't do it again. I'm likely to lose my position if Mrs. Clayton hears of it. And she could make it hard for me to work anywhere else."

"We'll see," he said, stopping at the high desk to speak quietly to the clerk. Then he took Mae's elbow as though she were a lady and escorted her around the building where the police wagon waited.

He let her sit in front with him. By now it was after nine, and nearly dark.

People weren't likely to notice her. And if they did, maybe they'd just think she was a friend of the lawman.

"Which way?" he asked, picking up the reins.

"Fifth Street, almost to M. The only street sign I saw called it 'Alley.' You won't tell Mrs. Clayton, will you?"

"You don't hear so good. I said we'll see about that."

"See what? If I cooperate?"

"Yes, ma'am." He turned his head, looking at her.

Something new had crept into his expression, something illuminated by the buzzing arc light on the corner of J Street. Just what it was she didn't know for sure, but thought it boded well that he looked at her with more than a lawman's interest.

30

As the wagon rolled across the busy intersection, Mae thought she glimpsed Butch backing into the dark recess of a store entrance.

At 5th and Alley, the lawman pulled the horses to a stop. Mae pointed at the dark shed-like dwelling. Helen would be upset, but that didn't outweigh the growing ire Mae felt toward Helen for getting her mixed up in grand larceny.

"I'd rather wait here," she said.

"How do I know you won't sneak off?"

"Well, if I do, you'll tell Mrs. Clayton and I'd lose my employment."

"All right."

She heard him knock on the door. No answer. The doorknob rattled, and then came the sound of a shoulder bashing the door open. Inspector Jones returned to the wagon and took one of the running lamps from its hook and carried it back inside. He returned in about two minutes and hung the lamp on its hook.

"Nobody home. You sure that's the place?"

"Sure as I'm sitting here."

"Nuthin' in there but a bare mattress," he said as he climbed up to the buckboard.

Helen was gone! "Honestly, Mr. Inspector, I don't have the slightest notion where she is. Last night she never mentioned leaving."

He flicked the ribbons and drove to the front of the building.

"Stay put," he told her. He hopped down and went to the door of the house.

A man answered the knock. A buggy and a wagon clattered up the road, and a bicycle with a carbide light streaked by. She heard the man say, "With the girl… well before noon."

Inspector Jones returned and ticked the horses to a walk. They were heading west on M Street, not turning the Black Mariah around as Mae expected. No doubt he would go around the block and back toward the Water Institute to drop her off. She was thinking through what to tell Mrs. Clayton and the girls and neighbors if anyone saw her in the police wagon, and her entire body was so ready to turn right on 4th Street that when he failed to turn, she had the sensation of missing a step and meeting the ground floor instead. He continued driving down toward the river.

"Where are we going?"

The silence lasted too long. She supposed this would be one way to go if he were taking her back to the station for more questioning, or to jail for believing she had lied about Helen. Mild alarm needled her scalp as the twin lanterns swayed with the gait of the team, swabbing light back and forth across the dirt road. A torn-off fingernail of a moon with a trace of red on the inside curve hung low over the crowded houses in this poorest section of the city.

With her mind jumping back and forth between the bad possibilities, she sat quiet as a mouse in full view of the cat.

"You're in harm's way," he finally said as the team clip-clopped through the night. "If I heard right, you was consorting with Robert LeRoy Parker, also known as Butch Cassidy. Did he mention bein' fresh from the hooscow in Wyoming?"

Shock bit into her. "What was he in for?"

"Horse thievin'."

Butch was hiding from the police, she realized. Other saloon patrons, not Butch, had told the lawmen about the red gown. They'd seen it on Helen before. At the same time, she knew that the man of her dreams would have spoken up for her and faced the consequences. Butch had acted like a coward. A long shot from California Joe. Her feelings for him slipped like a badly cinched saddle. She had been associating with two criminals.

"An' that's not all," the Inspector drawled, "you could run into the men chasing after Helen. Not a kindly bunch."

"What would they have against me?"

"Just like me, they'd think you know her whereabouts. That puts you in a deal of trouble. That hussy's the widow of the worst blood-letter in all of Texas. John Wesley Hardin. You'd oughta stay with me a while, to be safe."

Stay with him? "I never heard of John Wes—"

"Hardin's dead." The lamps washed over the 2nd Street sign.

Maybe he's taking me to his home. With a wife there. "Helen had more than one husband. Two were murdered, she said."

"Well, she's a skulkin' liar. That Hardin fella wasn't murdered. He was shot and killed by a police officer. Word is, she tipped the law off on 'im. Miss Duffy, Hardin has a loyal gang. A dangerous one. You don't want that bunch coming after you."

"She said a husband was tailing her."

"Heaven knows what trouble tails that woman! And as for Parker, he's wanted again here in California. Here we are."

The police wagon bumped across some railroad tracks and stopped at a black dead-end. He snuffed out the running lamps and jumped down. There was no house, only a two-story warehouse looming before them and extending far to the right and the left. Surely he didn't live here. Yet he unhitched and led the horses a few steps away. In the shadow of the building, it was dark as sin. She heard the hollow sound of horses munching hay and the restless river on the other side of the building. Something seemed wrong, but she couldn't run now. She needed to cooperate with the law.

"Here," said his voice. Pale in the scant light of the fast descending slip of a moon, his hand reached up for her. She hesitated, confused, but then took his hand and stepped down.

Ushered within two steps of what must have been a door on a small extension of the warehouse, she stopped in her tracks. "Sir, they lock up real good at night at the Institute. If you please, just take me back there."

Instead he opened the door. Stale, pent-up heat rushed out at her. Suddenly illuminated by a gas lantern swinging on its ceiling chain, the tall, broad-shouldered policeman stepped back outside and nudged her to the threshold of the little room, where she could see an unmade bed, a small table, a hand pump at a corner sink, and a countertop strewn with soiled dishes and rat droppings. Surprisingly, a telephone hung on the wall with the black ear tube hung up on one side of the varnished box.

He put a hand on her back, pressuring her to enter. "You have nothing to fear from me and everything to fear in a place where bad men can find you. Trust me."

Resisting his hand, "You aren't married?" She had expected to see a wife and children.

"Not'ny more." At least a foot taller and maybe twenty years older, he took her hands and looked down at her. "Trust me," he repeated in a tone of deep sincerity. "I'll sleep on the floor, on my bedroll."

She followed his glance to a saddle and a pile of blankets in the corner. *Maybe he'll find me better employment. A safe place to live. He knows so much about this city. I've got to let loose of that old rule about going into a man's room. I'll think of him as the law, not a man.*

She stepped inside. He guided her to sit at the table, and then opened a window to the night air, still warm but cooler than the stale air in the room. Somewhere there was a bad smell.

He took a fat bottle of wine and two jelly glasses off a shelf. "This here's normal procedure in these cases. I'm not at liberty to tell you everything, but this is the best we can do for now. We don't have a facility to put you in, unless you'd rather sleep in jail with some lice-infested ladies who ain't very nice." Pouring wine and smiling, he picked up the glass. "Here, this'll put you at ease."

He sat across the table. They sipped wine and talked like people just getting to know each other, which they were. The wine hit her quickly, and with every passing minute her joints loosened more. He said he'd fought in the Indian Wars and then came to California to hunt bears, which earned him good money before the grizzlies got cleaned out. She told him about her brothers expecting to find fields of gold in California. He laughed, and they laughed together over the many men still coming to California expecting to find a fortune just by bending over and picking it off the ground. She told how her family had come from Iowa.

"And you're here by yourself working as a maid?"

"Times are hard, and we're not what they call well-heeled. They know I can take care of myself."

He tossed a thick lock of hair out of his face. "They know where you are?" His dark eyes conveyed concern for her.

"Sure. I wrote them when I started working at the Institute." She swallowed wine and felt her face heating, over and above the heat in the room. The stained lace curtains on the window hung still. The evening breeze hadn't commenced, and maybe wouldn't this night.

Tossing back a swallow, "Planning to go back to your folks, are you?"

"Well, actually I'd like to find a better position. And continue to give piano lessons. I'm hoping to get by on my own here in Sacramento."

"You get along pretty good with your folks?"

A rush of conflicting feelings came to the fore. She shrugged and made a pained face to indicate maybe, maybe not.

He refilled her glass, dark hair looking soft in the gaslight. "What do you mean, a better position? More money?" He smiled, showing good teeth in a square jaw with a shadow of dark whiskers.

She smiled back. "Sure, money's part of it."

"What's the other part?"

She gave it her best effort, but it was difficult to explain considering that she herself hardly knew what she was aiming for, and she didn't want to sound like an idiot. An exciting life, she thought, a chance to rise to the top of whatever Sacramento had to offer—or better yet, San Francisco. Instead, she mentioned the difficulties of becoming a type writer at the Capitol Building. She flashed him a help-needed look that snagged most men's attention.

"Maybe you'd know of some position? Maybe at the police station?" She couldn't help but gaze into those wide-set eyes framed by that long hair. Few men wore it like that nowadays. Like a young Wild Bill Hickok or Buffalo Bill Cody. She was beginning to like being under his protection. Somehow there was a tickle of excitement under everything they were saying.

"I surely will think on that," he said, covering her hand, startlingly, with his large warm hand. The room began a slow spin. "I know this city inside and out. Many times a position will crop up."

He released her hand, patted it, and poured more wine into both their glasses, tipping the bottle all the way to get the last drop. Then he reached up with a long arm and retrieved another bottle from the shelf, clamped his teeth on the cork, twisted the bottle, and popped the cork out. "I'll keep my ears cocked."

"Say, let me show you something." He scraped his chair back and, in a stride, retrieved some things from under the corner sink and put them on the table, including an oboe-like object with an ear-like bowl protruding about two-thirds of the way down its length. Sitting down, he lit a strange little oil lamp and replaced the glass—conical with a small hole in the pointed top. Then he heated a needle over that hole, a needle large enough to sew grain bags. It turned red in no time. He then put the hot needle into a dark brown pile of something on a playing card, which had been folded to serve as a tiny tray. Some of the brown substance stuck to the needle, like melting tar.

Talking all the while about how he needed to relax after a long day of patrolling and catching criminals, the inspector turned and turned the needle over
the oil lamp, getting more of the brown substance to stick to it, and enlarging
the gob by manipulating it.

"You ever see this before?" he asked as he held the gob over the glass chimney, turning it as it bubbled like taffy and gave off a strange odor.

"No I haven't. And I don't see how this could relax you. It looks difficult,
like making candy one little piece at a time. What are you doing?"

He smiled at her as the gob cooked into a dark shiny ball the size of a pea,
which he then put into the ear-like bowl in the side of the oboe thing, and
withdrew the needle from it. This had taken three or four minutes. He held
the huge pipe to his mouth, the little bowl over the lamp flame, and sucked
hard four or five times, inhaled, smiled, and gave the pipe to her, nodding
for to do likewise.

"What is this?"

"An Asian treat. Go head. Don't let it cool." He was making sure the little
bowl stayed over the chimney hole of the lamp.

"The scribbling on that thing looks like Chinese writing."

"It is. Look, you're letting the smoke get away."

It was twisting up from the end of the long pipe.

"Suck it in and be sure to inhale. You'll like the feeling it gives you. Right
now under the floor," he stamped a heavy shoe, "Chinamen are puffin' on
this stuff."

She sucked on the pipe, felt the warm smoke go down her throat, and
coughed, handing it back to him.

Taking a long draw, he held his breath and as the smoke leaked slowly
through his words, he said, "There's an underground city down there, did'ja
know? Rooms, hallways, more rooms, underground alleys and roads that
used to see sun. So dark and twisted we get lost chasing after the criminals."
He threw back his head and laughed a rich rumble, then returned the pipe
to her, continuing while she inhaled the smoke.

"Once upon a time all that was above ground. Then they raised the city
and men down there made passages through to the next buildings and shoveled out the fill under the boardwalks, so the whole damned puzzle is connected where it ain't supposed to be, and blocked off where it's 'sposed to be
open. Mighty confounding for the lawmen."

Noticing her muscles going slack and loving the release of tension, she
drew in more smoke, handed it back, and, like he had done, waited before
blowing it out. Without coughing.

"Big business down there," he said as he passed the pipe back. "Gambling
dens, eating places, women of all kinds. A good deal more'n Chinamen down
there. Some call it the Catacombs of Sacramento. All the way from here to
the SP station and all along Front to about 12th."

Mrs. Clayton had told her about the streets being raised, but not about an underground city. The idea fascinated her. Nefarious things could be going on beneath her feet this very minute. She sucked and inhaled. A dreamy sensation was taking the floor out from under her chair, and she felt herself floating around and down into a dark labyrinth, yet the gas lamp continued to glow over her head like a shiny ornament on a Christmas tree radiating brilliant spikes of light.

She tried to explain how the lamp looked, with dark all around it, which didn't seem possible, and they laughed together. He stood up and turned the lamp down to a softer glow. "Chinese girls down there do things rich men pay a fortune for."

What kind of things, she wanted to know, but couldn't put words together. Nor could she imagine any of it.

His laughter invaded her body, and he shook the locks of his mane and his eyes were a warm smile that took her into his deepest confidence. He sucked and she sucked, and they inhaled and drank, and before she knew what was happening he was kneeling on the floor in front of her chair gently pinching her nipples through her dress and his tongue was licking at her throat. She ran a hand up his shirtsleeve, lingering on the strong forearm before moving to his muscled shoulder, while her other hand petted his long brown hair from heaven. She put her face in it. "This doesn't seem right," she said dreamily, inhaling the scent of him. "Is this procedure?"

"Oh yes ma'am. Here, let me help." He was between her knees with his hands up her dress, undoing her corset.

"Wait," she started to say, but the corset flopped loose and his big hands were on her hips, sort of lifting her as it fell around her shoes. He murmured something in her ear as his hand dragged lazily over a place no man was supposed to know about, and it came to her that maybe other girls had it too, and he knew and knew and knew. She wilted back in his arms while the lamp slowly orbited, trailing kaleidoscopic sparkle, and then he picked her up like Daddy used to and placed her upon the bed, which stood on the floor above the underground shadow world where strange people did forbidden things that no one could ever talk about. Ever.

31

Awake with a start in the middle of the night, Mae felt a naked weight flop over on her arm. Heavy. Twin blasts of nostril air shot into her face, an alien smell from deep within his body. Her head ached as though she'd been hit by an ax handle, but she pulled her arm free and started to put the pieces together.

I am not dreaming. It's the Inspector. I did with him what no unmarried woman ought, unspeakable things with a man whose first name I can't remember. Gave him what must have been my virginity.

People were always tightlipped about the exact nature of that, so she wasn't entirely sure, but she did know it was her fault. A girl was supposed to stop a man. She should have stopped him. Now she was a ruined for life. Crippled. Spoiled for marriage to a high-placed man. As Sister Delphine used to say about such girls, "A bird with a broken wing never flies as high." The enormity of it swelled within the small room, pushing out the walls and ceiling and pressuring her head until it was about to burst.

Her arm lost its feeling. She noticed a stickiness and soreness down there, and realized she was naked. Putting a hand on his shoulder she gave him a little shake. "You said you'd sleep on the bedroll."

"Oh! I'll get it." He moved off her arm but then was asleep again.

The narrow bed sagged into a gully and she lay hard against him. A sting of acid lurched up from her stomach to the back of her tongue. She swallowed and swallowed, head pulsing hot pain. She needed to lie on a level surface. Pulling back from the bond of perspiration that held them together, she climbed up and off the bed, and stood in the close room. It had never cooled off. Where were her clothes? She couldn't recall, nor could she see anything. All she could remember was the pile of folded blankets in the corner. Something to lie on.

Gambling that she could keep her stomach down long enough to find the blankets, she pushed her feet over the cracked concrete and waved her hands in the way of the blind—bumping a table, a chair, and a metal trunk, until at last her foot nudged a pile of woolly things. In a slow race against nausea, she shook two blankets open and dropped them on the floor, breathing fast, and then little by little lowered herself down to the blessedly flat surface. She closed her eyes, inhaling and exhaling long draughts of air, one hand on the extra blanket that would cover her if he got up. After a little sleep, she would feel better, then she would find her clothes and get out of here.

Through the muddle of head pain and nausea she addressed the next problem. *Should I leave before he wakes? No, it's dangerous out there. The Inspector is a nice man even if he did things he ought not. I just need to sleep a while more. In the morning I'll get him to drive me back to the Institute and promise never to mention what we did last night, not to a solitary soul. I want to live like this never happened. Maybe I can. And Daddy and Mom and the boys won't ever hear of it. Sister Delphine would be disappoint—*

I might be pregnant!

The shock of that opened her eyes. Faint gray showed beyond the curtain and open window. Moonlight? No. The waning moon had been about to set when she arrived here. Blinking, she elbowed up. It was early morning! The quicker she got out of here, the better. She'd have him drive her to 6th Street and let her off, with the solemn agreement between them. No one around the Institute must see her in a police wagon. She'd get Cooky to open the door, then tiptoe to her bed and pretend she'd been there all night. The cook must be sworn to silence too. This could never be explained to Mrs. Clayton.

"Inspector," she said in a moderately loud tone to wake him up, "Mrs. Clayton will think something's happened to me. She'll ring up the police station."

"Call me Oberon," he mumbled.

Sitting up, "Oh please, drive me to the Institute right away."

He didn't move.

"You shouldn't have done that to me, what you did last night."

A growl in his throat, "You was likin' it."

Yes, she admitted to herself, but it wasn't worth it. Far from it. "Still, you shouldn't have done it. Do you do that to every gi—"

"Shut the hell up!"

Rude! No man should talk to me like that, especially after—. She wanted no more of him. "I need to get out of here right now! I'll put on my—"

Exploding from the bed, he slammed down on her, hands around her neck, snorting air. His knees gripped her sides hard. She was pinned to the concrete with his thumbs pressing her windpipe. Panic roared in her ears and jangled in her limbs.

She tried to scream. No sound squeaked past his thumbs.

She strained to kick him, but failed. He was too high on her. She couldn't push his arms away. She tried to poke his eyes out, but he reared his head out of her reach. She couldn't get air. He was too big. She scratched his arms, long grooves through skin, fingernails full. She tried to punch his stomach, but couldn't get enough leverage for a good wallop. Nothing stopped him.

No air. Soon death. The knowing generated another round of fierceness. She would live! She wrenched herself back and forth like a flopping fish, carrying him with her, determined to slip from his grasp, kicking, scratching, hitting. She kept it up longer than she thought possible without air.

He was too strong, too heavy. Her strength gave out. Blackness crept over the window that had been gray. Now she would meet the Devil and the tortures of hell. Gone, her short life, down a black swirl—

She came to, his thumbs partly releasing her windpipe. With the revival of her lungs, she gasped and breathed past his thumbs.

He spoke in words smooth as steel, "Don't you ever tell me what to do. You will do exactly as I tell you. Or I'll scatter all the little pieces of your body in the Sacramento River and no one will ever know what happened. Understand?"

"Understand?" he repeated, painfully pinching off her windpipe again.

She tried to nod against the thumbs, tears of shock making warm streams down to her ears.

He lessened the pressure a bit. "What did you say?"

Sucking a thin bit of air, "Yes." *Oh God, and all the saints, help me!*
"I didn't hear you." He let the air return.

"I understand." Her heart was galloping like an oversized horse.

"All right, you can live, for now. But next time you tell me what to do, you'll be fish food. Same if you try to run away. I'll catch you."

Slowly he released her neck, put a foot under him, and rose to his full height, straddling her.

She lay on the blankets with the black silhouette of Oberon Jones towering above her, blocking the gray in the window. Gone was his pretense of protecting, even loving her, as in her delirium last night she had believed he did. She knew this man would kill her whenever it suited him.

He peed in the bucket. Then he reached down and helped her to her feet—weak, trembling, neck hurting. He sat on the side of the bed, drawing her to him, moving her legs apart. "Now there's a good girl," he said, lowering her upon him, adjusting himself within her.

Her mind locked itself away as silent tears ran down her face.

Quietly, he finished with her and then permitted her to wash at the sink and get dressed. Meanwhile he put on his trousers, and then from the tin cupboard under the counter took out bread, butter, and two peaches. They sat at the table while he ate methodically, Mae unable to swallow past the stopper in her throat—the windpipe pain nothing beside the horror of what might come next. She barely noticed that terror had replaced nausea and headache.

After eating, he stood up. "I'm going to the station," he said as though to a wife. "Can't say when I'll be back, but I'll drive by from time to time."

He inserted the revolver into the holster, shrugged on his shirt and long police coat with all the buttons, and stood over her as she sat at the table. "Someday I'll find you a position, but not yet. I want you to myself for a while."

Hope flared in her heart. He wasn't going to kill her. At least not yet. *I will escape.*

He pulled her to her feet, so tight against him that the pistol under the coat hurt her cheek. With his other hand, he raised her chin and kissed her on the mouth. She didn't dare resist.

Back at his open trunk, he rattled some things. "Turn around."

Automatically she obeyed, trying to peek over her shoulder, afraid of what he was doing. He pulled her hands together and snapped something on her wrists. *Handcuffs!* She tensed, resisted, as he yanked her by the joined cuffs, nearly causing her to fall backwards on the floor. He bent down and picked up a sturdy chain from under the sink, looped it through the handcuffs, and snapped a padlock shut. She was chained to the pipe! He had done this before.

With the flat stare of a snake, he dropped the key in his trouser pocket and, from a peg on the wall, took his police hat and put it on.

Ever since Nora's death, Mae had suffered from an unnatural fear of confinement. In her worst nightmares she was cooped up in boxes or buried alive. Now she was feeling the terror of those dreams. But this was real!

"Oh please, you're not going to leave me like this. You can't!" Warm urine leaked down her leg.

"Yes I can." Calm as could be. He took the pee bucket and set it against the wall near her, the chain long enough to reach. Maybe long enough to reach the telephone.

He cranked the telephone, turning to look down at her. "Sam, tell me the moment anyone calls to this number, or from it. Tell the desk to fetch me no matter what I'm doing."

As he listened to the operator, her panic-petrified mind considered screaming for Sam's help. But Oberon could kill and dispose of her before anyone could get here. Besides, it sounded like Sam, the operator, worked for him.

"Yeah," Oberon was saying, "I'm pretty sure I can get Jimmy out of that mess." He paused again, and then chuckled. "Whatdaya think friends are for?" He hung up the earpiece.

"You won't touch it if it rings," he told Mae, ripping a towel and talking as he pulled a length of it between her teeth and tied it behind her head. "But nobody will call. All forty-three people in town with telephones know to call me at the station."

He turned and left. Soon she heard the rattle of the harness.

In full panic, mouth stretched and already hurting, she sat on the floor determined to destroy the padlock or the link between it and the handcuffs. She banged the thing again and again on the concrete behind her, without benefit of sight. Without her best muscles. Before long, her wrists and hands couldn't take the awkward misses and bruising blows.

She turned her attention to the pipe, realizing she'd be free if she could break it. The wall angle from the corner sink made it possible to put her back against the wall under the telephone and push the pipe with her bare feet. The pipe moved a little, but it was stout, and with her hands behind her, she couldn't anchor herself, so she slid up the angle of the wall and lost leverage. Again and again she tried and failed. She tried the other wall, but the front post of the counter, with the cupboard underneath, was so close to the pipe that she couldn't squeeze herself in with knees up between pipe and post. She had no leverage on the pipe. So she went back to the first wall.

The more she tried to break the pipe, the more panicked and overheated and out of breath she became. The gag pained her face, and her head started to make crashing sounds like marching cymbals. Slobber soaked the cloth and dribbled down her neck. The sun blazed through the torn and yellowed lace curtain, striking her. Periodically she would go into another frenzy of fighting to get loose, and between times she listened. No one walked by the building, not that she could hear. She screamed into the gag until her throat was raw, hoping someone would hear the strange noises but fearing that someone would be Oberon. He had shut the window, the more to muzzle her. She kept an eye on the window in hopes a face would appear, yet frightened that if one did appear it would be his. No one came. He must have been correct that the warehouse was abandoned. Otherwise her gurgles and efforts to make sound would be heard.

She was hot and weak and hurting, but at least the sun moved and stopped frying her directly. However, it crept slowly across the tin roof like a monster torch upon a stovetop. She became sick with heat.

The settling barrel stood within range of the chain, but wasn't full enough for her mouth to reach when she stood up and leaned over its side. And if she fell in head first, she would drown. So she stood up, shoving her head under the pump handle to make it stand out, and then quickly slipping her armpit around it and doing knee bends to work the pump long enough to produce a trickle of muddy water, which she sucked through her gag. Each time she did that, the wide tongue of the pump-handle bruised her more but the water revived her a little. Then the panic would bloom again and she would pound the padlock on the floor until her muscles gave out, and then try again. Then she tried again to break the pipe. Perspiration soaked her frock from top to bottom. Sweat stung her eyes and mingled with the tears. How stupid she'd been coming here! And trusting!

Unable to think straight, she lay on the floor in a damp heap with her heart flapping its downy wings in her throat like a dying miller. She was trapped. Worse than in her nightmares, because she couldn't wake up and realize it was just a dream. The stench from the dark hole where the pipe entered the floor also sickened her—something rotten down there. That and the miasma from the bucket of rank urine brought the return of nausea. She retched repeatedly, dribbling out bursts of brown, gritty liquid, which added to the stench.

I toyed with my life and ruined it in but a few hours. If only I hadn't gone to The Old Corner with Helen! If only I hadn't gone back to see Butch!

Another hot room in which she'd been locked up floated up from memory. Back then she and Nora had a soft bed to sit on, not a concrete floor. Little Nora seemed to be with her again, her bony chest and hiked-up nightshirt, and that awful fecal slime with a streak of blood through it. The smell—

The Devil had Mae now, and all she could do was pray—to God, who had seen her sins, and to Mary, who was supposed to be merciful.

Oh please, please help me.

32

In the soaring temperature under the metal roof, Mae felt a mental lethargy as though her brains were cooking. The sound of hooves and wheels on gravel didn't register at first. But when it did, a little hope roused her from the stupor, only to be replaced by terror at the turning of a key in the lock.

Oberon entered and opened the window. He then pulled her up on shaky legs and removed the gag and the handcuffs. So intense was her fear that she didn't care about the pain in her face and shoulders from the release of her bonds. He took her hands in his, turned them over, studying the scrapes and dried blood. He ran a thumb over the purple bruises.

"Wash your face and comb your hair," he said in a husbandly tone. "Then we're going to the Water Institute for your things."

Mrs. Clayton will help. I'll get away from him.

That thought strengthened her trembling arms and legs as she dipped a pan of water from the settling barrel and drank, and then splashed it over her face. She drank more water, all the time thinking what to say to Mrs. Clayton, and when to say it. The captivity had erased all concern about embarrassment and shame.

Outside, when the two of them were on the high seat of the Black Mariah, the reins in his hands, he turned to her. "I'll be watching your every move. Leave this wagon before I say and you're dead. Don't even squirm around. Got that?" He patted the gun under his coat.

She swallowed the lump in her throat. *What if he's not taking me to the Water Institute after all?*

Snake eyes. "When we get there, I do the talking. Don't say a word. Understand? Not one."

She nodded, always in agreement. Whatever he said. Somewhere a foundry spewed black smoke over this end of the city, and a slaughterhouse emitted a choking stench. Peg, who had once been a meatpacker, had said that's where the stink came from.

He headed the horses up M Street all right, letting them walk while he kept his eyes on her. "And don'cha show your wrists to anyone. Keep your hands in your lap with the tops up, and that one on top." He reached over and touched her less wounded hand.

Sounds like he really is taking me there, but I can't let this hope blind me. Last night when he'd driven her past the expected turn, she felt herself drop like she'd missed a step. That had indeed been a bad stumble. This time, if he turned wrong or didn't stop at the Institute, she might be able to escape if she kept her wits about her. They were passing two women walking beside the road.

Maybe I should leap down now and zigzag hell-bent-for-leather past them so he can't aim, and hide in one of those broken-down shacks. If he shoots me in broad daylight, they'd be witnesses.

She came to a dead-end in her thinking, realizing that the word of those women in worn calico wouldn't stand up against a police inspector. He could kill anyone escaping from his wagon and get away with it. Besides, he was still going the right way. Better to wait and see what happens.

In the long blocks to the Institute, her mind kept circling, and perspiration had left salt swirls across the purple stripes of her dress. He stopped the horses before the Institute. Grabbing her hand in a crushing grip, he yanked, sliding her across the seat, then lifted her down over the steel steps to the mown grass between the sidewalk and the street.

He continued to grip her hand as he put the heavy ground-tie before the horses, with one hand. He hissed down at her as they walked to the front door, "Don't make me pull you. And not one word."

She stood with him as he rapped the brass knocker four times. Her heart beat at presto, her breath in short quakes.

Patsy opened the door, eyes widening. To his polite request to see Mrs. Clayton, she escorted them to the office a few steps away. Then at Oberon's request, Patsy left to get Mae's belongings.

Mrs. Clayton showed them the chairs and shut the office door. Mae sat down as though in a dream, on the same chair as on her first day here. Over the wide desk, the lady furrowed her brows at Mae, but her attention shifted to Oberon, who, with the demeanor of a caring uncle, introduced himself as Inspector Sergeant Jones.

Mrs. Clayton wondered aloud if she had met him before.

"In truth, I believe so. I'm obliged that a lady of your standing would remember a trifling thing such as that." *So polite. So like a pleasant visit.*

Mrs. Clayton smiled at him through her frown lines. "Well, in any case, I've heard good reports of your work."

Graciously he thanked her. Then an authoritative note asserted itself as he said, "It was that ruckus over at the SP shops, as I recall. A hysterical female shot her husband. You saw to the adoption of the children."

"Yes, that was it," Mrs. Clayton confirmed, her expression somehow turning inward. When she spoke again, it was with a shade less of her usual confidence. "Well, I've got a patient to see, so maybe we'd better get on with what you're here for."

Oberon nodded, explaining in a strong tone that he was still holding Mae for her own protection. *Still.* They had talked on the telephone.

"I'm not at liberty to say more," he admitted in a cozy tone, "but she can't work here any more. We've come to pick up her things. I'll bet she was good help; but you need to know, Mrs. Clayton, that she brought a criminal to your door a couple nights ago. You and your clientele could be in danger. Tell your girls to keep a sharp eye out for a skulking man."

Mrs. Clayton looked at Mae with hurt and disappointment. "You did that?"

Tears knifed the backs of Mae's eyes. She ached to blurt out the whole truth, but Mrs. Clayton would distrust anything she said. Later Oberon would sprinkle her parts in the river. Three weeks ago, in this very same chair, she had been impressed with her independence. Now, even without the handcuffs she was a prisoner; but unlike a jailbird who could shout through the bars, she had to sit in silence and listen to Oberon's lies.

Patsy carried in Mae's crate.

Back at his place, Mae having failed to convey a hint of anything wrong to Mrs. Clayton, Oberon fried pork chops while she stood at the bed weak with desolation, searching through her crate. Her hands trembled to see her old life before her—clothes, music, poems. She opened the cigar box and lifted the miniature burlap sack. It came up light and empty in her hand. Not breathing, she turned it inside out and stared at the emptiness. She searched through all the postal cards of her old boyfriends, and then each item of clothing, turning it inside out, shaking and spreading the music on the bed. But the money was gone. All of it. That forty-five dollars had made her think she could get along by herself.

The earth seemed to move from under her feet and she caught herself on the side of the bed. "Somebody stole my money," she croaked, hoarse from her day of trying to yell. She slipped her hand in the pocket inside her skirt. The fifty cents Mrs. Clayton had paid her for the week—generous considering the Wednesday off—was there, plus fifty cents from the piano lessons. She removed those coins and put them into the little sack so it wouldn't be empty, pulled the drawstring, placed it back in her cigar box, and covered it with the Schirmer Piano Exercises intended for teaching. Oberon had called the two ladies on the telephone and said she'd be unable to teach, so thanks to Mae, Mr. Pommer was out the money for the music. Now she was also a thief.

Turning the chops with a fork, Oberon asked, "How much did they get away with?"

She tried to subtract the cost of the stagecoach and sandwich at the station from the forty-five dollars.

Voice rising, "I asked a question: How much was stolen?"

Struggling to think, she said, "About forty dollars. No, forty-one or two dollars and ninety-five cents." Five cents for the trolley ride.

"Don't worry. I'll get it back. That's my business."

After supper he undressed her and did all that he had done the night before. He seemed kind, and she was so exhausted and foggy of mind, and so unable to keep fresh the horror of the day that her treasonous body actually liked it. Afterwards he allowed her to move freely around the room, which made her grateful to him, and then she lay in the gully of the bed, glued to him with sweat, on the wall side. His loaded Colt lay beside him on an upended crate.

As twilight darkened the small room, he told her about a recent case of a prostitute who had been tortured to death. He explained how he'd put together what had happened, from the burns and marks on her nipples and privates. By his rising tone and quickening speech, it seemed he relished the memory.

Despite that, and the sagging bed, and the man practically beneath her, she believed he wanted her alive. That eventually allowed her to sleep a little. The next thing she knew she was awake, lying in the dark and the quiet. His breathing was slow and regular, his back to her rising with each inhalation.

Fingers of fresh air from the open window felt their way up her legs, torso and damp brow. A distant dog barked. The Sacramento River on the other side of the warehouse moiled louder at night than in the daytime when other sounds competed. Sleep had cleared her mind. Oberon had locked the door and put the skeleton key in his trunk, but the open window offered escape. She would need to open it wider, push up the sash. He might hear the scraping of wood on wood.

There was a loaded gun on the crate. She could sneak around him and shoot him with it—if she could operate the mechanism. It might have a lock. She'd have to turn up the lamp to see it, but that would wake him. She couldn't try and fail. He'd wrest the gun away and kill her, or torture her to death like the prostitute. But on the other hand, if she succeeded, she'd be wanted for the murder of a lawman, and nobody would believe her story—especially not the police. They trusted him.

No one knew she was here. He hadn't told Mrs. Clayton where he was keeping her. That played in Mae's favor. Someone else might have killed him, and he, the city's top investigator, wouldn't be around to study the case. But she'd have to be clever about leaving town without any money. And there was also the possibility that he had told someone at the station where she was staying.

Like a tuba, his voice stunned her through the echo chamber of his back. "You awake?"

She jumped. "Oh, ah, I thought you were asleep." She couldn't breathe.

He flopped over like a whale in a bucket, now facing her. "Don't be stupid and get no i-deas about leavin' me. Remember the hungry fish in the river."

She lay waiting for her heart to calm down, waiting for him to go back to sleep. Maybe he'd never been asleep. She didn't know his breathing pattern, and realized she couldn't try to escape until she did.

She could neither sleep nor get comfortable. Twice he yelled at her to stop moving around, "keeping me awake," when all she did was straighten her cramped leg. Eventually she fell asleep, before he did.

The next morning, though she begged him not to, he chained her to the pipe and gagged her. Again he left the window shut. Her wrists were so sore she couldn't fight like she'd done yesterday. It was no use anyway. The padlock was heavy and strong, and she'd be starting with a fresh part of the chain. She could see the lightly scarred links she'd worked on yesterday.

As the long day heated up and slow-cooked her, a humming fuzziness built up in the room. It dulled the wild beating of her heart and her imaginings and fears. It stayed with her all day and remained during the evening when Oberon was there. After supper, it took her a long time to clear the dishes, wipe off the table, and heat the water so she could wash the dishes. She had moments of forgetfulness. What was she doing with the rag in her hand? Should she wipe this way or that? Why was that cup in her grasp? Her hand shook. Should she put the kettle on now, or wait for the stove to heat? She didn't speak to Oberon because it felt like she might not remember how to form words; and when he spoke to her, she had to think a while before she understood what he'd said. The hum persisted and the fuzz blurred her vision like a veil between her and everything else. This softened the room and made it tolerable. It allowed her heart a degree of rest. He acted as though everything was normal and ordinary. And indeed it was, in that fogged-in realm. She was at the table staring past him.

Plumping the pillow behind him, he lay back on the bed, rising a bit to flip the hair loose from behind his shoulders. Rows of muscle popped up across his abdomen, and then he relaxed back again. Pleasantly he asked, "Is your father a hunter? Your brothers?" He took a sip of wine and rested the jelly glass on his hairy chest.

Did she actually have a family? She couldn't imagine them nor recall what they might be doing. But no. "Not hunters," she finally answered.

"They have guns in the house?"

"A pistol." It seemed so very long ago since the landlord had shot Mr. Thompson. That had been real, but not this. This was happening to someone who lacked the courage to get up and run out the door. Part of her was paralyzed.

Oberon chuckled good-naturedly. "I'm a natural hunter. Used to love tracking a grizzly to its den. Why I'd smoke 'em out... pit my gun against all that fight and fury...." He stared fondly into space. "Raises your blood. You bet. Gives a man a feeling afterwards." He smiled at her. "Better'n opium." He chuckled softly to himself like he was making a joke. "Better'n you."

Through the fuzz and the hum, she couldn't think what to laugh at.

"Good money too. Eatin' houses paid dear for bear. That's the way it was when I first come to Californy."

He told of when he was her age, when bears would be shot many times in the heart and brain, yet would still attack the shooter. He described the fur flaming a little where the bullets entered.

"Human skin smokes too. Didja know?" He made a small circle with his thumb and finger. "There's a little hole, just the size of the bullet. The skin turns black around it and a little smoke rises from it. I'll never forget the time

I ran into a tent after a buck. Turned out to be a squaw." He chucked softly. "She tore her shirt open and bared her chest. Must'a thought I wouldn't fire at a female. I was closer to her than I am to you. Put a bullet right into her heart." He made the trigger motion. "At first there was just the hole in her teat—a teat of a paler color than a body'd think on a squaw—and around the hole a rim of burned flesh with smoke trailin' out of it. Then blood jumped outta that hole like it was bein' pumped. And then it gradually stopped." He looked at Mae like she was supposed to say something.

"You thought she was a man?"

"Dressed like one. Hair all up under a hat. Shot like a man too. That female was good with a gun."

His manner was pleasant, and he sipped more wine. Drinking slowly.

Something about the easy way he told about killing the squaw stayed with Mae. Over and over in her mind, she saw the surprise on the woman's face and the smoking hole over her heart.

When he was through with her that night, she was still thinking about that squaw.

33

One evening they were in bed doing it again when the telephone bell shrilled three times, making Mae jump. She'd never heard it ring before.

Oberon jumped up. Entangled in a sheet, he lurched toward the telephone, hopping on one leg. "Jones here. Sure…. All right." He listened a minute. "I'm coming."

He hung up the telephone, turned up the gaslight and beckoned. "Get over here. I'm going out." He picked up the handcuffs and padlock, waiting.

She dragged a blanket to the end of the chain. "Where are you going?"

"No time to jaw," he said, snapping on the handcuffs and lock. He threw on his clothes and shoulder holster, inserted the gun, turned out the light, and rushed out the door.

She was losing control of a runaway horse when strong light wakened her. Oberon was back. She covered her eyes. "Is it morning?"

"No. We got some sleeping yet to do."

"Did you go after a criminal?"

He explained as he freed her, undressed himself, turned down the overhead lamp, and lay back on the bed—all the time at ease and friendly. His boss had called, ordering him to get rid of a floater that a farmer had pulled out of the river weeds this afternoon.

"What's a floater?"

"Corpse."

"You investigating why it was dead?"

"Nope. Put it back in the river."

"Why do that?"

"They come down the river from time to time and get stuck in the weeds within the city limits. We give 'em a good shove, and off they go again."

"Why do that, so late at night?"

"No need to disturb the citizens."

"Maybe it'll get stuck in the weeds again."

"We got a long pole to poke 'em away from shore, out in the current. I drove this one a ways down the levee to a place with a strong current, put it in again."

"Someone'll be missing a son or a husband and won't know what happened to him."

He turned over, facing her, like he enjoyed this. "No claim of missing persons was filed in the city or county. We don't spend time and money investigating the identity of every floater. Most of the time it's from some upstream county. Sheriffs up there throw 'em in so they don't have to foot the bill. 'Less they know who it is. If we doan know who it is, we keep 'em moving downriver. Let somebody else pay. If we're lucky, they get all the way through the Golden Gate and out to the ocean."

That sounded barbaric. She'd thought Sacramento City was better than that. One night at the Institute Peg had talked about the Delta, where several rivers came together and then separated into what people around here called sloughs. A number of little towns hugged the banks of these channels. Franklin, Isleton, and Walnut Grove were three that Mae recalled. Maybe someone there would find the corpse that Oberon just prodded downriver.

By now he was into his heavy breathing again, asleep. Rested from having slept on the floor, Mae was sharp of mind, as she often was when she awoke in the middle of the night. She let her thoughts run, and found herself thinking that if Oberon Jones came up missing and his body were to be found in the river, there would be an investigation. They knew him and would pay whatever it cost to learn the identity of the murderer.

But I could strip him naked and beat his face in with something so they wouldn't recognize him, and hope he floats all the way to the ocean. If I could make myself kill him, and then batter him. I'm not very strong, but I'll bet I could put all my grit behind it and pull him into the police wagon a little at a time. At night that wagon would be a perfect disguise from a distance. I could wear his police hat and coat and drive down the levee road to a hidden place, pull him out of the wagon and roll him into the water—give him a poke with the rake he keeps in the stable. If I did it tonight, that long pole might still be in the wagon.

Exerting effort not to slip to the gully of the bed, which would wake him up—he probably outweighed her by over a hundred pounds—she turned over carefully.

"Fer crissake!" he yelled. "Lay still. Lemme sleep!"

When her heart stilled, she told herself again that sneaking out of bed would be the hardest part. Maybe she could do it with a knife. Figure a way to get it past him. He watched her undress every night and get into bed naked before he turned down the lamp. But maybe she could stash a knife under the mattress on her side and wait for him to go to sleep. She'd have to stab him in the perfect place in the back or he'd wrest it from her and kill her with it. Even badly injured, he'd be strong. If she aimed for his heart, the ribs might stop the knife. Or she could do it with him turned toward her, cut his throat. But didn't he usually sleep with his chin down?

There was too much chance for error. The gun was the answer. One shot in the temple. But however she did it, she'd have to dress and never return here. Maybe drive the team down the levee and leave the horses there, after Oberon was in the current. She could walk to some downstream warehouse and hide. There were supposed to be warehouses around Isleton. Oberon had mentioned docks for every kind of vegetable, all strung out along the main channel of the river, to be barged to Oakland and the City, which is what everyone called San Francisco.

Or maybe she should drive hell-bent-for-leather in the Black Mariah into the hills east of town. No, she decided it would be safest to drive the wagon back here, then light out on foot for the 28th Street station and take the Slough House stage in the morning. Oberon wouldn't be missed until they noticed his absence from work. He'd simply be gone and they'd have to find the body before they'd know he was murdered. He might never be found. And even if they did find the body, anybody might have killed him, such as one of the criminals he'd apprehended in the past. In any case, the delay would give her time to disappear.

What time was it now? Maybe three in the morning. Maybe later. Light started about a quarter to five, and she couldn't short herself on time, with all the dragging and getting the body in and out of the wagon, and battering him in the face. So it couldn't be tonight.

Shooting him presented another problem. Someone might hear the shot and come looking. She could conk him on the head with the cast-iron skillet before he could reach for his gun, and then beat on his face with the skillet until she knew he was dead, and drag him around the warehouse and roll him into the water right here, then run. That way she wouldn't worry about getting him up into the Mariah. Oh, how good it would feel to run!

Then again, maybe I don't need to kill him. I'd sure rather not. If I could hide in another warehouse on the riverfront, I could figure a way to stow away on a barge, hunker down between the goods. Surely I could hide from him in San Francisco. Or I could just crawl out this window and find a way to the underground. Oberon said the police had trouble following criminals down there. Butch might be there. He'd help me. All the entrances must be in the buildings, like at the Water Institute. But maybe all the doors are locked at night. It would be dangerous for a girl alone, hurrying from building to building, trying doors. Someone might notify the police. And even if I got into the catacombs, I wouldn't know my way around. All sorts of bad men are down there, maybe that gang of Helen's dead husband. I'll bet Oberon's on good terms with the criminals. They would turn me over to him.

No, killing him is the answer, and poking him into the river. The shooting would be hard, using a gun I'm not familiar with. And stabbing or beating him to death would be even harder. I'm not a natural killer—a liar maybe, but not a killer.

Just thinking about pulling the trigger at his head caused a sick feeling to ooze around in her. She could so easily imagine not operating the safety catch on the gun correctly. Then he would kill her. Her mind was running in circles. All she knew for sure was that she couldn't try and fail.

She was soaked from all the tense thinking. She went through it in her mind again and again, each time with fewer sharp images and believable connections. *Can't, can't* drummed in her head. She felt herself sliding back into the fuzz. How nice he had been tonight, like they were best friends. He was her only friend now that no other man would look at her, and all women would cringe from her. And he wasn't all bad. She liked seeing him when he came in at the end of the day. Her world revolved around him.

His back quietly expanded and contracted, and the monotonous dirge of the river mumbled and sang her back to sleep.

❅❆

Condor continues to dream in the cottonwood.

"That confinement changed me," Mae murmurs. "I used to think it broke my spirit."

"I don't know what that means, to break a spirit," I say. "I am a spirit confined in an oak tree, and I do not feel broken."

"Maybe that's because your spirit was always free when you were a human," Mae says. "Once I saw a performance of Lipizzaner stallions in the Sacramento Hippodrome. I learned that their training starts with severe confinement, snubbed day and night with their noses at a downward angle in the corner of a room so they can't move. They see nothing except a glimpse of the man who puts hay under their mouths. This confinement continues all their lives. A Lipizzaner loves the one man who releases him twice a day and leads him down the hallway to a showroom and trains him. The man punishes him when he fails and strokes him when he learns strange gaits and hops with his hind legs tucked into his body like a cottontail rabbit. He is not being a horse. His horse spirit is broken."

"Humans are clever," says Coyote. "If I had their grasping hands, I could do things like that."

"You would, too, wouldn't you," Mae says to him. "A pretty picture that would be, you riding a horse!"

"I've heard punishment makes you stronger," Coyote yips back.

"Fire-hardened," I clarify, recalling some of my people saying that about those who survived severe punishment.

"I don't know about punishment making you stronger," Mae says. "I was weaker after that. I lost my force of will."

I am remembering Pedro Valdez, my granddaughter's husband, and his horse Chocolate. "The Californios rode spirited stallions," I tell her. "They were proud men, and they wanted their horses to have wild male spirits, like theirs."

Mae chuckles. "Lipizzaners were bred and trained for European royalty, men who wore satin, lace and high heels. Hardly wild male spirits. They wanted a horse to dance the minuet and take a bow. Those horses arch their necks, but not from training. Their heads are tucked in close to their chests because the neck muscles have withered."

He-lé-jah saunters from the willows, greeting us with a mwrl. Coyote and Mae acknowledge him with a nod.

"Where are you coming from?" I ask in the way of my people.

"Hunting fat little dogs," he says, licking his bloody lips.

He leaps up to my branch, stretches out, and says, "My people have often been confined by Man. The best thing to do when that happens is sleep."

"That's what I did most of the time," Mae says.

"That's what I do most of the time," Rock Man calls out in his whispery voice.

34

Now," Oberon said, smoothing the disturbed locks of hair back from his face after cuffing Mae to the chain, "think on what I said. I don't like doing this, but it's for your own good. You're a stupid girl. When you get it into that thick head of yours to behave, I'll set you free. But not now, not by a long shot."

"I wouldn't go anywhere."

"No, and I wouldn't breathe air. Girls your age are all alike. You'd go out there an' coyote up real purty to the first man you see. Leave tracks all over the place. Finding you'd be like hunting a fat squaw in a snowdrift."

The moment the door clicked shut, Mae wept. During the long days, salt stung her wounded heart. The only noise she could force past the gag sounded like a dying animal. Sometimes, through the haze, she thought she saw the ghost of that Indian woman standing in the room with the smoking hole in her breast. Most of the time she felt certain that God was punishing her for her wickedness.

She couldn't think straight or plan anything so she slept. Often, when awake, she thought about why and when she started being such a sinner. She went over her life like a rosary.

She'd been mean to Nora, smiling as Mom combed her hair and Nora screamed. She liked being treated like the baby of the family after Nora died. She pretended not to hear Mom call for help with supper. She lied almost every day, claiming she'd been practicing a recitation for school when she'd been in the hayloft reading dime novels. She blamed Farley for bad things she had done, and the folks believed her. *Thou shalt not bear false witness.* Sometimes she'd snitched coins from Mom's jar in the kitchen. *Thou shalt not steal.*

She'd never offered to help Mom with the housework or laundry. *Sloth.* She'd been proud of her appearance. She made the boys use the outhouse in stormy weather when she was doing nothing more than looking in the bathroom mirror. *Pride and vanity.*

At St. Mary's she lied to the nuns, constantly bearing false witness when she went places with boys. The nuns were too innocent to imagine such deceit.

The sins with Jules and other boys and men were the start of her greatest sin. She shouldn't have gone to that saloon in that gown. Oberon was right. She was stupid. Now, in the heat and stench of that room, she understood the nature of that sin. That first kiss from Jules had been the start of fornication, even if she and Jules hadn't actually done it, and despite being chained up during the day, that same feeling came to her when she thought about being with Oberon. She shouldn't have let Jules kiss her like that. God didn't mean for people to do that before they were married. That's why she got that rash on her chest. It was a warning. That's what the Sisters tried to tell her. Her parents had forced her to go to St. Mary's Academy because of that sin.

And oh, how she dishonored her father and mother! She'd been haughty and disobedient. Refusing to give the watch back. The things she said to them on the way to St. Mary's, and the things she practiced saying to them made her skin crawl now. *Honor thy father and thy mother.*

All of that past had been a prelude. Now she was dancing a slow adagio with the Devil himself. What a worthless human being she had turned out to be! In the evenings she waded through the hazy unreality of her new life, cooking and cleaning for Oberon, and being with him like a married woman. Never speaking her mind. Just trying to make him happy.

Then one night he didn't return.

✽✽

Rock Man asks, "Howchia, did your men waste good women like that?"

"No," I say to the spirits around me. "Everything changed when the new people came. They had so many people that they could throw some away. They didn't know the parents and grandparents of those they wasted. Families were too small or too far away to help. It was a bad time for my little family too, with Billy away working for Mr. Swain."

✽✽

Flinging the door open, Isabella cried, "They took him to jail!"

Startled by the commotion, Maria Howchia looked up from the basket she'd been coiling and watched her sobbing daughter lurch across the room to the bed of her childhood. In the cold light from the window, the sight of her daughter by Pedro Valdez hurt Maria's stomach. One eye was purple and swollen shut. Her torn dress was streaked with something darker than the faded black fabric, probably blood. Her lumpy red face quivered as she wept. This wasn't the first time she'd come home beaten. Like a tree slowly releasing its hold on saturated ground, she tilted until she lay on her side, limp with weeping, an arm trailing from the bed to the floor.

Baby, Isabella's six-year-old daughter, who had been asleep against the wall, jerked awake, got to her knees and stared down at her mother. Her black eyes were surrounded by shadows that overflowed from the sunken sockets of her eyes to the other recesses of her sharp little face.

She punched her mother's head. It made a thump, and Isabella kept right on weeping just the same way.

"Is Cowboy in jail?" Maria asked, for her daughter had other men too.

A huge sob made Isabella hiccup. "Yes, Cowboy."

Baby scrambled over her mother, jumped off the bed, and screamed in her piercing way as she ran circles around the table. The fierce spirit was back in her. She kicked over the chairs and punched Maria on the arm. She swiped the basket makings off the table and kicked them asunder. Round and round the table she ran, screeching like a wild cat. On her next pass, she seized the tin cups Maria had been using to soften the sedge and hurled them both against the wall, all the while screaming.

Maria slid out of her chair, following close behind Baby in her circuit, but then turned with her arms wide and caught the child before she could change directions. She hugged the bony little girl, backside to her big belly to avoid her teeth, and lifted her off the floor pinning her arms down. Baby howled and writhed and kicked with sharp little heels that pummeled Maria's bruised legs through the long skirt, bruises from prior fits. Maria closed her eyes and called upon Oam-shu, her spirit-helper, to give her calm. This was like hugging Bohemkulla, the wild night spirit whose screams scrambled people's minds and made them crazy. Too often Maria needed to do this.

Baby dozed much of the time, a disturbed sleep full of twitching and moaning. Maria had never known a child like her, not when The People lived in the old village, and not during the long years since. However, at big times some said they had heard of this ailment, and no living doctor could cure it. So Maria couldn't do anything about it except hold Baby tightly against her until the frightening spirit receded from the child and went back where it lived.

She had no idea who would poison a child that young—Baby had displayed signs of this before she could sit up. Maybe it was meant to hurt Maria or Isabella, for this illness harmed anyone who cared for the child. She wished she could cover her ears. More than that, she wished her old teacher, Bear Claw, still lived. That man of knowledge might have been able to suck the poison from Baby. Maria would gladly pay everything she had to cure her grandchild, a child she took with her to work every day and dared not leave alone, a child who had caused more than one white woman to tell her not to come to work any longer.

The window framed a white sky against which the naked limbs of the oak were black and stark. This was the time of fogs and night frost. With Baby's high-pitched screams resounding in the little room and Isabella broken, Maria quietly wept tears of her own.

At long last the screams weakened to whimpers. Softly Maria asked Isabella, "Why did they take him to jail?"

Isabella wailed, "He killed Andy! Cut him!"

The child let loose an earsplitting yell and started kicking again.

Sorry to have spoken too soon, Maria took Baby to her own bed and crooned a low song that used to soothe Isabella when she was a young child afraid that her father's ghost was after her.

Baby finally went limp and began twitching and mumbling spirit words. Her mother slept with wine-colored spit trickling from the corner of her mouth. Grateful for the rest, Maria closed her eyes.

☙

It was almost dark outside when a knock on the door roused Maria and nearly woke Baby. Carefully placing the sleeping child on the other side of her, Maria got up from the cot and went to the door. Two white men stood there with a lantern. Her eyes had not adjusted to the light, and she didn't immediately recognize the sheriff's deputy whose laundry she washed every week.

"Is your daughter here?" he asked, raising the lantern to a height where it dimly illuminated Isabella on the cot.

"Yes," Maria responded with trepidation. A lawman at the door always boded ill for the People.

"We gotta ask her some questions."

Maria invited them in. She righted the chairs for them to sit. The deputy set his lantern on the table. The fire in the stove had gone out, so she took a handful of twigs from her neat pile and quickly stoked the coals.

She then shook Isabella's shoulder. "Daughter," she said, shaking her again. But she didn't move.

"I'll get her up," one of the men said. Pushing Maria aside, the deputy squatted down before Isabella. "Whew!" He jerked his head to one side and growled with disgust, "Breath's nigh strong enough to crack a mirror. Write that down, Ed."

The man at the table opened a book, dipped his pen, and scribbled in it.

The deputy grabbed Isabella's shoulder and gave it a hard shake. "C'mon," he all but shouted, "We ain't got all night."

Maria grieved that liquor, which was so plentiful, had the power to make people keep drinking it even when it weakened them and made them sick, even when they saw others die from it. Since before Isabella met Cowboy, she'd been drunk much of the time. She was drunk when Baby was born. And her lack of strength for the unborn child had made Baby weak at birth. She still hadn't spoken a word, and Maria thought it best not to name her until she was stronger. It would be bad to waste a name on a child who was so frail she might not live.

The deputy finally shoved and braced Isabella into a more or less upright posture in a chair at the table. "There. Mary, get some coffee into her," he said.

Silently praying all would be well, Maria fed wood into the fire bed of the nice new stove that Billy had given her.

"Tell us what happened over at Andy's place," the deputy demanded of Isabella.

Maria listened as she fed the fire, dipped water from the bucket, set the pan on the stove, and shook in grounds from the coffee can. The deputy had Maria's chair, so she sat on her cot, glad that Baby still slept. Every time Isabella uttered something, the white man named Ed scribbled on the leaves of a ledger book.

The wine had crippled Isabella's tongue. Normally she spoke better English than Maria.

"He come up. No see 'im."

The deputy probed, "You mean Cowboy come up on you and Andy?"

"Mmhmm."

"Where was you?"

"Andy's place."

"Where in Andy's place?

"Kitchen. Chair. By'm table."

"What was you doin'?"

She didn't answer.

"Was it jes' you an' Andy? Or was somebody else there?"

"No."

"Jest you an' Andy?"

"Uh-huh."

"Eatin', drinkin? Doin' what?

"Pokey."

Isabella flopped forward crying and moaning with her head in her arms.

"Look," said the deputy in a stern tone, "people been after us for not apprehendin' Injuns when they kill their own. You gotta tell me ever'thin' thet happened, or else you'll be sorry."

The coffee started to boil and Maria got up to move the pan a little to the side.

"Doan leave 'im in jail," Isabella wailed.

"It ain't up to me, but I'd say Cowboy's headed to the hangman in San Quentin. Now you talk to me or you'll go there too. We know you're his woman, so doan'chu hide nuthin' from us. Now what was you doin' when Cowboy come in?"

"Pokey."

This slow questioning continued while Maria poured the coffee for Isabella. She pieced together what had happened from what she already knew, the few things Isabella said, and from what the deputy said that Cowboy and the driver of the ore wagon had told him.

Isabella had been living with Cowboy, but she often went to Andy's place while Cowboy was shoveling ore for the New Chicago Mine—work he did when he needed money for liquor. Cowboy must have been suspicious, because last evening he asked the driver of the wagon to let him out at Andy's house. They were almost in Latrobe, where they would unload the ore into a railcar at dawn. It was just after dark when Cowboy crept up to Andy's house. The driver, wondering why Cowboy didn't go inside instead of standing in the bushes staring into the lamplit window, finally drove on. At dawn Cowboy didn't show up at the railroad station to help him shovel the coal into the railcar, so the driver went back to Andy's place and saw the bloody kitchen and Andy's body.

Maria *saw* what happened: Isabella astride Andy on a kitchen chair. Cowboy bursting in, shoving Isabella to the floor and slitting Andy's throat. She tried to stop him, and he beat her with his fists and dragged her to his place. They both got drunk. They drank all night and half the day.

According to what the deputy said, the driver of the ore wagon reported what he'd seen to his boss in the mine, and soon word of it got to the Amador County Sheriff. They questioned Cowboy, hauled him out of his shack, locked him in the police wagon, and took him to jail. Isabella had seen that from where she was hiding.

Now Isabella slumped over her coffee, sipping it. Baby, awake, lay quiet in Maria's arm as she sat on her bed. The deputy stood up with a click of his tongue and a wag of his head. As he closed the book, he turned to Ed and said in a low voice, "Ain't that just like Injuns."

They exchanged a knowing smile.

Standing, Maria spoke for the first time. "Doan take my girl." She couldn't make herself look the deputy in the eye, even though white people considered that proper.

"Well, guess I don't see no reason to haul her in. We got the testimony. It squares."

He scowled into Maria's eyes. "But you better git'er off that damned hair oil or whatever the hell it is."

Ed was snickering in his teeth.

Now that Cowboy was gone, Maria hoped Isabella would stop drinking wine and alcohol. Then she would be stronger and safer. In both worlds, coupling with the wrong person had always been dangerous.

35

Oberon burst through the door, smelling of life and fresh air. It was late morning. Mae grabbed him, when he freed her, weeping on his shoulder and trembling with a terrible need for human touch. He'd been gone for twenty-eight hours.

Her voice came in a spasm, her mouth paralyzed from the release of the gag. "You didn't come—"

"I'm here now," he said petting her hair. "There, there." Wrinkling his nose at the full bucket, he said with a touch of humor, "That piss'n crap's gitten' old enough to sell to the China gardens."

She couldn't speak for the dryness in her throat and the pain in her face. He dipped a full glass of water and handed it to her. She drank a second and third glass, sitting at the table while he cooked a noon dinner of black-eyed peas and ham. He'd also brought half a chocolate layer cake from the bakery.

He never explained where he'd been all night, but she was hungry and glad to eat in silence. She feared broaching any subject likely to lead her to a complaint or accusation. That would be as dangerous as asking him when he'd release her, or if he ever would.

Head tilted, hair softly bent on a shoulder, he put down his fork and asked, "Wanna come on my rounds today? Goin' to the SP shops."

Most of her rejoiced at the thought of leaving this place of fear and weeping, but the other part didn't want her hopes to be dashed. He had a way of breaking promises. "Yes, I'd like that," she said in a low monotone.

She spritzed off at the sink, brushed her hair, and donned her purple-striped frock, which he'd brought back clean and pressed from the Chinese laundry. As they were stepping out the door, he barred the way, brown eyes looking down at her, and asked in a soft voice, "You'll be good?"

She bobbed her head down and up. "I won't say anything to anybody, if that's what you mean."

He gave her neck a little squeeze from behind. "Wouldn't wanna hurt that pretty throat of yours."

Mae went out to the police wagon with him, and before her brains could catch up, they actually were driving up Front Street, the road along the river levee. Big red letters along the building on their left spelled out: Southern Pacific Company Freight Depot. A six-horse team stood dozing in their harnesses while men relayed bundles and bags of goods from the freight wagon to the depot landing. That big building blocked sight of the vessels in the river. Only the smokestacks showed, one of them belching smoke as it traced a slow circle. Strangely, she saw this without interest. Out in the air at last, yet the fog and fuzz of the last week followed her.

The horses pulled them along a set of tracks and they were passing two tall painted-brick buildings. The door of the first was marked City of Sacramento Water Works, and the second, Sacramento Justice Court. Another police wagon was parked beside it.

It hit her. This was the police station! She hadn't realized it was so near to the room of her imprisonment. She knew the jail was in this building, too, though no bars could be seen on the arched windows above. Probably on the other side, she thought, and when the criminals looked out the bars they'd see the river—nicer than where she spent her days.

The tracks they'd been following curved away in three directions, and before them stood the station, so enormous it made toys of the other buildings. But it seemed unreal, like a photograph from a book. Oberon was waiting for a streetcar to pass by, so she sat looking at the yawning maw where four trains could enter or leave the station at the same time.

Only three months ago she'd nearly burst with excitement stepping off the train inside that place with the high vaulted ceiling. She'd been thrilled to board the streetcar with Mom and Emmett and Farley, like the one dinging toward them. Now devoid of emotion, she noted that the turrets guarding the portals over the tracks were gray and sooty.

What was that word? The one Sister Delphine had insisted the class learn, describing the architecture of old cathedrals and castles? Only last April Mae had been able to write the answer on her test paper without a moment's hesitation. What had happened to her quickness of mind? Those sharply pointed towers with spires on top seemed to mock her stupidity, but at long last her groggy mind gave forth the word *gothic*.

What were such towers doing in the golden land of California? High above a center parapet waved not a king's banner, but Old Glory. All along the lengthy side of the station the noon sun blazed off giant, pleated steel fans, but that brought nothing but a dislike of being blinded by them and the tired thought that an excessive amount of machine work must have been required to make all those huge fans that were only for decoration. The glare obscured the passenger entrance. Parked in front was a worn stagecoach with a man standing beside it, and beside an elegant carriage, another man in a top hat. They and the women bustling through the door looked unreal. These people occupied another realm. She gave her head a little shake to clear her brain, but the fuzz wouldn't go.

Oberon reined up I Street alongside the station, pulling over to make room for another streetcar jingling toward them. He waited as it stopped and people stepped off, and then drove beyond the station. On their left, surrounded by tall buildings, a body of ugly water stagnated. About two city blocks in size, its turquoise color and floating foam islands made her want to vomit. "China Lake," Oberon reported.

It looked more like a sewage sump. They circled behind a brace of large, iron-roofed warehouses where the noise and clang of machinery came from open windows. Too warm in the noon sun, Mae watched four columns of black smoke rise slowly from the smokestacks of a building ahead, smoke that looked thick enough to spread on the ground and sleep on.

"The SP Foundry," Oberon announced, halting the horses. The sun sparked off broken glass in the parking ground. A row of tent-shops advertised beer, sandwiches, cakes, cookies, and something called pasties. She took this in without actually focusing on any of it, and hardly noticed the idle vendors staring at her.

"Come on," Oberon said.

Automatically she slid across the seat, took his hand, and stepped down the iron stirrup to the packed earth. She would have preferred to take a nap on the seat in the shade of the Black Mariah's roof.

He nudged her through a soot-blackened door.

In the heat and dim light, the smell of paint and axle grease woke her up some, as did the ringing of steel hammers on steel—a headache of atonal percussion. As her eyes adjusted, she realized that what she'd mistaken for a wall was actually a monster locomotive engine taller than most buildings. Men in overalls were riveting shiny steel plates to it, while other men with buckets and wide brushes stroked black paint on the new plates to match the rest of the engine. It was being built on a set of tracks that ran through the building and out an opening about a hundred yards away.

A large hairy thing moved near her shoes. Startled, it took her too long to realize that the black mop-like thing was a man's head. He was working on the underside of the engine, standing upright in a concrete pit beneath the tracks. She might have fallen in.

Taking her by the arm, Oberon steered her past the pit and the front wheel of the engine, which looked twice her height. An earsplitting clamor of steel scraping steel made her look up. There, attached to an overhead chain that stretched the length of the building, more steel plates came dangling and jerking through the hot air, to be received by men standing atop the engine. Wide belts turned up there, moving the equipment, and a slender boy with what appeared to be a bucket of tar was carefully picking his way along the girders. One false move and he'd be dead or crippled. "Grease monkey!" a voice demanded, "What's taking you so long?" The boy screamed over the hammering, "I'm coming, sir."

Oberon pulled her along a wall. On the left stretched a confusion of men working at countertops and manipulating pieces of steel. Beyond them, on the lakeside wall of the building, hot fires in huge upright burners radiated heat that she felt thirty yards away. Silhouettes of men moved before those fires. *Surely hell is like this.*

Suddenly a heart-stopping screech! She cried out in terror but heard no part of her voice in the hellish din. No one else seemed to be afraid.

Oberon continued pulling her along the wall, and men everywhere casually put down what they were doing, many removing apples and sandwiches from the pockets of their overalls. Others surged toward the door, not in a panic but with something like pleasure on their faces. The terrible whistle finally stopped, and the overhead chain jerked to a noisy halt. She saw the boy "grease monkey" picking his way back along the ceiling braces.

In the sudden silence Oberon's rap on a steel door echoed. The men passing beside Mae got an eyeful, but she felt as inert as the locomotive.

Oberon opened the door to a cooler place. The office door shut automatically behind them, clipping off the echoing murmur of conversation. Before a window, a man in suspenders and arm garters stood up from his desk and came around to shake hands with Oberon. Out the open window, workmen waited in lines before the tent-shops.

"Thanks for coming by," the man said. "I appreciate it." He looked at her.

"This young lady's from out of town." Oberon explained. "I'm showing her around. "This here's Mr. Tesla, foreman of the SP Foundry," he told Mae.

She nodded a perfunctory greeting, but Mr. Tesla seemed ill at ease, glancing back to Oberon. "I'd like to speak to you alone if you don't mind."

"I don't wanna leave her outside," Oberon said.

"Oh sure, noonday sun and all. Just outside this door would be fine." He pointed his head at the office door. Watching Oberon's face, he added, "Those are good working men, family men. Well, most of 'em. She'll be fine out there."

In the manner of a close chum sharing an intimacy Oberon said, "I'm not at liberty to say why, but she's gotta stay here and it can't be helped. But, Jim, ain't no reason we can't talk. She ain't gonna say nuthin'."

Mr. Tesla frowned at her, but she knew better than offer to leave. Oberon was in charge. She wanted him to trust her so she could come with him on more outings. Anything was better than being chained up like a dog.

"Oh, all right, but she'd better not let on to any of the men—"

"Jim, she don't *know* nobody here. Got no cause to know 'em either. Ain't that right, Mae?"

"That's right," she affirmed, moving to the window to give them space. She watched the men outside lifting beer mugs after they found places to sprawl in the shade of the vendor tents, dinner pails in hand.

Mr. Tesla muttered something she couldn't hear. They must have turned their backs and lowered their voices. All she heard was "trouble brewing." Mr. Tesla made a long speech, bits and pieces of which would have been audible to her if she'd the slightest interest.

"Well, I'll keep my ears and eyes open," Oberon said in a closing tone.

She turned toward them, Mr. Tesla thanking Oberon. They shook hands.

Oberon opened the door and nudged her into the hot workplace, causing her to stumble on the threshold. She couldn't seem to see little things like that.

Outside the building, she inhaled deeply to draw in the somewhat fresher air though it was overheated by the steel disk of the sun, which pulsed like a live thing in the white sky. Stepping in the stirrup of the wagon, she suddenly saw the boy—what was his name? The eleven-year-old woodcutter who had supported his family? Shirtless, he stood with a group of soot-faced boys behind a tent. She recognized him by his skinny rack of ribs. He waved to her, and she waved back.

Oberon grabbed the neck of her frock and the back of a thigh and threw her up on the seat like a bag of freight. Snarling through his teeth, "Make a liar out of me, wouldja! Right in front of that window!"

Her heart stumbled as she righted herself. Stark fear, her old companion, had returned. "I'm sorry," she said. "I forgot."

"Forgot! Why you're s'dumb you don't know sic 'em." He clucked the horses away from the foundry. "I'd oughta git rid a' you. Who is that?" He jerked his head toward the boys.

"A boy, used to live where my parents live now."

"You said your parents live in Cosumne. Yer lyin'."

"No!" Her skin was raw with fear. "His mother brought him and his brothers and sisters to Sacramento. To find work with the SP. Looks like he did. I don't know them at all. Really I don't."

"The father work here?"

"No, he's dead."

"Where do they live now?"

"I don't know."

About to mention that Farley had driven the Smith family to Sacramento, she didn't. It was too complicated. *Shadrack*, she suddenly remembered.

Slowly the wagon rolled through the vast Southern Pacific grounds, passing the butt ends of long iron-roofed buildings adjoined on the long sides, and bumping over tracks and chunks of wood and broken bottles. In the distance she could see the station with the four gothic turrets.

They passed more large buildings with metal spines along their roofs and groups of workmen eating as they leaned against the shady walls. There was a brick building four or five stories high, stout and perfectly square, with no windows. Men with sweat-shiny faces and tousled hair, some going in, some coming out, looked at her and Oberon, one man hooking the suspenders of his overalls.

"That there's the shit house," Oberon said. "Four stalls on each side of every floor. Fifty-four men can shit in there at the same time." The tone of that sounded less angry. He even chuckled a little.

She dared ask, "How do they get rid of all the—"

"Turds and piss? A hole to China, I guess." He laughed outright and her heart slowed down. His mind was somewhere else. Every moment since they'd left the foundry, he'd been looking around the grounds of the sprawling industrial place as though searching for something lost.

They passed many sidetracked cars. Oberon said that outlaws were blowing up baggage cars and damaging trains all over the SP railroad system. The cars were brought here for repair. New cars were also made here. Even the velvet chairs, gilded furniture, and fine sconces for the famous private cars were manufactured here, and the fittings for hospital cars. They were approaching the roundhouse, a circular building with tracks running out every direction.

Oberon suddenly halted the horses. She followed the flat lines of his snake eyes to a large group of men engaged in spirited discussion—hidden until the wagon advanced. One speaker's arms were waving. Others were shouting to be heard.

One of the men raised a hand to Oberon in a signal of friendship. Conversation halted as all turned and looked at the police wagon.

Oberon drove on with a wave.

By the time they drove full circle to the front of the passenger station and bumped over all the tracks, a long train had finished departing. Beyond the black spider-work of the bridge over the river, she could see the smoke in the distance and the backside of the caboose. *How I'd love to be on that train!*

He went back up I Street and over to H, where nice white houses with spindle-porches lined both sides of the street. At 7th and H, she jumped in her skin to see the Johnson house, where she'd given piano lessons. Oberon was turning right on 7th. She pressed her back into the warm wood of the

Mariah's seat and looked away so no one in the house would see her.

Two blocks farther on, he dodged men dressed like bankers crossing the macadamized intersection of 7th and K, then nodded toward a big pink-stone building. "This here's the new Post Office. Just built." He pulled across the street into a vacant space and tied the team.

This busy part of the city was a canyon of buildings, but to her it seemed another photograph. Oberon told her to come with him.

She stepped down like a mechanical thing. They crossed the street and went up the stairs of the post office, amidst a lot of people going in and out. In the back of the high-ceiling main room, where heels echoed and clerks behind a long counter waited on people, he took her through a door and up a circular staircase. Up and up they climbed until they arrived at a quiet hallway. A few steps away he stopped before a door with gold-leaf lettering that read Mr. James O. Coleman, Postmaster, City of Sacramento.

Oberon looked down at Mae and placed both hands around her neck. Though he exerted no pressure, her head went light and her legs felt about to buckle. "You gonna be better'n you was at the foundry?"

"Yes."

He leveled a stare, then opened the door and patted her bottom to go in.

A young man with round spectacles looked up from a desk. "Oh, good day to you, Officer." He stood up. "We got those posters in this morning."

The man walked across the room to a table, retrieved a packet wrapped in brown paper, and brought it to Oberon. "Would you like to see Mr. Coleman?" He gestured toward a door.

"No need to. Not today."

They left, went down the stairs and out the door into the fierce sun.

Untying the horses and joining her on the seat, Oberon opened the package. He rifled through a stack of wall posters, each with a photograph of a surly man. "Wanted" glared across the top of each poster.

"Ahah! Your friend LeRoy Parker." He showed it to her.

Butch. He had already told her Butch was a wanted man.

"Fresh from the printer," he said with satisfaction, returning the posters to the package.

She squinted into the sun while Oberon circled the team in the street and headed down K. Before long they parked in the side yard of the Justice Court, and Oberon steered her up the stairs to the desk. The beetle-browed officer was walking toward them, giving Oberon a look when he accepted the posters. She felt an undercurrent of humor. Did he know she slept with Oberon? Did they all? She tried to think through why that would be funny, and when she got to the fact that only a very loose woman would do that, the fuzziness came down and covered it up so she couldn't think at all.

It thickened as he drove her down Front Street back to the hellhole.

Inside the close gray walls with the bad smells, he waited for her to get out of her good dress so he could chain her up again.

"I'll leave the gag off this afternoon, if you promise to keep quiet," he said.

"Oh yes. I won't make a squeak. I promise."

"All right. Then if you're very good for a couple days, I might leave you off the chain. Then we'll go on s'more outings." Snapping on the cufflinks, he gave her look, eyes half closed, one she couldn't fathom.

Only one thing roared in her mind, and her voice sounded whiney as a three-year-old's. "You'll be back today, won't you? And not leave me alone all night?"

He said he would be back.

36

Oberon proved the truth of his words. By the next Tuesday he left Mae unchained in the room, and on Thursday uncuffed as well.

That first morning with free hands, she bundled up the bedclothes for him to take to the Chinese laundry. After he locked her in and left for the station, she tidied up the room, sloshed the mud out of the settling barrel, poured it out the window, which he now left open, and pumped a full barrel of new water to settle. She washed the greasy, dust-laden windows—the little one above the sink and the bigger one that looked over a narrow area with the horse stable. Front Street was out of sight beyond the stable. She swept the floor dirt down the cracks in the concrete, and tied the window-washing rags on the broom and mopped, pushing the muddy water down the cracks.

"Well, I see you been hard on the soap supply." Oberon said when he returned at the end of the day. He handed her the stack of bedclothes from the laundry, and she could tell he was pleased.

"Buy me the goods and I'll make some new curtains," she said.

"You a seamstress too?"

"Not a good one, but it'll give me something to do with my hands."

On her first Sunday of freedom, they walked along the river levee, Oberon nodding pleasantly to men working on the wharfs. He talked about police matters and crimes while they watched a paddle-wheeler churn downstream. Passengers crowded around the railings, some shouting and waving. She waved back.

She walked into stores like a wife. He bought curtain yardage, which she later cut to lengths and began to hem for new curtains. She never gave him cause to be angry, and a part of her believed she loved him despite his unusual behavior. His arrival was the high point of every dull day.

One day he lost his temper because she put the can of cooking grease in a new place and he couldn't immediately find it, but he restrained himself and later confided, "I wasn't always so quick on the draw, if you catch my meaning. It started when I was in the Army fightin' Injuns, back in seventy-nine." He wagged his head at the sliced potatoes he was frying. "Got in some bad scrapes. Thought I was goner. Saw things I'd rather forget. That changes a man."

She was beginning to like their lovemaking. He told her it was changing her, making her into a real woman. She felt part wicked, part in love, part wife, part proud when she cleaned up the place, part horrified at what little choice she had about anything and how sad her life had turned out to be. Mostly she felt unreal. Sometimes she prayed to Mary and the various saints, or to Jesus in more formal words, telling him she appreciated that he loved everybody, even prostitutes if they changed their ways. She promised to mend her ways when she could. If only the saints or Jesus or Mary would speak to God about her case! She would do her best to convert Oberon and they could get married and live like regular people. But other times she wanted God to help her leave him and even promised to go to a nunnery if He did. But then the rattle of the harness would make something inside her warm up for Oberon. *Which is it? Am I a whore, a prisoner, a wife, the Devil's handmaid, or a Christian trying her best—like Sister Delphine wanted me to be?*

Before supper one day she told Oberon it would calm her nerves if she could write poetry during her long hours alone.

"You write poetry?"

"You can read some if you like."

"Lemme see," he said, leaving the beans to boil.

She pulled out her cigar box and handed him a stack of folded poems. He sat at the table and read aloud from one:

> *The dance is awhirl like the stars in the skies—*
> *We girls in our gowns and young men in bow ties.*
> *The one two three, one two three measures my heart.*
> *As I whirl to the beat, I just know I could start*
> *And fly up to heaven away from these farms*
> *With love in my mind and you in my arms.*

"Well I'll be," he uttered.

"Childish. I wrote it years ago."

"What happened to the boy?"

"It wasn't anyone in particular."

"What about this?" He held up "Legion Are the Faint of Heart" and read it.

She watched his eyes dart back and forth across the page, his Wild Bill Hickok hair loosely framing his broad-boned face.

"So many people are afraid to try new things," she started to explain. "But we live only once, and—"

He burst out laughing.

When he quieted, she said, "I might go raving mad if I can't have some paper."

The next day he brought her a pink pasteboard box and set it on the table. Pulling the pretty blue ribbon, she opened the box and beheld very fine, pale blue stationery.

Like a father savoring the giving of a Christmas gift, Oberon slowly removed something from his shirt pocket and handed it to her—a new pencil, whittled to a fine point.

"Can I write with this? On this paper?"

"It's all yours. Go ahead."

She felt her face stretch into a smile. "Oh Oberon, I just can't tell you how happy this makes me! Thank you so much. I'll write small and use both sides so I won't waste any."

⤳

The arrival of paper brought new turmoil and fear. It made her think about writing letters, and that in turn made her think about the people who would read them. Of course letters about her situation would enrage Oberon, so that was out of the question. She tried poems, but nothing sweet and light came to her. The words tumbling to mind described the four walls, the pipe under the sink, the smell that came up from the hole, the cruel things he'd done to her, her foggy, contradictory way of thinking, and the river whispering at night *run away, run away.* Such poems cast Oberon as a villain, which wasn't fair since he was being nice to her. She would begin a poem, but by the third or fourth line it would turn grim and ugly, and she would burn it in the stove. She burned everything she wrote.

When Oberon asked to see what she'd written, she told him. "I don't want to spoil the paper, so I decided not to write anything until I have it perfectly in mind." On the heels of those words, fear caught her breath. He might inspect the stationery box, see it down in quantity and know she had lied.

But he did not, and the next day when he asked what she'd written she changed her story. Fearing that the waste would infuriate him, she almost choked getting it out, "I burned it. I want you to see my best, not my bad tries."

The fear remained all through the night and began to lessen when he left the next morning, not chaining her or taking the paper back. Every day after that she burned many pretty blue sheets. His apparent indifference to the disappearance of paper puzzled her, and it crossed her mind that her own money might have paid for the paper. *I wouldn't have bought paper this fine if I'd had a say in it. And if I'd been out talking to people I wouldn't have needed any. A few penny postcards would have kept the folks up on my whereabouts.*

Oberon never talked about her money or why he, a man with solid employment, still hadn't paid her back, or why he had also insisted she give him the dollar she had left.

She thought about writing to Hank and Sophie in Sutter's Creek. Maybe she could explain to them what had happened to her and get them to come and rescue her. She couldn't confess it to Daddy, a born Catholic, but Hank might see her as a person worth helping. He didn't hold grudges and had loads of friends wherever he lived. Now he had Sophie's Italian relations too. Or maybe she should write to Mr. Sheldon, who invited senators and the Governor to hunt pheasant in his Thicket. *No. No. No.* Explaining to that stalwart of Slough House would only prove to him that she was, after all, trash.

And this: if Hank and his friends came to rescue her, they would see that she was not completely locked up. They'd ask why she hadn't gone out the window and reported this to the police. *I could lock the window before they get here, but how would I know just when they would come? Or if they would come. No, that's stupid. I need the window open on these hot days, and I can't lie to the people I'm trying to tell the truth to. If they come here, they'll see I've been living in sin of my own free will. And if I tell them how afraid of him I am, they'll think I'm crazy. And even if they believe me, they'd make a ruckus at the police station, and those other lawmen would say they saw me with Oberon in broad daylight, and so would the storekeepers. All they'd have to do is ask around....*

No. If I try to explain it to anybody, no respectable man would ever marry me and I'll end up a ragged old maid or little pieces in the river.

The image of that overwhelmed her, and she lay down on the bed closing her eyes against it. The old Mae dissolved into islands of dirty froth floating through her mind like suds in mop water. And under that, the horror-stricken faces of Emmett, Hank and Sophie, and yes, Mom and Daddy, and the sneers of Farley. She tried to close off her mind's eye. She wanted her parents' forgiveness for being such a bad person.

This could never be explained.

Rousing herself from the bed at the end of the afternoon, she wrote a letter she knew she would not burn.

Mr. and Mrs. Edward Duffy
c/o Cosumne Store. Cosumne, California
My dearest parents,
   Please forgive me for not writing sooner. I just now got this nice paper. I have moved from place to place and had no address to give you. I quit my position with the Water Institute. They did so many colonics and I was the one to clean up after the loose bowels. I have taught piano in the homes of different families, nice people. You should see their houses! Almost like castles in Europe. I'll be doing more of the same and might even rent a room from one of them.
   All people need to pray for forgiveness. That's why I am writing. I

know we didn't do that at home, but you two and the boys should do it. You should open your hearts to Jesus and Mary and God. Get all the way down on your knees and pray every day—several times a day. I do it. This is the most important thing in life. Because we don't live for long. Be sure Emmett and Farley pray too.

Hope you are all fine.

By the way, I've made a friend in the Sacramento Police Station, so if you really need to get a message to me, you could write in care of—

She blackened that line out with heavy pencil, then closed: *Loving you, M.*

The folded letter slipped nicely into a little blue envelope, which she took from the beribboned bundle beneath the paper. That evening she handed it to Oberon to post. He glanced at the address, slipped it in his coat pocket, and left with it the next morning when he went to the station.

Alone again, she couldn't resist the guilty pleasure of writing a letter to Hank and Sophie, just for the fun of it, one that told the truth of her situation. She struggled over the words and sentences. Did they express the truth correctly? Just what, actually, was her situation? She rewrote and rewrote. Oberon had been so nice of late, behaving like a husband. Surely that would end and he would kill her if he saw what she was writing. Maybe she'd ought to take him up on his mention of getting married. That thought made her put the letter to the flames, and as the smoke hurried up the stovepipe the terror dissolved, and she wilted like a flower in a drought. Flopping on the bed, she napped. She slept more often now, while Oberon was away, and yet it didn't stop her from sleeping at night.

That evening he sat down to supper saying, "I didn't know you was religious. Me, I don't put any store in that crap." He buttered his bread as though nothing was wrong with reading other people's mail.

When he left for work the next morning she went back to bed and slept, wrung out by the experiment and the proof that he would open and read every letter she wrote. She sank into a murky, half-awake state, like Mom. Mom, whose only faults were marrying Daddy and spoiling her daughter—a daughter who had gone to Sacramento with the independence of a hog on ice. Dry-eyed, she stared at the water-stained beams holding the corrugated iron ceiling above. Twisted faces stared back at her, faces nested within faces, sufferers in Dante's *Inferno*.

And then out of nowhere, another image, this one in her memory. An old boot under the bed—back where the dust bunnies had been thick before her cleaning. It had no mate. She had searched. Now she got down on her knees and pulled it out—thin, cracked sole, frayed leather heel where a spur had ridden too many times. Too small for Oberon. Some other man must have left it here before he claimed the place. She doubted he knew it was there. A letter inside the toe might be safe. Then she could sneak it out to the Post

Office later. *I could bat my eyes at a clerk and maybe get him to post it for me.*

It would have worked in Iowa. She went to the table, lifted a sheet of paper from the box, and began to write to Hank and Sophie. The practiced words flowed like cream. She sealed the envelope and inserted the letter into the boot, pushing it back to the wall, dead center under the bed as measured from head to toe.

A tidal wave of fear and guilt swamped her. Not that she would post the letter. This was just another experiment, she told herself, to see whether she could leave it there and not burn it. The feeling of suffocation intensified all afternoon, closing in like the paws of a bear when Oberon walked in.

"Hey," he said, "You need a new gown. I'm gonna take you to meet a man who just might employ you. We've got a date to see him Monday. Get ready. We're going to a seamstress."

She blinked, barely comprehending.

"I said, get ready. Now."

Why a new gown? This purple one was a little soiled but looked all right, didn't it? Oberon hurried her out the door.

When they were side by side in the Black Mariah, the horses plodding up M Street, a good feeling started to rise inside her. Often she'd felt this way when going places in Iowa, but the cause this time was no silly thing. She had a prospect of employment! This she'd wanted from Oberon since the first moment she'd set foot in his place. She wanted to feel independent. While the horses lengthened the distance between her and the evidence that would put her back in chains, she breathed freely, lifting her face to the little breeze that brought clean air from the Delta, sometimes all day long.

"Looks like the seamstress lives in the same alley where Helen Rose was," she quipped lightly.

He looked at her, halting the rig at the other end of that alley.

A young woman with white skin and squiggly red lines in her cheeks opened the door the instant Oberon knocked. "Come in," she said, seeming to know him well.

In the clean, simple room, a sleeping child about two years old lay on a threadbare coverlet on the bed. Introductions made, the seamstress collared herself with a measuring tape and looked Mae over with level gray eyes.

Oberon sat uninvited at the table. He gave a flick of his wrist, a signal for them to get started. The seamstress measured Mae, writing numbers in a mercantile ledger. "What style?" she asked Oberon, not Mae.

"Make it red satin with those ruffles and frills around the bosom. Same as you did last time."

"Give me the money now and it'll be done by five o'clock tomorrow."

∽

"Red satin?" Mae asked when they drove away, Oberon two dollars lighter.

"A flashy gown for my flashy girl," he responded. "I recall that you like that color. We've got a man to visit on Monday."

Her ears pricked up like a horse straining to see ahead. "What man? I mean, what is his enterprise?"

He reached over and patted her knee. "It'll be fine."

The sky out the open window of the room appeared bluer than usual. She had slept in short stretches and lain awake most of the night—worried about the letter in the boot and very sure, in her nighttime clarity, that it was wrong to visit a prospective employer in a gown like the one Oberon brought home from the seamstress yesterday.

"Get up, sleepyhead," he said. "It's late."

She swung her feet down on the cool concrete and went to fill the wash-basin in the settling keg. As she washed herself he said something about this being the second week of September, with the California Exposition ending. There would be speeches at the Agricultural Pavilion. "I'm to keep the crowd behaving. So we're goin'. Put on your new gown."

"The red one?"

"Well now, you tell me. Is there a newer one around here?"

"I don't think ladies wear that kind in the daytime, in such a public—"

"I said, put... it... on." An icy tone.

Yesterday when he returned with the satin gown and a new corset and asked her to put them on, she'd seen right away that it revealed more of her than any of Helen Rose's gowns did. Why would a man want his special girl to wear that at the Agricultural Pavilion to hear political speeches? It didn't make any sense. But then last night, with a clear mind and the moon floating up the windowpane, she concluded that he was about to hand her over to another man, one who didn't love her at all. Such a man could be even more dangerous than he was. Maybe he expected the man to be at the Pavilion today, and that's why he insisted on her wearing the dress now.

A new thought germinated. This would be a big crowd, a possible chance to hand the letter to someone who would post it. It was not a perfect situation by a long shot, even if the person posted it, because if Oberon gave her to another man today, she would be gone and untraceable. *If and if.*

But it was her only chance. Drying herself, she made her voice sound casual, "Who will be speaking?"

"Oh, some politiker shovelin' out horseshit. Senator or some such." He pulled on his laundered trousers and police shirt.

She got an idea for carrying the letter. From the corner of her eye she watched Oberon sling the shoulder holster over his shirt, insert the Colt into it, and go to the sink barefoot. He dipped water from the settling barrel and put the coffee pan on the stove. Peering down into the firebox door, he squatted on his bare heels and struck a match.

While he inserted a series of long slivers of kindling into the stove, his back to her, she quickly and quietly retrieved the letter from the boot and shoved the envelope in the left breast of her corset, where it would be within easy reach from the low neckline. In the corner of the envelope where a stamp should be placed she had printed: *Very Urgent. Please forward.* Her heart was going like a kettledrum for fear he'd heard something. But he was scraping the stove ashes around with the poker, and didn't turn around.

With a deep breath, she backed up to him as he clanged the stove door shut. "Would'ja mind tying my strings?"

He tightened the corset hard around her. At first she feared he'd seen what she'd done and was killing her this way, but then he tied off the strings and turned her around, eyes and mouth calm. He did not suspect.

She already had an hourglass figure, but now she could touch her fingertips together around her waist. Her breasts mounded up in front, covering the envelope. The frilly new gown fit snugly over her improved shape, the small envelope stiff between her breast and the stays.

Later, when they were stepping into the sun, he said, "You're a tasty twist of cinnamon taffy."

In the rapidly heating air of the late morning, she tried to ignore the stench of the meat packing plant.

Queasy with fear and doubt, and short of breath from the tight corset, she rode beside him. What stranger would post the letter? And if a stranger did, and Hank charged Oberon with a crime, she would need to say things about him in front of his friends in the police station. A judge would hear of her walking around with him and would conclude that she was a prostitute, and if her case was dismissed she'd be dead in no time flat. *But he's up to something and not telling me what it is, so I've got to stick to my plan.*

All along M Street families and twosomes and family groups walked toward Capitol Park. On 10th Street, people poured off a streetcar and walked on the pathway across the gardens and lawns of the Capitol to the Agricultural Pavilion. Oberon drove to a livery stable on 11th and L. A blond and shirtless young man came out to help, muscles slick and gleaming, eyes on Mae.

Maybe I can give it to him.

Oberon handed him a coin and told him to care for the horses and wagon.

"Yes, sir!" he all but saluted, and turned to his work.

Not him.

Oberon turned a hard monotone on Mae, "If you say somethin' to anybody, or try to get away…" He made a circle with his hands and squeezed them into fists. Then he smiled. "Be good and we'll go to an afternoon dance when this is over."

A dance! He would he take her out with him like a real sweetheart. That's why he wanted her to dress like this. *Oh why did I put that letter in my corset! If it's still there when we get back to the room he'll see and I'll be back in chains—if I'm lucky.*

That thought strengthened her resolve to do it today, at the Pavilion.

A gambler's line floated at her all the way from an old dime novel. *The die is cast.*

37

Mae walked with Oberon, his hand unnecessarily grasping her upper arm, as they passed by a long string of vendor tents on 15th Street in front of the massive Agricultural Pavilion—high as the train station and vaguely Egyptian. In the road, a four-horse team of Percherons pulled a heavy roller behind a flatbed wagon, while a crew of men slowly poured a giant bucket of tar to be flattened by the roller. The sulfurous fumes reminded her that she could soon be in a worse hell than she'd seen so far.

A rounded beehive in the masonry above the building's entrance seemed out of place in this nightmare, until she recalled a Sister teaching recent history—the excavation of ancient Troy, man-high beehive structures, a wealthy antiquarian named Schliemann financing the expedition, a man made rich in Gold-Rush Sacramento. That bit of knowledge had helped fuel her excitement about this city.

Inside the cavernous hall a cacophony of disembodied voices rang in her ears and the high glazed ceilings cast eerie veils of light. Women glared their disapproval and men stared as Oberon hurried her past tables of fruits and vegetables—blue, red, or white ribbons lying across the winning peaches, apples, plums, jellies, and pies.

They ascended an open staircase with an ornate iron railing. Ashamed in her low-cut frock, she at first kept her gaze down but then forced herself to examine the strangers for someone who might be willing to help. On the upper level the railing continued around a wide balcony, keeping people from pitching to their deaths on the floor below. All manner of needlework hung along the wall.

Her solitary uncovered head among the diverse array of hats made her look the more like a prostitute, and Oberon's uniform added the impression that she was under arrest. A dowager in a day gown raised stemmed eyeglasses to be sure she was seeing correctly, but most ladies turned away, cooling their disgust with their fans. The place was crowded.

Men of all ages devoured her with their eyes, including another policeman standing between crocheted coverlets. He and Oberon exchanged a nod before Oberon prodded her to squeeze past the lawman with the bare mounds of her breasts scraping his coat buttons. Oberon didn't seem to mind. Somehow she knew he never intended to take her to a dance today.

People moved around finding spaces to stand in, looking toward a table with a white tablecloth, a pitcher of water, and a large glass. A royal-blue rope on stanchions kept the crowd from the sides of the table. Oberon pulled her to a stop with a hurtful squeeze. His dark eyes drilled her with the unspoken: don't budge an inch and don't say a word. He released her.

Lightheaded from the tight corset and the heat under the glass skylights, she nonetheless saw everything around her with stark clarity. The people standing near her pretended she wasn't there. The end of the speaker's table was about five yards away, with several men between. At the other end of it a policeman was relocating a pair of tall-hatted ladies, gesturing that people behind wouldn't be able to see. A man in a dark suit stepped to the narrow table, which fronted near the railing and gave those on the lower floor a ready view.

"People of Sacramento," he started, waiting until the noise upstairs faded to a rumble. In stentorian tones he listed the accomplishments of Grove Johnson, Congressional Representative from the Second District.

Mae suddenly recognized Mrs. Johnson and her daughters, Mary and Mabel, to whom she'd given piano lessons, standing inside the blue rope. Mrs. Johnson's husband was a Congressman. He and his wife were just the people to take the letter! Mrs. Johnson would know, surely she would, that Mae wouldn't dress like this of her own will. She might even read the letter herself, knowing Mae wouldn't write Very Urgent where a stamp ought to be unless she was in danger. This formidable lady could stand her ground with Oberon. It appeared that heaven had responded.

"And hence," the man intoned, "we are sorry to report that Representative Johnson could not be here today. But we are fortunate indeed to give you, in his stead, his right-hand man… his campaign manager… his estimable law partner… his brilliant son, and a credit to the Grand Old Party." He paused to let the quiet gather. "Ladies and gentlemen, a young man esteemed by his native city of Sacramento, Hiram Warren Johnson!"

Polite applause accompanied a low growl as people spoke to those standing beside them. Mae heard snippy tones: "…too busy to come," "…better things to do." But for her, the substitute speaker served just as well—the son of Mrs. Johnson.

A sturdy young man with a thick neck stepped to the table in a cream-colored suit. His middle-parted brown hair presented itself as he poured water into the glass, and then his large quick eyes surveyed the crowd on the upstairs balcony. The set of his mouth brought to mind a bulldog. As he began orating, Mae reminded herself that even if she succeeded in getting the letter into Mrs. Johnson's hands, she'd need to survive until she was actually rescued, and she had to be findable. She had to hope Mrs. Johnson would read the letter here, today. A slim chance. Very slim. Maybe a miracle.

The words soaring from young Johnson had a familiar ring. Soon the entire sprawling place quieted as people looked at the speaker, the ones on the ground floor looking up.

...that cause for which they gave the last full measure of devotion—that we here highly resolve that these dead shall not have died in vain, that this nation under God shall have a new birth of freedom, and that government of the people, by the people, for the people shall not per- ish from the earth

A new birth of freedom lingered in Mae's mind while *from the earth* echoed inside the vaulted Pavilion. All the time the speaker was quoting Abraham Lincoln, his mother gazed at the back of his neck, and Mae stared at that lady, trying to draw her attention by the mysterious force that sometimes makes the object of a stare turn to look at its source.

The clear tenor called out, "We Americans treasure the words of Abra- ham Lincoln...."

Mae noticed that Mabel and Mary Johnson were standing side by side with their hands clasped before them, searching the crowd with their eyes. One of them would probably see her before their mother did. That could work too. A few steps beyond Mary stood a slender woman in the latest fashion— bird-winged hat topped by a bouquet of curly feathers standing a foot above her head. She bounced a baby in a blanket while trying to subdue a fidgety little boy in a stiff collar and woolen knickers. Something about her said she bossed more than children. Mae could almost smell the dearness of every thread and bead and feather on her body. Probably the speaker's wife. Just then that young mother looked over her shoulder straight at Mae.

Confident, scornful eyes scoured her bare chest, and Mae looked down. This stranger was of no use to her, but the power of thought had worked, and she would focus it on the ones who knew her. She had about given up on the mother, the single-minded Mrs. Johnson obviously devoted to her son, but Mabel and Mary would see her.

"And I give you another quotation from that martyred president." Each line rose to a stinging height, followed by a short pause that made the idea stick in the mind, even Mae's, though she had a flapping bird in her throat:

I am not bound to win, but I am bound to be true.
I am not bound to succeed, but I am bound to live up to what light I have.
I must stand with anybody that stands right; stand with him while he is right, and part with him when he goes wrong.

Just then Mary looked straight at her, recognizing her!

Mae felt Oberon's line of sight crossing her like the throw of hot oil, but she blinked in Morse code, praying that Mary knew the famous distress signal, three longs, three shorts. Like a mad thing, she signaled SOS, again and again, believing that the puffy curly hair across her brow would hide her blinking from the lofty Oberon.

Mary appeared puzzled.

Looking out upon the upstairs and downstairs crowds, the speaker now paused for what seemed like several minutes, but must have been less. In the silence the people grew ever quieter, until the hush seemed to quiver with anticipation.

"People of Sacramento," the speaker lashed out, and Mary's gaze returned to her brother. "Freedom born in this Gold-Rush city and indeed all of California has waned. That robust democracy resting on the belief that a man could get ahead by his wit and the sweat of his brow has withered in our lifetimes, while a few men of the largest corporations in the United States live like kings. They select our political candidates and write our laws, and their influence permeates the three branches of government, at all levels, down to our city's governance, which accepts favors. Graft and corruption extend to our police force and the notorious houses of—"

Mary nudged Mabel, who leaned her ear to her sister.

Now tell your mother, Mae tried to transmit.

Oberon, who until now had seemed distracted, suddenly stared at Hiram Johnson as though he'd said something astounding. Something about the police—

"Let me be clear," Johnson continued, "it is no crime to make money, or to have money, but it ought to be a crime to—

Mabel touched Mrs. Johnson's arm!

"—allow companies to use their money to buy favored treatment from the government. For when there is no equality, there is no liberty, and without liberty we have no—"

Seizing her chance, while Oberon was still staring at the speaker, Mae carefully wiggled her fingers at Mrs. Johnson, but the lady didn't look at her. Instead, she frowned at the back of her son's neck and took a step forward. Disappointed, Mae let the flow and echo of words cool her wild heart as Johnson's voice rang over the stilled audience, the mass of faces gazing up through a haze of cigarette smoke in the slanting light from the glass above:

We have seen of late years the concentration of the wealth of this country in few hands and the alarming increase of poverty in our midst. We have seen perhaps an aristocracy rearing its head amongst us, not of blood but of wealth. We have seen perhaps this aristocracy arrogating to itself the rights and privileges that belonged to the aristocracies of the older world, and we have seen the poor becoming poorer, until in some parts of this country they are little better than serfs...

By now Mrs. Johnson had inched forward to the end of the table where she was level with her son and he would see her face if turned his head that way. All Mae could see of the lady was the rear of her black straw hat atop her gray bun. But then she turned her head toward her son and the look on her face conveyed the same awed disbelief that Mae saw in Oberon's. The two Johnson girls had clearly forgotten about Mae.

It may be that ere long, as the classes among us become more distinct, as the poor become poorer, and as hunger drives men to desperation, that we will be confronted with a problem again as serious as that which confronted the statesmanship of this country at the opening of the rebellion. It may be that men in this country, driven to desperation by the wrongs, suffering for the common necessities of life, will go forth from their starving families and engage in another rebellion against wrong and oppression that will eclipse in its bloodshed, in its fierceness, in its lawlessness and slaughter, any the world has ever seen... May God ward off from us any such contest as this... but if such a contest does come... may we found in the future, as you were in the past, struggling and if need be yielding our lives as you did, in the Right, in behalf of the equality in man."

It seemed to Mae that Hiram Johnson had warned of another Revolutionary War, but she had no time to think of that, for the oration was over and the recently stone-silent crowd now surged forward with a tremendous roar. People pushed up the stairs against those who stood on the upper level, and the entire sea of humanity was on the move.

"Stay with me," Oberon ordered Mae as he tried to keep a channel clear so that as people ascended the stairway, others could go down. He called out to the crowd, "Back. Stay back." But even Oberon in his imposing uniform was but a sinking post in an advancing river. Mae allowed the tide to carry her toward the man who had extolled liberty and freedom.

Glancing back, she saw Oberon looking at her. The next instant she struck the table and found herself standing before Hiram Johnson, squeezed from behind and on both sides by men leaning toward him, praising him. The table scraped back under the mounting pressure while Johnson back-stepped on the other side, hurriedly grabbing outstretched hands.

"Thank you. Appreciate that. Thank you. Thank you. Good. Thank you." Streams of perspiration ran down his face, and he seemed an ordinary man that she could talk to.

"I'm being held prisoner," she blurted out through the commendations being shouted around her, and reached for the letter.

Oberon's hand reached for her.

38

She ran before she could peel the wet letter from the underside of her perspiring breast. Head down against the wall of people advancing up the stairs, she squeezed between them before they knew what was happening, all the time seeing in her mind the blank expression on Hiram Johnson's face. Help was not to be had there.

Men muttered oaths as she pushed through, "What the… damned hussy!" Behind her, Oberon's "OUT OF MY WAY" boomed like a cannon. People would move for him. Her small size helped. No time to look back.

"Damned she-devil," yelled a man she knocked off balance. The first floor was just two steps away.

Brought to a halt by a shoe on her gown, she pitched forward into the arms of two men. Scrambling to her feet, she heard the whine of ripping satin and felt the release of it just when iron hands clamped her arms. She had the same feeling of suffocation like in the instant before striking the rocks in a nightmare plunge from a cliff.

Oberon's sour breath poured over her head and shoulders as he pushed her like a shield to deflect people. He forced her beyond the pie tables. She stumbled on the trailing satin caught between her legs. He stamped on it and deliberately ripped most of it off, and then pushed her forward.

A wave of darkness overcame her, on her way to death. She wanted to cry out for help but felt too weak. A hussy being arrested by a lawman. People would not interfere. Even Hiram Johnson, fearless enough to malign the police to their faces, must have doubted her sincerity. Soon she'd be alone with Oberon. He'd cuff her to the wagon—the end of a failed and stunted life. Her heart pinched in her ribs and she thought it might stop.

Then she spied Mrs. Clayton in a group of ladies leaving a tower of fruit— Mrs. Clayton who once helped President Lincoln stand for the Right and the Good, a woman who helped orphans—now coming toward her with a bowl of fruit in one hand and a closed parasol in the other. No free hand for the letter.

The lady stopped and stared at Oberon and his hands on Mae.

Jabbing a hand into her corset Mae grabbed the soggy letter and threw it at the lady's feet. "Read that! He's holding me prison—"

"She's a lunatic," Oberon drowned it out with, bending down towards the letter.

Mrs. Clayton was also reaching for the letter.

His grip slipped down Mae's damp arm as he bent nearly double, reaching.

With a violent twist, Mae wrenched free. She ran, gathering her skirts high. "Help me," she called to people who were gazing at sofas and chairs in domestic groupings under a John Breuner banner. But she was gone before anything registered on their faces. Asking help from strangers was useless when on the run.

Corset stays creaking, she fled with the strength of an animal fleeing powerful jaws. She saw no interior door to duck behind, so she headed toward the entrance. She zigzagged in and out of tables laden with pyramids of peaches and plums, and as she shoved through the people, in her wake came squeals, oaths, and fruit drumming on the floor.

Oberon's yell prickled the back of her neck: "Stop her! She's under arrest!"

That pushed her faster. Outside, the harsh sun and infant trees offered no shelter, no hiding place. She had to keep running. People turned and stared. She glanced behind, didn't see him, and kept running. She imagined dark hiding places in the back of that livery stable where they'd left the horse, and headed left on the concrete walkway along the street.

No sooner had she committed herself to that direction, than she recalled the young liveryman's admiration for Oberon. Where to go? People were bunched along the walkway looking at the wares of vendors in small pavilions. Behind the tents was the tarred street, where ladies and gentlemen were being dropped off or picked up in all manner of buggies and shays. She tried to blend into the crowds of customers waiting to buy things—sausages, beer, iced cream, hand protectors for hot items. Everyone stared at her like she was naked. One leg was exposed to the thigh, she realized, as she crouched inside a group.

She looked down and saw that one breast was partway out of the gown, perhaps pulled out with the letter. Not losing a step, she stuffed it back into her dress and infiltrated a bigger bunch of people listening to a man extolling the virtues of a cherry-pitting device. Looking back over the shoulders of taller people, she didn't see him.

A horse whinnied, drawing her eye through the spaces between the shifting people. He was there, between the walkway and street, looking for her on the other side. He would see her any second now—a bright cardinal in a flock of pigeons.

Walking swiftly—running would draw his attention—beyond the next tent and near the road where a tent would block his view, she found herself within arm's reach of an old buggy hitched to a swaybacked appaloosa. No people there, just a throw on the padded seat, like women used to cover rips. She whisked the large cloth around her shoulders, covering the flaming red with the pungent but nondescript wrap. Afraid that the owner, who might be any of the people around her, would put up a cry, she walked swiftly away, praying that no angry person would stop her. None did. The temporary relief was so profound that it brought a darkness that lifted in a few seconds, and then she hurried into the next crowd. Ahead lay open space, the end of the fair vendors. She had trapped herself as surely as if she'd been in a box canyon.

"Mae!" called a familiar female voice.

Jumping in her skin, she whirled toward the voice and saw Helen Rose stretched across the lap of the driver of a one-horse shay—reaching a hand toward her from the slowly moving vehicle. The gentleman holding the reins scowled down at the top of Helen's flowery hat.

Helen's childlike smile beamed and her hand beckoned. "Come on, gitcher self in. You don't look so good."

Like a drowning thing, Mae grabbed Helen's hand, her other hand clutching the throw to her neck. She boarded the shay, staying low, crawling over the gentleman's shoes in the small boot-box, and then curled into a ball on Helen's feet.

"What on earth!" the man bellowed.

"I'm in an awful fix," Mae explained from under the throw, the threads of which contained the stink of excrementitious fumes. "A police inspector's after me, but I didn't do anything wrong. He's been keeping me prisoner. Please don't—"

"Percy," Helen directed, "You best make that horse step out." She wiggled her shoes in a friendly way beneath Mae.

"I'm going fast as I can," the gentleman pointed out. "But just where're we supposed to be taking that, ah…" He cleared his throat and pronounced with some disdain, "her?"

"Please don't look around like anything's different." Mae could hear the pathetic sound of her begging. "Maybe he didn't see me get in." Then she remembered. "He's after you too, Helen. That's how he tricked me, had me at the station answering questions about you." She made herself breathe so she wouldn't pass out.

"You hear that?" Helen said, apparently to Percy. "Sounds like Oberon Jones all right. Let's hightail it."

"I'm doing my darndest to move this thing," the man grumped. "Too many rigs, too many horses." Traffic had stalled.

"Yes, it is Oberon," Mae clarified.

With a nudge of her shoe, Helen asked Mae, "Where you going to?"

"Be obliged if you could drive me out of here. Anywhere. I don't care."

"Oberon Jones won't mess with me," Percy stated. "Don't worry about that."

"Look at your mirror," Helen said. "You see 'im? A tall policeman with dark hair to his shoulders?"

"Yup. Tall enough to stand out in a crowd. From the way he's looking around, I'd say he didn't see her get in. But listen, we can't—"

"He'll kill me for getting away," Mae said from under the cloth.

"Oh, playin' that kill-you gaime, is he?" Helen drawled. "Percy, let's drive her to the hotel an' git'er into somethan else. Taik her to the raices with us."

After a while Percy growled, "Don'chu get notions about her staying on."

∽

Ever since leaving Oberon's place that morning, Mae's mind had been sharp and clear, making life and death decisions on the run. And now as she crossed the busy lobby of the Golden Eagle Hotel, having evaded him, she could barely lift her feet to climb the curving, carpeted staircase with Helen. Percy was tending to the livery and seeing about bringing noon dinner to the room.

On the second floor the emptiness of the long red carpet welcomed Mae, and the feeling of sudden safety left her wrung out. She closed her eyes and walked slowly. Ahead, a key rattled in a lock and Helen's sing-song floated down the hall.

"Why, you look tard as a tomcat walkin' in deep mu-ud," Helen said in a motherly tone.

Opening her eyes, Mae corrected her aim and moved faster. "I didn't get much sleep last night." *And that's not the half of it.*

Helen stood at the open door waiting, and Mae entered a room fit for a queen— green and maroon carpet with a border of gold, maroon velvet draperies on tall windows with golden swags, fine plaster moldings, and a ceiling medallion from which hung a stupendous brass fixture with many tiers of tiny lampshades. Golden curlicues and painted pink and red roses decorated the furniture, including the armoire, inside which Helen now laid her hat. But the bed ruled the room. Like nothing Mae had ever seen, this four-poster was draped with silk translucent curtains embroidered with nosegays of flowers and held back by little bow ties. It beckoned its beholder with mounds of pillows against the carved mahogany headboard, a far cry from the room Helen had lived in three weeks ago.

"Go ahayed, lay down," Helen said with a smile. "The girls here maik the bayed up real nice ever mornin', clean sheets n' all."

Mae sat down on the high bed, and then fell back into its heavenly embrace. "Ahh," she exhaled, resting her eyes.

"What was Oberon doin' with you?" Helen asked.

"I think he was planning…" But the future wasn't the question. Now that she was free, Mae didn't want to think of the past. However, she managed to get it out in a few sentences, slowly and with difficulty, like she was talking past a mouthful of marbles. Then she asked a question of her own. "How come you know him?"

There was a silence. Mae opened her eyes to see Helen perched primly at the dressing table removing hairpins. Their eyes met in a mirror surrounded by a frame of richly carved mahogany. The edges of Helen's curly lips turned up in a smile.

"Wayell, let's jes say they had me in the hoosecow, and Oberon come in that na'at to talk business. Real friendly like. We made us a deal, he b'lieved it was a deal anyhow, and the judge let me out." Helen giggled as she brushed her blond hair. "Y'see, Ah've met up with his ka'and before, an' Ah never do business with 'em."

Now she was pinning the loose curls on top of her head and giggling as she did it. "Ah gave him the slip." More giggles. "Betcha he were mad 'nough to eat the Devil with his horns on."

Mae had been trying to keep up with that, when she suddenly realized Eugenia wasn't there. She sat up looking around, "Where's your little girl?"

Helen flinched visibly in the mirror and her arms came down.

"Is she all right? Is she sick?"

Helen's voice was thin. "She's fa'an. Ah took her to San Francisco."

San Francisco!

"Ma baiby's better off with the nuns in that school. She needs schoolin'." She went back to her hair.

Nuns. Puzzled, Mae recalled that Sacramento had a Catholic girls' school around 10th and H Street, and Eugenia would have been able to see her mother every day. Recalling how she'd hated being dumped at St. Mary's Academy, she blurted, "I saw how much you and Eugenia love each other. It must be lonely for h…" She stopped, knowing this could sound like criticism.

"Mae, the way Ah'm living she woulda haited me 'fore long."

Helen went to the armoire and opened it. "Now, let's us see what to put on you."

Just then Percy came in, followed by a maid pushing a cart with three tall glasses and three plates covered by silver domes. The pitcher of iced lemonade made Mae crazy with thirst. The maid, surveyed Mae's torn dress as Percy paid her, and shut the door.

Helen held a brown and maroon paisley day dress up over her face. She stuck her head around it. "I'd say this's the perfect thang for the raices. Gitcherself over yonder and tra it on." She pointed her head at a flowery silk screen in the corner of the room.

"I don't think so," Mae said. "All I want to do is get out of this corset and sleep for a year. You two go on to the races."

A cloud came over Percy's features, and Helen obviously took note of it.

Mae pointed out, "I heard everyone in Sacramento goes to the Sunday races. Oberon could be there. But he won't find me here."

"Ah shore wouldn't bet on it," Helen said. "He coulda followed us to the hotel. Soon's Percy and Ah'd leave, he'd get the key from the clerk and be in here quicker'n hell can scorch a feather."

Shocked to hear that, Mae said, "But you said you looked back at every corner and didn't see him following."

"Guess you doan know much about lawmen."

Mae realized that Helen did, otherwise she'd be in jail. And she'd found just the day dress for Mae to blend in with a Sunday afternoon crowd, one that had not been in her trunk three weeks ago. This was no child, and Mae believed it would be safer at the races with Helen and Percy.

39

On the J Street trolley, Mae could hear Oberon in her mind's ear: *It'd be like huntin' a fat squaw in a snowdrift.*

The motorman cried, "Eleventh Street!" The trolley stopped in the middle of the road for people to get on and off. Mae's bench faced up 11th Street toward the Capitol Building. No police officer was in sight, only couples and families out for a stroll of a Sunday afternoon. Closer, just a half block away, soared the Cathedral of the Blessed Sacrament—glorious, massive, taller than the Capitol dome, as though God and His laws had bested mere government. Mae's predicament proved the truth of that. Secular law couldn't save her now. *I must go confess,* she thought, *when I get the chance. Oh, forgiving Mother Mary, thank you for getting me away from Oberon, and please help me hide from him. I promise to be good from here on. Please beg mercy for me from God and—*

The trolley bell dinged and the car jerked forward, nearly throwing her off the seat. She grabbed the pole and crossed herself. On the bench next to her, Helen and Percival Unstead, his actual name, had seen her arm move. They still didn't understand what Mae had gone through, except for the little bit she'd told Helen. Helen hadn't explained her end of things either, like what she was doing with Percy, as she called him, and how long he would tolerate Mae in his Golden Eagle nest. Probably not even tonight. Where would she sleep? How long could she last with an expert hunter on her trail? She could feel the beating of her heart over the clamor and squeak of the streetcar. The stench of fresh tar on the road made her stomach queasy. The beef sandwich with onion wasn't sitting well.

The driver sang out with the bell. "Sixteenth!"

The three of them stepped down with about eight others, apparently all heading to the races. Percy seemed a stiff-necked sort, but his presence might have kept Oberon at bay, and that's all Mae cared about. Beautiful new houses lined the other side of the street. On the near side, a single building and its grounds occupied the entire block. The three-story edifice with a bell tower stood amid a grove of trees so tall their leafy canopies shaded the mansard roof.

Helen put her mouth under the hat she'd lent to Mae, and whispered in her ear, "That's the grammar school. Eugenia woulda went there."

The whispering was a clue to why Eugenia had been banished. Percy didn't want the child around. Green lawns and flower gardens decorated the house fronts across the street, but not the school—a good thing. Tomorrow children would romp through those trees and no scold would threaten them about staying off the grass, as happened daily at St Mary's. *When I was innocent, just four months ago.*

Percy, perhaps noticing Helen's whispered comment, shot Mae a look, the rims of his eyes as red as the band around his straw hat—not a young man. He'd said nary a word to her during their hasty noon dinner nor in the streetcar.

Helen grabbed his arm and snuggled against him in broad daylight, shining her angelic smile up to him. Mae could practically smell the sex between them. She wished to rid herself of sin and not be walking down the street with it, especially not in front of a school. She looked through the very tall, vertical tree trunks, doubtless pruned high to discourage climbing children, but saw no sign of Oberon or his wagon.

"Say," Percy said to Mae—giving Helen a friendly shove to make her behave—"if you don't mind, just what was the nature of your problem today?"

Mae knew that help might be had in this quarter, and she had only one more block of privacy before the noise of the racetrack drowned them out. "I am very grateful for your help," she began. She told about being at the Agricultural Pavilion with the hidden letter. "I tried to give it to Mr. Johnson, just when he finished his oration. I couldn't get the envelope out in time, but I did tell him I was being held prisoner and needed his help. He didn't say or do anything. Just stared at me. I ran, barely out of Oberon's grasp. In fact he caught me, but I escaped and was running when I saw Helen."

"I take it you were disappointed in young Mr. Johnson."

"Well yes. I risked my life to do that."

"Do you realize, Miss Duffy, what Hiram Johnson said to the world today?"

"Yes, I heard it. Something about freedom. That's what I wanted. I thought he'd understand."

Percy stopped walking and looked at her with tired, red-rimmed eyes, "Well, let me tell you, young lady, a momentous thing happened today. The Republican Party of California began to break asunder." He resumed walking, Helen and Mae keeping stride as he expounded.

"A son breaking from his father is a common thing, but rarely has it been so public or carried such import. Hiram Johnson declared warfare upon the Southern Pacific Railroad and the titans of industry here and across the nation. So maybe with that on his mind, and the wrath of his father, being as how his father is a dependable mouthpiece for the SP, and all the hullabaloo it stirred up at the Pavilion, the poor fella was a little slow to become embroiled in a petty matter involving the local constabulary."

Mae felt her face heat up, being lectured to like that, and hearing him say that being saved from Oberon was a petty thing. But maybe it was true; her life wasn't worth a wooden nickel.

Those onions were making her sick.

They passed beneath the banner of the Agricultural Park. A noisy bunch of gamblers had congregated at a little building on the right, but Percy stepped to the front of their line and laid down some money. The man in the booth took his bet and said, "Thank you Senator Unstead."

Senator!

A few steps beyond a high wall, the track came into view—a mile-long track the Sheldons deemed suitable for their Thoroughbred. Never had Mae seen a track this magnificent or a covered grandstand this large.

Percy stood back while Mae and Helen seated themselves on a bench one row down from the top of the grandstand, covered on top and down the back against the afternoon sun. He sat at the aisle, his line of sight along the wire, always a coveted location at a race. Helen patted his nicely clothed thigh.

Mae scanned the backs, shoulders, and hats of the many people below them, the grandstand about a quarter full. She also studied the long row of stalls on the right curve of the track, well-dressed men walking back and forth, grooms with buckets and brushes, stable boys with pitchforks, jockeys in knickers. No Oberon. Trying to put aside the feeling of being disrespected, she told herself she had as much right to live as anyone else. Surely Hiram Johnson would agree with that. On the other hand, Senator Percival Unstead was probably right that Hiram Johnson hadn't been able to grasp what she was saying while all those men were speaking to him. And maybe Mrs. Johnson had been upset by what he was saying, and hence not seeing Mae's signals.

Mounted jockeys in white pants and high black boots walked their horses to the starting gate. Only two months ago she and Pal had defeated the Sheldon Thoroughbred, and she had won the purse. Now, neither the bugle nor the roar of the crowd as the horses left the gates produced the old tingle. The world felt colorless, the sky dull as the dust from the hooves. *Where will he catch me? On the street after Percy throws me out of the hotel?* Oberon always got his man, or woman. And yet Helen, cheering with the crowd as the horses streaked around the track, appeared to be living proof against that rule. Something about Percival protected her. Perhaps his power as a Senator.

A tall man in a white suit and straw hat came up the grandstand stairs and bent over Percy. They talked for quite a while over the roar of the crowd. The man in the white suit went down a couple of steps and stood in the aisle watching the race, arms folded.

"Why'ncha go down and git us a bucket of beer?" Helen yelled to Mae over the roar as the horses rounded the far corner and sped toward the wire.

"I… I'm afrai—"

"Charlie Rogue'll go with ya." Helen pointed to the man in the aisle. "He's a friend 'a Percy's."

The man in white with a full but trimmed mustache looked over his shoulder and smiled at Mae. His somewhat pockmarked face gave him a rugged look.

Senator Unstead reached across Helen with two bits in his manicured fingers and made it clear that Mae should take it. "Stay with Mr. Rogue when you're down there and Oberon will stay clear."

Mae took the coin, but made a worried face. "I don't know him," she yelled.

By then Percy was upright and intent on the horses approaching the wire. It felt bad and ungrateful to refuse to fetch beer for them after they had rescued her today.

"Wait 'til the race is over. He'll go with you," Helen, yelled from between them.

"Come on, Grey Boy!" Percy called through cupped hands.

Gray Boy didn't win, and the noise of the crowd dampened as Mae got up to join Percy and the stranger in the grandstand aisle.

"Charlie Rogue is as fine a gentleman as you could meet anywhere in this state," Percy asserted after introducing Mae. "In fact the state couldn't run without him. Charlie, this girl's afraid of her own shadow and I'd be obliged if you'd accompany her to get us all some beer."

"It'd be an honor, Senator." The tall man in white looked at Mae with a friendly twinkle in his dark brown eyes, like there was a joke and he was on to it.

Mae went down the stairs beside Mr. Rogue, feeling conspicuous to be parading where Oberon might be watching.

Down behind the grandstand, where the long line to the ladies' outhouse ran parallel to the long beer line, Mae figured she had nothing to lose by taking this man into her confidence. "Mr. Rogue," she said, "It's not my shadow I'm afraid of. It's…"

"I know," Mr. Rogue said. "The Senator told me." Planting his white shoes at the end of the beer line, he gave her a smile like a father would give a child. "Oberon's up to his old tricks again," he said.

Tricks was hardly the word Mae would have used. She peered though the parked vehicles and tents behind the grandstand, not seeing a police wagon. It occurred to her that Percy and Helen were handing her off to this man like they gave Eugenia to the nuns in San Francisco, for her own good. If so, she had to trust this man.

The grounds were abuzz with an incessant flow of people arriving at the track, and the betters near the entrance vied noisily for attention, holding up slips of paper. Among them she chanced to see a familiar young man with a boyish face and sandy hair around his ears. This time he wore a Western high hat, not a bowler, but it was Butch Parker. She was sure.

As though sensing her, he turned, and their eyes met. Criminal though he might be, she yearned to talk to him. There was a "Wanted" poster out on him, and she knew how it felt to be wanted by the police—the same police-man. She also realized that Oberon wasn't anywhere near, or he would have apprehended Butch.

"Mr. Rogue, sir, I've just seen an old friend over there. Would you excuse me to say hello to him?" She gave him the beer money.

His expression turned skeptical. "Stay in my sights. You're my respon-sibility now."

⌒

Butch pulled Mae a little outside the betters' ring, and she got her story out in about thirty seconds, all but the most sinful parts. "You were right about this being a den of iniquity," she said. "And I don't blame you for carrying a gun. Oberon's after me now, too."

His blue eyes were full of questions.

She got one in first. "How would you get away from here in a hurry, if you needed to?"

"Why?"

"Because I might need to." She recalled his way of sidestepping one ques-tion with another. "If I have to run, we could go together."

"I got wagers on some horses and leads on a couple more. But if Oberon comes in, I'll head over there." He pointed beyond the far end of the bleach-ers where some tents had been set up. "There's a raft over there to float me to the underground if I need it."

Cows grazed in the area where he pointed. "What water you plan to float on?"

"The American River's over there. You can't see it from here."

She realized that the long straight high ground behind the cows was a levee. This city had two rivers with levees. "You staying in the underground?"

"You might say."

"How do you get in? I mean which building?" Mr. Rogue was watching, but she felt no obligation to get back to him until she had an escape plan. She had prayed, and the Good Mother had responded by giving her Butch, a wanted man, an expert at avoiding capture.

"You know the Pacific Thomson-Houston Electric Light Company?"

"No."

"It doan look like much above ground. Right there on Sixth and I. You can't miss the smoke. Comes up through the boardwalk from the underground boiler room. It's how they make the electricity for them arc li—"

"But how can I find you?" She didn't mean to be rude, but Mr. Rogue had made progress in the beer line and she needed to get back, now that she knew Butch's plan. Besides that, she needed to go to the outhouse.

Butch continued, "There's a door to that basement. Give it a shave-and-a-haircut knock, plenty loud. Somebody'll let you in, day or night. That basement connects to the underground." He put a hand on her shoulder. "Poor kid, you look pale. I'll be there if you need me."

"Maybe tonight." She knocked the rhythm on his shoulder. "Thanks."

He stood for an instant looking the same as when he'd kissed her that night, but then vanished into the crowd of gamblers.

Mae waved at Mr. Rogue, now near the front of the beer line. She pointed to the ladies' outhouse line. He saluted back.

By the time she got to the front of the privy line, Mr. Rogue had been waiting for some time beside a giant barrel of Buffalo Beer in a vat of ice. He had two full buckets in hand.

Inside at last, Mae held her breath and tried not to look down as she gathered the paisley fabric and sat on the hole, but she'd caught a glimpse of the contents piled unexpectedly near the top. A stomach spasm doubled her forward. Again and again the minced beef and onion sandwich bucked up onto the floorboards. When the spasms subsided she rushed outside, faint and completely empty, her gaze avoiding the ladies next in line.

"You're white as a ghost," Mr. Rogue said, not without concern as he herded her along the bleachers and up the aisle. Several benches short of Percival and Helen, he said, "Let's sit here where we can talk. I'll wager some of that beer'll put the roses back in your cheeks." He handed her a bucket.

"You'll lose your wager," she said. While he delivered Percy and Helen's bucket, Mae washed her mouth out with beer and spat it down under the bleachers.

Charlie Rogue was polite and professional in a relaxed sort of way. The day was warm, and he removed his white jacket and folded it on the bench beside him, and then removed his bow tie, putting it in a jacket pocket. Another race was lining up, people shouting to their favorites. He put his mouth to her ear and told her that legislators in Sacramento were lonely for female company. Their wives and families lived in other parts of the state.

"Why don't they move their families to Sacramento?" she said into his ear.

He took a hefty draught of beer and fingered the foam off his mustache. "The men are visitors, here only a few months of the year. They need to live in the areas they represent, with the people who elected them. Their businesses are there too. Have a swallow?" He offered her the bucket.

She shook her head. "Are you a legislator?"

"No, assistant to the leader."

"Leader of what?"

"The Republicans."

"That's a lot of men to lead, all over the United States."

"No, just California, just the Assembly." His twinkle was back, and she knew she was the joke but didn't mind. She hadn't the first idea what that

Assembly did, but figured she'd better be sociable. And she liked leaning into him and talking mouth to ear. "Are there more Republicans or Democrats in the Assembly?"

"The former. A nearly unanimous preponderance of the GOP. This is California, my dear." He flashed her that twinkly-eyed smile. "Where are you from?"

She waited for the bugle and gun to start the race. "Iowa. Got here last May."

"Well, that explains it," he said over the crowd's roar.

The cragginess added to his manly appeal, a man probably in his early thirties. She leaned to his ear and said, "Is that the reason Oberon won't bother me when I'm with you—because you work for the leader in the Legislature?"

"Sure." His eyes followed the horses churning their way toward the left curve. "The city bosses don't wanna rile the state leaders."

Oberon worked for the city bosses. "Is Senator Unstead a legislator?"

He smiled at her like it was mildly funny, and nodded.

Elbows on knees, he was quiet in the loud stadium, fingering his mustache, the kind that filled the space from nose to lip, but then followed the lip down to pointed ends below the lips. The inverted V, a softened V, gave his mouth a somewhat unhappy expression as he watched the approaching horses, though his eyes retained their twinkle.

When the leaders crossed the wire the crowd exploded. Mr. Rogue waited until it died down a little, leaned over and said, "Would you consider accompanying a legislator to a supper dance on Thursday evening?"

"You want me to…"

Her face must have expressed her shock, because he leaned over and clarified, "…escort a lonely man to a party. That's all. A Welcome Back to Sacramento party. You are a very pretty young lady whose diction and grammar indicate that she'd fit with that higher kind of society. No spooning unless you want it. There'd be certain rewards."

Spooning wasn't mentioned in polite company, though some of the wiser girls at St. Mary's used the word when lights were out. "What rewards?"

"To start with, you'd be safe. Oberon would stay clear of you. You'd get a room in a respectable boardinghouse for ladies, beginning tonight."

That alone made her want to shout Yes!

"And what if I don't like the way the man acts?"

"Just tell me about it, and you won't be paired with him again."

"You're saying this is more than one time?"

"If you want, and reports are good, you'll get more dates. Otherwise we'll say our farewells and you'll move out of the boardinghouse."

"Is Helen Rose in on this?"

He put the beer on the floorboards between his shoes and moved his head from side to side. "Helen operates independently."

"What if the next day is too late?"

"I don't quite under—"

"I mean what if he, ah, you know, does things to me before—"

"Oh, on the first date. You will be paired with a gentleman." He looked at her like a worried uncle. "He'd respect your wishes, and if he wants a different girl next time, he'll let me know."

"What else would I get for doing this? You said safety was for starters."

"A dollar a date, and this time a gown of your choice. We'll go to Weinstock and Lubin to pick it out. Also, you get an evening at the most spectacular home in Sacramento, an evening most young ladies would give an eyetooth for. I understand Governor Markham and his wife will be there."

That sounded wonderful, except for the married man. "Aren't there any bachelors in the Legislature?"

His smile parted his mustache a tad bit. "One or two. But the vast majority of elected officials are family men."

The grandstand erupted in a sustained roar as the horses approached the wire. Mae saw that one of the lead jockeys was holding his mount back and the horse didn't like it. Some horses cared more about winning than their riders did. A boy in Iowa had told Mae that big city races were all fixed by gamblers. As the horses thundered under the wire, she couldn't tell which of two had won. The announcer on the other side of the track signaled a boy Mae had seen crammed into an angle formed by a brace under the grandstand. The boy must have signaled the number of the winner, because the announcer bellowed through the megaphone, "Sugar Girl by a nose!"

A man in front of Mae yelled, "Shit," a word she'd never heard spoken aloud except when Farley hit his finger with a hammer.

"Mr. Rogue, do you get paid for this kind of matchmaking?"

His eyes glazed dead and black. "Miss Duffy, I'm sorry if I've offended you. I assist my bosses in every way I can, and that includes making their stay in Sacramento enjoyable. It's not what you seem to be implying. If you'd rather not—"

More contritely, "In that boardinghouse, ah… you think Oberon could get in?"

"I'd alert the proprietress to be sure he doesn't. She handles herself well in all cases, I assure you. She has a telephone and would call me. I'd send the State troopers.

"Troopers?"

"The Capitol has its own state police. The city wants no truck with them."

"Can you take me to that boardinghouse right away?"

"Sure can."

40

It was a warm September evening, and the sky had turned royal blue by the time the driver reined to a stop at 1524 H Street. Mae stared at the tall white fairy-tale house. The rising moon, fat and yellow, lent a glow to the flounces on the arched windows and the fanciful gables. High above, lacy white grillwork fenced in the fish-scaled mansard roof, where fairies might dance of a summer night. Her gaze traveled higher, to the tower with a round nautical window. She counted six stories to the white tatting of grillwork on its rooftop and the curvy cupola with a cupid's arrow of a spire pointing heavenward. A little-sister carriage-house stood to the right of the mansion. Mae felt certain that this must be the most beautiful residence in all of California. And she was a guest!

"It's so pretty!" she exclaimed to Assemblyman Lubeck, her escort.

"Impressive indeed. The hardware business must be doing well." To the liveryman: "Please return for us at eleven."

"Yes, Your Honor."

Your Honor! Mae gathered her silvery sateen gown and extended her high-heeled shoe to the carriage step engraved: J. P. Steffens. The balustrade of the stairs flared out from the house gathering visitors from their carriages and ushering them up to the curved porch and open doors. She was Cinderella at the palace feeling the dark weight of her recent life lurking inside her.

"It is commendable," Assemblyman Lubeck said as she helped him slowly ascend the stairs to the main floor, "that Sacramento City raised all the streets above the floods."

The fringe of iron-gray hair beneath his top hat belied the youthfulness of his flawless skin. He had kind eyes. With a gloved hand, he cupped the sheath of black lace just below her elbow, while the other hand gripped a thumping cane as he swung his stiff leg up each step. He'd been wounded in the Indian Wars, Charlie Rogue had said. Perspiration showed on the sides of his face as he struggled upward. She wondered why he'd worn a cape over a woolen suit on such a warm evening.

They stepped through the double-width doors into a hall that extended all the way through the house. Scents of flowers and perfume enveloped Mae, while gaslight chandeliers hanging from medallions painted in graduating shades of pink, orange and yellow gave a feeling of sunlight to the house. A line of slender women of Mae's short stature welcomed them.

Mr. Lubeck swept his hat before Mrs. Steffens and her daughters, she in black crepe embossed with myriad silken violets. The three daughters in three shades of satin—dusty pink, aquamarine, and dove gray—also greeted them.

"Did I hear correctly," Assemblyman Lubeck playfully inquired of the lady, "You are Louisa Steffens, and these delightful creatures are Lulu, Lottie, and Laura?"

With a friendly smile Mrs. Steffens explained, "Mr. Steffens likes my name, and he insisted each of our children be similarly adorned with L's. I do wish my son Lincoln could have been here. He's in New York, back from post-university studies in Germany."

"Our loss," said Mr. Lubeck. "May I present Miss Mae Duffy. Recently of Iowa."

"Charming. Welcome to our house, my dear," said the blond Mrs. Steffens with a warm handshake and genuine smile. "Please make yourself at home." To Mr. Lubeck, "Laura will take your hat and cape." As he handed the hat to the youngest daughter and removed his cape, Mrs. Steffens was saying, "Joey, our houseboy, advises that supper will be served in about three-quarters of an hour. You'll be at the head table. Enjoy your evening." With the same smile, she turned to the next arrivals. "Why, if it isn't Collis Huntington! And Arabella, my dear. We're so delighted you could come."

Having progressed two halting steps up the hallway, Assemblyman Lubeck turned to look at Mr. Huntington, as did Mae. The man was bald as a boiled egg but for wings of wild white hair around his ears. The furrows between his eyes marked him as much older than the lady in red on his arm, perhaps also procured by Charlie Rogue.

Mae and Mr. Lubeck continued slowly through the ornate hall, past gilt-edged French tables with vases of roses and spikes of gladiolus. She'd never seen painted scenes on a ceiling before now, a ceiling so high that the tallest men looked small beneath it. Peering through bunches of elegant guests, Mae couldn't help but focus on the dining alcove at the end of the wide hallway, where gleaming silver, crystal goblets, and chandeliers doubled in the reflection of a wall-to-wall mirror behind the table.

A man seized Mr. Lubeck, thumped him on the back, and leered at Mae. "Why y'old cross between a horse and donkey, your girls are getting younger and prettier by the day."

Mr. Lubeck grinned. "This delightful young lady is Mae Duffy." To Mae, he indicated the men. "These are Assembly colleagues of mine from Solano County and Oakland." He gave their names. Tilting his head toward the door, he lowered his voice to the two men, "Did you see who just came in?"

"Sets the tone, doesn't it," one of the men rejoined.

"I doubt we'll hear about reform tonight," the other quipped.

"Good," concluded Mr. Lubeck. Mae stood beside him, smiling and dumb.

The back-thumper said, "That's Grove Johnson stepping out of, of—"

"—the Frenchiest damned privy in the United States," the legislator from Oakland finished.

Mae followed with her eyes as a slender man with wild black hair made his way through the crowd to Mrs. Johnson, the very same lady who lived several blocks down H Street. Tonight she was tightly confined in a gray lace gown with a number of gold chains swagged across her chest. Mr. Lubeck led Mae onward, people backing away from his swinging leg.

"I know that lady," Mae told him in a low tone, nodding toward Mrs. Johnson. "I gave her daughters piano lessons."

"You did?" He suddenly changed course and led her to the lady, cane thumping.

She could not refuse, though as she came face to face she knew that if Mrs. Johnson had seen her at the Pavilion in that scandalous red gown, she wouldn't want to talk to her now. The other life was intruding, confusing her. Congressman Johnson and Mr. Lubeck grasped each other's shoulders like old friends.

"Well," said the lady, stiffening her neck, "if it isn't Mae Duffy."

That sounded harsh and critical, and the old foggy feeling left her speechless.

"I understand she gave your daughters piano lessons," Mr. Lubeck filled in.

"One day only," clarified Mrs. Johnson.

"I'm sorry I couldn't make it to the next lessons," Mae got out.

"You might have called."

"I, ah, really... didn't have the chance." The bad feelings punched up so hard through the Cinderella veneer that it almost made her weep. Determined to push down that filthy girl chained to a pipe, she blurted out the first thing she could think of that would please a mother. "I heard your son speak at the Pavilion. He was excellent."

Somehow that didn't feel right.

Congressman Johnson and his wife stared at her. Too late, Mae recalled that Hiram Johnson had spoken in public opposition to his father. How could she forget that! Face hot with embarrassment, she wanted to bolt from the party.

Assemblyman Lubeck grabbed her elbow, bade the Johnsons good evening, and steered her through the crowd. She wondered if she might actually die from embarrassment. The only salve was knowing that Hiram Johnson wouldn't be at the party, a man likely to remember her ridiculous cry for help. But she feared seeing Mrs. Clayton. That would be worse. And worse yet if the lady had picked up the letter from the floor, read it, and forwarded it to Hank and the folks. Now that Mae had posted letters to her parents and Hank, posing as a normal girl, the very thought of that desperate, sweat-soaked letter shamed her deeply. It would remove every jot of respect they'd had for her. She hoped Oberon had retrieved and destroyed it. Her family knew nothing about him, and she didn't want them to know. She had written them that a state legislator would escort her to one of the best homes in Sacramento, and that she was living in a nice clean boardinghouse. That's how she wanted them to think of her.

All of this surged through her mind as Mr. Lubeck conversed with other men. Mae scanned the crowd but didn't see Mrs. Clayton. Helen and Percy didn't seem to be here either. A Chinese man circulated with a tray of fluted glasses filled with bubbly liquid. Mae took one for herself and one for Mr. Lubeck, who sipped and declared it to be "fine champagne."

She touched the cool glass to her hot cheek before taking a sip. "Mr. Lubeck, I'm so sorry... I didn't—"

He brushed it away. "Politics, my dear."

They advanced into an animated crowd around the base of the wide, graceful staircase curving upward. She liked Mr. Lubeck, and her face cooled a bit as he introduced her right and left. Slowly gathering her wits, she began to pick up a thread of conversation.

"...don't pay that any mind. C. K's still young, just lost his way is all. Can't prove a thing. The whole town's against him. We appreciate the Capitol being here. It's good for business."

"Graft, bah!" exclaimed another. "Business is business. What does that idiot know about anything?"

"*Der Bee* lost many subscribers over dat," said Mr. Ruhstaller, owner of the Buffalo Brewery. "Ve be heppy to see alla you beck. Und ve be hoping—"

Mr. Lubeck broke in. "Did you men actually believe we would abandon the Capitol Building and build a new one in San Jose?"

"Vell, you voted on da floor, at der end of session."

Smiling kindly at Mr. Ruhstaller, Assemblyman Lubeck said, "The state doesn't have the revenue to build a new Capitol. Especially not in this Panic."

"You mean dot vas not heppening? Dot vote?"

Assemblyman Lubeck turned his mouth down, shook his head, and with a wink at the lady on the German's arm, escorted Mae to the next group. She held his glass for him until he planted himself firmly enough to hang the cane over his arm and drink.

"I'm going to the—" She pointed toward the privy.

He bent down to her ear. "No need to tell me, my dear."

A real gentleman. If I stay around him I might learn to be a lady.

Large enough to be a bedroom, the bathroom sparkled with small white hexagonal tiles on the floor, a white porcelain bathtub on eagle's feet, and a gilt-edged sink and commode. Murals on the walls depicted lightly draped women emerging from pools or stepping into them—the same art style as in Mae's watch, except that here the rosy nipples showed through the veils and the women were almost life-size. The commode had a gold fob at the end of an actual golden chain—she knew by the feel—and it released water from the porcelain basin above. The idea of using gold in the privy!

She studied herself in a mirror framed by golden leaves. Her blue eyes, black lashes and brows appeared unsullied by her long ordeal. The embarrassment had colored her cheeks; no need to pinch them. The stiff swatch of black lace at her throat veiled her cleavage, which was good. As planned, she did indeed look decorous and reserved. The molded bodice was enough suggestion, the watch pinned on her breast the only ornament. The lamb-chop sleeves of the frock, though fashionably wide, didn't puff out ridiculously far as some gowns did, but narrowed down to her elbows and lapped over the black lace sheathing of her forearms. She and Mr. Rogue had chosen well.

Spitting on a finger, she shaped a curl near her face. The bunched hair falling freely down her back added to her demure appearance. Many young ladies here—in fact all of them with legislators—wore low-cut gowns and sophisticated nests of hair on their heads, one of them being Rowena, who also lived at Mrs. Swensen's boardinghouse. For all Mae knew, other girls from that house were here too, but she had spent so much time in bed the last three days that she hadn't met them all. She felt no embarrassment about being hired. This was what it was. And a lot of people here seemed to understand that.

Mae and Mr. Lubeck slowly toured all three parlors, one with a grand piano and walls of books. They visited with countless people, including Charlie Rogue, who squired a tall, pretty lady and gave no hint of a prior acquaintance with Mae. Mostly her Assemblyman Lubeck talked to other legislators about matters she knew nothing about—a horse racing bill, the Sacramento Bee's overreaction to corruption in the Legislature, womens' suffrage and whether the "ugly, unfashionable, obnoxious women agitating for it," as one man put it, destroyed its chances of passage.

By the time Joey, the Chinaman in a blue silk robe, rang the tinkling supper bell, Mae was giddy with champagne and high-toned people. She had even met Governor Markham and his wife. She'd also learned that Mr. Lubeck was Chairman of the Ways and Means Committee, which sounded important. Cinderella had returned.

Sumptuous food dishes stretched from one end of the table to the other in the long dining alcove, where painted walls depicted cooked game birds and bowls of fruit. While Mae and her escort had been conversing in the parlors, a much longer table had been set up in the hallway all the way to the front door, the tables now forming a gigantic capital T, with the top of the letter in the alcove. Sparkling glasses of red wine on the long table resembled two chains of rubies against the white linen. She helped Mr. Lubeck hunt among the place settings for their name cards, and found hers across the table and down a bit from his.

"My guess is there's two-hundred people here," the man seated next to her leaned over to say. "I'm Senator Smyth."

With his name before him on the card, that seemed unnecessary, and she was thinking it would sound even sillier to tell him her name, but the tinkling bell saved her. Blocky, square-faced Governor Markham stood at the head of the table, while Mr. Steffens rang the bell for silence.

The governor waited for the quiet to spread before he started. "Esteemed legislators... members of the Sacramento Board of Trade... and ladies and gentlemen, let us raise our glasses to our host and hostess, Joe and Louisa Steffens, for arranging this fine affair."

"Hear, hear!" The shouts went up. Mae drank with the rest, feeling like an observer in a royal court of Europe.

Mr. Steffens now stood at his end of the head table: "Governor and Mrs. Markham, ladies and gentlemen, legislators... welcome back to this fair city and to our home. Mrs. Steffens and I are honored by the presence of so many public servants who give of their valuable time to the Golden State. Perhaps enough has been said about the newspaper incident. Suffice it to say, *The Bee* has been soundly denounced at a special public event for that purpose, and as President of the Board of Trade, I have demanded a published apology."

The quiet deepened as Mr. Steffens went on. "I wish to thank the members of the Board, many of you here, for your help with the arrangements. Legislators, before you leave, don't forget to pick up your bag of gifts. Your names will be on them. Enjoy your supper."

As people cheered and talked, a squadron of Chinese men in black suits filed in with white towels over arms and large spoons in hand. They fanned out to serve the dishes, each staking claim to about six guests. They placed squab, slivered potatoes and green beans in sauce on every plate. Mae listened to the discussion around her about the Chicago Columbian Exposition. "Some are calling it a World's Fair," Senator Smyth said.

Mr. Whitney, opposite the senator, stood up dinging a butter knife on an empty glass. Lifting his wineglass he bellowed, "Here's to Collis Huntington, titan of industry, titan among men, President of the Southern Pacific Railroad, pioneer, visionary, head of the largest corporation on earth, and yet friend of the farmer. Permit me to register a public thank you for the SP's assistance in shipping our California citrus and other fruits to the exposition in Chicago."

Shouts and cheers echoed throughout the house.

Some time later, as Mae was savoring the delicious food on her plate, Mr. Huntington stood up. In the center of the head table with his back to the wall, the old man faced the people seated down the long hallway and turned this way and that to see those at the head table.

"Ladies and gentlemen, I'd like to introduce my bride Arabella to those who have not yet met her." He motioned, and the tall young woman in dark red stood up. "The Belle of San Marino!" he announced.

So, this woman wasn't in Mae's position after all. She should have known. Wives accompanied the businessmen. As people clapped politely, Arabella seated herself, and her husband continued:

"Sadly, I am here in the place of Leland Stanford, my recently deceased business partner, former Governor and U.S. Senator. In our young years he and I, with two others, also deceased, formed a company for the then audacious purpose of connecting this wide land by rail. Leland Stanford was my friend and a friend of many here. His service to the nation and the business will be sorely missed. I am grateful that the new university that bears the Stanford name will carry on his spirit and educate generations of outstanding Americans." He waited for the respectful murmurs to cease.

His voice lowered. "I know that some of you have read of a tiff between us—exaggerated in the newspapers, I assure you—" he shrugged—"disagreements between partners of twenty-five years can happen, but that in no way lessens my admiration for the warm-hearted individual he was. Please, let us observe a minute of silence for that great pioneer." Mr. Huntington bowed his bare scalp, the white wings around his ears stiff and still.

Mae bowed too, though she knew nothing about the dead man.

Mr. Huntington continued, not with the ringing tones of a politician, but the quiet voice of a businessman possessed of complete self-confidence. His tailored suit fit his burly frame as closely as the trim white beard followed his jaw line. His eyes, under wild brows, were those of a lion. The power of the man was evident in the silence of his listeners, nibbling with great care so as not to make a sound as he spoke.

"We at the SP welcome you legislators back to Sacramento. I'd like to introduce some of the new talent in the company. First, Mr. William Herrin has joined our political coordination office. That's right, stand up." He motioned to a man far down the long table. "Mr. Herrin is an attorney, eager to answer your questions and help with figures and reports that you might need. You'll find him around the Capitol or in his office in the Golden Eagle Hotel. His appointment frees up our previous political advisor to focus on the work he does so well—promoting agricultural colonies, subdividing and developing land, and handling the properties of our newly added railroads."

The other men Mr. Huntington introduced were also seated far down the long table. They also managed companies associated with the railroad. It felt improbable that she, and not they, sat at the head table. The next man was "reorganizing the companies of the SP to keep us out of receivership, which has been the fate of so many companies during this Panic." Another man was in charge of SP forests and lumber mills, which Mae thought odd for a railroad company, until she remembered Hiram Johnson saying that a few wealthy men owned all the important businesses. Surrounded by luxurious chandeliers, bejeweled gowns, and Chinese servants, Mae had to keep reminding herself that the dinner guests were real men and women, not actors in a theatrical performance. The flesh and blood man introducing his manager for the manufacture and repairing of trains and the "deployment of rolling stock" had created the railroad that brought her to California.

He introduced a man in charge of the SP hospital in Sacramento, "bringing it up to date with the most recent medical innovations. Ladies and gentlemen, while we're on the subject of medicine, I'll mention that I'm concentrating my own personal efforts on expanding our medical insurance program—connecting the country in a new way. This means working with hospitals across the land to provide care for our employees if they need help, but also caring for SP–insured people outside our employ." He paused. "I look forward to your calls. Here's to a fine legislative session."

The toasting, cheering people swallowed wine, all eyes on Mr. Huntington, the captain of the nation's transportation industry and its many related industries. All eyes, that is, except Charlie Rogue's. From the junction of tables he was looking at *her*. His mustache spread in a friendly smile, a mustache right at home in this crowd of stylish men. His eyes left her as the next man rose to speak.

"While we're honoring recently passed business pioneers," the new speaker said, a man probably in his thirties, "I'd like a moment of silence for my father, Horatio Gates Livermore, founder of the Natoma Water and Mining Company."

Mae bowed her head, pleased that Charlie approved of the way she was comporting herself. She doubted he knew about her gaffe with the Johnsons, and she tried to forget that by not ever looking at them down the long table.

Mr. Livermore continued, "As many of you know, I've taken the helm of the company. What you don't know is, I'm about to bust my buttons." His smile stretched his thin mustache almost to his ears, and Mae was curious to know what would so excite a businessman.

"Today I signed a contract with General Electric Company for a hydroelectric plant on the American River." People talked but he overrode it. "That means greatly enlarging the dam at our sawmill pond in Folsom. You'll hear from doubters and skeptics, but I assure you I've consulted the scientific minds of the country and I am confident that we *will … deliver … hydroelectricity … to Sacramento by 1895!*" Excited talk buzzed around the long tables. He waited for it to subside.

"We will do so through a twenty-four-mile transmission line the size of a man's forearm, carrying electricity sufficient to supply every business and home and government office in Sacramento with as much power and as many incandescent lights as their owners wish to use. Enough to power all the streetcars and all the machinery, including the SP shops, and enough to light every city street with clean, quiet lights operated by a fingertip. All at little cost to the user. This will render obsolete the boilers and steam-powered generators that darken the sky with coal soot.

"I also signed an agreement today with the arc-light company to acquire their facility at Sixth and I as our powerhouse, henceforth to be known as Sacramento Electric Power and Light Company."

Butch's entrance to the catacombs! Might the iron door be locked, now that a new company owned it? Or maybe they'd keep the coal-fired boilers in the basement until the new electricity arrived. In ninety-five, two years away. In the meantime maybe she could still use that entrance in an emergency.

"We need investors," Mr. Livermore was saying. "And we'll need help from you legislators. We have in mind using prison labor to build the dam and lessen the cost. My friends, we're making history. Hydroelectricity will put Sacramento at the head of the progressive manufacturing cities of this nation. This will boost the population and business of the entire area." He smiled in all directions. "Now my buttons are safe."

A roar went up as he seated himself, made noisier by the clatter of the waiters collecting plates. Mae felt awed that her tablemates could dam rivers, electrify cities, and connect the ends of the country with railroads and hospitals. They brought to mind the mythological gods that the ancient Greeks supposed orchestrated everything that happened on earth.

"They're doing that at Niagara Falls," Mr. Whitney yelled over the din.

Senator Smyth leaned forward. "Not with a line over twenty miles long. That's never been done, nothing close to it. Electricity loses something in the lines. That's why they couldn't get the arc lights out past Sixteenth Street." He glanced at Mr. Livermore, perhaps to be sure he hadn't been overheard.

A loud noise. The table jumped, startling Mae. Wine glasses sloshed. A man had slapped his hands down—Mr. Elkus, by the name card. He bellowed, "I tell you, I'm all for it! All I'd have to do is turn a switch to get my forty motors going. Why, I could hire twice as many seamstresses and double my production of overalls. I'll throw those hellish boilers in the river. I'm investing in the new electricity."

As Mae savored the fluffy pudding of whipped cream, minced fruit and ground hazelnuts, the table hummed with excitement. She kept thinking she'd ought to pinch herself, but feared she'd wake up. After dessert, all the men repaired to the nearest parlor for brandy and cigars, while Mae rustled along in the herd of ladies to the front parlor for coffee and candies.

"I have it on good authority," pronounced Mrs. Elkus from the davenport, "that nineteen of every twenty women in Sacramento favor women's suffrage." Several heads nodded in approval.

A sour-faced dowager in ivory silk declared, "Street ruffians and insolent boys in knickers think they have more intelligence than anyone in skirts, simply because they can vote when they're of age." She popped a chocolate in her mouth.

"You're right," said Mrs. Steffens as she poured coffee into dainty cups on the side table. "Lulu here is a nurse trained at Johns Hopkins. Lottie just graduated in Stanford University's pioneer class, and Laura's following her; yet my accomplished daughters are not allowed to vote. While ignorant men do."

"Uncivilized," a lady chorused.

The three L's, now distributing coffee, appeared unruffled by their mother's praise. Although Mae hadn't given any thought to this subject before, she now found herself incensed over her official inferiority to males, but wasn't about to say anything in front of Mrs. Johnson and the other matrons of Sacramento. Instead she savored a rectangle of caramel chocolate, still warm from the kitchen and lumpy with pecans.

Mae imagined that the younger ladies, perhaps all paid escorts, would hold their tongues too. But one strawberry blond jumped in. "The newspaper said suffragists are so ugly no man would marry them."

The dowager fired back, "All *thinking* people favor women's suffrage." The girl didn't blush, as Mae would have.

Another matron weighed in. "My husband objects to it on constitutional grounds. The Constitution says that men are created equal, and that's the reason the suffragists can't win in Congress. It has nothing to do with bloomers and strange clothing, just the fact that the Fathers of the Country did not include women in the voter pool."

"Pshaw!" the lady in ivory objected. "The fathers of the Constitution intended Man to mean Mankind. The real problem is that the WCTU publicly supports suffrage. The men of our state quail in fear that they'll be parted from their precious liquor if women are allowed to vote."

Mae knew that WCTU stood for the Woman's Christian Temperance Union, a large and powerful organization opposed to the sale of liquor in the United States. Talk shifted to the odds of passing a suffrage amendment in California. The discussion of committees about which she knew nothing made Mae drowsy, though she'd done nothing but sleep and shop for clothing for the past three days.

The clock on the marble mantel chimed ten o'clock. The driver would return in an hour. She had hoped to see the ballroom, but it seemed unlikely that Mr. Lubeck could climb to the third floor.

Charlie Rogue walked by the doorway. He glanced into the parlor, catching her eye, and beckoned with a finger as he vanished from her sight. She looked around the parlor. No one else had seen it. His lady friend hadn't been on his arm. Maybe escorted to a hired hack by him and on her way home.

"Excuse me," Mae whispered to the ladies beside her on the sofa before she rose to leave.

41

Charlie Rogue was so tall that, to get her chin above the middle of his chest, she had to dance on her toes, even in two-inch heels. Soft gaslight from the chandeliers gave sparkle to the diamonds and rubies and emeralds adorning the ladies on the dance floor. With thrilling vigor the talented twelve-piece orchestra served up a Richard Strauss waltz, and Mae skimmed the floor with Charlie, transported into a magical realm where the nightmare of Oberon vanished. She was Cinderella at the palace.

Charlie danced like a prince. He looked down at her with his brown eyes and spoke with a naturally resonating voice, a man who would never need to shout. "Nice place, isn't it?"

"Oh my yes! I've never seen such a floor." The intricate parquet pattern belonged in a Viennese palace. The high polish and wax of its geometric surface helped her glide. She had daydreamed of dancing in such a place when riding the train to California.

"This floor is famous in Sacramento."

"I was afraid I wouldn't get to see the ballroom, what with Mr. Lubeck's bad leg."

"The Assemblyman prefers to play cards with his friends after supper. I should have mentioned that."

The musical beat stretched and stretched, Charlie spinning her while her lithesome skirts flowed behind. They stopped spinning just in time to take a breath before plunging back into tempo.

As they whirled to the one-two-three, one-two-three she said, "The lady you came with, I'm surprised she didn't stay to dance."

"Truth is, I was hoping to dance with you. I gotta say it, you're good."

"I do love to dance." Flushed at the compliment, she told him about the dances in the Iowa farmhouses. "We'd all pick up the parlor furniture and carry it outside, and roll up the carpet. We usually had but one violin, or piano." she laughed with joy.

"People on farms know how to have fun."

"Guess so." She smiled coyly up at him. "But I was always hoping to get to a city."

"Me too," he said with a chuckle. "I grew up on a farm in Visalia, down on the other side of Fresno."

The mention of Fresno brought to mind Helen Rose living there for a time, after riding a horse from Texas with Eugenia on the saddle. "I guess Helen and Percy, I mean, uh, the senator, didn't come." She couldn't think of his last name.

"Senator Unstead. Yes. I noticed that too. Maybe he didn't want her out in polite society with him."

All but flying off her feet as they coursed around the perimeter of the ballroom, Mae thought about how he put that and said in her teasing way, "Are you trying me out? To see if I'm all right in polite society?"

He stopped the whirling as he said, "There's a big difference between you and Helen. She's a whore, a thief, a drunk, and a shameless liar. Yet men swoon over her like idiots. She hasn't been in the city long, but she's cut a wide swath through the grass. Poor Senator Unstead. He's under her spell—but apparently not enough to forget what she really is. I'm glad he didn't bring her here. Her appeal to men is contagious."

The wine and the whirling had gone to her head, and Mae couldn't help but play with him. "How do you know I'm not a thief and a liar?"

"Well," he said mimicking her light tone, "I don't see you on the wanted posters. And somewhere along the line you learned respectable grammar."

"Maybe my grammar's respectable, but am *I*?" *Oops, maybe pushed that a little too far.*

"There are different kinds of respectability. In you it's innate."

Relieved and not just a little flattered, "I'll bet I'm the only one in this room who really *is* wanted by the law."

He gave her waist a little squeeze. "There are flawed human beings throughout the legal system, from the making of laws to their enforcement."

"Will you ask me to a party like this again?"

"How could I not? Any country girl deft enough to squirm away from Oberon Jones deserves a chance at a better life."

She was thinking she owed her getaway to Helen, the whore and thief, when the waltz picked up speed in preparation for a grand conclusion. They whirled and whirled, and he ended with a dip, a hug, and a release—holding her hand high in triumph and smiling at her. She laughed with pure joy.

A tap on her shoulder turned her around to another man. Charlie bowed out, and she danced four more numbers with different legislators. Apparently all the escorts were being examined in what seemed a systematic exchange. The next partner, also tall but not as tall as Charlie, spoke in the respectful manner of a farmer. Right away she felt comfortable with him. He had black eyes, a dark beard, and thick dark hair that drooped over his forehead.

"I am George Wilder," he said, holding her at arms' length. "What's your name?"

She told him, and they danced in silence for a while before she asked, "Are you a legislator too?"

"No. I'm here with the local GOP."

"I'm ashamed to ask, but what does GOP stand for?"

"Grand Old Party. Republican. I'm on the County Steering Committee."

"Oh. We didn't talk politics in my family, but I keep hearing GOP. Thanks for telling me. "

"I hear you're new in Sacramento. Where were you just before that?"

"Out by Slough House, Bridge House, Michigan Bar."

"I've got friends out there. Maybe you know the Sheldons."

"Why yes I do. I went to a musical afternoon at their house just before I came to Sacramento."

They made squares around the floor for another couple of minutes. Then he said, "My mother is a friend of W. C. Sheldon's mother."

"I met a lady friend of that lady. Would you believe? She, I mean the friend, was in the Donner Party. Got rescued. Her maiden name was Donner."

They marched out more squares, the man regarding her oddly. Feeling a compulsion to prove herself, Mae added, "She was tall and quiet, dark hair about half gray. I think it's just amazing what those people went through. I came over Donner Pass with my family in early June, on the train of course, and it was snowing to beat the band—in June!"

"Yup, the weather can be unpredictable up there." He continued to look at her in that odd way. Quietly, "That was my mother. The Donner Party was named for my grandfather. He was George too. I'm named for him."

"Well, for the love of Mike! Olive must be your sister."

"She is." They danced in silence, Mae thinking what a small world it was.

"I appreciate your being respectful," he said. "So many people think it's funny to ask what we eat for dinner."

She had to think a minute, and then was appalled. "Do people really do that?"

"All the time. Some folks think they can turn off their manners when it comes to the Donner Party."

Mae wasn't about to say any more about it. "Is your whole family in farming?"

"Yup. We've been on the farm in Galt, down in the Delta, since fifty-five. M'dad's getting on in years, so us two boys run it now. The folks still live on the place."

This man was probably in his forties. As the music slowed and then stopped, he thanked her for the dance, adding awkwardly, "My wife's back upstairs."

Mae was about to hurry away to relieve him of any embarrassment when Charlie appeared, gallantly taking her elbow while exchanging a few words with Mr. Wilder about a farming measure being considered in a committee.

Then Charlie literally swept her off her feet. She came down on her tip-toes out in the middle of the floor. They danced skillfully together, and she felt safe and snug in his arms, pleased that he held her close.

He momentarily pushed her away to look at her. "I hope you didn't ask what he eats for dinner."

She laughed. "No, and I'm mighty glad of it."

"His dad's been a pillar of the local GOP for decades; now he's following those footsteps."

"His wife is here. He seemed a little jiggy about that, dancing with me."

"Uh-huh. Well, that's 'cuz you're a showstopper."

They stopped talking, Mae aware of the clean scent of Charlie's suit and another deeper scent she wanted to get closer to. She felt she could say anything to him. He knew about Oberon—well not the details, but he knew much more than anyone else did. Despite that, he'd said she had an innate respectability. Oh, how she loved that! And he appreciated her good grammar. The nuns had been right. Grammar was important. Charlie had started out on a farm but was already in a high place and on his way to greater heights. Anyone could see that.

∿

The full moon played peek-a-boo through the tree branches as the open carriage rolled along with the two men and Mae. She was falling asleep from the clip clop, clip clop of the horse. It had always been so. As a little girl when they'd been to town and Daddy drove the team back at night, the steady hoof beats always put her to sleep. Now her eyelids seemed to weigh five pounds each. If it hadn't been for the chill air keeping her awake, she would have collapsed on Charlie's shoulder—only an inch away. She wished she'd bought a coat or a cape, this being the middle of the night in mid-September.

At the Golden Eagle Hotel, Assemblyman Lubeck stepped down and Charlie and Mae bade him good night. The driver turned the carriage around and headed up J and then over to L toward the boardinghouse on 18th. Needing to know what would happen next, Mae shook off her drowsiness. "Do you mind if I ask about your plans for me?"

"Mmm. Let's see. How about I scout around for a day or two, then come over and lay out the possibilities. You're a comely girl, and you'll get your pick of the legislators."

"Mr. Lubeck's a gentleman. I don't mind going with him. Anytime."

He slipped his arm off the back of the buggy seat, down for a moment around her shoulders, gave her a squeeze, and then put it back. "Would you have breakfast with me on Sunday?"

She was about to say yes, but he twisted toward her. "No wait, now that I think of it, I've got to see a man in Rio Vista. We could eat breakfast on the boat and you could go down the river with me. Spend the day. Would you like that?"

She tried not to respond too fast. "Yes, that would be nice." *Divine.*

On the porch, with Mrs. Svensen's big shadow moving behind the curtain of the kitchen window, Charlie started to kiss her on the lips.

Gently she pulled away. This was confusing, so soon after Oberon, and with a man who arranged dates for her with other men. In the shadows of the trees she thought she could feel him asking a silent question.

His voice sounded soft, uncertain. "Well then, good night." Rapping loudly on the door in the Morse code he and Mrs. Svensen had worked out, he trotted down the steps and his dark form boarded the black carriage.

The door rattled, Mrs. Svensen working her key in the hole. An owl above the house hooted in slow triplets. The struggle to unlock the door intensified, accompanied by hushed Swedish curses.

A bad thought struck Mae in the stomach. Maybe Charlie wouldn't come for her on Sunday. He might have taken her rejection of his kiss to mean more than it did. Before he left, she should have told him again that she wanted to go on the boat.

Mrs. Svensen's hoarse screech came through the door, "I tink dis iss da bad key. You vait. I go look."

"I'll wait," Mae called back. Of course she'd wait—a stupid thing to say. She needed to visit the water closet. Waiting made it worse.

She could barely see the moving lamps from the carriage about three blocks down the road. Darkness had fallen around her like a shroud. She felt a chill, and in her heart a discordant sense of having upset Charlie.

Then came the prickly sensation of being watched.

42

Mae looked over her shoulder as she stepped into the house, the light from Mrs. Svensen's lantern slicing the darkness. The closing door cut it off, but in that brief light the ghost of what had been standing on the other side of the street stayed in her mind like delayed photography—two long columns of shiny buttons on a police coat and long hair under the hat.

"He's there!" she said aloud.

Mrs. Svensen, who had been quick-stepping toward the staircase, stopped and turned toward Mae, the lamp lighting the broad landscape of her face. "Who?"

"Oberon Jones."

"He follow you?"

"Yes. Or maybe he's watching this house all the time."

"Come, I take you in's bett. Please, qviet in da stairs. People sleep."

"But he's out there! He'll see where the light goes and break into my room!"

"Awk no, on dat high floor." Mrs. Svensen nodded for Mae to lead up the stairs.

Her heartbeat, pounding throughout her body, shook her voice. "If he can't get in up there then he'll come through a window down here and sneak upstairs. I'll be a goner." *Mrs. Swensen can't understand. She wasn't chained up by him. Nobody can understand. Charlie says she'll call the state police, but by the time they get here I'll be in the Black Mariah on the way to my death.*

She didn't budge. "Couldn't I sleep in your room?"

"Mae, dat man haff many girls. Vhat he vant vit you? Huh?"

A twisted love for me, I think, but you wouldn't understand. "I know him. It's the way he is. Please. He's out there. Tomorrow I'll talk to Charlie. Maybe he'll hide me in a different house."

The stubborn creases on Mrs. Svensen's face deepened. "Charlie's ladies dey stay here vit me, at my place. Understand? Charlie and I, ve do business. No udder place for you. You be safe in da room. You see."

"No. I can't sleep in that room. Besides, I can't unbutton my dress."

"I do dat in your room. Come, ve go up."

"Please, in your room. I'll get the pillow seats from the davenport and lay them out on the floor to sleep on. No need for sheets. Please, Mrs. Svensen. Just tonight."

"Awk no. Go upstairs."

"Then I'll come down and sleep in the water closet. I can lock it." It had a sliding bar on the door.

The good woman looked almost mean. "Oh vhat in Gott! One night only." Uttering the same curse she'd used when the key wouldn't work, she turned and led Mae to a downstairs room. "Stand back to da light," she ordered, setting the lamp on a small table.

Lamplight would pass through the ruffled curtains, which had been pulled across the windows. Doubtless the shadows of two women, one unbuttoning the gown of the other, could be seen. "When you get done," Mae said in a tone as pleasant as she could muster, "I'll take off the gown and go out like I'm headed upstairs, but I'll be gathering pillows. I'll crawl back here so he can't see my shadow through the windows." *But first I'll use the water closet.*

⌒

Mrs. Svensen snored like a steam engine, rumbling and whistling. It prevented Mae from detecting soft sounds. Her ears ached from listening for a man sneaking through a window. The horsehair sofa pillows kept moving apart, leaving an uneven surface, and stiff hairs poked through her drawers and camisole. Mrs. Svensen had given her a woolen blanket, which also felt scratchy. But uncomfortable as she was, she felt better here, next to this big strong lady, than alone in her room. And her hand never left the baseball bat Mrs. Svensen had fished from under her bed.

In the early morning light, the proprietress rolled out of bed. With her up and banging around the kitchen, Mae finally slept soundly for a little while.

"Awk zo?"

Mae opened her eyes to the towering landlady above her, elbows akimbo.

"Ve haff vaffles and coffee and runny eggs, yust as my girls like dem."

"I'm coming," Mae groaned, sitting up. *Runny eggs?*

The thought triggered an upheaval in her stomach. She raced to the water closet just ahead of the vomit. Fortunately, no men boarded in this house, and only Rowena saw her lurch down the hall in her bloomers.

She felt weak climbing the stairs to get into her everyday frock, and weak coming down to sit at the table. Covertly she glanced around at the other girls and Mrs. Svensen, who stood at the stove looking at her, spatula in hand. What had made her sick that suddenly? She recalled the sudden vomiting at the races, and yet she didn't feel feverish, as she would with the grippe.

Rowena, one of the girls rising from the table, raised her brows at Mae.

"And now eggs," declared Mrs. Svensen.

"No. No runny eggs," Mae said. "Just half a waffle and coffee with milk."

"You be pale. You be avake in da night. You need food." She slapped a stack of waffles on the plate and topped it off with two jiggling eggs.

Again Mae ran for the water closet.

❧

In the parlor, with the pillows restored to the davenport and all the other girls out of the house, Mrs. Svensen bade Mae sit opposite her. "And now," she said, "I tink you haff a baby in you. Ve cannot haff you in da house no more. You tell dat to Charlie Rogue. I tell him alzo."

"Oh no, I'm not pregnant." It simply couldn't be true, what she feared would happen.

The woman narrowed a very blue eye. "You tink I not see dis many times? Huh? Girl coming in here, running to vomit like dat? Girls vhat be wit men."

"But you're mistaken. I just *can't* be pregnant!"

"You bleed in da last munt?"

Mae had to think what she was talking about, and then think about the answer. She'd never paid attention to what day her curses were supposed to start. And it seemed too cruel that this would happen just when she'd finally slipped from Oberon's clutches—a baby of *his*. Just when she had a chance with Charlie. *Charlie!* She needed to tell him she still wanted to go with him on Sunday. And now she had to get to him before Mrs. Svensen did.

"I'll talk to him," Mae said. "Please, I want to be the first to tell him. I'll go now and find him."

❧

Mrs. Svensen's telephone was an enemy spy that could get to Charlie in a few seconds, while Mae had to hurry the whole seven blocks out of breath. She kept an eye on the many people on the sidewalks and in the streetcars to be sure Oberon wasn't there. He wasn't—at least not that she could see.

At the Capitol, a boy was dispatched to learn of Charlie's whereabouts. Waiting in the office of the Speaker of the Assembly, Mae noticed that the building was in disarray—men installing electric lights alongside the gaslights. "In case they don't work right," said the secretary behind the desk. "No," he said in response to Mae's question, "Don't believe I've heard of electricity from a dam. This incandescent system will run on a generator in the basement."

The boy came back out of breath. He reported to the secretary, whose face took on a hint of smugness though he spoke with professional courtesy. "He's on the sixth floor just now. Go up the elevator, or the stairs at the end of the hall, other side of the rotunda. At the top take a right. It'll be a couple of doors down. Agriculture Committee Office."

Thanking him, she walked through the high-domed rotunda on a floor that appeared to be tile but which softened the echo of her footsteps. In the center of the rotunda floor a concrete Grecian lady of heroic proportions sat enthroned, the word "Eureka" on her crown and gold-panning equipment and a grizzly bear strewn about her.

About a dozen men were waiting for the lift. She passed by to the beautiful curving staircase. A painting of Governor Markham hung on the wall at the bottom step, giving her a surge of pride to have met him personally. She climbed up and up, looking at paintings of former governors on the wall, and she continued upward long past the very first governor.

In the committee office Charlie stood in the back of the room over a man at a desk. The man at the front desk asked how he could help her, but before she could answer, Charlie came up and took her out in the hall. He looked at her closely. "What are you doing here?"

Out of breath from all the stairs she said, "I've got so much to say."

"Can it wait? I'll take you to noon dinner." He smiled with an air of distracted puzzlement. He wouldn't be wondering why she was there if Mrs. Svensen had called him on her telephone, and that much was a relief.

Mae felt a need to lie down. She felt faint, having had no breakfast and hardly any sleep. Not about to return to the boardinghouse without assurance that she could stay there, she blurted it all out quickly. "I *do* want to go with you on the boat on Sunday. Mrs. Svensen wants to kick me out, and I saw Oberon watching me last night after you left." Each part of her message deepened his frown, and she hoped he wouldn't consider her a troublemaker.

"Stay here a minute," he said. He went back and, just out of earshot, exchanged words with the secretary. Returning, he ushered her with a hand on her back toward a small door. On the other side of it, she found herself in a very narrow, curving hallway obviously not for public use. Charlie was too tall for it and had to walk with his head and shoulders down. They went

through another small door and stepped into the open air on a narrow balcony overlooking an expanse of treetops and rooftops.

"Where are we?" The bird's-eye view disoriented her.

"We're just outside the dome. Workmen use this to get up there and polish
the copper. I gotta go to a hearing in a couple of minutes. Speak up. What's
wrong at the boardinghouse?"

"Mrs. Svensen thinks I'm with child, says I have to leave her house because of it.

"Are you? Pregnant, I mean?"

Spoken by a man, that word caused heat to rise in her face. Such things
were not discussed between the sexes. Nearly whispering, "I hope not." She
looked at the toes of her black shoes.

"What do you mean, hope?"

"It just couldn't be!" She felt the prickle of tears behind her eyes. He would
believe she *was* pregnant, and yet he was looking at her kindly. Something
about that brought on the full flood, and she found herself bawling like a baby,
the wide streets and stately houses below awash through her tears.

"Now, now," he said pulling a handkerchief from his pocket, dabbing it
on her cheek, "Have you had... indications?"

"I don't know what the indications are," she sobbed.

A few moments passed between them, in which her entire life hung on a
thread. Then slowly, gently, he pulled her to him and patted her on the back
with the fingers of one hand. She laid her cheek against his suit jacket, and
then hugged him, needing him, a friendly man in a position of authority who
had said she was his responsibility.

His voice came from his chest, amplified as from a cello box. "I'll come
for you on Sunday at seven in the morning. By then things might be clearer.
In any case, we'll have a good time on the boat."

☙

Mrs. Svensen acquiesced to Charlie's reassurance that he would continue
to pay Mae's board and room for at least the next couple of weeks. With a
state trooper watching the house day and night she felt a little safer. She'd
also talked to Rowena, who told her that pregnant women feel nauseous and
emotional from the start.

But on Sunday morning Mae felt so healthy and happy in every way to
be spending the day with Charlie that she seriously doubted that she could
be pregnant. In a clear blue sky the early sun flashed through yellow cottonwoods along the shore, and the paddle-wheeler churned a wide froth in the
brown Sacramento River.

In his usual dark suit, white shirt, bow tie and straw hat, Charlie smiled
a lot and behaved as though he was there for a good time, not for business
with a man in Rio Vista or serious talk with her. That suited her just fine. They

climbed to the third deck to view the delta and the peak of Mount Diablo looming before them. Upon the flat land worked large groups of Chinamen in pointed straw hats—maybe a hundred in each group, some barely visible in the distance, one gang quite near to the boat. They were digging and piling dirt in high mounds.

"Eradicating the tules," Charlie explained. "The delta is being reclaimed for agriculture. Those tough tulares have to be dug out by the roots, along with layers and layers of dead roots below. It's extremely hard work."

Mae saw vast stretches of the marsh grass that hadn't yet been eliminated. "Looks like they hire all Chinamen for this work."

"Yup. They're good workers, and Americans won't do this kind of work."

That puzzled her. "With so many men unemployed I'd think lots of American men and boys would jump at the chance. My brother Emmett would. And he's strong from farm work."

Charlie smiled at her in his cozy way, like they were the only people in the world, and then his gaze went back to the piling of dirt. "You've hit on a touchy subject. A delegation of landowners recently went to Washington D.C. to testify before a congressional committee. They had to answer the very question you asked—why not American workers?"

She shot him a teasing, "So how did they answer?"

"Congressmen are like most people in this country. They think hoards of yellow men are driving down the cost of labor and causing this economic panic, but that's not actually the case." He rested his forearms on the railing, clasping his hands out over the water and easing his heels back—both of them watching the men moving around with wheelbarrows. "Congressmen from other states brought figures. It turns out that these men from China are paid higher hourly wages here in the delta than farm laborers in many states, a dollar an hour, almost twice as much as white laborers in the Midwest. But you see, they're worth it, because the landowner doesn't have to deal with each man individually. A China boss oversees everything. There are lower level bosses too, but the big boss is paid a lump sum. He distributes the money. The landowner gets no grief. The China boss also sees to it that the men are housed, and sick or injured men are treated. They've got top-notch medicine, and they have group kitchens with Chinese cooks. They're *organized*."

"American men could organize like that."

Charlie shook his head and then thrust out his lower jaw, moving it back and forth as though measuring the evenness of his teeth. The light spray from the paddle of the fast vessel delighted her.

He finally said. "American men are independent cusses. They don't want anybody between them and their money. They want to come and go as they please. Some just want to earn enough money for their next bash. They pound on the door at night complaining about things or demanding severance pay.

A hundred men doing that is untenable. Compare that to a simple payment at the end of the job, and a respectful bow and thank you from the labor boss. If the landowner has to be in D.C., the work still gets done—and done right too. That's worth a lot of money."

Mae loved talking to Charlie like this. It helped push the jitters about the other concern out of her mind. "If the work is so difficult, why don't the Chinamen quit?"

His shoulders moved. "They do quit, but the owners don't need to know about it. China bosses replace the workers. Where they come from and who pays their passage to this country is the business of the Chinese companies in San Francisco, the tongs."

"I thought Chinese people weren't allowed in the U.S. any more."

"Women and children are excluded. The law makes allowance for employers to hire the men, and we're trying to keep it that way. The farmers get blamed and they're called un-American for hiring the best labor available. I'm going to talk to one such man today. He thinks the Exclusion Act should be broadened to let more labor in."

"How do you know so much about this?"

"It's my work. Truth be told, I'm involved in everything controversial in this state."

They were churning past a tall white mansion with a landing flanked by perfectly round little trees in fancy pedestal pots. Behind the house she made out rows of Chinamen bent over a harvest and a pair of work horses hauling a load of full gunnysacks toward the dock. On the dock Chinamen were loading a barge, passing sacks from man to man.

"That farmer," Charlie said with a nod to the white man standing on the barge, "owns that steamer. He gets his crops to San Francisco without paying the railroad. His family goes along for the outing." He smiled over at Mae. "Their front yard's the river."

"Sounds nice."

"Speaking of nice," he said straightening to his full height, "My stomach's getting a bit controversial. Isn't that bacon and johnnycakes I'm smelling?"

The whiff of bacon grease almost undid her. But, fiercely determined not to be pregnant, she willed her stomach to stay put.

Over breakfast in the downstairs dining room, Charlie told her, "Most girls don't give a hoot about farm labor. You're a curious little lady, aren't you?"

Whatever interested Charlie interested Mae, but she couldn't say that. "You're more fun to listen to than most people."

Carefully he poured syrup from a tiny pitcher. "Any more thoughts about, uh, your condition?" He didn't look at her.

Neither did she look at him, but continued cutting her dry pancake into squares. "No."

"Have you calendar evidence to the contrary?" He forked a piece of dripping hotcake into his mouth, chewing as he gazed out the window at the spray of water and the trees along the shore.

"No." A little word quickly spoken, yet so heavily freighted. She had studied the calendar and seen that this vacation from the curse had indeed lasted too long.

In silence they finished eating, Mae guessing that he had talked to Mrs. Svensen about her vomiting. Unhappily, she nibbled another dry square of her hotcake.

He arranged the knife and fork on his plate, and then took a sip of coffee. "Mae, there are ways of handling this."

"What do you mean?"

"Ridding you of the condition."

Looking into his brown eyes, she grasped his meaning. He'd done this before. It was part of his work.

He leaned forward, placing his forearms on the ridge that kept the dishes on the table in rough water. His brows were slightly elevated, his voice matter-of-fact. "You see, I'm acquainted with knowledgeable people."

43

Two weeks after the boat ride with Charlie, she left the boardinghouse clutching the address Charlie had given her. Rowena walked with her. Mae barely noticed the dawn of another cloudless day or the few people out and about. She might as well have been walking a plank in the middle of the ocean. Whispers from way back rasped in her ears: Suzie dead at the hands of an abortionist, Charlotte giving away her newborn, girls returning to school with the life knocked out of them.

Disguised by a hair mustache glued to her upper lip, Mae wore the trousers and shirt left by Mrs. Svensen's son, her hair tucked up under an old pork-pie cap. This way she was less likely to attract Oberon's attention—if he were abroad this early. And Charlie had insisted she dress like a man. The abortionist had nearly refused to do it this time, claiming church people were spying on him. He didn't want publicity, and neither did Charlie.

"You'll be all right," Rowena said. "Just remember, it'll get over with fast." Her sister had gone through this.

"How do *you* keep from getting pregnant?" Mae asked.

"Not doing it."

"Don't the men want you to?"

"Yeah, but I don't let 'em."

"Because of what your sister said about this?"

They crossed 11ᵗʰ Street in silence.

Yes.

Rowena repeated. "It'll get over with fast. Don't worry."

At 3ʳᵈ and N, Rowena knocked on a door with a big white tooth painted on an otherwise blackened window. Mae felt short of breath. Perhaps the Nipponese warriors Sister Delphine had told the class about felt this way when they raised the knife to disembowel themselves. She was entrusting her life to a man of unknown abilities intent on slicing up her insides. Dizziness came and went.

A young man with frozen waves of fiery red hair opened the door. Mae's mind froze too. Rowena introduced her as Mel Johnson, who had an appointment with Doctor Rudi.

The red-haired man walked them through one room and then another. Sunlight from the street glowed through the pulled-down blinds of two windows, coloring the walls of the room sulfur. The empty room imprinted her mind like a ghastly tintype, possibly the last she'd ever see of the world. No picture hung on the walls. The room was bare except for a line of white plaster along one wall where the tops of four ladder-back chairs had scuffed it over a long period of time.

"Take a seat," the man said, giving no hint of being wise to the reason for their visit.

Lowering herself on the edge of a chair, Mae had the sense that she was made of spring-loaded parts that might at any moment catapult her through the window into the street. Rowena claimed the chair at the end of the line, picked a magazine off the floor, and wiggled herself into the chair like a nesting hen.

ꙮ

About an hour passed, judging from the shift of sunlight under the blinds. Why did it take so long? Mae wondered. Maybe testing to be sure no one had followed. Or giving her time to change her mind. By now her spine had reached the chair back. On the folded-back page of the magazine, she could see that Rowena was reading about Lillie Langtry. With all her men, how did that woman keep from getting pregnant? How had she gone to a strange city and made herself a famous actress without falling into a trap?

No one else entered the dim room. Only muffled street sounds could be heard. Mae continued to wait for the violence that could end her life, waiting because a truth had burned itself on her brain: She might as well be dead as to swell up with Oberon's baby and bring it to light in some dirty ally or back with the folks and Farley.

Rowena's quiet voice made her jump. "Gotta go now. Sorry. They must be seein' other people. Don't worry, nuthin'll go wrong." She dropped the magazine on the chair and left.

It seemed something had already gone wrong. But Mae waited. After what seemed another hour in that empty room her mind sank down to where she hadn't wanted it to go—imagining the thing inside her as a baby. *No*, she reminded herself. *It is nothing but a tiny clot in my blood. It is a parasite and I won't sacrifice my life for it.*

And this. In a way it seemed she was already dead, waiting with all the other tortured souls in purgatory, each in a separate room, waiting forever. But then she would stiffen as she realized that the butchery hadn't even started. *Any minute now.*

As the time crawled she revisited alternatives she'd gone over a thousand times—giving it up, never knowing whether it was adopted or leading the sad life of an orphan. As for herself, she couldn't imagine life in the gutter with a bastard child, making a living like Helen did with the child in the same room, and then giving it to a nunnery when it got old enough to understand. By then she'd love the child, of that she was certain. Sending it away would about kill her, and the child would be forever saddened by its mother giving it away. Try as she might, she couldn't force that kind of life to take shape in her mind. She was meant to be a respectable woman, maybe a famous one if she had a chance. The purpose of being in this room was to give herself that chance. Despite Rowena's assurances, there would be horrible pain and likely death, she was certain. At times she thought she should just get up and go kill herself. Unmarried pregnant girls did that all the time. But why do that difficult thing by herself when the man who was supposed to show up could do it for her? If he didn't come, she could always kill herself later. So she stayed on the chair.

Her mind circled around to the hope that she would survive. She might even come out whole like Rowena's sister. Sure, most men didn't want a used woman, and this operation would surely manifest itself to a husband. Men would fault her no matter what she said, but how to get around that problem *did* take shape in her mind. She had a way with men. She could talk to the one she would marry and get him to forgive her. She'd just have an extra hurdle to jump, compared with other brides. So there was some hope of a decent life, if she went through with this. And so she stayed in the chair.

The doorknob turned, startling her. A woman in a white nurse's cap stuck her head in saying, "Follow me."

Mae's heart flopped like fish on shore. Standing, she staggered in a swirl of darkness as knives flashed in her mind. She walked on shaky legs. "Oh God," she mouthed. "I'm a sinner. Save me. Let me live. I'll be good. I'll go to Mass. I'll have other children when I get married. I'll raise them right."

It seemed she was headed straight to hell as she followed the ghostly uniform through an unlit hall and down a steep dark staircase. Halfway down, the woman turned around and hissed, "You're a baby killer, and I'm helping 'cause

I need the work to feed my kids." The ghost continued to descend the stairs.

Something clenched in Mae's chest, making it hard to breathe. From the distant world above came the faint clanging of a fire truck, while with each downward step the roar of an engine grew louder, and the temperature rose, evincing her proximity to hell.

At the old first floor of the building she entered a hot room brightly lit by a hissing, sparking electric light—a wide Devil's eye glaring down on a vase of wilting flowers atop an oak cabinet. The room had been an office before the streets were filled with dirt. Dry packed earth pressed against the glass, just what a person buried alive would see from one of those little windows at eye level in expensive coffins.

"I'm Doctor Rudi," said a long-faced man with vertical creases down his cheeks. Standing near the cabinet in a checkered shirt and stained leather apron, he appraised her, a man who could as well have been a blacksmith or saddle maker. He held out a long hairy hand. "I get paid first."

Mae fumbled in the pocket of her trousers and handed him the money Charlie had given her. He counted out the gold pieces and then, moving the heavy apron aside, put them in his trouser pocket.

"Now, tell me why you want an abortion."

"He, that is the man, made me do it. It wasn't my faul—"

Wearily, "I've heard it all a hundred times. Just answer this question: Will he marry you?"

"I won't marry him."

"Well then, you should."

Oh God, must I explain everything? "He's a terrible man. He'll kill me."

"If you go through with this?"

"No, if he finds me. I ran away from him." She steeled herself against a question about Oberon's identity. For all she knew, Dr. Rudi did business with him.

He folded his arms. "How long since your last monthly?"

"Maybe two months."

"Maybe!" He lowered his arms and scowled at her. "I asked, how many weeks?"

"I-I'm sorry, I don't know. I don't keep track. I mean when things are normal I never know how much time between—"

He rolled his eyes. Pointing to the dark corner of the room where the generator roared, he said, "Go to the bucket over there and empty your bladder and everything else."

Timidly, "Isn't there a water closet in the building?"

He sighed like he had to repeat this time after time. "When this floor was built, people used outhouses."

She did as told, unstable on her bent knees and almost too embarrassed and afraid to make water. Meanwhile the nurse unfolded the oak cabinet piece by piece, transforming it into a short narrow table with oak slabs that pulled out from under the tabletop, obviously leg supports. At the other end she pulled up a back piece at an elevated angle with a wrought iron brace holding up a flat slab, perhaps a headrest. When Mae returned, the woman was adjusting the angle of the headrest by turning a wing nut.

"Take off everything from the waist down," Rudi said, "except your shoes."

"Everything?"

"Well, unless you expect me to cut through your bloomers."

All modesty had flown. Beneath the hissing light she unlaced and removed her shoes, dropped her trousers and bloomers, and then put the shoes back on the extremities of her naked legs, not lacing them. The man and woman watched, the latter giving her the evil eye as she stood in front of a cabinet of shelves enclosed by etched glass.

The man patted the table. "Get up here and lie down with your heels in the stirrups."

The varnished leg slabs hung straight down from the table like the wide trouser legs of a monstrous paper doll with iron toes jutting out to hold the patients' feet. But if she lay down on the table with her knees at table's end, her legs would dangle down, nowhere near long enough to reach the foot holders. Confused, she looked at the man's hard face, and then climbed on the table and lay down—knees over the end of the table, untied shoes dangling, and her head halfway up the table.

With a look of extreme disgust, Doctor Rudi stepped to the end of the table and yanked her roughly toward him so her privates were at the edge of the table. He then seized her shoes and jammed the heels into the ornate iron loops that jutted at right angles from the end of the table—the loops she'd thought were towel holders. Lying like that, knees akimbo, legs far apart, she trembled with the effort to close her thighs. To be seen like this by these people under this intense light brought tears to her eyes, until a bit of comfort came with the thought that she would soon be dead and not embarrassed anymore.

Standing between her legs, he poked and prodded her belly, and then held out a hand while the woman anointed it with oil. Mae could see this because the slab under her back angled slightly upward. He folded his thumb in and pushed his long fingers inside her, pressing on her belly with the outside hand. It hurt. Thinking maybe he wouldn't cut her open after all, she braced for a killing blow.

"Feels like about two months all right." He drew out his hand and wiped it on a towel supplied by the woman, telling her, "Bring the laudanum." At least there would be pain relief. From under the etched glass, the woman retrieved a dark blue bottle. He poured a small amount into a tiny metal cup and handed it to Mae. "Swallow that and stay here. It'll be about ten minutes. You can take your feet down."

Ten minutes for the parasite to live. Eyes shut against the harsh light, she forced herself to remember, while she still could, something good about her life. Running across the young green wheat in Iowa. She'd been about eight that first time she went with Emmett and Farley to catch the train. Willows along the creek had been heavy with silver pussies. The engineer waved when he saw them; the train slowed. They ran to it, the boys gauging the speed as the cars screeched past. Farley jumped first, and then Emmett. Both boys were on the caboose platform—Farley's hair blowing like an orange flag in the wind, Emmett's dark hair over his face as he leaned forward beckoning Mae. Scared nearly to death but not about to be left behind, Mae ran and leaped— a heart-stopping flight between earth and train. But she did not fall, was not crushed beneath the iron wheels. She felt a thrill to have saved herself with her speed and nimbleness. Now she lay waiting for the hard blow or the knife that would return her life to her, or take it all away.

"All right," said Rudi. "Feet back in."

She was too slow for him. Again he shoved her heels into the iron holders. The nurse was arraging strange instruments on a small table that she'd set near him. He invaded her with cold metal. Quickly he did something to widen the thing until she hurt from the stretching. Leaving it there, he picked another instrument from the tray. His thrust made her cry out.

He came around the table, bent down eyeball to eyeball and enunciated: "You are to make no noise. None. People could be on the other side of those walls." He jabbed a tobacco-stained finger in the direction of the street. "I can't chloroform you or give you more laudanum because I need you to walk out of here when I'm done. Walk, not stagger." He pointed that finger at her mustache, "No screaming. Is that clear?"

"I'm sorry. It just came out."

"Well *stop* it from coming out!" He cranked the back support down so she lay flat, and returned to her other end.

She couldn't see what he put into her. It stabbed through to her stomach, or so it seemed. He then manipulated something deep inside her, causing a bright pain to burn hotter. She bit her lip, knowing this couldn't go on much longer or she would scream. The pain ratcheted up and up until finally it paused where it was and stayed. Her heart beat faster, loud in her ears. Neck craned to see what he was doing, she saw him feeding a rubber hose into her like the ones used to inflate bicycle tires. He bumped around and then shoved so hard she felt it up to her tongue. She stared into the bright, hissing light, such pain never before imagined, yet clenched her teeth and made no sound. Perspiration ran down her head and stung her eyes. She shut them tightly, holding her breath to prevent any movement that would make the pain worse.

"Okay," he said.

She assumed it was over.

But something else started. She opened her eyes to see the woman's white cap bobbing in and out of view. Something wheezed in rhythm. The tire pump. They were blowing her up! A new pain, not quite as intense as what had preceded it. She squeezed her eyes shut and endured it, every muscle rigid. The persistent pumping sharpened the pain. *The wages of sin.*

It'll get over with fast, Rowena had said. But no. She was about to explode and they stood in relaxed poses staring at the wall and shifting on their feet as though weary of this. And then he began to scrape. Each abrasion went down to her toes and up into her ears. Methodically he grated the inner flesh of her, not moving to new places but continuing upon the same wounds. She couldn't stanch the moans.

He was at her face, eyes fierce. "Silence!" His jaw worked beneath the stubble, something bloody in his hand. Welcoming the pause in pain, she tried to tell him she had made only a quiet sound that couldn't be heard over the generator, but her mouth wouldn't work.

He went back to scraping. Blood rushed to her head and filled it like a stretched balloon. Her heart was in there too, drumming *accelerando*, each beat intensifying the sick pressure in her ears. She opened her mouth to breathe.

He was there again, at her ear. "Stop screaming!"

She worked to form words. "I… didn't…"

"You *was* screaming. SHUT UP or I'll gag you."

He went back to scraping, and she started to lose herself. Her heart couldn't go on at this rate, she knew, and her eyes felt bugged out, and yet he scraped on and on. Her entire insides would be gone. Her heart would burst and the blood would explode from her eyes.

Now he was holding one of her eyes open, looking in. She briefly looked back and then let her eye roll up where it wanted to go. She smelled his rotten breath. Her wrist seemed to be in his hand. Next would come somebody saying, *She's a goner.*

More scraping. This time her swollen head was dark and weak as it got sucked into the actual pumping of her heart, one monstrous heart screaming to live.

"Wake up," a male voice ordered. Hands slapped her cheeks.

Am I alive? She opened her eyes and saw the long, creased face, the dark eyes.

"You doin' more?"

"No. I'm done."

Alive.

Back between her legs he removed the metal from her insides and bent over so she couldn't see him. He straightened up with a basin of something heavy and carried it to the bucket. The loud slosh as he poured it into the bucket told her it was gone. Her belly was still in pain.

The man went to the water pump on the countertop. She could see brown water splash into the basin. He returned and wiped her thighs with a wet towel. Pushing something between her legs, he took her heels from the stirrups and told her to sit up.

"Hold the rags," he ordered, and then pulled her under-drawers up past her knees. Bright red blood on his apron was all she could see as he helped her to the floor. Dizzy in the heat of the sparking light, she nearly fell, but clutched a stirrup. Meanwhile he secured the drawers to her waist with twine, looping it around her groin so the rags stayed in place, and tied it off.

When she tried to walk, the floor was slippery with blood and her feet nearly went out from under her. He helped her away from the table. The woman, without looking at her, handed her the trousers and hat and then took the bloody instruments to the sink.

Mae stepped out of her shoes to get the trousers on, fumbling with the buttons like a palsied old man. With her insides in fragile suspension, she feared bending down to lace and tie her shoes—her innards might run out—so she left the laces untied. The woman set the washed instruments aside and began pumping water onto a mop.

"Go out this way," Rudi said, opening the door, different from the one she'd entered by. "And don't forget, you're a criminal, as guilty as I am for this. Don't talk to anyone about it. Now git. And be quick about it."

Pushing her hair up under the cap, Mae proceeded slowly through the door into a dark underground tunnel that might have been an alley before the streets were raised.

"Go about fifty yards," he said to her back. "There'll be a turn to the left. Don't take it. Keep going to the next turn and then go right, then left. It'll get darker. You'll see boards holding up the ceiling. That's where it goes under the road. Go up the stairs on the other side and you're on your way out. And remember, keep quiet."

As the door was shutting she caught a glimpse of the woman hastily mopping her blood off the floor.

It was dark with a little light far ahead. She put out a hand and felt rough brick on one side of the alley-tunnel. A warm sensation was soaking through her trousers despite the rags. She walked slowly, barely breathing, testing her new life like a hatchling walking into unknown dangers. This was the underground labyrinth from which the worst evils of Sacramento operated.

Gaslight spilled out some of the smudged windows. At the end of what might have been a block, she turned left into another dim corridor, and then right. Or maybe…?

She had forgotten the directions! Turning back to ask Dr. Rudi to repeat them, she bumped into a wall that couldn't have been thrown up in the last few minutes. Feeling with her hands she found the bulging mortar between the bricks to be hard and dry. The reek of old urine stung her nose in that frightening dead-end. She backed away, holding her breath. A sooty lantern leaked light through a jagged break in a window that otherwise would have been too dark to see through. It barely illuminated a tiny room and a ragged little man lying barefoot on a mattress sucking a tube. He held its attached ear-like bowl over the lantern, just as Oberon had done. With her tired heart pounding she turned down another tunnel. Dimly through other sooty windows she saw more dens, each with a similar occupant. An unearthly cry pierced the murky atmosphere. A banshee coming after her!

She hurried the opposite direction as fast as her delicate steps would take her. Suddenly she came face to face with a chalk drawing of a dog-like animal with pointed ears. It smiled at her with insolent lips and lolling tongue. Frightened and growing cold, she knew she was completely lost.

44

Coyote warbles with amusement at Mae's troubles.

"She had nobody to help her," I remind him. "No family."

"Ha!" he barks, "She had a big family. She brought her troubles on herself." Nosing around in circles to lie down the opposite way, he adds, "She went hunting on her own as soon as she could wobble out of the den. She got caught is all." He flops down and rips out another howl, this one long and musical—he isn't called Ki-yoo for nothing.

Mae speaks in a low voice. "That was you on that wall, wasn't it?"

Coyote lifts his muzzle. "I am a shape shifter."

✳✸

In the musty underground she watched a lantern approach but hadn't the strength to hide. Having wandered too long in a futile search for a way out, she slouched on the half-barrel and kept her face behind the hat brim. A little gray cat had crept out from behind a crate, but skittered away as the shadowy figure stopped before Mae.

"Me Ah Chin Chow. Wanee smoke? Wanee wheeksy?"

She shook her head.

"Wanee pray card? Goo' game. You wanee—"

"No, I'm just resting." Her deepest voice.

"Unnersan. You boy. Wanee grrra. Ah Chin ga rotsa grrra."

"No."

"Wanee boy? Rotsa boy—"

"No, but please show me the way out of here, up to Sacramento." Peeking at him, she pointed up to whatever kept the road and sidewalk from crashing down.

"Aahhh." He thrust a hand before her nose, rubbing thumb on fingers. "Wahn dolla."

She moved her head from side to side. "No money."

"You sick? Wanee meh-cin. China docta?"

Earlier she'd been thirsty but now felt only a sleepy weakness.

"Famree?" He pointed upward.

Family. "Yes," she lied. Charlie would wonder where she was. The thought brought tears. He wouldn't know if she was alive. "I can't find my way up to the streets." Head down, she couldn't stop the silly tears. She hadn't the brains to listen to directions.

He beckoned.

Before she knew what was happening, he pulled her up and was helping her walk. After a few steps he stopped, sniffed, looked at her brown trousers, but then continued. She knew she'd lost a lot of blood—the trousers felt wet and sticky, and she hadn't eaten since that half slice of toast in Mrs. Svensen's kitchen. Maybe that's why she felt weak as a—

∽

Startled to wakefulness, she had no memory of this dim room with a garlic smell. She fingered the edge of the little bed—canvas, a cot, like in one of the opium dens. Fear buzzed down her arms to the backs of her hands. A sooty lantern stood on a small table beside her cap, illuminating a Chinese girl on a poster. Wearing little, the girl looked at Mae with the sidelong tease Mae had used on young men. A lifetime ago, it seemed.

She heard a shuffling sound. It took all her strength to lift her head and twist against the pain in her abdomen, but she caught a glimpse of the Chinaman. He stood in a shelved alcove behind her. The lantern didn't reach all the corners of the room, but it appeared that she was alone with him. She knew she wouldn't be able to run. Once before she'd been captured. It had happened again.

Suddenly a little tug from behind on her hair. The man came around the cot and touched her breast lightly—through the man's shirt and the tight binding. "You no boy. You grra."

Oh God, help me!

"You famree?" It was a question as he pointed upward.

"Charlie Rogue is my brother. He works in the Capitol Building." That name and place had shielded her from Oberon. She prayed it would work here too.

"Ah Cholly Lo!" A smile bunched his cheeks. "Ah Chin Chow bling soup."

He knew him! That would help. Ah Chin Chow was in the alcove clanking a stove lid and rattling dishes when she noticed the same gray cat eyeing her through a grimy windowpane in the bottom row of panes that had once been a large storefront window. The cat was on its hind legs with a forepaw on either side of its head.

Mr. Chow returned with a sizeable bowl of steaming soup. Very slowly, motivated by the good-smelling chicken broth and vegetables, she got up to a sitting position. Three fat dumplings floated on top. The man watched her drink the broth and bits of chicken and onion straight from the bowl. With her fingers she picked up and ate two delicious meat-filled dough packets. Despite the anxiety, her eyes welled with tears to be cared for. She thanked him.

Seeing the cat's forward ears, its keen focus on the soup, she pointed to the window.

Ah Chin Chow charged to the door, threw it open, and made a loud noise. The cat vanished. Perhaps it was a frequent nuisance. While his back was turned, she put the third dumpling in her trouser pocket in case she needed it later.

"Thank you," she said again, handing him the empty bowl. "Maybe I can walk now. But I don't know the way up to the streets. If you could give me the directions, I'll memorize them this time and not get lost."

He looked dubious.

"You'll be paid. My brother will pay a big reward for me." She could only hope that would divert him from any bad ideas, this man who dealt in girls.

He said, "No. You stay bed, dlink tea. No walkee. Ah Chin commee baa. Show you way." He put a crate beside the cot and placed a small teapot and a cup without ears on it. "Tea for goo brud." He said.

Blood.

He took the lantern and left the room. Through the many-paned window she saw the light recede, and when her eyes adjusted, realized that a little light came from other windows outside this place. The soup and tea helped, and she sat up by stages. Waiting for the vertigo to dissipate, she drank the remaining tea in the pot. It tasted a little strange, but she was thirsty. Then she pushed to her feet. Helped toward the door by means of the table, she put on the hat, tucked her hair under it, and took two more steps to the door.

Not locked, thank goodness. She cracked it open and looked into the murky underground city. Dim light emanated from random windows begrimed by the constant pall of smoke—cigarettes, opium, stoves without chimneys, who knew? Now the thick air smelled of cooking as well.

Another Chinaman suddenly appeared from around a corner with a lantern swinging from a short mast on a four-wheeled cart, very near her. She stood motionless in the dark as the cart stopped in the middle of the tunnel that had formerly been a street. She backed up against the wall so he couldn't see her and slowly nudged the door shut. Through the window she could see some of the cart, including red lettering on the wooden slats in Chinese and in English: CHINA EATS. It was a vegetable cart with three or four roasted ducks on top.

The vendor called out one way and then the other. She couldn't understand him. As he was doing that the little gray cat bounded high to the side of the cart, clutching the slats with straining claws while biting into the hind end of a roasted duck. It got in a couple of gulps before the man noticed and slapped it away.

People came from three directions with lanterns, not all of them Chinese. Haggling went on for some time. She slid down the wall to sit, and wait. After a great deal of loud talk, silence and darkness returned. She slowly regained her feet and cracked open the door again.

Only a cabbage leaf marked the place where the cart had stood. A rat darted out and began to drag the leaf. Then she noticed the tail end of the little gray cat disappear around the same corner from which the vendor had come. It occurred to her that the cat was following the man. No doubt he had brought the cart from above and would eventually return to the upper city.

Mae followed the cat through the smoky, fungal tunnel.

It led to a noisy dead-end not far from Ah Chin Chow's place. Through the grimy windows she saw that the noise came from big engines in a large room lit by overhead gaslight. A man was shoveling coal from a pile and throwing it into a wheelbarrow. From the corner of her eye she saw the cat dash from one generator to another, for surely that's what they were. It must have made it through the door just behind the cart. Smart little cat.

Fortunately the door was hidden from the man's line of sight. She opened the door to the full blast of the noise and the unexpected heat. The cat vanished into a dark recess. She followed, hiding behind generators, and when the man had his back turned, quickly moved into what turned out to be an unlit stairwell, perhaps leading up to the outside. She flattened herself against the wall, hoping the vendor hadn't seen her enter. He might alert Ah Chin Chow, who might alert Oberon. Before her eyes adjusted to the dark, she heard the slow thump of the cart ascending the stairs and an occasional grunt. Somewhere between her and the cart was the cat. The thumping stopped.

A door opened. A rush of fresh air fell over her, but little light came down the stairs. Just before the door closed again, a small shadow slipped into the gloaming of evening. Mae realized she had spent the entire day underground.

Climbing as fast as her weakness allowed, she arrived at a landing and the bar of dim light under the door. She rested for some time, no longer needing to hurry behind the cat. Then she said a little prayer and felt for the doorknob. It turned. Unlocked!

Outside, she filled her lungs and tried to assume the demeanor of a man. Golden light on her left told her that the sun had gone down about a half-hour ago over the Sacramento River. She turned the opposite direction up the path beside a row of stores, where a number of people, many of them Chinese, walked. Thankfully, all seemed too preoccupied to notice her. She looked up at the sign on the corner of the two-story building she had just left:

SACRAMENTO ELECTRIC, GAS & RAILWAY COMPANY. She had been in the basement where Butch said she'd be able to find him.

Butch was a wanted man, and she needed to be on the right side of the law. That much was clear. Maybe it was a good thing she hadn't seen him down there.

Weak as a half-drowned kitten she continued up I Street, past 6th Street, thinking that Rowena should have stayed with her. Charlie had probably told her to. He would have sent someone to pick them up at the entrance she hadn't been able to find. By now he would know she was lost.

Suddenly a screeching yowl!

A ball of fur hurtled off a boot in a doorway. Landing on its feet in the middle of the road, the skinny gray cat that had guided Mae from the underworld stood trembling in the path of a team of trotting horses. Its tail, now held low in fear, was as perpendicular as a measuring square—perhaps an accident in a slammed door when it was a kitten. She hadn't noticed that in the darkness.

Sorry for the poor little thing, she was relieved to see it dodge the hooves and get back to the walkway. Pinching off a piece of pork dumpling she quietly called, "Kitty, kitty." People walked around her, perhaps mistaking her for a rheumatic old man. The cat didn't move. She placed the morsel where the brick wall met the ground and walked away. Looking back, she saw the cat hawk down the dumpling.

"Come, kitty, kitty," she called, holding out more dumpling. The cat came in furtive spurts, stopping to look around, but always moving toward her.

The boardinghouse was twelve long blocks away. Fortunately the onset of darkness obscured the bloodstains on her trousers. Each step brought her closer to a warm, soft bed. She would try to get Mrs. Svensen to adopt the cat with the bent tail. With her mind on the bed and the heavenly pillow, she had three blocks to go when a man's voice called from a horse-drawn conveyance.

"Mae, get in."

III
Charlie

Preceded by his hyponotic gaze, He-lé-jah pushes through the scrub oaks. With a short "mrowl" he greets us as he saunters our way, he of many names—cat, cougar, mountain lion, puma, catamount, panther, California lion. One of the few original Animal People, He-lé-jah is known for his unsurpassed hunting skill and also as husband of O-se-mai-ti, Grizzly Bear, whom the people on southern streams call A-zu-mati. Some say that He-lé-jah's later children with O-se-mai-ti looked more and more human.

"Humans are adaptable, like me," the big cat says as he arrives under my branches.

"Don't forget me," says Coyote looking over at him.

"Yes, you are adaptable too," but not as much as us cats. We can live alone or in colonies as thick as gulls."

By long habit, I use care when I contradict He-lé-jah. "We used to say you were the most solitary of the animals. Were we wrong?"

"In these hills it is efficient to hunt alone, but we take food and comfort where we find it. Your son saw my kind in the mission living in large prides. The mice were numerous enough in that granary to feed us all. We also received bowls of cream and tasty tidbits. Some of us gave up our independence to live with people."

Coyote has a gleam in his eye, "So you live the easy way, whatever that is."

The big cat stands thinking. "If it suits my fancy. And if it is safe."

In the quiet of the fog, Rock Man's strained voice can be heard above the plash of the river. "My people didn't feel safe with your kind around. We feared the long curved knives of your stabbing teeth."

"Our prey was bigger then," the lion explains. "Our teeth are not so big now."

"Do you eat smaller animals?" Rock Man asks.

"We must. The big ones are gone. Like I said, we are adaptable. Some of us are small enough to fit in a human lap."

The big cat leaps to a perfect landing and elongates himself on the branch, the tip of his tail twitching above Coyote's head.

In her Pierce-Arrow Mae is lost in memory. We all see her as she woke up in Sacramento.

✾✤

45

Mae floated beneath the surface, drifting until she heard a mournful baritone above the water.

South Coast, the wild coast is lonely, you may win at the game at Jolón
But the lion still rules the barranca, and a man there is always alone.
My name is Juan Hano de Castro, my father a Spanish grandee...

She tried to keep listening as the voice frayed like tissue paper in warm water, shreds of it floating away. Fainter and fainter the baritone whispered through the dreamy blue-green water. Her hair and skirts waved about her as she drifted in aqueous splendor, not caring where she was going.

After a time the distant song extended a sound tentacle all the way to her and wiggled into her head.

The lion still rules the barranca, and a man there is always alone.

That slowed her drift and changed her direction. She floated upward toward the light, gentled up and up through the shimmering ripples by an unknown force, and breached the surface.

In thin air she lay surrounded by a pale green room with white trim. Sunshine danced through yellow leaves outside the high arched windows, and the yellow invaded the room along one wall and down the brass chain and the arms of the gaslight fixture hanging from the ceiling. The real sunshine added luster to the painted sunlight within a work of art framed on the wall, and she dallied inside that flower garden at an English country house with a quaint thatched roof.

We came to my cabin at twilight. The stars twinkled out on the coast.
She soon loved the valley, the orchard, but I knew that she loved me
the most...

A singing man stood at a full-length mirror adjusting his bowtie. She saw his reflection, the slightly pockmarked face and mustache with a downward droop. *Charlie.* Still floating in the sheets, she noticed the crocheted coverlet undisturbed around her. On a small table beside the bed stood a ewer with pink roses painted on its fat belly, dew on the petals. A glass of water was there too, and slim rectangular bottles, one tall and indigo blue, the other half full of a yellow elixir, also a spoon in a saucer with a trace of purple syrup.

He was looking at her, breaking into a toothy smile.

Coming to the bedside he said, "So, you're back in the land of the living."

"Was I gone?"

"For quite some time."

She felt safe, having him near, and that fit with the floating feeling. "How long have I been out?"

"Well, let's see. You've come to time and again since I brought you here."

"I don't remember that."

"Not even my brave standoff with Oberon?" His eyes twinkled with that joke he was always on to, but the mention of Oberon opened her fears.

"This is the fourth day," he added more seriously.

So long. "Where are we?"

"I brought you to my place. Mrs. Svensen didn't want the responsibility for an ill girl."

His eyes followed as she looked at the medicine.

"I brought in a good doctor. He said you lost a lot of blood and then got a fast-moving infection. We thought we'd lose you." He sat on the edge of the bed and looked at her intently. "How do you feel? I mean down here." He put the weight of his hand on the coverlet, her abdomen.

Just how *did* she feel? He was presumptuous putting his hand there, but it felt all right and she was glad he'd found her in time. It might have been Oberon instead. "Um, sort of hazy," she said.

He grinned. "Well, that's clear as mud."

"Like I've been underwater. Floating."

He stood up and touched the yellow bottle. "This makes you feel like that. A wonder drug. The best doctors in Europe give it to eliminate pain."

"What is it?"

"Heroin."

That meant nothing to her.

His tone was light. "Similar to cocaine, the stuff that's in Coca-Cola—puts you in a good mood. But a lot more powerful." He walked toward the door, his tone changing to business.

"I'm on my way to work. Rowena'll look in on you."

She said to his back: "You fought with Oberon?"

"No, silly, just having fun with you."

"Oh."

He turned to her. "See you later."

"Where you been sleeping?"

"Davenport, in the front room. Now get some sleep."

He stuck his head back in just before shutting the door. "Oh, there was a cat tailing you. You wanted it, so I caught it in a blanket and took it to the basement. It's wild. The landlord wants me to get rid of it."

"You mean kill it?"

His shoulders moved. "Guess so."

"Please don't. I can tame it."

"Well then, you better get well in a hurry and start working on that cat before Mr. Harding does the deed himself."

He was gone.

ᴄ⃜

He sat in geometric angles, in white boxer shorts, the naked torso a firm wedge, one knee up, a long bare foot on the bed, forearm across the knee, hand hanging straight down. A lanky man with questions in his dark eyes. His expression pulled her to him. Tentatively she put her arms around his shoulders, her cheek against his freshly shaved face. But then she awoke in terror, afraid he wouldn't hug her back. It was Charlie in her dream.

ᴄ⃜

A cool hand on her forehead brought her up from turbid depths.

"Hey, you all right?" *Rowena.*

"Dunno."

All the color and light had gone from the room. The rocking chair between the bed and the door cast a tangled shadow on the wall.

Again the hand on her forehead. "I'd say you're still feverish. Maybe the doctor ought to see you again."

Mae looked at Rowena's unlined face framed by brown curly hair.

Rowena lifted the blankets from the side of the bed, sniffed, and wrinkled her nose. "Still smells putrid."

She reached under the bed and brought up the bedpan, pushed the cold metal to Mae's sensitive skin.

ᴄ⃜

The smell of beer on Charlie's breath and the cool out-of-doors scent of his woolen suit woke her. He straightened up as she opened her eyes.

"Doctor says you're to take a good broth several times a day."

He had a cup, and he tipped warm broth to her lips, holding her head in his hand.

She swallowed a little. "I'm a bother to you." It came out a whisper.

"Hush. Take some more."

She drank as much as she could before her throat rebelled.

"There, that's a good girl. Now have some more."

She gagged on it, sputtered, "Put me down."

First he spooned more of the yellow medicine into her mouth. He pulled the rocking chair to the bedside and sat down, unsnapping his collar.

"Ahh." He put the chair into motion, a mousey squeak.

"I 'spose you wonder what I'm up to in the state house all day."

"I sleep most of the time."

He moaned low in his chest and shut his eyes. "Sometimes I'm flat disgusted with my work."

She couldn't respond but was glad to have him at her side.

"A man would like to think his interpretation of the factual situation would bear upon the making of policy. A man in my position, that is—one paid to write up the analysis."

The complexity drifted past her.

"And yet I'm also paid to see to your care—no analysis of that public expenditure, of course." Squeak, squeak.

She started to say, "I'm a burden to y—"

"Stop saying that. Burden or not, this is what it is."

Squeak… squeak… squeak.

"A man came in today. A square Anglo-Saxon sort of fellow. Farmer, from somewhere near Modesto. Couldn't get through to any of the legislators so he poured it out on me. Afraid he'll lose his farm, with the SP's rates so high. Can't get his crops to market without the railroad." Squeak. "Asked me why the rates are so high. Hell, all I know is they charge what they think is right. Local agents know the situation… loan money to those farmers… pose as friends… notion of which ones to keep in business…"

Mae sank down through the layers of words. "…no freedom to ship on a different… buys the law… judges… unfair… man'd weep, if he…"

The sounds floated away.

A hand patted her shoulder though the covers, bringing her up for a moment.

"Mae, you got a tough break. Don't have the first notion what I'm talking about. I got no right to use you for a listening post."

⌒

They were bundling her in a quilt, and then carrying her down a flight of stairs. Charlie at her armpits, someone at her ankles. "Watch it… the door…"

A whiff of cold wind just as Charlie covered her face. The quilt slipped off when they laid her in the back of a buggy. Charlie at the reins, a boy at her feet.

"Where we going?" she asked.

The boy was somewhat younger than Mae.

"Marysville," Charlie said from the front. "Chinese herbalist there. The doctor says he's the best." He looked over his shoulder.

"Cover her up and give her more laudanum. We got a long ride and more agitation, getting on and off the train."

The carried her up into a caboose, and laid her in a bunk.

⌒

Strange scents woke her up. She saw shelves of big jars containing powders and leaves, twigs and reddish lumps. A Chinaman in a blue silk robe and skullcap leaned toward her with too old a face. She was afraid, lying on the cot. Charlie and the boy were back by a wall entrusting her to this strange being who was removing her quilt.

He sniffed over her like a dog, gazed in her eyes, told her to stick out her tongue. She did and he closely examined it, and then prodded her belly through the nightshirt.

Then the herbalist talked to Charlie on the other side of the small room. They nodded back and forth. The Chinese doctor removed a big jar from a shelf. A ghastly snake coiled vertically in a jar moved with the motion of the amber liquid as it was transported to her. She looked into the snake's dead white eyes. The man removed the jar's stopper, laid the huge cork aside, and dipped out some of the snake liquid in a small pottery cup. He put his hand behind her head and brought the cup to her lips.

She wrenched away, as she gagged.

Charlie held the cup to her and started lifting her head to it. She heaved again and again though only a bit of dark liquid and bubbly spit came up. Afterwards, all she could do was moan with the pain of that internal violence.

"You must drink it," said Charlie.

"It's snake juice."

"No," Charlie softly contradicted, "it's whisky. The snake is clean and pickled."

"Noooo!" She shook him off when he made another try.

He placed the cup on a table and returned to the other side of the room to quietly consult with the Chinese doctor. She couldn't hear what they said.

Tears made warm tracks to her ears, and she felt so shaky and awful that when Charlie returned, telling her she must drink it, she could only weep.

He picked up the cup, cajoling in patient tones and telling her that rattlesnakes make poison in their bodies but they also make an antidote so they couldn't accidentally poison themselves. The poison had been milked out before the snake was killed, and the whisky in the jar had been drawing the antidote out of the body for years.

"This'll work against your infection. Think of it as whisky," he told her, "because that's what it is, whisky with medicine in it."

When he tried again to get her to drink, she gagged and shuddered, most of the liquid running down her chin. The Chinaman refilled the cup.

Charlie's dark eyes pleaded as she looked directly into them. "Please, Mae, drink it for me. Don't you see? I'm trying to save your life." The abacus in the Chinaman's hands was going clickety-click.

Her flesh recoiled and her teeth chattered with revulsion, but he had said, "Drink it for me." She forced herself to get some of it down.

"It really is just whisky," he crooned as she coughed and tried again. "Alcohol is antiseptic. Anything bad on the snake has been killed. That's it. Swallow."

It burned up her nose and down to her stomach. Just before leaving Iowa she had tasted Daddy's whisky. This was similar but with a darkly alien aftertaste. Her stomach kicked a couple of times but finally lay quiet with the awful juice in it.

They worked together, Charlie coaxing a little more into her while she struggled not to look at the snake in the jar. With all her might she wanted to help him.

When the tiny cup was empty, Charlie lowered her head and she sank away from him, and the room.

⏝

On the way back to Sacramento, she was jolted awake as they put her in another caboose. And then she was back in Charlie's room again.

⏝

Over the next few days Charlie and Rowena made sure she drank a quarter cup of snake whisky three times a day. It helped that the snake wasn't present. The special tea Charlie had bought from the herbalist didn't taste too bad. And four times a day she had to swallow a piece of a huge tan spongy thing that Charlie swore wasn't an actual mushroom.

"What is it then?" She figured that people who would pickle a snake and drink its juice were capable of eating anything.

"Its exact nature is a mystery, forgotten. All I know is it's taken from a secret royal fungus discovered or created hundreds of years ago by ancient Chinese herbalists. It's kept alive in that special liquid, kept like sourdough starter over the centuries. They developed it to strengthen the emperors against illness. It's supposed to work wonders."

The morning oatmeal with raisins and cream, and later chicken soup with dumplings and crisp green vegetables from the local China garden began to taste better every day. By the time she'd swallowed the last of the snake whisky and the last of the mammoth "mushroom," she was walking around and taming Benty, the little gray cat with the bent tail—a young female with a difficult past.

Mae felt clear-headed now, except when she took more of the heroin and laudanum to enjoy the floating feeling.

One morning when she awoke to Charlie's singing, he turned to her and said, "You snore. Did you know that?"

Mortified—snoring was for old men—she couldn't think what to say. How hideous she must be to him! Unveiled to her ugly core, mouth open, horrid noise coming out. And how long and often she had slept in his presence! It seemed that lately all she could do was sleep.

⏝

Weeks passed. In the afternoon when he shrugged out of his greatcoat and hung his hat on the hook, Charlie smiled around the front room.

Relieved to see that he was pleased, Mae removed the pan of salted nuts from the tiles on the green cast-iron hearth and set them on the sundries table beside his upholstered chair. She had worried he might be upset that she had removed newspapers and other things he'd left scattered on the floor, newspapers that by their dates had been there three or four months. Lying down to rest between spurts of cleaning, she had put away the underwear and socks that he seemed to leave wherever he happened to be. She had folded and removed the bedclothes from the davenport where he slept, and dusted the front room. She had burned string and old paper wrappers in the kitchen stove, and organized the unlikely things he piled together on every surface—tins of unopened tomatoes and sardines, documents from the Capitol teetering on a sack of pinto beans, a section of lead pipe, postal cards from friends, and much more.

He seemed to appreciate the tidying up.

She had also kept the fires going all day, and he obviously liked the warmth. He smiled as he made a show of sniffing in the direction of the kitchen—oyster-potato stew simmering on the small gas range, one of his favorite suppers.

Benty, who had been dozing on the rug before the fire, stood in fearful alert as Charlie approached the upholstered chair. She made a hasty retreat to the far corner of the room when he sat in it.

"Ahh," Charlie exhaled, tossing a warm nut in his mouth and stretching his shoes toward the fire. Outside, the evening streets were damp and cold, the rattle of a passing trolley muffled by the fog. Reflected in the light from the cozy room, the heavy mist against the windows resembled cotton wadding.

Mae sat on the davenport opposite Charlie. "Have a good day?"

"Not bad. Things are slow in December. Just a meeting with the Governor and his cabinet, mostly over water in Kings County. And a legal tangle in the Delta. Oh yes, some of the fellows have arranged a party. Wanna go? Think you're well enough?" He sat up and leaned forward, rubbing his hands together near the little fire.

"You mean you want me to go with a legislator?"

"They've gone home 'til next session." He turned his gaze from the hearth and raised his brows at her. "I mean you and I go, together."

This jarred her. Could he be willing to let his friends believe he was sweet on the likes of her? Sometimes it seemed that his hand lingered a moment too long after patting her shoulder. He'd always been a gentleman, distant at times, but the kind she'd once hoped to marry—back when she thought she was worth marrying—a young man on his way up. At the risk of losing his rooms or having his rent increased, he had defended Benty's life against the landlord. And he had saved her life.

"Yes, Charlie, I'd love to go with you. When is it?"

"Tomorrow night. I'd have mentioned it before, but just got wind of it today."

"What should I wear? The dress I wore to the Steffens' place?"

"Oh, I don't know. That could be a bit formal. But it doesn't really matter with that bunch. I'm just glad you feel well enough to go at all."

For the first time in months the old Mae stirred in her, the one who had so loved parties and dances, the one who'd been attractive to men. But then the muddling haze invaded her again. While cleaning up Charlie's place, she had recalled cleaning up Oberon's stinking room. And she'd felt anxious about Charlie, suffering pangs of fear that he wouldn't return, just as she'd feared Oberon would leave her chained to the pipe. And below that thought lurked the most putrid thought of all—the want of a man who had hurt and humiliated her. The vile miasma of it rose in her now as Charlie stuffed tobacco in his pipe. It took all her strength to check the urge to go hug and kiss him, spilling his pipe all over the place in her filthy desire for him.

How God must hate me! And how ashamed of me Sister Delphine would be!

Charlie unlaced his shoes. "I think a social affair will be good for you."

He was a nice man. The only behavior that might be thought ungentle-manly was living with her in an unmarried state. They'd done nothing wrong. However, his neighbors in this small apartment house would suspect otherwise; and if she started attending parties with him, word would get around the Capitol. The men in novels would have arranged for a lady to move to another residence where she'd be spared the embarrassment. But that made no sense. A bad girl like her couldn't be embarrassed. Life was a tangle, like the string she'd tried to straighten today but finally threw in the fire.

One thing was certain, however. She didn't want to move out. And if Charlie's intentions were, well, ungentlemanly, she would figure out what to do later. She'd been sick and sore and unsteady in her nerves. In some ways she wanted to go on indefinitely like brother and sister, but his large pres-ence filled the room and was almost certain to pull her to him sooner or later.

Charlie would be shocked if he knew. He'd likely turn from her in disgust. Too many times he had seen her sick and snoring. Even with her improved health she slept half the day. She tried to pretend otherwise, but sometimes he came back for noon dinner and caught her still in bed. How many times could a person get away with saying: I must have overslept? She hated her sloth, but couldn't help it. Something in her needed to escape into dream. And Charlie knew about her and Oberon. That alone would repel most decent men. Yet despite all of it, she dared hope the reason he hadn't sent her back to Mrs. Svensen's rooming house was that he wanted her for himself someday, not as an escort for legislators. That he would see her not as a repulsive fiend of the Beast, but the girl for him. And maybe, just maybe, that was the reason he asked her to go with him tomorrow night.

To imagine marrying him, however, was beyond hope. Like a sleepwalker she went to the kitchen to dip him out a bowl of oyster stew with a dollop of butter and a dash of pepper.

46

She pulled the silvery gown over her head, stepped in her striped silk stock-ings and her pretty heeled shoes, and backed up for Charlie to button her.

When he finished, she gathered the loose material at the side of her waist, perplexed and disappointed.

"You've lost flesh," he said with a good-natured wink. "You'd fall apart if your hide wasn't holding you in."

"I could take a couple of tucks, if you've got a needle and thread."

His lips pushed out. "I don't have sewing gear, and it's too late for that." He frowned at her midsection. "Maybe we can do something quick. Just a minute."

He went to the kitchen and rummaged in a tin box.

"My purple gown's loose too," she explained, following him. She'd left all her things in Oberon's place. Clothes, poems, music, writing paper, money, her innocence.

The contents of the cracker-tin rattled onto the table as Charlie dumped it out. He pawed through old matches, nails, tacks, marbles, green pennies, skeleton keys, a coil of fine wire—

"Ahah! A Safety Pin. Just as I thought. This is a clever invention"

The pin wasn't big enough to grasp sufficient bunched fabric. "That's a little better," he concluded, "than letting it hang on you like on a scarecrow."

Like a scarecrow. Even this lovely gown, which had made her feel like Cinderella at the Steffens' place, was spoiled now. But it would have to do.

"Will there be dancing?" She hoped to dance with Charlie again, but with her arms up the pin and bunched fabric would show.

"I don't know what they'll be doing. We'll see."

She pulled on the long black half-gloves and wrapped herself in the black lace shawl while Charlie went to borrow the landlord's "talking box" to send for a buggy. Not a real telephone, he'd told her, but a device that could tele-graph messages to a couple of livery barns, and the hospital.

A buggy arrived in about five minutes. Mae feared she'd got her pale satin shoe in the mud as she stepped up. The driver urged the horse to a fast trot through the muddy streets, and then reined to a stop and handed the ribbons to Charlie before he jumped down at his livery barn. He called up to them.

"There'll be a man t'drive ya home when you gits back. If a smart rap don't rouse 'im, give a holler. G'night."

The November wind had stripped most of the leaves off the overarching trees, and the limbs clacked above them as the horse pulled the buggy through the maze of wheel tracks glimmering in the fractured moonlight. Trying to keep her teeth from chattering, Mae held the shawl on her head with a tight grip beneath her chin.

Charlie slowed the horses to a walk, struggled out of his greatcoat, and put it around her shoulders. For that she felt like kissing him. It was cold even with the coat. He urged the horse back up to speed.

"Charlie, why don't they light the streetlamps?"

He spoke over the sound of the sucking hooves and splashing wheels. "It's the third day of the waning moon. Day after tomorrow they'll light 'em again."

A dark conveyance hurtled toward them at full gallop, sped past and spat-tered the low windshield. Mud entered on Charlie's side, no doubt soiling his jacket and white collar and cuffs.

Guilty inside the coat that would have protected him, she wiped a drop of mud from her face. "What does the waning moon have to do with it?"

He threw back his head and hawed. "If you think that's daffy, you're in good company. For years folks have been agitating for the City Council to light the streetlamps every night and forget about the moon's schedule. In summer the leaves block the moonlight on many streets and it's black as sin."

He reached a long arm around her and pulled her toward him. "No need for you to keep all the warmth over there. We can share." One hand returned to the reins.

The shiny streaks of light reflected in the water standing in the ruts seemed to be mocking her as she sat against him pretending to be a sinless girl out for an evening's entertainment.

"The city saves over $4,000 annually on gas by granting the moon a monopoly on street lighting for four days before and after a full moon." He pushed his top hat lower on his forehead so it wouldn't blow off.

Dark lumps of farmhouses could be seen farther and farther apart. One place stank so bad she gagged—a rendering plant he said. The city was behind them, but U Street seemed to stretch on forever. Charlie had said the roadhouse was three miles out from the Capitol. She was anxious to get out of the wind, which blew into her side of the buggy.

She snuggled into him.

He spoke warm breath into the lace shawl over her hair. "I've been to this place before, out on Folsom Road. Oughta be coming right up."

By the time Charlie tied the horse at the hitching rail, Mae felt so frozen her hand could hardly hold the greatcoat together, nor could her other hand grip his with any strength when he reached for her. She felt sorry for him without a coat, but he didn't seem to shiver.

When he opened the door, warmth and music poured over them, and lamps glowed all over the room. A waitress serving food shot them an angry look for letting in the wind. In a corner, the pot belly stove beckoned. Mae removed the coat and handed it to Charlie. He hung it with his hat on a rack of coats along the wall.

He guided her with a light touch into a larger room where shouts and raucous laughter competed with a four-man band and a piano playing that new way—a steady oom-pah oom-pah in the bass and a lively counterpoint in the treble. It was too dark to see the walls, just the people bunched in the middle. A line of four women danced on a stage, their kicks not in step and their skirts so high you could see garters on pudgy thighs. Their bosoms bounced in necklines as low as the one on Mae's red gown. This surprised her. She had not imagined Charlie in such a place, but he was here and so was she.

Surveying the room from his commanding height, Charlie exchanged nods with a few men at different tables. Groups of people with drinks in hand loitered around a few popular tables, guffawing at jokes. The ladies were all young, wearing dark, wintry fabrics that hugged their hips and knees. Heaven knew how they managed to walk. Mae felt out of place in her summery Cinderella gown with the high neck. And she didn't recognize a single face.

Charlie guided her to an empty table and pulled out a chair for her.

"Are they all with your party?" A sudden burst of loud hooting drowned her out, and she repeated her question into the ear he offered.

"Don't know." He looked around the room. "I recognize about half of them. A couple of legislators, appointees of the gov—"

"I thought the legislators went home."

"They're from nearby—Amador, El Dorado, Sacramento Counties."

"Oh."

A waiter brought champagne. Mae and Charlie gave a silent toast and they each took a swallow. Mae liked it.

A man stood up, raising a glass and smiling at Charlie. His bellow could have been heard in the last row of an opera hall, "The Leadership is present. Here's to Charlie Rogue!"

Yells and whistles.

Charlie grinned.

A young man came over and sat in an empty chair at their table. Charlie introduced them, but Mae didn't catch his name in all the noise. It didn't matter. He directed his talk to Charlie's ear.

More champagne. More laughter. More bellowed toasts. The young man left for another table.

"Excuse me," Charlie said after a few minutes. "Be right back."

She watched him make his way through the tables, stopping to be introduced and to talk and joke. He laughed and slapped men's backs. He was popular.

He was still at it when the dancers tripped off the stage. The pianist stood up and yelled something, then sat down and directed, with one hand, the start of a lilting musical piece.

Onto the stage came a pink and white female mincing to the music in white shoes. She wore nothing but white silk stockings held up by white garters, short lacy underdrawers, and a white corset too tight for her ample pink body. The crowd quieted as she turned around to show her broad lower cheeks beneath the lace of her drawers, and then jiggled around to the front again with her breasts on the verge of bursting free. Her frizzy hair looked almost white, done up in a pink ribbon with a bow on top, and the round spots of dark pink on her face gave her a clownish appearance.

Smiling like an imbecile, she touched a finger to her chin and sang in a childish lisp:

> I am a Christmas dolly,
> You'll find I like to kiss.
> If a man should play with dolly,
> Methinks it's not amiss.

Grunting came from the darkened room. A hulk of a man hunched forward like an ape, arms swinging. Others grunted with him in time to the music as he approached the stage, and the whole room rollicked with laughter. He went up two steps to the stage, turning his head and flopping his mop of black hair from side to side, tongue lolling to draw more laughter from the crowd. As he headed across the stage to where Dolly stood swaying to the music, he got down and crawled on all fours up to and between her legs, turning crazed eyes and silly grin to the hooting crowd.

It seemed to Mae that she was dreaming, to see such a thing in a public place. Her brother Emmett's joke came back to her, something men repeated in slighty different words: Do your churching in Ione and your sinning in Sacramento.

"This is ridiculous." Charlie was back. "Let's go!" He pulled her out of the chair and grabbed her elbow, leading her out.

She had to watch her step in the dark room and couldn't look back to see what the man on his knees was doing, but just before they reached the door she looked into the teasing smile of Helen Rose! Seated beside an older gentleman, not Percy the Senator, Helen blew her a kiss as the door shut between them.

Then she and Charlie were back in the buggy on the ride home, his coat on her.

"Who was that man?"

"Which one?"

"The one crawling—"

"Oh, he's just one of…" He mumbled something she couldn't hear. "You might say he runs the crime rackets in Sacramento. Political boss of a sort. Cozies up to the state officials too."

"What was he—"

"Forget it. I never should have taken you there. It was all right, the times I've been there. Sorry about that. It was no place for a lady."

Me, a lady? The one person I knew there was Helen Rose.

❧

Two weeks later Charlie took her to a Christmas party at the Steffens house. She had regained a little flesh; but in spite of Charlie's constant good cheer, her mind remained, as Sister Delphine might say, a "slough of despond." She had lost her old drive and spunk, and believed she must be weary company for him.

He didn't want her to wear the same frock, so he took her to Weinstock & Lubin's Department Store, an exciting place that occupied the entire block between 3rd and 4th on J Street. The frock he bought was of a dark paisley fabric with a fashionably slender profile. In front, the skirt cut upward like folded wings, showing her ankles and her new maroon shoes. He also bought her a coat, a hat, and a brooch with gemstones of Christmas colors.

"Oh, Charlie, you mustn't," she told him. "This jewelry is too dear."

"Don't worry about it," he'd said, with a wave of his hand.

ᔐ

The strange tiredness continued to weigh on her even as they entered the magnificent Steffens home and Charlie introduced her to the first people they ran into: Mrs. and Mrs. David Lubin, half owners of that very same store. In a high-necked, finely brocaded black gown, pretty Mrs. Lubin smiled in a friendly way.

Encouraged, Mae told the Lubins her clothing had come from their department store, but then felt silly for saying that. She followed with, "What a grand place you have there, offering everything under the sun for sale!" That sounded even more foolish, a ridiculous overstatement or an obvious point. But Mr. Lubin, an earnest-looking man with large wide-set eyes and black hair, seemed pleased to hear it.

He launched into several reasons why department stores would one day put the haberdashers and corner dress shops out of business, mentioning the set price for everything and an end to haggling. "Don't you like it better that way?"

She had no opinion on that subject, and was relieved when a couple broke into the circle exclaiming over Mr. Lubin's good deeds for the city. Charlie was busy talking to someone else, so she made her way to the loaded dining-room table—silver trays and crystal plates filled with all sorts of cakes, pies and cookies. Many of the women had supplied their favorite Christmas cookies. Mae hadn't been asked to contribute, but then she didn't belong to this crowd.

She had to blink to be sure she was looking at the same man that Charlie had called the political boss of Sacramento—the man she'd last seen on his hands and knees! Many times she had tried to think what prurient act he'd been about to do on that stage, or pretended he was about to do. She guessed he wasn't the only one present tonight who'd been in that other place. Now the man appeared to be the top dresser in this crowd, and he was looking at her, but she couldn't bring herself to make eye contact. If shyness counted, she told herself, she might after all be something of a lady.

There was no dancing on the fourth floor, but rather drinking and visiting. Mae's fingers itched to play the magnificent piano in the library—one of the three parlors open to the broad hallway. However, the rest of her felt too shy for that. She tried to stay close to Charlie, but lost him for a time.

Nibbling a cookie from a plate marked "Mrs. Markham, First Lady," she watched a young man of slight stature arrive at the end of the table, still in his greatcoat and top hat. He threw his arms about Mrs. Steffens. The surprised lady pushed him back and stared at the laughing man. "Why, Lincoln, what on earth!"

The visitor removed his hat and swept it before the lady, bowing with humorous pretentiousness. "Thought I'd surprise you, Mother, with a yuletide visit."

She overheard Mr. Steffens say with a twinkle of his own, "Well if it isn't the prodigal son!" Quickly Lottie, Lulu, and Laura surrounded Lincoln. Yet a few of Lincoln's words came through, something about his taking employ-ment with a New York City newspaper.

New York. Of course people whose parents lived in houses like this would travel to Germany and work in New York. That was part of a dream that seemed ever more distant to Mae, though she stood in the midst of privileged folk.

And then all the lights dimmed and went out.

The buzz of talk ceased momentarily while eerie tips of cigarettes sketched jagged red lines in the dark. She felt disoriented, like the floor had tipped. Voices around her made guesses about the gas line.

A thunderous blast, and a streak of orange flame four feet long shot through the darkness. The wrong shape for a gas explosion. *Gunfire!*

A scream ripped out of her. Oberon was making good his promise to kill her for leaving him. He had tracked her, watched through the windows, shut off the gas, and fired. But missed. Next time he wouldn't.

She dropped to the floor and scuttled away as best she could, yanking her gown to free her knees. Heart in her throat, she surged with all her might to get to another corner of the room, pushing past gowns and trouser legs in the dark, someone yelping as she leveraged her shoe against an ankle.

The lights flickered and went all the way back up to their former brightness.

People loomed above her, looking down with faces distorted as in a fun-house mirror—revealing her location to Oberon!

He'd be getting a bead on her!

Darkness descended again, and the fear of death obliterated thought. She tried not to cry out but a scream somehow lingered in her mouth and in the air.

Hands grabbed her. Wildly she fought them, sobbing in horror and con-fusion. She needed to hide. Why wouldn't they leave her alone!

Charlie was there, lifting her to her feet. Her resistance melted. Support-ing her, he guided her, trembling and staggering, toward the front door, and she slowly began to realize that the lights had been up and the second dark-ness had existed only in her mind.

People were staring, some fascinated, some laughing at her.

Charlie opened the front door.

"No!" she said, shutting it, refusing to go out, "He'll kill me."

Somebody else opened the door and Charlie firmly walked Mae outside, down the stairs to the sidewalk, and around the corner into the dark recess under the stairs where Oberon might be waiting with his gun. In her shaking effort to walk, she couldn't fight or string words together. The sound of that gun remained in her, reducing her to a frightened child. Embarrassment piled on top of the fear and took away everything left in her. She blubbered shamelessly.

Charlie pulled her to him. "There now. Calm down. It's all right."

"I'm afraid he'll kill us both," she sobbed.

"Nobody is in danger," he soothed. "Friends of Lincoln pulled a gag, all in jest. They turned off the gas and fired a blank."

"A blank?"

"Yes."

She continued to quiver inside and out, despite what he'd said.

"It was a joke on Frank Rhodes, a reminder of a time long ago when Hiram Johnson and his father shut off the gas and stormed into a secret meeting of the Saloon Keepers League. They fired blanks and scared the wits out of Frank and his crowd."

Her frayed nerves refused to coalesce, and her mind stumbled over what he'd said. "A joke?"

"Yes."

She bawled like a baby, every part of her breaking down. She couldn't stop, and to make matters worse people from the house were standing around, watching.

"A stupid gag if you ask me," Charlie said with force enough to be heard by them. "I'll take you home."

⬿

She had embarrassed Charlie in front of people whose respect he needed. No other woman at the party had dissolved in fear. She never wanted to see those people again. Something inside her was broken, and like a wounded animal she wanted to be alone.

47

After supper Charlie poured himself a second glass of port—he normally had only one—and sat before the fire. "Mae, I'm going home for Christmas." His businesslike voice told her she wouldn't be invited.

"To Fresno."

"That area. We all go back to the farm for Christmas, my brothers and sisters. Their children. My folks expect it."

He'll want me to leave.

He pointed at her half-filled glass. "S'more?"

"No thanks." The wine was already making her lightheaded.

"You going home too?" he laid before her.

She tried out the word *home* to see what it meant to her. In her mind's eye she saw the farm in Iowa, her mother in the kitchen kneading dough, sleeves rolled up, arms dusted white to the elbows. This time of year Mom would make cinnamon rolls in addition to the many loaves of white bread. Daddy and the boys would be out seeing to the animals or sitting at the kitchen table playing caroms. Mae's thoughts floated upstairs to her room, her box of secrets, a *California Joe* novel borrowed from Myrtle. On the bed lay the quilt made for her by Grandma Duffy before she died. At night, tucked under Mae's chin it gave off the warm aroma. But then reality shut off that memory. That was all past. Gramps was under the ground in the family plot with Grandma and Nora. Uncle Ephraim's family had the farm and house. Even if a magic carpet could convey Mae to that home, she'd be seen as Daddy's spoor, disowned and unwanted.

She tried to imagine the stone house on Latrobe Road as a home. She'd lived there two days amid the chaos of the move and overflowing boxes with their contents rifled through. Surely by now Farley and Emmett had dug an outhouse. But even so, that place was no more a home to Mae than water to a sparrow. The folks were there in body only. Each of them had their own magic carpet that flew them out of reach—Daddy his whisky and Mom her melancholia. Emmett and Farley might go there for Christmas. Mae could fix them Christmas dinner, if Charlie gave her the stage fare, but the thought gave her an unpleasant feeling. Farley would pick her apart with pointed questions. They would quarrel. Daddy would leave for a saloon, and Mom wouldn't know the difference, or if she did she wouldn't let on.

"I'm not up to it," she answered.

"Not well enough to travel?"

"I guess that's it."

He took another sip of port. "Won't your family miss you?"

Letting her head fall back on the davenport headrest, she released her breath.

He pushed. "You said you had four brothers."

"Hank's married. He'll spend Christmas with Sophie and her family in Sutter Creek. George declared he'd never set foot in California again, and I believe he meant it."

"Why? What happened?"

"Oh," blowing out more air, "he worked in a deep gold mine. They caught him high-grading. Pocketed a few nuggets and the judge fined him $500. Last I heard George was working in a silver-mine, in Nevada. He doesn't stay in touch."

Charlie nodded. "I've had occasion to meet the owners of hard rock mines. High-grading is a serious offense. Judges come down hard on it." He looked at her. "That leaves two brothers."

"Farley and I don't get along. Never did."

"Well then, like the little Indians in that silly verse, *then there was one.*"

She flashed him a sad look. "Emmett and I are close. Closest in age too."

"Aha! Mightn't he be the reason for a Christmas visitation from a long-lost sister?" Brows raised hopefully, lips in a half smile.

She answered on the deeper level. "Charlie, you've been kind to me these last months. I can never repay you. And if you want me to move out, I'll be all right. Really I will, but only if I have some kind of employment so I can pay my own way."

In the fire's glow, his craggy face looked like the rock of Gibraltar.

She continued, "I realize you, well, sort of hired me to be, uh—" She didn't know the right term for what she was supposed to be.

Charlie got up and walked to the window, pulled the drapery back and looked at the rain-streaked pane backed by darkness.

Benty finally summoned the courage to leap onto the davenport. She was still wary after her life in the Sacramento underworld. Mae stroked her fur and thought she was getting a little fat. Charlie continued to stare out the window.

Mae soldiered on. "Sometimes I think about the Vaudeville theaters. The one on J near 11th, for example. Maybe I could see if there's employment there, you know, on the stage." *And get back to becoming another Lillie Langtry.*

He didn't move.

"But then I realize that Oberon could come after me there and—"

"Would you like that kind of life?" He turned to her. "Vaudeville?"

"Well, I like music and singing and dancing, so yes, I think so." Her tattered dream might buoy her up again, she thought, if she gave it voice.

"And if you were successful you'd travel all over the country, and live essentially on a train?"

"I suppose, and I'd have the money to hire a bodyguard, in case Oberon—"

He returned to his chair, looking at her. "You're asking me to go over there, to J Street? And talk to someone about hiring you?"

Please, just let me stay with you. I'll be your girl, your wife. I'll be more fun when I feel safer. "That would be nice," she said, "if you think it'd do any good. And if it would stop Ober—"

"I'm not all-powerful, you know. Far from it." With a sudden teasing smile he said, "Go ahead, sing and dance." He made a silly grandiloquent gesture to the open end of the parlor. "Entertain me. I'd like to see what you can do."

Never had she felt less like performing, nor did she have a scrap of an idea what to perform. "I can't, Charlie, not now. But I was thinking"—it just occurred to her—"Maybe I could stay here while you're in Fresno."

"Not Fresno!"

"I'm sorry." *What was that funny name?* "I could take care of the place until you get back, and we could sort it out later, I mean talk about what we do next."

"You'd stay here by yourself for five days, including Christmas?"

"Yes."

"It'd be lonely."

"That's all right."

∽

After delicate cajoling on her part and eyeball-rolling on his, Charlie carried two valises out the back door to hide the fact that he'd left—in case Oberon was watching. She knew that having him gone at night would frighten her, but being in his place was some relief. He'd promised to "do some thinking" on the three-hour train ride down and up the valley. Maybe he'd decide to keep her here, or move her back to Mrs. Svensen's and employ her as an escort.

He'd laid in plenty of firewood and stocked the larder with pastries, oranges, cheese, bread, Italian sausage, milk, and a tin of Pep Pills from the corner market. He also left her five dollars—enough to get to Slough House and back if she changed her mind. The first thing she did was to write a letter on Charlie's white stationery. She posted it to the folks, giving Charlie's address as her own.

To her surprise, a response arrived on Christmas Eve.

Miss Mae Duffy
1284 N Street
Sacramento, California
Dear Daughter,

    We greatly appreciate your Christmas greetings. Letters are a rare occurrence here, especially from you. Your mother and I are sorry you'll not be here to liven our spirits. You might not know that your brother Emmett left us October 29, ult. for Sacramento to seek employment with the Southern Pacific Railroad company. His work as Mrs. Miser's assistant with the flocks ended when he drove them down from the mts. and reported the demise of too many ewes and lambs. What with the coming of the rains and green grass in the home pastures, he isn't needed in that employment any more. We rec'd a postal from him and are tickled he did indeed sign with the railroad. Gave no return address. Try to find him at the SP foundry. The two of you might lift a toddy to the yuletide and to your loving parents,

                                    Edward L. Duffy, ESQ

    Post Script: We hear tales about that city of yours, some not to our liking.

We, we we. Does he actually talk to Mother?

ᔐ

Mae slept away Christmas day and night. She awoke so late the next day that the sun, or what could be seen of it through the fog, had reached its apex for this time of year. It was Wednesday. Emmett would be working, as men always did the day after Christmas. If she hurried, she might catch him on his noon break. No need for Pep Pills this morning. Mae slipped two five-dollar gold pieces into her coat pocket, made sure the front door and windows were locked and, locking the back door, used the back stairs. She went through the alley past 11th and 10th Streets. The chilly mist on her face sharpened her mind.

Charlie thought her terror of Oberon was ridiculous. She knew he held her in lower esteem on account of it, so to improve her chances with him, she silently vowed never to speak of Oberon in Charlie's presence. Walking alone on the streets where Oberon prowled daily was, she knew, dangerous in the extreme. Her lace shawl and new coat with the collar standing up over her ears disguised her somewhat, and the fog shrouded her. She turned up 8th Street, crossing M, L, and K, guided by the towering SP chimneys streaming black smoke. Even at this early hour the saloons were in full swing. An occasional merrymaker staggered out a door as she hurried by.

She located the SP Foundry backed up to the ugly body of water called China Lake, or sometimes Sutter Lake. The block-long building in the vast SP yard one one of many industrial buildings. Their roofs had tooth-like little windows on either side of their long spines, no doubt for ventilation. She remembered this place well and it gave her the shudders. The man who managed the foundry was Oberon's friend.

Careful to avoid the line of sight from that man's window, she hid behind the tents of the food vendors while she waited for Emmett. And if she didn't see Emmett first, but spied Shadrack Smith she'd ask him to find her brother for her. The noon whistle hadn't gone off yet, so before the lines formed she bought two ham and cheese sandwiches and two glasses of Coca-Cola from a vendor with a soda fountain.

∼

"Well, if you ain't a sight for sore eyes!" Emmett declared after Shadrack fetched him.

It felt so good to see Emmett! She looked him over, every detail from his dark wavy hair stiff with soot and his smudged face, down to his new black boots. He looked like a bona fide railroadman.

She raised the two sparkling glasses. "I got you a sandwich and a Coke. See?" She pointed her head toward the last table for the foundry men, out of sight from that window. "Let's go over there. Be quieter."

He took the glass and the sandwich and tromped sideways, keeping his eyes on her as they walked together. "Thunderation, little sister, I sure didn't expect to see you here. And with my dinner! You look so, ah, just real nice. Nice coat."

"Thanks." She couldn't tell him Charlie had bought her the coat.

They sat opposite each other at the sooty table with attached benches.

"Daddy wrote that you worked here."

"Well, that's a downright miracle—the mail bein' so fast, I mean. Why, I didn't know 'til last week I'd be here myself. Been hefting baggage at the station all November. Lucky this opened. It fetches more'n twice the money, a whole dollar an hour. What brings you here?" He tore into his sandwich.

The past jumped out at her as he wolfed down his food like he'd done at the table in Iowa. For Mae, Emmett was a big part of home. He acted and looked just the same. But she had changed. Things had happened to her and she wasn't a girl any more. Though she felt an urge to explain it, her need for his respect outweighed the desire to unload the awful memories.

Tears flooded her eyes and rolled down her cheeks. Turning aside, she wiped them. "I didn't have anything special to say." Choked by a lump in her throat, "Just wanted to talk to you, this being Christmastime and all."

"Well it sure is good to see you, Maezy. But now that I'm getting a close look at you, I'd say you're kinda bony around the eyes and cheeks, if you don't mind my saying. You've lost flesh."

"I've been sick. Didn't want to mention that to the folks. They've got enough trouble."

"You over it now?"

"Got'er licked." She couldn't help but use the warm old way of talking.

"What was it?"

She didn't look him in the eye. "A bad infection. I've been real tired, like I can't hardly stay awake. And, well, I just… uh." She swiped a coat sleeve across her face. "I uh… can't go into that now, without… getting all tired again."

Just the threat of explaining it cracked open a door that she'd been trying to shoulder shut, a door holding back a flood of degradation. Telling Emmett any of it would swamp her in it again, and she knew she'd quiver and flounder in the telling.

"I'd rather listen to you," she said. "Where are you staying? Daddy said you didn't give an address."

"Look who's talkin' 'bout no *ad*-dress." Emmett swigged his Cola and raised his brows in a way that let her know he was worried about her.

A little patch of blue sky showed through the fog. He looked at it, inhaling a lungful of air as though to give himself strength. "Well, I've moved around, sort of hopped from one spare room to another. You wouldn't hardly believe. At first I had a room with Shad Smith and three of his little brothers. All'ov us in the same bed. Them boys is so bony they woke me up all night with their sharp elbows and knees."

He took another giant bite of sandwich and talked through the chewing. "How in the world did'ja know he worked here?"

"I saw him when I was driving by."

"You got a rig?"

"No, I was with someone."

Emmett's knowing nod, his mouth pushed into an upside-down U, said he understood. But he didn't, no one could know. Starting to feel the rush from the Coca-Cola, she didn't dissuade him from thinking she had a gentleman friend. She hoped she did, a real gentleman.

He drained the last of his drink. "Daddy showed me that one letter of yours. September I think it was. Didn't have much in it." He looked at her kind of funny. "You gettin' churchy on us?"

Embarrassed to recall that letter and her plea for all of them to get on their knees and ask God for forgiveness, she laughed like she'd been joking and shook her head in a dismissive way. She bit off some of her sandwich and chewed like the episode was completely forgotten.

Under the clearing sky Emmett's sleepy gray eyes, almost blue, were underscored with purple circles. His long dark eyelashes curled up like those on porcelain dolls in the department store—not what an eighteen-year-old man would want to hear. Emmett's eyes had never matched the rest of his tough and compact body. He'd always had a lost boy look, she now realized. It seemed she was seeing through him, noticing that she wasn't the only one with secrets. But she couldn't probe his private life without giving back in kind, and her story would be worse, involving things no brother ought to know about his sister.

She finally asked, "How's Mom?"

"Well, I ain't seen the folks since the end of October, but at that time nothing had changed since you was there."

"I'm worried about that. Daddy writes like Mom talks to him. *We* this and *we* that."

"I know." He shook his head. "What the devil d'ya 'spose is wrong with her?" A furrow pinched his brows together. "You're a girl. Maybe you got a clue. It's got me stumped."

"Dunno. Truth be told, I couldn't stand going there for Christmas, with her like that."

"Me neither." Having finished his sandwich, he moved a finger around a knothole in the table. "Doan know what a body could do to git her out of it. Maybe if we knew the cause we could help. I send money every month, as much as I—" His voice trailed off.

Mae found it easier to talk about their mother than about herself. "I think it started when we got that letter about Gramps disowning Daddy. Both of them disowned. Maybe that was just too much."

He moved his head from side to side. "Don't think so. She was a tough lady when I was growin' up. Nothin' could get her goat. Not even Nora dying. I just don't understand it."

"I noticed a change in her back then," Mae contradicted. She'd seemed weaker in every way, now that Mae thought back on it. Spoiling Mae had been part of it.

"Nuthin' like she is now," Emmett argued in a rising pitch. "How the devil can a body cheer her up if'n she don't listen to what's being said to her?" His voice cracked.

"I doubt anything we do would make a difference," she said. "Maybe it's just that California isn't living up to what it was cracked up to be."

Emmett looked at her for a long moment. "It sure ain't. Not a whit like it was cracked up to be."

"Not for you, either?"

Anger flashed across his eyes. "Look at me! Glad to get wages workin' for somebody else. Why, we was 'sposed to be rich by now, all us boys! But we're all helpin' some other fella get rich. Hell, we coulda done that on a hay crew in Iowa." He spat the last out like bad pork.

"At twenty cents an hour?"

A cynical chuckle. "More like thirty. But 'stead'ov payin' high rates for a room here I coulda stayed and helped Uncle Ephraim. I got along fine with Uncle. Woulda been good help to'im too." His voice caught, and he looked away. "Woulda had my old friends."

Mae remembered when Emmett left to be a sheepherder. She'd thought such lonely work wasn't right for him. He needed people, and he wasn't good with a rifle. Probably missed when he tried to kill the wolves and coyotes.

"I'm glad you're working here," she said. "You can make new friends, and I can see you—"

The hellish screech of the whistle overrode all other sound, about knocking her off the bench.

When the noise stopped, Emmett said, "I gotta go. Where can I find you?"

"I might be moving in a couple days. Where can I find you, besides here?"

He made a giddy-up sound in his cheek. "That's just it. I'll be movin' too. Doan know where." He stood up.

She stood with him. "I'll come back and have noon dinner with you again. Unless you're thinking about leaving your job."

"Nope. I kinda like the work, you know, hammering iron, givin' it all I got." He spoke through clenched teeth while his eyes held hers. "Sometimes I see a face, all twisted and ugly in them swirls of red iron and I flatten it good and hard, I tell you, 'til every line in it's gone and I can't see it any more."

She understood. "There's a face I'd like to hammer too," she said under her breath.

He cast a steely glance at the men heading back to the foundry door and his shoulders relaxed. "Well, see ya. How 'bout a week from today?"

"Sure. Unless something happens. No—" She changed her mind. "I'll be here come hell or high water. Noon dinner next Wednesday."

"Next time I buy." He walked away, tossing over his shoulder, "If I'm still kickin'."

Pondering that, she watched him meld with the men pouring through the door. He was shorter than she remembered. Some of them were much bigger and taller, with ugly lines on their gaunt faces.

48

With her mind full of Emmett, Mae ambled back into the city. She was passing the Orangevale Colonization office at 214 J Street when the sun popped out of the fog, brightening the reflections on the windows. A buggy moved across the pane, and when it passed she saw a policeman in uniform on the other side of the street, looking down. In the glare of the window his buttoned coat mingled with the office furniture and "Lots For Sale" signs. Mae stared, all her senses prickling. He was just the size of—

His head jerked up. Their eyes locked in the window-mirror for an instant, and he lunged through the traffic toward her.

She knew he meant to kill her.

She whirled into the recess of the door, threw it open, hoisted her skirts, and ran past a surprised man at a desk. She ran to the back door. *Unlocked, thank God.* In the alley she quickly shut the metal door behind her.

Left or right? A canyon of brick buildings both ways. Too empty, too easy to see a person. She darted across the alley behind a small delivery wagon piled with vegetables. The back door of the adjacent building was ajar.

A clang of metal. He was in the alley!

She slipped through the door and ran up a narrow hallway. Numbers on the doors, both sides. A hotel. She tried a door. Locked. No time to try them all. She ran toward the light from the windows in the front of the building. Halfway there, a cloud of steam enveloped her, billowing from an open door. Through the steam, a Chinaman came at her with pole and baskets over his shoulders. In her haste to get around him she bumped a basket and it fell off the pole. All of it went down, but she couldn't look back. *Where to go?*

Not in the kitchen. Too many people. They'd point to her. Running up the hallway she stumbled on a wrinkle in the carpet, but caught herself and used the near-fall to propel herself faster. The steam behind would help hide her, so would the Chinaman righting his baskets.

In front now, no lobby. A stairway led upward, keys hung on a sidewall. No attendant. No place to hide. Oberon would be just behind her.

Out the door, she ran up the sidewalk. Fog again, a slight help. Maybe that saloon with swinging doors. No. Girls not allowed and men would tell Oberon.

Weaving in and out of shoppers she dashed into the traffic at the intersection of 4th and K Streets, dodging rigs, horses, wagons and hacks. Her shoe slipped in fresh manure, and she flailed to regain her balance. People stared. They would tell him.

She ran several blocks, to 8th and K. The Clunie Theatre stood catty-corner across the street. MAY HOWARD, AMERICA'S PEERLESS BURLESQUE QUEEN. It'd be dark there, but men were standing in line, paying. It'd take too long. Maybe a side door.

But then she turned into the recess of a dressmaker shop. She opened the door. Bells jingled.

A young woman not much older than Mae came from a back room. Colored threads streamed from several needles in the breast of her frock. Headless forms, two dressed in fine gowns, lined one wall of the tiny place.

Out of breath and trying not to alarm the proprietress, Mae said. "Hello, you make ladies' clothing?"

"Yes, I do. My, but you're winded." A hint of an Irish accent. "Sit yourself down and rest." She pulled out a chair and then sat on the other side of a consultation table. Her pale brown eyes searched Mae's face.

"There's a man after me," Mae gasped, dropping her coat on the chair so its flag of blackness couldn't be seen through the window and her blue day dress would be different. Heart pounding, she took a hat from a display and put it on her head. The wide droopy brim and the pile of pink roses on top would help hide her, but her shape was exposed to the windows.

The seamstress's face spoke surprise and puzzlement.

"I'm in awful danger," Mae blurted between breaths. "He's just behind me… Be here any second… Please… Let's talk in the back room."

The proprietress stared back, frowning.

"The hat's for disguise. Please…" Mae pointed to the opening in the curtain.

"Oh, I guess that'd be all right. Bring the chair."

Grabbing the chair that held her coat, Mae followed the young woman into a long, narrow workspace with a table reaching all the way to the back door and the alley.

Two large crates, one big enough to pack a small piano, lay on one side. A sewing machine stood on the other side, the seamstress sitting behind it. The long worktable started at the machine. Bolts of fabric filled the space under the table, and a dowel suspended from the ceiling ran above it, holding spools of laces, cording, bric-a-brac and tassels, a hundred tongues dangling the entire depth of the room to the alley door. High above, in the dark recesses of the ceiling, two gaslights provided insufficient light for needlework in this windowless room.

Mae put her chair behind the big crate, the top of which was heaped with scrap fabric. That hid her from the curtain, yet she was near enough to the seamstress.

"Is it your husband after you?"

"No. It's, uh… He chained me up in his room. For weeks." The woman was apt to throw her out if she told who he was.

"By Gory!"

"Said he'd kill me if I ran away." A torrent of tears interfered as she struggled to push out the words, "He's a policeman."

"Oh, no!" Fear showed in the wide pale eyes.

Mae knew the seamstress wouldn't want police trouble, a bad thing for a small business, but all she could do was weep and try not to make a sound in case Oberon came through the front door.

The young lady reached over the machine waving a piece of white fabric at Mae. "Go ahead. Use this."

At this gesture of sympathy, giant sobs engulfed her, and Mae pressed the soft flannel to her eyes. "So I can't… get help… from the police."

Bells jingled, the door shutting. Heavy footfalls rang on the wooden floor.

Before the girl could get through the curtain, Mae was on her knees inside the crate, bent over her coat. Stark terror halted her sobs. She removed the hat and quietly pulled a smaller crate in front of the opening of the big crate. *Please God, don't let her turn me over to him.*

The drumming of her heart drowned out the voices in the outer room, and it took a while before she realized the tenor voice was female, inquiring about a gown. "It will be finished by five o'clock," the proprietress promised. Again the footsteps sounded, the bells jingled, and the door shut.

Wrung out like a limp rag, Mae crawled back to her chair, and the release from the terror of imminent death brought a wave of false darkness.

The lady was back at her machine. "Where are you staying?"

"With a friend on N Street. I was at the SP yards visiting my brother. On the way back I saw… that detective. That's what he is. A specialist in finding criminals. But I'm not a criminal. He ran after me."

Again she was losing control. "I mustn't lead him to where… I'm staying. It's just that… I know he's out there… and I… just…"

In a storm of bawling she retrieved the flannel scrap from the crate and pressed it to her wet face. *I don't know what to do,* she wanted to say.

"Your brother—he's not helping you?"

Out of her tight throat, "I didn't tell him."

"You didn't? But then you came to me, a stranger…" It trailed off.

Again the door jingled. Fresh terror knifed Mae as she dove into the crate.

An alto voice made an appointment for a fitting the next day, and the seamstress returned.

"Why for the love of Mike didn't you ask your brother for help?"

"I couldn't tell him about the things—" *I was forced, or worse, not forced to do.* Sobbing overwhelmed her.

"I'd say you should get out of town. Or is all your family in Sacramento?"

"Only my brother… The rest are in Slough House."

"Your parents know about this policeman?"

"I can't tell them… They'd think it was my fault."

"Sounds like you need a priest. You a Catholic?"

"Sort of, but I don't know a priest."

"Well, I do. Bishop Patrick Minogue. He just got our cathedral built, and a glorious one it is. He'll advise you. And hear your confession."

"A bishop would talk to me?" Telling a bishop in a darkened confessional about something very wrong in his city might be possible. A bishop had power. He might be able to do something about Oberon.

"He's down-to-earth and compassionate," the young lady was saying. "In the forty-niner days he heard the confessions of the sinful miners of Nevada City. What's your name?"

"Mae Duffy."

"Hmm, Irish. I'm Mary Donahue. The Bishop's Irish too."

Now the Irish blood seemed to be helping. The terrible grip of muscles in her midriff relaxed, and her mind came into focus.

"That's a good idea. But right now I need a way to get to the alley behind 12th and N, without being followed. Is there someone who could give me a ride? So people won't see me running and report it?"

"Not that I can think of. I don't own a buggy."

Again the bells jangled and Mae ducked into the crate. This time it was a man's voice. The seamstress loudly greeted Mr. Johnston—a kindness that allowed Mae to breathe again. The man said something about an alteration in a waist. "The Missus will come for it tomorrow, late afternoon."

"It'll be done. Sorry about that," Mary Donahue told her customer.

The curtain rustled her return. This time she remained standing and addressed Mae with force, "Now I must get back to work. I'll get the boy upstairs to fetch your friend on N Street. She can figure out what to do."

"She's out of town, and I don't know anybody else in the house," Mae said.

That was a lie. But the landlord wasn't friendly and she didn't want him talking to Charlie about this. She didn't correct the assumption that Charlie was female because Mary would see her as immoral, and a girl had only one chance to be a worthy human being in the eyes of society. Oberon's stories about immoral women being tortured and murdered were a grim reminder that nobody cared what happened to them.

"Please, could you call a cab to your back door? I'll pay for the hat." She pulled it from the crate along with her coat.

Mary nodded. "Sure, I'll borrow the telephone in the Clunie Theatre. Don't worry, I won't tell anybody the police are after you. We Irish have to stand together."

Mae loved that. "How much is the hat?"

"Well, I have them here so ladies can get an idea what kind of hat would flatter their gown. That one cost me a dollar and I'll sell it to you for that."

"You're putting yourself out for me and I'm more grateful than I can say." Mae dug the money out of the deep pocket in her frock. "You're a saint."

"That's going a bit far," Mary sang out as she vanished through the curtain. *Thank God for Mary Donahue.*

"No need to hide," Mary called. "I'll lock the door behind me. Be about five minutes." The door jingled and shut.

Nonetheless Mae hid. Oberon had keys to all kinds of doors, and his determined face as he'd lunged toward her stayed in her mind.

∽

The cab was blinkered on the sides, the driver thankfully curt. Mae stepped down at the alley entrance, paying him five cents for a ride. She peered both ways. Children were playing on the otherwise empty street. She hurried up the alley, holding the new hat to her head.

Shaky and faint after climbing the back stairs, she fumbled with the lock. Inside, she checked each window to be sure it was locked. Extreme exhaustion pulled her to the unmade bed, and she lay on it fully clothed, shivering and pulling blankets around her. Benty jumped on the bed and curled up beside her.

After two quiet days indoors, Mae jumped when a key rattled in the front door. It was late afternoon on the day she expected Charlie to return. Until she was sure, she fled from the davenport with the book she'd been reading, went to the kitchen and stood at the wall beside the back door, hand on the doorknob.

The opening door sent a shudder through the walls. Then it slammed. Benty streaked past Mae's line of sight to the bedroom. Belated cold air reached her, but then a warm voice. "How's my girl? Back to her lively self, I hope."

Charlie. Going to the front room she wished to say, *I'd be a sight livelier if I knew for sure I was your girl.* Instead she used the manners the nuns had taught her, "I am well, thank you. How was your trip?"

"Quite pleasant." He shrugged out of his greatcoat and hung it on a brass hook between her coat and his hat. A lump of a gunnysack lay at his feet.

He squinted an eye her way. "Anything exciting happen?"

"No."

Looking her up and down, "You're still as slender as a desert grasshopper. Had any supper?"

"No."

He hefted the gunnysack and pulled out a huge thing wrapped in newspaper.

"My dad gave me a pork quarter. Let's fry some. In the morning I'll take what's left to the icehouse. Brought up some potatoes and turnips too, from the folks' cellar."

When they had the kitchen steamy with boiling potatoes, Charlie made a dash to the China garden on Q Street and returned with cabbage, scallions, and apples. The latter she sliced and spread on the pork slices sizzling on the little stove.

They worked together well, she thought, but underneath her polite demeanor she was on pins and needles about what he'd concluded on his train ride.

Over supper she found the nerve to ask, "Did you get any thinking done?"

His dark brown eyes went blank as he finished chewing a piece of meat.

"On your ride down and back, I mean."

"Oh, that."

He forked a chunk of buttered potato. "Getting down to brass tacks in a hurry, aren't we?"

"Sorry, I didn't mean to—"

"Stop being sorry."

They ate in silence, Mae wishing she'd kept her mouth shut.

The minutes stretched, and then Charlie laid his fork on his plate

"You're not a bad sort to have around. Most of the time, that is, when you're not scared of your own shadow. And I'm glad you recovered from the infection. Some girls don't, you know."

"I know." She put down her knife and fork.

"I had experience with a girl dying. Maybe that's why I was so anxious about you." He stood up. "Do you mind if we go sit on the softer chairs?"

Now it's coming. "I'd like that. I'll put more wood on the fire." She steeled herself.

Leaning back in his chair, Charlie stuffed tobacco in his pipe. She lit one of the long slivers kept for this purpose and held it over the bowl while he sucked in quick puffs. The tobacco ignited.

"Thanks. Did'ja notice I didn't take the pipe with me? My mother hates tobacco smoke."

He held the pipe out to Mae. "Go ahead, take a draw."

She took it, sucked smoke and blew it out.

"No, no," he laughed. "You gotta suck it all the way into your lungs. Try again."

This time she coughed so hard she thought she'd never stop, but managed to give it back, shaking her head. She curled her legs under her in the davenport corner nearest the fire.

Studying the cheerful little hearth Charlie said, "I do like having someone around when I get home at night. Gets lonely." He drew in smoke.

"Why aren't you married then? You'd always have someone."

"I'm not the marrying kind."

Not permitting that to linger between them, she forced a casual tone. "Been married before?"

"No."

"Oh. I thought maybe you'd had a bad experience."

"Mae," he said turning towards her in his chair, "I dislike intrusions into my private life by people who think they know better than I how I should live."

Whatever that meant, the sharp edge cut her.

He continued. "Social pressure upon people to marry is unjust. It's a mass hysteria that in many cases prevents the pursuit of happiness, which we Americans are supposed to be entitled to. I don't believe the state has any right to legislate or adjudicate my procreative behavior or force me to utter public vows or sign documents that promise from death do us part etcetera. If a man decides his liaison with a woman has lost its charm, he ought to be free to leave her. This is more than a constitutional matter. I would argue it's a need of human beings to live freely."

Feeling slapped, she watched him suck on his pipe and blow out smoke. He did it again, and she waited to be sure he was finished.

"I'm not pressuring you to get married," she finally defended.

"But you expect it, and that's the same thing."

Everything he said hurt, but yet they weren't in an argument as she understood arguments. They weren't yelling and hitting each other. "I guess you're what they call a confirmed bachelor."

"I despise being called a *confirmed* anything. I am simply an unmarried man."

The start of tears stung her eyes. How she wished to dam that salty spigot forever! Luckily he was looking at the fire.

She took a chance. "Does that mean you might get married some day?"

"It means I hold the right to change my mind about my private life. All I'm saying is, it's my business and nobody else's. But that in no way expunges the logic of what I've just said about marriage."

"Marriage is a sacrament the world over, in the Church." The instant that left her mouth she knew he wouldn't like it.

He rolled his eyes. "Better not get me started on religion." He looked back at the fire.

The silent spigot overflowed, and she looked away. Well, she'd better set herself a new course in life. Maybe vaudeville.

Suddenly he was speaking in a softer tone.

"Mae, I just came from five straight days of defending my unmarried state, and it must have perturbed me more than I knew. My mother, my sisters, even my nieces and nephews are all bent on getting me married—especially my mother. Forgive me if I sounded a little short."

She rubbed her face as though in thought, actually wiping tears. The silence between them lengthened as the little fire crackled and Benty purred on her lap. Trying to put herself in his position, she realized she didn't like her family making assumptions about her either. This time she gave more thought to her words before speaking.

"It must be hard for you to be romantic toward a lady, lest she expect marriage."

He looked at her with surprise. "As a matter of fact it is."

He added, "You see, I dislike living within the strictures of convention. I hate speaking polite untruths, although I must do it all day and every day in my work. But at my own hearth it's too much. I want to be honest with you."

"I couldn't want anything more, Charlie." *God, give me strength.*

Laying the pipe in its cradle, he got up and poured two glasses of port. He handed her one. "I would have preferred to eat at the State House Hotel this evening and stayed for a theatrical performance, but I knew you'd worry about Oberon. Your fear controls me too, and I don't like it."

With you at my side I'm not afraid. I would have liked to go to the hotel too.

He continued, "If we decide to cook here instead, I would like you to fetch things from the China Garden. Do you see what I mean? *I* went there and made the purchases because of your fear."

"Which you don't think is warranted."

He sat down and dipped his head like an actor making sure the nod was seen all the way to the back row, and then he sipped his wine.

"Furthermore, I don't like to take advantage of a girl in a delicate state, in her health or her nerves, though I might have wanted to." The last came as a low mutter.

"Did you? I mean, want to?" She held her breath.

Quietly, "Yes."

He added, "I would like you, without the expectation of marriage or the talk of it, to live with me and share my bed."

49

It was one of those nights when the lamplighters didn't make their rounds because the moon was supposed to light the town, but a fog came up and shrouded the moon. Nonetheless, Mae pulled the draperies shut.

In the dark of the familiar bed she said nothing to Charlie about her doubtful insides but let the silence meld with the darkness in a spell she was loath to break. His hand on her felt hesitant, even awkward and a bit shaky, but she had no idea how normal men behaved, or if this was normal for Charlie. It certainly wasn't to her. Despite that, and despite being female and fifteen years younger, she found herself conducting a tentative exploration of the mysteries of him. She didn't mean for things to go any further—there were medical doubts. But she did want him to love her.

Mumbling something about "…good to be in my own bed," he flopped over, away from her. The sheet, taut on his tall shoulder, let in the cold air. Within a few minutes his even breathing told her he was asleep.

She stared into the black void. Would he ask her to leave his apartment? She tried to think where to go, but found no answer. For a long vacant time she listened to him breathe, but then she turned the question around and asked herself how she felt about him as a man, and whether she felt disappointed, for reasons other than the terror of leaving him. She didn't know the answer, and she couldn't hook into anything like a feeling. Elusive strands of emotion floated into her mind and slipped away before she could fully identify them—guilt about Oberon's use of her while she battled fear, sorrow about her lost virginity, curiosity about how it would have been on her future wedding night had he not captured her, distress that Charlie found her unattractive, and bewilderment about her own feelings. All of it paraded round and round in her head.

Hours passed. She reviewed the evening and what he'd said about marriage, and exactly what moves she'd made before he turned over. And then in the honesty of the quiet night, or perhaps the lunacy of exhaustion, she believed she felt disappointed in a physical way that he had turned over. But there was also a sense of relief. God had saved her from further sin.

Sadly, however, she might have lost the chance to grow on Charlie. He could well send her away. This led to a debate with herself about what to say in the morning to make him like her better.

Then suddenly it *was* morning. The curtains were open to the blank upper wall of the house next door and a triangle of blue sky above the roof. The fog had lifted. She smelled coffee and heard Charlie singing in the kitchen.

And her golden hair was hanging down her back...

"Ah, you're awake," he said from the doorway. "How'd you like to accompany me to Oakland this afternoon? I've got a meeting there tomorrow." He was wearing his heavy black business suit, complete with vest and bow tie.

"Oakland? Where's that?"

"A nice town on the Bay. We could take the five o'clock train and dine aboard. Or we could eat noon dinner and catch the boat at two-thirty and be there about the same time as the train, but for less money. You'd see more water and some pretty sights along the way."

Groggy from a dearth of sleep she could hardly construe what he was saying. But he sounded happy. He wasn't telling her to leave, and was inviting her to go on a trip with him. Her night torment lifted like the fog.

"If it's the boat," he said, "you'd better get up. It's almost noon. I've been to the office and back."

He didn't even frown about her sleeping so late.

50

Sitting beside Charlie on the viewing deck as the Daisy churned up the strait, Mae wondered why he had brought her with him. But ask him she would not. He wasn't an easy man to understand. In public he liked to appear bluff and hearty, but at home could be angry. As for her, every nautical mile from Sacramento lifted more of the gnawing fear that had for so long warped her conversations with Charlie.

At the moment he was imparting knowledge to the silver-haired gentleman on his other side. Touching a map, "We're about here now. Port Costa's just ahead." He reached over the man and put a finger on the window. "See the railroad trestle over there? Just visible along the water's edge. It leads to the wharf, at those buildings. See, the grain barn back behind the trees? In volume it's a big little port."

The man put his nose to the window.

They'd been on the boat for over two hours, but Mae never tired of the panorama as the paddle-wheeler plowed up the widening Carquinez Strait with hills on both shores. On the north, a gnat-sized dray indicated a road, and a train resembled a miniature toy. Through the window near the prow of the boat she watched the January sky clabber with color.

"After a while we'll veer to the left," Charlie said to the man, "and go south."

The gentleman on Mae's right had his head in a newspaper, as did the men in front and behind, all dressed like bankers. The view meant nothing to them, but to her it looked like another planet, one principally of water.

The silver-haired man stood up. "May I?" He looked at Charlie's long legs.

Charlie stood to let him pass, and then smiled at Mae. "Say, wanna go too?"

"Sure." His jovial manner buoyed her.

The wind on deck tore at her hat pins. Giggling, she grabbed her hat and raised her voice to be heard over the roar and splash of the boat, "Charlie, I'm taking my hat back to the seat. Find us a space at the rail."

On the seat her wide black hat topped with pink roses looked nice beside Charlie's top hat. She turned up her coat collar and returned to the foredeck, away from the smudged and water-streaked windows. The vastness of the bay thrilled her. Huge brushstrokes of orange and gold in the western sky now spilled over the water. Charlie's backside stuck out farther than those of the other men as he squinted into the wind, forearms on the rail, hands clasped.

"I'm glad you asked me to come," she said, moving in beside him.

"I'm glad too." He put an arm around her. "We're in the Bay now."

Snug against him, she liked the spray of tiny drops on her face as the boat rode the choppy waves.

He pointed. "Can you see it now? The City?"

She followed his finger across the restless orange water to what looked like a dark encrustation at the base of a mountain, the sun starting to dip behind it. "I think so."

"That's the powerhouse of the state you're looking at." He glanced at her, perhaps seeing her high spirits. "The tycoons, the money over there—" He shook his head like mortal man couldn't put words to it. "I'm meeting with one of them tomorrow. But in Oakland. He had a business meeting there so we decided to meet at the Tubbs Hotel. He likes to stay there, and we've got a reservation for a room."

He continued. "I've given thought to what produced men like him."

"Well, what did?" She loved him talking to her like this.

"The Gold Rush. You see, it was like a giant sieve that stretched 'round the world. Hundreds and thousands of men jumped into that sieve. They dreamed of riches—young lads for the most part, eager for the unknown. The first shaking came on the journey—the tramp through the Nicaraguan jungle thick with disease and mosquitoes, rickety vessels on both oceans scared up to replace the regular ships that were stuck in this bay without crews. For months passengers baled and pumped water, sleeping like kippers in a tin. Ruthless men cheated them out of space and money. Those who came overland suffered too. The poor buggers walked every step of the way through storm and dust and thirst, dogged by cholera. Boys and men of fragile health died, and those with weak wills gave up before they ever saw the gold fields."

Suddenly straightening to his full height, Charlie threw back his head and laughed. "I can hardly believe I'm telling you the same old grist my dad dished out to us when I was a boy. How he did go on! All I wanted to do was go shoot quail with my friends. They heard the same litany from their parents. My whole generation was sick to death of the Gold Rush. And now—" He wagged his head and chuckled.

"I've never heard of that jungle before. Nica—"

He raised his brows at her. "Believe it or not, California businessmen are talking about digging a shipping channel across that steamy neck of land, to connect the Pacific with the Atlantic." He snorted a laugh as he leaned again on the rail. "Some are the same men who suffered through it."

"In Iowa, we thought all you had to do was go to California and you'd get rich."

"The whole world's been thinking that for forty years. But most of those miners didn't make a dime, when you figure food and necessaries. Old-timers like my dad puzzled over it. Couldn't figure out why, when all those capable men started out with equal hardship and equal opportunity, only a few ended up richer than lords. Lady luck, they claimed. But I don't agree."

Charlie moved his lips around like he was cleaning his teeth with his tongue. "In a way, all of life is a great sifting. But the Gold Rush accelerated it. Something of an unintentional scientific experiment the scope of which has never been seen before. The man I'm meeting tomorrow is one of the handful who profited colossally from the it."

He smiled at her.

"Charlie, what's that over there?" She pointed to something huge and dark rising from the water with lights flickering on the near side.

"That's Angel Island. The government established a U.S. quarantine station there about a year ago—you know, for people with smallpox, plague, cholera and so forth."

"Oh, I didn't know such places existed. I'm glad they do that."

"Me too." He paused. "You know, Mae, all day long at the Capitol I dicker over words and phrases, but I much prefer to think about big things like what I've been talking about." He gazed over the water, his tone confidential. "You won't remember, but I talked to you about things when you were too sick to hear."

"Well, I'm listening now."

He smiled at the water, his hands clasped again. "That giant sieve shook like a son of a gun all over the canyons and gorges of the Mother Lode. Kept it up for five, ten, fifteen years. Heaps and piles of men were eliminated—the fainthearted, the ones who broke down physically after digging from dawn to dark with their feet in icy water, those who couldn't stand more sickness, broken bones, sciatica, bullying and cheating. Keep in mind there was no law. Droves of them went home, and quite a few good men made a clever switch from mining to the provisioning of miners. They built this state. Mr. Levi Strauss with his canvas attire, for instance."

"You don't mean the overalls my brothers wear, Levis?"

"The very same. The Levi factory's over there." He nodded at The City. "When the surface gold was picked over, the digging went underground. Some of the men, like the one I'm meeting with tomorrow, rose to be mine owners. But most found themselves digging in someone else's mine."

"My brother George is doing that, and is not happy about it."

"Some got angry. They blamed everyone else for their failures. They quarreled and shot each other to death, or turned robbers and were hung. You'd be surprised how many were hauled to the Stockton Asylum for the Insane and Habitual Drunkards. But a lot of good strong men stayed on as farmers, like my dad. Or they're working for the railroad or wielding picks in the mine tunnels, if they're not too old. Some are still angry over how things turned out. A few became labor leaders in the mines."

"My brothers were sifted out in a hurry," Mae put in, "But I'd say it was on account of our coming too late. The gold was all sewed up."

"You're right about that. But a determined and inventive man can still make a killing in California. Just not in gold."

"Do you think Emmett could work his way up to the top in the SP Railroad?"

"Umm, probably not with them. Those are college men, or have long experience. I'd say he'd have to start a business of his own to make real money. But not every man is inclined toward business. And that brings me to the final sifting.

"The few who survived all those trials *and* understood business remained in the sieve like big shiny jewels. Their fortunes are too great to count. I'd say Lady Luck had little to do with it. While lesser men drank their troubles away, those special men worked harder and thought smarter and learned faster, and invented new methods and machines to extract the earth's treasure. Next, they invented new ways of doing business and worked the Legislature to change state law to allow the accumulation of capital. They saw to the loosening of the rules of finance, and they created monopolies and bank trusts. Their fortunes multiplied like rabbits."

Mae didn't understand *accumulation of capital* or *trusts* and she knew her brothers wouldn't either. Schools didn't teach about making money. "Maybe the tycoons came from money," she offered, "and they learned those things from their fathers."

Charlie was shaking his head. "Many of the winners came from poor families. They had little schooling of any kind, and yet they're savvy gamblers who calculate in their heads the risks of complex business deals. It seems like everything they touch turns to gold, but they're actually making sure that it does."

"You say they're gamblers?" Emmett didn't like to gamble.

"Decidedly. But they don't squander their money in gambling halls. Their heirs'll do that soon enough. No ma'am, the fists of those tycoons are as tight as their minds. I'm talking about the creation of stock companies. You see, they built the investment system of California—their own gaming table— and they place their bets with solid knowledge about the enterprises. Old as they are, they're still shaping the marketplace of the world. I tell you, those men are the strongest of the strong and the smartest of the smart. Working with them is more than I could have imagined as a boy—though it's a tad disquieting at times."

He turned to her with a concerned expression. "I've gone on too long. Are you warm enough out here?"

"My coat's warm, and I love to hear you talk." She now believed Charlie had brought her with him because he liked her. Not since that first night on the train, when she and Mother and the boys had high hopes for California, had she felt this good. More keenly than ever she realized that marrying a man such as Charlie was her best *chance.*

"I was wondering," she dared venture, choosing her words, "if those tycoons have nice homes, and families, and wives."

He leaned over the rail moving his mouth around, and then spoke in a dismissive way. "All they think about is business. Marriage doesn't hold up under it." His shoulders bumped up. "Or maybe convention doesn't apply to a breed that rare."

His enthusiasm had returned, and Mae breathed easier.

"Thunderation, I wish Anthony Chabot still lived! He stayed at the Tubbs Hotel. Didn't wed 'til his mid-fifties. The girl died in childbirth a year later. He gave the baby to his dead wife's mother back east. Years later when the mother died he married a spinster—to get care for the child, people said. Anyway the three of them moved into the Tubbs Hotel. I guess she finally divorced him and took the girl away with her."

That didn't sound very nice. Hardly the family life Mae would have envisioned for a tycoon. "Did you say we're staying at the Tubbs Hotel?"

"Yes." Charlie went on about Mr. Chabot, how as a boy he'd walked to the United States from a poor farm in French Canada. "Spoke no English. Had but a couple years of grade school under his belt and not two coins to rub together. The Mother Lode taught him about water. He hated digging dirt and carting it to streams to wash gold, so he figured out how to bring the water to the dirt. In other words he invented hydraulic mining."

"They're doing that in Michigan Bar. My brother Farley worked those hoses." *Before they laid him off.*

"They're hydraulicking in other places too. Technically it's illegal now."

"Why?"

"Farmers and shippers seeing red over the silted streams. As a matter of fact the first lawsuit was filed out in Michigan Bar." He smiled over at her.

"Aren't those companies punished for law-breaking?"

"Not always. But that's another story."

"Oh, sorry. Go on." It pleased her no end that Charlie obviously enjoyed this, and she was getting a pleasant feeling that he knew many of those rich men personally. Surely that boded well for his future.

He put an arm around her shoulders and squeezed. "Mr. Chabot never stopped moving water. He built San Francisco's water system. My guess is the City'll be using his waterworks for a hundred years. Before he came, people were drinking from polluted wells or paying men to haul water by boat, donkey and bucket. Next, that little man went to Oakland, San Jose, Benicia and built their water systems, reservoirs up in the hills, flumes, pipes, ditches, always figuring water flow better than any certified engineer."

Charlie opened his hands to the glorious reds and gold that colored sky and water. "People on every shore here are paying Chabot companies for their water. The Water King, we called him. Had a hand in a lot more than water, too. When he needed pipes, he started an ironworks. When he needed wood for his flumes, he became a timber man with many sawmills. He even raised cranberries to the north of us."

"What happened to him?"

"Died a couple years ago, liver problem I heard. But before he went, he gave a fortune to charities."

"And to think he came from such a poor family! I hope they got a piece of it."

"Oh sure. And his wasn't the only family to become rich because their boy ran away from home to seek his fortune. As we stand here those same men over there are still moving mountains and building skyscrapers." He nodded toward San Francisco.

She turned that in her mind, but had to ask. "What on earth is a skyscraper?"

"A tall building. A word I'm hearing of late." He lifted a brow at her. "Say, if I finish my meeting by eleven tomorrow, maybe we could take the noon ferry and pay a visit to the Imperial City. Would you like that?"

"You mean San Francisco?" Seeing his smiling nod she almost squealed. "I'd love it, Charlie! Can we go early?"

"That'll be up to Mr. Fair, the Bonanza King."

In the next few minutes, as the colors deepened and Charlie leaned into the wind, she learned that Mr. Fair's bonanza was the richest gold and silver strike in the history of the world. Others abandoned what they thought was depleted ground, but "that cussed Irishman just kept drilling six hundred feet down. Invented a stamp mill to process the ore quicker. Played fast and loose with the stock market, and kept the lion's share of profit. Day in and day out for years he shipped trainloads of high-grade ore out of Nevada. Was said to make $700,000 a month."

"My word! How much money has he got now?"

"Estimated in multiples of millions. Hundreds of millions. Only he knows the multiples."

"Is he married?"

Charlie closed an eye and gave her the histrionic look of a comedian.

In the same feigned manner, she clapped a hand over her mouth. "Whoa, my horses ran away with me and let that bad word get out."

He hawed, and then turned again to the spectacular sky and water. "Is my girl planning to prospect in Oakland?"

"Maybe. After I see what Mr. Bonanza looks like."

"You think that would be fair? For you to size up a man right under my nose? And a geezer named Fair at that?"

"So we've got rules now, have we?"

"Well, if we don't, we'll have to establish them forthwith."

She had never felt so good about Charlie. "Ahh," she exhaled, gazing at the sunset. "It's so grand! We never had sunsets like this in Iowa."

"Never?"

"Never."

"When a gale scours out the smoke in Sacramento the sunsets are a deal paler, so I think it's smoke that makes them so fine." He grinned. "Not a romantic analysis?"

"No. But with this much wind, I'd think things'd be good and scoured out."

They stared at gaudy slashes of red with golden dust ruffles.

"I'd say what looks to be clouds over there is mostly smoke. Day and night San Francisco burns thousands of tons of coal. Sacramento's a piker by contrast. Not to mention the electric lights in those buildings, each with its own coal generator. That's a lot of smoke."

"Don't forget the fireplaces," she quipped.

"That too. In about every room."

Looking at the nearer shore on their left, he pointed. "I just caught a glimpse of the University of California. Do you see it?"

She stared at a darkening forest. "No."

"It's behind the trees now. Only yesterday the legislature was debating the construction of a 300-foot campanile on the campus, one that travelers could see way out here. I'm for it, but in this Panic it's looking doubtful."

"What's a campan— What did you call it?"

"Campanile, a bell tower. Like the tower of Pisa. But ours wouldn't lean."

"You talk like you own the place."

318 ⌒

Rest for the Wicked

"I work on the state budget. All the people of California own the college."

"Well, what do you know. I own something after all!"

He raised a brow as though to say her joke fell short.

"Is the university new?"

"Hardly. Berkeley's been churning out graduates for twenty years. Three of those years it was shaping me up for life in a business suit."

"Hmm. Looks good on you too." She peeked at Charlie, surprised at herself for flattering a man. "Isn't Mills College on this bay someplace?"

"Yes, in Oakland."

"Katy Irene Sheldon goes there. Polly Sheldon too."

"Perchance daughters of William C. Sheldon of Slough House?"

Charlie knew everyone of importance! "Katy's a niece. They treat her like a daughter. The Sheldons are friends of mine." A prideful bit that Sister Delphine would have admonished.

The water had gone dark, the sky on the starboard side deep purple. Across the Bay, the last of the sunset outlined in bright gold the crest of the black mountain beneath which San Francisco nestled.

"Mr. Sheldon grows experimental fruits," Charlie said.

"Funny, those plums tasted mighty real to me."

He granted her a chuckle.

"He's experimenting with corn too," she supplied. "Katy Irene told me he's developing a hard variety that can be milled easier."

"I believe he's working with Luther Burbank. A genetic scientist. Crosses fruit trees to make new varieties on his own little farm in Sebastopol, over there near Santa Rosa." Charlie turned to point northward and then continued looking south. "He'd be in the gilded city living like a king if he'd file patents on his varieties."

"Guess he doesn't give a fig about the money."

That yielded a guffaw, after which Charlie looked at her appreciatively. "You're right. Burbank's no businessman. But he works hard. Visits growers to check the progress of his special trees. I think his name will be remembered. Watch for him when you get back to Slough House."

"*When?* Fixing to get shed of me, are you?"

"Not at all. I'm liking you more by the minute."

51

When the Daisy tied up to the wharf and Oakland twinkled against a backdrop of dusky hills, Mae and Charlie joined the little crowd of passengers bouncing along the floating dock. On firm ground, he strode with the bags to one of the parked hacks, Mae trotting to keep up.

"Seventh and Broadway," he told the driver.

Mae climbed into the back seat ahead of Charlie. The horses stepped out smartly, and already she liked this city, so distant from her fears. The gentle air, not sooty or cold and damp like Sacramento, was more like Iowa in May, though this was January. As the last of the light faded, they drove along the waterfront where stars sparkled over the black water. The driver turned up the wide maw of a lighted street.

"This is Oakland's Broadway," Charlie said.

Well named, Mae saw. It was wide enough for several sets of rails down its middle, with room for buggies and wagons on both sides and boardwalks to boot, both sides lined with streetlamps. A horse car plodded toward them pulling a streetcar, which seemed behind the times for a city like this. But soon afterward a streetcar with no overhead electricity—and seemingly no means of power—overtook them, stopping and then whizzing to life again.

"What on earth makes that coach go?" she asked Charlie.

"You never heard of a cable car?"

Stung by his amused tone, she recalled someone saying something about them. "Maybe."

"They hook into an underground cable that keeps moving all the time."

Watching that car stop to pick up more people and then move alongside them again, Mae was even more puzzled, but didn't ask how it stopped for fear of sounding stupid. Anyway, it didn't matter. No one could understand all the progress these days.

Charlie looked like a million dollars in his suit and high hat, and she felt like a real lady to be with him. Modern buildings on both sides of the wide street stood flush against each other, the lower levels closed and dark. In the lamplight she made out some of the lettering: REALTY, INSURANCE, DENTIST. The out-thrust windows in the upper story were lit up, and she saw people moving around inside, this being the supper hour. Charlie called the new style of three-sided windows "bay windows."

"Seventh Street Station," their driver called, pulling the horses to a halt.

After paying, Charlie escorted her inside and studied the chart on the wall, the long list of arrivals and departures. "Look at that." He put a finger on San Leandro and Haywards Electric Railway. "Last I was here, it was called the Tubbs Line. Mr. Fair must be peddling property in San Leandro and Haywards."

"The Bonanza King?" Mae inquired, the rest of it going past her.

Charlie was on his way to the ticket counter. "Yes, James Fair," he remembered to say when he came back with the tickets. "Didn't I tell you I'm going to talk to him about streetcar franchises?"

"Yes, you did." She told herself to listen more carefully in the future. If he stopped talking about his work what *would* they talk about? And then how *would* she ever get him to marry her?

They sat on a bench to wait with about a dozen other people.

"I'm surprised they still have horse cars here," Mae remarked to Charlie. "Sacramento's ahead of Oakland." This, she thought, was his kind of conversation.

A lady of girth turned towards them, the yellow plume of her hat quivering above her severe countenance.

Charlie whispered, "People don't take kindly to rebukes of their city." In a normal tone he added, "All the streetcar tracks are laid by land speculators for the convenience of their customers. In Sacramento too, but Sacramento's got only two or three lines, so it wasn't hard to get them consolidated and electrified. Oakland's got at least fifteen different lines, so that's more complicated. I'll wager by the turn of the century they'll all be electrified and consolidated under one banner."

Chagrined, Mae peeked at the dowager's stern, double-chinned profile. Outside, another cable car made a jerky departure. To redeem herself, Mae said in a loud voice, "The cable cars do look nice with no wires."

"They're a bit slow," Charlie said. "And it's costly to dig up the streets and lay cable so, if you ask me, the future is in overhead wire."

The clock on the wall ticked to 6:50 when a half trolley, half indoor car, screeched to a halt with feelers sparking on the overhead wire. The man behind a desk trotted out to help the motorman push the car around on its turntable, its electric light sweeping over the buildings. "Here we go." Charlie said, grabbing the bags. "About time too. I'm hungry as a wolf."

They sat in the open end of the car to enjoy the nice air, the lady with the yellow feather inside. Humming up Broadway for a few blocks, they jerked around a corner. Mae grabbed her hat as she was thrown against Charlie.

"Twelfth Street east," the motorman called. They passed blocks and blocks of stately homes, stopping to let the yellow-plumed lady off. Through the windows of those homes Mae caught glimpses of people at the supper table, the soft gaslight spilling over gracious lawns.

Suddenly they sped into darkness, leaving the homes and streetlamps behind. A cow gave forth a round moo and a sewer smell added to the scent of marsh and salt air. Then they were rattling over a long bridge.

"We're crossing an inlet of the Bay," Charlie explained. "Lake Merritt. The pride of Oakland." Points of light formed a necklace around the darkness, reflecting on the water.

On the other side they passed several blocks of mansions before the motorman called, "Tubbs Hotel." Hearing a name like that, Mae had expected something squat and ordinary. Instead, a broad gateway lined with trees opened to them and myriad electric lights gave daylight to the enormity of a three-story, two-block palace bristling with towers, turrets and gables.

Sotto voce as they walked though the open doors of the massive hotel, she said, "This is like the country home of an English baron. My schoolbook had a picture of one like this."

"You're entering the largest hostelry in California." He led the way across a vast lobby with fine furniture. A red velvet seat mimicked a bench around a tree, but instead of a tree stood a tall vase of gladiolus and snapdragons spiking upward. Flowers in January! A young man at a grand piano was playing something that sounded like Debussy. Sister Delphine, fond of modern music, had taught Mae to recognize the fluidity of it.

"Wonders never cease when a girl is with Prince Charming," she said under her breath when he couldn't hear her.

Setting the bags before the mahogany counter, Charlie signed the ledger, and a bellboy about Emmett's age picked up the bags. Mae was scanning a list of entertainments: vocal recital, poetry reading, séance by a Madame, and a demonstration of thaumaturgy. That puzzled her, but she caught up with Charlie and the bellboy.

A uniformed man operated an iron cage of a lift, and the three of them rose like angels to the third floor. A few steps down a hall she found herself inside a suite of rooms at least as elegant as those in the Golden Eagle Hotel.

The bellboy deposited the bags in the bedroom. "Sir," he inquired, "would you like to have supper here or in the dining room?"

Charlie looked at Mae. "What do you think?"

"Dining room." She wanted to see more of the hotel.

"The lady's wish is my command," Charlie informed the boy, who had another question at the ready.

"Would you like me to notify Mr. Fair that you'll be in the dining room?"

"I think not. If it's convenient for him, an early breakfast meeting would suit me. Oh, and there'll be a shirt outside the door for laundering, and shoes to be polished."

The young man bowed and left.

"A body'd think Mr. Fair lived here," Mae quipped, opening her valise.

"He stays here when he has business. Many businessmen do." He shook a clean shirt out of his bag. "Ladies and children frolic while papa conducts business."

Mae pulled on her new gown.

"I wouldn't mind living here," Charlie said, helping her with the buttons in back. "The employees would make my bed, summon me to the telephone, and serve brandy to my visitors. Not a bad way to live."

She couldn't imagine living in a hotel on a permanent basis—not that it would be bad, but such a thing had never crossed her mind.

⌒

A prairie of tables stretched before them—mostly filled, as Mae and Charlie followed the host across the expanse. She felt stylish in her new gown. Charlie had purchased it "in celebration of her reasonable decision." The saleslady had emphasized that it was suitable for both day and evening. More memorable, Charlie had said the dark red fabric set off Mae's "raven tresses and rosy cheeks."

Seating them, the host handed them over to a Negro waiter dressed in tails.

The waiter gave Charlie a menu card and bowed away. Mae looked around and noticed that all the waiters moving about the dining room were spotless Negroes. This was exotic, thrilling to be in such a fabulous place, so very far from the cabins of Michigan Bar.

A man two tables away extinguished her euphoria. Looking down so the brim of her hat hid her face she said, "Charlie, that's Mr. Miller, the owner of the main hotel in Latrobe. Let's move to another table." She didn't add that if Mr. Miller saw her with a man in Oakland, the folks and Farley and Hank and Sophie would hear of it, and she'd never be able look at them again.

Charlie looked puzzled. "Where?"

"The other side of that lady with the red hair." Surreptitiously she pointed.

"How do you happen to know him?"

"He was on the train to Latrobe when we first came to California. He offered to talk to my father about employment. Please, let's move."

"Did that work out? Employment, I mean"

Maybe he won't remember me. "We told Daddy, but he never did talk to Mr. Miller."

"That's too bad, not to meet an important man of that area." Charlie didn't seem to care a whit that she wanted to move to another table.

"Guess he'd rather be dirt poor," Mae remarked. In her distress she'd let the bitterness out, and Charlie looked at her strangely. *After this I won't mention my family except in short replies. Now that I'm with Charlie I must think like a lady.*

"Do you know his girls? They look about your age." He was staring at the Millers!

"No, I don't know them. Charlie, please stop looking at them."

Mr. Miller's head jerked toward Charlie, and he smiled. They both smiled. They knew each other! Mr. Miller said a word to the older lady, doubtless his wife, and in a thrice the man stood before them grinning a toothy smile at Charlie.

"Well, old man, who the devil would've thought you'd be here? And with a lovely little lady." He studied Mae. "Say, I think I've met her before."

"You did," said Charlie, stunning her with his carelessness. "On the train from Sacramento to Latrobe."

Mae felt her face burning and she had to look down, feeling like a freak in a circus show.

Mr. Miller snapped his fingers. "That's it. Well, we'd be doubly honored if the two of you would join us. We haven't ordered yet."

Charlie, of course, accepted. To refuse would have been rude to one of the rich men he so admired.

Waiters brought chairs and pushed another table against the Miller table. Champagne was poured. Mae drank three large gulps, glad for the almost instant slowing of her heart that it bestowed. She drank more and felt her muscles relax.

Soon she seemed at home with Mrs. Miller, whose diction and grammar were those of an unschooled farm wife. The young boy turned out to be a grandson. By the time the fricassee of California elk arrived, Mae's fears had dissolved and her tongue loosened ever more with each tiny flute of sparkling wine. The Millers seemed to accept her, never asking embarrassing questions. It felt like she'd known Harriett and Frankie, the girls, all her life. They chatted about their school, and Mae made sure they knew she was almost a high school graduate.

Suddenly it seemed there was nothing more for the girls to talk about, so they listened to the men at their end of the table.

Mr. Miller asked Charlie, "What do you think about the U.S. annexing the Hawaiian Islands?"

His shoulders budged. "The capitalists are licking their chops."

James Miller's mustache spread. "So's the military. This puts the United States in the Pacific as a major power. Did you see where C. K. McClatchy at *The Sacramento Bee* is railing against it, calling it a great wrong to the natives?"

"Yes, I did. He marches to his own drummer."

"Getting back to California," Mr. Miller said, "are the Delta landowners going to Washington to testify on coolie labor?"

"Yes. P. J. Van Loben Sels and George Roberts are there now. They'll make their point. Congress isn't quite so awash in the Anti-Chinese hysteria as is California."

"No? They passed the Dog Tag Law."

"It's my understanding," Charlie said, "that the Chinese tongs took that to the Supreme Court and it's supposed to lose. Meantime, the tongs are telling their men not to register for the ID tags. Anyway, it's ridiculous to even discuss deporting all those people, especially in these bad economic times. It'd bankrupt the government for years to come. From what I've heard, there are still about two hundred thousand Chinese workers here, despite all the violence against them, and a quarter of them are illegals. Can you imagine the cost of shipping them all the way to China? Congress should step up the enforcement of the existing Exclusion Law, rather than pass a measure that is entirely unenforceable. That just invites illegal immigration."

Mr. Miller agreed wholeheartedly. "They're pandering to the fear-mongers who scream about the yellow hordes taking over America. I believe the Delta farmers when they say they've tried trainloads of white men from the Midwest and South, but they can't do the work. Or won't. The reclamation effort requires Chinese labor. Period. And I do wish journalists would stop their endless whipping up of hatred for little brown men. McGlashan in Truckee is the worst. Though I always liked him personally. He's gone crazy over this."

"Well, at least the Sacramento papers aren't so bad on that," Charlie said.

After a few more comments back and forth, Charlie turned to Mrs. Miller and said in a personable manner. "So you're living here permanently? In Oakland?"

"Yup, we've dug in for good. Gave Sacramento a try. People claimed summers there wasn't so danged hot as Latrobe." She shook her head. "I sure's heck didn't hardly notice that nighttime breeze everybody's so all-fired wild about."

Mr. Miller put a hand on his wife's arm and continued the story. "Eliza had a violent heat stroke. Every summer she gets hit harder by the heat. We thought we'd lose her. I took her to the hospital in Sacramento, and bought a house there while I was waiting for her recovery. The SP hospital's the best in the United States, but a year later, the doctor took me aside and said Eliza mightn't make it through another summer, so we'd better get her out of the valley altogether. So we bought a place here in Oakland, not far from this hotel. The summer was grand." He smiled at his wife and she smiled back.

Harriett said, "We overlook Lake Merritt, right across the road from a livery, so we can drive around town anytime we want."

Mr. Miller continued. "We're not far from the railroad, so I get to Sacramento and Latrobe regularly. Keep a room in our hotel." He turned to his daughters. "Oakland suits you two, doesn't it?" Harriett and Frankie nodded. Little Jim piped up, "Me too."

"But I do miss the ready access to the Capitol," Mr. Miller admitted to Charlie. "That's the one drawback. I like to keep my toe in the water." The corners of his mustache spread as he lifted a finger to the waiter for another bottle of champagne.

By the time the pear dessert with scorched-sugar arrived, Mae was floating. Mrs. Miller invited her to breakfast at their house while Charlie met with Mr. Fair.

"Oh, do come," Frankie begged. "Harriett and I'll take you on a ramble, won't we?" She looked at her sister, who was nodding with a mouth full of pear.

"That's a nice offer," Charlie told Mae. To Mrs. Miller he explained, "We're planning to take the noon ferry to The City."

"Don't worry," Eliza Miller said, "She'll be back by then."

ᔍ

Everything was easy for a girl on the arm of a man with connections, Mae was thinking as they strolled through the lobby. But the floor refused to stay put. It circled like a merry-go-round and she giggled about needing Charlie to keep her upright. A Strauss waltz emanated from a string quartet that had replaced the pianist, and she wanted to dance with Charlie right then and there, regardless of what anyone thought.

He was staring at the far side of the lobby where a man beckoned. "Looks like Mr. Fair, the capitalist himself. With Hiram Tubbs and some other men."

He took the room key from his pocket. "Here. Go on to the room. I won't be more than a minute."

"Oh, no you don't! You're not getting rid'a me that quick." She tugged him forward. "I wanna meet the Bonanza King." Her tongue tangled over it.

Charlie stood his ground. "Mae, that's a saloon full of men over there, and you're in no condition to talk."

She gave him her sweetest smile. "Oh please. It's wide open to the public." Half of the wall was missing, allowing people in the lobby to see inside.

He frowned for a while, and then said. "Only if you let me do *all* the talking."

She promised, and they proceeded. Gentlemen were seated at most of the tables. Four snifters of brandy stood around Mr. Fair's table, with three gray heads and one light brown head hovering over them. The four men looked up at her like she was a young lovely, and she was aware of attaining a height to which she'd only dreamed—being social with possibly the richest man in the United States.

"We're on our way out," Charlie declared, motioning them not to stand for introductions. "This is Miss Mae Duffy. I'm taking her home."

He continued, "This is Mr. Fair, the Bonanza King," indicating a boulder of a man with trimmed gray beard and overflowing mustache, an old man clearly pleased to be introduced as such. "This is Mr. Hiram Tubbs, the hotel owner. He and his brother sold so much cordage that they built Tubbs Resort Hotels in two sunny cities on the Bay."

Mae was about to ask where the other hotel was, but Charlie squeezed her arm. Mr. Tubbs was introducing Daniel Stein, a capitalist, and Frank Smith, also a capitalist.

"Borax Smith," Mr. Fair added with a malicious grin.

Borax is laundry powder. Younger than the others, Borax Smith had a tidal wave of sandy hair above his forehead. He raised his snifter to Mae. They all did, and drank to her beauty. She felt she had just gone to heaven.

The Bonanza King told Charlie he'd meet him in the lobby at seven o'clock in the morning. While that was coming out of his mouth, the old man's black eyes moved up and down Mae, one glittering orb the keener for the accent of the bushy black brow lifted above it. It felt rude, but maybe nothing was rude for a millionaire a hundred times over. Or maybe a thousand.

Charlie acted like he didn't notice, although of course he did. Quickly agreeing to the time for the meeting, Charlie took her elbow and led her away while Mr. Stein, the picture of genteel amusement, sipped his brandy. With the room tilting, she couldn't think what was funny.

∾

She entered their suite waltzing to the strings now faint in the distance of the first floor. Charlie closed the door and shut out the music.

"Oh, Charlie," she said dancing to the waltz in her mind, into the bedroom until she fell back upon the bed of puffy quilts and pillows, "I had such a grand time tonight!" She closed her eyes and felt herself floating in circles around the ceiling of the room.

"I liked seeing you so lively." He was there with her.

The side of the bed sagged under his weight. His fingertips traced a path from her forehead down her cheek and neck and shoulder, down the sleeve of her arm. Soft lips met hers and the scent of pipe tobacco in his mustache engulfed her. She opened her eyes. His were closed as he kissed her, and his mouth was more and more urgent. No hint of hesitation or awkwardness.

52

Mae opened her eyes to sunlight pouring into the hotel room. She stretched, feeling dreamy and a little sticky. From the other room a melody soared like a sweet bird—Charlie whistling in the way of men raised on farms. She sat up and looked out the window. Over the green treetops water glistened about a half-mile away, a spit of land beyond that, and then a vast expanse of blue slate dotted by sailboats almost too tiny to see. Not a cloud in the sky except a bank of smoke hiding the distant shore of San Francisco.

The whistling stopped.

She looked at the doorway. Charlie was there naked above the waist except for red suspenders and a towel around his neck. The wet spikes of his hair grazed the door frame as he walked toward her.

"Mornin' Skeeziks. You sleep well?"

She gave him a coy glance. "Yes. You been to the bathroom?"

"Had me a hot shower in a merry row with three other men." Dropping the towel on an upholstered chair back, he came to the side of the bed and leaned down to kiss her.

She reached up and felt his baby soft cheeks. "You shaved too."

"Men do that in the morning, you know. How do you feel?" He put his hand on the covers above her abdomen.

"I'm fine. Very fine." She ran her fingers through his dark, silky chest hair.

"Is there any place where you're not so fine?"

"Maybe my soul. It feels wicked to be in a hotel room with a man I'm not married to." *Oops, not supposed to say that word.*

He straightened, pulled an undershirt from his valise and walked out to the front room.

Needing to get back on his good side before he went to his meeting, she got up and poured water into the basin, lathering the washcloth. Quickly she washed herself, doubting he'd wait for her to go shower.

"Guilt," he said returning to the room as he worked on the last buttons of a freshly starched shirt, "is a false feeling which has been drummed into people for centuries. We are handed a list of sins. Some are behaviors hurtful to others; some are not. Nonetheless, we're told that if we commit any of these sins we'll be consigned to the devil and his tormentors for all time."

He shoved his shirttail into his trousers all the way around. "I've given thought to this, as have other thinking men. One of the more vocal is the genetic scientist Luther Burbank, of whom we were speaking. It is obvious that religious commandments are made not by God, but rather by men as a way of keeping the masses in line with age-old precepts. Did you know there are places of the world where people have never heard of sin and guilt?"

His back was turned, and she hooked her new corset down the front. "They'll all go to hell," she said lightly.

"Hogwash." He snapped on his collar, and then picked up his comb to part his hair in the center. "For argument's sake, let us assume that god exists. Answer me this: Is God good?"

"Of course." She wiggled into the frock she'd worn last night.

Combing his hair, "Is God powerful?"

"All-powerful." She sat down and pulled on a silk stocking.

"Is God wise?"

"All-knowing." Pulling up her other stocking and hooking it on the garters, she backed up to Charlie. "Would you mind buttoning me?"

He bent to the task, and as he talked she felt his fingers working. "So. All-knowing and all-powerful, and yet this god condemns millions of people to suffer eternal fire and torture because they had the bad luck to be born in a place where nobody ever heard of him. That's not good. As a matter of fact, I'd say that's unfair, as well as petty, vengeful, bloody, and barbaric. Such a god might well be called evil."

Something pinched in Mae's chest. She looked out the window half expecting to see a dark cloud with God throwing spears of lightning into the room.

"If it's so important for everyone to know this all-powerful god," Charlie continued as he finished the buttons and stepped before her with whimsically raised brows. "Why wouldn't he speak to all the peoples of the earth where they live? Instead of telling a handful of lost Jews in a remote desert? That would have been good. That would have been wise."

He reached for his vest. "And why would he depend upon fallible men to get the story straight and leave their cozy homes to spread the news to the far corners of the earth, in a babble of tongues? Unwise and ineffectual in the extreme, I'd say." He finished buttoning his vest.

Never had Mae heard anyone talk like that. Anxious to get out of this room with the rumpled bedclothes, she quickly twisted up her hair and secured it with her combs. Beside her, Charlie straightened his bow tie in the mirror.

"I'd like to go downstairs with you," she said pinning on her hat, "if you don't mind."

He had that twinkle in his eye. "You mean you can stand being seen in the sinful state of morning togetherness with me, after I supposedly drove you home last night?"

"They don't know me."

"Oh, I *see*! It's not a sin if they don't know you." He shrugged into his coat and topped himself with his hat. Smiling, he touched his hat, bowed, and opened the door for her.

He waited outside the women's water closet, perhaps ready to pounce with a reminder that she had been introduced to the owner of the hotel and several other businessmen, not to mention the Miller family. But he didn't.

In the lift with the operator, all three of them looked straight ahead; but when they stepped out on the first floor with no one else around, she said lightly, "Most people would call you an evil man, to have such ideas about God."

"Of course. They're in the thrall of a medieval religion. I consider myself an ethical man. I believe it's wrong to behave in a way that harms people."

Where they entered the lobby, three respectable looking ladies stood talking. He leaned toward Mae and lowered his voice. "Do you think anyone was harmed by what we did last night?"

He had pulled away before completing his act and used a handkerchief on himself so she wouldn't get pregnant. "I guess not."

Perversely, talking like this in a public place with Charlie dressed up and ladies standing around in fine clothing made her want to go back upstairs and do it again. Sister Delphine would weep. And Daddy would wash his hands of her, especially after thinking he'd rectified her by sending her to a Catholic school. *I really am wicked, she thought. Oberon gave me a taste for this, and I'll never be a normal girl again.*

Charlie smiled in that coaxing way of his, "I consider what we did to be good behavior, don't you?"

She couldn't look him in the eye because God was waiting for her to say *no*. And to stand here and say *aloud* that what they'd done was good would be telling him what kind of a girl she had become.

"Your soul ought to be content," he said leading her by the elbow and holding his head high as they entered the lobby. "Mine is."

She walked beside him like a wife or a sweetheart or a harlot or whatever she was, telling her mind to erase feelings of tawdriness and guilt. She must rise above it like Lillie Langtry. Charlie wanted her that way. She had to agree with him that no one had been hurt, and what people didn't know wouldn't hurt them. For about fifteen minutes she had lived with the idea that guilt and sin were fabrications, and as she walked close beside Charlie, seeing behind her eyes what they'd done in the dark, just upstairs, the very secrecy and sin of it warmed her nether region. She glanced at the other men and women, seeing little smiles on their faces. Some laughed with abandon. What had they been doing last night? This very hotel, where such things must regularly transpire, gave her the sense of being in the heart of a large and delicious sin, but without guilt. Just wicked pleasure.

As they approached the Bonanza King, Mr. Fair painfully pushed up from a blue velvet sofa in the lobby. Her skin remembered his eyes, and she stopped.

"Charlie," she said quietly, "I've already met him. I'd rather look around the hotel until the Miller girls get here."

"Very well." He released her elbow. "See you in the room at eleven." He winked.

She locked eyes with him, feeling their connection. With a tiny wave at Mr. Fair she went to the board to read about the entertainments. From the corner of her eye she could see Charlie and Mr. Fair leaving for the dining room, the latter shuffling along a head shorter and twice as broad. Charlie looked like a tall and gangly Abraham Lincoln.

At 10:30 A.M. Mr. Robert Louis Stevenson would read from *A Child's Garden of Verses,* and at 7:00 P.M. the thaumaturgist would perform.

"Are you staying at the hotel?" asked a female voice beside her.

It was a girl about twelve years old, with a slight foreign accent and the face of a stern librarian.

"Just last night. I'm waiting for friends to pick me up for breakfast."

"I've been here for a year." The sloe-eyed girl wore her dark hair in a bun that looked too old for her.

"My, that is a long time."

"It'd be all right if there were more people my age. They don't stay long enough for me to know them. How old are you?"

"Sixteen, seventeen in April."

"My brothers and sisters are older than you. They live in Baltimore."

"So it's just you and your parents living here?"

"My mother died. Father and I and my nou-nou moved here so the hotel staff could take care of us."

Nou-nou? Mae changed the subject. "My friends will be here in about fifteen minutes. Would you mind giving me a very fast tour of the hotel? I haven't seen the central court." She touched the last item on the board: Central Court Croquet and Badminton. Ask at desk for Equipment.

"I'd be glad to." The girl cracked a little smile and stuck out her hand, "My name is Gertrude Stein." She gave a distressingly firm handshake.

Introducing herself, Mae followed the military stride of the young lady up a hall and into a shallow lounge room, the long side of which consisted of windows and windowed doors, all looking over a green lawn about half the size of a city block. The girl went out one of the windowed doors, held it like a hotel employee, and shut it behind Mae.

Children were playing croquet in this interior courtyard. Not very far away four young ladies batted a small white thing back and forth over a net—all in sporting white dresses. Flowerbeds made a summery border around the green, flowers that would have wilted in the Sacramento frosts and geraniums that in Iowa would grow only in indoor pots lovingly tended by people schooled in art of horticulture. Oakland was an oasis of warmth, easy life, culture, and beauty. Gertrude was watching her.

Mae made a connection. "I met a man named Stein last night."

"Was he drinking brandy with Mr. Tubbs?"

"Yes."

"That's Father."

"Did your father come to California with the Gold Rush?"

"No. We haven't been here very long."

"Is he American?"

"Yes."

"But you have a little accent."

"I try not to have one, but I grew up in Paris and all my family speaks French. I've always had a French nou-nou. You would call her a governess."

"Is your father a businessman?"

"Yes," she sighed. "Railroads, properties, streetcars, and finance. I hope you're not interested in those things."

"No, I'm not. I like music and theater."

"I do too."

"I'd like to see where the readings and recitals are held."

"Follow me." The young lady led the march over the lawn. They crossed a pathway circling the green, upon which three women in white nursing caps were pushing perambulators on different stretches of the lap. Gertrude opened a door and waited for Mae, and then led her up a long corridor, turning right and left several times.

"There," she said pointing through an open door. "Mr. Stevenson will read here later this morning."

"What a cozy theater! It must be fun to have so many entertainments going on where you live."

"I like most of them. Sometimes actors recite Shakespeare or perform skits. Sometimes vaudeville actors perform here after they've finished with shows downtown."

"Do you know what a thauma… I don't know that word. I'm from Iowa."

"A thaumaturgist performs magic. I'm getting tired of them because they all do the same old tricks."

"I appreciate your showing me around, but I'm afraid it's late and I'm turned round. Would you mind showing me the way back to the lobby?"

"A pleasure. I'd like you to see the thaumaturgist with me tonight."

Walking at a brisk pace beside the lonely girl, Mae felt sorry for her. She explained about going to San Francisco and then directly back to Sacramento.

Something was wrong in the lobby. Excited talk crackled. People hurried alongside men in white, who were carrying something on a stretcher. A clerk from the desk rushed over and grabbed Gertrude's arm. "My dear, I'm sorry to say your father is ill—"

Gertrude ran into the crowd, where a woman put an arm around her.

A short time later Mae watched with others while men inserted the stretcher into the back of a white conveyance lettered in red: AMBULANCE. The horses champed at their bits while Gertrude and the governess climbed in through the back to ride with the sick man.

God, it appeared, had struck the hotel but hit the wrong person.

Then she saw the Miller girls waving from a buggy in a line of stalled rigs waiting for the ambulance to get out of the way.

⌒

Breakfast with the Millers in their home at 857 Fallon Street went by in a haze of wonder at the gracious two-story house, the beautiful gardens of Oakland, and the easy life of the Miller girls.

The high point was the ramble up the Oakland hills to the silo of a building that turned out to be the Chabot Observatory. Mae didn't expect to see any stars on a bright day like this; however, it alarmed her to see the daytime half-moon pockmarked, and so near. According to a plaque on the wall Anthony Chabot, the Water King, had donated the observatory to the City of Oakland, including money for its upkeep in the future. From the vantage point of her secret life, Mae observed more than the moon. She saw order and beauty and married decency all around her.

After the observatory, they ran the horse on a hat-grabbing ride along roads that made them bounce and laugh. Then they threaded their way down through Indian Gulch, which had no Indians, just green grass and gnarled oaks with spreading branches. For a moment those trees brought fear and wickedness to mind, and she couldn't think why until she remembered where she'd seen such trees—in a book of Grimm's Fairy Tales, an illustration of the scary forest where Hansel and Gretel had lost their way.

The name of the winding, rutted road changed to Trestle Glen, named for the trolley line through it, Harriett said. Teams of workhorses and steam-puffing equipment leveled the ground for new houses. At a lower elevation carpenters hammered. By the time Harriett Miller reined the horse to a stop before the hotel, Mae's sinful breast-watch pointed to 10:50. She snapped the lid down before the others saw the naked Greek maidens.

Saying her good-byes, she was anxious to get back to Charlie and go to San Francisco.

⌒

When Charlie answered the door of the suite she rushed to him. On her toes with her arms tight around his high chest she puckered her lips. He leaned down and gave her a long kiss, and then returned to packing his valise in the front room.

"Have a nice time?" he asked.

"Yes. A wonderful breakfast and then we looked at the moon through a telescope." She bantered from the bedroom while she packed. "Did you know? It truly is full of holes. And the Water King gave that observatory to the people of Oakland."

"That's right," he called back, "for the education of children as I recall."

"Did you hear about Mr. Stein?"

"No. I just came in from my meeting. What happened?"

"He was taken to the hospital in an ambulance."

The silence lasted too long. She peeked out and saw him staring at nothing. Then, like a sleepwalker, he reached for the fringed silk rope and gave it a yank. She buttoned her valise and took it to the outer room, excited about going to San Francisco despite Mr. Stein.

A knock sounded at the door. Charlie lunged toward it, stepping into hall to talk to the bellboy. Then he put his head in and said, "I'm going downstairs to make a telephone call."

"To find out about Mr. Stein?"

"Yes."

"I want to come. His daughter showed me around this morning."

In the lift, the three again rode down in silence, Mae puzzling over Charlie's reaction. Until last night he hadn't even known the man.

In the office of the concierge Charlie ordered central to connect him to Fabiola Hospital. A silence. "I'd like to speak to the doctor seeing after Mr. Stein." A longer silence. "Yes," he said. "I see." He listened a while. "Thank you."

"He's dead," he told the concierge as he hung the mouthpiece on its hook.

"Oh that poor girl!" Mae said.

The concierge had a kindly expression. "Gertrude has a governess, and I'm sure her father has arranged for her welfare."

"Sir," said Charlie. "Please get an urgent message to Mr. Fair." He reached for a piece of hotel stationery on the concierge's desk and scribbled fast. A minute later the bell boy raced away with the note.

Mae and Charlie headed back to the suite. "This could change things," Charlie said. "I've asked Mr. Fair to come to our room. I hope he isn't already on the ferry."

"What's Mr. Fair got to do with Mr. Stein dying?"

"There is a connection—roundabout, as far as I'm concerned. Mr. Fair wanted me to do some work for him here in Oakland, work that would take several weeks. I agreed, if I get leave from the Legislature."

"You'll stay here in Oakland and work for him?"

"After seeing to some things in Sacramento."

"You mean you can leave just like that, and get your employment back later?"

"I'm willing to take the risk. He offered a good sum of money."

What will I do if he doesn't want me in Oakland?

Charlie was unlocking the door of the suite. "Mr. Stein's death might change his mind. I want to find out before we leave. Before he leaves."

"Are we going to miss the noon ferry?"

"Possibly."

A rap at the door.

"There he is." Motioning her to sit down, Charlie opened the door, but it was the bellboy telling him to go to the main hotel entrance. Mr. Fair was down there.

Again Mae hurried downstairs with Charlie, this time running through the lobby to keep up with his long strides.

Mr. Fair, at the door with a piece of luggage at his feet, spoke curtly. "I'm late for the ferry so this'll be short. The deal's off."

Charlie looked frozen. "Oh, what—"

"We wasted a good morning." Mr. Fair turned his accented eye to the bellboy and pointed. "Put my bag on that hack." It was just pulling in and the old man shuffled toward it.

Charlie, who seemed momentarily dazed, called to the tycoon's back, "It's never a waste to talk to you, sir."

The Bonanza King ignored him, and it hurt Mae's heart to see her Charlie, who knew so much about everything, treated in that rude manner.

53

On the windy foredeck of the ferry, watching the City approach, Mae made her voice light and casual. "Mr. Fair wasn't very nice to you, was he?"

"Everyone calls him a son of a bitch. And he's the first to tell you that. He's proud of it." He glowered over the rail of the ferry.

She didn't dare ask whether he'd have brought her with him to Oakland if the deal with Mr. Fair had gone through, but she loved it that he showed her his wounded heart. She restrained her hand from stroking his back. "If he's so bad, why would you want to work for him?"

"Maybe it was my main chance. For that I'd have worked with a rattlesnake. Made myself a nice nest egg too."

He was thinking of his future. She inhaled the salt air and watched the rapidly enlarging buildings, wondering if she'd be part of that future.

He moved his lips around in that way of his. "One competitor dying doesn't mean others won't enter the fray. But I don't give a damn."

Charlie would have stopped Mr. Stein's bid for streetcar franchises, whatever that meant, but that was behind them now. Eight to ten vessels lay anchored in the bay, some with three and four masts, some steam-driven with big smokestacks. Behind the vessels, the flounces and mansard roofs of the buildings were gaining visibility. On the left of the wharves a forest of chimneys belched a black cloud over the warehouses and soot-blackened houses.

"You were right about the smoke in San Francisco," she said.

"You're looking at perhaps the largest ironworks in the United States. They make millions of tons of equipment for the mines, dredges, head frames, rail-roads—you name it. And now they're making battleships."

"Battleships! Whatever for?"

"Modern steel battleships. The owners talked Congress into a contract." Obviously, this talk was helping Charlie come up from his dark place.

"But we're not at war," she said to keep him going.

"The European countries are stockpiling armaments, so a lot of men think we should too."

"Do you think there's going to be a war?"

He shrugged. "Who knows?"

The ferry sidled up to the dock and they stepped out upon a wharf with coiled ropes and seagulls on tarred posts slowly painting them white. Other gulls bickered over scraps of fish guts left by fishermen.

At the foot of Market Street, hotels overshadowed the Norwegian Sea-man's Church. Big drays and wagons delivered heaps of goods, while carriages picked up people at the Ferry Building. The gold filigree hands pointed in the direction of 2:30. "Think we'll have enough time to see San Francisco?"

"There's never enough time to see San Francisco." Back to his old self.

She smiled as she walked up the boardwalk of Market Street on the safety of his arm. Posters on theaters displayed women with half-closed eyes and revealing garb. Accordion music wheezed out of a saloon. Charlie ignored the drunks and blind men and the one-legged man extending his hat for money. "Most of them are just pretending to be blind and crippled," he said.

Young men in working clothes looked her over. She couldn't help but stare back when a gang of ebony Africans passed by, speaking in a strange tongue. A threesome with swarthy skin and turban-wrapped heads came laughing out of one of the buildings. Traps and buggies rattled over the cobblestones, and a cable car parked in the center of the street disgorged a dozen or more men dressed in sailor suits. They talked in British and Scottish accents, and stared at Mae as they chattered and softly whistled.

Charlie ignored that. "Take a gander at the Ferry Building," he said. "It'll be dark by the time we get back and you won't see it like this again."

She turned to look at it. "They're not tearing it down, are they?"

"Yes and no. They're going to build a new one."

"I don't see why. It looks nice to me."

"Gothic's out of fashion now. The SP wants to be modern. Plus they need more space. This embarcadero is mobbed during commute hours."

"What are commute hours," she asked as they walked up the noisy artery of the fabled city.

"Hours when men come and go to work. Hundreds of them work in the City and sleep in Oakland."

"You mean their houses are over there?"

"Sure. A city of sinful pleasure palaces isn't for raising a family." The twinkle in his eye reminded her that he didn't believe in sin.

She surreptitiously pointed at two tough-looking females with garish makeup standing in a doorway. "Are they ladies of the night?"

"Yup. The Barbary Coast's teeming with 'em. That's what they call this area."

She pointed to a structure standing taller than the others. "Is that building up-to-date?"

"No. Too Frenchy. The new trend is masculine and squared off, like the buildings of ancient Rome. There, see that?" He pointed up Pine Street where a street angled to the right. Men were slowly raising a heavy granite stone with pulleys up to a third floor. Extensive scaffolding hid most of the new building. "San Francisco is the new Rome," he said. "As in 'all roads lead to Rome.' In fact all roads and waterways lead to this embarcadero." Charlie led the way up Pine Street.

Would she ever know all his words? "Embar—?"

"Waterfront in Spanish." He reached under her hat and tapped her temple. "Skeeziks is curious."

With a twinge of peevishness about the way he said that, she hugged her coat against the wind. The city had gone gray and austere.

After a couple of blocks they turned right on Montgomery Street, and she couldn't help but gape at the narrow canyon of buildings. She counted seven and eight stories. Globes of streetlamps marched in neat rows on both sides of the street, where purposeful men in dark coats and pipe hats strode the sidewalks with their heads down and long coattails kicking behind. She could feel the urgency of money on this cold gray street where not one inch was squandered to grass and flowers. Ahead, a light mist veiled the sharp edges of the buildings but they seemed the more powerful for it, like the secret minds of the men who made fortunes here.

Charlie flicked a hand upward. "Mr. Fair lives up there. That's the Lick Hotel. Wouldn't be surprised if he's looking down at us from behind those curtains, but he won't invite me up for an explanation and a drink. That—" He paused.

Son of a bitch, she silently completed. "Does his family live there with him?"

"No. I'd say he's a lonely old man."

They walked to the next block. Across the street, shiny brass letters above a doorway proclaimed: San Francisco Stock and Exchange.

"Isn't he married? Mr. Fair, I mean."

"Divorced long ago, with everyone in several states reading the details of how she got away with half his fortune. She took the daughters to New York, and he kept the sons. Let 'em run wild. The ongoing saga of a miserly millionaire."

"Do his daughters care about him?" They were rounding a corner.

"Not if the Hearst paper has it right. Those young ladies are busy in New York social circles."

Suddenly a man burst out of a door and nearly bumped into them.

Charlie sidestepped. "Sorry sir."

The slender man about Charlie's age stared at them with ice blue eyes.

Thinking him impolite, Mae started to walk onward, but Charlie spoke. "Say, could you be William Tevis, son of Lloyd Tevis?"

"Do I know you?" The frozen syllables crackled. Charlie had been rude.

"No," Charlie said, apparently undaunted. But I met your father at the governor's inauguration. I'm an admirer of your family and I saw your photograph in a newspaper." He extended his hand. "I'm Charlie Rogue, staff to the Republicans in the Assembly."

Shaking his hand, a bit hesitant at first, Mr. Tevis thawed some. "This is a business day at the Capitol, is it not?"

"As a matter of fact it is." Charlie seemed confident in a situation that would have flattened Mae.

The stranger glanced at her, then back to Charlie. "Would you think it presumptuous if I asked what you're doing in the City?"

"I met with James Fair about doing some work for him."

"Oh, I see. Has he employed you?"

"No. It's an odd circumstance, but the reason he needed me died in an Oakland hospital this morning."

The blue eyes digested that, and then the ice turned on Mae.

She did a slight curtsey as Sister Delphine had taught her.

Charlie said, "Allow me to introduce Miss Mae Duffy."

Mr. Tevis touched his hat and tilted his head at Charlie as if memorizing his face. "How long have you worked for the Republicans in Sacramento?"

"Three years."

He stroked the point of his reddish Vermeer beard. "Would you allow me to make amends for nearly running you down? I'll buy you a drink in my club." He nodded toward the door he'd just come through.

"We'd be honored," said Charlie without asking Mae. Not that she would have objected.

Mr. Tevis opened the heavy door and allowed them to precede him into a high-ceilinged, half-dark lobby. An old man behind a counter offered to take their coats. Following Mr. Tevis' lead, Mae and Charlie removed their coats and handed them over.

Mr. Tevis led the way upstairs and into a room with Greek columns for a doorway. Golden draperies hung along one wall. Incandescent light bulbs in a chandelier provided bright light over a mahogany bar and gentlemen conversing at several round tables. Mae was the only female in the room.

The three of them took seats at a table. A man in tails came and bowed slightly, his accent British. "Mr. Tevis, what can I bring you and your guests?"

"Have you had your noon dinners?" Mr. Tevis inquired of Charlie. Seeing Charlie's lips say *no*, he ordered the special of the day for Charlie and Mae.

The man vanished, and then returned with whisky and sodas for the men and a flute of champagne for Mae. She'd never had spirits in the daytime, and didn't want to act silly like she'd done last night, so she determined not to have more than this one glass.

"How is your father?" Charlie asked.

"Getting on in years, but doing all right, considering."

Mr. Tevis then questioned Charlie about matters before the Legislature. Charlie answered in his usual bluff and hearty manner.

Most of it went over Mae's head, and she lost herself in the paintings on the walls, mountain scenes with gold prospectors and mining head-frames poking up well above the tallest pines. One depicted men in slickers and rubber boots shooting water cannons at a torn mountain, creating a gusher of brown water down a gulch. More captivating was a framed photographic portrait of a seated Indian girl about Mae's age. Her chiseled cheekbones conveyed the stoicism of her race, and heavy black hair draped over the shoulders of her rustic dress. In her lap lay a bawling white infant, skinny arms flung out to the sides, but the girl's upturned hands lay inattentive on her thighs as she stared into the distance with the flat eyes of anger. A story Mom once told came to mind, about a man fathering an Indian baby at the same time as his legitimate child, and when the Indian baby died under suspicious circumstances, the white couple benefited by having a wet nurse so the wife could travel with her husband. People said the baby had been conceived for that purpose. Mae wondered if something like that happened to the girl in the picture.

Just as Mae was trying to catch up to the men's talk—something about the drinking water of San Francisco—talk ceased. The waiter set full plates before her and Charlie. Filet of sole, rice, green beans in a buttery sauce. She was hungry.

Mr. Tevis had already eaten, so he talked while Charlie ate. Neither of them took the slightest notice of her. She was the invisible eater.

The City's businessmen, Mr. Tevis was saying, anticipated a future when San Francisco would enfold all the towns and cities around the bay into a single metropolis, like New York City, all under a charter government. Greater San Francisco it would be called. "Water's the key."

He watched Charlie eat his salad. "So, what do you think? Would you be interested in seeing to those options for me, discreetly?"

Charlie looked up. "Why discreetly?"

Mr. Tevis turned his eyes to Mae.

"Miss Duffy has my full confidence," Charlie said. "She's with me now."

Words that warmed her down to her toes.

Mr. Tevis nodded. "I'm sure you understand that I can hardly show my cards now. But once they're all in place, the Board of Supervisors will see the value of the project."

338 ~ Rest for the Wicked

He lit a cigarette and blew out smoke. "No doubt you'll need to see a map of the water sources."

Charlie chewed and swallowed. "Yes. And I'd need the records of property ownership so I'm not stabbing in the dark."

"That would be arranged." All the frost had melted. This well-spoken man seemed eager to work with Charlie. Already Mae's life was up in the air again.

The waiter removed the empty plates, served the men another round of whisky, and brought dishes of iced cream with chunky strawberry syrup for Mae and Charlie.

Charlie took a few mouthfuls of dessert, and then leaned back in his chair.

"Mr. Tevis, your family name answers any questions I otherwise would have been concerned about." He smiled in his friendly way, eyes a-twinkle. "It's uncanny that just after the deal fizzled with Mr. Fair, fate led me to you."

"I must say, it strikes me as uncanny too, nearly colliding with a man of your experience. My business partner, James Ben Ali Haggin, owns land bordering Sacramento City. He raises thoroughbreds there, but he's too well known to do this work. He and I were just talking last night about where to turn, and then you show up right here at the door of the Pacific-Union Club."

"Obviously we've got more talking to do." Charlie wiped his mustache with the napkin and looked at Mae. "But the two of us are doing some sight-seeing."

"Oh, I see," said Mr. Tevis, "I don't mean to break into your tour." He pulled a gold chain from his vest pocket and flipped the watch open. "I'm about late for a meeting, but if you'll come to my home this evening we could finish up the details." Slipping the watch into his pocket, "I live in Burlingame, a bit of a ride, but I'd send a man for you. Where and when?"

"That's generous of you," Charlie said. "But we were planning to head back to Sacramento on the eight o'clock ferry."

"My man will see that you're on the earliest ferry in the morning. Needless to say, you'll spend the night at my place."

54

The cable car dinged. "Let's go," Charlie said, starting to lope.

Mae grabbed her hat and sprinted with him to the corner of Pine, two quick steps for each of his strides. In the nick of time they leapt aboard laughing. She had a good view of the motorman, who yanked a lever jutting from the floor.

The car jerked forward. Charlie tipped his hat to the ladies on board, but his special smile was for her.

"Sounds like you're going to work for Mr. Tevis," she said smiling back.

He deadpanned. "If I'd sent prayers to heaven, I'd be on my knees thanking God."

"What will you be doing? For Mr. Tevis, I mean? I missed that part."

Charlie moved closer and lowered his voice. "Mayor Phelan has his cap set on damming the Sierra rivers to increase the City's water supply. Mr. Tevis wants to do it before Phelan moves ahead with a plan of his own. You see, Tevis is part owner of Spring Valley Company, which now supplies water to the City."

"I thought Mr. Chabot's company supplied the water."

"Spring Valley bought Chabot's system some years ago. They started bringing extra water to the Peninsula so they could develop San Mateo County. But the Mayor wants to get control of that."

That was clear as mud. "You mean the City can get new water and bring it in if the Spring Valley Company doesn't?"

"That's the idea. And leave the bad old monopoly out in the cold." He threw that out with a wry grin.

"Bad old monopoly?"

"A good number of San Franciscans are peeved at the current high water rates."

A man in workman's clothing and porkpie hat inserted, "If you'd excuse me, sir, peeved ain't the right word. But with a lady present I won't say t'other. Why, we pays more for water than bread. An' that ain't right." He stuck out his bristly chin.

Charlie nodded soberly at the man, but then he leaned to Mae and whispered, "That's why it's a bad old monopoly." His eyes twinkled.

She also dampened her voice. "Didn't Mr. Tevis say something about damming the entire Cosumnes River?"

In her ear, "That's right. Also the American River."

"But Mr. Livermore's damming the American River. Can they both dam the same river?" She recalled the huzzah after supper at the Steffens place, when Mr. Livermore announced he'd deliver cheap electricity to Sacramento City.

"My little skeeziks has a quick mind." He patted her knee. "If that'd starve the planned Folsom reservoir, I'd have a problem with it. I'll find out tonight. Tevis is in a rush to get started." His breath in her ear warmed her. "Else he wouldn't take us into his Burlingame inner-sanctum."

The trolley tilted alarmingly upward, creaking and grumbling up a hill so steep it scared the wind out of her. People walking up the sidewalk had to bend forward like mountain climbers, stopping to rest and catch their breath. "Oh, Charlie," she grabbed him, "If those hooks slip off the cable we'll die!" She visualized in her mind those underground hooks missing their targets.

"Impossible." Again he looked like he was onto a silent joke.

"But look!" She pointed at the shrinking city below. "We'll be pitched to our deaths. Maybe we should jump out now while we have the chance."

"Nonsense. This design was developed for vertical ascents in the mines. Compared to that, this is a walk in the park for Old Dobbin. Not in twenty years has such a cable slipped or broken."

People were smiling at her.

"Nob Hill," the conductor called a few minutes later.

They stepped out on top of the world.

"I thought we'd stretch our legs a little up here," Charlie said. "The richest of the rich live here, up out of the smoke."

"The ones not in the Lick Hotel," she quipped, woozy with relief to have her feet on solid ground.

He chuckled. "Or the ones in Burlingame Park. Some wives prefer to live in a hotel where others do all the work. Did you know? A smart man wrote in the *Examiner* that hotel life is the cause of moral degeneracy in the women of California."

She glanced at him sidelong, "I'd say it's the other way around. Degenerate women move to the hotels." Helen Rose came to mind.

He hawed, patting her shoulder with the fingers of his hand, the one comfortably steering her along the walkway beside the rails.

The pale gray sky held no warmth and the cold wind came through her coat, but the homes on Nob Hill stood against it like European fortresses. They bristled with towers and cupolas, porticos, and fancy grillwork. Wide green lawns with copses of trees and gardens of blooming flowers surrounded them. "These places make pikers of Sacramento's best," she said using one of his favorite words.

"Did you meet Mr. Huntington at the Steffens place?" he asked.

"No, but I remember him." A big old man, mostly bald, with a young wife in a red gown.

Charlie pointed at one of the mansions. "That's his house."

She stared. "How could two people live in a place that big? Charlie, wouldn't you feel lonely rattling around in there?"

"Oh, I might be able to tolerate it." He grinned. "Wait'll you see the Tevis place."

"You been there?"

"No."

"Then how do you—"

"I don't think Skeeziks realizes just who that man is." Charlie chuckled. "His father has been president of Wells Fargo for twenty years. Does that company mean something to you? Nationwide shipping and banking? Every few years the Tevis family fortune grows by leaps and bounds. They're into forests, timber mills, mines, iron, and the Kern County Land Company, which runs far beyond Kern County now, even to Arizona and old Mexico. They're interested in water because they want to develop Greater San Francisco. They're married to the Sharon banking fortune and many other enterprises, including Spring Valley—"

"Charlie, you've studied up on these people! Are you going to be rich someday too?" *And take me along with you?*

"I don't see anything wrong with that. Do you?"

"Not at all!" In her mind she could see him rich. It fit him.

He pointed to another mansion. "That one's a lot bigger than Huntington's. The dining room seats sixty. How'd you like to feed that many people?"

"No thanks!"

Hiram Johnson, she recalled through a fog of fear and time, had said that a handful of men lived like kings and controlled the government.

"Mr. Hopkins, Mr. Huntington's partner in the SP, built this house," Charlie was saying. "What material do you think the outer walls are made of?"

"Stone." That was plain to see.

"Wood, cleverly painted to look like stone. Remember, railroad magnates own forests and timber mills to make railroad ties and resort buildings at the end of their lines. I've heard the master bedroom in this place has walls of ebony inlaid with precious stones and designs of African ivory. Can you imagine the diamonds and silks and satins and four-horse carriages that have pranced up to this place? All bought with the gold of the Sierra Mountains."

He pointed out each one of the four mansions belonging to the Big Four: Stanford, Hopkins, Crocker and Huntington. "They're all dead except Huntington, so he's got control of the whole thing now. Fortunately, he's a good manager. Healthy, too—not a drinker like Mr. Fair."

"Just curious. How old is Mr. Fair?"

"Mmm. Late sixties I'd guess."

"He looks eighty."

"Limping and shuffling and a big belly age a man. People say he goes into drinking bouts, locks himself in a room for months at a time with a servant bringing brandy and rich food. I suppose that takes a toll."

"Why didn't he build a house up here?"

"Actually he did, years ago when he was married. Come see."

Mae hurried beside Charlie at a fast walk. They stopped near the edge of Nob Hill, overlooking the City. The sun bronzed the mist in the far distance, seemingly the end of a desolate earth. "There," he said pointing at a modest house, at least for Nob Hill. "He built it across the street from Mr. Flood's place, his partner in the Comstock Lode mines."

She surveyed the lavish grounds of the Flood mansion, and then looked back at the plain yard of the Fair house. "It's not kept up like the others."

"But it's a fair view up on this mount." He smiled at his pun. "A honey of a spot for a hotel. I don't know who lives here now, but whoever it is, you can bet they're paying him plenty of rent."

"I'm surprised the Bonanza King didn't build a grander home."

Charlie shrugged. "Like I said, he's a miser, not interested in show. I doubt any of the Big Four were interested in show. Their wives had these homes built, each vying with the other for the grandest place."

"Well, what else could they do to occupy themselves? You said their men were gone all the time."

He raised a brow at her, but then grabbed her hand and they were running before she realized another cable car had stopped at the end of the short block. Charlie waved his hat at the motorman, who waved back and waited. They leapt aboard as the car lurched forward. They were on their way to the ocean and the place called the Cliff House.

"We'll have supper overlooking the sea," Charlie said. "Maybe catch the setting sun. I do hope the Sutro Baths are finished. I hear they'll be the eighth wonder of the world. Sutro owns the Cliff House too and a lot more property out there. I won't bore you with how he made his fortune in the mines."

Glad of that, she got out what had been niggling at her all day. "If you had worked for Mr. Fair, where would we have lived?" *We*.

"The Tubbs Hotel. My work would have been in Oakland and the surrounding areas."

She waited a few heartbeats. "Would you have wanted me with you?"

"Sure. We're pals now." Holding his hat in his lap to keep it from blowing away, he snuggled her to him with his free arm.

Warmth coursed through her despite the damp wind, for she was safe with Charlie. Her mind rested. She needed him like she needed food and water. That he had his arm around her in this trolley, where other couples sat silent and apart, told her he loved her too. At this moment she understood what he'd meant when he'd said marriage wasn't necessary. It was just another age-old practice grown rigid over the centuries. Love, however, was fresh and powerful.

"We're on the outskirts of the City now," Charlie said, "but someday all these dunes will be filled with houses." They had just stopped at an immense lumberyard to let the workman with the pork-pie hat get off.

She moved closer into him, oblivious of the people around them.

"I'm told that James Fair owns sixty acres downtown," Charlie said, "but he lets the buildings rot. The bastard makes the tenants pay for repairs. Some of those places are an outright disgrace to the city. And I don't mean just in appearance."

"Is that where the sinful goings on go on?" She tossed up.

He chuckled in his chest.

Soon they jerked to a stop at a flattened area where men were hammering new houses together. Several more workmen debarked.

Continuing westward up and down the sand dunes with low vegetation, there were no more stops. Some areas were being flattened by teams of horses pulling mammoth graders, some by steam-powered equipment, engines puffing out black smoke that vanished quickly in the wind. Between the dunes she started to catch glimpses of the vast gray ocean, and that excited her as much as the mansions of Nob Hill.

"So? Will you be a business tycoon someday? Become a partner of Mr. Tevis?"

With an amused smile he smoothed back the dark hair whipping about his face. "It's too late for anyone to become his partner. The top owners were picked long ago. The businesses of these second-generation tycoons are so vast and diverse that, well, nobody can comprehend it."

"But you said Emmett could succeed in a business if he tried. Don't you believe that?"

"I said a man can still succeed in California, but the degree of his success will never be on a plane with the wealth and power of the Builders. I meant that if a man takes note of how the land lies—economic and political—and he works with certain men, he could prosper in his business and might rise quite high. It's just that nowadays raw ability and hard work aren't enough to equal the Builders. That's what I meant."

It came to her that she'd ought to invite Emmett to supper to meet Charlie, but then she remembered that she didn't want Charlie to hear Emmett's bad grammar. She felt in herself a growing interest in how wealth was achieved, despite what she'd told Gertrude Stein.

"We'll be at the ocean soon," Charlie said. He jabbed his thumb over his shoulder. "The Sutro Heights development was back there. Too bad we won't be at the Cliff House in the morning to see the aerialist jump off and steer his balloon over the Pacific. But we'll come back another time, spend the night and swim in the Sutro Baths."

We.

She smiled into the wind. She had risen from the bowels of hell to the fabulous, exciting, and just plain wonderful.

55

After a sunset repast in the Cliff House, a colossal structure built out over the astounding ocean, Mae and Charlie stepped off the open cable car in the cold damp wind. They were back in The City. Beneath a streetlamp she saw the man in a tall hat and frockcoat, waiting beside a sleek carriage—Mr. Tevis' man.

Inside, the carriage was cozy and private, the lap fur warm. The pair of grays set a fast pace, and all Mae could see of the driver through the eye-level opening was an oval piece of his black coat. Then Charlie slid the glass over the porthole, shutting that out too. Modern springs floated them over cobblestone and crack, and the isinglass windows in the two doors admitted eerie light while the scent of fine leather surrounded them. All day Mae had resisted the pull of Charlie, but in the industrial area south of Market Street where the streetlamps came to an end and the windows went black, she advanced her hand beneath the silk lining of the lap fur and gave his thigh a little squeeze.

He was at her throat, nibbling her neck and undoing the buttons, not caring that his hat fell on the floor. "It's a long ride to Burlingame," he murmured in her ear.

Blissfully unaware of anything but him, she would remember only the abandonment of time and place in that floating booth. Later she laid her head against him and closed her eyes, thinking back on the day that had passed too quickly—a day of playing the part of Charlie's wife.

She melted into his shoulder.

In her dream she stumbled around an abandoned building. Somewhere there was a horrible stink. The floorboards gave way as she stepped on them, seeking what she hoped would be stronger footing, but it kept caving in beneath her until she was running to keep from falling in a black abyss below. Scrambling for her life, she chanced to see a broken-down privy in a dark corner and knew it was the source of the stink. Drawn to it as if by some powerful force, she stared down into it, trying to make out the nature of the large shiny blob, when a sudden push from behind pitched her into the wooden seat, shattering it to rotten splinters, and she was falling, heart in mouth, down into a shapeless frightening thing, worse than death—

Screaming in her nightmare, she must have made a noise.

Charlie yawned and rubbed the corners of his eyes with finger and thumb. He'd been sleeping too. She snuggled into him, the smell of good tobacco and fine wool. In a few minutes the coach stopped.

Straightening up, she hastily rearranged her frock while he pushed the isinglass window down into the door and stuck his head out. "Are we at the Tevises?" he called.

"Yes sir," the driver responded.

Pleasant night air flowed around Mae, fanning away the nightmare with the scent of jasmine.

She put down the window on her side and saw the coach driver in the headlamps as he fiddled with the latch of an enormous wrought-iron gate, perhaps fifteen feet high. Lacy tree foliage drooped down over both ends of the gate, trees of a kind she hadn't seen before.

Laboriously the driver pushed the heavy gate open. A little later he was back at the reins with the gate closed and locked, driving them up a narrow driveway that curved out of sight like a pale snake entering a leafy burrow.

Charlie pulled up the window and fished around on the floor for his hat. Then he stood up, bent almost double as he tucked in his shirttail.

"That gate was big enough for a whole city," Mae remarked.

Seated, Charlie snapped his collar in place. "Most of the Gold Rush wealth is now behind gates like that. Where corporate secrets are hidden from prying eyes."

"Even groggy from sleep you use five-dollar words."

A low chuckle. "Mae, I really am liking you."

That woke her up a bit more. They stopped before a three-story house with porches vanishing above the reach of the gas lamps.

As Charlie guided Mae on to the carriage step and up the walkway to the entrance of the house, the door opened. The slim silhouette of a gentleman in a suit stepped toward them, backlit by a huge chandelier inside the house. Mae recognized Mr. Tevis' shape. After a word to the driver, Mr. Tevis spoke to Charlie.

"I hope you haven't had your suppers."

"Only a salad," Charlie lied. Mae realized it had been hours since that light supper and she looked forward to eating again.

Mr. Tevis led them into a lobby where a young lady in a lavender gown and a black bun at the nape of her neck stood waiting. "May I present my better half, Maybella Ramona." He slightly bowed to her, and after Charlie and Mae were introduced, they all walked in as male and female pairs past the floral arrangement on a table beneath the chandelier.

Maybella Tevis had a nice alto voice. "You've had a long ride," she said. "May I show you the powder room?"

Gladly Mae followed her while Mr. Tevis led Charlie in another direction.

Before long, restored and daintier, Mae stood in a room decorated with huge wall tapestries. Charlie was there looking at a long gleaming table with four settings of silverware, fine plates, and crystal goblets.

"Mr. Rogue," said William Tevis, "normally we'd all enjoy supper together, but unless you object, I'd prefer if you and I ate in the library. The maps are there." He looked at his wife. "They're leaving early in the morning, and we need to talk."

With a pleasant nod, the young lady spoke a foreign language to a middle-aged servant in a black and white uniform. Quickly two assistants arrived with covered dishes, and the men followed them to another room. A third servant removed two of the place settings and trailed the men. Now the oversized table held only two place settings on either side of a corner.

Glad to be eating with the lady of the house, Mae took the chair indicated and felt some of her old confidence buoy her up.

Mrs. Tevis' smooth apricot cheeks glowed in the overhead gaslight, and her straight black lashes partially veiled her dark eyes giving her a pleasantly mysterious look.

"Where are you from?" the lady asked.

"Iowa, but recently Sacramento."

A servant arrived with a bowl balanced on stiff fingers, the other hand skillfully manipulating two large spoons that delivered a stew of meat and vegetables to the plates. She then poured red wine into the goblets.

Maybella Tevis was saying, "Sacramento is a city of trees. I have nice memories of that place." She ate daintily.

Thankful that Mom had taught her manners, Mae nonetheless followed the lady's lead in selecting a fork. "You have nice trees here too," she said.

"My grandfather loved the native oaks on his rancho. He had the pepper trees planted, as well as other varieties. He liked the beauty of the pepper trees."

As the servant returned with a puffy food that collapsed in a cloud of steam when she spooned it to the plates, Mae asked, "Are those the big trees at the gate?"

"Why yes. Aren't they lovely."

Mae felt certain that the land had been inherited from Mrs. Tevis's side, and considering that rancho meant farm in California, she thought she are Mrs. Tevis had something in common. "We didn't plant shade trees in Iowa, only apple and plum trees. My father and brothers were too busy with the farming."

Mrs. Tevis looked at her with lash-veiled eyes but didn't follow that lead.

Mae tried the other thing they had in common. "Did you say you were in Sacramento when you were little?"

"Yes. We lived there for a time."

"I live on 12th and N."

"Hmm. I don't recall the name of the street where we lived." She looked at Mae with a bite of the egg-spinach dish suspended partway to her smiling lips. "I do remember the horse cars running along the rails. And the rough men on wagons driving mules into town." She laughed. "My parents didn't want me near enough to see them clearly."

She sounded so completely American, and yet she had spoken a foreign language.

"Are you from another country?"

The lady chuckled like it was a joke. "No, everyone else is. Actually, I'm fourth generation. My father was the first Californio governor of the state after California joined the Union."

Governor! "Oh my, I wish I had learned more about California in school. Is Californio another word for Californian?"

Mrs. Tevis shook her head. "It's what the people who settled here were called before we lost it to the United States, before the Treaty of Guadalupe Hidalgo." She sipped wine, blotted her lips with her napkin, and smiled gently at Mae. "I am a proud Californio."

Mae had forgotten that California had once belonged to Mexico. The foreign language must have been Spanish. "I have so much to learn," she admitted. "What was your father's name?"

"Romualdo Pacheco." A pause. "And he's still living. Not far from here." Apologizing for the blunder, Mae asked, "Is that why you were in Sacramento? When your father was governor?"

"Yes. For two years. Actually my father had been State Treasurer, and then was elected Lieutenant Governor. When the governor died he became governor. My mother meant to stay on the rancho, but when that happened she moved us to Sacramento. We rented a house there."

During the rest of the supper, and the fruit and cheese dessert, Mae learned that California aristocrats spoke politely to upstarts from Iowa who pretended they had something in common.

Mrs. Tevis offered to show her the guest cottage where she would stay. Mae hoped Charlie would be directed there too, when he and Mr. Tevis were finished. But maybe not, if it were known that they were not married.

The hem of Maybella's gown rustled along a path of stones while her lantern flashed past the night-fragrant flowers. It was warm here, as in Oakland, after dark. They stopped at a cottage overgrown with vines and half hidden by the lacy foliage of the pepper trees. In the exposed areas Mae saw that the whitewashed walls were of large bricks with rounded edges. Mrs. Tevis opened the latch of a heavy oaken door and raised the lantern illuminating a bed, chest, table, and two chairs, all of hewn wood. She then opened a door to a second room with another made-up bed. "Mr. Rogue can sleep there," she said, closing the door.

The decision belonged to Mac and Charlie!

The servant, having followed, placed a stack of light blankets and towels on the bed, and put two small jars, a silver-handled hairbrush, and two tiny brushes with ivory handles on the bedside stand. She shook out a silky cream-colored garment and laid it over the pillow.

Maybella Tevis explained. "I've taken the liberty of bringing you one of my nightgowns. "I think it'll fit." She touched a jar. "This is my favorite night cream. Mr. Tevis said you hadn't planned to stay the night, so I thought you could use these things." She touched the smaller jar. "This is our favorite tooth powder. The pitcher in the bowl contains fresh water. Just toss out the excess."

"This is very thoughtful of you. And I'm grateful." Mae had heard that rich people brushed their teeth, but she'd never seen a special powder for that purpose. The Duffys had always used toothpicks and rubbed their teeth with a finger dipped in baking soda.

"Now that you've seen the adobe," the lady said, "feel free to accompany me back to the house. We could continue our conversation over a glass of aguardiente?"

Her friendly smile and offer were nice, but in this cozy place Mae wanted to ready herself for Charlie. She could hardly wait to get out of her corset and put on that silk nightgown with all the eyelets and pale embroidery.

∿

By ten the next morning the train to Sacramento was whizzing past houses and farms and poplar windbreaks. Mae relaxed against the velvet upholstery on her high-backed seat. On their left stretched the Strait of Carquines. A few passengers on that side of the aisle had opened their windows to let in the fresh air.

Charlie, who had signed on with Mr. Tevis, couldn't stop smiling as he gazed out the windows.

"So what exactly will you be doing for him?"

"I'll collect options on the water rights and the land to be flooded. That way the costs will be known when he presents the project to the City officials. Some of the landowners live in San Francisco, and Mr. Tevis will talk to them; but a number of them live in El Dorado, Amador, and Sacramento Counties. That's where I come in. I'll explain what a good deal it would be for them to sell to Tevis, and perhaps use the money to invest in the system."

"By system, you mean ditches and reservoirs?"

"Uh-huh. And big pipes."

Charlie scrunched down in his seat, crossed a leg, and put an arm over her shoulders. He told her more about why the City might want to do it themselves, something about jumping on the Progressive bandwagon. She wanted to understand it.

"What is a Progressive bandwagon?" She imagined a float in a parade with a brass band tootling in a wagon-bed.

"Just a political tag. It's considered Progressive when the users pay for the systems and set their own rates. Supporters say it's cheaper for the customers because it eliminates the profits of the businessmen. But if San Francisco buys the existing water system and capitalizes a new system, they'll need help raising all that money. Businessmen know how to do that, and can do it more simply."

Mae hadn't the foggiest notion what he was talking about. Exhaling a long breath, she let it go. She felt almost secure with Charlie. They would live together in Sacramento, and he would work for Mr. Tevis in his spare time. Oakland would have suited her better, being away from Oberon, but she had come a long distance with Charlie in more ways than one. She loved him; that much was certain. Moving into the future with his arm around her like this made it seem possible to forget about Oberon. Charlie was better than the California Joe she'd dreamed up as a girl. She ran her fingertips down his slightly scarred cheek, across the shoulder of his suit jacket and down his arm. Her hand came to rest on his hand, which was on his thigh.

He turned his hand over and squeezed hers.

She leaned on him, secretly wanting him.

He removed his hand and snapped *The San Francisco Examiner*, causing her to sit up straight as he read the paper.

After several miles of that she said, "Did you know? Mrs. Tevis is the daughter of a governor."

He lowered the newspaper and looked at her. "My, my. Which one?"

Pleased to be telling him something he hadn't known, she said, "Pacheco. I can't remember his first name."

"Ahah! An old Californio. The Pachecos had a Mexican land grant. The town of Concord was originally called Pacheco. There's Pacheco Pass near Hollister. And Ignacio, named for Ignacio Pacheco, in Marin County. That was a big family. Big landowners." Clearly he like that she'd ferreted out such information. "I think their land grant was originally in Contra Costa County."

Mae added, "I'm not sure but I think her family originally owned the place where they live now."

"That's possible. Interesting too, considering Tevis' role in Spring Valley Water Company, which opened San Mateo County to development. Those old Californios had dozens of children and their women came with dowries of land. So land got splintered as it moved into the hands of American husbands and their children."

He had a habit of saying more than she wanted to know, but she took it as a compliment and a sign that he cared for her. Her seams were about to burst from the love of him. "I'm so happy we're, you know, together."

With a little smile he went back to his newspaper.

She wanted him to understand that she had changed. "From now on I promise to go to the China Garden for our fruits and vegetables. And I'll make friends with the neighbor ladies." Friends would help her avoid Oberon while Charlie was at work. She would befriend the landlord's wife and maybe go shopping with her. And she'd go visit Mary Donahue, the dressmaker.

With the train clicking past wire fences and flocks of sheep grazing in green pastures, she dared ask, "Are you happy too?"

After a long moment, "Wha—oh, ah, happy? We'll see."

He returned to the paper.

Her heart contracted, the only moving muscle in her. She finally managed to breathe but the words sounded feeble. "What do you mean, we'll see?"

Still looking at the paper, "Just that. Time'll tell. But one thing you can count on, Mae, I'll always tell you the truth."

He snapped the paper again to make it stand up before his face.

One more thing I must never utter again—are you happy?

The list was growing.

56

Billy laid the packet of meat on the upended crate next to the cookstove. "Brought you some ground pork," he said.

He knew Ma wanted him to pretend. She was a woman of power, and yet pain showed in her eyes because he never honored that Indian practice. He wanted to ask where Baby was, but didn't. Absently he fingered the big amole brush that Ma used for whisking dirt away. He was glad to be in the house alone with her, without Isabella and Baby, but it didn't do any good when Ma wouldn't talk to him. Well, he'd just have to wait.

She put another plate and fork on the table, and he saw with satisfaction that she was stoking the stove and heating up the frying pan. She wasn't ignoring the meat.

The door banged against the wall, admitting a gust of cool wind.

Baby stood in the doorway staring at him from the black pits of her eyes. She took mincing steps to the wall until her back touched it, staying as far from him as possible but staring at him the whole time. She sidestepped along the wall in the direction of the table, never taking her eyes off him, her uncle who had never lifted a hand to her. What the hell was wrong with her? Obviously Ma hadn't taught *her* to pretend people weren't there. The pretending time was supposed to get people accustomed to each other again so they could hear each other's music. What a joke! Baby's music was screams and howls. Many a time he'd turned from the path to Ma's house because of that girl.

Now Baby dashed to the table. She shoved her chair next to her grandmother's, and pulled her plate over. Thus protected, she sat down on the chair staring at him. That's another thing Ma didn't teach her. Indian people weren't supposed to stare.

Figuring he'd better get it off his chest before the girl started screaming, Billy said. "Ma, I think I'll go work at the mill in Railroad Flat. I heard they're hiring. So I won't be around here no more."

He saw her absorb that with a sad heart, though she seemed to ignore him, and he knew that she wanted him to know she was grateful he wouldn't just leave without telling her. All this knowing, despite the silly time-of-pretending! Maybe back when the home place was full of the People, this custom had made more sense.

"I might get goin' tomorra," he said.

The light of the window gave shine to the moisture in her eye as she flipped the pork patties. She spoke in the tongue of the People while spooning greens and acorn mush onto Baby's plate.

"What kind of work will you do up there?"

As always, he answered in English. "Push yellow pine into a saw, makin' railroad ties."

"Steam saw?"

"Yup."

"Don't cut your arm off." She pressed the spatula down on the sizzling patty.

"I'll be fine."

"Some men do that. Cut off hands, fingers, arms."

"They're dumb. I watch what I'm doin'."

"Keep watching."

She nudged the patty onto his plate, hesitated a moment, and then slapped a gob of nu-pah on it—the sticky acorn pudding of the People.

"Ma, you *know* I don't eat that."

"It makes you strong."

"Thunderation, I'm forty-five—" *and don't need you telling me what to eat.* He was a head taller than Ma. She'd told him once that he had his grandfather's height and his big shoulders and arms, the grandfather who had been headman of the People before the massacre.

Ma ate in silence. Billy too. As usual he tried not to look directly at Baby because her shadowy eyes unsettled him. She never spoke a word, except the noisy mutters and gibberish in her sleep. Often it went on all night. Even Ma couldn't make out the strangled sounds, but she knew the dream visitor was spirit. Baby would wake up screaming and shaking with fear like someone was trying to kill her. Billy slept elsewhere on account of it. Ma would pick her up and rock her in her arms and try to get her to tell her grandmother about the dream before it vanished. She always said that Baby needed guidance in her dreaming. She also said the girl spoke in a normal way and asked questions like a normal girl when the two of them walked in the river bottomland gathering medicine. So maybe the girl *was* able to learn things, and the only problem was spirit.

Half the time Isabella didn't come home until daylight and then slept like a dead thing until afternoon. A ranch hand had told Billy his sister had a lot of men. She stayed away for weeks at a time. So Ma continued to take Baby with her to clean houses and help ranchers' wives give birth. She also showed the white women how to gave their sick children the medicine of the People. Baby, exhausted from her noisy, active nights, slept most of the day.

Baby's father was still in San Quentin for killing Andy and wouldn't be released for another ten years. His absence didn't make Isabella stop drinking. She drank with men she hardly knew, whenever one of them got a bottle. She drank every kind of strong rot. Billy had seen that before in other men and women, even children. As a young boy he had watched Iris Flower in her last days, and knew that old Efren and Antonio were correct when they said fermented drink had poisoned her. Most Indian people didn't listen to the elders any more, including the ancient warning against food and drink that had turned. But on the matter of fermented drink Billy listened. He also refused to eat cheese.

He was finishing his supper when a rude knocking sounded on the door.

Loud. He exchanged a glance with Ma. Friends would simply enter. He knew that some ranchers said Baby should be sent to an Indian school hundreds of miles away. Not the schoolhouse where white children walked in the mornings and returned to their homes in the afternoons, but a place where Indian children were locked in and not allowed to leave.

Ma's eyes glazed over, anticipating trouble. Billy scraped his chair back and went to the door. Two white men stood there, one the deputy sheriff with almost no chin.

"Howdy," Billy said, inviting them to come inside.

By now Baby was standing on Ma's bed as far in a corner as she could get, staring at the visitors from those coal pit eyes.

"Take a seat at the table," Billy said, lowering himself to the edge of Isabella's bed.

The deputy pushed the dishes to the center of the table and sat staring at Ma as he sat down. "Sorry to bother you at suppertime," he said, "but nobody's home here most days and we got to get this done. We have reason to believe that girl is at least seven years old. It's our duty to send her to the Indian school. It's the law." He pointed at Baby.

As though jabbed with a stick, Baby let out a scream so quivery and long that Billy could feel it in the bed frame. He almost laughed when the eyes of the white men went owlish. They didn't know that once Baby got started, she could scream for an hour.

The deputy's mouth moved, but Billy couldn't hear his words.

Baby flew off the bed, leaped to the table, and jumped on the man, plates crashing to the floor. She screamed as she kicked and hit and scratched him.

Ma grabbed at her, but Billy could see she held back a little. Baby was defending herself from being sent to that school, though Billy doubted she understood that. One thing he knew for sure. No white teachers in that school would be able to quiet her like Ma did. This girl was the rare filly that couldn't be broken.

Baby kicked the man's knees and pounded his balding head. Her scratches drew blood. The other man tried to grab her, but she jumped down and bounded across table and floor, back to her corner. The deputy touched his wounds and looked at the blood on his fingertips. "Damn her hide! Get her!" he ordered his helper.

"Ain't nobody can stop her," Billy yelled over the rattling screams. She was like the night spirit Ma had warned about in his boyhood, the noisy one that scrambled people's brains and made them crazy.

Maybe the men were going crazy. Both of them headed for the door. Baby ran at them and jumped like a mountain lion on the deputy's back, pummeling with feet and fists. This time the younger man punched her in the back, and she fell to the floor.

In the quiet while the wind was knocked out of her, the men hurried out and mounted their horses.

"Needs a real good whuppin, I'd say," the deputy yelled from the saddle.

Billy couldn't help but smile to himself as Baby regained her breath, gave out a bloodcurdling scream, and ran after them. They kicked their mounts to a lope.

Billy captured his niece and brought her back to Ma, who took her in her arms and rocked her back and forth, humming through the shrieking and kicking. There would be no peace and quiet in the house for a long time, so Billy left for Railroad Flat.

He was halfway over the bridge before the screams became too faint to be heard. He would begin a new life, passing for a white man. As his steps fell into the cadence of distance-walking, he thought how nice it would be to be paid again. Nobody around the home place could pay for work now. Even white men worked for food.

A year ago Mr. Swain had given Billy a sad look and a straight razor for a good-bye present. "You're a good man to lose," he told Billy. "Hope you find more reliable work." They shook hands, both callused from all the work they had shared over the thirty years. Since then he'd been doing odd jobs from ranch to ranch.

〜

On the road up through the foothills Billy was feeling hungry and tired when he came alongside a man about his age lying against some saddlebags. It was still light enough to see the bright chestnut color of the horse grazing on the first grass of autumn. The man wore good boots with spurs. What kind of an Indian would have a horse and good boots? And if he were Portagee or Mexican or one of the other kinds of darker skinned men he wouldn't wear his straight black hair down to his shoulders with a length of red cloth tied around his forehead. Hair like Billy allowed himself to grow since it was easier and everyone around his home already knew he was Indian, hair he must singe short before he got much higher in the mountains.

"Howdy," Billy said raising a hand.

"Howdy," the man said. "You're a long ways from any place."

Billy stopped walking and smiled. "On my way to Railroad Flat."

"Set yourself down a while," the man said, sitting up straighter.

That was a nice offer of companionship.

While Billy lowered himself to the ground and leaned back on a clump of bunchgrass, the man said, "Travelin' light, I see. Got anythin' to eat?"

"Nope. Been lookin' but ain't seen nuthin' yet. There's a little creek over there, so figgered I'd find some frogs or somethin'."

The man turned on his knees and rummaged in a saddlebag. "Try this," he said, extending a thick sandwich toward Billy.

Billy took it, nodding in surprise and appreciation. A large hunk of bread, meat, and tomato slices occupied so much room in his mouth, he couldn't get words through it for a while. He rubbed his belly in the way of the People to show it tasted good.

The man looked at him with interest in the fading light, realizing that he was Indian.

"Where you going?" Billy asked.

"Down to Sheep Ranch."

"You live around there?"

"No. Used to, but most of the time I'm on the road."

Billy was curious to know how this Indian made his money. He limited himself to, "You have a nice horse."

"Yup. He's a good'n all right."

"Where you comin' from?"

"Kirkwood's. You know that place?"

"No. But I've broke horses for them that drive cows and sheep up to summer pasture around there."

"Well, you're talkin' to one 'at does just that—drives cattle that is."

Billy was thinking it must pay good money when the man reached a hand over and said, "M'name's Raul Martinez."

As they shook hands Billy said, "Mine's Billy McCoon."

"What're you doing, going to Railroad Flat?"

"Lookin' to get paid work. There's a sawmill up there. Heard they make rail ties."

"You say you break horses?" Raul held a bladder of water over to Billy.

Billy drank deeply of the full bag and handed it back, wiping his lips. "Been doin' it all my life." He stuffed the last of the sandwich in his mouth and savored it before he said, "I do anything needs doin' on a ranch."

"Cows?"

"Sure."

"You know how to rope?"

"Sure do. Catchin' runaway cows an' horses. That kinda thing."

By now a blood-red strip of color lay like a ribbon over the crest of the mountains on the western side of the big valley, and Billy could see the parts not hidden by the near hills and patches of tall forest. He could no longer read his companion's expression, nor see what the man was getting out of his saddlebags, but Raul was friendly and obviously glad to have company too.

"I don't understand," Raul said after a comfortable silence, "why a man would want to work in a sawmill when he can ride and rope."

"Well, how 'bout if a man's got no horse to ride and nuthin' to rope."

A warm chuckle resonated in the dark. "You like some hooch?"

By now Billy's brain was going down like a lamp out of fuel. His eyes were closed, and he laid himself on the friendly ground between the bunchgrass clumps like a baby in a bikoos. His body thanked him, and he drifted past the place where someone had mentioned hooch.

At first light a horse nickered in Billy's ear. Startled, he sat up to see the big nostrils looming over him. He shoved the nose away.

Raul sat up, rubbing his eyes. He spoke softly to the horse in a language Billy had heard before but knew only a few words. From this, Billy knew that Raul had been born to one of the Maidu peoples forty or fifty miles to the north.

Billy had slept soundly and now his side and back ached from being in the same position too long. Raul was up peeing, a man who had ridden this road many times.

Billy joined him. "How many days from here to Railroad Flat?"

"If you walk fast, maybe one whole day."

Looking up toward those hills, Billy inhaled the cool damp air of morning. "Think I can pass as a white man?"

"Cut off that hair and you'll pass for a Norwegian. What are you, quarter Indian?"

"Half."

"I'm full-blood."

They returned to the saddlebags where Raul again offered Billy part of a sandwich. Grateful, Billy ate it.

"I didn't bring no coffee pan," Raul said, "seein' as how I'll be in Sheep Ranch in a couple hours." He lifted the saddle and put it over the Chestnut.

"I'm surprised," Billy now felt comfortable saying, "a man can make enough money to buy a fine horse and saddle drivin' cows up this road."

Raul pulled the cinch strap, held it while the horse let out his air, and looked at Billy with a smile playing in his eyes. "Well, that's not 'zactly all I do."

"What's the other thing, if you don't mind my askin'?"

Raul changed his voice to sound like an announcer: "Raul Martinez, wonder of the world, riding Lightning!" He grinned. "I do rodeos and competitions. They think I'm Spanish."

"Sounds like I shoulda been ridin' rodeos all these years."

Raul studied Billy. "Mebbeso. *Hasta luego, amigo.*" He swung into the saddle with the lightness of a disembodied spirit and pranced down the road, but then turned in the saddle and reined to a stop, sitting the horse crosswise on the road as he provided advice.

"Next June when it's hot in the big valley, go up and camp by Kirkwood's Inn. You'll meet all the vaqueros and ranchers that use the summer pastures. Mebbe get work. Tell 'em you're a friend of Raul Martinez."

With a merry laugh he went on his way.

57

People said the Panic of '93, which had spiraled into a serious economic recession in '94, would soon be over. But this was June and it seemed to be getting worse. Just about every day *The Sacramento Bee* ran stories about the "depression" or "recession." There were reports of over a thousand banks locking their doors while angry customers waved papers at the windows.

Today, sad about Benty—the little cat had never returned after being locked outside while Mae traveled with Charlie—Mae walked through the downtown in her big hat with pink roses. There were more men than usual asking for alms on the corners, and more haggard women and children begging for ten-cent pieces. One woman had a tot as well as a dog half-naked from mange and showing its ribs. The sad brown eyes of the boy and the dog just about made her cry. She hurried past them, sorry she couldn't give the woman a coin. All she had left of her weekly allowance from Charlie was thirty-five cents, and she needed most of it for her noon dinner with Emmett. Besides, if she gave money to these people, the next beggars wouldn't get any and they'd all be just as hungry a few hours later. So what good would that do? *Not the way Jesus would think.*

Out of Business signs were nailed to two doors on Mary Donavan's block. In addition, the furniture-maker had printed: I Give Up.

The bell tinkled as Mae entered Mary's store. "Hello!" she called out.

Mary came smiling from behind her curtain, her pregnancy showing. "You're right on time. And I'm so glad we're doing this!"

She removed the threaded needles from her bodice and stuck them in a pincushion. Bending her knees to see herself in the table mirror by the hat rack, she put on a wide hat with big flattened bows of a crinkly red material. She licked a finger and ran it over an eyebrow. Studying the effect, she pinched her cheeks, bringing up color.

"I like this hat I bought from you," Mae said, "It hides my face."

Mary stepped to the window of the door and looked out both ways. "Let's make tracks," she said, "No policeman that I can see."

When Mae was outside, Mary turned the key in the lock, dropped it in her pocket, and reversed her sign to Closed For Noon Dinner. "Now that you mention it, maybe we should switch hats so you aren't always in that one. That'd help fool him."

They changed hats and headed for the railroad shops. There they'd buy food for Emmett and Rob, Mary's husband, and split up to eat with their men.

The Metropolitan Theatre had gone out of business. "Would you look at that!" Mae said as they walked by. "I noticed two more places closed on your block too."

"It's a wonder anybody can pay the downtown rents anymore," Mary said. "You're still in business."

"Not for long. Customers aren't coming in like they used to, and I haven't paid the May rent, much less June, so I'm about to get evicted." Seeing Mae's shock, "You see, prices of ready-wear clothes have gone down and people expect me to lower my prices to meet that. But—," she sighed. "Actually I did reduce my prices, but it didn't help. Ladies are wearing their old gowns to parties. But Rob and I have the house, and when it comes right down to it, that's more important than the shop."

Saddened by this turn of affairs, Mae looked ahead to Chinatown with the SP smokestacks smudging the sky behind it. "Will you stop your dressmaking?"

Two young Chinese boys ran past them on the dusty street, playfully looking over their shoulders at other Chinese boys gaining on them. The smell of chicken and garlic was everywhere. Noon dinner in Chinatown.

"I'll sew in my house," Mary was saying. "Our place is cramped, though. Just one bedroom and a little front room, and with the baby coming I won't have the space I need. I'll keep some of it up though. What a time for this to happen! You're lucky Charlie isn't in business."

Two weeks ago Mae had told Mary *everything*, not meaning to, but once she got started she hadn't been able to stop, what with Mary glancing up from her sewing and treadling with that keen listening expression. She had occasionally cut into Mae's monolog with, "Oh my stars," "Saints preserve us", or "For the love of Mike!" More than once she took her hand off the machine and crossed herself. And though she frowned at the part about Charlie not believing in marriage, that hadn't stopped their friendship. Mae had the impression that Mary rather liked having a friend who'd been through all that. And The Irish did love a good story.

"Is Rob proud of you, I mean for having your own business?" To Mae that seemed a high degree of female freedom, and she doubted most men would tolerate it.

"Yes, I'm lucky to have such a husband. He's proud even when I'm tired and don't feel like cooking." She looked over at Mae with a devilish smile. "He sure liked my income too, when it was coming in good."

"Well, for all we know the *Sacramento Union's* right. The Depression will end and your landlord'll let you pay the back rent later."

The big Chinese Theatre appeared to be open. They crossed several streetcar tracks on I Street and approached the vendor tents in the SP yard, a city within a city. As planned, they arrived before the noon whistle and were the first ones in line. Quickly they placed their orders.

By the time the whistle went off, Mary was on her way to Car Shop Number 9 with beer mugs and sandwiches, and Mae was wiping soot off one end of a table in front of the foundry.

The instant the first bunch of foundry workers shuffled out the door Mae knew something was wrong. This was not the eager bunch that had lined up at the tents and dug joyfully into beer-pails for their dinners, as they had done last Wednesday. The life had gone out of them, Emmett too. She flagged him down with her sooty handkerchief.

He dropped himself on the bench like he weighed five hundred pounds. Soot had worked its way into the small lines around his mouth and eyes, ageing him far beyond his nineteen years.

"You look like you've been whipped. What's the matter?" she asked.

Emmett groaned. "We was just told there's gonna be a heap a' layoffs and nobody's gettin' the raises and promotions we was promised. Here I'd figgered to get a room of my own and git outa that hellhole with... well, you don't wanna hear about those, those—. Damn! They'll likely fire me too. Just when I was set to be raised to apprentice." He sounded like he might cry. "Just when I found work to be proud of."

"Oh, Emmett, that's vile!" A word she'd picked up from the ladies at the Water Institute. "Here." She put his sandwich and Coca-Cola mug in front of him.

"The master machinist just told us in there." He jabbed a thumb over his shoulder. "Said orders've slowed way down. The last engines we tore apart and rebuilt went for a pittance. The company can't keep a-goin' like that." He chomped off a third of his beef sandwich and chewed, his troubled eyes bluer in that blackened face. Two other men came to sit at the table.

"When will you know about, ah—"

Garbled through the mouthful, "Gettin' the ax?"

She nodded, watching him chew.

"Dunno. Hell, they're givin' my kind 'a work to the crippled class, hardly paying 'em a thing." By now three other men with store-bought food had squeezed in between bench and table. Mae didn't lower her voice.

"What? They take cripples off the street to work—?"

"The *crippled class* is what they call men who got theirselves hurt workin' for the railroad. You'd oughta see 'em draggin' around on crutches. Workin' with one leg or one arm. One poor bugger was blinded by the steam. Got a face like ground meat. Eyes all white." Emmett chased the first half of his sandwich with the Coca-Cola.

A man in clean work clothes sat down on Mae's side of the table.

"Howdy ma'am," the clean man said as he handed a folded sheet of paper to Emmett and the others. "Sidle up and give a listen," he invited a couple of men walking past. They hesitated but joined the table. With a glance at Mae, "Sorry to break in on you like this, but I don't have long." He continued.

"Brothers, I'm from the American Railway Union. Anybody at this table already belong to it?"

All were silent.

"The ARU's growin' fast in Sacramento, and now you know why. The SP's set to lower the boom on the working man. Us shopmen can't fight this alone—not in Los Angeles nor Oakland. The Brotherhoods won't help us."

"Where're you from?" demanded one who'd moved his rump up the table to be straight across from the stranger.

"Los Angeles."

"You in the running trades?"

"Nope, boilermaker."

A man with a cockney accent asked, "What's a bloke like you doin' up here then, midweek and shiny as a new penny? 'Ow're we to know you ent the brass dressed down an' trickin' us into sayin' we's soft on the Union?"

"Here," the man said, passing circulars to everyone at the table. "I wouldn't pass this around, would I, if I was a spy? Our shop in Los Angeles's been fighting to get our grievances up the SP chain of command. We joined the national union in January, but in numbers we're pikers compared to Sacramento. We need you, and you need us. Best as can be figgered, thirty-five hundred men are employed here, and you put out more rolling stock than any center west of Chicago. You got the power to cripple the whole damned SP. Just think how long it'd take 'em to get it all up and runnin' again, without you."

As Mae drank her Coca-Cola, feeling the instant pep it always gave her, the man provided more arguments for joining the ARU. He told them about the leader, Eugene Debs, and yet managed to eat his dinner at the same time. "Well, that's about it," he concluded, brushing the crumbs off the table with a big hand. "See Joe McDougal in Car Shop 9 about signing up."

"Hold your horses there a minute, mister," an older man piped up. "You sayin' this costs money to join in. How much?"

"Two dollars. It's all in the circular."

"Oh, I see. You figger we're gettin' so all fired edga-cated 'round here, we c'n read that crap. Sorry ma'am."

"Look men, I gotta visit ten more tables before the whistle blows. My brother 'n me, we're up here on the lam. For your own sakes, for the sake of workingmen all over the country, talk to Joe McDougal." He tipped his cap at Mae. "Ma'am.

Emmett was pointing his finger along a line of words in the circular. At that rate he'd finish reading it next week. The visitor was already at another table.

At their table a bass voice asserted, "I joined last month. The ARU's the only way, far as I'm concerned. All you shopmen should join up."

Another man said, "I got talked into joining one of the Brotherhoods a year or so ago. They're sayin' the ARU's takes too hard a line. The Brothers won't consider a strike. They say we should soft-soap it like they do."

Emmett cleared his throat, keeping his place with his finger. "I'm just a

Helper, so this is new to me. What do you mean by a strike?"

The basso profundo answered. "It means stop working. Stop the trains 'til the SP guarantees our pay, guarantees no more pay cuts. If you been working a set time and doin' good, you get promoted and git paid more. Period."

A new man spoke up. "Them so-called Big Four wants their trains runnin' so's they can live like oriental potentates. Well, I say they can damn well pay the people who make the trains and see that they run. Or else."

Had Charlie been there, he would have informed them that three of the Big Four were dead. Wanting to be on the side of the men, Mae said, "I've seen the mansions of the owners, and you're right. They live like kings."

Ignoring her, the basso screwed his face into something like a smile. "A strike'd make 'em take note all right. We might disable the tracks fer an extra sweetner."

Talk moved from man to man, Emmett listening closely.

Another man said, "They'd likely fire us 'n fix it so's we can't never work for no railroad agin. That's too much gamble for me, with my kids and all. Just when I'm gunna be a machinist. Maybe we'd oughta stick it out and wait till this depression thing gits over with."

"Earl, I'll take bets they cut your pay a good healthy percent. Unless we join the union we got no strength to fight 'em. That there's the kinda thinking that keeps the Brotherhoods from striking."

The basso again. "Don't compare us to the running trades. The engineers and firemen and conductors and such all got contracts. We boilermakers, machinists, sheet metal workers, blacksmiths and car-men got no power at all. We're out here twisting in the wind. They c'n poke us ever which way they want. But Eugene Debs, that's the head of the ARU, can help us. He's the best."

Somebody pounded his fist on the table "By damn, I'm joinin'. The threat of a strike'll open their ears."

"Does the ARU sign up helpers and apprentices?" Emmett wanted to know.

"Sure boy," a new voice answered. "We all started in your shoes. You need protection same as we do. A man has to fight for what's his, and railroad work is worth fightin' for. A man can be proud to make it his life's work."

"Proud? That's crap in a bottle," said another. "Don't forget, they make the government jump around on strings. They sent the railroad agents to kill those good men in Mussel Slough. I say we band together with our working brothers around the country. If it takes a strike to talk sense into 'em, I'm for it."

"Me too," a new voice said. "I'll do anything to keep from losing my little house. First time the Missus ever had a place of her own."

This kind of talk continued until the whistle blew. Mae had wanted to talk to Emmett alone, but she was glad to understand the turmoil he was living in. "I'll come again," she told him as the other men left for the foundry. "Two weeks?"

"The pay train's supposed to get here any day now," Emmett said. "We never know when. They stagger the days to fool the bandits. Come next Wednesday, before they fire me. I'll buy your lunch."

She loved seeing his old smile.

∽

Mary looked hollowed out around the eyes, and her cheeks needed to be pinched again. "Rob is certain to be laid off," she told Mae the moment they met to walk back through town. "They've got no orders in Car Shop 9, not even a promise of one."

"Did the men talk about joining the Railroad Union?"

"Yes, but anarchy won't save his job." Mary's pale brown eyes were wide with fear. "It'd just hasten the fall of the ax. Now we'll lose the house." The last words made her voice crack. She pressed her lips together like she was squelching tears.

Mae ached for this able businesswoman who could soon be begging in the streets with a baby in her arms. She put an arm around her and patted her shoulder. They walked in silence. *At least she has Rob and whatever happens they will face it together.* To say that could sound uncompassionate, so Mae kept it inside.

Charlie might have secure employment, but the slender thread connecting him to her was of fiber so fragile as to break in the attempt to tie it.

∽

A letter from Daddy waited on the floor under the letter slot. Mae tore it open and went to the sofa to read it.

Hank's pay at Knights Foundry in Sutter Creek had been cut by twenty percent, but he and Sophie and the baby were living with Sophie's parents, so they would get along. Farley was home again, laid off from the Ione Brewery for starting a fight. "If any work should have been secure," Daddy wrote, "it ought to have been the making of beer." Mae felt her face make a sad smile.

That evening as she sat at the kitchen table snapping the ends off the amazingly large green beans that she'd got at the China garden, Charlie entered the little kitchen and sat opposite her, pipe in hand. His suit looked rumpled from the long stage ride and the train from Folsom. He'd been gone since dawn. She itched to get his opinion of what Emmett should do, but Charlie ran with the crowd that managed the railroad, and she felt she shouldn't mention what she'd heard today. *One more subject not to mention*

"Guess I'm not much of a salesman," he muttered, looking at her with the expression of a lost boy.

Such a thing from him! She'd assumed he'd be good at anything that hinged on thinking and speaking, and she'd never seen him admit to failure. She continued snapping the beans. "What do you mean?"

"Just can't seem to talk those tough birds along rivers into selling options. It's getting me down."

"Maybe they don't want their land to go under a lake."

"It's not that. You see, many of them are selling out anyway on account of the hard times, and they don't want to burden the sale with any obligation that a buyer might not want. No thank you, they say, and shut the door in my face. Today I had to report to Mr. Tevis about it."

Thank heavens Charlie had his regular work at the Capitol. "What'd he say?"

Tamping tobacco into his pipe, "Well, he surprised me by not batting an eye, so to speak, if eyes can be batted over the telephone. He called back a couple hours later and said the Board decided to offer more to the sellers."

"Is that the incentive you were talking about?"

"No." He sucked and puffed on his pipe, the sweet smoke blossoming until it filled the kitchen. "Just a higher price tag on the options. The incentive is what goes to the San Francisco Supervisors."

"How much goes to them?"

He drew in a lungful of smoke and let it out with his words. "I wouldn't know. Maybe half a million dollars."

Half a million! So vast a number, Mae couldn't think how many zeros. It was outside the universe of her understanding. What a strange day, seeing skinny people begging for small coins, and then hearing about people earning that much for a single vote.

And to think she hadn't given that street woman a nickel! Silently she vowed to go back and do it tomorrow. If she was clever about haggling, she could "earn" it back and Charlie'd never know the difference.

"Will Mr. Fair pay the Oakland supervisors that much for his streetcar lines?"

"It's a city council in Oakland. He didn't say how much. Plenty, no doubt. A businessman unwilling to give incentives loses. But Fair needs to do a lot of work besides that."

"Sounds like you should get yourself one of those city positions."

Rising, he gave her a funny look and went to his soft chair in the front room.

〜

A few days later *The Sacramento Bee* reported "fears of revolutionary violence felt across the United States, roused by the spectacle of thousands of unemployed and homeless men organizing in all sections of the country to march on Washington." Coxey's Industrial Army, it was called. James Coxey was at its head. Many thousands of men, and some women as well, camped at the nation's capital city to pressure Congress to provide "Government employment on public works and emergency relief aid for their destitute and starving families."

That evening Charlie brought home both newspapers as usual. *The Sacramento Union* denounced Coxey's Industrial Army as evidence of a "frighteningly radical trend in the country." A Congressman was quoted as saying that such an "army" was un-American. "It is the time-honored place of churches and charitable groups to provide alms to the poor. It is not the government's place to give handouts to indigent and homeless people." Coxey responded that the "traditional sources of aid in the United States are overwhelmed by the magnitude of the relief problem, and if the government won't step in, this country just might see a revolution."

That's what Hiram Johnson had predicted on that awful day last year. And now federal troops were arresting campers in the parks of Washington D.C. for trespassing. Maybe a revolution was starting.

At the end of the same article, George Pullman, the man whose Illinois company made the famous sleeping cars, was quoted as saying he'd reduced his workforce from 5,800 to 1,100, and had cut the wages of the remaining workers by 25 percent. He admitted that was a big cut, but said it had to be done or his company would fail and shut down.

The following Wednesday when Mae opened her eyes, Charlie had already gone to El Dorado County. This was Mae's day to meet Emmett for lunch. She felt a gnawing worry that he'd been fired for joining the union. And as she made her way to the water closet another worry niggled. She didn't feel quite right. There was a wishy-washiness in her insides, and a slight dizziness.

58

O h, it's you!" Mary exclaimed as Mae opened the jingling door of the dressmaker's shop. "I'm so worried about the men. You still want to go? I sure do."

"Of course. But Mary, I thought they'd terminated Rob."

"They did, but he goes there every day to help."

"I don't underst—. You mean he's still working?"

"No. Nobody's working. Just a few scabs. He's helping to keep 'em out of there—workers from the streets, men who don't know the first thing about the equipment."

"How do they keep, ah, scabs from getting in?"

"Rob says there'll be fights."

"Let's go," Mae urged. She worried about Emmett. He was a scrappy boy, but not very big.

She had slept in, quickly eaten some uncooked oatmeal with milk, swallowed a half cup of lukewarm coffee that Charlie had made before he went to work, and left the apartment without reading the newspapers from last evening. It was late June, a hot day, and the bodice of Mae's frock was soaked by the time they arrived at the SP foundry. Worse, she felt a return of queasiness, which she'd assumed, hoped, prayed would go away. The curse was late, but it couldn't be happening again! They had been careful. Except maybe once or twice, now that she thought about it.

A lone wisp of smoke wafted from one of the towering smokestacks rising from the foundry. The other chimneys stood like petrified trees surrounded by blue sky. It was nine in the morning, when on a normal day the men would have been inside working. Now hundreds of them moved about the earthen yard. A line of toughs strode back and forth before the entrance, making tight turns. Some of them carried signs Mae couldn't read from her angle.

"That's the picket line," Mary explained.

Many strikers stood watching the picketers, talking among themselves or shifting around. She didn't see Emmett, but thought she recognized a man from the lunch table last week. Off to one side stood the "slim and hungry men desperate for work" described by the *Sacramento Union* in yesterday's paper. The SP had put out a notice of "help wanted, all comers." The haunted gazes of those silent men stayed fixed on the picket line.

"Look, the militia's not lifting a finger," Mary said in low voice not to be overheard by the many people crowding around.

Mae didn't see them. "Where are they?"

Mary pointed toward the vendor tents, and now Mae saw about a dozen brown-uniformed men in boots and gaiters lounging on the ground or squatting in the shade of the tents. Some were upending mugs, one wiping his forehead and putting his stiff-brimmed hat back on his head.

"There's Joe!" Mary said, pointing toward the militia. "He's Rob's best friend. He's for the strike."

Mae knew the volunteer militia was there to stop the strikers from preventing scabs from entering the buildings. Joe and his pals sure didn't appear to be doing that.

The vendors were doing a brisk business serving drinks to the strikers, the militia, bystanders, and, Mae was horrified to see, lawmen coming from police wagons. Oberon would surely be one of them. He had an arrangement with the foundry boss. Afraid of giving herself away, she didn't stare long enough to identify him, but tilted her hat over her face and elbowed Mary. "Look over there." She pointed surreptitiously.

"Uh-oh," Mary said, pointing to the back side of the foundry, "let's go." She stepped away smartly, explaining over her shoulder, "There's a back way to Car Shop Number 9."

That's where her Rob was. Mae, wishing she'd seen Emmett, lifted her skirts and followed Mary around the narrow end of the very long building. Then they were alone on a faint path through brittle grasses and stickers, some of it shoulder high. It choked the area between the windowless length of the foundry and the reeking little lake. Bits of oily garbage floated on the blue-green water along with scraps of putrid meat and poultry feathers. The stench was awful. Her stomach lurched. Swallowing it down again and again, she kept her eyes on the path, where foxtails jammed her shoelace eyelets and stabbed her feet and ankles through her stockings. Queasy and losing ground to Mary, she noticed the accumulating weight of the heavy brown burrs that matted her skirts.

Something big was rotting in water. This time she didn't try to suppress the gagging reflex, but bent down in the burrs and heaved up her oatmeal and coffee.

Her hat dangled before her, attached only by the loosened hat pins. Weak and faint, she straightened up, picked the thumb-sized burrs off the collar of her dress, and re-pinned her hat. The sun felt like an anvil, and she thought Hell must feel like this. She walked gingerly, Mary far ahead, clearly hurrying to get to Rob. Mae let her go.

A deep-throated roar of mostly male voices on the other side of the building momentarily stopped her. It sounded like an exciting moment at the city racetrack. But she knew something awful had happened. She thought about going back to see—maybe Emmett would be there now—but she was halfway to the end of the building and couldn't go back where the police were.

The shouts of the crowd continued, and the littered ground at the opposite end of the structure contained all manner of discarded items and broken bottles. She came to the corner and peered around it—the strikers about a hundred yards away and no people blocking her view. A fight was underway, a dust plume rising around it. The police stood watching. She was alone here, with the sour reek of urine cooking in the sun. Feeling faint and worried about Emmett, she leaned against the corner, the red bricks of the building radiating too much heat though it was only about 9:30 in the morning.

The crowd of strikers shifted around as they bellowed encouragement like spectators at a boxing match. Behind them, the militia watched as a group, ignoring a man in a straw hat screaming at them. Even from where she stood, she was able to make out the red of the man's face.

A stray movement of air carried the acrid odor of many unwashed bodies, adding to the smell left by men unwilling to wait in line at the company shithouse.

Stepping back where nobody could see, she bent over again, and let loose. Her stomach kicked like a horse, but heave after heave produced only foamy spit. Feeble as a hatching bird, she wiped her mouth and returned to the corner. Leaning again on the hot bricks, her burr-laden skirts scratching against it, she noticed that not even weeds grew in this area, probably not for years. Too much pissing.

As the fighting men stirred up dust, a heraldic voice bull-horned through the noise and the distance: "Employees of Southern Pacific, return to your work stations and you will not be arrested. I repeat. Return to your work or go to jail."

Everyone appeared to ignore it.

"Ohhh," the crowd exhaled, intent upon the fight.

Even in this excitement Mae longed to lie flat on the ground. Only the dangerous broken glass sparkling in the sun stopped her. It seemed that one of the fighters was swaying on his feet. She knew how he felt. Another man staggered off the grounds, parting the bystanders like the Red Sea.

Two or three men made a head-down run, like human battering rams, toward the foundry door. They collided with the picket line, and all collapsed in a fighting melee. The crowd roared again, and Mae made out the louder yells:

"…teach 'em a lesson!"

"…at 'em, boys!"

A gunshot cracked.

Mae held her breath. Someone had been shot. The crowd turned as one, everyone looking at the blue uniforms of the lawmen. The officers held guns before them. One lawman was tall, his hair giving him away even at that distance. Oberon!

Knees melting, she shrank back out of sight. If he had followed her around town lately, when she visited Emmett, he would recognize this hat with the pile of pink roses. He might think Emmett was her sweetheart. Maybe he'd just killed Emmett! He assumed he was above the law, and his promise echoed in her head. *If you ever leave me I'll track you down and chop you into little pieces to feed the fish in the river.*

She removed her hat, put it behind her, and peered around the corner again, heart banging louder. Angry men and woman now had the police surrounded, and from the demeanor of the crowd—not hovering over anyone on he ground—she doubted anyone had been shot. She exhaled. Perhaps the gun had been fired into the air to scare the strikers.

"Lay off!" She heard clearly.

"We're not criminals."

A woman's voice pierced the distance. "Shame on you!" Others joined the cry.

At that moment Mae spied a small man with Emmett's easy stance, hands in pockets. She thought she could see curly dark hair springing out from under a cap. She felt sure it was Emmett! He was all right. Just watching the people of Sacramento scold its police force.

After sagging against the wall for a moment of rest, Mae hurried back down the prickly trail, limping from the poking foxtails and powered by an intense need to get far away from here. She nearly blacked out several times but kept putting one shoe ahead of the other. At the end of the building she rushed into the crowd of bystanders and wove her way through them, heading back to 12th Street.

It felt like a thousand miles.

ᔕ

Back in the apartment with the doors locked, she stepped out of her frock and untied the laces of her corset. In her knickers and Charlie's old shirt, she lit the pilot light and boiled hot water for tea. Then she was in the front room sinking into the davenport pillows with tea steeping on the sundries table. She closed her eyes for a long time. When she felt strong enough she picked up the evening newspapers, which she had left to Charlie last night. The headline blared: *Strikers Threaten Mail Stoppage.*

The story said that on Monday, Eugene Debs, the head of the American Railroad Union, had telegrammed leaders of all local unions at every railroad center in the United States to boycott the Pullman cars.

She got up and went to Charlie's glass bookcase, pulled out his dictionary and looked up b-o-y-c-o-t-t. Reading the definition twice, she decided it meant that Debs had ordered the union members all over the United States not to allow the sleeping cars to be coupled to the trains. Curled in her nest, she read that Debs had also telegrammed top officials in the railroad companies, requesting that they voluntarily join the Pullman boycott. If they did, Debs assured them that the passenger and mail trains would run. But the companies refused. It surprised her that other railroads existed in the United States, besides the SP.

She rested her eyes. The tea was helping. She continued reading. "The SP management underestimated the anger their refusal would provoke. Within twenty-four hours the workers controlled all the major rail yards in the country." She was fascinated to learn that SP employees across the country had stopped work and set up picket lines. In Redding, not far north, they had set a trestle afire. Around the nation people had their eyes on Sacramento, the largest train center in the West, to see what would happen here.

Both local papers endorsed the "historic" strike, supporting the workers in Pullman, Illinois, but they also advised the strikers to keep level heads. Sacramento was a "critical nexus of the national railroad system," the *Union* stated, being the original terminus of the transcontinental line as well as central to the north-south line from Los Angeles to Seattle. C. K. McClatchy, the editor of *The Bee,* wrote in his special column that labor's check on the "monopoly of the Southern Pacific" could be a good thing. He noted, however, that most of the newspapers around the country, including the *Los Angeles Times*, viewed the strike as "tyrannical anarchy" that should be stopped by federal injunction and, if necessary, stamped out by the regular army. This was because the U.S. mail must go through, and also because local militias tended to side with the strikers, as they did in Sacramento. President Grover Cleveland's telephone, McClatchy wrote, was ringing constantly as businessmen urged him to immediate action.

A separate article caught her eye. Sacramento residents were offering board and room to the strikers. Hundreds of sympathetic people had contacted *The Bee*. "These are brave men," one homeowner was quoted as saying. "We owe it to them to help in their time of need."

∾

A half-hour later, feeling proud that Emmett was part of an important national event, Mae was at the drain board assembling a sandwich for Charlie from last night's lamb roast. The tea had calmed her stomach but she still couldn't eat anything.

Charlie came in for his noon dinner, throwing off his suit jacket and talking about the strike.

"I read all about it in both papers," she told him.

Having thought about Emmett's predicament, Mae had decided to end her personal boycott on conversation with Charlie about Emmett. She cared about her brother and saw no reason why Charlie wouldn't like him too, even if he used "ain't" and "we was."

"I have a brother in town," she began.

"Oh, which one?" Charlie dipped himself a glass of water from the settling keg.

"Emmett, the one just two years older than me."

"Older than I," he corrected, sitting down to his sandwich.

Hot rage flashed through her. He didn't give her credit for three years in St. Mary's Academy. Why must he always act the teacher? But she stopped short of reminding him that he too reverted to his farm-boy way of speaking when he felt like it. Not so long ago she had habitually corrected the grammar of all her brothers. Oh how they'd hated it! And mocked her for it—their little sister who'd been privileged to go to school while they worked in the fields. Now she yearned to take it all back.

Charlie finished chewing a bite of lamb sandwich. "Well, what about him?"

She sat down across from him. "He's one of the strikers. He needs help. I don't want him going hungry and sleeping on the ground like so many are doing. We have the davenport in the front room."

Charlie took a swig of water. "I find it strange you've said nothing about him before now."

"I've been visiting with him at the rail yard, at noon dinner." This was difficult because Charlie worked closely with SP in fashioning laws.

"He know about us?"

"No, but maybe it's time he did."

Charlie regarded her with a lopsided smile. "Sometimes big brothers get touchy about little sisters living out of wedlock like we do."

"I think he'll understand. People all over town are taking in perfect strangers to help them over the crisis. This is my brother. The one I'm closest to. The newspapers favor their cause. The strikers will win out, and soon. He'll be promoted and have a place of his own, so it won't be for long. Please Charlie."

Charlie ran the palm of a hand down over his face like he was tired. In the light of the kitchen window she noticed the start of lines on his forehead and around his eyes. He looked all of his thirty-two years.

"It wouldn't set well with my bosses," he said.

"You don't have to tell them."

Charlie bit into the second half of his sandwich, and when he spoke his voice had the ring of finality. "It's summertime. I don't think there's anything wrong with a young man camping by the river. It's nice down there, pleasant at night. Why don't you just take him some extra vittles. That'd tide him over."

"All right," she conceded too fast. Rage flared in her heart to realize that she had no real say about helping Emmett. These swings of emotion upset her. She hardly knew herself anymore. But at least she wouldn't need to explain Charlie to Emmett, as she would have to do if Emmett slept on the davenport.

That last thought brought a heavy melancholy, right on top of the smoldering anger. "I need to talk to you about something else, too."

"Go right ahead. This is a free apartment."

No it's not. "You've been careful and I'm grateful for it. But, well, in spite of it I'm, uh, afraid I'm in a family way. Again."

She couldn't look him in the eye, but from the dead silence knew her words had hit him hard and in some strange way evened things.

He finally spoke, in his matter-of-fact way. "That why you're not eating?"

She shrugged.

He rearranged his face, returning to the calm Charlie she knew. "Well, this isn't unprecedented, and as you well know there is a cure."

No. Not again. She loved him, and he wanted her to live with him—he'd told her that a number of times and it counted even if she'd had to pry it out of him. Since their return from San Francisco he had escorted her to dinners and other gatherings of Capitol people, always treating her as a gentleman would treat a wife. Somewhere she'd read that a man needed a little push in these matters. It was time she pushed.

The teakettle whistled.

She got up, turned down the gas, and poured the boiling water from the pot, agitating the curly Chinese leaves. Almost in a whisper, "I don't think I could live through that again."

"Now, Mae, you've got to remember that your case was unusual. I've, um, heard of many such operations. Your degree of trouble was rare, the infection and all. You'll be all right next time. Of that I'm certain."

"It's more painful than childbirth."

"Oh pshaw. What do you know about childbirth?"

She had promised him never to speak of marriage, but circumstances had changed. Low and steady, she said, "You and I live together. We love each other. And now we have reason to be married."

He stood up so fast his chair clattered on its back. He stared down from his height, tight-lipped, big eyed. "Mae!" he shouted, "I will *not* marry you or any other female. We've been through this quite enough!"

He whirled and strode to the front room.

She sat there with a heavy stone on her heart, hearing his footsteps thump around the carpet, expecting him to go out the door and never return. Her chance of a decent future hung in the balance. A thought flashed in her mind: Mom had married Daddy and been disinherited because she was pregnant. Babies were dangerous and powerful.

Charlie returned to the kitchen, sat down, reached across the table, and covered her hand in a fatherly manner. "This time," he said, "I'll see to it that you get a good dose of chloroform."

59

On the fifth of July the sun came up bloody and big. The silent birds hid in the trees as Mae made her way into the bottomland of the American River. It was only about nine in the morning but the night had brought no relief, and already it felt like the hundred-and-five degrees that had tortured Sacramento the past few days. Not a leaf stirred.

The stench reached her before she saw the scattered encampment of the homeless—a vast area where the beggars of the downtown mixed with the strikers from the SP rail yards. Emmett and his friends would probably be at the foundry by now, but she hoped to find him here so they could talk. She'd brought him some food, and she wanted his advice. She wanted the closeness they'd had as children. She felt a wall of secrets between them, on both sides.

She watched where she stepped. Makeshift shade had been erected all over the place—moth-eaten blankets draped over tree limbs, webs of tattered towels, shirts, and sheets tied together catawampus between stakes, a sheet of corrugated iron propped up and shading a glowering occupant. If he'd looked sociable she would have inquired about Emmett.

But she spotted two women. Picking her way past a big oak under which bedding lay open to the droppings of birds, she avoided the discarded cans, bottles and greasy newspaper wrappings, and went to the women sitting with knees akimbo in the swales of their skirts. A coffeepot stood on the coals of a spent fire. A frizzy redhead nursed an infant, and a dirty tot peeked from behind a hard-looking woman with black hair falling over her face.

"You lost?" asked the redhead.

Mae gave back a sweet smile. "I'm looking for someone. Do you happen to know Emmett Duffy?"

They exchanged blank looks and shook their heads.

"He'd be with the railroad strikers," she added.

"Oh. Over there." The redhead pointed toward the river, downstream.

"Much obliged."

In the denser trees by the water's edge, she found herself beneath the squeal and laughter of children. They were swinging like monkeys on the grapevines that festooned the cottonwoods and oaks. How they thrilled to the danger! Mae had been that kind of child.

Emmett was coming toward her, obviously as delighted to see her as she was to find him. With relief she saw that he was uninjured. He looked her up and down. "Well, well. You found my lair. You're a sight fer sore eyes, little sister."

"Brought you something to eat." She offered the flour sack with the hunk of wurst, a tin of crackers, a jar of grape preserves, and two cantaloupes. "You got plenty of company, I see." She looked around at the many bedrolls and other gear.

"Yup." He seemed anxious to leave, but took the sack.

"Do you have a place to store that?"

"Sure." He looked inside the bag. "Say, thanks for this, Maezy. I can sure use it." He pointed his head. "C'mon, I'll stow it before I go."

She followed him to a pile of neatly folded blankets and watched him shove the sack between them. Another stack of folded blankets stood adjacent.

"You trust these people not to steal your things?"

Emmett shrugged. "Most of 'em'er all right. That's brother George's roll."

"George! Our brother George?"

Emmett grinned. "Showed up at the foundry a couple days ago. Outta the blue. I couldn't hardly believe my eyes. Walk with me and I'll fill ya in. You see, there's big doings afoot today and I'm a little late."

They walked single file down a beaten path, "This is the quickest way to the SP grounds," Emmett said as he led the way. On their right the surging river seemed to cool the air a bit. The water beckoned, and she wished they could play in it like the children they were now passing. It didn't seem possible that a city the size of Sacramento or a gigantic rail yard could be so near to this wilderness.

Emmett said he'd sat up late last night listening to the men talk about the strike. George had carried on about the miner's union and their tactics. "A real stem-winder George is. All fired up too, I'll say. He come all this way to help us out. Didn't even know I was here. Guess he didn't talk to the folks."

Following, she waited for more.

"Lord only knows how late it was 'fore we called it a night. Then I couldn't sleep with all that talk runnin' around in my head. Dozed off at first light, with every damn bird in creation awhistlin' to beat the band."

"I haven't seen George since the trial in Jackson," Mae said. "He was madder'n a rained-on rooster." She felt herself under the sway of Emmett's grammar and her grammar school years.

"I'll say. Like to'ov killed that judge. When he left for Nevada I doubted we'd see him again. And here he turns up at the foundry! Can you beat that?"

"Is he the same old George?"

"Nope. Not a prankster any more. More like a mean bulldog. But that's all right, long's he's fightin' fer the workin' man. You know, I b'lieve the miners' union or somebody in it paid his fare to come out here. He claims there's gonna be a mighty rising up in this country. The entire world. And he's not the only one believes that. There's foreign men standing with us, names you can't hardly git your mouth around, men as worked in European steel mills. They call us workers of the world. Their idea's to get all the laborin' men in the same big union. George is for it. They claim we can take the reins outta the hands of the mines and railroads and such, an' our committees can run the business theirselves."

"Just imagine, my two brothers working on a thing like that!"

"Whoa now, lil' sister. I didn't say I was joinin' up with 'em. Hell, the first I heard about 'em was last night. But it sure spins yer head, don't it?"

"Yes, it does." *And Charlie mustn't hear a word of it.* Just as she was about to mention that a lawyer named Hiram Johnson had warned of an uprising, a great blue heron whumped out of the rushes. Mae stopped and watched it flap skyward, squawking something awful as its dung splashed in the river. The bird landed on the opposite shore. The high trees on both shores supported massive cascades of grapevines that draped from the lofty heights to the ground. This made for deep shade and a sensation of being very small. A stand of herbs smelled like sage. The place brought to mind The Thicket at the Sheldon ranch, except on a larger scale—the river, trees, width of the bottomland, everything was bigger.

Emmett looked back. "You comin'?"

She hurried to catch up, and asked as they continued walking, "Do you wade out in the river, to wash I mean?"

"We all do. It's tricky. There's a drop-off a few feet out. Folks drown in there all the time. That current's swifter'n it looks to be."

Emmett's short strong legs moved like pistons in coveralls, going faster than she wanted to go. She felt too warm and out of breath. Her corset was too tight. Perspiration soaked through her gingham frock, making dark circles on her chest and under her arms.

"You said big doings are planned. What?"

"An Army battalion come in Tuesday, just before the Fourth. Seized the cars n' engine right out of the hands of our brothers in the Oakland yard. They come here on a train, occupied the rail yard and let the scabs in. Had us in their gun sights so we couldn't stop 'em. There'll be some action today. Yessiree. We'll show the bastards what we think of Washington nosing in our affairs."

She watched his dusty work boots striding ahead. "The Army?"

"The *You*-nited States Army."

"Emmett, that sounds like real trouble." Every step sapped her strength.

His reply squeezed through clenched teeth. "They're not keepin' three-thousand-five-hundred working men down like a bunch 'a rats. Not with the en-tire city behind us."

They rounded a bend and saw several other men going their way. There hadn't been enough time to talk, she realized. If only they could have sat in the shade dangling their feet in the river, she might have found the nerve to tell him about her condition. Now they were in full sun, climbing a steep levee.

On top, gasping for breath in the sunshine, she viewed the arid waste-land ahead—pale weeds, faintly purple swaths of foxtails, oak trees spaced too far apart. On the far side of it stood the massive SP "shops", warehouses in tandem, the peaks of the roofs making multiple Ws. In the distance and haze, the city was a clutter of toy blocks. Always before she had approached the shops from town. Now she felt jittery walking toward all those angry men without a ghost of an idea what to do when she got there.

Emmett turned and frowned at her. "Maezy, I think you'd best go watch with them other looky-loos. Skirt around that way." His finger traced a half circle and settled on the crowd along I Street. He looked at her again. "The men mean business. You could get hurt. Anyhow, I need to go in alone."

"I can't go over to I Street. I see police wagons."

"That's good, fer *you*."

"No it's not."

He screwed up his reddened face and squinted at her, his freckles dark in the sun. "You in some kinda trouble?"

"Yes, but it'd take all day to explain, and I'm gettin' lightheaded. It's the heat. You see, I've been unwell for several weeks, actually longer."

"Wh—Why in heaven's name didn't you say nuthin'?"

"I wanted to, but that man from the railroad union was there when we ate together last, remember? Not to mention your friends from the shop."

He put his hands on his hips just like Mom used to when she was exasperated. "You could'a said *somethin'*."

Smarting behind her eyes, she blinked to stop the tears. This subject was quicksand, and yet part of her wanted him to know about it.

"The law after you?"

"Only one policeman," she said quietly.

He turned away, blew air, and when he turned back his jaw was set. "Give it to me straight. Right now."

First she had to recover from a wave of vertigo. Her breath came fast and shallow. "We should'a talked back there in the shade, but you was hell-bent on getting to the—"

"We're not goin' one more step 'til I git the whole damned story. Now shoot."

"All right, but it'll have to be fast. *Before I faint.* An inspector tied me up and used me like a slave. Said he'd kill me if I ran away." At the sight of his shock, she couldn't block the tears any longer or stop her voice from going high and squeaky. "I got away, but I can't tell the police, on account 'a, they're on his side. I went through awful… had an operation. About killed me, infection 'an all. Not so long ago. But a *very nice* man saved my life. I think he'll marry me and I'll be—"

"And where is this *very nice* man? I'd say you need him now."

She blurted it out in short quakes, the grammar of her childhood suddenly friendly in her mouth. "He don't believe me… when I say Oberon'll kill me. He gets riled."

"Oberon! Inspector Oberon Jones?"

Another wave of vertigo. When it started to lift, "You know him?"

"Just by name. The men hate his guts. He patrols the yards huntin' down organizers."

"Emmett, I can't stand any more sun. You see, I'm in a family way." *Again.* There. It was out.

He stared at her with his pupils shrunk to mean pinpricks. "When you gettin' hitched?"

Between sobs she blubbered, "Charlie don't wanna get married."

"The hell he don't! Just wait'll I get my hands on him. George and me'll go after that sonova—"

"No, no. Charlie's good to me. It's just gonna take time with him is all. I gotta lie down." Turning back toward the river she staggered, the world gone momentarily black. The sweat had stopped, and she felt goose-bumpy, almost chilled in a strange sort of way.

Emmett's arm was suddenly around her shoulder, guiding her back to the shade and the river. His tenderness as he took the pins out of her hat and laid her down in a thick patch of soft plants with a sage scent brought emotion too deep for words. He still cared for her. In her mind's eye she saw him long ago putting up his little-boy fists to fight a much bigger boy who'd pushed her down. Mom had grabbed him by the belt and the scruff of the neck—later laughing whenever she told how his feet and fists had churned in the air.

Now he removed his shirt, dipped it in the water, and swabbed Mae's face. "Stay here 'til you feel better," he said. "Then go back to where you're living. This heat ain't fit fer man ner beast."

He stepped a few paces away, leaped up, grabbed a grapevine and bought it down. He yanked down more of the giant leafy strings, hacking the vines with his pocketknife. "There," he said, laying them over her, "now the rowdies won't see you. Sorry, but I gotta go." Sweat streamed off his nose and chin.

A loud crack came from the SP yard.

"Gunfire!" Emmett said, pulling the sopping shirt over his overalls.

Three more shots cracked.

Mae sat up and touched his leg. "You better not go."

"I'm a-goin' all right." He pulled away and left at a trot.

"You got a gun?" she called. Nobody had said a strike was a war.

He called over his shoulder, "No. But some'a the men do. Doan worry, we got numbers on our side."

Afraid for him she lay back, breathing in the strong aroma of grape leaves and sage. The noon whistle at the foundry went off, though it was only about ten. Despite the distance that eerie finger of sound wiggled in her inner ear. Everything felt out of kilter.

Cool off, she told herself, then go watch from the levee.

Still lightheaded, she took off her shoes and went to the water, waded through the mud and stood in the edge of the river. The bottom didn't drop off. She sat down and scooped the mossy-tasting water over her face and hair and down her neck.

Hat and shoes back on, she sloshed up the levee in soaked shoes and clothes. The whistle had stopped. So had the gunfire. The small blue sun pulsed high in the white sky. Across the wasteland black smoke boiled out of the little windows along the spine of the foundry roof, also out of several other buildings. The workers were setting the place afire! With all that tar and coal and oil inside, it would go fast. The men's chances of keeping their employment were nil, she reckoned, and now they were trying to destroy the SP, the biggest corporation on earth.

More gunfire. Men yelled in the distance. She made out the ding-ding of fire wagons, saw the red paint and glints of brass as the horses plunged into what appeared to be a swarm of stick figures running helter-skelter. All hell was breaking loose, and Emmett and George were in it!

I've got to do something. Go ask Charlie to help? Idiotic. Besides, those are federal troops. Charlie works at the state level, a difference he keeps pounding into me. He's not in charge of anybody around here. He couldn't help if he tried. So there's nothing I can do but pray.

She beseeched God, Jesus, and Mary to keep Emmett and George safe.

Occasional gunfire popped as the buildings burned and little knots of soldiers ran crouching across the yard. Not a single blast of water could she see directed at the fire. Could the silt in the city pipes be clogging the fire hoses? She'd heard about that problem from Mary Donahue. She felt stymied. It wouldn't do any good to follow her instincts and try to help. It could make things worse for the boys.

The first time those bright colors swooped at her, it scared her. Then she noticed that it happened only when she blinked. With open eyes she saw nothing but smoking buildings, stick figures, and the steel marble of the sun. But every time she blinked, blocky things swooshed at her faster than a through-train. It was in her head, she knew. She blinked longer and longer to get a better look. Chunks of vividly painted things, big as houses, splintered apart just before striking her, and the shower of red, yellow, green, blue, and purple shards magically missed her. Those blocks came from a distant place in the sky, a colorful, multi-tiered city, from which parts constantly broke off and zoomed at her. Fascinated by the kaleidoscopic color and near misses, she closed her eyes to watch.

When she opened them she was on the ground being picked up by a strange man, his arms slick with perspiration. The sun was still high and yet she felt cold. Little girl voices talked around her.

"Look, she's dirty."

"Maybe got heat stroke," the man said as he walked with her in his arms.

Half dreaming, Mae felt herself as a child being carried to her bed, except that now when she closed her eyes, the bright things flew at her. Many more of them came now. They came faster and faster, the colored shards exploding around her.

"Look, somebody made a bed." A child's voice.

"A leaf bed. And somebody's been in it."

The man laid her down.

Water landed on her face. She spluttered and blew it out her nose and mouth. A girl about six years old was standing above her head with a dripping skirt. Before she could say anything, a smaller girl came to the other side and unloaded another skirt-ful of water on her face.

She sputtered and coughed it away.

"You all right?" The man knelt beside her head and tipped a cap to her lips.

Water with a taste of salt went down her throat. "More. Please," she croaked.

"You had anything to eat today?"

"I dunno." She couldn't quite remember where she was.

The man returned with more water in his cap.

She drank it in gulps. She couldn't feel anything under her, it was so soft, but heard the river trying to say something as it moved in its depths and lapped on the shore. The little girls took turns bringing the filled cap. Each time, most of the water had leaked out but not before Mae got a couple of good swallows.

"You campin' down here?" the man asked.

Emmett's in danger!

"I asked, you campin' here?"

"He's at the foundry." She meant to explain but her head didn't work right. Neither did her tongue. "He'll get shot."

A little girl whined. "Pop, you said we could have a soda."

"Is he on strike from the SP shops?" The man was asking.

She saw the high tops of scuffed shoes, the kind a banker would wear if they weren't so scuffed.

"Oh Emmett!" A moan sounded all around her, coming out of her.

"We wanna soda. *You promised!*" Shrill as a whistle.

"You'll be all right now. Get some rest." The man had a calm voice.

She heard footsteps walking away. She tried to sit up. The three were leaving. She let herself drop back in the leafy bed. Leaves all around and underneath. Layers and layers of leaves in the sky. She was a small thing in a quiet world, with the highest leaves sun-bright against blue pieces of sky. The heat had got to her. That's all.

Emmett! He'd been angry at Charlie and Oberon, both of them. He was on her side. He had made her this bed. He wanted to protect her. And now he was at war with the soldiers of his own country. *Oh please God, keep him safe.*

If he lived, and if she lived through another immoral operation, she vowed not to keep any more secrets from him. They were two Duffys off the same branch.

In the moil and plash of the river she heard the half-words: C'mere, it's nice. Slow-rolling off the leaves she crawled on all fours to the water, pulling at her skirts. The sage-scented plant was everywhere, tall green spears snagging on a buttons of her bodice. Warm moss and mud squished through her fingers as she entered the water. Carefully she moved through the mossy submerged rocks, up to her elbows. The water helped to hold her as she cupped it to her mouth. When slaked, she turned around and lay back in the eddy with her head on the muddy shore.

The trees were so tall. The vines so thick. The water lifted her legs and skirts and cooled her thighs. She inhaled the medicinal scent of the torn leaves at her throat, and while she gathered her strength a decision formed in her heart. The baby should be born. Whether or not Charlie married her. It was the right thing after the love they had shared. Even if that love was over. Even if he didn't want her. He was the best man she'd ever known, and the baby was half his.

And surely he would marry her.

60

That night, not yet brave enough to face up to Charlie about keeping the baby, Mae scanned the newspapers for the daily report of injuries at the rail yards. She was shocked to see that workers had been killed, but relieved that neither Emmett nor George appeared on the dead or injured list.

With a quieter heart she pored over the articles about the Army troops in

Sacramento. A letter to the editor called it an "unwarranted invasion." Troopers had been creased by bullets. Four had sustained injuries from broken bricks hurled at them. It was not known when an agreement would be reached. Eugene Debs had telegraphed *The Sacramento Bee* thanking editor C. K. McClatchy for supporting the working man. McClatchy wrote in his editorial that the strikers should seek a peaceful end to the dispute, because violence rarely wins arguments. The tone of that sounded like the workingmen might be losing. In her heart Mae hoped it was true because then the strikers would give up the fight and find work elsewhere. Emmett and George would be safe.

At noon dinner the next day Charlie said he was bringing Lincoln Steffens to supper—the first time he'd invited anyone to the apartment since she'd been there.

Steffens, she knew, was a wealthy man.

Afraid of making errors of etiquette, she cleaned and polished while racking her brain over whether she'd been introduced to that young man at his parents' house. She recalled him talking to his mother Louisa and his sisters Lottie, Lulu, and Laura; but at the time she's been scared out of her wits that Oberon had her in his sights, and she couldn't think straight. Now, after dusting everything, she put on her men's clothes, tucked her hair under Charlie's old hat, and went shopping at the China Garden and the butcher shop. Back in the apartment, she had everything done and was wearing her day-dress when Charlie's key rattled in the door.

She pasted on a smile and went to greet them.

The slight, immaculately dressed man standing beside Charlie looked Mae up and down before he growled at Charlie, "Why you old horse-face! She's as pretty as a picture."

"This is Mae Duffy," Charlie said with a chuckle. He clapped the man's shoulder and gave it a shake. "My old college pal, Lincoln Steffens."

Mae curtseyed slightly. "Nice to meet you."

"Enchanted," said Mr. Steffens. If they'd been introduced before, he seemed to have forgotten, ending one of her worries.

The man had an amused, aristocratic look in his pale blue eyes, and he seemed to look down his nose at her with an air of superiority. But he did that to Charlie too, though Charlie stood much taller than he, so it was just the way of him. Jauntily he tossed his hat on a peg next to Charlie's. Mae showed him the davenport.

Charlie was pouring whisky at the cabinet. "As you can see, Lincoln, we live a simple life. The salary of a political hack isn't so great."

Mr. Steffens nodded his thanks for the drink and said, "I live a simple life myself."

Mae had the feeling she was supposed to disappear into the kitchen, but couldn't let that stand. "You have a grand house on Sixteenth Street," she said.

That tall white house couldn't possibly be part of a simple life.

The guest wrinkled his small nose. "That's my parents' place. They bought it while I was doing post-graduate work in Germany. I married over there, and now inhabit modest quarters, quite like this, in New York City. My wife, her mother, and I."

"Congratulations," Charlie said, lowering himself to his upholstered chair. "Nobody told me you were married. Didn't your wife come along on this trip?" He sipped his whisky.

"As for marriage, it happens to the best of us." Steffens lifted a bemused eyebrow at Mae. "And no, my wife despises California."

Charlie looked surprised and a bit hurt that anyone felt that way about his beloved state. "Did she have a bad experience here?"

"She has never set foot in this state and claims she never will."

"That's odd," Charlie said, speaking for Mae too. "Droves of people tramp into California from every corner of the world, most of them all agog."

"That's just what my wife detests, the endless hullabaloo about the Golden State." His indulgent smile somehow conveyed that the subject was finished now, if you please.

Charlie amicably returned to the previous topic. "I would have thought with your contacts you'd have pull with a number of fine companies, and would not be handicapped by finances."

"Pull, as you call it, is the bane of civilization. A man ought to be judged on merit alone. When I told my father I wanted to be a journalist, he had a letter of recommendation sent to me from the editor of Southern Pacific Publications—those monthly magazines, weeklies, and daily newspapers owned or subsidized by the Railroad"—to introduce me to the *Century Magazine* editor. I'm proud to say that my wife and her mother encouraged me in my refusal to use it."

Charlie looked quizzical.

Mae repaired to the kitchen to see if everything was in order—carrot tops and other waste removed, table set for three, silverware placed correctly. She lifted the lid and touched the roast, finding it still warm at the back of the stove. The shiny golden domes of the brandied peach dessert, surrounded by a fence of ladyfinger cookies—a recipe from the ladies' section of *The Bee*—looked exquisite in its oval dish. But had the green-bean dish turned out too thick? She'd decided not to boil the corn because there wasn't another serving dish and she didn't want to put the pan on the table. And most important, had she cooked the roast properly? Charlie was a better cook, she knew, but ladies were supposed to prepare the food—homemakers they were called, gracious creatures who brought civilized manners to the coarser males.

Listening for a break in the front-room conversation, she crossed herself, and called into the parlor, "Supper's on."

Charlie and Lincoln seated themselves at the table, bringing a bottle of wine with them. She set the roast before Charlie and laid the long sharp knife beside it. He began to slice the meat while Mr. Steffens continued what he was saying about New York.

"The *Evening Post* put me on Wall Street duty, but at the time I was living near a police precinct headquarters, and that changed my career. Each morning as I walked to work I saw the night's criminals being hauled in. I began chatting with certain officers, and some of the criminals, and before long I was delving deeper into the affairs of the precinct, its hierarchy, and its own private world of crime."

He scooped a heavy glob of beans to his plate, looked at the roast beef Charlie laid beside it, and seemed to be searching for something else.

Horrors! He wants more. I should have boiled the corn. Then she remembered the bread rolls from the bakery. Scraping her chair back she pulled the rolls from the cupboard and put them on a plate in the middle of the table.

"Oh, many thanks," Lincoln Steffens said, buttering a bun.

"So is that what you're reporting on now?" Charlie asked. "The police beat?"

"Precisely. For a reason unknown to me, I was given license to examine police corruption in New York City. I'm getting to the bottom of it, so now I have to worry that the truth won't sit well with the powers that be. My first articles in the *Post* are giving indigestion to a number of city leaders."

"I can imagine," Charlie laughed.

Police corruption. It has a name.

Glancing up from cutting his meat Steffens said, "Yes, old man, no doubt you understand. Anyway, I was despairing over how to keep my job, considering certain links to the Post's owners, when as fate would have it, a new Police Commissioner by the name of Theodore Roosevelt thundered into the precinct headquarters. I tell you, Charlie, there's a man who cuts to the heart of the graft system. He and I have frank discussions. He is fearless. Encourages me to draw aside the sable veil from the hallowed subject of police crime."

Police crime.

"Are you talking about money paid to the police for concessions?" Charlie inquired.

"Bribes for privilege yes, but think higher up to those who hire the police. The police get their cut, but so do their bosses. They're supposed to protect the public, and they do it well—unless protected illegal businesses are involved, and perhaps a convenient murder or two, depending on the circumstances. Or when they're paid to come down hard on union men." He toyed with his beans and stopped eating them.

Too thick.

Charlie caught Mae's eye and looked sharply at the center of the roast. She saw with dismay the uniform brown color. He had instructed her to roast it so that the center stayed pink. How on earth was she supposed to see the color inside a hunk of roasting meat? She felt like crying.

Steffens went on, "As it turns out, Commissioner Roosevelt and I see eye to eye on cleaning up the graft. In fact, he's bully about it. Sees it as the beginning of change throughout the country, New York being the flagship city."

"What you call graft exists in every city and state, and Washington DC," Charlie pointed out. "How can you hope to change all that?"

"As a journalist. It's my duty to tell the story of why some men get off free while others are punished for the same behavior. After I finish with the police I'll move my sights up a bit and write about how the business bosses persuade the cities to operate for the sake of business. It's up to us scribes to lay this bare and explain it to the people, the system of bribe-givers and bribe-takers."

"Reform," Charlie said.

"In a word." Steffens sawed through his meat, took a bite and chewed for a long time.

Too long. Mae found gristle in her slice too.

"I appreciate the power of the pen," Charlie filled in while his guest was chewing, "but it would take a thorough rising up of the people to bring about significant change."

George had talked about *a rising up of the workers of the world.*

Lincoln looked down his nose at Charlie with that amused tilt of his head. "Would you mind edifying me about how privilege is purchased at the state level in California? For example, do you find, as I do, that the boss grafters are singularly pleasant men and more intelligent than anyone else in the political landscape?"

Charlie pushed aside his plate with uneaten meat and beans. "That's an interesting way of putting it. I will say this, though: The head of the SP's political office once told me something in a private moment—not to appear in your writings, old friend, not if you value our friendship."

The halves of Lincoln's slim mustache separated in a tight smile. "Don't worry, old man. No quotations from good friends, I assure you. Think of me as the outcast little boy who once rode his pony around Sacramento talking to miscellaneous men and learning by stages how the grown-up world works—while other boys played their eternal ball games. I'm still sorting out the contradictions between what we were taught to believe about a democratic government and the realities of it."

Charlie relaxed in his chair. "You say the business bosses are pleasant men. Well, the head political man in the SP truly is. He philosophizes about democracy with the best of them. And he's a fan of it. In that private moment he told me this country couldn't run at all without the wise infusion of money from business. To him it's like walking a tightrope, paying what's necessary but not too much to smudge the gloss of democracy."

"Fascinating," Steffens said as he dabbed his napkin on his mustache. "Do you find this man to be unusually intelligent?"

"The brightest."

"More so than the *takers* of the bribes?"

"Oh, absolutely. But I wouldn't call them bribes."

Incentives, Mae supplied in her mind.

Lincoln was smiling. "But that's what it is, is it not? Bribery?"

Charlie chuckled and moved his meat around with his fork.

"Are you ready for dessert?" Mae asked, turning in her chair to grab the pretty peach dish from the counter.

"I must say, that looks scrumptious," Steffens said.

Mae removed the soiled dishes, replaced them with small, clean plates and then ladled out peach halves with brandy pudding and ladyfinger crust.

Meanwhile Charlie sounded thoughtful. "This system, as you call it, whereby elected representatives are helped and guided by business, is not always as I would like it to be. Nor, I should say, as I once believed it was. No doubt it does to some extent warp the government of the people, by the people etcetera. We were silly idealists back in college, weren't we?"

Mae could see that they both liked the dessert—a success! She herself could hardly believe how delicious it tasted.

"I'm not sure that was idealism," Steffens responded, pushing the plate away and lighting a cigarette. "I name it ignorance. We weren't encouraged to be curious in good 'ole Cal. Before I went there, my father sent me to a private tutor who opened my eyes to the way schools stunt the minds of the young. They don't let them in on the failures of knowledge, the intriguing unknowns, and the frequency with which the facts don't fit the cherished beliefs. Instead we were force-fed stale facts. Our enthusiasm wasn't engaged. It is my belief that those professors lacked the personal confidence to whet the appetites of the young about the mysteries that they, the high and mighty and old, hadn't been able to solve. Heaven forbid that the young might leap ahead of them! But I digress. My point is: our civic lessons were watery porridge, Charlie. And I would bet a pile of money that you've learned the same thing in your position, exploring as you must the unseen government behind the façade. Mind you, I'm not interested in dividing good men from bad—a false and simplistic business though popular and entertaining—I'm searching for the right relationship between business and democracy, as is your intelligent friend in the SP lobbying office. The extent to which a government of the people can be run by the agents of big business, for business interests, in the name of democracy."

This was over Mae's head and growing tiresome. She felt uncomfortable being looked through like the clear pane of a window glass. She had ideas too, didn't she? Maybe if she added her two bits they'd respect her more. But first the coffee. She got up to see to that, and removed the dessert plates.

Lincoln mentioned that the East Coast was older and more "mature in its graft," better at hiding it, whereas in young and innocent California, the graft was visible."

"Innocent?" Charlie chuckled. "I wouldn't describe California that way."

Pouring coffee, Mae spoke into the pause. "I heard Hiram Johnson give a speech. He said this city and state were full of corruption, and a handful of businessmen ran everything important."

Charlie turned his eyes to her like she was a curiosity of nature and not a welcome one at that. A hot flush burned up her neck and face.

Steffens' gaze had lifted to the upper reaches of the high ceiling, and he drew in a long draught of smoke, letting his breath form smoky words. "Ah yes, Hiram Johnson. A pugilistic fellow. I knew him well. His father, when in public office as he often is, is a lackey of the SP Corporation. Just elected again to something or other, isn't old Grove Johnson?"

"Congress," Charlie supplied. "He pushed through a bill to extend the SP's three-percent loan for eighty years."

Lincoln hooted out smoke and coughed and sputtered through a violent outburst of laughter. He struggled to get out, "And we the people pay the interest. Wouldn't you like a deal such as that?"

So unexpected was this outburst of laughter that Mae went dumb again. She set the sugar and creamer on the table, and got out a clean spoon for each person.

"Hiram talks against the railroad now," Charlie said.

Lincoln stubbed out his cigarette. "Isn't Hiram a partner in Grove's law firm?"

"Not now. He and his brother started their own firm."

"No more Johnson, Johnson & Johnson?"

"The old Johnson remains on J Street; the two young Johnsons have a firm of their own a few blocks away. As a matter of fact," Charlie added, "Mae is right. Hiram delivered a speech at the Agricultural Pavilion last fall accusing the SP of being part of the ruling oligarchy of the state and the nation. He predicted a popular rebellion if democracy is not returned to the people. Talk is, his father has never spoken to him since, and never will."

"Do you believe Hiram is sincere about this?"

While the men drank coffee and talked politics, Mae noticed a heavy feeling in her middle. In her zeal to make them enjoy their meat and vegetables, she had overeaten. She shouldn't have taken that second helping of dessert either—a dish swimming in twice the amount of peach brandy the recipe called for. She shouldn't have drunk two glasses of wine either. Needing air, she opened the kitchen door and went outside to the small landing.

The glittering stars were nice, but the air was almost as warm as the overheated kitchen. The first inkling of a gag gave warning, and she crept down the stairs to the dark jumble below—the landlord's stabled horse, empty crates, the barrel of reeking garbage, and an abandoned, broken outhouse so old it didn't even stink.

Now she wished she had shut the kitchen door behind her, because her insides were in spasm. Too late. Her supper came up, every particle of it, spraying over the dry weeds. Mortified to have Mr. Steffens hear it, she realized this was worse than usual. All that wine and brandy! Oh God, she promised, I will never eat another brandied peach, ever again.

Emmett! Would he be safe tonight? She had been so preoccupied with the dinner and how she looked to Lincoln Steffens that she'd forgotten her brothers.

61

I'll be there the whole time," Charlie promised as he knocked on the door with the big white tooth painted over the blackened window.

In spite of her plan, Mae felt her insides shiver as she stood on the threshold of the torture chamber.

The red-haired man ushered them inside, and Charlie gave him a stack of paper bills. This procedure differed from the previous visit and Mae hoped it wouldn't ruin the plan. Thanking him, the man seated them in the mustard-colored room with drawn blinds, and then quickly left.

"You are brave, Skeeziks," Charlie said, turning to Mae. "I appreciate how you're taking this. It won't hurt this time, the doctor assured me."

Like a Gordian knot of nerves she sat on the ladderback chair. Last night, after Mr. Steffens left, she had tried again to get Charlie to say he'd marry her, but he'd become angrier by the minute. The pitch of their voices had doubtless penetrated the walls. She imagined the neighbors in the other three apartments smiling at each other like an audience at a vaudeville production. Defeated as always by Charlie's logic and fine words, she had wept and finally agreed to the abortion, but only if the same doctor performed it. She convinced herself that if she could survive once she could probably do it again. And if the infection returned they could go to the Chinese herbalist, and sooner.

Charlie had used the landlord's talk box. He left in a rented hack to make this morning's arrangements, and returned an hour later. So here she was once again, afraid that if something went wrong she'd soon be dead.

All night long her life had paraded before her eyes. She asked herself at every turn what she'd done of any importance. Nothing. Zero. She'd come to Sacramento hoping to become somebody. She'd learned two things: she was too easily fooled and too easily pregnant. She was like a leaf twisting in the wind. Then sometime before dawn she began to imagine being the wind instead of the leaf.

The wait was short this time. She stood up when the steely-eyed nurse entered the room—the same one, she was glad to see—in her puffy-sleeved white blouse, winged nurse's hat, and long black skirt.

On his feet, Charlie turned Mae to him and gently kissed her on the mouth. Not a passionate kiss like they'd shared in the carriage and in the Tevis adobe, but she clung to him as long as possible memorizing the feel of his lips and the comfort of his arms. He had saved her life and kept her safe for almost a year. She loved him. They broke apart looking into each other's eyes. Strangely, he was looking at her in the same way. Like he wouldn't see her again. An awful thought struck. In an illegal operation it would be easy to arrange for a girl to die of too much chloroform.

Following the nurse, she looked back at him, and he wiggled his fingers in an awkward little good-bye. Her skittish heart flailed in her ribs. This nurse had called her a baby killer and said that only the money to feed her children kept her working for this "doctor." Mae would use that information.

The nurse was leading down the stairs to the hellish underground room when, close behind, Mae put a hand on the woman's shoulder to stop her and whispered in her ear. "I'm *not* having the operation. I want the baby."

The nurse stopped and turned, her face unreadable in the dark stairwell.

"If you could please fetch back the two hundred dollars that Mr. Rogue just paid the red-haired man," Mae said. "I'll give you fifty. I need the rest to get out of Sacramento and support myself while I have the baby. Would you be so good as to go back and get the money—without letting Mr. Rogue catch on? Then I'll go out through the underground and he won't know."

The nurse put a finger to her lips, and quickly went back the way they'd come.

With her back to the wall, Mae listened to her pounding heart. It would have been easier if Mae had the money in her pocket like the first time. Making the red-haired man give up the money added extra risks. He might have taken it from the building already. Charlie might question him or the nurse passing back and forth through the waiting room and learn of the plan, and the "doctor" downstairs, thinking this was taking too long, might come to investigate and find Mae alone in the stairwell. She rehearsed what to do—a quick and agile dash past the man to the door of the underground.

A door closed above her. Footsteps in the hallway. Mae looked up and saw the ghostly white uniform, the nurse returning. She came down the few stairs, took Mae's sleeve, and tugged her to follow to the upper landing. "I'll show you another way out," she whispered urgently.

Weak with relief, Mae followed the woman through a different door leading to another stairwell. They hurried down the steps, and when they reached the underground labyrinth, the nurse counted out twenty and ten-dollar bills and kept fifty dollars. Mae put the hundred and fifty dollars in her pocket.

"Stay with me and I'll take you up on Fifth Street," the nurse said. "I'm finished working there."

In the dim world beneath Sacramento City, they lifted their skirts and ran quietly along tunnels that had once been streets and alleys. The smell of mold, garlic and unclean dwellings revived Mae's memory of her failure to find a way out last fall. But this time she had a guide. They alternated between a fast walk and light jogging, sometimes glancing behind. They didn't pass the opium dens or the storefront where Mae had followed Benty.

Shortly, Mae was back on the sunny streets of Sacramento, gasping for breath. "I can't thank you enough," she said, giving the woman's hand a sincere squeeze.

"Godspeed," the woman snapped. She pulled off her nurse's hat, folded and stuffed it inside the waistband of her skirt, and then briskly walked away.

Mae got her bearings from the gothic towers of the SP station, visible above the hotels and other buildings. Knowing that the strike involved some of the streetcars, she was wondering which route to take on her long walk to 28th Street and the Amador Stage Line, when the unlikely sound of a train wheezing out of the station grabbed her attention.

A train! Sure enough, in the clear sky above the buildings puffs of black smoke started making a giant dotted line. Trains weren't supposed to be running, but this one was audibly chugging, and now rattling, across the trestle bridge. The strike must have ended!

A loud boom compressed her chest. Followed by a rolling cascade of crashing noises. Then silence.

Mae and businessmen on the street stopped to stare at the gigantic plume of dust or smoke rising above the buildings. People came out of shops and offices, running toward the noise. They spilled out the door from the underground. All hurried toward the river.

Mae went along, hidden in the crowd. Not until she pushed past a row of men in tall hats, up to where she could see across the Sacramento River—City Buildings and police wagons on her right, the SP warehouse on the left—did she see the demolished train that had been hurled from the trestle. The engine lay upside down and half submerged on the opposite side of the river, wheels up. Other cars lay in the water overturned and on top of each other, like a huge toy train kicked off the tracks by a bully. Ducking behind the men in case Oberon happened to be at the police station early, she peered through little gaps between elbows and shoulders. Something had derailed the train, possibly an explosion. Soldiers and newsmen with heavy cameras were hurrying across the bridge, watching their step between the ties.

"They've wrecked the Army train!" an excited male voice declared.

A laconic male voice added, "Doubt if a soul survived that."

"It's just a tragedy," said a woman shaking her head, "this whole sorry mess."

A man thundered: "It's the work of anarchists! They ought to be strung up by the toes and skinned alive!"

The vivid image of George and Emmett strung up flashed through Mae's mind. And then, while everyone watched the soldiers picking their way down the embankment to the rubble of the smoking train, she decided how best to get to 28th Street. The entire city was coming to see the wreck. She'd go the opposite direction through the SP shops, take the trail along the American River and follow it to 28th. That way she'd go through Emmett's camp and might be able to warn him to get out of town. There would be retribution for this wreck. She could pay his way on the stagecoach. George's, too, if he wanted to come.

She made her way up G Street through the oncoming crowd. Although Oberon would probably be getting dressed several blocks downstream of the wreck, she watched for police wagons, but never saw one. The wreck had occurred within view of the city building, and the police must have stayed there. As she walked, her mind went back to last night when she'd imagined opening a little business of some kind with Emmett, using her money. "Uncle Emmett" would be a father to her child—if Charlie didn't come for her. On the stage she'd talk to Emmett about such a business. Maybe George would have an idea about it too. A new kind of life was forming in her mind.

The rail yard still smoked from the fires, fires uncontrolled due to silt clogging the pipes, the newspapers said. The place appeared to be vacant. She hurried past the devastated foundry building and out the back way on the path beaten by homeless strikers. Today, with the delta breeze sweeping the bad air toward the mountains, the wasteland wasn't so daunting. She ran up the levee and down, anxious to find Emmett, catching her breath at the leafy hiding place he'd made for her. Then she fast-walked up the shady trail to the encampment of the SP homeless.

A few grim men were rolling blankets or slinging packs over their shoulders. Two of them shook hands and departed in opposite directions. With nearly all the bedrolls and clothing gone, the place looked trampled and different. The stacks of blankets looked lonely: Emmett's and George's. Rummaging, she found a small piece of the wurst and about half the crackers left. Good. They had been eating.

The last man was leaving. Catching up to him, Mae inquired, "Do you happen to know Emmett and George Duffy? They're my brothers and I need to find them."

The middle-aged man with a dark visage stopped and said, "Emmett? Curly dark hair, a foundry helper?"

"That's him."

"Brother from Nevada, in the miner's union?"

"Yes. Where are they?"

The man's black eyes held her for a long time, the furrows deep between his eyes, before he said, "Ma'am, they got shot."

"No! That's not true!"

He laid a heavy hand on her shoulder.

She wrenched away, "I saw the newspapers." *Why is he lying?*

"Sorry, lass. We lost our work and some lost their lives. That's all that's come of this." He turned and walked up the path.

"Wait! Where are they? In the hospital?"

He turned to her. "The SP Hospital?"

She forgot. That was the only hospital, and it probably wouldn't accept strikers. "Maybe the Sisters of Mercy," she suddenly remembered.

"Ma'am, them boys is dead. Sorry." He continued walking.

"No! That isn't true!"

He didn't slow down and she called after him, "At least tell me where they ARE! "

He kept on walking.

Maybe shot this morning.... No!

A sharp whimper surrounded her, like a wounded rabbit. She crumpled to her knees and put her face in Emmett's blankets. *Dead.* She couldn't think or move. All was pain, her heart cored and raw. Time vanished. The old fog began to dull the edges of the trees and bushes. She folded Emmett's blankets and waited for him, the brother who had always been her best friend.

When it seemed that sunlight was coming from the opposite direction, the first thought took shape. She might miss the last stage to Slough House. Steadying herself, she pushed to her feet and began to walk, but then stopped and returned to stare at the blankets. Shouldn't she take them and keep them safe? But then again, he would want them when he returned to this place. He would need them. Trembling, she stacked them neatly like she'd found them, his and George's. The only blankets in the campground.

She started walking away again, and as she stepped over tree roots and fallen branches, oblivious of the cheeping of the birds, she began to imagine what Charlie would say when he looked her up in Slough House. When he would hold her in his arms and tell her he had come to marry her.

IV
Billy

He-lé-jah leaps smoothly from my branch. He steps forward, leaving one hind leg stretched back to his toes, and gives his other leg a good stretch too. Then this mysterious Animal Man—one of a handful who helped create humans—comments on Mae's predicament.

"Females can tend to their cubs without a male hanging around."

"You're right about that," Old Man Coyote lifts his snout to agree. "And we males have a lot more fun if we don't have to feed the yapping pups. Charlie Rogue knew how to live."

"He should not have tried to kill his cub," He-lé-jah disagrees. "My wife would have taken his life as well as his money. She fights to the death to protect her cubs."

"Where *is* you wife?" I ask. "I haven't seen O-se-mai-ti for a long time. She used to stop here on her rounds."

"She doesn't live around here any more."

"She's extinct," Coyote supplies.

"No, she's not," says He-lé-jah. "We're just separated. Mother Grizzly's range is far to the north now, and in Yellowstone and Montana. But we were together for a long time and we had many children."

It is a rare honor to talk with He-lé-jah, and I venture to ask, "Did you get along, being so different, you and your wife?"

"We are alike in the important things. Both of us are independent. We always had separate ranges. My wife is a strong mother, very competent. I like that. We saw eye to eye on most things, and we both enjoy deer meat."

"Don't you get lonely with your wife so far away?"

"I don't bother about that. Raccoon is my wife now."

"We humans," I tell him, "grow attached. We feel a painful hole when we pull away from someone we love, even if we do the pulling."

Already leaving, the big cat turns his head to say, "It didn't bother Mae when she left Benty on that back step with nothing but a saucer of milk. The little cat found another lap."

He goes to the river and crouches down for a drink.

Still behind the wheel of her Pierce-Arrow, Mae quietly says, "I did too. It began in the churchyard."

❦

62

Only a scattering of people attended the funeral in the tiny frame church on Jackson Road. Most of them stayed for the burial in the churchyard, including two of Daddy's drinking friends. The others had gone home. John Dunaway was there looking more respectable than Mae remembered, but his presence disturbed her, reminding her of their previous encounter, after she forgot about her date with him. She looked beyond him to the two Parker women who attended all local funerals. They'd been at Emmett's burial too, after the coroner finally shipped his remains home in a lead-lined box. Now the Longs, Pratts, and Isabella Miser and Agnes had come, and, surprisingly, the two Indian Marys and their little girl. Near them stood a man in bare feet, the brim of his work hat shading his face on this warm Sunday afternoon.

George wasn't there, but even if he still lived, as Daddy had insisted he did, nobody knew where to find him. No corpse by the name of George Duffy had turned up at the Sacramento County morgue.

The itinerant priest had ridden his horse from Sutter Creek. Now, as the sun bore down upon him in his black robe, he sprinkled holy water on the closed pine box in which Daddy was laid out. The cuts and bruises on Daddy's face had looked gruesome through the funeral paste, while the skin of his forehead matched the white rose in his lapel. Her eyes strayed from the rectangular hole in the ground that gave forth an earthy smell. The next grave over was a fresh mound marked by the cross that Daddy had carved for Emmett. That cross, Mae realized, commemorated both of them better than the marble stones she considered buying. Daddy had begun whittling the cross immediately after reading the coroner's telegram inquiring where to send Emmett's body. He never stopped carving until it was done. The scrollwork and cross were as good as any she'd ever seen.

Now, the priest intoned, *"In nomini patris et filii et spiritus sancti."* Farley and Hank, and, to Mae's surprise, John Dunaway and another man helped lower the coffin into the grave. Watching it descend she felt herself pulling apart, fraying, unwilling to let go of the man who had given her life.

There had been no wake. Nor had there been one for Emmett, because at a wake the coffin was uncovered so the guests could raise toasts to the deceased. But since some of Emmett's face had been blown away and nearly a week passed before the morgue shipped the body, it wasn't possible to have a proper wake. As to why there'd been no wake for Daddy, Mae and Farley just flat out couldn't stand any more grieving than was necessary, possibly the first time they'd agreed on anything in their entire lives. With Mother's melancholia, it hadn't felt right to invite Daddy's drinking friends to the house, and to stand face to face with the same befuddled brains and whisky that contributed to his death. But now Mae was thinking they'd made the wrong decision, to deprive his friends of a good drunk in his honor.

So, here she was again in the churchyard with Mom at her right elbow and Hank on her left next to Sophie and the baby. This time Farley stood at the foot of the grave, where Daddy had been at Emmett's burial. The service seemed too perfunctory, like a stripped-down necessity for getting rid of a body instead of an ancient ceremony filled with mystery. The priest's dusty shoes under the hem of his white mantle made her aware of him as a man, perhaps impatient to go home. She turned her mind from that to the shifting patterns of shade under the big oaks, and then back to the events of last week.

Burying Emmett had broken Daddy. That afternoon he'd ridden away on Belle, and now Mae could hear the hoofbeats in her mind, fading up the road toward Michigan Bar and his favorite saloon. No moon had lit the road that night, and she had sat up late with Mom, letting the house go dark. Farley was gone with Hank and Sophie back in their home in Sutter Creek. Mom hadn't uttered a syllable. Mae was lining up the words to tell her she was pregnant, when a horse and wagon rattled into the yard.

It was Mr. Long, the landlord, at the door. He said there'd been an accident. Mae went with him as he drove hard through the inky night. About two miles up the road they stopped. Mr. Long lifted his lantern so the light spilled over the embankment and illuminated the dark shapes in the dry, rocky streambed below—Belle on her side, head back, teeth bared, and Daddy's leg sticking out from under her.

Mr. Long broke the awful stillness. "I was a-settin' on my porch when I heard the filly cry out. I run over an' seen what happened."

Mrs. Long, coming from her house, stepped into the circle of lamplight. The two Indians stood outside the light as Mr. Long continued, "That filly was a-thrashin' some'um fierce, an' ever time she tried to right herself, she done more damage to your pa. So I run back for my rifle, went down there and put 'er out of her misery." He paused. "Didn't find no pulse on yer dad."

Believing Daddy could still be alive, Mae had slipped and slid down the cut bank. The others followed in a cascade of dirt and rock. She put a shoulder to Belle's backside. The others joined her and they rocked her until Mr. Long was able to yank Daddy free. It was too steep to carry him, so they had to drag him up the embankment, wrenching her heart. In the wagon on the ride to Dr. Walker's house in Michigan Bar, she held his still hand, and the smell of blood and whisky traveled with them.

Before the horses stopped she had jumped out and pounded on the doctor's door. The tall old man finally came out in his nightshirt, lantern and stethoscope in hand. He listened for a long time to Daddy's chest, and then said, "He's a goner all right."

On the dark ride back to the house, Mae's childhood with Daddy jerked through her mind like a kinetoscope turned by a slow hand, and she realized that he had bequeathed her his love of music, story, and laughter. The Indian began a mournful dirge in his native tongue, to the rhythmic clatter of hooves on slate and the whoo-whooing of owls in slow triplets. She had returned to her parents hoping, in spite of the tragedy of Emmett, for a more adult acceptance within the family. She had wanted to close the painful space between her and Daddy, he growing distant and she thinking of him as a drunk. She had ached for his forgiveness and his love, though she was pregnant and unmarried. But it was never to be.

Mr. Long and the Indian laid the body on the kitchen table and left. Mom creaked out of her rocking chair and shuffled to the table. What followed seemed, looking back on it now from the sunny churchyard, a macabre theatrical performance.

Under the hanging lamp they had stripped and washed him, and straightened his broken limbs, every touch a caress. Mae felt grateful to have had at least that intimate good-bye. The last she'd seen of Emmett was his back as he walked toward the rail yard. She wished she could have worked with Daddy on a song, she on the piano, he singing, laughing together as two grown people for once in their lives. Instead, she was washing blood off his face, shaving him, and trimming his beard and mustache. She took her time, perfecting the lines while Mom sponged his Sunday suit.

When he was fully dressed for burial, Mom tied his shoelaces in bows, and then leaned over him and spoke. Mae remembered every word of it.

"Ed, when we came to California we were a happy bunch, the boys all eager for their main chance. That was one year ago, and now you're gone. Emmett too, and George in all likelihood." Here she paused, and when she spoke again her voice had gone high and reedy.

"I loved you so, Edward Duffy. I gave you everything." Her cheeks glistened with moisture in the lamplight. "And you gave me love."

Now in the sunlight that miracle of speech seemed unreal. Mom hadn't spoken since. She still didn't know that Mae was pregnant, didn't know that St. Mary's Academy had failed to make her a good girl. Not about to spoil a miracle, Mae hadn't told her any part of it—not that night nor, as it turned out, ever.

The priest was saying the last words over Daddy's coffin, and Mae made the sign of the cross with him. This service had seemed too stinting for so lively a man, one who'd sung the Irish story-songs with such delight, a man who awed his listeners with wild tales of driving stage in the Black Hills—none more enthralled than Mae and the boys.

We should have had a wake, Mae told him in her thoughts. Should have bought whisky for your friends so they could take turns toasting you. That's what you would have wanted.

She stepped to the lip of the grave and, in the dust raised by dirt being shoveled on the pine box, lifted an invisible glass of whisky and called out, "Here's to the best stagecoach driver in all the West."

"Amen," said Mom a step behind her and loud enough to be heard by the entire assembly. "Amen," Hank and Farley added. Mae couldn't help but throw her arms around the mother she had so admired before the melancholy set in—the smart schoolteacher, the woman the neighbors praised. Daddy was gone but Emma Duffy was back. Tears melded their cheeks together. Now the baby would have a real grandmother to love. Mae squeezed her mother's soft bulk, and Mom hugged her back. The lips that had been still for so long moved the hair at the back of Mae's neck as she spoke again.

"I'm going back to New York. Come with me, Mae dear."

Mae looked into those moist blue eyes with the heavy lids. "I-I don't know. Let me think."

"Yes, you think." Mom took her hands in hers and continued looking at her like she hadn't seen her for years. "It'll be a fine life for us there."

People had been walking away, Hank already on the buckboard waiting for the family. Alone in his harness, Pal loosed a heartbroken whinny for his lost Belle. Hank and Sophie climbed aboard, and as Emma and Mae waited their turn, the barefoot man walked past lifting his hat.

Sunlight flashed across a pair of moss-green eyes.

∽

The mill in Railroad Flat had shut down and Billy McCoon was back. Since his mother and sister were going to the funeral he had come too, in case they needed help with Baby. Immediately he noticed *her.*

She stood at the graveside, a shapely little woman in a dark red dress. A wide straw hat piled with pink roses shaded her face, but he could see that her eyes were swollen and red. Even so she was beautiful. All through the ceremony he couldn't stop looking. Never had his stomach, the source of Indian emotion, talked to him as surely as it did then. This was the woman for him. He had been interested that first time they'd met, but now her presence made him forget that women always brought him trouble.

He was a half-breed, and old for her, but the Duffy family marked the graves of their dead with wooden crosses like the poorest of the poor. They lived on a rocky place with no outhouse, next to a creek that was dry most of the year. So maybe he had a chance.

John Dunaway, Billy's foreman at the Grimshaw Ranch, a man working his way up as only white men could, was looking at her too. Billy waited until Dunaway and everyone else had left before he walked past her. Their eyes caught for a moment—china-blue eyes, like his long-dead father's. Ho, she was the one.

Back in the cabin he told Ma he wanted to marry the Duffy girl. They were sitting outside on chairs enjoying the shade, and he saw the little smile that she tried to quash.

"Her name is Mae," Ma said in the tongue of the People.

Billy was glad that his mother knew her. It was a good sign. In the tongue of the People, he said, "I want some old-time medicine to make her love me."

"You? Saying that?" Now her smile stretched from ear to ear, to have him ask her for something that she alone could give

"I need all the help I can get," he said under his breath.

"Maybe I forgot how to make it."

But she was teasing. Her eye had a shine in it.

63

Mae had nothing to pack. Everything she owned was on her body, all of it in need of a good scrub, but that was the least of her worries. The big problem was whether to go to New York. The very thought of it made her hands go to her heart as though to keep it from leaping out—starting over again as a Hamilton! Mom was slowly packing in the bedroom, so Mae went out for a walk. Sometimes her mind worked better when her feet were moving.

On the road in the warm September air, she let her thoughts settle where they might. They went first to her new gowns hanging in the closet of Charlie's apartment. He'd have time to haul them to her, because Mom wouldn't leave until tomorrow. A telegram from the Cosumne Store would reach the Capitol right away and he could rent a rig—

Stupid, stupid, dolt! She shook her head thinking someone ought to knock some sense into her. Charlie'd be madder than a rained-on rooster over the abortion money she'd taken. Might even drive out just to get it back, and she would hand it all over. She repeated to herself as her feet kept time with the words, "Those gowns and gloves are gone. The shoes are gone. And Charlie is gone, gone, gone." Just like her music and poems and crinoline underskirt and everything else that she'd left at Oberon's place. Daddy was gone. Emmett was gone. George too. All gone. She could hardly figure out how to think about herself now that she couldn't see herself in their eyes. The only thing California had given her was the seed of a bastard child folded up deep inside.

And she was about to lose Mom, if she didn't go with her. She still hadn't said a word about being pregnant. She needed Mom, almost herself again, but telling her now could bring on the melancholia again. So that would have to wait.

She wanted to go to New York so bad she could feel the velvet on the Hamilton upholstery. How restful it would be in a place where Oberon couldn't find her! New York was perfect. She'd be safe for the first time in over a year. Just imagining it slowed her heart down. She would worm her way into the Hamilton family, and her baby would be raised in high society.

But a big chunk of that picture wouldn't fit no matter how much she moved the pieces around. She would die of shame swelling up with a bastard baby in the home of a lady like Aunt Phoebe. Men would never call on her, not even after the child was born. Not respectable men. She'd be a black eye. She would shame her mother. Aunt Phoebe would rue the day she'd accepted Mom back in the family with a bad girl like Mae in tow. Mae would serve as proof that marriage to an Irishman had lowered the family. Mom would be disgraced again. She let out a long breath of air. Maybe she should go for a couple of months and then make an excuse to leave. They'd never know. No, no, and no! Stop being stupid! That'd just waste the train fare, her precious money. At a time when even men couldn't find gainful employment, she needed every penny of it to raise her child.

The situation just wouldn't straighten itself out. It was like trying to fold and sort a huge pile of laundry with no surface to work on. Her brain wasn't working right. She was dazed with loss, unable to grasp the whole of it. The vivid sense of dirt falling on a coffin hammered her as she meandered along the edge of the road. In the sun's hard glare, glimpses of the dry creek bed below came into view. She felt drawn to the place where Daddy had breathed his last.

Tears clouded her vision as she pointed her feet to the opposite side of the road. The oaks on the hill were dropping little brown leaves that drifted over the road. In the speckled shade and cooler air, her mind flew her to a better place—Charlie coming for her, not when she'd be big and ugly, but after the birth of the baby. She could almost see him, almost hear his cheerful voice.

My, what a dandy boy he is! Smile lines would radiate from his eyes. She would smile and say, *He sure is. Just like his daddy.*

Mae, you were right, we should be married.

Oh yes, Charlie! I'm so happy you came for us.

She'd snuggle the baby to her and give his daddy a coy look.

Charlie would suck on his pipe in his thoughtful way and say, *I saw the newspaper account. So sorry about Emmett.* He'd reach out to pat her shoulder, making that giddyup click in his cheek. *Tough break for my little Skeeziks.*

Yes, but we've got each other, Charlie, and our boy. That last she'd say with a smile because Charlie liked her happy.

He faded away, but one thing stayed sharp and clear in her mind. That conversation would never happen if she moved to New York. And it just might happen if she stayed here.

So intense had this fanciful exchange burned in her mind that she hadn't noticed the sound of a horse and wagon. It didn't pass her by like it should, but lingered behind. Her heart came to her throat as she slowly turned to look—perhaps Charlie… or, God forbid, Oberon.

⌒

Billy had just driven by the stone house. He was on his way to deliver four bushels of plums to the grocer in Latrobe, and then he was supposed to stop in Michigan Bar on his way back to see if Mr. Heath wanted plums for his store.

No one was in the yard, but something moved behind the window. Believing it was *her,* he'd let the horse almost stop. But even dallying, he was too soon leaving the air that she breathed. Slowly he drove along the road, up the hills and down again across the gully that flooded in winter. The oaks had turned shades of brown. The gray pines among them leaned like tired old men, taller than the oaks and shaggy with the long needles that his mother used for making tiny baskets.

And then as he came around a bend, as though materializing from his thoughts, there she was! The lush dark hair curling freely down her back thrilled him. Her shoulders in that dark red dress seemed too narrow beneath all that hair, and the modern dress showed her narrow middle but also the movement of her hips as she walked along the shady side of the road. She seemed a creature of the forest, free and young. He pulled the horse closer.

She hesitated in the way she turned and looked at him. Sparks of sunlight through the oaks glinted red in the hair that framed her face. At the funeral her hat had obscured her face, which now took his breath away—cheeks the delicate pink of a pale rose, mouth wider than most and full in the center but disappearing into a down and up curve at the corners, dark blue eyes pulled down slightly at the outside corners, and swept-up lashes. This face printed itself on his soul. He wanted to see those lips part in laughter, those eyes sparkle with fun. He wanted to kiss away the redness and swelling on her eyelids.

He felt lucky to be here with her, but unlucky too. Ma had made the elixir and he hadn't swallowed a drop of it for fear he'd see the wrong woman first.

Pulling the wagon alongside, he lifted his hat. "Howdy, ma'am. Wanna ride?"

"No, thank you." She looked straight ahead and resumed walking, fast.

"Sorry about your brother and father." He flicked the horses ahead so he moved alongside her again.

She slowed down and glanced over at him. "You were at the funeral."

"Yup." Covering his excitement, he fixed his gaze over the horse's ears.

"I forgot your name."

"Billy McCoon."

"Where are you going?" The old Indian greeting, though she wouldn't know she had used it.

"Haulin' plums to Latrobe."

He kept his eyes on the road ahead. "Say, how 'bout keepin' me company. I'll drive you back. Won't take long."

She continued walking.

Feigning a casual demeanor while his wild heart rocked him, he slumped with the reins and waited for a response.

She stopped walking and looked at him. "Who do you work for now?"

He tugged the horse to a stop. "Grimshaws. I was doing a little work for Mr. Driscoll that day I met you. Before that, I worked a long time for Haskin Swain. Dairy cows."

"Where you from?"

"Born a stone's throw from here. You're new here. But my mother knows you."

"Who is your mother?"

This could end it, but sooner or later she would learn who he was, so despite the fist in his chest pinching off the blood, he said, "People call her Indian Mary. My father was white," he added.

Waiting to see what she would do, he gazed at the house-sized boulders on the hilly side of the road, and forced himself to think about the gray lichens that splotched the boulders and how Ma used to chew them into a liquid to spit into Baby's mouth when she was newly born. It was supposed to cure gas, though Ma believed that spirit, not gas, made Baby scream even back then.

"Would you bring me right back?"

His heart skipped a beat, but he kept his outward calm and dropped his chin down and up like giving her a ride was an ordinary thing to do.

She climbed up and sat on the buckboard beside him, and his pulse leaped like a boy gaining ground in a footrace. A magical silence enveloped and wrapped them together, bouncing them to the same cadence as the horse pulled along the road. And when the grasslands opened up in every direction, they would have been able to see all the way to Latrobe but for miles of rolling hills ending in Onion Mountain, now called Ben Bolt. In the distance the white mountain peaks hung suspended in thin air. The space between him and Mae pulsed thick with power, a colorless gel that if he elbowed she would feel. The Basque sheepherder's dog rushed out barking furiously, but the horse trotted along without fear, not wheeling and overturning the wagon, as happened to so many people. Instead they floated like peaceful spirits above the surface of the world. All of this confirmed that she was the one, at long last.

In Latrobe, he saw her watching him from the shade of a locust tree while he carried the bushel baskets into the store. His feet never touched the ground. On the way back over the same bumpy road, down the shoulder of Ben Bolt through Miller land, her presence salved his itchy soul. She was the good girl he'd been wishing for. He could see in her unlined face the absence of splotches and dark circles under her eyes that drinking would have put there. He was over forty-five years old—he could never remember exactly how old—and had let his old dreams dry up. Until now.

"What are they doing?" Mae asked, pointing at the People in the distance.

"Rounding up grasshoppers." She must have missed seeing them on the way up.

"Why? To save their crops?"

At first he couldn't think what crops had to do with it. That was open grassland. The People were doing what they'd done for thousands of years. But then it came to him.

"No, they're Indians. They eat grasshoppers, roasted."

He knew that most white people gagged at the idea, and it was against the law for Indians to burn the dry grass like they used to, so he surprised himself by explaining all about the grasshopper roundups, and how they used to set the grass afire and roast them in a pit. Something made him tell her about it, despite the possibility that it would disgust her and stop any further interest in him. They were approaching Kangaroo House. Mr. Silva's fiddle music could be heard out into the road, and the place looked full with four freight wagons pulled up in front and down the road. This was the intersection of Latrobe and Michigan Bar Roads. He was supposed to turn toward Michigan Bar, and he wanted to—not just to talk to Mr. Heath about the bushel of plums in the back, but to stop at his mother's house and gulp down some elixir. He needed it now. But it would be a detour.

Spoiling the magic with a lie, he stumbled over his words. "I wanna, er, see a man in Michigan Bar 'bout the plums, but it'd take some time—uh a little longer. All right with you?"

She was quiet for a disturbing length of time.

"How much longer would it take?"

He shrugged. "Mebbe add two extra miles."

"No, please drive me home now. I live in the stone house on this road."

As if he didn't know.

The silence of the rest of the drive prickled. He stopped to let her out at the opening in the low stone wall, and now would drive back to Heath's Store.

"S'long," he said, unable to smile from the hurt of her vacating the buckboard.

"Good-bye. Thank you for the ride." A sweet, sad voice.

∽

Mae went in the house and stood at the window watching him leave, amazed that she'd done that, but relieved he'd brought her back as promised. Mom was wrapping a rag around the little wooden horse whittled by Daddy long ago, a decoration on a shelf in the Iowa house and here on the fireplace mantle.

"You came in a wagon," Mom said.

"Yes. A man who works for the Grimshaws gave me a ride home."

"I'm going to leave most of this stuff here. The next woman can use it." She put the padded horse in the crate as gently as if it were made of crystal, and then waddled into the bedroom.

Mae sat down at the table and laid her head in her arms—praying silently for the help of the Virgin. She didn't want to stay in this house with Farley, and she couldn't go to New York. Now she had gone for a ride with a half-breed stranger. That was about as stupid as going to that saloon with Helen. Whatever possessed her to do such things? She must stop trusting people. Yes, Charlie had turned out to be good, but this man could have slashed her throat. Half-breeds were unpredictable and dangerous. Oakland and San Francisco were fine cities, but she mustn't forget that this area was still something of a frontier. But even if safety were assured, no self-respecting white girl would ride with an Indian man, or buck as they were often called. Thinking back to her state of mind at the time she got in the wagon, she recalled feeling weak with relief after the fright about Oberon, and then extremely disappointed that it wasn't Charlie stopping to pick her up. Somehow that mix of relief and sorrow caused her to do it. Or was there more?

She saw in her mind's eye the planes of Billy McCoon's tanned, clean-shaved face, and the beginnings of crow-feet around those green eyes. He seemed calm and strong, and the way he'd held the reins tugged at her, bringing Daddy to mind. Fortunately, Billy had turned out to be harmless, at least today, but riding with him could have made him think she liked him. She was in no danger of wanting a man, any man, much less an old Indian. Maybe that made her feel safe, being that he didn't count as a man.

She picked up her head and stared out the window, barely seeing the sweep of yellowed grass across the road and the shadowy tracings of the meandering cut banks of Crevice Creek, now dry. More to the point, she wasn't a self-respecting girl. Why have pretensions? That time was gone. Not a day passed that she didn't realize something inside her had broken. It had never righted itself, not even with Charlie. Much of the time with Oberon she had not even tried to run away, and had done Oberon's bidding. She had not burned at her stake like Joan of Arc did. She was tested and found wanting. She was of low character. So why shouldn't she get in a wagon with an Indian she didn't know? She needed to pee but put if off, hating those trips behind the big tree, always worried that someone would see her. Besides, it stank back there. She lived like an animal, not washing her clothes for lack of anything to wear while they dried. She smelled bad. She had sunk to a low she couldn't have imagined back in Iowa. She also felt the loss of Emmett and Daddy like herheart had been cored.

But that grief had eased on the ride with Billy McCoon, and she had forgotten the grating and gnawing of the New York dilemma. She had even forgotten her guilt over being pregnant. She hadn't thought of Charlie on that ride either. She had stepped outside of the world somehow. She'd been curious about the man who ate roasted grasshoppers, a man whose white father had given him those green eyes.

64

Early the next morning Billy walked four miles out of his way to pass the Duffy place. She was there, in the yard! So was the young man with red hair springing out from under his hat—he'd also been at the burial. The two of them were boosting the big old woman up to the buckboard of a wagon. Billy willed the man to be a relative, not a husband. Mae wore the same wide hat with pink roses that she'd worn at the funeral, and the same dark red dress. Then he saw two wooden crates and a large traveler's trunk in the wagon bed.

She was leaving! His insides compressed into a tight space. He tried to resume walking against the flow of his blood.

She turned and looked at him. He couldn't help but stop and look right at the little rose of a woman. She opened her hand to him, then went to speak to the old woman, clearly her mother, who now sat on the buckboard. He looked up the road and took more steps.

Her voice called, "Where are you going?"

He looked again, cleared his throat, and pushed out, "Grimshaw place."

"We'll give you a ride."

He moved toward her as in a dream, forlorn but invited.

"You gave me a ride yesterday," she said privately to him, "and now we'll drive you to the Cosumne station."

Stagecoaches stopped there.

"That's my brother Farley." She pointed to the man with red hair, now on the buckboard holding the reins. Billy's stomach noted that. "And that's my mother, Mrs. Emma Duffy. This is Billy McCoon," she told them.

They turned their heads partway, nodding.

Mae stepped up the wheel axle and climbed in the wagon bed and beckoned to him to do likewise. She sat on the trunk. Billy vaulted in, glad to ride with her if only for two miles. He settled himself against the side slats where nothing blocked his view of her. This morning he'd drunk a big dose of the elixir and luck was with him, or had seemed to be until he saw that she was leaving. Accustomed to life's setbacks, he told himself it was a good thing he had doubted the effectiveness of the old medicine. This way he wouldn't be as disappointed.

He didn't stare at her as the wagon jounced along the pitted road, but took her in in little gulps as they rode up over the high hill on Stone House Road, heading straight toward Yellow Snake Peak. The People claimed it still had some power left over from when that monster snake had coiled itself there, squeezing the earth so hard you could still see the pointed cone with rocky ridges marking the snake's loops. The teacher in the schoolhouse just across the road from it liked to hike with the children up to the peak each day to eat their noon dinners. Indians never went up there. They figured they had enough bad luck without stirring up that old snake poison.

At the schoolhouse Farley turned the wagon right onto Jackson Road.

Billy asked Mae, "You goin' away?"

A furrow creased the tender place between her perfect eyebrows. "I don't know."

He looked down to cover the rush of his blood. Why didn't she know? And if she left, how far would she go? Would she stay away forever?

"My mother's going to New York," she continued. "I couldn't make up my mind about going with her, so I have to make up my mind between here and the station."

He had a chance! He wanted to blurt out, *stay*, but couldn't think of a reason except to please him. So he said nothing and felt dumb as a post as the wagon closed the distance to the station.

Too soon they pulled up in the little town of Cosumne, at the stage stop in front of the store, beneath the roof. Mae put a shoe over the side of the wagon. Billy jumped out and reached up for her. As her soft hand closed over his work-scarred paw, lightning shot through him. He hadn't felt that since he'd loved Lizzyanne. It made him young again, and if she left he'd be an old man forever.

Quickly she pulled her hand back. Farley was coming around the wagon toward them. Farley took a crate out of the back and put it down in the passenger's waiting place.

Quietly, while Farley's back was turned Billy said, "Don't go."

She looked at him with wide blue eyes.

Farley returned for the other crate, and Billy realized he should help. He eased the trunk out of the wagon—big, but light for a man who daily hefted heavy equipment and fruit crates. When Farley was out of earshot he whispered, "I want to show you places, like where the old-time rock people lived."

There hadn't been time to think that through four times. It would sound superstitious to her. His face heated up, and he carried the trunk to the waiting area and set it down beside the crates.

She followed and stood beside him. He stared up the road, amazed that he'd had the nerve to say that, hoping she wouldn't sneer and taunt him. What would she care about the rock people? What did *he* care about them?

Farley went to the old woman on the buckboard and helped her climb down, one slow move at a time. Meanwhile, Billy glanced at Mae, her blue eyes connecting to his stomach, as powerful as the lightning of that touch.

"I'm pregnant," she said in a quiet voice. "They don't know."

"You married?" It fell out of his mouth.

"No."

"But you got a man."

She turned her back to her family so they wouldn't see her mouth moving. "No. I left him. He doesn't want the baby. Doesn't want me if I have it. I left him in Sacramento."

Billy stood sideways to her so he could see her and her approaching mother at the same time. Quietly he said, "You want the baby?"

"Yes. I guess."

"He's a bad man, the one in Sacramento."

"No, no, he…"

He whispered, "If you stay, where would you live?"

"With Farley, but I don't like him… er, that is we don't get along."

The old woman halted toward them with Farley's help, but wasn't yet within earshot of a whisper.

"Stay with me. I wanna take care of you and the baby," he said turning away, trying to act natural though his insides clenched with the shock of asking a white woman he barely knew to marry him. Seeing the questioning faces of her people, he put up a hand in a wordless *hasta la vista* and crossed the road to the Grimshaw place.

The men were gathering to hear what their day's work would be. He felt the relief of having spoken the truth. Now it was up to her.

He sat on the bare earth with the others, mostly boys and relatives of the Grimshaws, but his stomach remained across the road. He had nothing to offer her or her family, nothing white people cared about. He worked for food at the Grimshaws. In bad times, that's the way it was for Indians and boys and poor whites. He had come back to the home place after the mill shut down because his people were buried nearby. Even his father lay in the ground at Vyries Brown's place. But with her at his side he would die trying to earn money for his work so he could support her. It wouldn't be much, but he would kill any man who laid a hand on her, and he'd be a father to her baby. He closed his eyes, opening himself to power and hoping for a miracle.

John Dunaway, the new foreman, came out of the house. "Mornin'," he said. "We got corn to pick." He pointed. "You, you, you…"

A team of six rattled and stamped to a stop under the roof, the stagecoach blocking Billy's view of Mae. Mr. Dunaway continued assigning work, but Billy's ears were stopped up, his stomach caved in with sorrow. Men were tying the trunk and *both* crates on the top of the stage. She was leaving. The coach jiggled on its springs—people inside making room for new passengers.

With a loud "Eeyaw!" and a crack of the whip, the stage rumbled away. Billy blinked to squeeze the tears from his eyes, and when the dust cleared he blinked again. But he was not seeing things.

Mae was still standing under the roof!

Farley gestured to her, and she climbed in the wagon without crate or trunk, and was on her way back up the road. The medicine had worked.

65

"Who woulda thunk!" Farley flung his hat into the bedroom that used to be Mae's. He'd just come in from putting Pal to pasture.

She knew he didn't like living with her any more than she wanted to live with him. The bedroom Mom and Daddy had slept in was hers now.

"You mean you and me here alone?"

Rolling his eyes, he flopped down in Daddy's corner of the sofa.

Mae was in Mom's rocking chair pushing herself with her toes. Like in a horrible nightmare, they had taken the places of their parents. *No.* She could still go. She had the fare. She might even catch up at one of the train stops.

What did Billy McCoon say? Strange. Frightening how she'd blurted out her secret to him of all people. She had no self-control. Outlandish that he offered to take care of her. He didn't know her from a rock in the road, and she sure didn't know him. She understood men now and was well aware what the payment would be, and yet the very thought that someone who knew the worst about her wanted her, and said he wanted to take care of her baby, made her eyes flood with tears. She wiped them away, glanced at Farley and saw the menace in his glare.

"Now, donchu go gittin' no notion of poor lil' Mae needin' me to earn her keep."

She told herself not to jump to his bait. They had to get along now. "I'll cook the food," she said, "and drive to the river and fill the barrels." Trying to please Charlie, she'd learned a few things about cooking. "And I promise to help as much as I can with digging the outhouse."

"That again! You think we ain't picked at every damned inch of this place tryin' to poke a hole in the rock? Oh! Poor thing, you didn't know. You was livin' in *style* in Sacramento."

That bit into her like a rattlesnake. She could never tell him about Oberon, or even Charlie. He was too full of spite for her. "Every inch of ground?" she asked, keeping a placid tone.

"That's right. It can't be done, 'less mebbe over in Miser property 'cross the road. Rocky as hell over there too. But poor lil' you wouldn't know nuthin' about that."

"Mrs. Miser's a friend of mine. I'll talk to her."

"Tell you what. You go an' do just that, go talk to Mrs. Miser and tell her to feed you while she's at it, an' send diggers for the outhouse. Meantime, I'll keep *workin'* fer my vittles." The ugly sneer on his pimple-scarred face said, you're a spoiled brat and can't do a lick of work without complaining.

He thought she was the same Mae she had been two years ago, not a seventeen-year-old fighting her way out of hell. True, she couldn't dig an outhouse by herself. But they simply had to stop bickering. This was serious. With him eating at farms and ranches and not bringing in money, she'd draw down her stash of abortion money just to keep body and soul together, and when the baby was born, what—

A loud crack.

She nearly dropped to the floor, assuming it was a gunshot. But he had slapped the leather sofa and now was yelling, "Why'n tarnation din'cha go with Mom? You said you was goin'!" It exploded out of him like toxic gas that had been stoppered since they'd left the station.

Still jumpy inside, she snapped, "Well, why didn't *you* go?"

"Hah!"

She knew his reason. He didn't want to live with high-tone ladies telling him to wash his hands and use table manners and correct grammar. He'd rather be taming blast hoses and sloshing around in the mud with the mining crew. He liked working with rough men, and he expected the hydraulic company to return when the Panic was over, if it ever ended. He wanted to be here when it happened.

"Farley," she said, "I've changed."

"Oh sure! And frogs grow hair."

"No, really, I'm different than what you think."

From habit she'd been talking without actually looking at him, but now she stole another glance, only to see his upturned gaze as though beseeching God to save him from the pain of living with a selfish idiot.

"I need some air," she said.

༄

She took the bridle from the wagon bed. Pal came to her call and she stroked his white nose and soft lips. It had been a long time since she'd ridden him. He seemed eager, so without saddling him she pulled up on his back and yanked her skirts around to free her legs.

The height and freedom of being on a horse helped a bit, but her insides stayed unsettled from the quarrel and, she supposed, the sorrow of losing a chance for a fresh start in New York, in addition to losing Mom. She kept thinking there might be a way to get shed of the baby in New York. There, she wouldn't miss Charlie so much. And Oberon wouldn't find her.

No, no, no, she scolded herself. She'd made the best decision she could, and now she must live with it. This was hard, with Farley nursing a hatred of her from a time when she used to blame him for things, like the time she left the gate open and the neighbor's cows trampled the corn. He sure got a good whuppin' in the woodshed. But she'd been very young then. She expected him, being four years older, twenty-one-and-a-half to be exact, to chalk that up to bad old things that happen when you're growing up.

She rode up the road at a gentle pace. The world looked pretty. *Looked.* She didn't *feel* it like she would have if she'd been her natural self. She had all her money in the inner skirt pocket, but had become a bird with a broken wing, like the two girls who had lived in the basement of St. Mary's—cast out by their families. With insides so tight they hurt, she passed Cathedral Rocks where, on the other side of the road, Daddy had fallen and died.

She rode to the Miser place hoping a visit with those cheerful people would settle heer nerves again, as they had in the past. Maybe, she thought, it would settle her nerves to visit with the lady who'd been so kind to her before she went to Sacramento. She tied Pal to the hitching rail and knocked on the door. Yellow leaves floated down from the towering cottonwood, piling up in every nook and cranny of barn, stoop, and the pretty rock well.

Agnes opened the door and her hands flew up. "Well, if it ain't Mae Duffy. C'mon in and set yourself down."

Before Mae could sink into the striped cushions of a match-stick chair, Agnes was at the back door singing, "Yoo-hoo, Isabella. Company!"

The two women quickly returned, Mrs. Miser smiling and brushing her hands on her dirt-stained apron. "Well, my dear, how *are* you?" Right away her smile turned to concern as she studied Mae's face.

Of course she couldn't give a real answer to that question, and so they exchanged comments about Daddy's funeral and how Mom had gone east today, having come out of her melancholia, at least a little.

"And you stayed!" Mrs. Miser observed with wondering eyes.

This would have been the time to mention the baby-to-be, but Mae couldn't face telling her about that. Her gaze stopped at the piano. How her fingers had missed dancing on those keys!

"Go ahead, dear," said the lady. "Play the piano. We haven't heard anyone as good as you, have we Agnes?"

Agnes shook her head.

"It's been so long since I've played. I won't be any good."

"Nonsense. Git-cherself on over't the stool," Isabella Miser shoved the air in her direction.

But with the two of them folding their hands and looking at her with rapt attention, Mae felt self-conscious, and she stumbled when she got a few chords in. She tried another piece, but twirled around on the stool, shrugged and said, "I can't just now. I need my music."

"Well, I think you sounded just fine," Mrs. Miser softened that to a motherly coax. "But next time bring your music and leave it here so it'll be waiting for you."

She couldn't tell them why that was impossible, couldn't pour her nasty secrets over these gentle ladies. "I had an accident," she lied, "A crate with my things slipped off a wagon and—" Her chin started to tremble. What a liar she'd become! She tried to relax her tight chest and stem the tears.

"Oh, you poor dear!" Mrs. Miser came over and laid a hand on her shoulder.

That triggered big bawling convulsions rising up from the bottom of her being. She ran for the door. They came after her and tried to get her back inside, offering cookies, but she wrwenched out of their grasp and ran through the front yard. Jumping on Pal and shaking her pinched and twisted face. "No thanks!" she called to their entreaties.

She galloped away sobbing. They'd think her a dolt to cry over a lost crate. She'd never be able to explain to anyone respectable what was wrong with her. She couldn't even explain it to herself. Out of their range she slowed Pal to a walk and collapsed under a sudden overpowering fatigue, leaning forward, cheek on his warm neck, hugging him with both arms as she sobbed.

She mourned the girl who used to be able to control her emotions. Now she didn't belong in polite society. Quite on his own Pal walked down the road toward the stone house, the rhythm of his shifting withers too friendly to leave, but when he turned into the opening of the wall, expecting to be put back to pasture, she sat up and reined him back to the road. She couldn't be in the house with Farley, not now.

Turning left on Stone House Road she had no idea where she was going. It just felt good to ride somewhere, anywhere. Up the high hill she rode, and then down the road straight as a string toward that odd little pointed peak. At its base she turned right onto Jackson Road, just as they'd done earlier in the day with Mom, and passed fields of grazing cows. She rode past the stage stop and past row crops where field hands shoveled irrigation ditches. A man stood watching her, his legs apart, possibly Billy McCoon. She continued up the hill with no idea of a destination. On the high ground she reined left at Slough House Road, and then left again down Sheldon's lane. This brought back those innocent days when she'd hoped to beguile Jared Sheldon into marrying her. How idiotic she had been! And how far she had fallen!

Where the road turned right, she looked down it and was glad nobody was coming toward her. She didn't want any Sheldon to see her. There was a rough pathway into the bushes and trees. She reined Pal into it, ducking the low-hanging branches and walking him across dry Deer Creek. To her surprise she came upon a cluster of little frame cabins perched on the river levee with long poles supporting them on the downhill sides, none of them painted. They looked deserted, with dry overgrown vines and bushes all around. Except for the cabin lowest on the levee.

It had a tended garden and curtains at the windows. A large number of hens and roosters pecked and scratched around the place. They came and went from under the cabin in a space that a short person like Mae could stand up in. There was an outhouse beside the garden, and Mae needed to use it.

A plump Chinese woman ducked out from under the house with an apron sagging from the weight of something, likely eggs. Her gray hair had been cut, it seemed, to the length of an inverted bowl placed over her head, and then trimmed straight across her eyebrows. She had a round face and a round belly beneath a colorless old quilted dress, perhaps red in a long-ago time, that hung in a bell-shape down to her high-top farmer's shoes. Squinting at Mae she spoke.

"You ross?"

"Pardon me?"

"You ross?"

Mae realized she meant lost. *Am I?* She felt weak from all the crying and knew her eyes would be red and swollen. "Sort of lost." She tried to smile. "May I please use your outhouse?"

The woman gestured to it. "Rater, you com-ee. Makee tea."

Another stranger was inviting her in, this time an old woman—the first Chinese woman Mae had ever seen, though she'd seen countless Chinese men. She tied Pal to one of the small trees that grew there. They had huge yellowing leaves, each comprised of about twenty little leaves attached to the center-vein, a tree Mae hadn't seen before coming to California. As she made her way to the outhouse, the eyes of the old woman followed.

In the outhouse she checked for black widow spiders, gathered her skirts and sat forward with her head in her hands. She lingered there with the words of a poem learned in St. Mary's trailing through her disorganized mind.

> *I remember, I remember*
> *The house where I was born,*
> *The little window where the sun*
> *Came peeping in at morn;*
> *He never came a wink too soon,*
> *Nor brought too long a day,*
> *But now, I often wish the night*
> *Had borne my breath away!*

She understood that wish. Good poems were all sad. Her own poems used to be light and happy. She had enjoyed fitting them to the rhythm of a waltz. Gone. Everything was gone now. It seemed she was crawling through a desert knowing the worst was yet to come, having the baby without friends or a man.

Trudging back to Pal she saw movement behind the screen door up the levee. She should get back to Farley. He'd be upset about her taking their only horse without asking him.

"You com-ee," said the woman opening the screen and holding it.

In the grip of that overpowering fatigue, she decided to put off returning

to Farley and visit with this old woman for a little while. She looked safe. And
if not, Mae judged that she could overpower her in a fight. How low she had
fallen to be thinking like that. She stepped up the sandstone block that served
as a stoop, and the woman opened the screen to her.

The same garlic and herb smells surrounded her as in the Chinaman's
place beneath the streets of Sacramento. Two small windows in the room
didn't admit enough light. Most of it came through the screen door. When
her eyes adjusted she saw that the room was well kept, four simple wooden
chairs around a heavy table. In the center of that table stood a large basket of
little green melons piled too high for seated people to see across. Two small
beds with pretty quilted coverlets lay along the walls on opposite sides of the
room. In the shadows on the back wall an open cupboard held ceramic jars
and ewers and bowls, and bundles of herbs hung from the rafters. Next to
the cupboard an odd little stove had the shape of a wide, shallow sink. How
on earth could she cook on such a surface?

"You sit," the woman said, pointing to a chair.

Mae obeyed.

"Ah Sen," said the woman, thumping her chest.

"Mae Duffy." She placed a hand over her heart.

With a polite nod, the old woman took two handle-less cups from a shelf
and set them on the table. "You got man?" she asked, coming shockingly to
the point as she stoked a fire in the metal box below the sink of a stovetop.

"No. Do you have a man?" Mae worried that one would burst in.

Dipping from a settling keg and pouring water into a steaming kettle, the
old woman said, "Ah Soon Chin my man. He dead. Bone bury in Sherdon
glave." She lifted the lid of a blue ceramic jar with high shoulders and pinched
out tea leaves for their cups. Sitting opposite Mae, she asked, "You sick?"

Mae wagged her head, no, she was not sick.

Tilting her head, Ah Sen's voice became very kind. "Wy no happy?"

"My brother died, my father died, my mother went away for good, and
my man doesn't want me, so I'm living with a brother who hates me. I need
to live someplace else and work for my food." All pulled out with difficulty.

Ah Sen gave an almost imperceptible nod at each part of that, her eyes
like polished onyx.

Mae hadn't mentioned the worst of her troubles for fear this woman would
tell the Sheldons. Ah Sen took the teakettle out of the hot sink and poured
the steaming water into the cups.

Inhaling the rich aroma of the tea rising from her cup, Mae inquired, "Do
you work for the Sheldons?"

"No. Biness rady now. Sellee chicken, sellee egg." Her English was so bad
that Mae now doubted this woman would talk to the Sheldons about anything
as complicated as a stranger's troubles.

"I'm going to have a baby." It felt good to just say it. Again.

"Ah so!" the woman nodded vigorously like she understood everything. "No wanee babee?" She sipped from her cup, watching Mae with a keen eye.

Mae put her elbow on the table, the wood softened by years of chopping and scrubbing, and cupped her forehead in her hand. "I don't know. Maybe I want the baby. Maybe Charlie will come for me and the baby, and maybe we'll get married."

Sipping her tea, Ah Sen seemed ever more interested. "Ah mebbee," she said bobbing her head up and down. "Mebbee Challey come."

There was something about this woman from a strange land. Mae felt a wordless bond with her, one that invited secrets. Ah Sen had also lost a man she loved. Mae felt she could talk to this lonely old woman in this dimly lit house. She told her about Mom returning to New York, and why she couldn't go with her, and as they talked the tea calmed her jitters.

"Do you plan to go back to China?"

"No. Chinee no wa me, Ah Soon bone in glound, Sherdon prace. I stay."

Her husband's bones were in Sheldon ground. "Why doesn't your country want you?"

Ah Sen shook her head. "No flen, no famree. Dead now."

"How old were you when you came to California?"

Ah Sen stood up and held her hand half a head shorter than she was now, and she was already short. "Dlinkee tea," she ordered, replenishing the hot water in their cups.

"Did you come here with your parents?"

Ah Sen closed her eyes, sighed, and then sat down again opposite Mae. "Fawer die. Momma sellee me in China, rotsa money, feed numba one son, numba two son."

"Your mother *sold you?*" Mae was beginning to forget her own troubles.

Ah Sen nodded. "Young girra, rotsa monee." She rubbed her thumb against her fingers. Many girra comee Gold Mountain. San Flisco."

"San Francisco?" Affirmative nod. "Did you find friends there?"

Ah Sen stared at her with the blank expression of the dead. "China boss rady." She rained her fist in the air, miming fast punches. "Say go wi man, rotsa man, alla time. Unnerstan? No go out. Doorra lock." She indicated a room the size of the table and mimed writing. "China rady book. How many time man. Pay ship."

Mae was horrified. "How long did it take you to pay back your fare?"

A huff of scorn. "Young girra no can pay. Man ara day, ara night. Girra die. Rotsa China girra die. San Flisco rong time. Rotsa yeawa."

Years! Recalling her own time of terror Mae couldn't imagine being locked in a tiny room with strange men coming in. She recalled what Charlie had said about San Francisco's dens of iniquity, but she had not imagined it to be like that for the girls, lititle girls—

"But you're alive, here in this house. How did you get free of that bondage?"

"China rady pray card" A big smile stretched across her face. "Wite man win. Take me. Comee Delta. Ireton."

"So he won you in a card game. Was he nice?"

Ah Sen took another sip of tea and shrugged. "Betta. Ownry one man."

"But you married a Chinaman. How did you get away from the white man?"

Ah Sen's face lit up. "He mawwee wite girra. Say Ah Sen, go."

He told her to leave. "So how did you get here?"

"Ah Soon Chin wa me. We comee dis prace." She opened her arms to the scrubbed walls and smiled. "Goo house. Ah Soon Chin goo man." She smiled at her cup like she shared a secret with it.

Mae was glad this mistreated woman had finally found happiness.

"Rong time dis house. Ah Soon die. Mista Sherdon say, go China. I say no. Ah Soon bone here. I stay. I biness rady." She was obviously very proud of that.

"Aren't you lonely?"

The shoulders of the quilted smock moved. Mae noticed a double-barreled shotgun standing in the corner.

"My house," she said gesturing around. "In China, Ah Sen got no house."

Mae understood, she might be lonely but at least she had a place of her own. "Do you have any children?"

A shadow shut down her proud smile. "Rong time sick, no babee."

Remembering her own sickness, Mae supposed infection could scar up a woman's insides. "You're lucky you didn't die when you were young."

Bobbing her half-gray head, Ah Sen said, "Rotsa China girra die."

That could be one reason Mae hadn't seen other Chinese women, plus the fact that most of the men who'd come for the gold came without women and children. Charlie had told her that, and said their women were now banned from entering the United States.

Ah Sen set her cup down and looked Mae in the eye. "Ah Sen o rady. Loo-mi-tiz in ba." She placed a hand on her lower back. "O rady need hep, chicken biness. You young girra, you workee me?"

Ah Sen tilted her head to one side and asked again. "You stay my house? Ah Sen make dinna?" She pointed at one of the beds. "You bed."

66

Mae shooed the chicken off the nest and took a warm egg in her hand, but stopped gathering at the sound of footsteps coming up the trail. Carefully placing the egg in the swale of her skirt with the others, she flattened herself against the rough wall of the chicken house overhang.

She could hear Ah Sen talking to somebody, but no clear words. The talk faded behind the slam of the screen door, and she waited in the gloom. She'd been at Ah Sen's place for about a week, but wasn't herself yet and didn't want to talk to any Sheldon, the most likely visitor here. They'd ask questions, and she'd get weepy like she did at the Misers. Pretty soon the whole countryside would be gossiping about her. As it was, nobody knew she was working here, not even Farley, and that was to her liking.

The short visit with him came to mind, when she'd taken Pal back to him. What he'd said or rather how he said it, kept returning to her—soft, almost apologetic. She'd told him she had room and board in Slough House and thought he needed Pal more than she did. He'd looked at her funny and said, "I can sure use him. Mr. Long'll let me stay in the house if'n I work for him, but the work's up the road a piece. An' there's talk of a hard rock mine fixin' to open up around Dry Town, so I *do* need a horse." She could tell by his expression that he could hardly believe that, for his sake, she would give up something she wanted. He added, "I surely mean t' thank you fer bringin'im."

The voices moved outside again, this time louder. "Thank you, Ah Sen. We all love the melon candy." It was Katy Irene Sheldon!

Nonetheless Mae stayed hidden like a bear in a den about to give birth, but in her case she was considering *not* giving birth. Ah Sen had told her about herbs that ended pregnancy. Just like that, simple and safe. The mind-opening wonder of it had got her thinking. Maybe she had run away from the "doctor" in Sacramento just to save herself from pain and likely death, not because she wanted the baby that much. With a simple and safe solution she'd be able to get on the train and go to New York and no one would know the difference. The very thought made her giddy. Yes, she had loved Charlie, but he hadn't come for her, and when she looked at it clear-eyed she doubted he'd ever loved her, really loved her. Still, she needed to know more about what those herbs did to a girl before she decided what to do. So she couldn't explain, especially not to a Sheldon. So far, only Billy McCoon and Ah Sen knew her secret, and neither of them had any cause to gossip about her to white people.

The footsteps faded back toward the Sheldon place, back to where strong boys did the farming, Mr. Sheldon conducted his business, Mrs. Sheldon cooked and cleaned, Grandma baked pies, and the young people went to college and played music. No longer did Mae expect such a life. She had become practical.

Gathering the rest of the eggs, she took them in the house. Ah Sen had put all the melons in a gunny sack. Many more of the softball-sized melons lay in the garden ripe on the vines. Tomorrow she would hitch a ride to Sacramento, where she would sell melons, chickens and eggs to Chinese markets, and Mae would stay to watch over the place.

"Want me to pick the rest of the melons?" she asked, knowing that stooping brought misery to Ah Sen's back. Ah Sen dipped her chin down and up in her militaristic manner.

Mae filled a crate with the small round melons, and when she returned to the house, Ah Sen had nested the cleaned eggs in a crate of dry grass on the table. With a long-handled spoon she lowered the last of the biggest white eggs into a pickle jar of brine. Salt lengthened the shelf life of eggs and some merchants wanted them that way.

"Ah Sen stay Saclameno mollow nigh," she said.

That meant Mae would be alone overnight. She couldn't help but fear that, but this was part of her work and she would do it.

∽

The iron door on the firebox clanked shut, waking Mae. She cracked an eye. It was early morning, Ah Sen stoking the fire. Mae turned over on the mattress filled with a sticky plant that grew in tangled masses around the deserted cabins. She and Ah Sen had yanked up piles of it and then, under Ah Sen's supervision, Mae had stuffed the ticking sack with it and sewed up the open seam. The vine left air throughout, which made the mattress resilient. They had also washed Mae's colorful bedspread, dried it in the early October sun, and re-stuffed it with down. The finely woven ticking and coverlet admitted no poke from vine or feather. This little house may have appeared crude from the outside, but its wise owner made it civilized inside.

The steady thump of the butcher knife on wood announced that breakfast would soon be sizzling in the wok, as Ah Sen called her stovetop. Mae sat up and stretched.

Ah Sen handed her an old tunic that would fit a person of any girth. "Today kirr chicken," she said, returning to what she called "wedgetabos."

Mae remembered quite well that they would kill chickens this morning. Pulling the faded smock over her camisole she caught a whiff of garlic, and it gave her a twinge of nausea. She made a dash to the outhouse.

Her employer understood. By the time Mae returned and sat at the table, Ah Sen had steaming tea in her cup, a special tea from Sacramento for calming her insides.

She had learned that offering to help cook was useless.

Ah Sen stirred the chopped onion, potato, carrot and dark green cabbage into the leftover shreds of chicken from last night's supper. After more sizzling and stirring, she poured whipped egg over everything and stirred a little more. Scooping a pile of it into Mae's bowl, Ah Sen handed the bowl back. The steam smelled of the peppery red oil and the sesame seed oil, both of which Mae had learned to like. Ah Sen sat across the table with her own bowl, drizzling the dark liquid all over it, the kind she used at every meal.

She extended the black ewer to Mae. "You rikee."

They'd been through this before, Mae always declining. But this time to placate her friend and employer she splashed a couple drops on one side of her breakfast and, with the flowery ceramic spoon—she couldn't master the sticks—placed a little of the mixture on her tongue and rolled it around. The dark sauce gave it a salty flavor. She sprinkled it over everything.

"Now, you China girra," Ah Sen said with a round-faced grin. She scissored and clicked her sticks from plate to mouth in what always seemed to Mae a feat for a sideshow in a county fair. How on earth did Chinese mothers teach little children to do that? White children had a hard time with forks.

Mae had adjusted to eating vegetables in the morning, drinking tea instead of coffee, and seeing Chinese script on bottles and crates. She was still in awe of the way Ah Sen's fingers flew over the beads of her abacus in an incomprehensible way of doing arithmetic. After breakfast Mae wiped out the wok and washed the bowls, cups, chopsticks, and spoons while Ah Sen stowed things away, and then hefted the wash bucket to the wok-stovetop. She added wood to the fire and then beckoned Mae outside, where forty to fifty unsuspecting chickens pecked and scratched around the house.

As a young child Mae hadn't been able to watch the beheadings. She'd been protected from it after that shocking first time—bawling in horror when the chicken she'd once tended as a fuzzy yellow chick staggered across the yard headless. Farley had howled with laughter when the poor thing finally keeled over. Mae had been angry with him ever since.

Ah Sen waited with her hatchet, an empty crate beside her. "You catchum," she said, standing beside the stump in the front yard. "You hord 'em. Ah Sen chop."

Mae chased pullets all over yard and garden, but the young birds must have divined her murderous intent. Protesting loudly they fluttered up out of her grasp and then glided into the trees. Mae redoubled her efforts, but they all evaded her.

Ah Sen dropped the hatchet on the dry ground. "You watchee."

She strolled around like she was out for a walk, tossing grass seed from her pocket. The chickens returned and pecked at it. Soon they were crowding around. In a quick move she caught a squawking hen. Holding the feet in one hand and the head in the other, she stretched the flapping bird over the stump with its neck centered. "Chop!"

Mae chopped so hard the blade sank into the stump. Warm blood sprayed on her arm and smock, a small geyser of it pulsing out the severed neck.

Ah Sen dropped the bird in the crate and yanked the hatchet from the stump. "Now you catchum; I chop." Putting a hand on her lower back in explanation, she transferred seed from her own pocket to Mae's.

Mae did her best to imitate Ah Sen. It worked. She caught two more pullets. They flapped their frantic wings, scratched her with their claws, and tried to peck her as she held the scaly legs in one hand and the heads in the other, careful with the beak while Ah Sen chopped. She hadn't counted on the astonishing strength of young life trying to survive against something much bigger than itself, struggling with every fiber of its being to get free of a betrayer who had seemed friendly but was beholden to a force beyond the ken of those picked to die. All of that showed in the terrified round eyes. This struggle, though fought with wing, claw and beak, touched Mae, and she felt a kinship. That, and the mounting odor of blood as the headless pullets stumbled around the crate bumping into each other and clamoring over the fallen—made her breakfast lurch up. Three times. Ah Sen waited.

Mae wiped her mouth on the hem of the tunic, determined to be a better helper. But they had seventeen more birds to kill and she couldn't conceive of lasting that long. Nonetheless, it was with determined effort that she made it to eight, with pauses for ejecting "wedgetabos" and more tea than she possibly could have drunk. After each episode her head felt lighter, her legs weaker. Finally Ah Sen handed her the hatchet and, despite her aching back, did the catching and holding while Mae chopped.

By the time twenty headless pullets were dying in the crate, Mae had to lie down on the dirt, arms outstretched, eyes closed against the brightness. Everything smelled of blood, even the dirt. She had failed Ah Sen, just as she failed Mary Granlees, and failed Mrs. Clayton at the Water Institute.

She opened her eyes to see Ah Sen standing over her with red hands and blood-spattered tunic, her cheeks and graying hair spotted with blood.

"I'm sorry," Mae moaned for about the tenth time this morning. "I'll be all right now. I can pluck fast." She knew this had taken longer than Ah Sen had figured. They should be half finished plucking by now. The driver she'd hitched a ride with would come before noon.

The old woman went in the house and returned with warm water in a large ceramic bowl. She washed her arms and hands in it. "Comee," she said, extending a hand.

Mae felt ashamed—a young girl being pulled up by an old woman with back pain. It was in this posture, pushing herself up with one hand, Ah Sen pulling on the other, that she saw Billy McCoon emerge through the trees on the path from the road, barefoot as usual.

"You in trouble?" he called.

"No," Mae moaned. Kneeling at the bowl, she immersed her arms to wash away the blood, vomit, and dirt. Billy was looking at the vomit on the ground.

"I'm drivin' Ah Sen to Sacramento," he said.

She hadn't known that they knew each other. He, on the other hand, didn't seem surprised to see Mae there, only that she'd been on the ground.

"I came early," he said, looking at the headless birds. "To help."

"Tankee," Ah Sen told him. "We pruck now. Need mo wata."

"Got a bucket?" he inquired.

Ah Sen pointed to the back of the house.

Billy fetched large bucket made of woden slats and headed to the river. By the little lines around his eyes and neck, Mae had judged him to be in his forties, but he strode up the steep levee with the grace and bounce of a young boy.

Inside the overheated house Ah Sen removed her stained dress while Mae opened the windows. The old woman had no modesty. Her bare body looked pale, none of her yellow—her face, neck and lower arms brown. Undressing and putting on the clean dress her employer tossed her, Mae waited until Ah Sen turned her back to stoke the fire. The shapeless tunics had no buttons, just two hooks at the shoulder. Pulling it on made her lightheaded again, and she was glad to sit at the table. One thing seemed certain. If Billy had any notions, seeing her smeared with blood, vomit, dirt and feathers would have put an end to it.

From a tin box, Ah Sen shook out a bunch of soda crackers on the table. As Mae nibbled a crisp cracker, Billy came through the door with water. Ah Sen rinsed her face in it, as did Mae, feeling Billy's eyes on her. He and Ah Sen would have long hours to talk on the drive to Sacramento, perhaps about her. But fortunately no white people were likely to hear of her secret from either of them.

Billy brought in the crate of dead pullets and a bunch of gunnysacks from under the house, some for the regular feathers, others for the down. Then he sat beside Mae, rolling up his sleeves. Ah Sen took a hammer from her shelf and tacked the gunnysacks to the edge of the table, two before Mae and two before Billy, so they hung open between their legs. With the water now boiling, she scalded the first bird, loosening the feathers. She left it in about two minutes and then laid the first steaming bird in front of Mae.

Having plucked many a chicken Mae knew to pull with the grain. She plucked as fast as she could, careful to get every stubborn feather, including the down, and to put the feathers in the right sacks. The next bird went to Billy. He was surprisingly skillful despite hands hardened by farm work. He seemed to be catching up with her. She dropped her first plucked bird into a pile just a little ahead of him. Ah Sen scalded chickens faster than they could be plucked, so the pile of steaming birds grew.

"You taking Mr. Grimshaw's produce to market?" Mae asked Billy as they worked.

"Yup. Corn and tomatoes." When he dropped his pullet in the crate his glance met hers. It told her that he'd felt no disgust at all at the sight of her today. The plane of his cheek caught the light from the open door, and his blunt hair hung straight and black around his face, shorter than it had been when he'd told her he wanted to care for her and the baby. She couldn't pretend that hadn't been said. And the constant weight of it hung between them. Also the mystery of him—an older man from a primitive people, as Indians were called. This situation seemed wildly out of kilter.

When the last scalded bird lay on the pile, Ah Sen sat across the table.

With three people plucking, the feathers were soon removed. Now came the gutting.

"I've never done that before," Mae admitted.

"Birry and Ah Sen cut," her employer said. "Git brue bowl." She jerked her head toward the door.

Mae went outside, threw the rust-colored water across the dry ground and brought in the ceramic bowl to receive the innards. The two of them worked fast with their knives, slitting the birds down the front, careful not to nick the organs, which would also be sold. They cracked the backs and spread the ribs to get their hands inside to pull out the entrails, which sometimes came out in a pale sack that included the other organs. The pile of cleaned birds grew on the table.

"I'll go wash the crate and get more water," Mae told them. It wouldn't do to transport the washed birds to market in a dirty crate.

Ah Sen's sharp nod sent her on her way. She threw the steaming dirty water into the yard and hurried over the levee with bucket, bloodied crate, and the scrub brush. Pulling off her shoes she waded into the river made warm by the summer heat and gave the crate a good cleaning. For some reason there wasn't much sand and silt in the water. When she returned, Ah Sen looked up with a smile, obviously pleased.

Mae laid the cleaned crate on the table and washed the gutted birds in the fresh water, cutting away any dung left in their hind ends. She laid the finished pullets in the wet crate, six abreast and five bird-lengths down the long side. As Billy helped wash and arrange the birds their fingers touched. That touch seemed to linger, and it made him suddenly more real to her, less primitive.

"Were you close to your father?" Mae asked. Your white father.

"I can't hardly remember him."

"So your mother raised you?

"Yup."

He remained a mystery.

Ah Sen stood up groaning and stretching her back. "Pi-up," she said to Mae, wiggling a hand at the feathers that had escaped to the floor. She went outside and around to back of the house.

Mae stuffed errant feathers into a sack and took the puffy sacks under the house. Billy did too. When she returned, he opened the screen for her, his green eyes on her while his shoulder and arm momentarily sheltered her. That feeling of shelter also seemed to linger.

"Thanks," she said quietly.

"You pluck good," he said. He pushed his sleeves down over muscular forearms.

"You too. Do you always help Ah Sen with her chickens?"

Eyes half-shut and standing about four feet away, his expression was hard to fathom. The male solidity of him unsettled her. Not that she'd been at ease for a single moment since this day began.

Ah Sen's voice was muffled, "Bling chicken."

Mae looked through the screen at what appeared to be a haystack on ill-fitting farmer's shoes with the tops flapping open—Ah Sen under a load of straw. Billy and Mae both smiled to see that, and she noticed him watching her smile.

Ah Sen told him to cover the double layers of pullets with cloths from her shelf and to follow her to the wagon. "Keep chicken coor," she explained walking down the pathway with the huge pile of straw in her arms, carefully steering it around tree limbs that she knew from memory.

Billy and Mae were draping the crate when Ah Sen returned. She went inside and returned with the shotgun. Thrusting it into Mae's hands, "Shoo man, boy, dog, coyo stea chicken."

"You mean shoot anything that steals chickens or eggs?"

Dipping her chin, Ah Sen pulled her trigger finger in the air. "Shoo!" She dropped a handful of cartridges into Mae's pocket. "Mo burwet." She touched the firing mechanism with her index finger. "Gun leady."

With the shotgun in her arm, Mae watched Billy carry the crates of melons and pullets up the pathway to the road, two trips. Ah Sen stayed at the wagon packing the straw around the pullets while he returned for the five-gallon jar of brined eggs.

As the wagon rattled away, Mae turned back through the trees and bushes. She doubted she could shoot anyone for stealing eggs, but she would scare them. She liked the feel of a gun in her hands. Now, if Oberon came for her, she would shoot him point blank in the face, drag him to the river, and push him out in the current.

And something else was new. Billy. The way he'd stood in the middle of the house and filled it up. He wasn't just a half-breed. He was a man.

67

Mae had the gun upright between the bed and the wall where she could whip it out fast. But all that long night nothing stirred but a fat harvest moon floating past the window, accompanied by screech owls and the long-winded warbling of coyotes, fugues that Bach himself would have admired for their convoluted complexity. How on earth, Mae wondered, had those hated livestock-killers survived ten years of government poisoning? Charlie claimed hundreds of thousands of coyotes had been exterminated across the country, and yet here they were, loudly proclaiming their whereabouts.

Marveling at the resilience of life, she finally let go and slept.

At about noon the next day Billy and Ah Sen returned. He had to get the wagon back to Mr. Grimshaw right away, so Mae waved good-bye and helped Ah Sen stow away the Chinese food from Sacramento. Late in the day when the chickens hopped to their roosts and she shut their door, she went up the trail to sit on the levee and think. It wasn't easy talking to Ah Sen. A couple of times over the last week she'd tried to ask whether the herbs that got rid of a baby would be harmful to a girl. Ah Sen couldn't seem to find the words to give a satisfying answer. She said something about the Indians knowing about that medicine, but finally quit with a shrug.

The wind died down taking the chill with it. It had blown most of the leaves off the trees and Mae could now see parts of the river, brassy in the low sun. There was something moving on the trail, in and out of the tangle of bare branches. The black mop of a man's head, Billy McCoon. Finished with his work. He looked up and beckoned her.

"Wanna come walk?" he called.

She made her way down to him, glad to walk that river path with a man, not by herself as she was often tempted to do. It wasn't just the fear of Oberon. Ah Sen had seen a puma down there.

For about half an hour she followed Billy on the trail softened by the newly fallen leaves. The scent of moisture in the air brought out the nice smell of something akin to sage. They didn't talk and their steps made little sound. The vultures circled the half-dead cottonwood tree where they would roost. Those strange silent birds were said to vomit on those who approached their eggs, but yet in some ways they were like chickens, staying in flocks. Now they were finding roosts in the bare branches where they always slept.

She thought Billy might say something about her being pregnant—surely he and Ah Sen has talked about it on that long ride—but he said nothing. She felt safe and comfortable with him, and she loved the feeling of being small under these tall trees with the river whispering by. This was how she'd felt in that beautiful Sacramento cathedral, with God present.

Billy stopped, said it would soon be dark, and led the way back to what he called China Trail, where he'd found her. She agreed to meet him there the next day after his work. She looked forward to it, even though she hadn't spent a single moment on what she ought to be thinking about.

The next day he showed up again just after sundown and they walked again in the gloaming. This time she told him how she'd run away from Charlie, but mostly they just shared another evening walk and enjoyed the good weather while it lasted. On a detour around a blackberry bramble he said the river was low on account of the rains being late, and with the downstream farmers irrigating pastureland the flow was down even more. Salmon were in trapped in pools.

Ahead of her on the narrow path Billy placed his bare feet with measured care yet with balance and speed. His shirt stretched across the wide wing bones of his shoulders but bloused loose from the waistband of his worn and faded trousers. "They're swimmin' round and round," he said, "waitin' for rain."

"A lot of them?"

"Fifty, sixty."

"How do you know that?"

"I go look."

A self-appointed overseer of the river, Billy thought nothing of walking twenty miles. She imagined those salmon swimming in circles. "Do you take a bucket and catch them, I mean for your supper?"

"Yup."

The small birds were leaving for their nests. Overhead and all around, the red leaves of grapevines fell like bunting from the trees, cascading red against yellow in the cottonwoods and down through the naked alders. Orange-red rose hips blazed on both sides of the trail. An autumn poem came to mind, one that Sister Delphine had loved. Mae recited it to the tempo of her steps.

> *The morns are meeker than they were,*
> *The nuts are getting brown;*
> *The berry's cheek is plumper,*
> *The rose is out of town.*

Billy turned toward her. "What's that you sayin'?"

"A poem by Emily Dickinson. Here's the rest of it:

> *"The maple wears a gayer scarf,*
> *The field a scarlet gown.*
> *Lest I should be old-fashioned,*
> *I'll put a trinket on."*

He'd kept his head tilted as though corraling every word in his ear. Then he smiled.

"That last line makes me smile too," she said.

"I doan git some of it," he said, "but I like it. You a friend of Emily Dick…. Er, what's her name?"

"Dickinson. No I don't know her. I memorized that in school, from a book." She sighed and looked around them. "Oh, how I'd love to have a gown of all these browns and reds and golds. It's so beautiful!"

His chiseled cheek was turned to her as he gazed across the darkening water, his voice quiet. "I didn't know they learned that kinda thing in school. Guess I only heard 'bout the bad stuff."

"Didn't you go to school?"

"No."

Likely, he couldn't read a word.

He turned to her, voice scratchy with emotion, "Mae, you're beautifuler than all this." He opened his arms wide.

Her face burned hot, this being so unexpected. She had Ah Sen's old dress on and hadn't even brushed her hair. Yesterday she'd seen how he loved this river where his mother's people had lived from time immemorial. But for him to say that! It caused something to melt inside her—a wall, she realized, that she'd built up to keep him out. It slumped like warm beeswax.

"It's getting dark," she said. "I think we should go back."

Now she walked in front and his soft footfalls behind her went straight to her heart. His silence, and hers, felt strained, so she returned to the subject of fish. "Will all those salmon die? Seems like they wouldn't have enough to eat."

"They doan wanna eat. They wanna lay eggs 'an make baby fish."

"Why don't they just lay their eggs where they are?"

"They don't feel like doin' it there. They wanna feel the water movin' just so. They wanna see the rocks and pebbles on the bottom just so. When they get to their home place the bucks chase the doe fish around. That's how they do it. In the spring thousands of eggs hatch."

"And the parents swim back to the ocean?"

"No. They have a big time and they die right where they are, upriver. Indians have a big time eatin'm too. So do eagles, gulls, bears—" He stopped for a few moments, and then continued, "before the grizzly bears all got killed."

"That's sad. I mean, the salmon dying after they mate."

"That's how they do it. Only one time. They want it perfect."

He told her that the hydraulic mining in Michigan Bar had flushed whole hillsides of clay into the river and covered up the salmon's pebbly nesting places, so nowadays most of the salmon died without mating or laying eggs. "They can't find their place."

She was thinking about that when his hand came down on her shoulder, stopping her. "Shh," he said at her ear.

After a while she heard a slight rustle in the bushes ahead.

"Mebbe deer," he whispered softly.

Night was falling fast. She couldn't see a thing.

The crack of a gun stopped her heart.

Oberon! With shock shooting down her arms and legs, she lunged into the leaves beside the trail, her shriek having given them away before she could stop it. Now the noise was coming from her booming heart.

Something crashed through the brush.

A gruff man demanded, "Who's there?"

After a silence, "Billy McCoon."

"What in tarnation you doing in my Thicket?" It was only Mr. Sheldon!

"Nuthin'."

Between the leaves she saw the dark figure with a rifle loom into view. He jabbed it at Billy. "G'on! Get off my property."

"Yes sir."

"Who's that woman you got there?"

In her mind she begged him not to give her away. But she'd never known Billy to lie.

"Just a girl."

"Billy," Mr. Sheldon said with steely determination, "I asked you a simple question and I expect the courtesy of an answer."

Billy's voice dropped half an octave. "Mae Duffy."

Acute shame withered her, her heart not yet recovered from the fear. But she understood that Billy sometimes worked for Mr. Sheldon and he had to stay on the good side of a man like that.

"Miss Duffy," Mr. Sheldon directed toward her, "I'd have thought you had more sense than to crawl around in the bushes at night with an Ind—" His anger shaded to exasperation. "Go on, both of you. You damn well know the rules Billy. The Thicket's off limits to all but my family and guests. Next time you could get killed."

The leaves rustled and she felt Billy's probing hand. She couldn't think how to get out of the brambles with the thorns digging at her from all directions.

Billy murmured, "Come." Gently he tugged her arm.

When she got to her feet and yanked the tunic free of the brambles, Billy said, "Sorry, Mr. Sheldon, we musta passed China Trail a ways back. Won't do it again."

Billy walked her back the way they'd come. Her face was hot with shame, not just on account of what Mr. Sheldon must be thinking. Billy had seen her wild fear of Oberon, something he wouldn't understand. He might think less of her, like Charlie had.

A few minutes later they walked past Ah Sen's lamp-lit window framing the old lady as she sewed at the table. Mae lifted the door latch. "Come in a minute," she told Billy. "I got something to say."

Inside, Ah Sen got up from her chair, frowning at the sight of her. "Oooh, brud," she said tracing a line down Mae's forehead and cheek, and down her arm and hand. She dipped a clean rag in the wash bucket and dabbed at the blood, saying, "Ah Sen heaw gun."

"Just Mr. Sheldon out hunting," Billy said.

She frowned at Mae. "Burret gitchu?"

"No. I was scared and fell in the berry bushes." Ah Sen was finished with her.

"Sit down Billy. You too, Ah Sen. I need to tell you something." She walked to the dark window, gathering strength as the two sat at the table. Her reflection was frightful—hair standing on end, blood still trickling down her face.

"You see," she said, walking back to the table, "I'm afraid of guns more than most people, and I think it's because of what happened to me in Sacramento."

Seating herself at the corner of the table looking at both of them, she started at the beginning, telling how she'd gone to the saloon that night but not revealing her intention to meet Butch. Her jaw tightened more with the words that brought her nearer to the long and humiliating time with Oberon. The stove kept the house warm and yet she shivered like she was freezing. She hurried past the part about Oberon tricking her into staying at his place. She'd been such a fool! The muscles in her face grew tired and stiff with the effort to talk, like she had lockjaw. Of a sudden her calf muscle started twitching.

"I was there for weeks. Chained to a pipe like a dog," she blurted out. "He said he'd come after me. Kill me if I got away. And I did, get away that is. Ran away."

They only looked at her. They did not say they were sorry to hear that.

It occurred to her that she hadn't been able to look them in the eye, and with all she'd left out, her story sounded untrue. Like a child telling a lie. Not about to tell them what Oberon used her for, she tried to relieve the tightness in her mouth and throat by telling the easier part about how clever he was as the Inspector for the Sacramento Police, and how good at finding people. She spent some time on that, but continued to shiver, and still couldn't look them in the eye.

Ah Sen kept sewing as though hearing an ordinary story.

Billy also seemed to take it lightly. But they were both good at masking their thoughts, she reminded herself. Billy, after an awkward pat on Mae's shoulder, pushed up from the table, stretched, and said he was tired and his bed was three miles away.

With clamped jaw Mae got up and followed him out the door. She couldn't let him leave thinking she was a lily-livered liar fabricating a story to make them pity her. The screen door banged behind her.

In the cool blue light of a quarter-moon, Billy turned toward her with indistinct features. She couldn't tell what he was thinking. Why should she care? Why was it so hard to explain? God only knew what half-breeds and Indians had lived through. Maybe things far worse. She hugged her arms to stop the shivering. "I just wanted you to know *why* the gunshot scared me so."

Suddenly she saw herself the way she was at the Steffens' place when that other gun went off—on her hands and knees quaking with fear and crawling around trying to hide among the hems of the ladies' gowns and the shoes of powerful men. That gunshot turned out to be a joker sporting with the guests, but she'd made an awful fool of herself. Was it any wonder Charlie wouldn't marry her after seeing that, in front of his friends and colleagues?

"You do believe me, don't you? I mean his coming to kill me." *Unlike Charlie.*

Billy stepped to her and put his arms around her like she was made of fragile glass. He gentled her ear into the cushion of warm muscle beneath the fabric of his shirt. The steady thump of his heart, startlingly near, spoke its own language and she understood it. It was pounding for the love of her. In the wonder of it, her jaw let go its tightness and she stopped shivering. She hugged him around the chest, his heart booming faster and louder. His words resounded through the drumming, bellowed by his lungs and amplified by the nearness of his voice box.

"If that man comes to git you, I'll kill 'im."

The door squeaked open but did not shut. "Birry, you wan stay. It's awlight."

Mae looked up at his face as he continued to hold her, his eyes closed as if silently praying to the moon. His heart shook her to the bone.

"Yes," she whispered, "Stay."

68

As the coyotes wove their eerie preludes that night, and the moon moved across the sky, all she could think about was what a sweet man Billy had turned out to be. He'd tried not to tell Mr. Sheldon who she was. He understood her embarrassment. He'd said she was more beautiful than autumn, and his heart had told her that he cared for her more than Charlie ever had. And he wanted to take care of her and the baby.

Now she couldn't hear him breathing and suspected that he was lying awake too, on a very hard floor that a thin old quilt wouldn't much soften. She imagined him naked—those strong arms and shoulders, and strong legs. Did he wish to be holding her, as she wished to hold him? For sure, living with Oberon and then Charlie had made her shameless.

Ah Sen, just across the room, was breathing steadily in her sleeping way, a little rattle at the upbeat of each breath.

Mae slipped off her cot in her loose camisole and long cotton underskirt. She could see the table and chairs in the moonlight from the window, but not Billy. He was down in the shadow on her side of the table.

She kneeled at his head whispering, "You awake?"

"Yes."

"It was selfish of me to ask you to stay. If you want to go back to your mother's house, go ahead. I'm all right."

He was silent for what felt a long time.

"You want me to go?"

"Oh no. I'm just saying I'll be all right if you do. The floor's hard."

Ah Sen's breathing was the only sound in the chilly house.

He got up on an elbow, high enough for his eye to glisten in the moonlight. "You're awake 'cause I'm here," he said.

That was true. "It was unfair of me to ask you to stay."

Billy's hand touched her arm and slid slowly down to her hand, leaving goose bumps along the way. He lifted her hand and kissed her palm with soft lips, whispering, "I just wanna be where you are. Doan care where it's at."

That from a man who'd seen her lying in vomit and chicken blood. She wondered if he wanted her because she was white. Or maybe, just maybe, he could feel the way she felt about him. That frightened her. Life didn't work that way. You didn't run from one man to another and love them both. She'd never heard of such a thing, not even in dime novels. And what did it mean to love a person? In spite of all the Iowa boys who'd sworn they loved her, in spite of her feelings for Charlie, she still didn't know the answer. People talked a lot about love but never explained it. All she knew for sure was that with Billy she felt like a small flake of iron beside a powerful magnet.

"I'll go, if you want," he whispered.

"If you did, I wouldn't be able to do this."

She surprised herself by quietly lifting his quilt and lying down next to his warm body, her head in the crook of his shoulder, and pulled the quilt over them. Another surprise: the floor wasn't hard at all, and Ah Sen's breathing, of which she'd been so very aware, disappeared. She felt safe and secure with Billy, loving the scent of his neck and the beat of his heart. She realized that a baby must feel this way wrapped in its father's arms. And come to think of it, Billy was old enough to be her father.

"Let's just hold each other," she whispered, moving an arm over his chest. "Then maybe we can sleep. You have a long day of work tomorrow."

"Yes." He turned to her, put his arm over her, and kissed her forehead.

ᔤ

In the morning when Ah Sen lit the fire, Mae was back on her cot, Billy gone. Out the windows dark clouds hid the sun. It looked like rain. Maybe the salmon would be freed from their watery prisons.

"Won't you let me help you chop the vegetables?" Mae said.

This time Ah Sen agreed. They worked together on the little table next to the wok-stove, and it felt right, both of them weeping over the onion that Ah Sen was chopping.

"Did Billy work for you before I came here? I mean like driving you to Sacramento?" She wiped tears with her sleeve.

Ah Sen shook her head, no. "You in house, Birry come."

He must have followed her that first day. Saw her from the field.

Ah Sen gathered Mae's sliced carrots and dropped them in the wok with her sizzling onions and Chinese cabbage. She doused it with a new bottle of dark liquid, whipped four eggs, poured them over the vegetables, and stirred. By now the wok seemed to Mae a very sensible stovetop.

"Did he talk about me when you were driving to Sacramento?"

Filling Mae's bowl, Ah Sen nodded. "Birry rikee you."

"How long have you known him?"

She shrugged. "Rong time. My man say Birry goo boy. Inyan mamma."
"Billy's likely forty years old. Not a boy."

On her chair, just clamping the first mouthful of breakfast between her sticks, Ah Sen looked up with a grin that showed the missing teeth behind her eye teeth. "O rady say, he boy." She popped in the food and chewed, her mouth open and still smiling at Mae as it rolled around.

The next three nights Billy slept on the floor. Ah Sen invited him to live with them. She wanted him to build a fence around her yard and garden. But Billy told Mae in private that he didn't feel right living there. She agreed. Even though Ah Sen had spent years as a plaything for men, it didn't feel right to do things under her nose.

That didn't stop them from going to a hidden place in the river bottom when there was a break in the rain. There they gave in to a force as old as creation. It felt new and different with Billy, almost like they were learning together. His hands were slow and gentle. Absent the worry about getting pregnant, she opened completely to him, and he took her to a place in her soul where she'd never gone before, a secret garden far from the real world. And though that place would be judged wicked by the rest of the world, to her it was more than good.

In the mornings she hated to see Billy leave for his work, and in the evenings she loved watching him eat at Ah Sen's supper table. At night it tortured her to have him on the floor beside her bed, so near and yet so far. Billy said it was hard for him too. But they couldn't lie together without igniting a fire neither of them could put out. The problem was, Billy had no house. From the time he was seven years old he'd lived away from home while working for ranchers and dairymen. Lately, he'd been staying with his mother some of the time. Except for Farley, he might have worked for Mr. Long, and then he and Mae could have lived in the stone house.

She felt herself rushing headlong into something again, not danger or rejection—what more rejection could there be?—but the end of a dream, the one she'd hoped would come true when she attained the name Mrs. Rogue. She had loved rubbing elbows with the wealthy leaders of California. She'd liked hearing ladies discuss whether women should be allowed to vote. It had tickled something inside her to hear Lincoln Steffens and Charlie talking about whether there was any democracy left in the country. Billy couldn't talk about such things. In her wildest dreams she had imagined living on Nob Hill with servants and a nanny to look after her children. She and Charlie would have sipped port in the parlor and read newspapers. She would have arranged fine affairs for the rich and famous of San Francisco, including the Tevises from the Peninsula. She'd loved visiting with Mrs. Tevis, the daughter of a former Governor. That's what she was throwing away, the chance of socializing with such people.

With Billy, she'd always be an outsider. He didn't have a dollar to rent a room.

Yes, she still had a hundred and fifty dollars in the pocket of her day dress, folded inside an old crate left by Mrs. Smith and pushed under her cot. But that wasn't enough to get by on for long, and she couldn't bring herself to mention it to Billy. Something in her had changed when Oberon forced her to give him every cent she had. Not that Billy was anything like Oberon. Not that she didn't trust him, but maybe he would spend it all for something she didn't want. And it was more than that. It just felt wrong to hand all her money to a grown man, unless it was back to Charlie after he came to marry her. She'd seen how things could change in the twinkling of an eye, especially for a poor person. The money could be stolen from Billy. He could get in an accident and lie unconscious while someone picked his pocket. Selfish or not, she cared about that money more than anyone else did, and that's why she kept it a secret from Ah Sen and Farley and Billy.

On Saturday, Mae put a handful of gold five-dollar pieces in her left pocket when Ah Sen wasn't looking. Then she talked Ah Sen into letting her deliver the day's eggs to the Cosumne Store. Her employer was grateful; the mile walk made her hip sore. So Mae took the small wood-partitioned crate of straw-packed eggs to the clerk in the store. He paid her and gave her an empty box for tomorrow. She put Ah Sen's money in her right skirt pocket.

"I was wondering," she told the clerk, "If I could look at some guns."

"What kind?" Standing there in his black suit and stiff white collar, with tufts of unruly hair pointing straight up from his head, he looked surprised. A few boxed rifles were on the shelf behind him.

"I want one I can put in my skirt pocket and not have it be seen."

"Hmm. Well, how about a Smith and Wesson Safety Hammerless revolver, in .32 caliber. They come in three-inch or three-and-a-half-inch barrels. Good size for a lady. Easy to conceal."

She asked to see one.

"We don't keep all those specialty models on hand, but I could order anything you want."

"Would I need to pay in advance?"

"Uh-uh."

"How much are they?"

"About ten dollars, a little more depending on the model." He reached under the counter and pulled out a small catalog. He thumbed through it and ran a finger down several pages of handguns. Mae could see the drawings. "Most ladies like guns with three-inch barrels. Here's one," he said turning the catalog around.

Very different from the Colt she'd fired from the roof of the moving train.

The man was saying, "You press down on that latch there with your thumb. See it?" He seemed to be pointing to a small metallic thing on the grip. "That makes the gun drop open and the barrel tip downward. You put the cartridge in there. Pull the barrel back up and you're ready to fire. If there'd been a spent cartridge in there you'd have to throw it away."

"Where's the hammer?"

"This model doesn't have one. So you don't cock the revolver. You simply pull the trigger. A long, firm pull. A hammer would stick up in your pocket and give the gun away. Or it could snag on your skirt."

"My heavens." They've thought of everything.

He pursed his lips and jiggled his head up and down. "And that's not all. There's a safety grip. See it?" He took a pencil from the counter and pointed with the lead to something behind the grip on one of the guns. "When you pull the trigger, this lever unlocks the safety lock. That's supposed to keep children from firing it. That's why you need to squeeze hard and firm to make it work."

"You mean squeeze harder than a child could?"

"That's right."

"What if I was so scared I couldn't squeeze hard enough?"

He shrugged. "No squeeze, no bang." He looked at her like she was daft.

Maybe she was. Every one of those guns seemed to have a different way of working.

"Here's a dandy one with pearl grips." He pointed. "Some ladies like to show off. And there's this little one too. They just started making this last year. It's got a two-inch barrel, easier to conceal. It's called the Bicycle Model."

"A bicycle gun? Why that name?"

"They're popular with bicyclists. You know, to shoot dogs."

"How does it work?"

A lady was standing behind Mae waiting with three children and looking at the clerk, who was giving her signals to wait just a little longer.

"You'd buy special cartridges," he said to Mae.

By now Mae's mind was running over all the ways these guns could fail. Oberon was no dog, and she knew enough about guns to know you needed the right caliber bullet to kill a big animal, especially if you didn't aim well. And she wouldn't want to be opening the gun to throw away a spent cartridge when he was injured and coming after her. She might fail to squeeze the trigger hard enough on the first try, and then she'd be a goner. She'd have to buy a lot of cartridges and practice shooting.

One of the children waiting behind her cried out, "He kicked me!" There was a thud and another child screamed loud and long. The mother started scolding them.

Raising her voice to be heard over that, Mae said. "If I buy one now, could you take it back if I change my mind."

"No, ma'am."

"How long would it take to get here? After I ordered it?"

"At least six weeks. Maybe longer for the Bicycle Model. I think they sold out the first batch, and it could be a couple of months before they make a new batch. Like I said, they're popular now." He gave her a look. "Well, you ordering one?"

"I'll think on it," she said, relinquishing her place to the woman. She didn't know where she'd be in six weeks. Anywhere but this area would be safer. Even going to the store today had been dangerous. Oberon would come here to ask after her.

⌒

On Sunday Billy led her up the river trail to his mother's place. It had been raining for days and pouring all night. Now it sprinkled on the trail, on and off, and the overhanging trees pelted them with occasional big splats. They laughed like children, trying to dodge them. When the trail widened they held hands, swinging as they walked and laughing when they slipped in the mud, each trying to keep the other upright. Once they stood like statues when a coyote with a full coat of reddish fur trotted toward them on a trace to the left of the main trail. Fear jangled through Mae seeing the large size of this animal—she'd heard they were small. It passed within a few feet of them with a hank of dripping, furry meat dangling from its mouth. Intent on its footing, it never looked up, never saw them, but ducked into an opening in a tangle of brush.

Awed, Mae turned to Billy.

"Feedin' her pups," he said with a smile. He resumed his lead up the trail.

"I'm surprised she didn't smell us."

"We was upwind."

"I hope that meat wasn't poisoned."

"Naw, she's savvy to that."

"Then you don't believe they'll all be poisoned to extinction?"

He was quiet for a time. "Doan unnerstand that, exti—"

"Oh," sorry for making him feel bad, "it's just another way of saying all of that kind of animal has died out."

He nodded, taking that in as he continued walking in his balanced way.

Determined never again to make him aware of his lack of schooling, she tried to sound lighthearted, as before. "So, do you think the coyotes will all die out on account of the government poisoning?"

"Coyote don't never die."

That was an odd way of putting it.

The cool drizzle persisted, and by the time they reached Indian Mary's cabin they were drenched to the skin.

The unpainted cabin stood on the north bank of the river just downstream of the bridge. It tilted slightly on little rock piles that kept it out of the mud. The Pratts and Driscoll-Granlees called this the north side of the river, but Billy made a point of it being on the northwest bank. One thing about Indians, they knew their directions.

As Billy stepped on the flat rock of a stoop, a skinny little girl in a flour-sack dress came out the door and ran past him and Mae without a word. She seemed not to see either of them. "My sister's girl," Billy explained as he opened the door for Mae.

The warm, neat house smelled of everything old. It was smaller than Ah Sen's, but also had cots on opposite sides of the room and a table and four chairs in the middle. Hanging on the wall, on nails, were a man's hat and patched trousers.

Old Indian Mary oddly pretended they weren't there. Mae felt tongue-tied looking at this dark-skinned woman in the steamy warmth of the cabin. She wore the same black frock, the hem of which brushed the tops of her callused brown feet. In the dim light her black eyes sparkled with interest, perhaps pleasure, as she glanced past Mae. Billy had warned that his mother wouldn't look her in the eye when she talked, and she wouldn't talk to him at all for a while. Mae recalled that awkward conversation with old Mary on that summer day long ago.

As she and Billy warmed up at the kitchen stove, Indian Mary shook dried berries from an old can into three tin cups and poured hot water over them from a blackened kettle. Billy explained that he slept here when his sister was gone for long spells.

"Baby likes me 'cause I sleep in her bed and then she can sleep with her grandma."

Mary set the three steaming cups on the table, and they all sat down. She said nothing to Billy as he introduced Mae, but, glancing past him, said to Mae, "Good you come. We talked before."

"Yes. And I want to thank you for telling me about Mrs. Miser. She's become a friend of mine. You gave good directions."

She smiled as Mary nodded, "Good lady."

"Yes. I like her a lot. Agnes too."

"Lotsa sheep."

"Yes. They own a lot of land."

The hot berry tea tasted sour and almost lemony. Good.

Billy spoke directly to his mother. "Mae and I want a place to live. And I wanna work in a place where they think I'm white so they'll pay money." He looked at Mae. "She has a baby in her."

Old Mary didn't seem a bit surprised, nor did she seem upset with her son, as Mae thought other mothers would have been if their son brought in a pregnant girl.

There was a note of respect in Billy's voice when he spoke to his mother. "Mebbe you know a place for us."

Not looking at him, Mary said, "Omo Ranch Mine is open. Linnie Hickey wants a man to work. Mebbe doan know you my boy."

"She Indian?"

Mary wagged her head, no. "Tall. Red hair. Her man beat' er up. She gave 'im his pants and said get out." She had an engaging twinkle in her eye, and Mae realized she liked this old lady. She'd liked her before she knew Billy.

"Mebbe Omo Ranch," Billy told Mae. "Bout thirty-five miles from here. In the hills."

"Yes, maybe there, if there's a room for us."

"Linnie Hickey got lotta rooms," Mary said.

The door opened and the same skinny girl came in and stood staring at Mae with strange black eyes enlarged by the deep shadows around them. She couldn't have been over seven or eight, but her bony face looked old.

Mae leaned toward Billy and whispered, "What's her name?"

"Baby," he said in a normal pitch. "She'll get a name later."

That was strange. Baby continued her hollow stare from the door.

"She's a little tetched," Billy explained.

"Scary spirit comes at night," his mother added. "She don't sleep much. Talkin' to that spirit."

The child went to the wall, faced it, and sidestepped along it feeling her way and peeking over her shoulder now and then at Mae, clearly afraid of the new person in her house.

Mae averted her eyes, hoping to relieve the girl's fear. She asked Billy, "Does your sister come back often?"

"Sometimes." With a wink he added, "Then I sleep on the floor."

Mae smiled too, reminded of their tormented nights.

"Your mother go away," Old Mary said to Mae. Not a question.

"Yes, she went to New York."

Billy spoke the Indian language, and the two of them exchanged a couple of sentences. "Mebbe," he told Mae, "we oughta go." He started to get up.

"I'd like to ask her a question first."

Billy sat down again.

By now the strange little girl had made her way around the wall to the nearest point to her grandmother. She made a dash and climbed into Mary's ample lap and snuggled her nose into her grandmother's big bosom.

"I was wondering," Mae said, "if you know of Indian medicine to make the baby come out?" She put a hand on her abdomen.

Mary's eyes went there, and she nodded a definite yes.

Heartened, "Does that medicine do anything to harm the girl's health?"

Two faces looked at her—one big and dark, one small, pale, and bony.

"I mean, does that medicine make the mother sick? Could it kill her?"

"Mebbe. Too much, you die."

Away flew the hope of a harmless cure. "Maybe you could make her understand, Billy," she said to him, "I'd like to know exactly what that stuff does to a girl, *besides* getting rid of the baby."

He spoke to his mother in their tongue, Billy halting and slow.

"She says it depends," he said to Mae. "Some girls're strong. If the girl doan take enough, mebbe she gets a little sick an' the baby stays inside."

"But how sick does a strong girl get if she takes enough to make it work?"

He talked to his mother again.

"She doan know," Billy said. "Depends on the girl, and how strong her spirit is."

Mae sighed. It seemed nobody knew the answer. "Thank you, Mary." Then she added for no particular reason, "The baby isn't Billy's."

"She knows," Billy interjected. "Says all babies is blessings."

"Does she think I'm wicked if I get shed of it?"

"Not wicked. Mebbe you just doan want that blessing."

"Maybe I don't. And I don't want to go to Omo Ranch until I figure it out one way or the other. Your mom's the only one who can help me if it's what I decide." She loved it that they didn't see her as evil either way. That took half a load off her.

Standing up, he put his hands on her shoulders and said again, "I wanna be daddy to your baby."

"Yes, I know." she said, getting to her feet. "That's one thing I love about you."

There, she'd said it in front of his mother. Another thing she loved about him, he always meant what he said.

69

They walked back on the river trail toward Ah Sen's place, where Mae had promised to pluck chickens for the evening meal. When they were almost there the rain clouds parted, unveiling a red sun on the horizon. Red-gold light flooded through the trees, enchanting the bottomland. The masses of bare outer twigs on the oaks were a mauve halo around each tree, and the long bony fingers and gnarled limbs and trunks, normally pale gray in their lichen sleeves, now glowed a bright yellow-green. The scene was a stained glass window with sunlight blazing through. Mae felt herself inside a fairy tale with the oak trees smiling to have surprised her so.

"Billy, just look at these colors!" she gestured around.

He pointed up behind them.

"Oh, a rainbow. A double rainbow!" she cried. Two giant arches stood out against the rain-dark sky to the north and east.

Billy put an arm around her and said quietly, "Some say it's Coyote peein'."

That struck her as a crude desecration. "How can you say such an awful thing about rainbows?"

"Old Indians say that." He kept smiling. "They say Coyote made people, so I guess he can pee where he wants." He squeezed her shoulders. "Some white people doan open their eyes to it. Workin' too hard I guess."

His smile was so warm, his arm so friendly, that she couldn't help but hug him back despite what he'd said. But she corrected him on one point. "White people do too see rainbows. They look for them. Everyone loves a rainbow."

They resumed walking, hand in hand in the enchanted wood, and she told him about Noah and about God's promise not to drown the world again. She also told him that the leprechauns of Ireland put a pot of gold at the end of every rainbow.

He chuckled. "An folks doan never find that gold."

"No, but every boy and girl sure goes a-looking."

"So leprechauns like to fool people?"

"Yes, they do it all the time."

"Like Coyote. Is a leprechaun a shape-changer too? Changin' into other things?"

"Yes, I think so. Sometimes a rabbit or a bird, or a rock." The similarity in folk tales surprised her.

Avoiding the wet bushes, they walked single file again, Billy in front. Mae recalled how Gramps had loved his "emerald isle." But no green could be brighter than the lichens on these trees in this light. The sun was half gone now but still suffusing everything with magic. The trail took them to the river's edge, where brassy wavelets rose and fell on their way to the ocean.

Billy stopped, pointed, his voice high with excitement. "Salmon. See there?"

"You mean that ripple over there?"

"That's a fin pokin' up. Look. There's more! See 'em comin'?"

She caught his excitement. They were swimming against the current like faithful sailors, near the surface, fins breaking through now and again. She counted five, no six, seven!

He turned to her, the last of the sun crowning him with a reddish halo. "I'll sleep at Ma's tonight an' catch some salmon for her. Come mornin' I'll bring a big'n to you and Ah Sen."

He wouldn't be there tonight and it felt like pain. "Will you help me pluck the chickens when we get back?" Actually she wanted to talk to him about his mother's herbs.

"Yes." He kissed her tenderly, then passionately.

The earth made a quarter turn, like a merry-go-round under her feet.

"We're about at our lovin' place," he murmured.

༺ ༻

That evening they ate chicken pulled by Ah Sen into bite-sized shreds. She stirred it with some new vegetables from Sacramento, including delectable juicy things called litchi nuts. She also steamed some rolls made of rice flour, a soft and silky texture that neither Billy nor Mae had eaten before. Inside each one was a little surprise, a piece of seasoned pork or cucumber.

Ah Sen said, "My mamma make." Her lips pressed in a shy smile.

This was a feast, Mae realized, a gift that dated back before that awful time of starvation when Ah Sen's mother sold her. For dessert they had chunks of bitter melon and red beans sweetened with a special syrup. Ah Sen didn't hide her joy that they'd smacked their lips and gobbled everything down.

When Billy was leaving, Mae went out on the stoop with him. She hadn't found the right moment to talk about what had been bothering her. Shivering from the cold, she said, "Maybe I should take that medicine and get rid of Charlie's baby."

Billy hugged her in that tender way of his. "The baby ain't his, it's yours," he said in a low tone. "Mine too, if you want."

"But, Billy, if we're going to be together maybe you'd rather not—"

"Doan matter none to me." The first time he'd ever interrupted her. "The baby'll come from you. I'll be poppa."

"But maybe it'd make me keep thinking about Charlie."

"Mebee," he said, but added in a thoughtful tone, "I never knowed my real pa much—that were Perry McCoon. I called Pedro papa."

She knew his mother had married a Pedro. "Did you grow up with him?"

"I growed up all right. My real dad died on a buckin' horse. Dragged to death. Lotta folks watchin'. Pedro won that contest. I saw it."

"How old were you?"

"Six. After that Pedro 'as my Papa."

"How old were you when Pedro died?"

"Eight or nine when he left, I guess. Said he'd come back from drivin' horses to Mexico. Never did."

He told her a story about people getting Pedro mixed up with a bandit named Joaquin Murieta, a man whose head was put in a jar, and he said he still didn't know if it had been Pedro's head, despite what he'd told Isabella.

"Oh, heaven forbid!" Mae said. "It would'ov rotted."

"Not in brandy." He pulled away a bit. "They took it to the towns 'round about so folks could look at it and say if it 'as Joaquin Murieta. Got a dollar to say yes 'an wrote their names on a paper."

Her insides quivered. "Ugh! What a horrible story!"

"I dug around some to get it. Ma wouldn't talk."

"Why wouldn't she tell you about it?"

"Indians doan never talk about their dead."

Another of their strange ways. "Billy, you had an awful time when you were young, didn't you?"

It was cold and she was glad his arms were around her. She couldn't see his face but felt the vibration of his voice. "My pretty rose, alla us get stormy times sooner or later. Everbody. But them storms pass by. Mine did. Yours will too. We just gotta look forward, not to the past."

That brought tears to her eyes. She'd never known anyone like him, unschooled and yet so wise. It was dark now, clouds covering the stars and moon. A chilly wind whipped the bare branches of the trees-of-heaven, the seeds brought from China in the pockets of miners so they'd feel at home. "You'd best get along now," she whispered, kissing him on his cheek. "Don't want you to get hurt."

He kissed her on the hair. "I'll take the road."

That would add a mile, but he'd be less likely to meet up with a mountain lion. She watched him disappear into the darkness, and by the time she went back in the cozy house, Ah Sen was setting the last dishes on the shelf. Mae felt guilty after such a nice meal. "Sorry I didn't help with the dishes," she said.

The old lady pulled off her tunic and wiggled into an old nightshirt, a gift from her dead husband.

"O rady wan shut eye," she said climbing into bed. She pulled the coverlet to her chin and closed her eyes. In the lamplight her tan scalp showed through the gray hairs. Ah Sen wasn't sure how old she was, but thought she was probably about sixty-five.

"I don't mean to disturb you," Mae said, "but I was wondering if I could ask you a question."

"Ah Sen shut eye. Talk."

"Do you think I'd get sick if I took the medicine Billy's mother knows about, the herbs that get rid of, you know, the part in me that turns into a baby if it stays there?"

"Ahh, you talk Indian Melly 'bout dat."

"Yes. We talked a little about it. Could that medicine kill me?"

"Mebbeso sick. No baaad sick."

"You've heard about other girls taking it?"

"Some. Me too. San Flisco."

"Oh, you took it!"

"Six, sev time. Man no wan big girra." She patted her belly under the quilt but kept her eyes closed.

Six or seven times! And yet she had lived to be an old woman with rheumatism. "Was that medicine the same as the Indian herbs?"

"Mebbeso. China boss rady bling medcin. Mebee same."

Why did Charlie put his girls through that stabbing torture when the Chinese doctors had an easier way? Especially when he knew the best herbalist in California. But then it occurred to her that maybe Americans knew about the infection-stopping mushroom, but not the baby-stopping herbs, because they never asked.

"I think I'll do it," Mae heard herself saying, her heart stumbling a bit at the thought of another risk to her life.

The rattle at the upbeat of Ah Sen's breath said she was asleep.

I'll do it right away, then Billy and I can go up to Omo Ranch... She interrupted that thought with another. *I could go to New York.*

If I could pull myself away from Billy.

∽

Two days later Mae was back in Indian Mary's house. Mary had collected the herbs and was working at her stove. Mae watched her separate the enlarged and deformed purple-black seeds from stalks of spent grass. It was some kind of smut, like the kind that ruined corn in Iowa.

Billy was there too, this being Sunday and his day off from work. Baby was staring at Mae. Jumpy as a grasshopper on a hot stove, Mae left the cabin and walked up and down the pathway that led to Jackson Road. She could feel every thump of her heart.

Billy came out to get her, and when they went back inside the house the big woman sat her down at the table and began a quiet chant. This continued for some time, and it calmed Mae a little, reminding her that from times long ago countless women had taken this medicine and survived. Then Mary handed Mae a tin cup of warm black liquid, nodding for her to drink it.

Mae looked at Billy, who also nodded for her to drink it. She gulped down the awful stuff. It had an aftertaste like a dead mouse. She gagged a little but kept it down.

"You stay my house," Indian Mary said. "Two, three days."

"Oh." That came as a surprise. Ah Sen might need her to weed her winter garden. But without her saying that, Billy said he'd go see if he could help Ah Sen after his work at the Grimshaws. He was amazingly thoughtful, for a man.

The four of them roasted fresh salmon on pikes over an outdoor fire. Mary fried bread dough in a pan over the same fire, and they ate that and the fresh tender fish, and Mae managed a few bites of a tasteless acorn pudding. So far she felt nothing unusual. Soon after supper Billy and Mae curled up together in the cot he normally occupied by himself, while Baby slept with her grandmother.

"Baby's good with you here," Billy whispered.

Whispering back. "She never talks."

"But she's good with you here. No screaming."

"Does she scream a lot?"

"All night, sometimes."

"Why?"

"Spirit, Ma says. Indian superstition. Listen."

A quiet mumbling came from the other bed in a child's high pitch.

"Keeps up most'a the night," Billy said. Screams sometimes. Like she's scared or mad at that spirit."

"So she *does* talk."

"Not Indian. Not English. Not Spanish. Ma says its old-time Indian talk."

"Well, for the love of Mike!" She'd heard of speaking in tongues, but never imagined Indians did it too.

Mae had been noticing a pain in her belly, and it was getting worse, like she'd eaten something bad and might get diarrhea. Maybe it was only gas. "I need to walk around," she whispered in Billy's ear, quietly getting out of bed in hopes that movement would settle the gas. She had convinced herself that the medicine would be painless, or willed it to be so.

As she circled the table in front of the stove, the diminishing warmth told her the fire had died out and the room would soon be as cold as the out-of-doors. The rains had gone, and moonlight glistened on a white lacing of frost around the windows. There was no outhouse. They did their business in the bushes and covered it like cats. But she didn't want to go out in the cold and dark, so she hoped it wasn't the start of the runnies. As Baby mumbled, Mae padded round and round the table in her bare feet, increasingly uncomfortable and knowing that she had been fooling herself.

Lulled by the fact that Ah Sen had gone though this six or seven times and didn't mention belly pain, she'd talked herself into the belief that a tiny bit of something would slip out unfelt. But the pains grew stronger, causing her to moan as she walked, her voice blending with Baby's murmur.

From the darkness Billy said, "You all right?"

"Just some cramps."

Actually she was feeling dizzy, and a tingling itchiness had started on her arms and legs. She couldn't help but scratch. It was like ants crawling under her skin, and spiders running after them. Scratching didn't alleviate the itch. Increasingly frantic, she tore at her skin. Colorful things started sweeping before her eyes, like that day the soldiers attacked the railroad workers. She felt thirsty too. Her hands and feet were cold, and the stomach pain had become almost unbearable.

She lay down on the bed again, hoping that would help. Billy pulled himself to the head of the bed and got off there so as not to disturb her. She heard him whispering across the room, and then Indian Mary was at her side.

"Hurt?" she asked laying a hand on Mae's abdomen.

"Yes!" The weight of a hand increased the pain, and as she tried to push Mary's hand off, Mary came down with her considerable weight behind the heels of both hands.

Mae yelped and turned toward the wall to keep that from happening again.

"Get up. Jump," Mary said tugging her elbow until she was sitting up.

"Jump?" Spots before her eyes like black sand almost obscured the moon, and she felt dizzier than before.

"Up, down. Jump." Mary pulled her to her feet.

"It'd wake Baby," Mae said, swaying with lightheadedness.

"She talkin' to spirit. Jump."

Mae couldn't make herself jump. Colorful things swirled at her and she staggered into a sucking vortex, grabbing the table to slow her fall to the floor.

Mary lit the kerosene lamp and turned it down to low light. "Here's chair," she said, pulling Mae up until she was sitting again. "Go stand on chair. Jump down."

With Mary's help Mae managed to get up on the chair seat, and teeter there, but when she jumped and landed on the floor she kept going and crashed hard. The room circled around her. She didn't know which way was up. Mary's feet were coming out of the wall as she pulled on Mae's elbow.

Mary said something to Billy and he went outside.

"Jump more," Mary ordered, trying to pull her up again. "Many time."

Mae staggered inside her whirlpool and fell hard against the table. "I can't," she said, having been sucked down to the floor again. She was drenched with sweat, though a short time ago it had been cold in the room. The ants and spiders had expanded their runs all over her, even inside her ears. The itching came from deep down where she couldn't scratch. Baby began to howl in long incomprehensible word strings. Outside, coyotes joined the fracas.

Mary finally got Mae on her feet, but she fell again, the chair skidding away.

She was suddenly about to throw up. She got to her knees and forced her voice to work. "Pan. Bring a—"

It was too late. Up came everything like somebody siphoned it out effortlessly.

"Go in bed," Mary said.

Mae staggered that direction and fell on the bed, helped by Mary. The colors swept past her and sweat ran down her face and stung her eyes. Mary pressed again on her abdomen.

Mae yelled like a stuck pig. She grabbed the pan, her breathing fast and shallow. She heaved again.

Mary brought the lamp and pulled up Mae's skirt, pressing Mae's hurting belly and looking between her legs, probing with her fingers. Weak, Mae couldn't stop her, though she was ashamed.

"No come," Mary announced. "We wait. Mebbe morning."

Mary set the lantern back on the table and started cleaning up the vomit. Mae grabbed the pan, sat up and out it came again and again. As she wrung herself inside out she marveled that her stomach could hold up in the violence of it.

"Mebbe baby wanna stay in you," Mary said. "You sleep."

But sleep was impossible. She thought the retching, far beyond the last grain of food in her stomach, would surely vault all her insides up to the light. And between episodes she lay still as a rag doll with a hard and steady pain in her stomach.

70

In the morning Mary poked and prodded and looked at the bedclothes. "Baby still in there," she said. She then gave Mae's hands and feet a brisk rubbing, one at a time, while Billy toweled himself off, having returned from bathing in the river. He pulled on his old work clothes, gave Mae a look like he wished the pain were his, and left for work.

Mary took Baby with her to clean somebody's house, leaving Mae alone in the little cabin. Her head and muscles ached like she was getting the grippe. Her hands and feet tingled. She stayed in bed though the stomach pains had lessened. They would return with a vengeance, she knew, if she ate anything. Mostly she dozed, waking briefly to drink from the dipper, which was in a bucket beside the bed.

She dreamed a flesh-colored maze of loops and folds, in which she was searching for something she couldn't see or understand. She was walking through tunnels, soft passageways, pushing through heavy, moist folds as she made her way deep into the maze, becoming increasingly frustrated at not finding what she was looking for.

She began to hear a distant sound, like a mouse squeak at first. She listened, straining her ears. Every few loops and tunnels she would stop and listen again, hearing it just a little louder, and then she would keep groping through the maze. The sound grew ever louder. After more struggle, it dawned on her that it was an infant crying, far away, screaming in terror. She continued toward it, and the scream was a word, *Mommy!* That stopped her. Should she continue? Every step took her closer to it. And why was that baby calling for its mother with such a heart-wrenching pitch? Then she knew.

It was dying. Its mother had abandoned it. It screamed sorrow, anger, fear, and hurt at so great a betrayal. Only that could cause a child to sound that desperate. Horror prickled her skin and she shrank back from the cries. In panic she now struggled to go the opposite direction, fighting through all those confusing loops and dead-ends, trying to get away from *Mommee! Mommeee!* Away through those fleshy passages where heavy flaps thumped her on her head and held her under their weight and she struggled with all her might to continue in the opposite direction. Exhausted but ever more panicked, she wiggled and pushed forward, feet slipping under her, again and again, until she found herself pinned down and unable to move at all. She could hardly breathe in her panic, and the deafening screams intensified. The frantic baby was just around the corner! *Mommeee! Mommeee!*

The *eee* stabbed her ears, and her heart. She flailed in her terror. She must get away from—

"Wake up," a man's voice was saying. "You was dreamin'."

"Oh, Billy!" She was out of breath. "Oh, it was bad." She sat up and took his hand. "I'm glad to be awake."

When Mary and Baby returned at the end of the day, Baby sat on her grandmother's bed and stared at Mae across the dim room. Elbowing up on her bed, Mae winked an eye and smiled at the child—just as frail and bony as Nora was at the end. Baby continued to stare in her eerie way from the shadows of her deep-set eyes, but she didn't seem afraid.

"Do you go to school?" Mae asked.

Baby stiffened. Mary turned from her cooking with a quick, "No school."

Baby's face quivered on the brink.

School was a sore point, Mae understood, not to be mentioned. Acting on instinct Mae wiggled into her covers and pulled the blanket over her head like *she* was afraid. Actually she was—afraid of a blood-curdling scream about which Billy had warned her. Hearing none she moved the blanket enough to peek out with one eye.

Baby was staring at that eye.

Mae yanked the cover over herself again, acting afraid. Playing this game, she had the pleasant feeling of being a child herself.

Silence.

She peeked. Baby's staring eyes. She whisked the covers back over her.

More silence.

Next time she exclaimed in mock fear, "Oh no!" and dove back under.

In the darkness of the covers she could see the ghost of a smile on Baby's face, just now registering in her mind. Recalling the joy of making Nora laugh in what later turned out to be her last days, Mae this time uncovered her whole head and, with mimed fear, flopped back into the bed shaking and moaning under the bedclothes.

There was a squeak. An odd little giggle?

Uncovering her head she saw Baby actually smiling! Mae would have liked to keep playing but she had made herself dizzy again. Mary stood at the stove with a big spoon in one hand and eyes round as saucers.

The door slammed. Billy came to the bed and looked down with two deep worry creases between his brows. "You all right?"

"I'm fine. Just playing peek-a-boo with Baby."

He looked at Mae like she was out of her mind. "Peek—"

"A silly game."

Behind him, Indian Mary spoke in her language.

Listening, and then kneeling at the bed, Billy searched Mae's face. "You made her laugh."

"A little laugh, yes."

"Good." He patted her hand and turned to Baby and then to his mother.

"*Cudja*," he said. Looking back at Mae, he asked, "You sick?"

"Yes, but getting better."

"Still got a baby in there?" He pointed at the blanket.

"Your mother says so."

Billy stood up and went to his mother at the stove. They talked quietly for a while, Mary in her language. Then Billy returned to the side of the bed, petting Mae's hair as he talked. "She says you had a big dose of that medicine but the baby's holdin' tight. Wanna try again? Ma says sometimes it takes three, four tries."

"No." Mae spoke directly to Mary, surprising herself with the certainty of it. "No more medicine."

She couldn't take any more pain. Her stomach was too fragile, and she could only imagine how much worse it would be next time. Most likely it wouldn't work anyway. Three or four tries could kill her for sure. No part of this was easy.

With a nod, Indian Mary took the bucket of split salmon to the door. "Billy," she said before she opened it, "take Mae walkin' after eat. Lotsa walk. *Cudja* for foots."

"What does *cudja* mean?" Mae asked when the door shut behind the old woman.

"Old time talk. It means good." He patted her again. "We'll walk after supper."

Mae asked him the question she assumed any man in his position would answer in the affirmative. "Did you want that medicine to work? I mean the true feeling in your heart?"

He sounded exasperated. "I keep tellin' you, I wanna be poppa to your baby."

A thought zoomed into her mind and paused like a hummingbird. Before it could zigzag around any more, she saw it clearly, a thing she'd been pushing away. Billy must know that her pregnancy, and the future baby kept her from going to New York or marrying a respectable white man. The baby was his ticket to her. She was trapping herself with him by having the baby. What was the tenderness and love she felt for him? Was it actual love or only a need for his help, a temporary thing? She'd never been able to envision herself living a long life with Billy, as she had with Charlie. And when she forced herself to see this in the long term she saw herself as a sad, bent woman old before her time with too much work, and still living in a tilting one-room cabin. In fact, at this very moment she seemed to be tipping over a cliff with rocky ground below while at the same time smiling at Billy and rubbing the backs of his work-scarred hands with her thumbs.

Baby watched this with the keenness of an owl fixed on its next furry meal.

Billy gently pulled Mae to her feet and helped her outside. Baby followed. The cold had dissipated and the air felt surprisingly warm for December. Billy gazed with joy on the sizzling slabs of salmon roasting on willow stakes, and Mae realized he had labored hard all day and would be hungry.

On an old chair, Baby snuggled into her grandmother's lap, and Indian Mary absently petted her granddaughter's hair.

"I can't eat now," Mae told them. Her insides felt too precarious. "I'll go for a walk by myself—not far, just a little up and down the river trail. Be right back."

Mary nodded her approval. So did Billy as he twisted a stake to cook the fish from a different angle.

Mae walked carefully down the trodden path through the winter-bare willows, past the big gnarly cottonwood tree, turning to the right on the river trail. Still a bit shaky, she paid attention to the ground so she wouldn't stumble over roots and burrows. Her mind kept returning to whether she should open herself to more suffering by trying to dislodge the baby, considering it might fail again. Apparently, she wasn't brave enough to face pain for the chance of a better life. Men at war were braver than that. But then again, they didn't willingly submit their bodies to it in the same way. No one asked, "Will you volunteer to be shot in the belly today?" The agitation was back upon her. For well over a month she'd been jumping from yes to no and back again, every day worrying that she'd waited too long for the medicine to work. Mary said babies could hold on and make it more difficult to dislodge them, especially when they had been in there too long. That meant a bigger dose and more pain.

Things had changed. She had hoped that having the baby would bring Charlie to her. But he would have come by now if he'd had any desire for her. Only a fool would think otherwise. Logic told her she just needed to be braver and face more pain for the sake of her future, and that she must be more clear-eyed about the realities of starting a life with Billy. He was the path of least resistance, a beguiling path because of the way he loved her, but shortsighted. This would be the major decision of her life. All else would follow from it.

Only a year and a half ago she'd set out to find her fortune in Sacramento. She now understood why girls in this situation killed themselves. Trudging slowly between the trees on the river path, she came to a sudden opening of wide blue sky.

The pure blue of the sky pulled her into it, like she was flying, but then looking downward from that, through the trees there was a brilliant pink band of cloud coming out of the west where the sun was setting. That broad ribbon of hot pink had wrapped around the world. She followed it, pivoting toward the east and saw where it boiled and curled upward four times higher than the Sierra Mountains. Light gray shadows defined the edges of those lavish pink billows. This, she realized, laughing out loud, was a colossal pink bow on a gigantic gift. The sense of dreaming still hung thick around her, but it appeared that the entire world was a gift for her baby, wrapped and tied up in a magnificent pink ribbon!

She couldn't help but laugh. Never in the most fanciful artwork in paintings had she seen anything like this gift-wrapped world. If an artist painted this exact scene it would look so improbable as to be laughable. And she was laughing full out! In Bible stories, troubled people often asked God for a sign. This was her sign. She had been mired in her dilemma, and now this! If only Sister Delphine could be here! She would laugh too. Indian Mary was right. The baby wanted to be born. God was telling her that the baby was willing to take its chances in a wicked world with a mother ill-suited for the job and a father born into poverty. The more Mae gazed at the amazing sky, the happier she became.

Peace settled over her, replacing the worry and fear. She felt herself in the lap of something much bigger than herself. She wouldn't question her love for Billy, or his for her, or whether they could have a good life together. He was a thoughtful and good man. Her job was to do what she could to make theirs a good life. She would help him live in a white world, and teach him to read and write. Like a cork that had stopped bouncing topsy-turvy on stormy waters, she would sail this powerful, smooth current over which she had no control—her body holding onto the baby and the very sky celebrating. She didn't have to make any more decisions. She was free! She need only wait, and the baby would come in its own good time.

A blessing, Indian Mary and Billy called it.

∽

That night, minding his mother's orders, Billy slept on the floor not doing anything with Mae. That suited her fine, but she dangled her hand over the bed. He reached for it, and they squeezed hands both happy in the bargain they'd just made. She would live with him.

In the morning Indian Mary was at the table eating acorn porridge left from last night—breakfast in this house was whatever could be found, and not necessarily eaten together. Baby lay quietly in her grandmother's bed facing the wall, and Billy was in his work clothes, about to leave for the Grimshaw place.

Mae felt less dizzy than yesterday. Maybe she didn't need to stay another night under Mary's care. Baby turned over and sat up, staring at Mae.

She winked and smiled, and their gazes locked. All she could think was, you poor little thing, abandoned by your mother. She got up and moved toward her, seemingly without the aid of her feet, which were too numb to feel the floor.

She sat down beside Baby, both of them looking into the other's eyes, inches apart. Baby put a hand on Mae's hand. The sweetness of that brought a lump to Mae's throat. She gently squeezed the frail hand, and then slowly, carefully, put both arms around the child and hugged her the way Billy sometimes hugged her—like she was fragile.

Baby allowed it.

"Poor baby," she said as she petted the girl's tangled hair, "you had a bad dream."

Billy and his mother looked like they were witnessing a miracle.

"If Baby wants, she can stay home with me today," Mae said, smiling down at the child. "Would you like that? To stay here with me?"

Baby nodded.

The day passed easily, Baby and Mae in beds across the room, sleeping for hours at a time and then smiling at each other in between. When Billy returned he announced that no farmer or rancher around Bridge House or Slough House would pay him money for work, not when they could get it for free from other men. Billy said he wanted to leave for Omo Ranch as soon as possible. He offered to go back and pick up Mae's things from Ah Sen.

"I'll go with you," she said, needing to thank Ah Sen personally and say good-bye.

"That'd add six or so miles for you, down and back," he said. "I'll wait 'til you're ready to go."

On Monday the sun was out and Mae felt as good as new. They were all leaving at the same time, Baby looking at Mae as though she understood they wouldn't see each other for a long time. Mae laid a hand on Baby's head and said to Mary, "If you need my help with her, don't hesitate to send for me, or bring her to me. I think the two of us got ourselves an understanding." She smiled at Baby.

Baby touched Mae's forearm, light as a dragonfly. Her black shadowy eyes didn't frighten Mae any more. This child, too, was a blessing, and Mae felt sorry to leave her. But her work was to help Billy, and Baby was in good hands with her grandmother.

∽

Back in the cabin that smelled of garlic and ginger, Mae explained to Ah Sen why they were going. "It'd be good for him, and me too, to be away from where Oberon can find me." She got down on her knees and retrieved the hat with pink roses from under the bed, and then she pulled out the crate with the red day gown. Feeling the wadded lump inside the seam, she knew the money was where she left it, and wasn't surprised.

Ah Sen, who'd been watching, suddenly dove deep into the crate of her belongings, throwing things out on her bed. She came up with a crumpled bag the size and shape of a carpetbag, misshapen after years of being in the bottom of that crate.

"You takee," she said, thrusting it at Mae. "Ah Sen no need. Die heew." She pointed at the floor of her house.

Mae accepted the bag with care. It was made of very old, very stiff golden silk. She ran a finger over the Chinese writing embroidered in paler gold threads. Under the horn grip, a thick weave of gold thread looped over the big button that served as a clasp. "Is this from China?" she asked.

Ah Sen sharply dipped her head and pointed at her chest. "My mamma."

"Oh, she gave it to you and you brought it with you all those years ago?" Seeing Ah Sen's misting eyes, Mae started to hand it back. "It must be precious to you. I can't take—"

Behind Ah Sen, Billy was making a no sign, telling her the lady would feel bad if she didn't take it.

"I mean, it's beautiful! Thank you. It will always remind me of you. Thank you for this, Ah Sen, and for taking me into your house and being so patient." Just then she remembered that she was wearing one of Ah Sen's tunics. She started to take it off, intending to wear her good frock, but Ah Sen stopped her. "You takee."

"Thank you, again." Mae said. She folded her red frock and put it in the silk bag.

Ah Sen, having made tea, convinced them to stay a few minutes more. She opened a box of sweet shortbread from a Chinese market in Sacramento. As they talked of the weather and other inconsequential things, she didn't ask if Mary's medicine had worked. Neither Mae nor Billy brought it up either. When it was time to say good-bye, Mae gave the stout old woman a hug. It felt awkward. Clearly her people didn't hug each other. Mae's family didn't either, but nonetheless it felt right to do it.

Ah Sen turned to her shelves and took down some soft rice buns. Wrapping them in waxed paper, she indicated Mae should put them in the bag. "You walk, eat," she said. She turned to Billy, stabbing him in the chest with her short finger. "Mae-Mae goo girra. You be goo man."

71

The cold mist on Billy's face felt clean and fresh as he and Mae hiked up the river trail toward Jackson Road. He liked everything about the morning, and was so puffed up with happiness to have her with him, *with* him, that it seemed he would burst if he didn't breathe carefully. And if he exploded and shouted his joy, all the flying pieces of him would give cheer to every living thing for miles around. Still, he kept a straight face from long habit. But things were different now. The white side of him was taking wing, and he'd better watch out when he got to Omo Ranch or he'd work himself to death without even noticing, so eager was he to provide his pretty rose with the best of everything. It all circled back to joy. For once in his life Luck walked with him.

After a couple of miles on Jackson Road they came to the old Swain place, now owned by another man. Black and white cow rumps were lined up under the eave, and the pinging of milk in a metal bucket made him happy not to be young and crazy. He told Mae there had been a rancheria on that place when he was a boy.

"What's a rancheria?"

She was so sweet and fresh in this tired old world! "It means old Indian living place. There was a lot of 'em up and down the river before white people came."

He recalled the strange way the Cosumne came to live at Old Sheep Corral. It seemed remarkable that the entire river and this particular district was named for those people, and yet only old Indians knew the story. Most buyers of supplies at the Cosumne Store did not. "Someday I'll tell you about the people who lived here," Billy said.

"Why don't you tell me now? We'll be walking a long time."

He wasn't sure he could do it and stay happy. But he decided to tell her a little of it. Oddly, when he was young he wasn't much interested in the People and their stories; he wanted to be white. But now that he was about to become a white man he wanted her to know about the Indian side of him, and he hoped she'd be interested.

"In the old times there was a big rancheria down river, in the Delta. Called Cosumne. The people was the Cosumne. 'Umne' means people. A sickness come and killed 'bout half of 'em. Them folks was sad and crying, and they believed their spirits wasn't powerful no more, so they all walked away from their home place and went to where there'as supposed to be spirits with more power, in Mission San Jose."

"What do you mean by power?" Mae asked.

He grinned over at her, "Spooky old Indian superstition."

"You're funny, Billy McCoon."

"You wanna hear this story?"

"Sure, but Cosumne is back there," indicated by a thumb over her shoulder. "So how can it be in the Delta?"

"'Cause you ain't heard the story yet." He smiled at her to let her know he wasn't upset that she didn't listen quietly. White people were an impatient people. He knew that.

"So they went to the mission in San Jose. After a time of workin' and prayin' to those spirits, the headman did some'um the padre didn't like, mebbe gettin' up late in the mornin' or some such, and the guards tied 'im up at the church door and whipped 'im naked, with all of 'em watchin'. They did that all the time, to make people work."

"Did they whip the white workers too?"

Billy had to chuckle to himself. She was so innocent. "No. Back then there wasn't no white people in the mission, 'cept for the two padres and all the guards. Indians did all the work. No white man woulda lived there."

"Why not? Isn't a mission like a monastery?"

He kept looking over at her just to see how pretty she was. Her big words didn't bother him now. He was feeling stronger with her than at first, and it felt good.

"I don't know nuthin' 'bout monastery, but the mission was where they teached Indians how to work hard all day and live like Mexicans. They wasn't 'sposed to leave 'less they got paseos. Lotsa Indians got shot dead by Mexican soldiers chasin' after 'em. Indians had to stay in the mission, like a jail."

"Oh, I didn't' know that."

"Well, that old chief, after the whippin' was 'sposed to put on his mission shirt and pants and get on his knees and kiss that padre's ring and then go back to work. 'Stead, he threw them clothes at the padre's feet and said, 'You take 'em back, and take your Christianity back too. I doan want 'em.' That man and all his people walked away. They walked up the rivers to Sutter's Fort—"

"Did the Mexican soldiers go after them?"

He laughed good-naturedly. "I shoulda said, alla that was goin' on *after* the Indians fought some big battles 'gainst them soldiers. After that no soldiers came huntin' for people to take 'em back." Billy's grandfather had played a major part in those wars. Antonio and Efren had told him about it.

"It's a wonder any of them stayed in that mission," Mae said.

Billy smiled to recall people saying how shabby the mission got after so many Indians left, and he remembered the story of peoples from many different home places and languages leaving the mission and building a big dancehouse in Pleasanton. Later, some of them left Pleasanton and went to Jackson Valley.

By now they were on Jackson Road, a busy thoroughfare flanked by green rolling hills. All kinds of rigs and freight wagons traveled the muddy road today. Mae walked on the outside, ducking behind Billy for protection from splashing mud.

"Well, anyhow the Cosumne people walked up to Sutter's Fort and told Captain Sutter they wanted to live there and work for him. He said all right. They could build their houses and a roundhouse for dancin'. So they lived at the fort 'bout ten years. Some were real good vaqueros from their times at the mission. Well, Indians like to—"

"What's a vaquero?"

"Some say buckaroo." The image of Raul Martinez flashed through his mind. "Good horseback riders, good ropers. Good at tendin' the cattle."

"Sounds like a cowboy."

Billy had heard that, the nickname of Baby's father. "Those was men," he said, "not boys."

"Well, I think they're called cowboys."

"Okay. Anyhow, Indians like to have big times. They like to dance and sing all night. One mornin' when they was all laid out on the ground too tired to get up, Captain Sutter come out and started yellin'. He were mad as hell 'cause they wasn't in the fields workin'. He set fire to their dancehouse and told 'em to git off his land.

"Mr. Sheldon was at the fort. He told them Cosumne he needed vaqueros on his rancho. By then, Mr. Sheldon's Omochume vaqueros was away gittin' gold for him on Weber Creek."

"You mean the Mr. Sheldon I know?"

"The papa of the one we know."

"The one that died in the shootout over the dam?"

"Yup. Anyhow, Mr. Sheldon brought the Cosumne people to live on his rancho. They built houses at Old Sheep Corral, at Daylor's place. Some of the elders still call it Sheep Corral. I worked there for Mr. Swain. So that's how the Cosumne people came to this district."

"I have a feeling there's more to it."

Billy was remembering Pedro's relief at getting more vaqueros to help watch the cattle at night. Back then, Pedro had been Mr. Sheldon's major-domo. Miners shot cattle like they were deer. They stole plenty of horses too.

"There's more," Billy said, "But I'm too happy to talk about it."

Those son-of-bitch white men killed the People, and Mae knew nothing about the bad times that gnawed at the soul of everyone with Indian blood. It would take a lifetime to explain it.

"That's funny," she said, "most people like to talk when they're happy."

Getting back to being happy he said, "You asked me what power is. You have it. Sometimes I see a light around you, pretty as the sky with the sun comin' up. You have a secret place inside you with the power to grow babies. Strong power." He glanced over at her and saw that she felt uneasy hearing this, but he continued. "Men fight to the death for such as that."

"I don't see anyone dying for me."

Her joke and nervous chuckle told him she didn't understand. In time maybe she would. He'd been wanting to tell her this for months, and now seemed the right time.

"You hafta be careful. Power goes good or bad. You could die young. I'll watch over you and see that doan happen. But you hafta live careful and think what you do afore you do it. If I die, think careful about what man you give that power to. Don't waste it on weak men, or bad men."

Mae started to say something but a freight wagon rolled by and she jumped to the side, not quick enough to dodge a wave of muddy water. It splashed all over Ah Sen's tunic, but Mae just laughed.

Billy realized he should be hiding behind the brim of his hat. He felt lucky today, but some of those teamsters were Indians, and Indians knew each other. It wouldn't do to have them tell their friends all up and down the chain of peoples that Billy McCoon and a white girl were going to Omo Ranch together to live at Linnie Hickey's place. That could ruin his new life. He needed to hide who he was until he got to where no one knew him.

A wagon long as a barn gradually overtook them, loaded with steel trusses and pulled by twenty-four oxen. The big iron wheels deepened the ruts in the rain-soft road. A one-horse white-top pulled around the freight wagon, whipped to a run by a man in a suit trying to beat an oncoming stage with four galloping horses. With all these people around, Billy kept his hat well over his face.

Barking dogs rushed out from the farmhouses along the road. He gave each dog a calm, stern look, and they all went back to their porches. They could feel his power.

They were approaching the junction of Stone House Road where the little schoolhouse stood on the hill on the left and Yellow Snake Peak poked up much higher on the right. He didn't give a second thought to those layered ridges supposedly left by the coils of the giant snake. They walked down the little hill to where children on their way to school waded through the marshy creek with lunch pails in hand and shoes tied around their necks.

Sitting down to take off her shoes, Mae looked up at him. "Remember when you drove me to Latrobe, when you were delivering plums?"

"When I'm laid out dyin' I'll remember that."

Her mouth tightened in a tease. "You didn't seem that interested in me at the time."

He grinned to recall how hard it had been to keep that much joy a secret.

"Remember, we saw Indians rounding up grasshoppers?"

"Uh-huh."

She waded with him across the water. "Did you ever do that?"

"Helped my ma when I was little, sure."

As they continued up Jackson Road, a freight wagon loaded double-deep with whisky kegs rattled past, and the driver looked back at them. One glimpse told Billy that the young man in the Union cap was Frank Isaminger. Billy waited with his hat down for the wagon to move onward, because Frank was a man who liked to talk and he knew all the teamsters.

"Hey Billy, that you?" Isaminger called out.

Billy acted like he didn't hear.

"Whoa!" Frank halted his team of six. "You ain't foolin' me none, Billy McCoon. I can see you got a purty gal. That Chinee garb doan fool me none."

Always the joker.

"I'm givin' you two a ride. C'mon." He made a round motion with his fist.

Billy saw Mae's delight at the prospect of a ride, and he realized she must be footsore walking in those shoes. She needed a ride. Anyway Frank had already seen them together, and Billy needed the chance to tell him not to tell anyone what they were doing.

In the white world it was polite to let the lady go first, so Billy helped Mae up into the high buckboard. She sat next to Frank, leaving Billy on the outside with a barrier between her and him, the toolbox, often called a jockey box.

"The name's Frank Isaminger," he said to Mae, lifting his cap between the tiny stub of a thumb and a fingerless hand. He had no fingers on either hand and yet he controlled a six-mule team as well as any freighter by wrapping the reins around his wrists and moving them just so. He told friends he kept his hands in his pockets when interviewing for work. Now he was talking real soft to Mae, saying he'd loaded the kegs at Eagle's Nest Station and was driving whisky to Bridge House, Kangaroo House, Latrobe, and eventually to Dry Town.

Billy, leaning forward as though to watch Mr. Granlees ride out of his road, caught the tail end of a flirty look from Frank to Mae! Strong emotion boiled in his stomach. Everyone knew Frank Isaminger had girls all over the place, and he was storied to be in trouble with more than one husband at a time. Some said women were curious to know what it was like with a finger-less man. It steamed through Billy's mind that Frank might try to steal Mae. He was younger than Billy. His clean-shaven face had no weathering, like Billy's. In fact it was quite good-looking. And Frank already had paying work in these bad economic times, something Billy only hoped to find.

Billy wanted to get Mae off the wagon but couldn't think how to explain it.

Frank was saying to her in that jovial way of his, "Wonderin' about my hands, ain'tcha?"

"Well, it is unusual. For a teamster, especially." Wonder and admiration in her voice!

Frank's smile showed his even teeth. "I'll bet you wanna know if I was born like this."

"Well, sure," she said sweetly, "if you don't mind."

"Ever'body wants to know that," he said guiding the team by the wrists around the creaking oxen-pulled wagon. "Well, I was a year and half old when it happened. Me and my folks was visitin' friends in Dry Town. I can't remember it, but the men was burning piles of old grapevine cuttings. I stumbled into one of those fires with the white-hot coals underneath. And there you have it. Burned my baby fingers clean off." He laughed like wild man, as joyful as Billy had been today before meeting up with him.

"You never told me that," Billy said from his edge of the buckboard.

"You never asked."

Neither did Mae. He was buttering her up.

"Did they heal up pretty fast?" Mae asked in a sorrowful tone.

"No ma'm, and 'twern't just my fingers. Nosiree. I owe my life to an old squaw livin' nearby. Ma said I was far gone. Couldn't git healed up for the longest time. Kept gittin' infected, skin crackin' open agin and agin. That squaw said Indian medicine would work, so Ma let her try. She wrapped my hands in bandages soaked in a special salve. She changed 'em a lot." He leaned forward, around Mae, and gave Billy a teasing grin. "Mebbe on thet account

I got a soft spot in my heart fer Injuns." He tee-heed as he looked up the road, handling reins like the best of them.

What a disgusting Coyote trick that would be, Billy thought, if his own mother saved Frank so he could steal Mae! "There's an old story about Coyote," Billy said. "He burned his hands when he was carryin' fire to the world, and that's why coyotes got short fingers."

"That doan stop Old Man Coyote, do it?" Frank bantered, reaching right into the heart of the matter, Coyote's exploits with women.

"No mor'n it stops you," Billy seethed. "You're always after purty women."

Frank loosed a bellyful of laughter, like he loved hearing that, and then looked at Mae with a closed-mouth smile that belonged in bed. Not that she was leading him on; she was staring straight ahead with her hands on the silk bag in her lap. Billy couldn't think what to do, so he sat there trying to suppress something like panic that was robbing him of power as the wagon bounced over the bumps and dips in the road.

They rolled noisily across the iron truss bridge, which had recently been painted yellow. Billy and Mae both looked over their shoulders at the little house beneath the big oak. He didn't see Ma there, but felt a part of his life ripping away like a scab not quite ready to go. He turned forward, reminding himself that Indian blood had given him nothing but trouble. It was time to leave it behind.

Frank delivered whisky kegs to the Bridge House Store, where they all used the outhouse, then drove to Michigan Bar where he stopped the wagon and delivered whisky to three different saloons. While Frank was doing that, Billy was glad to see Mae had pulled her wide rose-piled hat down over her face. She leaned over the jockey box and quietly told him, "I know people here, and don't want them telling Oberon they've seen me. Don't want Farley to know either. He doesn't know about Oberon, so he'd tell Oberon anything he asked."

Good. She wouldn't want to go inside the Kangaroo House either, and she would support Billy's refusal to do it. He explained that to her, and she understood. This helped smooth away the fears, as did a look from her that went straight to his stomach. She wasn't falling under Frank's spell.

Leaving Michigan Bar, Frank slapped his pocket when Mrs. Ruman came out at the bridge. Avoiding her eyes, Billy and Mae looked down while she reached into Frank's vest and picked out the right coins. The wagon then rolled over the slightly swaying bridge. Billy looked to the east where heavy clouds hid the mountains. Passing Chinatown on the opposite shore, they rode onward, up and down the hilly road with open grasslands on both sides.

Every so often Frank probed them about where they were headed, and Billy sidestepped it. Clouds were moving quickly across the sky. A few groves of ancient oaks remained here and there, and a few pines. Billy could remember when this whole area was mostly forest—before the woodcutting and the overgrazing and drought years. Now it was all grassland, and mostly sheep grazing.

The wagon creaked to a hilltop, and in the distance Billy saw Kangaroo House, where Michigan Bar Road intersected Latrobe Road. Three freight wagons were parked in front of that roadhouse. All teamsters stopped to water their horses and use the outhouse. And most of them were looking for food, drink, and a good time. Even from this distance Billy recognized Skinny Joe walking his horses to the trough, a bandy-legged fellow wearing tight pants. All kinds of people there would recognize Billy.

"Billy, you ever dance with Ida?" Frank asked as the team started down the hill.

That told Billy that Frank planned to stop. The Kangaroo House always had fiddle music spilling out on the road, and teamsters danced with any available woman, including Ida, the daughter of the owner.

"I'm not dancin'," Billy said. "We're gettin' off here."

"What the hell! 'Scuse me ma'am. Whoa!" Frank pulled the reins and stopped the wagon at the side of the road. "Where you headed?" Frank turned and asked.

"I can't say," Billy said. First he planned to cut across the open ground to Latrobe Road, rigs and buggies on it looking like tiny toys from here. That would bypass Kangaroo House and the unnecessary right angle of the two roads. Then they'd go through Latrobe and north to Omo Ranch. Lambs Crossing would have been more direct but they needed a ride, and it didn't matter if Latrobe added a few miles.

"Whatsamatter? You runnin' from the law?" Frank asked the two of them.

"Naw. Just lookin' for payin' work," Billy said. "Mae an' me needs to live somewhere's they don't know I'm Indian, and I'd thank you for keepin' that under your hat."

"Well don't that beat all! You two gettin' married?"

"If she'll have me." Billy pretended not to see the surprise on Mae's face.

"Well, just how d'ya 'spect to keep your old pal Frank from tellin' folks you's marryin' a white gal? A looker too." Regret showed behind those joking eyes.

"I'm askin' you to keep your mouth shut."

"Never heared'a such a thing."

"What? Keepin' your mouth shut?"

"Injun buck marrying a looker of a white girl."

A chilly breeze had blown up across the unprotected hills, and a twenty-mule team with a load of clay pipe came rattling and creaking around them as they sat at the side of the road. The teamster waved as he went by.

"You never heared of a squaw man?" Billy said when the noise died down.

"Thet's different."

"No 'taint."

"Well, I'm gunna hop to the Kangaroo House," Frank said.

Mae was hugging her arms. "Let's go, if we're going to," she said to Billy.

"First a drink to love." Frank flipped his wrists free of the reins, reached over Mae, pushed a fist up through the leather loop of the jockey box. It opened and he pinched a tin cup between his knuckles and the stub of his thumb, then twisted around to the keg behind him in the wagon and punched the spigot with the knuckles of his other hand. The amber liquid streamed into the cup. He punched the spigot off and handed the cup to Billy. Then he reached back in the box for another cup, wiped it out with his shirt, twisted around again and poured himself a drink. While he was doing that, Billy flicked the contents of his cup over his shoulder.

"To love eternal." Frank raised his cup.

Billy raised his cup and pretended to drink. This was a white man's ritual he didn't want to spoil, but he needed all of his power. Frank raised his cup again. "Doncha worry none. I ain't gunna open my yap. And I think you're mighty brave to do this. Course you don't wanna galoot like me telling people where you are, so I won't ask you any more questions. But I'll say this. A whisky driver knows where the mines is good and where they're shutting down. There's a place not far from Shingle Springs where they're lookin' for more men. It's Big Canyon Mine. Out of the way of all the roads. A good place to hide."

"We ain't goin' there," Billy said.

※❈

"This is a good story," Rock Man says in his strained voice. "I haven't been asleep for quite a while."

Mae sits in her Pierce-Arrow with her kid gloves on the wheel, going nowhere. She is seeing Billy those last few months. "Everything would have been different," she says, "if we had gone to Omo Ranch like we planned to. If Frank Isaminger hadn't mentioned Big Canyon Mine. If Billy hadn't gone into the company store that day—"

Coyote warbles his delight, "If, if, if, if."

"Mae," I remind her, "any of those ifs and you wouldn't have had the kind of life you wanted, or that motorcar."

"Back then I didn't know what kind of life I wanted."

"Remarkable," mrowls He-lé-jah, "how people are so dim-witted and yet so cunning."

About his own wants, a cat is never in doubt.

All of us settle into looking back. It was the time of early flowers.

72

Billy stepped into the tram, sat back against the sloped backrest, and turned off his hat-flame to save acetylene. Exhausted and too tired to talk to the other miners after the long day of blasting, shoveling and picking, he closed his scratchy eyes. Last night after his shift he'd volunteered for the day shift with only a two-hour rest between. Now, in total darkness, he felt the bumps in the concrete as the tram rolled up the steep angle from the bottom of the mine. They relaxed his back muscles. Quickly he melted into a dream of running scared, fleeing for his life.

He awoke to two bells. The tram jerked to a halt. Six miners from Level Two crowded in, and the cable cranked to life again. The square cement opening at the top gave some light now, and the crushing, grinding noise of the stamp mill outside grew louder as the tram rose higher. At Level One all the miners shuffled off. This level had been mined out, but it contained the locked, wire-mesh rooms where the miners hung up their company clothes and showered.

Fatigue vanished under the brisk water. With the Level Two foreman watching like a hawk, he and the other miners scrubbed their bodies with soap, including between their toes. A pan of quicksilver under the central drain attracted and congealed any gold that had stuck to their skin.

Dressing himself, Billy reflected that Mae's baby would come to light in about a month. Sometimes she joked that "Baby Emma" might turn out to be a boy. Or she would wonder aloud if the baby would have straight hair or curly, brown eyes or blue. More and more she was thinking about things like that. This was natural.

After the back-to-back shifts, he ached to see her. Dressing quickly, he caught the next tram to the top. As they all stepped out on the concrete under the towering head-frame, most of the men went to the right toward Shingle Springs, about three miles away, to escape the constant racket of the mill and be with their women. Billy turned the opposite way, heading toward the little cabin that he and Mae rented from the company for a dollar a month.

He opened his lungs to the fresh scent of grass and trees—the sap running again in the oaks and pines. How pleasant it would be if the stamp mill would stop for just a little while. His ears had been hurting much of the day with all the blasting, and now this awful noise drilled into his head. They had agreed that after the baby was born and the miners were given two days off on the Fourth of July, they would take a stagecoach ride up to Kirkwood's and talk to the ranchers up there about Billy being a drover. The idea of working in the sunlight again tugged at him. But in the meantime he was with his rose, and he was happy.

The temperature outside was perfect, the same as in the belly of the mine. Back in January the mine had felt warm compared to the outside and he'd thought there must be an unseen fire burning in the middle of the earth. Old-timers said that in the summer the mine felt cold compared to the heat of the outdoors, and miners were the luckiest of workmen to get out of the scorching heat. They maintained that no matter how it felt, the temperature in the mine never changed at all.

The sky was dark blue for a little while yet, and he smiled at the fanciful wisps of thin white cloud stretched like cobwebs across it, and the coral sunset beginning on top of Mount Algore. The hawk soaring over the eastern ridge of the canyon was happy, he could tell, and he felt like that too—floating over his own domain knowing that all he ever wanted was waiting for him in the cabin.

She would have supper waiting. Everything from her hand tasted sweeter. Later they would lie together and hold each other while darkness gathered in the windows. No need to waste lamp oil. They would fall asleep in each other's arms. Tears came to his eyes, he was so happy. He was earning money like a white man. Just this morning the foreman complimented his work and told him he'd probably get a raise of ten cents per hour, a big jump. The other miners were polite to him as he worked beside them.

Spikes of lavender lupine bloomed beside the pathway, a peppery sweet scent, and on the right, in the mouth of the old mine tunnel, two big yellow slugs were mating. All life was joy, from the high heavens to the earth.

Smiling, Mae came out the door of the cabin to welcome him home.

∽

"I love the way your skin smells," she said snuggling up to him in the dark after they had eaten.

"Must be the soap."

"What?"

He preferred to speak softly, but the thin boards of the cabin didn't keep out the racket of quartz rock being crushed beneath steel stampers. It forced them to raise their voices. He repeated, "Must be the soap."

"No, it's your natural smell." She was lightly running her hand in slow circles over his chest. He never wanted her to stop.

"Today," she was saying, "when I was in the store, two dirty men came in. They stunk."

"Must'a been farmers."

"Umm. Then I'm glad you're a miner."

"I'm glad too." He leaned over and kissed her accepting lips.

"You know, Billy," she said pulling away but not so far that he didn't feel her lips move, "What I love the most about you is that I trust you. You always tell the truth. And you're a good man. That sounds common, maybe, but—"

He tried not to squeeze her and the baby too hard. "I'm runnin' over with love. Mebbe we oughta give the baby s'more blood to grow on." That old Indian belief was their little joke.

"It sure is working, isn't it?" She unbuttoned and opened the extra large miner's shirt she'd bought in the company store to use as a housecoat.

He ran his hand over the ripe fruit of her.

With a bubble of laughter tickling her voice she said, "If Baby Emma has green eyes, we'll know Indians are right."

∽

The day shifts passed and then the night shifts, and by the time the day shifts were back again, a second shift of wildflowers spread over the hills. The days were longer too. Billy never tired of lying with Mae, both of them telling the stories of their lives. He felt her disquiet when she told him about being locked up with her little sister, when Nora died. He felt her joy as she told about going to dances in the houses and barns when she was a girl. She had a way of talking that made him feel like he was there, and he felt himself giving her an extra push when she jumped on that train with her brothers. The sense of being lucky never left him. She told him more about Oberon, which made Billy burn to crush the life out of that man. She also told him a little about Charlie, and Billy reflected on his good luck that Charlie had saved her life and then pushed her away.

He told Mae about Iris Flower, his first love, and how she died. He told about the boys he played with when he was little, and how it didn't matter to them that he was Indian. He told her about the change in his friends when they came back from high school. He tried to explain it. "It was like a wall between us, even if we was pickin' hops or plums side by side."

"What do you mean, a wall?"

"I knowed I'd stay a picker. They'd have land of their own some day and be the boss-man. That's how it turned out."

"Didn't any other Indian boys live around there then?"

"A few. Most of 'em moved to Auburn. The Cosumne people had bad luck. Many died in the Big Sickness, and they kept on dyin'. Ma's people was killed by miners. Oh, Indians came on the train to work in the fields. Mostly growed men."

Mae snuggled closer to him in the last light from the window. "Did you have girlfriends? After Iris?"

Lizzyanne jumped to mind. The old anger sparked through him and then, as always, the sadness.

"Go on, tell me."

He didn't want to ruin this peace by opening that up again.

"I wanna know everything about you, Billy. Come on. I told you my secrets."

Thinking he'd tell just a little, he started in on the worst part, the wheat harvest on the Dixon place. He told about those men circling like wolves and getting Lizzyanne, and he told how he got away and went after them on a Percheron. He told about being arrested and Mr. Swain becoming his guardian.

"How old were you?"

"Hmm. Mebbe seventeen. She were fifteen I think. They was lookin' to kill me, fixin' to claim I come after 'em. Indians doan get a fair shake from the law. Everthin' gets twisted 'round to make 'em look bad. I figgered those men'd kill Lizzyanne when they was done with her to keep her from talkin'. I seen she was gonna die on account'a me."

For a long moment, the skull-crushing noise was the only sound in the room.

"Did you and Lizzyanne keep seeing each other?"

"She never looked at me again. Mebbe scared to be with an Indian."

"Oh, Billy, I'm so sorry that happened to you, and sorry it's like that for Indians."

"Indian life is shit," he said. "I brung you this far away so's you doan gotta be scared 'a that kinda thing. I'll keep you safe by being a white man."

"You must hate white people."

"Oh, there's some is all right." He rolled over, smiling at her. "My favorite is you." He kissed the tip of her nose. Mr. Swain were good to the Cosumne people. Let 'em live in Old Sheep Corral after he bought it. Let 'em go work on other ranches if they wanted, so long as they tended to his cows. There's some white people like that. An' there's some I'd like to hurt."

"What would you do to them, if you could?"

He hesitated, but then felt he trusted her enough to say it. Rolling to his back and looking at the ceiling, he told her what he'd thought about many times but had never said aloud until now.

"First I'd stand 'em up in a trench. All in a row. Feet tied together and hands tied behind backs. I'd take me a shovel and fill the trench with sand so's only their heads was stickin' out. Like cabbage in a row. Then I'd borrow me some boots with iron toes and go down the line and kick their heads clean off."

Her hand had stopped moving on his chest. Maybe afraid of him. He should have thought that out four times before speaking. The noise grated his nerves.

Finally she spoke. "Did you have another girlfriend?"

"You like hearing such as that?"

"I told you. I wanna know everything about you."

But her hand didn't move.

He'd told her too much already, so he drew the wider picture. "There ain't 'nough Indian girls to go around. White men take 'em when they're young and toss 'em out like trash when they're done with 'em. I got my fill'a that kinda girl, that kind what steals my money to go drink. I stopped lookin' at 'em. Then I seen you."

"Oh Billy!" She turned to him, all soft with the hard lump in the middle. "And here you are over forty years old. That's sad."

"No it's not sad. I am a happy man."

"But how did you earn that money? Back then. The money that got stolen."

"Times wasn't so bad back then. Ranchers paid wages. And when I wasn't needed at the Swain place in winter I went trappin' in the mountains. Sold the pelts." He laughed. "Like to got my toes froze off."

"Did you go barefoot up there?"

"Learned my lesson a couple times."

"I've been thinking we'd oughta find us a place without all this noise," she said. "I heard there's a good cabin over the ridge to the west. It'd be a long walk for you, to get to the mine, and you're already so tired when you get back from work, so if—"

"If you want that place it's all right with me. I'm used to walkin'."

The next morning after Billy left for the mine, Mae put on her red frock and buttoned the top buttons, leaving the middle section open in the back as always. She threw the oversized miner's shirt over it, pinned on her watch, and left the drafty cabin.

She took the old trail used by miners years ago, angling up the mountain toward the saddle in the high foothills separating Big Canyon Creek from French Creek. Heavy in front, she took her time, loving the warm day and the green hillsides with puddles of yellow, pink, and purple wildflowers. It was an Easter fairyland. As she climbed, the trees and bushes grew thicker. She passed two abandoned mine tunnels with ferns dripping down over the mouths, watered by seepage from the mountain. All would have been idyllic except for the stamp mill, which echoed off the opposite ridge and bounced back in dizzying cacophony.

At last she passed the high point of the saddle, but even going down the other side she still heard the mill, as well as other mills echoing across the wider canyon of French Creek. She also heard the train whistle in the distance, on its way from Latrobe to Placerville. That meant it was about noon.

She continued on the trail, thinking how proud Billy was of his pay increase. No question had arisen when he'd passed himself off as the son of a Portuguese farmer. For this work he even wore boots, oversized. Her mind returned to that shocking thing he'd said about kicking men's heads off. She hadn't imagined that such a sweet man could think such a thing, like he had the savage in him that people feared in Indians. It puzzled her.

In the shady places, the round leaves of miner's lettuce crowded together in bunches, the shadier the bigger the leaves. She snapped off a handful to munch on as she walked. Crisp and cool, tastier than most lettuce. She waved at a crew of woodcutters. They had a fire going with a black twister of smoke rising into the blue sky, no doubt burning green twigs and leaves. The big branches and split trunk pieces they had harvested filled half of their gigantic wagon, strong oak destined to support mine tunnels and city buildings. Eight or ten draft horses, free of their harnesses, munched in the meadow where the oaks had previously been cleared. Stifling the urge to go over and pet them, she continued on the path.

Woodcutters had no advancement opportunity. But miners did. Experienced miners had told Billy that the Big Canyon leads would produce a good yield for many years. She hoped Billy would work his way up to foreman or higher. The raise in pay meant they believed he had a future with them. She looked forward to visiting the high mountains with him this summer when he had the Fourth of July off, but she doubted drovers had advancement opportunities.

There it was! Rounding a bend she saw the cabin made of massive logs just like Mr. Gates had described. Three logs laid one on top of the other were high enough for the entire wall. This was old-growth yellow pine, he had said. Only young trees of that variety remained in the harvested areas. It looked funny to see a cabin made of such fat trunks, like a fanciful house in a children's book. She knocked to be sure the place was still deserted, and then lifted the latch and went inside.

Quiet. The massive logs shut out *all* sound. A back window let in the morning sun and a front porch faced the afternoon light. It would be cool in the summer and easy to heat in the winter. Not far away was a natural spring, so all they'd need to do was dip out a bucketful each morning. This sturdy house seemed to put its arms around her.

Getting off her swollen feet, she lay down in a warm rectangle of sunshine on the floor. White curtains with a little pink pattern would be nice on the windows and they could afford to hire a mule team to haul a cookstove up here. It would be a long walk for Billy in the dark of the early mornings, but maybe the foreman would allow him to take the carbide hat off the grounds. Billy had told her how that brilliant light worked. Under the hard hat a little lever made water drip down from a tiny reservoir into the acetylene container. The mixture created a gas that came out a hole in the front of the hat, which the miner lit with a match. If the flame shot out too far, the miner changed the amount of water with the tiny lever. A cougar would run from a man with a flame shooting out of his forehead. Luckily grizzly bears had been killed off years ago. She'd read something in *The Sacramento Bee* about the last grizzly bear being killed in the state.

Even with Baby Emma bumping around inside, sleep overwhelmed her.

She awoke in shadow. Fuzzy with sleep she looked at her watch. The stew had been simmering at the back of the stove, and in an hour and a half Billy would be home! The fire would need to be stoked, and she had to get to the store before it closed, to get more flour for the dumplings.

Back on the chilly trail mosquitoes whined around her. She slapped at them on her arms and face and tried to clap them out of the air. As she topped the ridge and walked down the dark side of the mountain, the noise hit her like the devil releasing a damper on a colossal noise-maker from hell.

Long rows of curdled clouds over Big Creek Canyon blocked the sun.

73

This was payday, and the men in the washroom joked and flipped towels at each other like little boys. Under the showerhead next to Billy, Ian Burnett stood on one leg, bent over, lathering between his toes.

He looked up at Billy and said, "Store's got a lady's cape at a low price." He thumped his foot down and stuck his chest into the water, pushing off soap. "Louise said redheads like her oughtn't to wear pink, but it'd look good on

Mae." He turned away to rinse his backside. Stepping out of the shower he shouted over the melee, "Two whole days!"

Billy had heard of Easter but never imagined it to be a holiday, and he had forgotten to mention it to Mae. He stepped out and grabbed a towel. In the clean-room the men were dressing when Ian lowered his voice to Billy, "Clem and me's goin' down canyon to get us a buck tomorrow. Wanna come?"

Billy didn't let on that he had no gun. "Mae's time's comin'. I'd best stay."

"Sure, man. See ya." Ian dashed out to the cage that was about to go up.

As Billy knelt over his bootlaces, he thought he just might buy a surprise for Mae, if that cape was still there and didn't cost too much. With only three women on the grounds full time, the company store didn't normally stock ladies' garments.

On top he stepped into a cool, cloudy evening. Across the road the stamp mill hammered full blast, as always, amplified by its nonstop echoes in the narrow canyon. He walked to the mine-house a long stone's throw away, where the pay line was moving fast.

Still joking and laughing and punching each other's shoulders, the men ahead took their money and started up the road to Shingle Springs, a three-mile walk. Billy pocketed the coins and stepped one door over to the store, which occupied the end section of the building.

Inside, the pink cape hung on the shoulders of a curvy wire frame. Louise Burnett was right. It would be pretty on his rose. He couldn't read the note pinned to collar so he'd ask Mr. Gates the cost. One of these days Mae would teach him to read. He smiled to himself. They never could seem to find the time.

Mr. Gates glanced up to acknowledge Billy but continued listening to the tall customer at the counter. Meanwhile Billy examined the shirts, woolen stockings, leather gloves and postal cards. A stack of shiny little beer buckets stood beside a keg on the counter, and a hand-written sign. He didn't have to read to know that miners weren't allowed to buy more than one bucket of beer per day. The limit on alcohol applied to all men, not just Indians. Billy had never seen that before. The store didn't even stock whisky. The men had to go to Shingle Springs to get drunk.

The customer in the business suit wasn't the mine superintendent. Billy's sense of privacy blocked what the stranger was saying until—

"…name's Mae. Dark curly hair, small of stature and, uh, in the family way. Be obliged if you'd tell me where I might find her."

It was Oberon! Punched in the solar plexus by those words, Billy darted out the door and ran back to the head-frame, dodging the last men leaving the cage. He slipped behind a big steel leg watching the mine house through holes punched in the metal.

Oberon had promised to kill Mae, and Billy promised her he'd kill him if he came after her. This man was tall, broad-shouldered and dark-haired, just like she'd said. It couldn't be one of her brothers. They were both shorter than Billy. This man was a great deal taller. His hair wasn't long like Oberon's was supposed to be, but any man could cut his hair, and naturally he wouldn't wear a police uniform to do his dirty work.

Mr. Gates would tell him that Mae's husband had just left the store in a big hurry—everyone in camp thought they were married. Oberon would be armed. If Billy succeeded in killing him, and the body was found, Mr. Gates would point to Billy's strange behavior.

He looked around for a length of iron, a hay hook, a rope, a broken wine bottle, anything. All he could see in the shadow of the hill was an old tobacco tin. Then he recalled the windstorm two days ago. Woodcutters hadn't yet cleared that area behind the cabins, and early this morning on his way to and from the outhouse he'd seen some downed branches. With a little time he might be able to find a good club. But first he needed to know for sure that Oberon would go after her. He glanced at the orange clouds on the western ridge-top. Sunset in the canyon didn't last long. Soon darkness would help him.

The tall man came out of the store placing a bowler hat on his head. He didn't turn toward the livery stable as any other man would after conducting his business. Instead, with that bounce in his knees that Billy recognized as the confident walk of a bully in search of a smaller, weaker victim, he headed directly to the three cabins, toward Billy.

Billy skidded down through the loose gravel of the slag pile, the cascading rattle covered by the stamp mill. Then, at a run, he circled around to the back of the little clearing with the three cabins and ran into the trees behind them. He'd have to find a club in a hurry because Oberon had a direct route.

Relieved to see the pale streaks of downed branches in the dark of the grass, he realized the weather had been warm, stoves unused except for cooking. The deadfall hadn't all been collected. He ran from branch to branch, the first ones too brittle or weakened by rot. Some were too long and unwieldy. Fearing that Oberon had reached the cabin before him, though it was highly unlikely at the slow pace the man had been walking, Billy went to the back of his house and sidled around the corner and along the wall to the window. He released his breath to see Mae calmly working over the stove. No Oberon yet. He didn't want her to see what he had in mind, nor did he want the Burnetts and Smiths to see.

Running back to the trees, with one eye on the path, he continued looking for the right branch, trying them, gripping them, testing their weight. He found one that fit his hand. He swung it back and forth. It was good and heavy.

Still no Oberon.

Billy considered striking him from behind when Oberon faced the door, but it wasn't dark yet and the neighbors might see. For some reason the man still wasn't coming down the path. He needed to find him and see what he was doing. One side of the Smith cabin had no windows.

Billy raced past it, then bent low and made a beeline across the clearing. He ducked into the greasewood on the little hill opposite, staying low as he crept parallel to the path, back to where he could see the head-frame. Long ago an old mining tunnel had been pecked out of the solid rock of the little hill he now stood on.

He had crept most of the way to the tram when he spied Oberon sitting on an stump. Just sitting. Puzzled at first, Billy then realized the man was also waiting for the cover of darkness. Well, that was good. Billy waited, club in hand, nose filled with the coal-oil odor of the greasewood. The tram-tender's lantern on the top of the head-frame wasn't throwing much light yet, but it would as night descended.

Billy dropped his head for a moment to stretch the tight muscles in the back of his neck. The old tunnel, he realized, would hide the body for a while but not serve as a grave. The floor was solid rock, as were the walls and arched ceiling. Where then to put the body? Any grave dug around the camp would leave a telltale patch of fresh dirt. The best place would be in the loose barrow dirt of one of the two deserted mine holes on the side of the mountain.

The canyon darkened slowly. The head-frame lantern now cast ghostly light around Oberon and the mine entrance.

Oberon stood up, stretched his arms out to the sides, and brushed his backside. He turned and looked at the last of the purple-red cloud over the ridge and then began walking straight toward the cabin! All doubt vanished. Billy must act because Oberon intended to make good his deadly promise.

Billy let him pass by on the path below. Then he stalked him, parting the greasewood and allowing the branches to whip behind him, unheard in the mill noise.

In the darkest place, just entering the little clearing, several strides before Oberon would enter the lamplight from the cabin windows, Billy ran forward.

His blood was up, the club raised. With all the loathing he'd ever felt for bullies such as this, he swung at the ear. The impact lifted him momentarily and he heard the hollow sound of a ripe melon over the noise.

Oberon fell like a tree.

Breathing hard, Billy came around the front of the sprawled man. He raked his gaze across the windows and doors of the three cabins—no one there—and again raised the club and struck down across the man's face.

Knowing it took a lot to kill a large animal, he straddled the body and aimed the butt of the club over the heart. He brought it down sharply, the way a deer would kill a man, rearing and punching down with the front hooves to stop the heart.

Billy's shoulders and arms pulsed with the fierce pumping of blood.

He wouldn't be able to hear a heartbeat if he got down and tried, and it was too dark to see the extent of damage. He watched for a sign of life but the man lay stone still. Three hard blows, he realized, delivered by the arms and back of a man made strong by the swinging of a pickax ten hours a day would have killed him.

He trotted to the edge of the wood, swung the club up and back and then let loose of it so it would fly high and land in the willows of Big Canyon Creek. Now the enormity of what he had done and the sudden change to his life crept into his stomach. His mouth was dry. He returned to the body and fast-dragged it into the old tunnel, a temporary hiding place. Ducking under the trailing plants over the entrance, he continued about halfway into that blackest of caves and dropped the legs. Then he went to the cabin, trying to calm himself.

"Billy!" Mae stood up and smiled when he opened the door. "I've got stew and dumplings on the stove." Her smile faded. "What's the matter?"

"I killed Oberon. He come askin' for you. Tailed him and killed him out front." He pointed with his head. "We gotta bury him and get out'a the canyon."

She stared at him with blank eyes, and then said, "Yes. We'll put him in that old mine tunnel across the way and cover him with dirt."

"He's there now. But there's no dirt. 'Cept outside the tunnel where it'd be seen. Let's wait 'til the lamps go out in the other cabins and take him up to one 'a them old tunnels in the mountainside. Plenty dirt there."

He searched her blue eyes for assurance that he'd done the right thing. They were blank. "We gotta get out of camp," he said, thinking that he had paid one man back for what he'd done to Mae, and for what men like him had done to the People, and now his life had turned from white and respectable to one more Indian running from the law.

"It would look suspicious to run just when he went missing," Mae said.

"It's already suspicious. Mr. Gates'll say he saw me run outa the store when Oberon asked after you."

"The Sacramento police will come looking."

They talked in bursts. About Nevada and other places to hide. After a time he was able to sit down on the edge of the kitchen chair.

"Billy," she said coming around and laying a hand on his shoulder, "I never knew a man who would go so far as to kill a police inspector for a girl. I hardly know what to say. Except thank you."

He breathed a little easier.

"You won't be scared no more," he said, but the instant that left his mouth he knew it wasn't true. Now she'd be afraid of all policemen, not just one. They were in this together. He had made a criminal of her too.

She set the pan of stew in front of him. He nibbled a little and saw that she ate nothing. "We need to get clean outa California," he said.

"I remember those wanted posters in the Sacramento Post Office. Lawmen telegraph each other. We'd need to change our names..." Her voice trailed off.

"Mebbe Mexico."

She went silent. They didn't undress. When the lamps went down in the other cabins they turned their lamp off too.

He'd taken a blanket off the bed to wrap the body. She had a lantern and the twig broom to cover the tracks and blood. "Don't light it yet," he told her. "Here, put some matches in your pocket."

They agreed to continue over the ridge to French Creek after burying the body. They could catch the train. From Sacramento, the tracks fanned out in all directions to anyplace in the country or Mexico or Canada. He had his pay in his pocket.

"There's an abandoned cabin over the ridge," she said. "I went to see it today. I'd be a good place to stay the night."

"We'll see how long it takes to bury him. Pro'bly we otta walk all night. Get to one of the stations for the first train in the morning."

He helped her tie the Chinese bag on her back with a long twist of muslin sheeting left by the previous renter. Then they stepped into the deafening clamor of a black world. Even those pinpoints of light, the stars, were cloaked by cloud, and the thumbnail moon was on the wane, almost at the mountaintop. He smelled a hint of rain. Mae waited outside the tunnel while Billy found the body, rolled it in the blanket, and picked up the ankles wrapped in the cloth, one in each hand on either side of his waist, and then dragged the dead weight into the night.

Mae followed behind, brushing back and forth across the trail with the broom while Billy pulled the body. Going straight up the steep hill they cut across the road that traversed the hill and kept well out of the tram-tender's lamplight. Billy knew that when an accident happened in the mine, the tram-tender rang an alarm that could be heard over the stamp mill. But the tram-tender was said to take naps at night, and Billy hoped he was napping now.

It took strength to pull the body through brush and rock. At last his feet found the level road higher on the mountain. Now on the road they could move faster. Soon they rounded a hill that blocked the view. The tram-tender could not see them.

"Light the lamp then come on up here and help me find a tunnel," he told Mae. Coyote holes, some men called those abandoned mining tunnels.

The lamp flickered on behind him, and he started to pull again, but Mae's voice cut through the mill noise.

"Oh no!"

He looked back. She had the lantern just over Oberon's face, the blanket having come undone. He understood the shock of seeing a smashed face for the first time. She dropped to her knees, feeling up and down the body.

"We gotta hurry," he said, beginning to pull again.

"It's Charlie!"

The words paralyzed him.

"You killed Charlie!"

He stammered something about Oberon being tall.

"His hands. His smell. He's a lot taller than Oberon. I tell you it's Charlie!"

He had the sensation of being punched in the stomach. Not once had she said a bad word about Charlie, just sorrow that he wouldn't marry her. And he was the real father of—

"Go," Mae said, getting to her feet. "Get out of here. I'll hide him."

"He's too heavy for y—"

"Go! I don't wanna know where you are. Charlie's got friends. They'll follow. Maybe coming right now. Go now!"

Her voice knocked him back. He dropped the legs and staggered away, his stomach in a noose. He'd killed the wrong man. He shouldn't leave his rose to clean up after this ugly mistake, but he could tell that she couldn't stand the sight of him. Dizzy with horror he lurched backwards out of the lamplight.

He turned up the trail and shuffled into a slow, awkward trot. She didn't want his help. He'd ruined everything. He had to remove himself from her, from this vicious Coyote trick.

With all his blood in his stomach he couldn't feel the ground and could barely make his legs move. But then his heart exploded from too much love and hurt, and the force of it gave strength to his legs. He dug his toes in and flew over the earth like a wild wind. Sometimes he stepped off into the brush but his feet corrected and found the trail again. He ran faster and faster, putting distance between himself and that bad place where he would never see Mae again, and never be father to Baby Emma. He would leave El Dorado County and California and the United States.

74

Billy disappeared into the night and already she missed him. She loved him. He knew all about her, even the bad parts, and still he loved her. But he must vanish without a trace because he'd be held responsible even though he didn't murder Charlie. *She did.* She'd said too much about Oberon and too little about Charlie. She'd done Billy a great wrong and now must not slow him down by traveling with him. Powerful men would be searching for Charlie. His secretary at the Capitol always knew his whereabouts. They could be waiting for him in the mining camp this very minute.

Kneeling with the lantern, she stared at Charlie's mangled face. Not long ago she'd prayed for him to come and marry her. Now he had finally come. She set the lantern on the dirt and touched his cheek, the blood wetter than expected. She spoke to him, feeling the vibration in her throat and mouth but not hearing herself through the clamor of the stamp mill.

"You came too late, Charlie. And you were right. Oberon can find plenty of girls in Sacramento. He wouldn't hunt me down in a place like this. If only I'd believed you, this wouldn't have happened. If only I'd had some sense." He'd seen her as a hysterical female, and maybe he'd been right about that.

Poor sweet Billy had listened to her and taken her at her word. He trusted what she believed and gave weight to her fears. He respected what she wanted, whether to have the baby or not. His downfall was trusting her. Now the law would try to kill him for it. The law didn't know the goodness in him. She must hide Charlie for Billy's sake. And the baby's. She mustn't grow up knowing her mother helped kill her father, a good man. Everyone would testify to Charlie's good character, including the Governor himself.

She lingered longer than she knew, until she felt ready to act. It wouldn't be easy to find either of those old tunnels. One had loose barrow dirt spilled down the hillside at the entrance, at about this elevation. Struggling to her feet, she bent down to pick up the lantern.

Charlie's eyes opened!

The blood jumped in her veins.

His unblinking eyes glittered in the lamplight and seemed to stare into the starry sky. She shrank back in horror. Was it a twitch of the eyelids, like a headless chicken walking? A ghost rising to slay her, as in the story of Ichabod Crane? She glanced around half expecting to see a banshee screaming out of the forest to whisk her away to hell. Anything seemed possible on such an unnatural night.

The eyes turned in their sockets and looked at her!

A sound came out of her, unheard in the din of the stamp mill but felt in the back of her throat.

Heart knocking in her ribs, she tried to think. He could be alive. She knelt beside the lantern and put her mouth to his ear. "Charlie?" Quickly she flattened herself, as best she could with that extended abdomen, against his shoulder so her ear was over his mouth. Baby Emma moved and she realized he might have felt it.

Warm air puffed into her ear. He was trying to talk. Charlie was alive!

∾

The steep downhill pull toward the cabin went fast except for her efforts to un-snag the blanket when she failed to avoid the bigger rocks and brush. She had to hope the wool of his suit padded him a little. She hadn't been able to lift his upper body, so she dragged him by the ankles, downhill easier than Billy's uphill pull. The closer to the canyon floor the stronger she felt the mill vibrations up her legs.

She had wanted to run up the road to tell Billy he wasn't a murderer after all. He would have appreciated knowing that, but he could have been a mile or more away and she knew she couldn't catch up to him, especially not in her condition. Nor could she leave Charlie alone in an area with mountain lions and coyotes. Besides, it didn't change anything that Charlie was alive. Ambushing and severely wounding a man was also a serious crime, especially an Indian attacking a white man. Billy needed to get away just as much as if Charlie were dead.

Back in the cold cabin, out of breath and fearing he was dead, she pulled him to the space between the bed and the table. Her hand shook so much as she tried to light the wick that she needed another match, but finally got the light on him. He lay still, a bloody lumpiness where his face should be, except for a pale and sheer something in the middle. Trembling inside and out, she set the lantern on the table and stoked the fire, put in more wood, and then kneeled down and pressed her fingers into his neck under the bristly jaw. She waited. Yes, still alive. The smell of blood was thick in the confines of the cabin.

Pulling the blankets off the bed, she laid them over Charlie. He needed protection from the cold hard floor. She yanked the under-bedding off the mattress, folded it into four thicknesses, tucked the edge under his back, and then got behind him and pushed him on his side away from the padding. Tucking it far under him all along his length, she rolled him to his back onto the folded material. Now he would be warmer.

She held the lantern to his face to get a better look. Even two handed, it shook so much that the shadows moved and jerked and she couldn't see any more than before. Solid blood! She didn't dare try to wash it away, though the water in the pan would have heated some by now. She felt for his pulse again. *Weak.*

He needed the doctor from Shingle Springs! She must go to the tram-tender. In case of nighttime emergencies the tram-tended opened the mine office and telegraphed the doctor, who came by buggy to care for any injured men, or in her case, to help with the birth. Taking the lantern she opened the door and stepped into the cool dampness and louder din. But her chest wasn't cooperating. She could hardly draw breath. In her mind's eye she could see Billy running for his life in the dark. Dear, sweet Billy who had tried to help her by doing this. What would she say to the tram-tender? The doctor? They would ask about the cause of it. If she told them Charlie had fallen down on one of those jagged outcroppings, they'd wonder why Billy hadn't reported it instead of her. Then tomorrow they'd notice his absence from work.

She needed to think this out. Billy wasn't far enough away yet. He had to take the morning train to Sacramento. He'd get there at noon, and he need until about midnight to get out of the country, north or south. Lawmen, she knew, used the telegraph in apprehending criminals. Her mind jumped from Charlie to Billy and back again. Should she keep Charlie alive and let Billy hang? Or should she let Charlie die and save Billy's life. That's what it boiled down to, But she could not make that choice! She didn't know how to think about it. She couldn't seem to think at all. Too much had happened in a short time. And the lantern! The Burnettes and Smiths would wake up and think the baby was coming. They'd come over to help and see Charlie! They mustn't do that. Turning out the light, she went inside and quietly shut the door, her heart working too hard—for hours now.

She felt her way to the table, put down the lantern and carefully moved around Charlie's shoes. *Whose life should I save? Charlie's or Billy's.* Maybe Charlie was gone. Again she kneeled and felt his neck. *Alive.* Each time it surprised her.

I'll rest here a little while and won't need to get up and down all the time. Just stretch out alongside him. It feels so good to get off my feet. Two times up that mountain in one day. I'm not used to it. Maybe now I can think. Maybe it's not so clear cut a choice and I can keep Charlie alive long enough for Billy to get away. One full day. She tried to slow down her shallow breathing. It was making her faint. Then she remembered God and Mother Mary.

Taking a deep breath, she folded her hands on her chest and prayed. *I'm sorry I've been such a sinner. Billy did this because of me. He doesn't deserve to die. Show me the right thing to do. Please guide me. Amen.*

In the grinding noise she waited patiently for an answer, and the next thing she knew she was waking up, stiff and cold. Nothing had changed. It was dark. Possibly only a few minutes later. She felt Charlie's neck. He moved his head a little! *Definitely alive.* She covered herself with his blankets and moved closer to him to share the warmth. Again she prayed and It became a chant in her mouth: *Help me, guide me, dear Heavenly father and mother, Show me the way. Help me and guide me...*

She drifted by small jerky stages, away from the cabin to a place where Baby Emma, quite big now, stood outside a little blue door knocking, smiling wanting to come in. Or was it out? It didn't matter. Mae gladly went to the door...

⌒

Mae awoke to a different world. At first she couldn't think what made it so. She was lying on the cold, hard floor with her back aching and the wind whooshing around the eaves. Charlie lay beside her. The loose slats that once sealed the vertical boards of the cabin walls clattered and tapped. She could hear! That's what had changed. The stamp mill had stopped for the first time since she and Billy had come to the mining camp.

She put a hand on Charlie's chest, still rising and falling. *Thank you, God and Mary Mother of God.* Up on an elbow, she spoke softly to him. "You awake?"

He opened his eyes—bright red where they should have been white! His blood crusted face had no nose, but a paper-thin bone cresting out of the oozy gore. But he was still among the living.

"I'll be back in about fifteen minutes," she told him, struggling against her ungainly body to get to her feet. She would go to the headquarters and figure out what had stopped the mine. Maybe an investigation into Charlie's disappearance! If so, it'd be God's will. She'd decide what to do then.

His eyes rolled back. She dropped to her knees and listened for a heartbeat. It was there. Maybe the pain knocked him out. Intending to get laudanum at the store, if they had any, she almost reached for the coffee can on the shelf where they kept their money. But she'd spent the last penny on flour for the dumplings and Billy's weekly pay was in his pocket. She took the Chinese bag from under the bed, fished out two dollars and slipped it in the pocket of the large miner's shirt that she wore over her dress. Shrugging into Billy's old sheepskin coat, she buttoned the top buttons until it wouldn't fit around her middle. The wind pushed, and she had to fight to get the door closed behind her as she went out into a skittering of rain.

Steeling herself for what would transpire, she went to the outhouse— fortunately no Louise or Adair at this hour—and then hurried to the mine headquarters. On the way she passed the mill, motionless and silent, several steel elephant feet raised in various degrees mid-stomp. On her right the head-frame towered over everything, but she saw not a miner or mill worker anywhere. She continued up the road to the mine house and found a hand-printed sign on the door:

MINE CLOSED APRIL 13 AND 14
HAPPY EASTER

She tried the store door. Locked. She knocked on the windows around the entire building. Not even one lamp on this gray day. She backed up but saw no light in the upstairs windows. The telegraph wire attached to the roof draped from pole to pole along the road to Shingle Springs, but the men on this end weren't there to turn the thing on. The doctor couldn't be reached, and any help for Charlie would come from her alone. But at least no investigation was underway. That much was clear.

Back behind the cabin, she gathered wood of a size that she could break to fit the tiny stove. While she worked she recalled the good care Charlie had given her those months when she'd been so sick, how gently he'd spooned in the medicine and broth to her lips. He'd given her his bed and slept on the sofa, and he even hired a nurse to watch over her while he was at the Capitol. It was her turn to help him. And as to the question of marriage, for surely that's why he'd come for her, it must wait until she had her brains collected. It was hard to think when faced with the wretchedness of knowing she'd done terrible wrongs to two men that she loved.

Inside the cabin Charlie awoke for short stretches but faded into an unconscious state most of the day. She lay beside him many times to feel if he had stopped breathing. His regular breaths let her sleep.

The next morning she dabbed at the coagulated blood on his face and head. The purple swelling of his face was worse, so bad she couldn't tell if he was wincing in pain. Faint moans were her only clue.

He opened his red eyes a slit and said in a weak and raspy voice, "Wha… what happen?" Had the mill been running she couldn't have heard it.

"Don't you remember?"

"No." Reedy like a weak old man, "Where'm I?"

"Do you know me?"

"Uh-uh." He moaned. "Wh… where?"

"At the Big Canyon Mine. In El Dorado County."

He looked at her with those awful eyes saying something she couldn't hear. She put her ear closer to his ruined mouth. "Why… here?"

"You had an accident."

"How?"

"You fell down. Maybe landed on one of those shale rocks standing on end."

"Uuuuuh. Head hurt."

"I know. You've got a big goose-egg here." She pointed at it in a way so he could see her finger. "Your nose is broken, and your lips are split and swollen. It's bad. At first I thought you were dead."

"Who you?"

His loss of memory would give her time to think. She'd heard about people forgetting everything after a head wound. They often remembered later. She didn't want to tell him what Billy did, but knew she shouldn't lie about her name, which he was likely to remember later. "Mae," she said.

He shut his terrible eyes and faded away again.

Just in case he could still hear, she said, "I'm going to cut willows to make you a special tea. Be back in about twenty minutes." Billy had told her willow bark tea took down swelling and pain.

She took the water bucket and her sharp knife and walked up the road past the deserted mine house to the livery barn. A sign on the barn said, "Closed for Easter." They must have locked the horses in with their feed and water. She turned off the road at the brick building that people called the powder magazine, and made her way down through the bunch grass and lupine to Big Canyon Creek. On her first day alone in the cabin, when the men were at work, Louise Burnett had come to visit and warned her to fetch drinking water upstream of the mill because quicksilver and arsenic were constantly being washed from the stamp mill into the creek. "You could get sick," she'd said. So Mae often took the extra time to fetch water from this more distant place. However, she so hated the crude remarks of the men around the mine headquarters that she frequently dipped water from the little eddy downstream of the mill. When Mae told Adair Smith, the other neighbor, about what Louise had said, Adair scoffed. She said she and Clem drank from that nearby eddy all the time and hadn't been sick a day. But today Mae needed more than water. The gray willows were thick here, and she cut a good many young switches covered with pussies, as Iowans called them.

Back on the little flat she waved at skinny, red-haired Louise. Louise smiled, raised a hand and strode away on her morning constitutional. Clearly not suspicious.

Charlie's heart, she thanked God, was still beating, though he was unconscious. She peeled the outside bark of the switches, making sure the underlayer was exposed, and boiled a pan of it. Next time he awoke, she kneeled and supported his head while she spooned the acrid smelling tea into his mouth, careful not to bump his torn and swollen lower lip. He swallowed just fine. She also spooned in broth from the two-day old stew. When she removed her arm, he sagged down and slept again.

She ate the rest of the stew with the soggy dumplings.

Charlie woke up for short stretches. Each time she spooned in more tea, and she began to believe he would recover. However, his rugged good looks would be gone unless the doctors in the Sacramento hospital tended to his nose real soon and performed a miracle. An ugly face would hurt his ability to work with the public and the Legislature.

Taking care of Charlie took most of Mae's thoughts and energy, leaving less time to worry about Billy. The next morning she was removing Charlie's trousers and shorts when he opened his red eyes and spoke in his weak, slurred voice.

"Wha... doin'?"

"Cleaning you up. Can't have you lying in your pee like that."

"I... go... outsi'e."

Outside. He wanted help. "Now?"

He tried to nod.

"I can't lift you."

He was trying to move himself.

After a lengthy struggle, she got him most of the way to his feet leaning over her bent back. "Oow!" he said, sliding off to his knees and then crumpling to the floor. His poor damaged head got knocked again, but fortunately on the other side.

She left him where he fell.

"You're in no condition to get up," she told him. "I'll get you something to pee in."

She went to the cabin on the right. Louise wasn't back from her constitutional, and both men were still away hunting. Adair Smith had an empty whisky bottle. Thanking her profusely and making up an excuse about brewing a quantity of tea, Mae hurried back to Charlie.

He was still awake. She helped him use the bottle. He closed his eyes, and they disappeared into the folds of his swollen face.

She gathered all the stinking blankets and trousers off the floor, went to the creek and washed the pee out of them. Back in the cabin she stretched the heavy woolen materials out to dry over table, chairs and headboard, and then rolled Charlie over on his back, which seemed to be the least uncomfortable position. She also put the pillow under his head.

She lay down on the bed thinking about Billy. Probably he wouldn't ever get in touch with her again for fear of being traced. By now he could be in Mexico. There could never be a trial, with his only defense being that he'd intended to kill Oberon, a policeman, who would possibly be in the courtroom. She hoped he'd find a happy life and marry a woman worthy of his trust and love, one who, unlike Mae, wouldn't cause him any more grief.

75

On the third morning Mae opened her eyes again to the eerie silence. She could hear Charlie snuffle in his sleep. She'd slept better in the bed and hadn't heard the morning whistle. No doubt they'd start the mill again after a cart or two of ore came up from the ground. The whole place would be back in action, without Billy. The quiet was a hole in her heart—Billy gone forever and permanent damage to Charlie. Both of them hurt terribly by her.

The light from the windows told her it was afternoon! She lay in the quiet, immobilized by that awful knowledge; but when she heard Charlie move and saw that he was awake, she swung her legs out of bed and returned to the task of healing him. She forced her stiff body into an upright position and onto her bare feet. Then she squatted to kindle the stove, dipped water from the bucket, added half a cup of rolled oats to the pan, and put it on the stove.

Seeing Charlie's eyes open, she helped him use the whisky bottle. Black and yellow hues added more color to the red, maroon, blue and purple of his swollen face.

"You'll need some more willow tea," she told him. He nodded in his almost imperceptible way. "We both slept in half a day. Musta needed it."

Kneeling on the hard floor she spooned the rest of yesterday's tea into him. He took it dutifully, as he'd done every few hours yesterday. She had tried letting him hold the cup and drink by himself, but he couldn't tolerate the touch of it on his lips, and he hurt too much when he tried to sit up. While he took the tea like a grateful baby bird, she recalled Billy's answer to her question. She had asked what he meant when he called Baby Emma a blessing. He'd said something like: Love matches love, and it comes out of the earth, like all things do, and it finds another piece of itself that fits like a glove. Love matching love between male and female is the dance of life, like the love between mother and child, or a father and a child. All are blessings.

He had been a blessing to her. He had saved her from going out of her mind with grief and loss. And he would have been a blessing to Baby Emma. But now Charlie had finally come for her. Bringing him back to life to be a father to his own baby would, she knew, also be a blessing. All of them would be blessed—mother, father, and baby.

Charlie slowly pointed to his chest when the last drop was gone. "Wha... ha'en... ee?"

What happened to me? "You had an accident." She went to the door and dumped the steaming contents of the bottle outside.

He'd forgotten what she'd told him yesterday. "You fell down the hill."

"Uuuh."

"I'm just guessing that's what happened. I wasn't there."

"Who dere?"

She added water and willow bark strips to the tea pan. "I don't know. I found you in this condition."

He slurred, "Aullet gone?" He slowly patted the place his pocket should be, unable to make the *w* sound.

"I didn't find it." That was a lie, but a beating and robbery made a good story too, being closer to what really happened—in case he remembered something. She threw the miner's shirt over her gown and stepped into her shoes without lacing them. "Be back in a minute."

On her way to the outhouse, she realized she must hide the wallet in a better place. She'd taken it from his trousers pocket before washing them.

Back in the cabin she stirred sugar into the oatmeal. It began to bubble.

"Look in ay 'ocket," he said.

"Which pocket? In your jacket?"

"Uh-huh."

She went to the line of nails on the wall and felt around in his jacket, though she knew it wasn't there. She shrugged and tried to get him to think in another direction. "Can you remember coming to Big Canyon Mine?"

"Mm." He closed his puffy purple eyelids and shook his head in that barely perceptible way.

"Think. Did you come alone? Or did someone drop you off?"

"Dunno."

"Do you know your name?"

"Chollee 'ogue."

"Where were you raised up?"

He tried hard to make sounds that she could understand. Clearly, his memory was improving.

"Your memory is better," she told him. "I'm so glad. Before long you'll—" *remember everything*, she almost said—"be up and at it."

He surprised her by making a long speech in his halting way, missing the consonants his lips couldn't shape, giving chest force to the *w's*, and saying *n* instead of *m*. "I grateful… fer yer hel'. Hurt, hurt, hurt…" He pointed to his eyes, nose, mouth and head, and then his ribs on one side. "Hurt. Wanna kill sel'. Wan heart ta' sto'. Wan laudanun. Get laudanun." He closed the slits of his puffy eyes and sagged back.

He felt like killing himself because of the pain. *Oh God, help him.*

Stirring and lifting the boiling oatmeal off the stove so it wouldn't overflow, she told him that's where she planned to go, to the company store, right after she gave him some breakfast. "I tried to get you some laudanum yesterday, but the store and mine were shut down for two days, for Easter. Don't you remember? I told you that."

"Oh."

When the creamy oatmeal felt cooler in the cup, she spooned five or six mouthfuls into him, little drops at a time. He moaned and moved his head in that way that meant no more. "Laudanun," he said.

She buttoned Billy's jacket down to where she couldn't make it come together over her big belly, then left for the mine headquarters with two dollars from her Chinese bag, Charlie's money.

⌒

From behind the bushes she saw that the turn-around area in front of the stamp mill contained a freight wagon with a gang of four horses and a bunch of men. Two men unloading large-sized containers of quicksilver sidestepped up the hill with one between them and set it beside others, next to the sluice frame. Water normally spewed from the pipe that came out of the hill. It hadn't been turned on yet, but when it was, it would gush over the crushed ore, and the fine gold would amalgamate with the mercury to form clumps. Two other men were pouring the gleaming mercury from one of those lead containers into the sluice apparatus.

Taking a deep breath, she stepped out of the trees. The idle men gawked at her. They jabbed each other in the ribs at the sight of her walking up the road. She knew she looked like a freakish hippopotamus.

"'Bout to explode there, I'd say," a man called, haw-hawing to his friend.

Another looked her up and down and shouted in mock horror, "My God, girl!"

Only a few months ago such men would have looked at her with whistles. She hadn't told Billy about this. He didn't realize that decent ladies in a family way were not to be seen in public, and she hadn't wanted him to be angry at his workmates.

Ignoring them, she stepped over the open ditch, now mud, where the waste-water from the stamp mill would run downhill into Big Creek, and made a bee-line to the mine house. It occurred to her that laudanum would be dispensed, like whisky, by the office and not the store. So she knocked on the office door.

"Come in," sang a tenor voice.

Having composed her speech on the way over, she entered a room of maps and stacked papers. Three men stood up behind desks. "How can I help you," asked the tenor. He offered a chair. One of the others sat down, but the mine superintendent continued to stand. She recognized him.

She sat down. "No doubt you know that Billy was called to his mother's deathbed," she said laying a hand across her big belly. "Well, the pains might be commencing. I'm not sure yet. Mrs. Smith and Mrs. Burnett will help when it comes to that, but I'd sure be grateful for some laudanum, if you've got it."

Odd-shaped red islands blossomed on the young man's cheeks, the pan-handles climbing into his sideburns. Intimate female subjects were not to be mentioned in the presence of men.

The lower half of the mine superintendent's face was framed by a carefully shaved, narrow border of dark whiskers. He walked over and stood beside the young man as if to provide support. "I'll handle this," he said clasping his hands behind his back. The younger man went back to his desk and hunched over his papers.

"Mrs. Rodriguez," boomed the superintendent, using the name she and Billy had invented, "your husband failed to inform us he was leaving. This was disappointing to say the least, and I've already replaced him." Pushing up ever so slightly on his toes, he came down again and cleared his throat. "I see you didn't go with him."

"I didn't think the bumpy ride was a good idea."

"I don't like to do this, but I must ask you to vacate the company cab-in. It is there for the convenience of miners who live on site. I'm sure you understand. I was about to walk over and tell you, but you've conveniently come to me instead."

"I will, that is *we* will move out as soon as possible. But if I might, please, buy some laudanum I'd be much obliged."

He narrowed his eyes. "As soon as possible is too long. I want you gone by tomorrow morning. I don't believe your lying-in time has come or you would have sent a neighbor lady. Our supply of laudanum is for injured men. You're not an injured miner. Please depart at once." He pivoted and returned to his desk.

Trying to stop the tears in her eyes from running down her face, Mae didn't blink. She got up, went out the door, and closed it behind her. Then she let them run. She almost didn't go in the store on account of it, but she wiped her face with the shirtsleeve and opened the door.

Mr. Gates stood alone in his cluttered store. She asked for something for pain.

"What's the ailment?"

"Just pain."

"Well, some people swear by these." He took down from a shelf a tin of Pep Pills. "The main ingredient is cocaine."

She remembered those pills. Charlie kept them in his apartment. Just about every store in the country stocked them, but she hadn't known that in addition to giving energy they also alleviated pain. She bought three tins for thirty cents and turned to leave, but a lady's cape caught her eye. Dusty-pink, it had an appliqué pattern of the same fabric around an upright collar. This was the perfect thing to replace the ugly miner's shirt, and the color would complement her hat and the paisley of her red dress. The note pinned to it said: SPECIAL SALE: $2.00 OR OFFER.

"I want this," she said removing the cape from the wire frame. She spilled all her coins on the counter. "I owe you forty cents. I'll go get—"

"You're the first taker and it's yours for this amount. We're not stocking ladies' wear any more."

Thanking him profusely, Mae took the cape to a back corner of the store and turned around so her naked back couldn't be seen—her camisole, petticoat and under-drawers no longer fit so she'd not been wearing them. Careful not to reveal any of her skin, she removed the shirt and threw on the pretty cape. She re-pinned her watch to the cape. Now she had more courage to walk that gauntlet.

"By the way," Mr. Gates said as she headed for the door, "The other night a gentleman came asking for you. Did he find you?"

Her heart skipped a beat. "Nobody came calling. Do you know his name?"

"He didn't say."

Breath ragged, she went outside and drew air. Three buggies were parked beside the livery barn, which stood catty-corner across the way. They looked like well-used hacks. It occurred to her that one of them might be rented to Charlie.

Yes, the more she thought of it, the more certain she became that he had ridden the train to Shingle Springs and hired a hack to the mine. If so, she could drive him back to Shingle Springs in his own hack and take him to Sacramento by train. This was the way out. Charlie had friends in the Southern Pacific Company, which owned and operated the best hospital in the United States, and she would take him to be cured there.

She had just entered the livery barn when the first steel foot smashed down on the gold-bearing ore, immediately followed by the next and the next—eighth notes from a massive instrument of torture looping around and around with an offbeat echo grating from ridge to ridge.

"Sorry to bother you," she called as she walked up behind the only man in the barn. Tongs in hand, he was holding a piece of red-hot iron inside a small triangular forge that stood on a metal table. The upper point of the forge emitted an acrid coal smoke. The horses munched silently in their stalls, seemingly unaware of the sudden resumption of noise.

The man's voice blared through the din. "Say what you've come to say."

"Sorry to interrupt," she yelled, "but a friend of mine took a serious fall. He's been out of his mind and forgetful. He thinks he left his rig here but isn't sure. Name's Charles Rogue."

"Yup, it's here all right. You got the voucher?"

She'd guessed right! But hadn't thought about looking in his wallet for a voucher. "No, it's back at the cabin."

The man drew the now white-hot bar out of the forge and turned the tongs so it lay on an anvil. "Stand aside," he ordered.

He released one hand, grabbed a ball-peen hammer, and began to pound the glowing metal. The round head of the hammer bounced a little with each blow.

"I need to get to him to the hospital... in Sacramento," Mae called between blows.

"'Bout wrote 'im off," the man said after the next pound. "He was to git back here Friday afternoon. Owes me for three extra days."

He turned the hot metal with the care of a surgeon, and before the next round of hammering, she cried, "Could you let me drive the buggy to the cabin now? To get the voucher and the money? I'm in a company cabin just up the way." She didn't want to walk back and forth in front of the men more than necessary, or risk another encounter with the mine superintendent whom she never wanted to lay eyes on again in her entire life.

"I'll pay when I drive out," she added over his pounding and the mill noise, "On my way back to Shingle."

He pounded like a mad man, changing the straight bar into a horseshoe shape.

"I'll be driving out right past you," she yelled. "I'd appreciate it very much... if... if you'd let me take the hack... now so I can load Charlie in it... and get on the road as soon... as possible."

He suspended his blow and looked her in the eye. "You won't be drivin' t'nowhere 'lessen I see that voucher and that money. For all I know you'd go out the Nashville Road or down to Amador by way of Lambs Crossing."

She wanted to scream, *Look at me. Do you think I'm a thief?* He would make her run the gauntlet twice again, four times including the drive back and forth. But his face was hard.

"All right," she conceded, hot with anger but trying not to let it show. "And when I bring you the voucher, can I drive the buggy to the cabin?"

"After you pay, I got nothin' more to do with it." Pound, pound, pound.

"I'll be back soon. When do you close?"

Now he carefully placed a plug on the pliable iron and pounded it into the horseshoe for the shoe nails. "Six o'clock," he said after a blow.

"Do you happen to know what time the next train leaves from Shingle on its way to Sacramento?"

"First thing in the mornin'."

They'd have to spend the night in Shingle Springs.

Back in the cabin, Charlie was awake and moaning.

"They wouldn't let me buy laudanum, but I got you some Pep Pills," she said. She put all but one tin in the pocket of his suit jacket. "I'd like to throttle the mine super, and would 'ov if I'd been bigger. The cocaine is supposed to help with the pain too. I didn't know that." Charlie was a big man with big pains, so she figured three to one would be about right. She put three pills in his open mouth, and took one herself, to make her feel better.

Now the problem of the wallet. It was under her pillow. *Damn*, he was watching with unusual interest as she stood in her muddle. If he'd only just shut his eyes and go back to sleep. *Oh what tangled webs we weave.*

His red eyes seared her like the molten iron. "Gotta new cake," he said, pointing his finger.

Cape. Charlie, an intelligent man, was getting his memory back, perhaps remembering her, knowing she hadn't had this cape before. Her heart bounced like a pinball down a washboard and then skipped a couple of beats—fear perhaps, or the Pep Pills having an effect.

Throwing caution to the wind, she said, "I found your wallet." She went to her pillow, pulled it out, and opened it, not giving him time to ask questions. "Here's the voucher. You rented a hack. It says right here the Shingle Springs Railroad Livery. I'm going to pay the liveryman man and come back with the hack. Then I'll drive you to the train station and we'll leave early tomorrow morning. I'm taking you to the Southern Pacific Hospital in Sacramento. We'll be there by noon."

She hurried out the door and returned to the livery, ignoring the men in the turnaround area, and paid the liveryman for the extra days.

The horse balked as Mae drove him back past the stamp mill. If the men made rude remarks, she didn't hear. Maybe they noticed her nice cape and her wherewithal to rent a horse and buggy, not to mention her skill with the reins. This horse acted every bit as fractious as most rented horses. It took a firm hand to drive him.

Back at the cabin, the horse went down on the spring grass like he'd never seen it before, and Mae engaged the brake.

Louise and Adair came out of the Burnetts' cabin, staring at the buggy and Mae. More than likely they'd had their heads together over her comings and goings. She went to them. Before they could say anything, she explained that Billy had gone to his dying mother, and the mine super had replaced him and told her to leave. "Also, I've got an injured man who I'm taking to the Sacramento hospital. I'm on the way now and won't be seeing you any more."

At each part of that, the women looked more taken aback.

Mae hurried inside. Clearly Charlie felt some better, even tried to get up a little on an elbow. The furnishings and bedding belonged to the cabin, so the Chinese bag was all she had to pack. She pulled Charlie's trousers and jacket on him, a struggle with her awkward body, and tried not to hurt his sore chest. The trousers looked the worse for the wash in the creek. They had shrunk, but she got them buttoned halfway up, with only two sharp cries from him. Then, short of breath, she pulled his black silk stockings and his shoes onto his feet, leaning over her big belly to tie the laces.

Out of breath, she willed away the kink in her lower back, and realized she needed the help of her curious neighbors. Still outside, Adair and Louise came quickly.

It took all three of them a very long time to carry Charlie to the buggy and get him by degrees up into the back seat where he could lie down.

Despite all the sleep this morning, Mae was done in. "I gotta go lie down for a bit," she told Louise and Adair. "He'll sleep back here. Just help me pull his legs through the bows to make him more comfortable." By now the day had turned very warm, but the hood of the buggy shaded his face from the hot sun, and the horse wasn't about to leave the fresh grass.

Mae surprised herself by dozing off for a few minutes in the cool cabin, but she felt much better. Louise and Adair came back outside when they saw her, Adair with a man's hat in her hand.

"You've both been good neighbors," Mae said. Thank you for everything." She climbed into the driver's seat and took the reins. Even that made her feel out of breath.

Adair was handing her the black bowler hat, but then gave it to Charlie, who had awakened. "Yours?" she asked. "I found it on the ground over there." She pointed to part of the wide-open little meadow.

"Uh-huh," he said, putting it on the floor.

She flicked the horse into a reluctant trot, worried that a room in Shingle Springs mightn't be available. This was risky, but she couldn't stand one more minute in this hellish place. It had been tolerable with Billy's arms around her and the tenderness and love between them, but now she had to keep moving or fall apart, and Charlie needed help.

76

Mae drove up out of the mine with Charlie in the back seat, legs dangling through the bows of the buggy bonnet. She passed the junction of French Creek Road and, shortly, the little village of Frenchtown—whitewashed houses, spindle porches, blooming flowers. Looking at those houses she wondered if the inhabitants went through one shock after another like she was doing. She didn't think so.

At each turn of the road the noise receded a little more, and her spirits lightened a bit. She congratulated herself on getting out of the camp so fast, despite the voucher trouble, and Charlie hadn't said a word about the wallet's sudden appearance. At the same time, the warm day became downright hot, and she felt tired after running back and forth and bending and lifting for three days. How nice it would be, she thought, to take a nap while the horse took you where you needed to go. This animal behaved as though he'd never been in harness before. She worked hard to stop him from bolting. Weary of that, and the pain that kept gripping her insides, she could hardly wait to get to Shingle Springs and rent a room.

The horse calmed down a little on a stretch of road beside a small graveyard and through some tall pines. Mae almost nodded off with the steady clip-clop. Charlie's voice brought her up short. His voice was stronger, though the consonants made by lips were missing and some normally made by lips growled from his throat.

"Why'd a nan thrash ne and not take 'ay aullet?"

She interpreted: Why would a man thrash me and not take my wallet?

"There uz a nan that night. Where'd he go?"

He remembered a man there! "He was called to his mother's deathbed," she said.

After a long minute, "You 'arried?"

She had two seconds to think through the desirability of a future with Charlie, now that Billy was gone. "No," she said. "He's not my husband." That left it open.

Several minutes later, "Why'n'cha go, to his nother?"

"Too much traveling, being in this family way."

Pauses separated the forced words, "You're travelin' now."

The Pep Pills were sharpening his mind.

"You know how I got hurt," he barked behind her head.

That was the snapper. He was grilling her like a police inspector. She tried to be light. "Whatever makes you say that?"

Forced and breathy, "I know you."

She stopped breathing at the reins. The game was over.

"You called y nane when I dint know it. I father a' that child you carryin'.

Yes, she had used his name when she thought he was unconscious. And he remembered the baby! She couldn't hear what he said next because at that moment she turned left onto the main road to Shingle Springs and the horse lunged forward nearly wrenching the reins out of her hands. She braced her feet on the board and pulled back with all her might, blinded by the sun sitting on the road straight ahead. She tried to make a filter of her eyelashes.

"Pull my hat brim down over my eyes!" she shouted, desperately trying to navigate at this unruly pace through the slower rigs. Harnesses rattled as a gang of mules came at her out of the sun. If it had done any good, she'd have used the quirt on the horse. Another pain started up.

Gritting her teeth as she squinted into the sun, she concluded that either Charlie hadn't heard her request about the hat, couldn't do it in his condition, or wanted her to suffer. She squirmed, seeking a more comfortable position, and on her right caught a glimpse of a train platform under a yellow roof. That explained it. This jug-head horse knew the livery barn was just beyond the station and was hell-bent to get there.

With the pain mounting and nothing blocking the road, Mae let the reins go slack. The horse galloped headlong, and the buggy bounced over the tracks, nearly overturning as it whipped around a sharp turn and careened into the barn. Wet, frothy and heaving, the horse now stood like an angel with a halo over his ears.

Mae stayed in the buggy, waiting for the pain to subside.

A scowling man came out of a back room, assessing the buggy and staring at Charlie in the backseat. The pain made her speak in short bursts.

"He's been hurt in an accident. Can't walk without help. We need a place to stay... 'til the train leaves in the morning."

The man scowled at her. "I'm not in the hotel business."

Out of patience in the pain and the heat, her voice flared, "Well, if your goddamned horse hadn't acted up so bad, I woulda drove around and found us a place!" She closed her eyes and took a deep breath as the pain began to ratchet down. Never had she used such language. She hadn't thought she was that kind of girl.

Managing a sweet smile, she asked, "Would you be so good as to direct me to an inn nearby where they serve a little supper?"

Suddenly the man was as nice as the horse. He pointed and she looked out the open barn doors up a road with no sun at its end. "See that two-story building there, on the left? Big trees? That's the Murcheson's boarding house. They drive infirm guests to the station. I'm not saying they have a room, but I'll drive you on over to ask. If they don't, there's always the Anderson place."

She paid him for the three days, with an extra nickel for taking the reins for the short drive to the boarding house.

The horse wouldn't leave the barn until he felt a quirt on his rump.

The liveryman drove the short distance and then held the horse in front of what appeared to be a large house while Mae inquired inside.

Yes, they had a room on the lower floor, in a closed-in porch. She signed for it as Mr. and Mrs. Duffy and led Mr. Murcheson back to the buggy. The liveryman acted like he expected Mae to get under one of Charlie's shoulders while he drove away with the buggy.

"Sir," she told him, smothering her exasperation, "I can't lift any part of him. Please help Mr. Murcheson get…" remembering not to use Charlie's name, "him to the room and I'll hold the horse."

She watched the two men struggle to keep their feet under them as Charlie started to fall one way and then the other as they walked him up the path and the two stairs to the door. Charlie yelped a couple of times. Later she thanked the liveryman, took her Chinese bag, and inhaled the scent of the cascading blossoms of honey locust trees. Their sweet fragrance competed with the blooming lilacs and huge pink roses climbing over the white grillwork of the porch. It had been a long time since she'd see flowers.

The room had screens instead of windows. Charlie was lying on the only bed, a small one. She shut the door, realizing she'd have to sleep on the floor.

"They'll bring us some soup, she told him as she sank into the eiderdown pillows of the overstuffed chair, the only furniture in the room besides the cot.

Charlie said, "You'n I are a sorry 'air."

Sorry pair. "Yup." A far cry from when they were at the Tubbs Hotel. At the end of her strength, she was about to fall asleep when another of those pains grabbed her. She moaned and stood up, hoping that would give relief.

She opened the door to the backyard. A path led to a big white outhouse. "Be right back."

With the pain tightening its vise-like grip, she slowly put one foot in front of the other on the path that bisected the lawn. Overhead, the gnarled boughs of an ancient oak provided shade, and lilac bushes bloomed everywhere. Being off the main road, this inn was beyond the rattle and bustle of the freighters. Inside the four-seater, stood a vase of lilacs. It didn't cover the smell, but she appreciated the effort. Pulling up her cape and dress she sat down, determined to get rid of the gas that was causing those pains.

She waited a long time with dim light filtering down through screened openings high on the walls. Another pain started up, but nothing came of it. The door opened and a woman's head poked in, delicate features, a skillful blonde updo. "May I join you?" she asked.

Mae nodded.

The lady did her business in short order, then pushed the door a little open like she was leaving, but turned to ask, "You all right?"

"I'm fine, thank you."

"I saw you come in. That was some time ago. Thought I'd check, you being in a family way and all."

"Thank you, but it's just gas pains."

She shut the door but remained inside. "Could it be your time?"

"No. That's not for about three weeks. I'm finished now." Mae got up, dabbed at herself with shreds of a half-gone Sears Catalog, and pulled the cape around her. Embarrassed to have no underdrawers to pull up, she added, "Nothing fits me any more."

The woman waited as Mae went out first, and then she walked beside her, speaking in a quiet ladylike way. "The lilacs are beautiful this time of year, aren't they? Smell so good, too."

"Yes. You staying here?"

"Uh-huh. I'm from Carmel, actually San Francisco. Hunter's Point if you've heard of it. Came here to visit a friend. I leave for Carmel on the morning train, by way of Sacramento, of course."

Mae hadn't heard of Hunter's Point or Carmel. "We'll be on the morning train too," she said, "for Sacramento."

"Then we'll be on the train together. Will I see you at supper?" She appeared to be in her thirties, an entirely poised and friendly woman in a businesslike way.

"No, I'm taking care of an injured man. We'll eat in our room."

By now they were at the door of the former back porch. The lady looked at Mae with friendly blue eyes and put out her hand. "I'm Abbie Jane Hunter."

"The Hunter of Hunter's Point?"

"That's right. A beautiful place on the ocean, but not as lovely as Carmel." Her handshake was firm.

"I'm Mae Duffy."

"If you ever get to Carmel-by-the-Sea—that's what I'm calling it now— look me up at the Ladies Real Estate Investment Company." With quiet pride she added, "My company. Anyone there will know the way to my cottage. I'll show you around. It's a place to win your heart."

"I'll remember that," Mae said, astounded that a woman would own a company with the word "investment" in it. She turned the doorknob.

"This is your first, I imagine."

"First?" Mae looked back at Abbie Jane Hunter.

"Baby."

"Oh, yes. My first baby."

"Well," said the lady, "see you in the morning."

Abbie turned away, the back of her head bobbing around the side of the house.

Another pain started. Mae stood for a while, and then slowly retraced her steps to the outhouse, determined once more to put an end to it. She figured she hadn't been eating right, with Charlie in the cabin, and had become constipated. She probably needed a colonic, but none would be had at this hour, and possibly no such establishment existed in this small town.

As she sat waiting, a loud knock sounded on the door. A man called, "All clear in there?"

"No. Just a minute."

She gave up and went back to Charlie.

"What took s'long?" he rasped. "It's co'd." He pointed at the tureen of soup.

"Sorry. I talked to a lady from a place called Carmel-by-the-Sea. You want me to spoon the soup into you?"

"Uh-uh. I can do it now."

She watched the way he avoided his lips, the lower one craked open in two places and jutting out farther. "I'll be glad when I get you to the hospital. When's the last time you had some Pep Pills?"

He moaned. "Dunno." He put the spoon down and carefully laid himself back against the pillows, eyes closed.

She dug in the pocket of his jacket and pulled out a tin. It had only six left. She gave him four and took two. Then she spooned more soup into him, bending over him in an awkward way that put strain on her back. He took it slowly.

Afterwards she pulled off his shoes and eased him out of his jacket. "You need the thunder mug?"

"Okay."

When she finished helping him, in the grip of another of her pains, she took the mug and walked slowly to the outhouse and dumped the contents. She sat down again. Nothing happened. After a while, another man knocked and she gave up and returned to the room.

Charlie was still awake. He took up the entire cot and then some, his large bare feet hanging over the end. She fluffed his pillow and covered him with a blanket. With no glass on the windows, it was getting cool. She lit the lamp and yanked the dark, patterned draperies over both windows.

The lamplight shadowed and somewhat neutralized Charlie's gruesome face, the purples and blacks blending with the curtains. Days ago she'd developed the habit of not looking at him when she spoke to him. By his voice, she concluded that the Pep Pills made him sharper, though he continued to slur his words and drop consonants.

"On the road, I said 'reciate your takin' care'a ne. You coulda jes' rolled ne down the hill."

He remembered that too!

"Oh Charlie, no." She scooted forward in the chair, wanting him to understand. "I never would hurt you. Don't you know that?"

"You 'ere draggin' ne," he said.

"Yes, to the cabin."

"I heard you talkin' t' a nan." The last blasted out of his chest.

Oh God, what did we say? "You were unconscious when we found you."

"Why'd he lea'e you alone?"

"That man is... more than a friend."

"Uh-uh," he objected. "Lef' you with ne. Not fhiendly."

He remembered everything! Fortunately, Billy could be in the heart of Mexico by now with Pedro's people. Even Charlie's state troopers couldn't find him. So there was no need to lie any more. "You see, he's the one who accidentally attacked you."

"Wha—? Accidenta—. Ow!" He cried out as he started to sit up, but groaned and sank back.

She lowered her voice. "He thought you were Oberon."

He looked at her from the puffy slits of his eyes.

"My friend made a terrible mistake. He didn't know it was you. It was dark."

"Why'd he think I 'as O'eron?"

He even remembered Oberon! And no doubt their arguments about him. She told him what Billy had heard in the store, and reminded him that Oberon had promised to hunt her down and kill her—something Charlie had forbidden her to talk about when they were last together. If he didn't like it now, too bad. She told him how, thinking he was dead, they dragged him up the mountain intending to shove him into an abandoned mine tunnel, before she realized who he was.

"Charlie, I'm not going to tell you his name, but he took me at my word. He told me he'd kill Oberon if he came after me. And when he says something he means it."

His face had a new crimp in it. Even behind all that color and swelling she recognized anger. She supposed he had the right to be angry. She settled back in the chair with a sigh, realizing she hadn't answered his question. Why indeed had Billy attacked him without knowing for sure who he was?

"You're both tall," she said.

"Hah!" came out of his chest. "'Eans what he says. Huh! Dint get it done."

"He almost did. You're tough, Charlie."

"So you're gonna shove ne down a shaf' t'die."

"We didn't know it was you! Charlie, I'm so happy you're alive. When I saw it was you, I told my friend to run away and hide. He's a good man, he really is, and doesn't deserve to be hung."

Again the huff of disbelief from his chest. "Good, is he? Out tryin' t'kill—" He couldn't seem to put the words together.

The start of another pain made her irritable. "Are you telling me you think he should hang?"

"You's in nai skin you'd think so too." The slurring didn't even cover the heavy sarcasm. "He dint kill, so he on't hang." Charlie was back with all his sharp edges.

Under her breath she said, "The law wouldn't treat him fair."

She knew he'd be rolling his eyes with disgust if he could. "Wy not?"

With the pain mounting, she blurted, "'Cause he's half Indian." There, she said it. If Charlie thought an Indian had sullied her and made her untouchable, then she didn't want him. What did he expect? That he could push her away and not marry her when she was pregnant and she'd be just fine? That people would feed and care for her and her bastard baby? Breathing hard, she turned her head away so he couldn't see the anger and sorrow and tears, and the physical pain.

"Injun attack," he growled.

She hated the way he said that.

"That's the way judges think, Charlie. That they're all the same. He wouldn't stand a chance."

"I doan either. Set'sis settin' in. Gits too far gone, the hos'ital can't cure."

He was right about sepsis. Maybe she'd waited too long. If she had notified the tram-tender that night Charlie would have been in the hospital's care for two days by now.

The gradual release of pain bolstered her resolve to finish this conversation, which had festered so long in her mind. She looked up at his burning eyes, about to ask why he came for her, but he was quicker on the draw.

"You love 'in?" Through the shadows and the puffiness she saw his distaste.

She wouldn't even try to explain the love between her and Billy. It wasn't any of his business. "Charlie, I told you something you wanted to know, what happened back there. I told it straight. Didn't want to, but I it did anyway. And now I'm asking you to tell me something I want to know."

"What?"

"Why did you go to the Big Canyon Mine?" In his anger over Billy, he might lie about this. Still, she hoped he'd follow her example and tell the truth.

He closed his eyes. "Gotta think."

A train whistle blew, the freight train. She could hear it start to slow down. After a long minute he spoke in a neutral tone. "I talked to the 'ine su'ertendent. 'Ater rights."

"Water?"

"Uh-huh. You 'orget? 'Ister Te'is hired ne to do it."

He had come about water rights! "I don't understand. Why did you ask for *me* at the store?"

"Dunno." He slurred something. "Saw you at the store."

It had the ring of truth. He hadn't come to marry her at all! He must have seen her leaving the store with the flour. He'd had no change of mind since they'd parted in that "dentist's" waiting room. But she had changed. She had learned what love is.

77

They couldn't sleep. Charlie, fully clothed and lying on his back, blamed the Pep Pills for making him jiggy.

"Does cocaine do that?"

"All nerves. 'usinessnen give 'em to 'orkers so's they kee' goin' all night." He moaned. "Hurts 'ad. Need laudanun."

His slurred speech was worse again. Why on earth hadn't she gone looking for a pharmacy instead of spending so much time in the outhouse? She might have found one open. Now it was too late. And she couldn't wake up the Murchesons to borrow their laudanum because a sign on the wall forbade ringing the office bell after 9 P.M. or before 6 A.M. for any reason other than "fire or death."

She felt jiggy too. Until another cramp would start. And then she couldn't think at all, and she'd moan in response to anything Charlie said.

She was between pains when he asked why she was taking him to the hospital.

"Coulda telegraph 'ai office. A nan woulda co'e for ne."

She answered in a lighthearted way. "I thought you'd come to marry me."

"Ugh! Doan wanna g' 'arried."

"Don't worry, Charlie. I'm not asking you to." She was onto his speech impediments and could fill in the missing sounds better.

He took his time before saying, "You gonna 'arry that ..."

"Man," she completed, believing he would have said Indian or half-breed or no-account. "He wanted to marry me."

"Is he comin' back for you?"

"No. I hope he stays away so the law won't get him. I couldn't bear it if they hung him."

Charlie took a long time to make a small shift on the cot. Then he slurred, "He won't hang or get 'unished atall 'less I 'ile charges."

Just beyond the screened windows, owls hooted back and forth, one in a slightly higher pitch. With everything so quiet she could hear the grind of a distant stamp mill. "Will you? Bring charges I mean?"

He moaned.

He would.

"Would I be part of it, in the eyes of the law, if you charged him?"

"You hel'ed."

Yes, I helped. In a cloud of hopelessness, she said under her breath, "But I helped you live when I saw it was you."

"Shoulda rolled me down the hill and lennne die in 'eace."

Shocked, she thought it must be the pain talking. "Charlie, I had to save you. It was my fault, what happened."

He turned his head a little toward her like he was surprised to hear that.

"It was my fault as much as if I'd clubbed you, because I told him too much about Oberon. He listened to me and sacrificed his future trying to protect me. He *respected* what I was telling him, that I was afraid." Suddenly she was in tears. "I *had* to save you, Charlie, whether or not you came to marry me. And I wish to God I'd gone looking for laudanum before the stores closed. I'm so, so sorry you are suffering!"

Another pain had started up. She stretched her legs out in front of the chair, slightly arching her back, and gritted her teeth. If the Pep Pills were doing any good she couldn't tell. In her mounting agitation, she decided the doctors in the hospital should look at her too. No telling what was wrong with her. Something sure was. She flipped open her watch and held it to the lantern. Ten minutes after four in the morning. The train would arrive at six.

During the pain Charlie drifted into a half-unconscious state, mumbling unintelligibly. After a couple more pains Mae nodded off too, until a new pain would wake her.

The sun wasn't up yet when Mrs. Murcheson knocked and handed Mae a tray of buttered toast, jam and boiled eggs. Mae explained the urgent need for laudanum. The proprietress returned with a bottle and a tablespoon. Mae took a couple spoons of it and Charlie took four. She paid forty cents in addition to a dollar and a half for the room and breakfast.

At 5:45 Mr. Murcheson drove them the two blocks to the station and let them sit in the buggy until the train came. Abbie Hunter, waiting on the platform, stared at Charlie's face with round eyes and parted lips. His lips and nose had swollen into a colorful and inhuman snout. Mae tried not to look.

A black steam engine pulled two passenger cars to a stop, the same little train Mae had ridden to Folsom when she and Mom and the two boys first arrived in Sacramento. Abbie Hunter, Mr. Murcheson, and a gentleman passenger practically carried Charlie down from the buggy and into the train. They seated him so he could lie back against the window on pillows brought by the conductor, so his long legs had some room. Abbie and Mae sat in the seat behind him. A minute later the train whistled up the tracks and Mae felt the knifepoint of another pain starting deep inside her. It would spread hideously. By now she thought she might be dying.

She couldn't help but writhe in her effort to find a more comfortable position. Either the laudanum hadn't taken effect or she needed a lot more of it. Abbie looked at her watch.

Fortunately the pains came and went. If they continued without pause, she doubted she could bear it without screaming aloud. As the train clicked and jerked down the west ridge of French Creek, trees whizzing by, the conductor called out three stations. One they stopped at, the others they slowed down for the mail hook. Mae gripped the armrests.

Abbie looked at her breast-pin watch, stood up, leaned over the seat, and said to Charlie, "Mr. Duffy, I think your baby will be born right here on the train." She turned to Mae. "He's asleep. Did you have those pains all night?"

Mae nodded.

"My dear, I've been through this before and I know. I'll talk to the conductor."

Mae wanted to hold her back but all her energy was devoted to keeping a scream inside her. She twisted and turned and moaned with the clacking of the rails. Well, all right, she said to herself. Maybe I *am* having the baby. All the more reason to get to the hospital as soon as possible.

"Brandon's Corner," the conductor called.

The train stopped. The conductor, in a black suit and white shirt, came down the car with Abbie. They stood looking at her.

"The baby isn't due yet," Mae got out with a shallow breath.

The man asked with skeptical brows. "You got relations or friends along these tracks?" He nodded toward the window, "Where you could stay for the lying-in?"

"No. I'll get help at the Sacramento hospital."

The conductor looked at Abbie. "Me and my wife got four youngins. With a first, the pains go on a long time, maybe days. I think she can wait 'til she gets to the hospital. What happened to him?" he asked, pointing at Charlie.

Abbie explained that he'd been attacked and beaten.

With a sympathetic click in his cheek the conductor continued down the aisle, punching tickets. Abbie returned to her seat beside Mae. A man had just boarded in a western high hat of the kind Emmett liked. He seated himself in front of Charlie. The train began to roll again, chugging slowly and jerking around the corners as the tracks snaked around a hill. Then the view opened out to green pastureland, oak groves and ranch houses. After another big pain, they jerked to a stop in Latrobe.

"We'll be here about five minutes," Abbie said. "You must be tired. Here," she pointed at her shoulder, "Lean against me while you're resting between pains."

Mae felt herself in the hands of a wise woman. She laid her cheek on the puffy pleating of Abbie's ivory blouse and closed her eyes. After they left the Latrobe station and the train made a turn northward toward Folsom, another pain stabbed, gripping her harder and harder. The lower half of her body remained in the vise for a long time, her belly like a boulder, and then, bit by bit, it left and she could relax her limbs and shut her eyes. Again she put her cheek on Abbie Hunter's shoulder. The totality of what she knew about childbirth was that God punished Eve for her sin and made all women suffer in childbirth because of it. That was unfair of God. Charlie would have agreed, though he was sound asleep and the real cause of this. But of course she had brought this on herself too. Now for the first time she understood the overheard whispers between her mother and Mrs. Yoder in the kitchen in Iowa, something about women not doing it any more.

"Cothrin Station," the conductor called.

The train lurched to a stop. Mae couldn't help but let out a crescendo of "oh, oh, oh, oh" as another pain started. If only she could just get into a better position—

The conductor came to her once more, staring down. "This is Mr. W. S. Cothrin," he said, nodding at a man who had just boarded the train, a wiry old gentleman with the keen look of intelligence in his eyes. "His family lives here. He's offered to let you lie in at his son's house."

"Mr. Duffy," the conductor said, reaching down to Charlie, "Wake up."

"Huh, wha—"

The stilled train wheezed on the tracks, and a big man in a cap and pin-striped overalls came through the door, joining the huddle in the aisle. The engineer. A moment later he announced in a loud voice, "I'm not allowing this on my train."

"All right then," Mr. Cothrin said. "Some of you get holda the girl and git her to the ground. I'll lead the way. Just don't let this train leave without me!"

Abbie Hunter added, "I'll see to it that Mr. Duffy gets to the Southern Pacific Hospital."

Three men started to lift Mae off the seat.

"No!" She knocked their hands off her. "I will not get off while Charlie stays aboard. I need to get to the hospital too." Surely God wouldn't be this mean to every woman on earth—give them so much pain they thought they were dying. But then she recalled the pain of lying on that high table while that "dentist" grubbed around inside her with a sharp tools. She remembered the moment when her head felt like it was exploding. That was worse pain and she had lived. It gave her the strength to grit her teeth and bear this.

Everyone was gawking at her—Abbie, the conductor, the engineer, the man in the high hat, and the lady across the aisle with two young boys. The lady said with a twist of her nose. "It's scandalous! Right in front of my boys. Get her off the train."

The engineer looked down at Charlie. "I've got a schedule to keep. As her husband, you should order your wife to take advantage of this nice offer—and quick! Either you go with her or accompany Mrs. Hunter to the Sacramento. Which is it?"

"All right," Charlie slurred, slumping back into the seat. "Take her off."

In short order Mae was in a yellow house of a kind used for train stations, so new she could smell the fresh paint. The men laid her on a bed against the far wall of the parlor. Old Mr. Cothrin said to a younger woman something about handling emergencies being the duty of the train station. Then he and the other passengers left.

Mae gritted her teeth against the worst pain yet, and hardly heard a lingering scream in the room until she realized it must have been hers. She couldn't think about Charlie on the train, chugging up the track to Folsom as the whistle blew.

Mrs. Cothrin tried to give her another dose of laudanum, but Mae waved her away until the pain was over. Then she lapped it up.

"It'll make you sleepy," Mrs. Cothrin said. "I've sent for the Indian woman up the gulch. She's good at birthing. I'm not." Then she went out the double doors to another room and shut them.

Several pains later, Mrs. Cothrin came in again followed by an Indian woman gasping for breath. Droplets of sweat glistened on her brow. "This is Mrs. Craig," Mrs. Cothrin said.

Mrs. Craig pulled up Mae's frock and poked and prodded her privates. "Baby's coming," she said.

This body-ripping pain, beyond anything a human being could bear, one after the other, frightened Mae. It was almost as bad as the abortion. Women died of childbirth all the time and she thought she would too. She slipped from keen awareness and fear to a kind of sleep, in which she barely knew they were taking off all her clothes. But the short rest ended when the vise gripped her again.

They covered her with a sheet.

The Indian woman told her to bite down on a twist of wet towel. "Open yourself and let the baby come out," she said.

Mae bit the rag nearly through, and it stopped some of her cry from scaring the children she'd seen peeking through the crack of the door.

Mrs. Cothrin came in with a tub of steaming water.

At the height of a pain, the Indian woman pushed gently on the top of Mae's bulge. "Push it out," the woman said, pulling a chair beside the bed. "Push hard. The pains help the baby come. You gotta help."

Mrs. Cothrin got behind Mae and pushed her to a sitting position on the edge of the bed. Mrs. Craig was there, on a chair facing Mae. She opened Mae's knees and put them in an unladylike position on either side of the armrests.

Another pain ripped into her and stayed and stayed. She cried out in long, unending agony, the rag dropping as she implored God to stop this.

"Push hard again," the Indian woman said.

Mae had no strength left but she tried. This time she felt a slippery wiggle like a fish being taken off the line.

"Baby's here," the woman said with her head down under.

A thin little cry sounded in the room.

Mrs. Cothrin gently pulled Mae back and laid her down on the bed.

Closing her eyes in a haze of disbelief, she felt warm towels mopping her, and heard the two women talking in low tones.

"Here. You take him," Mrs. Cothrin said after a little while.

She put a wet baby boy in the crook of Mae's arm. He smelled of the secret world inside her. Tears of relief ran down her face. In a short while, she slept.

⌒

The last rays of the sun over Ben Bolt Ridge washed golden light across the wallpaper. Mae got up on her elbow and looked closely at the baby. He had fuzzy dark hair and the face of an unopened rosebud. She pulled the cover down and saw again that he was a boy. She counted ten toe buds and ten perfect little fingers, all there. He was starting to seem real now, his tiny chest rising and falling. He had a seductive, musky scent of his own—an independent person who would be five years old when the twentieth century arrived. How strange that sounded. He would write 1901 on his first school papers.

A girl of about thirteen came through the double doors with a mug of hot broth on a plate surrounded by warm buttered bread. "I'm Carrie Cothrin. Mom sent me in," she explained, setting the broth on the sundries table. "Mind if I look at him?"

Mae pulled the sheet down, which made the baby's doubled-up fists fly up in the sudden light.

"Aww! He's *so* cute," Carrie said. "Have you named him yet?"

"William Rogue." *For Billy, and his real father.*

Still smiling, Carrie started for the door but then turned back with an embarrassed giggle. "I almost forgot, lookin' at him and all. Mom said to tell you the birth went good. Not much ripping. I'm supposed to bring in soap and water morning and evening so you can wash yourself. She says in a few days you'll probably be able to follow your husband to Sacramento."

78

Four days later, far less than the usual lying-in time of ten days, the distant whistle announced the train's departure from Latrobe, on its way to Cothrin's Station, bound for Folsom and Sacramento. Mae felt she could manage the trip, and she didn't want to be any more trouble to the Cothrin family.

Torn about going to Sacramento to see Charlie, Mae wrapped little Billy in her old miner's shirt. Part of her wanted to go directly to Indian Mary. Not only was Mary a wise older woman, knowledgeable about birth and newborns, but perhaps she had word of Billy's whereabouts, or a way to get a message to him. Mae ached to tell him that he wasn't a murderer. On the other hand, she needed to see how Charlie was doing in the hospital. She hoped that they'd be able to fix his face. And maybe she could glean a hint of whether he intended to file charges against her. If so, the sooner she knew the better. And she believed he might change his mind about that if she could talk to him face to face, with his baby in her arms. Besides, a contrary corner of her mind dared her to walk the streets of Sacramento and test the new mettle she felt within her. She felt ready to face the scorn of being an unwed mother. She even believed she could stand up to Oberon patrolling in the Black Mariah. If it were daylight. If other people were around. She could feel herself more grown up, and she could understand Charlie's point about Oberon probably not being interested in killing her any more. Likely he had some other girl chained inside that warehouse. Poor thing.

Mae felt stronger in spirit if not yet in body, like men were said to feel returning from war, tested by fear and pain. She doubted few had suffered to the extent she had in trying not to have a baby, and then in having one. People said it was a natural thing, to have a baby. But nothing in a man's natural body reared up against him to deliver anything like that pain, unless it really was killing him. She felt certain that Eve and her daughters must have kept secret the inhuman pain of it, or Mae would have heard more about it. Mother, for example, never spoke of childbirth.

The whistle blew again, now closer.

Mrs. Cothrin came into the parlor. "Good luck with the baby," she said, accompanying Mae as far as the front porch.

Mae smiled her thanks, snuggling the warm little bundle to her. Little Billy had a fat padding of Cothrin rags around his bottom. "I appreciate your taking me in at a time like this," she said. "Not everyone would have done it."

"It was nuthin'." Mrs. Cothrin was a tough little lady who, like so many of the pioneers, had a generous soul beneath a stern mien.

On horseback, Carrie and her younger brothers, Roy and freckle-faced Harry, were leaving for school in Latrobe, Harry behind Roy. They looked back at Mae.

With one more smile for Mrs. Cothrin, Mae followed them under the branches of a massive oak tree twittering with birds. An old well with a wind-up bucket stood near the empty building that had once been the Cothrin Store and Station when the rails had first been laid. The grandfather who had offered his son's home for Mae's lying-in had settled here early in the Gold Rush, and she had learned that his original mine was still worked every day—a hole leading underground just uphill from the house. However, the Cothrin family income came mostly from dairy cattle and wood off the ranch. She saw the platform Carrie was pointing at below the road, which had been a major thoroughfare before the railroad was extended to Latrobe. She waved them on, and stepped over rails and ties onto the wooden platform. She thought of the rancor she'd heard about the SP and its unfair practices—there had even been a theater play in Sacramento about that. But as she stood here waiting, she now saw the railroad as a friend.

When the engine puffed to a slow stop, Mae recognized the smiling engineer waving at her out his open window. Mae took a window seat in the rear of the first car where she could nurse the baby. Now he was sleeping like an angel. She laid him gently on the seat beside her. The ruddy-faced conductor came down the aisle—bracing himself against seat backs as the train wobbled up the tracks, whistle screeching.

"Boy or girl?"

She grinned, uncovering the baby's face. "Boy."

"Ah, a fine looking little chap. Goin' to see his daddy at the Sacramento hospital?"

"That's right." She dug in her Chinese bag for fifty cents, which she tried to give the man.

He waved it away. "You paid for this trip once and that'll do." He sat down across the aisle and settled in like he intended to visit. Last time she'd seen him, when he helped carry her off the train, he seemed a villain. Now he was more like a friendly uncle.

"You were right to take me off the train," she admitted. "The baby didn't waste much time coming after that. The Cothrins are nice people."

The conductor moved his grizzled head up and down without taking his bright blue eyes off her. "Railroad people are like a family. At one time old W. S. was one of the two big landowners in these parts. Him and James Miller, Cothrin north and east of Ben Bolt Ridge, Miller south and west of it. We've been haulin' Millers and Cothrins around the countryside since these here tracks was laid." He tilted his head. "You new to the area?"

"Yes." She told him how her family came from Iowa on the transcontinental, adding that she knew Mr. Miller personally.

"Ah, a fine man he was too," he said, oddly in the past tense. Just then the train angled away from the old wagon road through a more forested area, and the conductor mentioned that this railroad line had been the first in California, which Mae already knew, and that Mr. Miller and Mr. Cothrin had expected it to be a transcontinental railroad, which Mae did not know.

"Mr. Judah, originally with this railroad, had the route planned before he jumped ship and planned out a different route for what became the SP. Anyhow, the Millers and Cothrins was both settin' pretty on land along the tracks. Their land woulda been worth a millions." He made a click in his cheek. "Why, they owned land all up around Lake Tahoe too. Summer pasture for their sheep, on wide stretches of lakefront. They sold it for next to nuthin', and I'm talking about the same ground the captains of industry are building on up there now—a summer playground for them. Guess you know what happened to Mr. Miller."

"You mean his wife getting heatstroke every summer?" Mae recalled that was the reason the Millers had moved to Oakland.

He looked at her. "Maybe you didn't hear."

"What?"

With a sad shake of his head he told the story. "It was early February, this last winter. Froze 'round here for days on end. Damp and cold in Oakland too. Jim Miller got up early. Put on his robe and slippers and went downstairs t'start the fire in the parlor before the family woke up. He was like that, always thinking of his family. Musta got a good'n going in the fireplace. I can just see him turning around to warm up his backside."

The conductor twisted his face in tragic lines and wagged his head again. "His robe caught fire and he didn't know 'til it was too late. They figgered he musta run around trying to free himself of it. Ended up settin' the draperies and the whole gol dern room afire. By the time those that was upstairs heard his screams, the whole place was goin' up in flames."

Mae listened in horror. She knew that house, that fireplace, those upstairs bedrooms. She held her breath. "Did the girls make it out, Frankie and Harriett? The little boy?"

"Everyone got out alive and mostly unhurt 'cept Mr. Miller. They run down the stairs and outside, but they couldn't go into that fire in the parlor to drag him out."

"Thank God they didn't all die! Where are they now?"

"One stayed in Oakland. One went to Bakersfield, or was it Fresno? I think one of the daughters lives there. Don't rightly know the details."

Little Billy started fussing.

"To think that such a thing would happen to such a fine man!"

"Yup, a reg'lar on this line too. Came back ever so often to check on his Latrobe enterprises. The property changed hands I hear, like it does at a man's death."

By now the miner's shirt was jerking like little Billy was trying to fight his way out of it. His muffled cries started the pinch of her internal pumps priming themselves. Soon she'd be leaking. "Excuse me," she said picking up the squirmy bundle. "I've got to feed him."

The conductor blushed and made a hasty escape as she threw the old shirt over her shoulder.

ᔆ

Mae stepped off the train at 12ᵗʰ and R with her Chinese bag and Billy in her arms. She walked all the way across the east end of Sacramento to C and 13ᵗʰ, reciting the alphabet backwards every time she came to another corner. Springtime in Sacramento meant pink and white camellias, bright pink quince bushes, and all shades of tulips making the houses gay. The white, four-story Southern Pacific Hospital occupied half a block, an imposing sight. Patients were taking the air in the deep balconies along the second and third floors. She stepped aside when an ambulance pulled by two horses entered the circular drive and stopped under the covered carriage port. Men rushed from the building to help move the stricken person.

Mae had never seen a hospital before. She entered through a small gate in the picket fence surrounding a mowed lawn and passed by a row of junipers pruned into stiff cones. Everything in this place had the look of being well tended. Charlie would be in good hands.

Inside, the smell of lye soap was everywhere. Shoes tapping on the tile of the long hallways and high ceilings, and echoes of those receding shoes, made her feel small. A nurse behind a desk listened to the ambulance driver and scribbled notes in her ledger. Meanwhile, Mae read a plaque on the wall. It said that Dr. Thomas W. Huntington had been the first in the United States to have an anti-septic operating room, and that this as well as other life-saving innovations had brought the Southern Pacific Hospital national acclaim. When it was her turn, Mae went to the nurse at the high mahogany desk and asked to see Charlie Rogue.

The woman looked like a weathered man in a nurse costume. Her tenor voice asked, "A patient?"

"Yes. Came in four days ago."

The nurse ran a finger down a ledger book and stopped on a spot, silently reading. Mae wondered if Charlie had been dismissed.

The nurse looked up at Mae and the baby in her arms. "Are you Mrs. Rogue?"

Brought up short, Mae was about to say no, when the woman explained. "The lady who brought in Mr. Rogue said his wife almost had a baby on the train and sent the injured husband ahead to us."

"Yes, that's me. Mrs. Hunter was wonderful to bring Charlie in. Is he still here? If so, I'd like to see him."

The starched white hat tipped downward as the woman read aloud. "Expected to live." She looked up. "I'll have to speak to the doctor before I can let you see him. Take a seat over there." She indicated a row of straight-backed chairs against the wall, and walked briskly down the right-hand corridor, heels ringing.

Surprised at the grim words, Mae worried for the first time in days. She had seen him improve quite a bit, except for the infection setting in. But they had anti-septic medicine here. Her main concern had been disfigurement.

After a while a middle-aged doctor in a white jacket, accompanied by the admitting nurse, came toward her from the right wing. Mae stood up to meet him.

The nurse said, "This is Dr. Huntington." She opened a hand to Mae. "Mrs. Rogue." She returned to the desk.

Mae saw no reason to clarify her relationship to Charlie. Possibly they wouldn't allow her to see him if they knew they weren't married.

The doctor said, "Your husband has suffered serious injuries. The blow to his chest resulted in broken ribs and ought to have killed him, but luckily the fractured bone didn't puncture his heart or lungs. He also has a concussion that would have killed many people, but in that too he was lucky. The infection in his face is our most serious concern now." He checked the notebook in his pocket. "We soaked his face in carbolic acid solution all of Tuesday, Wednesday, and yesterday, and gave him sulfur. I can't try to put his nose back together until the infection is down. But there was progress this morning. I'll be removing the bandages again this afternoon about four o'clock. If it looks good enough, I'll operate on his nose and lips early tomorrow morning. Somewhat of an experiment, you understand. Your husband wanted me to try. If you want to talk to him, come back at four. His face is bandaged now. He can't see or talk. He's also had a lot of laudanum. It knocks him out."

"I'll be back at four."

The doctor drilled her with flinty eyes. "You should have got him here sooner. By the time he came in the sepsis was galloping. I gave him, at best, a five percent chance of survival."

Horrified, she couldn't keep the tears from her eyes. "I was stuck in a mining camp and it was closed for Easter. No telephone or telegraph. I gave him willow bark tea."

He regarded her with naked scorn. "Nobody to run a message out of there?"

She didn't answer. Ian or Clem would have done it, if they'd known. And Louise might have welcomed a jaunt to Shingle Springs as part of her morning constitutional. Mae couldn't bear to look into the doctor's accusing glare. Sister Delphine would be disappointed, and God would add this to her long list of sins. Instead of saving Charlie, she had given Billy time to run from the law.

Sick with guilt she dallied as she walked to Charlie's apartment on 12th and N. She didn't want to pay for a hotel room for one afternoon. She'd have time, after she saw Charlie later today, to catch the late stage to Slough House.

Robins and other birds fluttered around young elm trees along the neat walkways. What simple lives they led! The baby began to squirm and fuss. Hungry again.

The landlord—the man who'd so hated Benty—answered her knock. She could see that he remembered her well. His eyes went to the fussy baby punching inside the miner's shirt. She explained that Charlie was in the hospital and she needed a place to rest for a few hours before she went back to see him.

"Mr. Rogue's secretary at the Capitol sent a messenger," he informed her. "Said he'd been attacked. Sounds like he won't be on his feet for a long time, and they aren't sure if he ever will be. I don't know about the apartment, needing the rent money and all. Got some people who want to move in on May first."

"Oh no! I just came from the hospital. The doctor says Charlie has made good progress. He'll operate on him in the morning to make his face look better. Then it'll be just a few more days before he's back here. He has plenty of money to pay the rent. Did you know? He's been doing work for a capitalist in addition to his work for the leader of the Legislature. He's saving a nest egg." Seeing his eyebrows go up, she went on, "But for now, please let me rest here and feed the baby."

Little Billy gave out a mournful howl.

"His baby?"

That made her angry. Of course this was Charlie's baby. But she only nodded when she saw that he was unlocking the door for her.

A sinner in every possible way, Mae leaned against the pillows on the bed and sobbed as the baby sucked. Here she was with Charlie's baby in her arms, angry with a man because he asked whether the baby was Charlie's when in fact she loved and missed another man. The baby lagged in his sucking. She changed sides.

Oh, how wicked she was! Charlie could lose his work and his apartment because of her. In these bad times he wouldn't find employment quickly with a ruined face. The horror of helping to drag him through a dark night intending to bury him in a deserted mine tunnel kept returning. Little Billy paused again, sucked two or three times, and then his tiny red lips opened, releasing the suction. Bluish milk washed over his tongue and leaked out the corners of his mouth. He was fast asleep.

She removed his soaked rags—his body as limp as the rags—and put Charlie's towel around him on the bed, covering him with Charlie's blanket. She couldn't help but look in the closet to see about the clothes she'd left there.

Gone. She looked in the drawer and saw that her corset and gloves and other items were also gone. She'd been the last thing on Charlie's mind when he went to Big Canyon Mine.

She curled beside the baby and cried herself to sleep, knowing she had no call to weep. She meant nothing to Charlie. And she had nearly killed him, twice. Once when she'd talked Billy into acting on her behalf, and then by not getting him to help fast enough. She truly was a wicked person.

Yet beside her slept a perfect little human being with miniature fists balled up beside his ears like he was ready to box the big bad world. She would protect him.

With that thought she drifted into sleep.

❧

Back at the hospital at four o'clock, Mae sat where Dr. Huntington pointed, in a straight-backed against the wall of the small room. As the doctor and nurse unwound the gauze from Charlie's head, the nurse held his head off the pillow while, each time, the doctor slowly bought the gauze around.

They had shaved his hair off! It became more evident with each strip of stained gauze lifted away.

"There," the doctor said to Charlie. "Let's take a look." Bent down with his hands on his knees he studied Charlie, his white coat blocking Mae's view until he shifted to a different angle so the sunlight from the window fell directly on Charlie's battered face.

The bruising was darker, almost black. His slit eyes looked out at her.

"Much better," the doctor said to Charlie. "The carbolic acid is clearing it up. One more night under wraps and I'll be able to work on your nose. Nurse, prepare another soak."

The nurse went out.

"Mrs. Rogue, don't get near him," the doctor said on his way out. "Stay on that chair. I'll be back in a few minutes." The door shut behind him.

"How're you feeling?" Mae asked when they were alone.

"Uuugh. In and out. Is that—"

"Your son," she filled in. "I named him Billy."

"Can't see."

She took him out of the shirt and held him up. The towel fell off him as he kicked and wiggled in the open air. Suddenly, an astonishingly long arc of pee shot out of him nearly reaching the bed. "Oh!" she exclaimed, quickly wrapping the towel around him.

Charlie's black puffy lips twitched in what might have been a smile. "M'son."

She didn't know what to say.

"Glad to see 'ay son."

"They think we're married. Abbie Hunter told them that. It's in the hospital record. She told them I'd be coming. I don't know how she knew that, 'cause I sure didn't."

She wondered if he would file charges, but couldn't bring herself to ask yet. "I'm glad you wanted to see the baby."

"I wanna hold 'in, when the doc says I can."

Relieved that he approved of some aspects of her, for the baby was part of her, she dared admit, "I hope you don't mind. I needed a place to feed him and went to your apartment. Just for today. Your landlord let me in."

He flopped a listless hand on the outer bedclothes. "Stay there. I doan care. And co' see ne again."

The doctor entered with a vial of medicine and the nurse hauled in a basin heaped with steaming gauze.

Mae hadn't talked to Charlie like she'd wanted. Sore of body and soul, she shuffled back to his apartment. Billy would have taken her in his arms and made her feel better. She ached to see him again and wondered if she could outlive the hurt if she were never to see him again. The heat of the sun bored into the back of the cape. She couldn't take it off. The buttons on her frock were still three inches from their buttonholes. She'd expected to be slim again by now.

Mrs. Cothrin had set her straight on that: "It'll take several months to get any kind of a waistline. And maybe you'll never be the same again." She knew that would lessen her in Charlie's eyes, but not in Billy's.

79

At eight that evening Mae was about to retire early with the baby when a man called her name and knocked on the front door. Terror ripped through her until the man identified himself.

"It's me, Gerald Harding."

She closed her eyes and calmed herself. Only the landlord.

"Just a minute." She threw Charlie's robe around her and nearly stumbled over the excess yardage as she hurried to the door.

Beside Mr. Harding stood a tall, broad-shouldered woman in a bird-wing hat and an apple-blossom frock, brown eyes underlain by dark leathery flaps. She surveyed Mae as she spoke. "I'm Charlie's mother."

"My land! I didn't—"

...*expect you* hung there as the landlord left and they studied each other.

"I didn't know about you," Mrs. Rogue supplied in a tone that said it was just like Charlie to keep secrets from her.

Something of Charlie was in the lady's smile, the flat lids and slight up-curve of the lips, reserving judgment. Her face was a road map of crisscrossed lines.

"I'm Mae," she finally got out. "Come in, and I'll fix you some coffee."

The lady talked as she followed Mae to the parlor. "No. Just hot water or I won't sleep tonight. Been on the train all day. Couldn't pick up and leave 'til this mornin', what with all the work around the place. Neither hell nor high water coulda kept me away though. The mister had to stay t'home to keep things a-goin'. Spring's our work-round-the-clock time."

Mae felt uneasy acting the mistress of the house, turning up the lamp and gesturing toward the sofa. The moment the woman sat down, her hands flew to her hat and began removing hat pins—large hands reddened by decades of sun and strong soap.

She had a farmer's twang in her voice.

"We got some catchin' up to do, you and me."

"About Charlie. I assume you know—"

"Oh, good lord! The store proprietor come up and fetched me to his telephone. Like to'ov fainted to hear that doctor tell it. Why the brute that done it oughta be strung up by the toes and *horse*whipped to death." The lines between her eyes deepened as she shook her head. She placed her hat on the sundries table and smoothed her gray hair. "I been prayin' night and day for my boy."

In the shadows of the lamplight she looked fierce, and Mae felt certain that this woman would have horsewhipped her too if she knew her part in it.

A tremulous little cry came from the bedroom.

Mrs. Rogue reacted like one of those wooden figures that, when you push a rubber button underneath, stand up straight and fling their arms out. "A baby! You and Charlie got a baby!"

She raced to the bedroom with her big black shoes thumping the floor.

Surprised that the landlord hadn't told Mrs. Rogue about the baby, Mae came in behind and turned up the overhead lamp.

Charlie's mother leaned over little Billy with her mouth agape and tears filling her eyes. "I prayed for this," she intoned in a half-whisper. Turning the cover down, she lifted the wet towel that served as a diaper. "Oh, you sweetum iddo baby boy. Come to gwama."

She gentled him up to her shoulder, cupping his sparsely haired scalp. "Oh, oh, oh, oh," it came out half laugh, half sob as she moved around the floor with her cheek scrunched up to his head. She looked past him to Mae with an expression of naked joy.

Little Billy stopped crying.

"Iddo sweetums like his gwama," Mrs. Rogue crooned as she walked out of the bedroom with him.

Feeling bereft, Mae followed to the parlor where the woman continued her steady croon and walked slow circles with the baby. A surge of something like hurt and outrage reminded Mae of how she'd felt in grammar school when an older girl grabbed Gramps' violin out of her hands and strutted around the room pretending to play it, after Mae had brought it to show the teacher. Her arms ached for the baby. He was hers and hers alone. How dare this woman come in and claim him!

Then it hit her. Mrs. Rogue believed she and Charlie were married. Mae recalled that after his Christmas visit with his family, Charlie returned quite upset because everyone kept asking him when he planned to get married. Especially his mother. Maybe the lady had wished it for so long that she believed it was true.

Still, the sense of being violated continued as Mrs. Rogue walked little Billy back and forth around the room, her demeanor saying what a shame it was that he had nothing but a green girl as a mother, and now an experienced and superior mother had come to his rescue.

Then, just as Mae hoped, he resumed crying, this time with more vigor. Mae got up and pried him out of Mrs. Rogue's arms. "He wants to be fed," she said with authority.

She sat down and opened the robe to him. He latched on, immediately silenced. The familiar relaxation softened Mae from head to toe, and she felt again how much she and little Billy were of one flesh, bound by his need for her milk and her need to be milked by him. And something else bound them. Every day she talked to him, all day, about everything, and no matter what she said he gazed upon her with awe, never disappointed. She could tell he loved her. Love, however, was too soft a word for the intense protectiveness she felt for him. The grown-up Billy had been right that this mutual love between parent and child was a blessing. So rich a blessing, she added in her mind, that it made up for the lack of marriage and lack of house and home. Well, almost.

As Billy slaked his hunger, Mae thought about tomorrow and realized that the woman sitting across from her would accompany her to the hospital. And if Charlie could talk after his operation, he'd tell his mother what had happened in Big Creek Canyon. He'd say that they would never get married, and Mrs. Rogue would hate Mae for what she'd done to him. Then, as sure as shooting she would try to take the baby away!

Sacramento was a dangerous place again. Mae could almost feel Ah Sen and Indian Mary beckoning from Slough House and Bridge House. Either one of those old women would take her in and hide her, and never want to steal the baby. She would leave Sacramento first thing in the morning.

But then she remembered Charlie asking her to come back so he could hold Billy. She wanted him to do that, and she wanted to see him on the mend before she left. She also wanted his reassurance that he wasn't bringing charges against her and Billy. She wouldn't be able to rest until she had that. And so, she'd have to accompany Mrs. Rogue to the hospital and somehow finagle a way to be alone with Charlie before his mother went in and learned the truth. How best to do that required some thought.

⌇

At two the next afternoon, they learned at the desk that the operation to fix Charlie's nose and lips had taken five hours. Much of the procedure had been experimental. The nurse fetched the doctor to the lobby to provide more detail.

"It went fairly well," Dr. Huntington said, directing a decided glare at Mae as he added, "under the circumstances. But you can't see him. He's in a drugged sleep, and his entire face is bandaged. Come back tomorrow at nine when I change the bandages. You won't be able to visit, but..."

"We'll come," Mae broke in.

Mrs. Rogue wasn't about to let him get away that easy. "What do you mean, 'under the circumstances'?" She held the doctor with her glittering brown eyes.

Mae girded herself for the blow, but the doctor said only, "she'll explain," and walked away.

"Well?" Mrs. Rogue demanded.

"Well, you see, we couldn't get out of the mine area for a couple of days. The livery stable was closed, everyone gone for Easter." That sounded weak to her, so she added, "I would have needed a magic carpet to get him out."

Charlie's mother seemed to accept the explanation, at least for now. "Well, I'm mighty glad to hear the operation went good," she said.

Sooner or later she'd be accusing Mae of nearly killing her son. But for now, Mae knew she must stay in Sacramento another day, and maybe tomorrow Charlie could talk to her in spite of what the doctor said.

Mrs. Rogue insisted on carrying little Billy back to the apartment. She sounded hurt as she said, "Well, dear, now tell me about your secret wedding."

"It was nothing," she said, "only a couple of Charlie's friends there." The last thing Mae wanted to do was embark on another lie, but she had no choice. The truth would put the baby in jeopardy of being taken by Charlie's mother; and the law, after Charlie filed charges, would see Mrs. Rogue as a superior mother, not to mention a law-abiding citizen.

Much to Mae's relief little Billy started fussing. That caused Mrs. Rogue to concern herself with getting him into a better position—over her shoulder, over her other shoulder, lying flat in her arms, all the time making quick little moves up and down.

"We've got to hurry," Mae said, "or he'll be screaming. He's hungry again."

Back in the apartment, after feeding the baby in the bedroom and claiming she needed a nap with him afterward, Mae knew she must get out of close quarters with Charlie's mother or something would explode. She needed to go someplace to fill in the afternoon, then come back to the apartment and say she was too tired to talk this evening.

Taking a deep breath, she burst into the parlor telling the lady, who was reading an old newspaper, "I almost forgot an appointment with an old friend. It'll take a couple of hours so I'll take the baby." She had looked in the City Directory for Robert Donahue's address.

Before the lady could argue, Mae went out. "I'll be back by suppertime."

The lady eyed her and said something about doing a little shopping.

Mary and Rob lived on 8th Street, near M. It was up a steep stairway, a three-room place on the second floor. Mary answered the knock, exclaimed over little Billy, and led Mae into a room with bolts of cloth standing along the walls. Fabric scraps and spools of laces and bric-a-brac littered the floor. In the center of it all was a wooden cage, inside which stood Mary's baby—a huge and alien being, accustomed as Mae's eyes were to Billy's tiny pink face and body. Patsy wore a short tunic that didn't cover her diaper. She had a cap of yellow hair on her outsized head. Gripping the rail of her cage with both fists, she stood on fat feet and very fat legs. Mae stared at her, and Patsy stared back with round blue eyes, her skin smooth and devoid of lines.

Mary brought one of Patsy's old blankets and spread it on the floor for Billy. Mae laid down the sweet wrinkled rosebud of a boy, and he went straight to sleep like a perfect infant.

Obviously glad to interrupt her sewing, Mary told Mae about Rob working at a livery barn. This made him melancholy after being laid off from the SP. He now did the work that any raw boy could do while his car-building skills went unused. She went to the kitchen and returned with coffee and cake, putting a cube of cake in Patsy's grasping hand. Patsy sat down with a thump on her padded behind, stuffed the sweet in her mouth, and as Mae and Mary updated each other on their lives, amused herself for a long time by picking crumbs from between her fingers.

Mary made a mournful face and said she'd seen the notice in the newspaper about Emmett's death. "I wanted to send you a note, but I didn't know where to send it."

Mae told her about the funeral and Daddy's death. She also told her about Billy and tried to explain why she'd come to love him despite his being a half-breed. She was about to describe the Big Canyon Mine, but Mary cut in, making a face.

"Oh, but they have that *coarse* hair! How could you stand to touch it? Indian hair's like stubble where it's cut off." She shuddered like some people did at the mention of a snake.

"His hair is no coarser than my own," Mae said, feeling hurt. "And he's very sweet. I know that's a word not used for men, but it's true." The disgust remained on Mary's face and Mae felt like crying.

She tried to get beyond Mary's hurtful reaction—like Billy wasn't human—tried to make Mary understand her feelings for him. She retold the events of that awful night and, in spite of herself, broke down sobbing as she summed it up. "He did it to save me from Oberon! A hanging offense, for my sake. I never thought a man would do that. For me!"

"They hanged him!"

"No, no. But they will if they find him. I'm sure he left California for good, the place he loves like life itself. Where his people are buried. I never thought a man would do that for me."

"Glory be!" Mary said, riveted as always on Mae's perils and troubles. She picked up a half-done garment and began pulling a needle through its layers. "Hope you don't mind if I do a bit of basting. I sew all the time. Rob's work brings us so little."

Mae told about how she got Charlie out of the canyon and about that night in the Shingle Springs boarding house when she learned that Charlie hadn't come to marry her. She told about Abbie Hunter's Woman's Investment Company in Carmel, and the baby nearly coming to light on the train.

Little Billy woke up and fussed. The clock on the wall pointed to four forty-five. Mae took down her frock. How easy it was to nurse here compared to doing it in front of strangers or Mrs. Rogue. Watching Billy, Patsy reached toward her mother, crying, "Mok, mok!" Mary set her basting aside, opened her blouse to Patsy, and listened to Mae's story of the hospital and Mrs. Rogue appearing on the doorstep.

"I think you're right," Mary concluded. "Charlie's mother might take the baby from you. You know, she has the right to consider what's best for the baby."

Mae gave back with some alarm, "I don't own a house and farm, but I'll be a hired girl or muck stalls or whatever it takes to keep my baby and raise him up." *Like Indian Mary did with her granddaughter.*

If Mary had more to say, she kept it to herself. She stood Patsy back in her cage and went to an open crate. Lifting out a strange-looking mechanical thing, she kneeled before it on the floor. "This is my new button machine," she said. "It makes a row of tiny buttons in no time flat. I'll show you."

Mae kneeled beside Mary as she inserted a small sheet of tin, from a stack of them, into the machine and pulled down hard on a lever. She opened the lid to reveal a punched-out line of small tin discs. Mary handed one to Mae. The backside had two tiny raised slots, to allow the needle through so they could be sewn on a garment. Mary took it back and returned it to its place in the line in the machine. Then she cut a length of cloth of the fabric she was sewing and placed it over the discs, pulling down on a second lever. The machine did its magic, and when Mary opened it this time, there lay a row of perfect cloth buttons framed by edges of bright tin that crimped the cloth and held it taut.

"Another modern marvel!" Mae said.

"I was thinking," Mary said, "You could come here for an hour each morning and make all the buttons I need for the day. I could use that hour to sew. The more buttons on the dresses, the more my ladies pay for them. I'd give you ten cents a day. We could visit together. Would like to do that?"

Mae had to think out loud. "If I lived in Sacramento with someone else paying my rent, I'd do it in a minute. But I've learned that a girl can't live in a city on dreams alone. I'd be on the streets, with Oberon on patrol. Then I'd be in worse danger of having Billy taken from me. Thank you for asking, Mary. I hope you understand, but I just can't do it. I have to go back to Slough House." Actually she would go to Bridge House and Indian Mary, but she couldn't say that to Mary.

The very best thing about Billy McCoon, she realized, was that she could tell him all the truths in her heart. She missed him sorely.

"I wish I could offer you more money," Mary said, "but we're barely getting by now. Every penny helps." She blew out air. "I'll just have to sit up nights making buttons."

Mae knew this had been a sincere attempt to help her, and she felt a surge of warmth for Mary.

The doorknob turned. A man in dirty work clothes stepped in, looking at Mae.

Mary introduced Rob. "Have supper with us," Mary said.

"Thanks, but I can't have Mrs. Rogue worrying about me. I gotta get back."

As Rob went to the kitchen, rolled up his sleeves and started pumping water, Mae wished she could hug Mary good-bye, but people didn't do that.

Why she was so teary she couldn't fathom. Perhaps it was the thought that she wouldn't see Mary again. Or what Mary had said about Indian hair. Or both.

Sadly she walked the six blocks to Charlie's apartment, girding herself to fend off questions from his mother—how she and Charlie got married and exactly what happened to him that night. She'd been dancing around the truth and making the woman suspicious. Mrs. Rogue was a strong adversary—smart like Charlie, a married woman with house and garden, milk and pork at all times. So Mae must bear false witness again and again, or run away, again, into hiding.

80

Entering the hospital the next day, Mae knew this could be the last time she would see Charlie. The night before had worn her out. She'd managed to deflect Mrs. Rogue's questions about why she and Charlie's father hadn't been invited to the wedding, but so much lying felt awful. Indians were right. Lying weakened a person. Now she had to be blunt.

She stopped in the big lobby and turned to Mrs. Rogue. "I need to talk to Charlie alone, so I'd like you to stay here and wait." She gestured to the chairs along the wall.

Mrs. Rogue said, "I was about to say the same thing to you." The flaps under her eyes were now red, like she'd cried last night.

Mae hadn't slept well either, on the sofa with little Billy. "I really do want to talk to him first."

"So do I." The firm line of Mrs. Rogue's mouth looked just like Charlie's when he was being stubborn.

The fight dissolved inside Mae. After all, Mrs. Rogue hadn't seen her son since the accident, and Mae's visiting credentials rested on a lie. "Go ahead," she said. This meant that Mae wouldn't be able to sneak out to the stage station while Mrs. Rogue was in the room with Charlie. But Mae figured she'd just look her in the eye when she got back and tell her she was leaving town for good. She rather liked the idea of being bold and strong, and if Mrs. Rogue tried to take the baby, Mae felt sure she could outrun her. A grim but determined thought.

Present during this exchange, the nurse said, "Mr. Rogue needs his rest, so the two visits can't add up to more than a half hour."

"I won't take more than fifteen minutes," Mae said, looking at Mrs. Rogue, "but I want all of my minutes."

Mrs. Rogue laid an exhausted gaze on Mae, turned to the nurse and said, "Take me to him."

Their footsteps rang up the hallway.

Mae sat down and tried to be calm despite worrying that at any moment a guard would come out to nab her, having heard what Charlie was surely telling his mother. She walked Billy around the lobby, checking the watch on her cape every so often. Ten minutes remained of the joint visit when the nurse returned with Mrs. Rogue.

The woman appeared to be sadder than ever, not angry at all. She smiled weakly at Mae and said, "I wish you all the luck with him."

Luck? He must not have told her much. Could it be that she hoped Mae could talk Charlie into marrying her?

"I'll mind the baby," Mrs. Rogue said, stretching out her arms.

"No. I'll take him. Charlie wants to hold him."

"He can't do that," the nurse said.

"Oh, all right. But I still want to show him off." Mae strode up the corridor with the baby and the Chinese bag—containing everything in the world that she owned, including infant nightgowns and diapers bought yesterday by Mrs. Rogue. The nurse, marching beside her stopped at a door.

Before opening it she said, "Microbes fly in the air. Don't touch him or breathe on him. We're strict in this hospital."

The bandages were off, and Charlie's bald head was painted bright orange. No doubt iodine. Fat black lids covered his eyes, and his horribly swollen face contained every dark color in the rainbow. Turkey tracks of black stitches wandered down his head. He looked like a stuffed monster with edges of raw flesh poking through the black stitches all over his nose and lips. Occasional tufts of tied-off threads stood up stiff as burned bushes. His bruised arm lay outside the gleaming ironed sheet folded neatly over his chest, which was bulging from unseen bandages.

"Hi Charlie."

He opened the puffy slits of his eyes. The whites had previously gone yellow but were now bright red again. She glanced back at the door and saw that the nurse wasn't peeping through the little window. "They told me not to let you hold him, but his breath is pure as the driven snow. It couldn't possibly hurt you." She unwrapped Billy from Patsy's blanket and threw it over her shoulder. "He sleeps most of the time." She said, extending the sleeping baby toward him.

"So do I." His voice was nasal due to the cotton stuffed up his nose, and his hands reached up toward the limp baby in the new lacy nightgown. She laid Billy on his side, on the undamaged side of Charlie's chest. Charlie put a large hand over him, covering almost all of his tiny body, all but the dark head and the hem of the gown gathered by a slender blue ribbon.

No hint of expression registered in Charlie's monstrous face. Was he feeling the miracle?

"Mm," he said. "Nother loff 'in."

Mother loves him. Mae's stomach tightened, realizing they might have made a pact to take him away from her. After a few seconds more, she took Billy back and wrapped him in the blanket again.

"Wish I c'd talk," Charlie said, fixing his red eyes on her. "Si' down."

She sat on the edge of the chair near the bed, ready to say good-bye.

"Nose is nailed an' 'ired."

"Wired?"

He nodded a little.

That sounded gruesome but she tried not to show it. "When'll they take the wire out?"

"Go'd wire. Stays in."

"You've got an expensive nose." Jumping to her purpose, she asked, "Did you tell your mother who attacked you? And my part of it?"

"No."

Something inside her slid back to normal. "Why not?"

"Har' t' talk."

Indeed.

With a slight head movement toward Billy, Charlie initiated talk of his own. "I thinkin'. S'hard fer you t'nake it on yer own. Y'need a nan." He lay on the pillow breathing through the mouth and resting from the exertion.

Digesting the surprising sympathy, Mae began to feel more relieved; he must not be bringing charges. Before she could ask for assurance, he spoke again.

"Let's g' narried."

Shocked to the core and staring at him, she wondered why he shut his eyes when he said that and didn't look at her. This was her dream, marrying a man like Charlie who was well up in the world and destined to rise higher. And for a long time she had dreamed of marrying this particular man. The baby started fussing, perhaps feeling her stunned heart.

"Did your mother talk you into that?"

His head moved back and forth, red eyes on her again. "She dint say it, 'cause she wants me to." The "w" forced up through his chest.

Mae had to think about that. Those two stubborn people must have been at awful loggerheads when they lived in the same house. "Charlie, why would you want to marry me, after what I've done to you? You don't even believe in marriage."

"I hurt you too. You hel'ed me. I 'reciate that." He closed his eyes.

She supposed it was true; he *had* done harm to her, though she'd never thought of it that way. He'd had all the power over her, and made her love him. It pained him to talk so she tried to do it for him. "You feel like you owe me something?"

"Uh-huh."

"And you think you should be a father to your son, now that you've held him?"

"Uh-huh."

"Any other reason?"

"S'enough." The *gh* came as a huff from his chest.

No, it was not enough. She still loved big Billy in a way she could never love Charlie. Billy was like a kind father to her, a devoted brother, and a sweet boy that she wanted to hold in her arms all rolled up into a body that electrified her. He respected her. Charlie had dismissed Billy's motive in a tone that said: *Well, he's a savage Indian.* The thought of being forever tied to a man who thought like that made her stomach feel like she was falling down a well. Clearly he didn't love her like Billy did, and she'd never be up to his standards, especially after she'd *known* an Indian in the Biblical sense. Everyone had heard stories about white men rejecting their wives after they'd been rescued from Indian captivity. A white woman in the arms of an Indian made those women dead to their husbands. Charlie wasn't different enough in his thinking. Bad scenes of a future with him flashed through her mind: Charlie resenting her for making him a married man; her crying bitter tears when he went out with other women; she, like Mom, sinking into a melancholia. And it would be only a matter of time before little Billy displeased and angered Charlie—all boys upset their fathers sooner or later. He didn't think of children as blessings. He would say scathing things to the boy, and to her when she stood up for him. So she had to put away her dream. It wasn't possible to marry Charlie.

A year ago she would have married him with two minutes notice. But she'd learned a few things. Charlie's big oval mirror had told her that at eighteen, despite all she'd been through, she'd kept her good looks. More important, she had seen herself through Billy's eyes as having power. It had to do with her connection to the universe and her ability to bring forth new life. He saw an aura about her and said that men fought to the death for such as that. He warned that she should be careful. If he died, she should not waste herself on weak or bad men. Charlie saw her as a disobedient girl who refused to rid herself of the baby, and now he must do his duty and saddle himself with her—no doubt for a short time, given how he felt about marriage.

She'd also learned that regardless of skin color all people are the same. So if Billy could love her, it was conceivable that she could meet another man who would see her not as a slut or an unwanted responsibility weighing him down like an albatross, but as a rose, and she could love such a man in return. Furthermore, she'd come to know two old women who had supported themselves for many years. If Ah Sen and Indian Mary could do it with the heavy disadvantage of race and lack of schooling, surely she could too. And even if she had to fend for herself for the rest of her life, that would be better than being legally bound to a disgruntled man.

"Charlie," she said, "that's a nice offer, but I'm not taking it. I came here to see if you'll get better, and I'm very glad to know you will. I want you to go on with your career in spite of this terrible thing that I helped do to you. I think you know I didn't mean to do it, and I'm very sorry I didn't get you to help sooner."

Feeling the weight of unshed tears behind her eyes, she stood up and turned away. The weeping never stopped.

"Whur'ya go?" Charlie said.

"Slough House or Bridge House. I've got friends there."

"I'd send noney, reg'lar."

Through the slurring, she could hear his relief.

"Thank you very much, Charlie. I sure could use any money you could send. Send it in care of the Michigan Bar postmaster, Mr. John Heath. If that changes I'll write and let you know. And I'll tell you how the baby's doing. Maybe we could be friends through the post. I'd like to know how Mr. Tevis's water plan works out too."

He pushed a hand toward her on the white blanket.

She grasped the large soft palm and squeezed. The only man she'd ever known without calluses.

The nurse came scolding through the door.

Mae whirled to the woman. "Ma'am, I held a piss bottle for this man when he was worse off than he is now, and it didn't kill him. Anyway I'm leaving."

When the door shut behind her, she realized she hadn't asked Charlie to defend her if his mother tried to take the baby. On second thought, she ought not plant the idea in his head. Come to think of it, marrying Charlie and then divorcing him for any reason was a sure route to losing little Billy to that woman.

The nurse was still in the room, so Mae hurried in the opposite direction from the lobby. She turned down a second hallway toward the back of the building. At a sign that said SERVICE ENTRANCE ONLY, she exited into the alley and made rapid tracks to the 28th Street station.

81

In the stillness of the late afternoon the ancient oak sprawled over Indian Mary's cabin with its crooked little smoke-pipe. The quaint place welcomed Mae. The tree had its full complement of leaves, some of them hanging in clusters almost to the earth like a surfeit of jewels suspended from slender chains. If oak leaves were a crop, Mae thought as she shifted little Billy to her other arm, these would fetch top dollar. She had dreaded coming here but now the beautiful place eased her mind a little.

The river's roil and the subtle oak scent gave a healthful feeling, and as the late sunlight slanted through the branches she saw tiny moving particles. Charlie's nurse had cautioned that bad microbes had been discovered in the air, too small for the human eye to see. Maybe good microbes also lived in the air. Somehow, the idea that human beings lived alongside not only thousands of stars orbiting in the heavens but a world of tiny beings moving to their own aims put her troubles into perspective and dampened her trepidation for what she must do.

She had not stopped to see Ah Sen in Slough House, but rode on to Bridge House, drawn as by a magnet to Billy's mother, the woman who had nursed him and taught him so much about life. It had taken only minutes to walk across the yellow iron-truss bridge and up the path to the cabin. Now she stood a stone's throw from the door, drawing a long breath and knowing she must tell Indian Mary what had happened to her son. If Mary hated her for it and sent her away, so be it. Mae needed to get it off her chest or she'd never be able to look at herself in a mirror. She must apologize and, if given a chance, atone in some way for her part in Billy's exile.

And there was more. This was the wise old woman who had convinced her that the baby wanted so badly to be born that he'd clung to life through the poisoning, as Mae now understood the medicine to have been. This was the woman who'd taught big Billy that babies were blessings even when their mothers were unwed. Such a woman would surely want to see little Billy, a sweet child named for her son.

She also had her own reason. If big Billy returned it would be to see his mother and his beloved home place. Maybe he was in the cabin now. The thought tripped her heart until she thought through the impossible odds. She needed to be on good terms with Indian Mary so if he came for a few fleeting hours in the dark of night, his mother could tell him that he was not a murderer. He needed to know that, and Mae wanted to tell him in person that she was certain Charlie wouldn't bring charges for the assault. Because this was only a hunch based on what Charlie had said in the hospital—difficult to shape into words—she didn't want to leave it for Mary to explain unless absolutely necessary.

Furthermore, she wanted to see Billy again.

Desire for him lived in a bittersweet place in her heart. She might yet marry him. The thought worried her because no matter how much she loved him, his chances were limited and that in turn would limit little Billy. Would love bought at such a high cost last? She felt wicked to weigh worldly things against love. Sister Delphine had taught her that God loved and cared for the smallest sparrow and robed the lilies of the field. Jesus in his wanderings had met a wealthy man who wanted to get into the kingdom of heaven, and Jesus replied that it was harder for a rich man to get there than for a camel to pass through the eye of a needle. Jesus had advised the man to give up worldly things and follow him. Mae wished she could remember how that story ended.

Something big moved behind the dark of the screen-door, which Billy had bought and installed for his mother.

"Mary, is that you?"

The screen opened and old Mary emerged onto the little stoop, her black blouse loosely tucked under the waistband of her full black skirt, her shoulder-length hair half gray. As Mae approached, she saw Mary's blank expression, that of a person trying not to show emotion. She had seen Billy's absence.

Mae stepped to the stoop, aware that Mary ignored, for a while, people who had been gone. The uncertainty of that made her voice sound halting and awkward. "I need to tell you what happened to Billy. That's why I've come."

Indian Mary, a statue of mourning, spoke in a dull voice from the chest, like the flow of a creek beneath snow: "Where my boy?"

"He's gone but not dead." Mae hoped that was true. "I want to sit down and tell you about it. Would that be all right?"

The stone figure cracked slowly, her black eyes crossing Mae's as she turned and entered the cabin in small steps. Her glance had told Mae to follow, and it also conveyed relief, sadness, fear and hope for what would be said.

In a dark corner of the cabin, Baby—skinny as ever, eyes like smudged coal oil—kneeled on a bed staring at Mae.

"Hello," Mae said to the girl, glad to postpone for a moment the awful tale. She turned to Indian Mary, now sitting down at the table. "Here's my baby." She extended the sleeping baby in an asking way.

Mary reached for him and gently folded him into her big arms.

Sitting across the table, Mae said, "I named him for your Billy."

Little Billy winced in his sleep, and a smile flickered over Mary's lips.

"You were right," Mae said. "He sure did want to come into this world."

Baby went to her grandmother's side and stood staring at little Billy.

"And he is a blessing," Mae added.

Mary closed her eyes as she settled back in her chair with little Billy, the wrinkles relaxing on her old face. After a time she looked past Mae again. Waiting.

Mae told the entire story—her fear of Oberon, and Billy earning white man's wages for his work at the mine. She soldiered through the events of that terrible night, telling how, after she urged Billy to flee, she discovered that Charlie was alive. She told about Abbie Hunter taking Charlie to the hospital while Mae gave birth at the Cothrin place, with the help of Mrs. Craig."

"Mrs. Craig good," Indian Mary agreed.

"Oh! How do you know her?" Any subject but the other reduced the tension in Mae's shoulders.

"She good doctor. Inyans know her." Mary moved her fingers across little Billy's scalp, pushing a wave of velvet wrinkles.

"This morning I visited Charlie in the hospital. The doctor put his nose bones together with gold wire, and it looks like he'll mend. I'm pretty sure he won't charge Billy with a crime. That's what I came to tell you. So if Billy comes to visit, you can tell him he's not a murderer and Charlie won't send the police. But I want to tell him that last part myself. I want him to understand why I believe it's true so *he'll* believe it. Then he can live around here as a free man."

"He comin' back?"

Mae took a breath. "I'm sorry but I don't know. I'm afraid he won't. He thinks he'll be hanged for murder. But I do wish he would come back." Tears trickled down her cheeks and blurred little Billy's face as he blinked with wonder at his new world.

Baby, now sitting at the end of the table, reached toward him with a pleading look to Mae.

In truth she worried about this child holding the baby, but a thought was springing to mind. Maybe she could live here. If she did, the two babies needed to be introduced to each other and now was as good a time as any.

"Yes, you can hold him," Mae said, "if it's all right with your grandmother." Indian Mary knew the child inside and out.

With a nod, Indian Mary stood up and placed the trusting infant into those sticklike arms while showing Baby how the head must be supported at all times, just as Mrs. Craig had explained it to Mae.

The shadowy black eyes lit up. For the first time in Mae's presence, Baby seemed like any other young girl thrilled to hold a real baby. Mae recalled that she too, as a little girl, had yearned to hold a real baby, and she understood Baby's obvious joy to be trusted with a being so precious.

"I was thinking," Mae said to Indian Mary, keeping an eye on Baby, "you could help me raise up little Billy. Help make him a good boy."

In the meager light the shadows seemed to darken in the old woman's face. After a time she said, "No."

"Oh," came unbidden from Mae. "Why... if I may ask?"

"You say, make him good boy. What Old Mary say good mebbe bad to white peoples. My people say fighting bad. I tell Billy doan fight. Doan hit people. He fight. I doan raise him up good. He no listen to Inyan momma." She pointed to Baby, whose eyes were locked in a stare with little Billy. "That girl no listen to old Inyan gran-mamma."

Mae was thinking how to answer that when Mary continued.

"I say Isabella, doan go with man drinking whisky and wine. She go. She drink all time. She no listen to old Inyan mamma. Nobody listen." Her big shoulders nudged up and down. "Old Inyan mamma no good no more."

"Oh no, don't say that. You kept working and made a living for your children and your grandchild, and you did that through terrible times. *Daddy didn't.* You didn't break down and quit, *like Mom did.* Your children and grandchildren can lean on you when they're in trouble. You are a good person and you raised up a good boy, a wonderful man. That much I know." The pesky tears had been damming up in Mae's eyes. Now they spilled down her face.

"Old Inyan mamma no make Baby go school far away. White man say bad."

"Nonsense. This little girl needs you. Those white teachers couldn't begin to understand her." A thought struck with such force it gave her goose bumps. "I could teach her to read and write. Geography and spelling, and music too. And if the sheriff's deputies come for her again I'll tell them I'm a teacher and she's learning all she needs to know. I could raise chickens and sell eggs, if you wouldn't mind them pecking around your place, and wouldn't mind me living here." The last was the main thing, and she plowed on.

"Baby could stay and help me while you're cleaning houses. She could learn the chicken business." Billy had said some ranch wives stopped using Mary because of Baby. Mae's strength sagged as she realized she had no bed to sleep in tonight and that too was behind her desire to stay.

"You see, I have no other place to live." She supposed Ah Sen might…

"You wanna live in my house?" Mary met Mae's eyes for a long moment, though Billy had said Indians considered that rude.

"Yes. And I'll help you any way I can." Mae turned to Baby. "What do you think? Would it be all right if little Billy and I stay here with you?" Having said that, she hoped Mary wouldn't consider it presumptuous for her to address such a question to the child.

Baby continued staring at the tiny baby.

Indian Mary poured tea from the kettle into three tin cups, and set them on the table. She sat down again, and with a quick glance at Baby told Mae, "She wan you stay. Me too."

Baby's lips moved into that awkward position that had so little practice, a smile.

Yes. For some reason the strange little girl liked her. Big Billy had told her that the only time Baby had ever remained home while her grandmother worked away from the house was when Mae was there recovering from the abortion poison. This would be a challenge for Mae, but it was the least she could do to help this woman whose son she had driven away.

Mae felt like she'd been holding her breath, and now released it. Here she would wait for Billy. With the the $104 left from her freedom money, as she now thought of it. She would buy laying hens and a rooster from Ah Sen, and would buy other things Mary and Baby needed. And if she was lucky, maybe old Mary would teach her about Indian medicine.

82

The day after moving into Billy's old home, Mae took little Billy and Baby to the Stone House School. She waited in the yard until the bell rang and happy children spewed out the door into the warm spring day. Jack and Bert Granlees, big boys now, paused to look at her; she waved at them and they continued their dash toward home.

Mae explained to the teacher that she needed a book to help teach Baby, an Indian girl, to read. She touched Baby's shoulder. The teacher, the recipient of Baby's dark stare, went to a shelf and selected a reader with a broken spine, which she laid in Mae's hands.

"It was left here by a child," the teacher said. "That boy had no idea his folks was leavin' these parts. Why, they barged in here like the law was after 'em, grabbed their son, and was gone before he could think to take his reader. I'll lend it to you." She smiled at Baby, who continued staring. "When you need the second reader, bring that one back and I'll see what I can do for a trade."

Mae thanked her and was turning to leave when the teacher added, "If the Office of Education asked me, I'd give 'em an earful. I see no cause to send Indian children to schools so far away when they could just as well attend regular schools. Money spent up there in Mendocino or down in Los Angeles could help us out right here. Particularly when we're short on pupils. But who am I to say? Nobody asks me."

～

On Indian Mary's next washing day, Mae took little Billy to Ah Sen's place. She carried him in a sling cut from a blanket so moth-eaten that its owner didn't want it back after Mary washed it. Baby pouted, wanting to come too, but her grandmother wisely convinced her that Mae would return in the afternoon, and Baby was needed to help with her favorite task, stretching the clothes over the bushes.

Every bit of the trail down the river brought big Billy to mind. The elderberries in bloom, the huge creamy umbels that his mother dipped in hotcake batter and fried. He would have loved seeing the water clear of mud now that the High Hill Mining Company was shut down in Michigan Bar. She sensed mamma coyote watching as she passed the den, and she paused near the place where she and Billy had first made love.

Angling up the levee on what Billy had called China trail, she was pleased to see the chickens thick as thieves all over Ah Sen's yard.

"Hallo," she called, knocking on the door. "It's me, Mae."

A grin stretched Ah Sen's round face. She opened the screen door exclaiming, "Oh! Numba one babee." She put tea leaves in cups and poured hot water from her ever-steaming teakettle in the wok. Meanwhile Mae told the story of what had happened in Big Creek Canyon, continuing as she prepared to nurse the baby.

Ah Sen looked over her shoulder as Billy latched on. "Number one babee make house happy." Her brows lifted to learn that Mae was staying at Indian Mary's house.

When asked if she would sell Mae some hens and a rooster, Ah Sen narrowed an eye. "You in chicken biness?"

Mae explained that she would sell eggs and pullets only to the Bridge House Store, not to the Cosumne Store, so they wouldn't be in competition. When Ah Sen agreed, Mae paid the going price. They put four hens together in one lightweight wooden cage, the rooster in the other. Then they rigged up a harness so the straps went over Mae's shoulders with the cages stacked on her back, Billy's sling in front. Mae would return the cages later so Ah Sen could use them for selling live pullets.

After hearing her friend's warm "See you rater," Mae headed home.

The chickens lived in the house until Indian Mary got Mr. Driscoll to drive over with some scrap lumber for a lean-to. Every day Mae and Baby went out to gather grass seed, beating it into a carrying basket with a flail woven for that purpose. Soon the chickens knew their new home, and knew to come back to roost at night. The hens laid enough eggs daily for Mary, Mae and Baby to eat, plus a few extras to sell to the Bridge House Store. When Mae let one of the hens raise a batch of chicks, Baby was so fascinated she didn't seem to miss her grandmother, though she was always happy to see her at the end of the day.

One day, the chinless deputy sheriff came to the door to take Baby. While Baby screamed from a back corner in a bone-rattling pitch, and a terrified little Billy wailed in her arms, Mae shouted to be heard. She lied a little, saying she was a high school graduate and "guaranteed" that Baby would be reading from *McGuffey's Reader* by next spring. For emphasis, she picked the book up from the table and showed it to him. She invited him to bring over the teacher from Stone House School to check on Baby's progress. The deputy, who remembered Mae from the murder investigation, seemed confused, amazed and wordless to see a white girl living with an Indian and teaching the screaming child. He promptly left and never returned.

Mae liked Wednesdays, when she helped Indian Mary with her five washtubs of laundry. Mary wove a bikoos for little Billy, insisting on a board to keep his back straight, and then laced him in with twine. A deadfall stake whittled to fit into the weave behind the board made it possible for little Billy to "stand" and watch his family. The bikoos had a sunshade to protect his delicate skin when the sun shifted. On the washing days, with Mae rinsing and Baby stretching towels and shirts over the shorter bushes, Indian Mary told stories about Coyote's exploits, or how the People came from an ancient home place in the land of ice and snow, or about unusual happenings in the ranch houses where Mary cleaned. Now that Baby stayed home, the ranch wives paid Mary five cents a day, plus all the leftover food she wanted.

By September, five-month-old Billy had grown so much that Mary wove him a much bigger bikoos with a sturdier stake. The chicken and egg business had also grown, with at least one hen raising chicks at all times. Each morning after breakfast Mae took Baby across the bridge to the store—the highlight of their days. She carried the straw-packed tray of eggs before her by means of a strap around her neck, and little Billy rode on her back.

Baby watched Billy as he surveyed the out-of-doors like a straight little soldier while Mae delivered the eggs and received her payment from Mr. Warren. With the money, she bought a twist of sarsaparilla for Baby and a loaf of oven-warm bread—baked by an enterprising woman up the line and delivered by the Amador Stage driver just minutes earlier.

It was sunny and pleasant outside, so instead of leaving immediately, Mae sat on the store's porch and read the newspapers left there—*The Sacramento Bee*, the *Sacramento Union,* and the *Amador Ledger-Dispatch.* All three papers blared front-page stories about the Great Electric Carnival to be held in Sacramento on Sunday, September 9.

While Baby pantomimed skits to little Billy's rapt attention and Mr. Warren hurried out to collect bridge tolls, Mae skipped the schedule of picnics, speeches, and concerts and went to the main article about the Carnival. A man from Stockton and another from Jackson wrote that they would attend "to be part of history." People from outlying areas wrote that they "wouldn't miss being there when the lights were switched on for the first time." Strings of incandescent bulbs had been draped up and down the streets. The Capitol Building, including all the ribs of the dome, would "shine as though with diamonds." Businessmen were decorating doorways with painted bulbs or hanging "colorful paper lanterns" over them. When the master switch was pulled at dusk, the streets would be "one grand poem of color." Green, gold, and crimson lights would hang from the trees in the parks, in private yards, and in the Capitol grounds "like fruit in a fairy tale garden." Bands would play and people would dance all night on J and K Streets. Darkness, that scourge of ages past, had been conquered. Progress was on the march!

Mae folded the papers on her lap and looked unhappily at the scattered, dusty structures around her, left from an earlier time. It had been five months since she'd seen Charlie. Perhaps he would escort a lady to the Carnival. Or maybe, not being as attractive to ladies as before, he would go with friends from the Capitol. She recalled his eager face at the dinner party when Mr. Livermore promised legislators and merchants that he would deliver electricity to Sacramento by 1895. Now it was 1895, and he was delivering. She recalled the naysayers who claimed the power line would leak. She missed the excitement of being with Charlie, missed being in touch with the mainstream of life and knowing about important things that were happening. How nice it would be to stroll on Charlie's arm and dance in the streets in the blaze of all those lights!

With a sigh, she got up and took the newspapers back to the store's proprietor. The counter doubled as a bar, and the dancing area occupied most of the space in the building. They were alone. Behind the counter a new sign proclaimed: MR. ROBERT LELAND WARREN, PROPRIETOR. She tilted her head at the papers. "I hope the lights work on Sunday," she said.

"Me too. I'm taking Katy Irene to see it." The nice-looking young man continued while Mae recovered her equilibrium. "It'll be something to behold. The Folsom Powerhouse'll be all lit up too. But Sacramento City's the real show. I'm hoping to get the whole Sheldon clan to come with us."

The shock of hearing Katy Irene's name flow smoothly from the man's mouth, followed by the Sheldon name, posed the problem of how much anonymity Mae still wanted. For two years she'd been isolated socially, in Sacramento, with Ah Sen, in Big Canyon with Billy, and now in Mary's house. The deputy sheriff knew her name, but the teacher at the school didn't. On the whole she'd escaped notice. Fortunately Indian Mary was a tight-lipped sort. But now every part of Mae burned to query the man about Katy Irene—Married? Sweethearts? If married, Katy lived right across the road in that peaked-roof "bungalow" where the previous proprietor had lived. A kitchen window looked directly at the store, which Mae entered and left each morning. If Katy lived there, the odds were small that she hadn't seen Mae with Baby and little Billy looking like a papoose. Yet she had not come out to talk.

Casually, Mae said, "I used to know a girl named Katy Irene—a relation of the Sheldons, I think."

"She's my wife."

The ease with which he showed such pride took Mae's breath away, and her response came without conscious thought. "Congratulations. She's a beautiful and talented girl."

"Thank you, I think so too."

Suppressing additional questions, she bade him good-bye and left.

She pulled up the stake of little Billy's bikoos, turned it around, and shrugged into the straps. She kept her head down as she and Baby paraded past the brown bungalow with the white picket fence and gladiolus in lush bloom.

That afternoon Mae took little Billy and Baby for a long walk to the Cosumne Store's post office. At the Western Union counter she sent a telegram to Charlie. Telegrams cost a penny a word, so she discarded anything extraneous or hinting of a change of heart about marrying him:

Coming Sacramento Sep 9 afternoon stop Maybe talk stop Mae

The next day the Western Union delivery boy, perhaps a young Grimshaw, came to the house with the reply:

BUSY ON 9TH MAYBE COME OFFICE 3-4 THURSDAY NEXT STOP CR

She didn't go. And she was glad she hadn't mentioned wanting to see the Electric Carnival with him.

Charlie continued to wire ten dollars approximately every two months. That plus the chicken business allowed Mae to take the stagecoach to Sacramento once in a while to shop at Weinstock & Lubin's for diapers and clothing for fast-growing Billy, and some warm blankets for winter. From her remaining freedom money, she bought a few things for herself and Indian Mary—aprons, better pots and pans, a pretty dress for Baby, who wasn't looking so skeletal any more. Mary continued to bring home leftover food and very ripe fruit and vegetables from the gardens of the homes where she cleaned. She also salvaged clothing her employers didn't want any more. Most of the dresses needed a good deal of mending, but Mae was glad to have them for everyday wear.

A year went by, Billy growing into ever-bigger bikooses.

A winter pleasure was Chinese bitter-melon candy. Ah Sen provided melon seeds and taught Mae how to grow them in the early summer. She also shared the procedure for making the candy. Mae bought the sugar with her egg money. For three days, they boiled melon chunks with sugar, and then for three days cooled them, then boiled and cooled them alternately for three more days. Since the kitchen range had to be kept going all day in the winter anyway, this treat seemed to be provided by God.

Mae continued to be a recluse, not lingering at the Bridge House Store in the mornings. If Katy Irene knew about her, she sent no messages.

Neither did Billy, wherever he was.

⌒

By May of 1897, when Billy was two years old, Baby was reading aloud at the second-grade level, though no sheriff or teacher came to see that miracle. For the first time she was talking—in English and Miwok—a related miracle for a girl of about ten who had never spoken in a language anyone living could understand. Indians didn't put much store in age as white people did, and few of them knew their exact ages.

Indian Mary—and Baby, surprisingly—taught Mae about the plants along the river and their medicinal qualities. Mae learned the remedies for ague and coughing, stinging nettle, poison oak, toothache and headache, and now used native mint for stomachache and other maladies. In the tangle of vegetation in the river bottomland, Baby came alive like Mae had never seen her. If Mary left anything out about the individual plants, Baby filled it in. Clearly she was destined to carry on the legacy of Indian Mary's doctoring.

One day as Mae read *The Sacramento Union* on the porch of the store, she was fascinated by a back-page article reporting that Gugliano Marconi had sent a wireless radio message in Morse Code from his native Italy, and it had been received in Wales. This new invention, according to the writer, would make it possible for people to communicate around the world, and from ship to ship at sea. It would forever change the way people lived. Mae was marveling at how narrow her own world was, when footsteps caused her to look up.

Katy Irene stood there smiling, with a baby riding her hip. "M-M-Mind if I sit a s-spell?" The baby looked about a year younger than little Billy.

"Oh, please do," Mae said moving over, too amazed to say more.

"I'm s-sorry I haven't c-come over to talk sooner," Katy said, looking at Baby as the frail girl backed away from little Billy into the scrub oak growing rampant from the base of the blue oak.

"This is R-Robbie," Katy said. She petted the hair standing straight up from her baby's head. "That's George." She pointed at a little boy shyly lagging behind her, having just come across the road.

Mae went to the staked bikoos. Bringing him back to the bench, she said, "And this is little Billy." She set him on her lap. "He's two and a half."

"Robbie's a y-year and a half. G-George's three."

The two youngest, Billy and Robbie, eyed one another, both obviously glad for the protection of their respective mothers.

"I really am s-sorry for not…"

"Oh, don't worry about that. You probably thought I had gone crazy, living with an Indian and all."

"I uh… well, d-d-don't know what I thought. Anyway, you l-look just the s-same… except for him." Katy glanced at little Billy and looked down, her embarrassment standing between them, but she was trying her best to be friendly. "I have to a-ask. Is his father I-Indian? Is he Indian M-Mary's son?"

"No. Billy's father is white, living in Sacramento." Billy had been struggling to get free, and Mae put him on his feet.

"Oh," Katy said.

She looked so uncomfortable that Mae grasped the back of her free hand. "Please don't think anything of it. I can't tell you how much I appreciate your coming out to visit." She felt like hugging her old friend.

Katy Irene must have seen the tears in Mae's eyes. She set her wiggling baby on his feet too, and they both watched him back down the step of the porch after Billy, who being twice Robbie's age had done that with confidence and haste. Robbie lost his balance and rolled in the dust at the foot of the step. He didn't cry but made a terrible face as he tried to tongue the gritty dirt out of his mouth.

Mae and Katy Irene laughed at him, and Katy picked him up and brushed him off. She stood him on his fat legs, and when he got his balance, returned to the bench. "Isn't that the g-g-girl who screams all the time?" She pointed at Baby, who surely would have seen that point but didn't let on.

In her hawk-like way, Baby was watching the three little boys, Robbie barely able to walk, Billy running barefoot on the uneven ground where countless horses and rigs had made powder of the dirt and dry manure, and older George standing shyly at his mother's knee. Katy jumped up to retrieve Robbie before he went too far. He was still trying to get the dirt out of his mouth when she sat down with him on her knee.

"She used to scream a lot," Mae told her, "but she's a lot better now. I'm teaching her to read. Teaching her music too." She smiled at Katy's obvious astonishment. "We started by sitting near the river. I would draw a treble clef in the sand and put the notes on the lines, and then sing them to her. She picked it up very fast. Now I can draw a very long staff and put a song on it. She walks from one end of it to the other singing the melody as she goes, not just from memory. She *reads* the notes."

"Oh my! I had n-no idea. Everyone says she's, well, uh s-simple, and mute."

No doubt people called her a moron or an idiot.

They visited for about twenty minutes, every minute a little more comfortable for all of them. When Billy climbed the step and returned to the bench, Mae decided it was time to take him and Baby home. She felt light as a feather for the visit.

After that, Katy Irene came out each morning. In November, after a cold windstorm blew in, she opened the door as Mae and the children were passing by and called out an invitation to come inside for a cup of coffee. By now the three little boys were fast friends, and George let Billy ride his little hobbyhorse.

One spring day when Billy was almost three, the Western Union boy came to the door with a telegram for Mae. The instant she saw the name Phoebe Hamilton Payne, she knew it was bad news.

EMMA DUFFY PASSED APRIL 18 STOP PLEASE INFORM FARLEY STOP

That ended her hope of taking little Billy to visit his grandmother "someday." Obviously Hank and Sophie had been in touch with Mom, and that's how Aunt Phoebe knew to send the telegram c/o the Cosumne Store. But where was Farley? Suddenly Mae was bawling in the doorway of Mary's cabin. Though an adult of twenty-one, she felt like an orphan.

Baby's expression mirrored what Mae was feeling, her light hand pulling Mae to lie down on her cot.

"My mother died," she sobbed to Baby.

Baby patted her lovingly. Little Billy caught on, and hugged her like she hugged him when he was crying.

⤳

Billy was nearly four when Isabella returned to the house looking old, ragged, and thin. Her mother wouldn't acknowledge her presence for a long time, but Isabella waited. By then little Billy was in Mae's bed for the night, recharging his little body for a tomorrow filled with more running, jumping and twisting like an acrobat. Baby pressed herself into the corner and stared at her mother, but when old Mary began exchanging words with her daughter, Baby came out and approached the table, where Mae was also seated. Mary offered Isabella acorn pudding mixed with blackberries left over from breakfast.

Spooning that in, Isabella stared at the wall. "I'm done with men," she said in English. "I wanna be mother to my girl."

Indian Mary looked at her daughter with kindness and a bit of skepticism.

Baby came over to Mae and stood so close that their arms touched.

"What are you doing here?" Isabella raked Mae with. "I've heard of Indian pets in white houses, but not white-girl pets in Indian houses."

Mae felt her face burn with the insult, but by now she had learned to withhold retorts until she'd thought them through four times, as Indian Mary taught. "Nobody's a pet here," she finally said. "We're all helping each other."

"We teach each other too," Baby added.

Isabella stared in amazement to hear her daughter talk.

"She's right," Mae affirmed from the bottom of her heart. "But if you're home now and you don't want me here, I'll leave." She had hoped to wait for Billy, but he hadn't returned or sent a message. Now, she knew she could work as a hired girl if necessary, and she would do it willingly rather than cause trouble in this small house.

Then she imagined herself in Isabella's place, returning home to find a stranger living there, and knew she would resent that person. This realization prompted her to put her own truth on the table. "I know what it's like to be hurt by men and have your body and soul torn up. I was lucky that your family took me in and saved me. Each one of them helped, and I'm sure your family can save you too. I'll get out of the way to make that easier."

"Mae's in my family now," Indian Mary said.

That declaration, Mae knew, had been thought through four times.

83

During 1898, the depression that trailed behind the Panic of '93 finally ended. The *Sacramento Union* credited the war for the recovery. The government was paying for steel battleships and ever more guns and munitions. A Bay company and Sacramento steel works had received big government contacts. Unemployed boys and older men flocked to the thriving factories all over the United States, while young men of soldiering age signed up for military service, glad for the work. Farmers and ranchers made good money again as the government purchased meat, grain and woolen uniforms.

Mae's eggs and pullets didn't bring in any more cash than before, but the roosters saw to the increase in their numbers, and she acquired new store-customers in Amador County where the hard rock mines had reopened. Even the one in Plymouth started up again, though the hydraulic mining in Michigan Bar stayed shut and most of the merchants there were closing their stores. Mr. Heath decided to relocate his store to Jackson Road in the sprawling and ill-defined community now called Live Oak. Already under construction, the new store would serve travelers on a road predicted to become the main road as Michigan Bar and Latrobe receded in importance.

Mr. Ferris, the Amador Stage driver, delivered Mae's grass-packed eggs to bakeries and stores in Dry Creek, Amador City, and Sutter Creek, and the storekeepers returned the crates to him for the afternoon stage run. Mae picked them up each morning at the Bridge House Store.

Isabella took an interest in her mother's laundry business. She kept the chickens off the drying clothes on Wednesdays, and that led to her idea of erecting a series of permanent clotheslines and building a roof over them for drying clothes on rainy days. She turned out to be good with a hammer. Charlie's money paid for tin sheets and tall four-by-four posts. The cabin supported the roof on one side. But when the chickens decided to roost on the drying laundry, and Baby couldn't keep them from dirtying the lines, the four of them quickly realized they needed to wall off the laundry room. That way, they could put a stove in there and dry clothes on even the wettest, coldest days. Isabella, who seemed more energetic every day, tried to collect scrap wood from abandoned cabins and houses, but she needed a horse to expand her range and haul the materials.

"I'll see about finding Pal," Mae said. She'd been missing him terribly ever since moving to the river's edge where a horse could feed himself. She also wanted to teach little Billy to ride him. So she wrote Farley in care of the Sierra Railroad Company in Jamestown, where Hank had traced him when Mom died, and asked Farley what he'd done with Pal.

"If you sold him," she wrote, "I'd like to buy him back. Please let me know who has him and how much you got for him so I can dicker with the new owner."

Two days later, when she delivered her eggs, Mr. Warren handed her a postal card addressed to "Mae Duffy c/o Bridge House Store." On the front was a photograph of Farley grinning. Behind him a joker on a little railroad service wagon pretending to pump his side of a two-bar contraption that made the wagon move up the tracks. Mae figured Farley worked opposite that clown when not mugging for the camera. She knew that photographers nowadays went all over the country taking pictures like this one for twenty cents. The customer received twenty printed cards with markings on the back for message, address, and stamp. She read the cramped hand:

> Dear Mae, heres one for your collekshun good workin here frens all over we's putting in a rail line had to get rid of pal. Dint no were you was. got $2 for him, bad times. forgot the mans name. Sold him in Ione big brik livery. Hope you get him bak.
>
> Farley

The next day Baby stayed home with her mother while Mae and little Billy took the stage to Ione. Right there on the main street stood a tall redbrick building with an arched opening for the hayloft. "He could be in there," she said to Billy, "but don't get your hopes up." The sign above the entrance said: LUDGATE AND SURFACE LIVERY.

The cooler interior smelled horsey. She looked in the stalls, most of them empty. No Pal. "Where is he?" Billy asked.

A man in a leather apron spoke from the entrance. "Need a buggy?"

"No thanks. Just trying to find a horse I used to have. My brother sold him to somebody here. I want to buy him back."

The man beckoned. "I'm workin' outside just now. Let's talk out here."

Billy in tow, she followed to the side of the building—a forge against the brick wall and a roof to keep the coal and forge dry. "Hope you don't mind, but I gotta get a shoe done quick," the man said.

"No, please go on with what you're doing."

Billy watched intently as the man heated a horseshoe and then hammered the hot glowing iron on the anvil.

"Pal's his name," Mae told the man. "He's a dark bay with a shiny black mane, tail, and black socks on three legs. Big pretty eyes."

"Hm. Uncommon color. Let me think. How old?"

"He'd be twelve by now. Trained to saddle and harness. A real good horse. Gelding."

"Hmm. Don't believe we got 'im now. When did we buy 'im?"

"Don't know for sure. Maybe two years ago. Paid two dollars."

The man was hammering, thinking.

"He was trained real good," Mae added.

"Sounds familiar now that I think back," the man said. "Tryin' to recall that doctor's name. Funny name. We rented him for buggies, the horse that is. That doctor'd just come to town, rented a buggy and the horse was injured on the road. We was about to put him down, but the doc thought he could save the leg. So we gave him to the doctor. Let's see now, what was his name." The hammer bounced on the hot iron.

"How many doctors you got in Ione?"

"One, but that other one with that horse moved on. Heard he went to Moke Hill."

"How far is Moke Hill from here?" She'd often heard of that place.

The hot iron sizzled in a water bucket, held by tongs. On the other end of the tongs the man was thinking. He finally said, "You new around here?"

"Uh-huh, sort of."

"Well it's on the Forty-niner Trail south of Jackson, crost the Mokelumne River."

"Can I get there by stage?"

"Sure. Take the stage to Sutter Creek or Jackson. There's two of 'em. Forgot which, but one of 'em leaves pretty quick."

She thanked him and started to run with Billy.

The livery worker yelled after her, "Schoneburg or Shonenstein or some such funny name. Pretty good doctor. A dutschke by the accent."

Billy assumed stagecoaches were invented for his entertainment. He put his head out the window and grinned with the wind in his teeth and his hair blown back as the six-horse team galloped hell-bent-for-leather. Mae was glad the ride took less than an hour. The steep grade down to that river with the Indian name snaked around and around, and the horses had to walk, much to Billy's consternation. But the road cut through a dense forest of oak, pine, and other trees and made for a shady ride. Mae felt enlivened by this search for her lost horse, with high hopes that she was on the right trail.

The business end of Mokelumne Hill, called Moke Hill for short, clung to a fairly steep hill. The stage stopped at the large Ledger Hotel. Inside was a fancy bar with velvet walls and a long mirror that reflected more kinds of liquor that anyone could imagine. First, Mae took Billy out the back door to the outhouse where they waited in line, and then went inside to the room that served as bar, waiting room for stage passengers, and eating house.

"I wanna get one like that," Billy said pointing to an alcoholic drink being served to two men dressed like bankers.

"Do you have something wet and sweet for him," Mae inquired of the bartender as she claimed one of the stools. Billy struggled to climb up on the next stool, and she let him do it himself because he loved challenges. "I'm hungry," he informed her when he'd reached the summit.

While Billy happily consumed his drink with the clinking ice, made pink by a fruit Mae had never heard of, she told the bartender she wanted a quick noon dinner that a four-year-old would like. The man went back to the kitchen and fetched a woman wearing a splattered and smeared apron. She said she had a peanut concoction that children loved. She'd read about women making it and now produced it in the hotel kitchen—pulverized peanuts made into a paste. "It's good with preserves," she said, "plum or grape or any kind. Truth be told, it's good by itself. I eat it all the time."

Mae worried that such a thing would be too alien for Billy's taste until she remembered that he ate Mary's acorn pudding. And what were acorns but nuts? Then she inquired about the town doctor.

"I hope it's not an emergency," the bartender said. Assured it was not, he told her that Doctor Schoenenmann had a house on the road into town. "It's lettered on the shingle beside his door. South side of the road."

Suddenly excited, Mae could hardly bear the wait for the strange sandwich. Billy was finishing his drink, so she gulped down a glass of water and studied the stagecoach schedule: Departure 4 P.M. Jackson, Sutter Creek, Amador City, Michigan Bar, Bridge House, Slough House. However, she would ride Pal back home *if* Schoenenmann was the right doctor, *if* it had been Pal that was injured, *if* Pal had recovered and still lived, and *if* the doctor would sell him to her. A lot of ifs to be getting excited about. The clock on the wall said 2:45.

She liked the peanut sandwich, and Billy wanted more, but it was gone and they needed to be gone too. Billy had fun running down the steep boardwalk. At the bottom where it dead-ended into another street he stood wondering which way to go. She caught up with him and they hurried to the left, and sure enough, after a short walk, on the left side of the road stood a pretty house with a garden in front and a shingle beside the door. CHARLES W. SCHOENENMANN, M.D.

She knocked. Nobody answered. Disappointed, she stood on the porch with Billy, wondering what to do. The trees and shrubs along the road were tall and lush. "Come on," she said to Billy. "Let's take a peek in the back."

A driveway led into an empty stable, and a path continued to the back of the house. A fenced pasture stretched behind that, a pasture with good grass and plenty of shade, and in it were two horses. A black and a dun. Lucky horses to live in such a place, Mae thought. Maybe Pal was pulling the doctor's buggy.

She became aware of an older woman on the back porch. Embarrassed to be snooping on someone else's property, she went to the woman and saw that her chair had big wheels.

"Hello, little fella," the woman said to Billy. "What's your name?"

Billy looked down and mumbled. He lived with a woman who believed it was extremely rude to ask a person to speak their own name, and Mae realized that Billy had probably never been asked to do so.

"His name is Billy Rogue," Mae said.

"Cat got yer tongue?" The lady angled her head toward him.

"No cat gots my tongue," Billy said loud enough for the neighbors to hear. He stuck the whole tongue out for her to examine.

Obviously taken aback, the lady asked Mae, "Are you a patient of the doctor?"

"No. But I'm looking for him. Is he expected back soon?"

"Oh my land! A body never knows when that man'll turn up." She checked the watch pinned on the front of her dress. 'Sposed to be here now, for my exercises."

Thinking she might be a patient instead of a wife, Mae asked, "I wonder if I could wait here for awhile. I'm looking for a horse he might have bought a couple of years ago. Not one of those in the field."

"Suppose you could set a while. He's got the other horse out with him. My name's Ruby Miller."

Not the wife. "I'm Mae Duffy," she said, hoping Pal wasn't the doctor's favorite horse. The price would be dear, but she'd come with ten dollars just in case. "Is his other horse a bay?"

"It is at that."

With mixed emotions, Mae sat down on a step of the shady back porch and watched little Billy run along the fence line to get a better view of the horses. A honey locust provided shade, a tree that settlers had planted in Iowa as well as California. As a girl Mae used to eat the sweet blossoms that cascaded down into reach. Shaggy white daisies and spotted orange tiger lilies bloomed next to the porch. This, Mae thought, would be a nice place to raise a little boy.

The rattle of a harness and hooves, not out on the road but closer, drew her up to her feet. "Excuse me," she said to the lady and went around the corner of the house.

There in the drive, headed to the open carriage house, was Pal with blinkers on. He didn't see her. All the love for this horse rushed back, and her eyes teared up to see him so bony. Many people believed a horse was healthier bony, but she didn't agree. She wanted to run up and hug him, but instead half-curtseyed to the old gentleman seated in the open buggy. It had a shiny black leather seat, four big black wheels and a canvas dashboard. The man wore a black suit and bowler—the very picture of a doctor.

"I'm sorry to be late," the man said with a German accent, obviously thinking Mae had been sent here to wait for him. "I be yust a minute, putting da horse away."

"Doctor," Mae said, "it is the horse I came to see." She walked up to Pal, peered around the blinker, and stroked his neck. "It's me, boy," she said. "Remember me?" Her smell would remind him if nothing else did.

Pal answered with a low nicker. That opened a well of tears as she continued to pet the warm and wonderful horse from the happy part of her past. She tried to tell the doctor that her father had died and her mother had gone to New York, and Farley had needed to work in a place where he couldn't care for a horse.

"I was stuck in Sacramento," she continued, "and my brother didn't know where to find me. We lost touch with each other, but now I've got a place where a horse can graze, and I need him back. Could you possibly part with him for three dollars? I brought the money with me."

Little Billy came running up to her, looking shyly at the doctor. "This is my son Billy," she said. And to Billy, "This is Doctor Schoenenmann. And this is Pal!" She ran her hand down his twitching wither.

Billy squealed and jumped up and down. "We found him! He's gunna be my horse!"

By now the doctor was out of the rig and Pal was nuzzling Mae, his nose to her neck. She wept to feel that again. "I love this horse," she sniffled. "We brought him on the train all the way from Iowa, and I won a horse race on him. I want to teach Billy to ride him."

"He iss mine bestes horse," the doctor said. "I save him ven he been injured. He iss mine Schatze, my sweetheart."

"He is my Pal, my best friend," she sobbed. "The man at the livery in Ione told me you saved him and I'm so, so grateful to you for that."

Mae wasn't aware that a woman had been listening from an open window just behind her: *"Gott in Himmel, Karl! Lass mal die Frau dem Pferde kaufen, und komme herein. Eure Patienten wahrten!"*

The doctor threw back his head in a short laugh, and extended the palm of as hand. "Please, tree dollars and you take him avay. But first, water and hay in the carriage house. He need dot. I go to my patients now. Good-bye and good riding."

∿

Now they had a four-legged friend to help them find and deliver building materials. Mae bought a used harness, a cart for light hauling, and a small used saddle. Now, having spent more of Charlie's money, and for a good purpose, she was beginning to feel stronger in spirit—a woman who didn't need to cling to money as though it were the last she'd ever see.

Everyone in the house loved Pal, and he seemed to love them back. He didn't have horse friends like in Moke Hill, and he didn't have a fenced-in pasture of grass, but Isabella and Mae took turns moving him around to areas near the river where green grass grew. But in the hot days of summer, she paid Robert Warren to board him in his rented field behind the store, where drivers delivered loads of hay for the horses and mules pastured there.

One day as Isabella was measuring boards and nailing them to the roof structure, Mae asked, "Where did you learn to build?"

"In jail," Isabella said, taking a nail from her mouth.

That's the last thing Mae expected to hear.

"How on earth could you learn this in jail?"

"Lookin' out the window."

Isabella finished sawing the board and held it up to a post, indicating Mae should hold it in place while she hammered.

Mae didn't want to pry into something Isabella had never talked about, but her curiosity was piqued. "How can you learn to do this by looking out a jail window?"

"Men building a barn right outside. Nuthin' else to look at all day."

"How long were you in jail?"

"Doan known." Lightly she brought the hammer down on the nail to make sure it was straight, and then hammered four firm blows directly on the nail head, pushing the nail all the way in.

Mae couldn't imagine a person not knowing how long she was in jail. All the the inmates of storied dungeons scratched the days on the walls. Isabella continued her work, Mae and Baby helping.

Mae couldn't resist another question. "Why don't you know?"

Isabella took a little break to look at Mae.

"Doan know how long I 'as yellin' at the spirits. Mebbe two, three, four months. Them spirits turned into snakes an' spiders, an' all kinds of things, all tryin' to kill me. I warn't lookin' out the window then. It were bad." She went back to nailing.

Mae figured she'd pried enough out of her for one day.

"I saw bad spirits too," Baby said after about five minutes.

"I know," Isabella said. She put down the hammer and went to her daughter. Deliberately, almost as though she didn't know how, she knelt beside Baby, where she was straightening nails, and put her arms around her.

Mother and daughter stayed that way for nearly a minute, Baby's hands still on the hammer and nail, and then Isabella went back to nailing the wallboards.

By now another question burned in Mae's mind. "Was that a long time ago, that you were in jail?"

"It were just afore I come back home. Figgered I gotta Ma who knows how to heal people, and I needed some healin'."

⤳

Isabella found a bent little stove someone had thrown in the community dump and fixed it up with pieces of an old chimney pipes so the new room could be heated in the winter. The new drying room and the additional pair of hands made it possible to do the wash for more customers. And the clearer water, now that the hydraulic mining had ended, made the clothes cleaner. The customers were more satisfied.

Isabella increasingly managed the laundry business, and Mary got more rest.

Between them, Mae and Isabella agreed that any time Isabella wanted Mae gone, she would go. But they got on well now, and Isabella sometimes watched little Billy if Mae had to visit customers in Amador County.

The three little businesses—laundry, housecleaning, and eggs and pullets—plus Charlie's contributions, kept everyone fed and clothed. Mae took pride in her part of it, and was surprised how good it made her feel to know that she could survive on her own if she had to. It seemed to her that if the three women of this household could make a living, anyone could. She knew, of course, that the house and the land by the river made it all possible. Baby gradually warmed up to her mother, and that was another good thing.

"Auntie Mae," Baby said one warm Sunday near the end of August 1898, "Let's go to the picnic at Dixon's Grove."

84

Mary never went to picnics unless one of the ranch women needed her help. Her outings were the big times at Captain Maximo's place in Ione or Captain Oliver's at the Buena Vista rancheria, and she always took Baby.

"Sure you don't want to come?" Mae asked Isabella, who looked less haggard than when she'd first come home. Isabella shook her head.

Mae understood. At her low point she hadn't wanted to see anyone either.

At the Grove, Mae hobbled Pal, and with Baby on one end, carried the willow hamper to the shallow place in the river where Billy liked to play. Other young children were already there, and Mae told their mothers she and Baby would watch them. Mary Granlees, with baby Arthur on her hip, was grateful to be able to leave Georgie and Hilda in their care. Georgie was older now but still unpredictable.

Baby watched all little children with the same intensity she had watched Billy. "She knows her spirit helper now," Mary had assured Mae some time ago. Baby's nights were calm, with only a few exceptions, and she could read aloud from *McGuffey's Third Reader*. However, she never stepped into the river here. She had her own quiet relationship with the river spirit in a special place near the cabin. Now she sat on the old quilt against a cottonwood in full view of the children at the river's edge.

Mae didn't mind watching other people's children, since she'd be here anyway. An outsider in the community, she came to give Billy an outing and to hear the music.

The Sheldon boys were in the bandstand tooting and sawing, George on his trumpet and Jared on his violin. The band swept into Mae's favorite waltz, *A Ride through the Vienna Woods*. Thrilled to hear it again, she recalled Sister Delphine explaining that Mr. Strauss had been inspired by an afternoon carriage ride with a lady friend. Mae could almost see a fancy trotter pulling a carriage through a forest of trilling birds, the horn of a distant sheepherder providing a second theme. The 1-2-3, 1-2-3 of the horse's gait delighted her. She sat on the other side of the old quilt, the hamper between her and Baby. Her white summer gown was a bit frayed at the hem and stained on one side if a person knew where to look, but the shadows masked that and Mae no longer cared much about stains. She moved her fingers on the piano of her thighs, imagining playing with the band as she watched happy little Billy splashing with his friends. She missed the piano like a drunkard missed his liquor.

Billy's belly laugh cut through the squeals of the children, all wildly slipping around in the mud and then splashing through the water. Suntanned and tall for his age, he had a strong little body that had lost its baby fat. She saw Charlie in him, especially in the wide shoulders and the easy way he got on with others.

She became aware of the approach of a whistler helping the Strauss tune. John Dunaway stretched out on the ground beside her. Casual on his elbow, he wore a black western hat and black angora chaps, the height of manly fashion. She realized he'd climbed a rung or two up the ladder of success since she'd first met him.

"Good to see you again," he drawled.

John had talked to her at previous picnics, starting in June when he'd brushed off her apology for leaving him in the lurch five years ago. At the Fourth of July picnic he'd told her about growing up on a farm in Tennessee. He smiled as she told him jokingly about the lessons she'd learned expanding her chicken and egg business. He had a wry wit and she enjoyed sparring with him.

"He loves playing with the older children," Mae said with a nod at little Billy.

"They like him," John said. "I do too."

For some reason that pumped so much pride into her heart, it almost hurt. Her little boy didn't have a man in his life, his only male relative being Hank. But though Hank and Sophie invited Mae and Billy to visit a couple of times, they were busy with babies born every two years and Mae didn't think they felt comfortable around her, an unmarried mother living with Indians.

John twisted his compact body to extract a tender wild oat stalk from its sheath. Back on his elbow he nibbled the end of it, one knee up under his chaps, grass wiggling as he spoke. "Would you let me drive you home in my new surrey?"

"You? Got a surrey?"

"Yup. Even a chucklehead like me gets a sore hind-end riding a pony."

No doubt about it, he was doing well—not really a surprise since he worked so many odd jobs in addition to his main work for Mr. Grimshaw. She turned to Baby, now a frail eleven-year-old sitting a few yards away. "What do you think, Baby? Should we ride home in Mr. Dunaway's new rig? Tie Pal to the back end?" Baby never appeared to listen or answer questions right away, so Mae turned back to him. "What color it is?"

"Raspberry with black upholstered seats. Double seat in front and two single seats in the back."

Eyes intent upon the frolicking children, Baby looked past Mae and dipped her head in a nod that most people would have missed.

"Yes, John," Mae told him, "We'd be glad to get a ride in your surrey. I'd like to see it."

The grass stalk jumped with his words. "Good. Cause I got somethin' to say to you."

"Well, for Pete's sake, tell me now. I don't bite."

"I'm savin' it."

"Oh, come on," she grinned at him.

"Nope. But I'll say this. You're a real purty woman."

That disturbed her. They had an unspoken understanding not to be on those terms.

She gave John a sandwich and they ate in silence until the band launched into *Stars and Stripes Forever*. She couldn't help but clap to hear that rousing march again. She'd heard it last month in Sacramento with little Billy. It had been a fluke. She'd taken him to see Charlie, to pick up money before going to Weinstock's to get Billy some new trousers. As they were saying good-bye in his office, Charlie snapped his fingers like he'd forgotten something and gave her two tickets to a John Phillip Sousa concert at the Hippodrome. He couldn't go, but somebody in the Capitol had given them to him. The concert fit the stagecoach schedule, so she took Billy. He seemed to like the music as much as she did, though he grew tired and about went to sleep during the last half. The entire way home she couldn't get this march out of her head.

"I love this," she yelled at John over Sousa's trills and booms.

"I can see that."

The dripping children emerged from the water marching like sober troopers with their bare chests thrust forward. They aped the grown ups who were full of beer and cavorting before the bandstand. Billy followed the older children in a high-stepping march to join those people. It was irresistible, with the piccolo chirping, cymbals crashing, and the bass drum punctuating every musical statement. All the picnickers were on their feet.

"Come on, John," Mae said, trying to pull him up. Everybody in the whole place was marching like drum majors gone berserk.

John declined, so she followed the children to where old and young were high-stepping and strutting. The music shook out all her kinks. She laughed with Katy Irene and Bob Warren, and Polly Sheldon and Jack Granlees, a boy who had grown up to be a good-looking young man. The flutes and tinkling triangles *were* the stars, and they trilled up her spine. The newspapers said that bands all over the county had been increasing their numbers as a result of Sousa's most recent tour, this composition being his newest. Music stores and teachers were doing better business. At the final boom of the drum, Mae added her cheers and applause to the roar of the crowd, and in the racetrack the older boys ran their horses as they whooped and fired guns in the air.

When she returned to the river with Billy and other children, neither John nor Baby had moved. John jabbed a thumb toward the racetrack. "They'd oughta quit that shootin'. They'll spook the horses."

"You sound just like a grumpy old man," Mae teased. "And you're hardly any older than they are."

The musicians were putting their instruments in their boxes and cases. Not ready to end the fun, little Billy threw himself into the shallow water and made huge splashes. A couple of others joined him. John brushed off the splashed water and struck his hat against his knee. The low sun across his eyes made them momentarily transparent, though they were a rich brown color.

"The whole gol darned country's gone silly over that Spanish War," he said, "That marching music pumps it up. Won't be long 'fore them boys on the racetrack is shootin' off their guns in Cuba, gittin' theirselves killed. They're shipping our boys off to them Philippine Islands too, so there's no end to it, even if Cuba breaks free of the Spaniards. All that killin' for no good reason I can see." He wagged his head. "What do we want with them foreign countries anyway? Half way 'round the world?"

His opinion of the war was unpopular, Mae knew, but he was not alone. "Old men talk like that," she reminded him. "All grumpy about keeping us out of the business of the European countries."

"Makes no sense. All them boys goin' to Cuba! I think they been hearing all their lives about the heroes of the Revolution and the War Between the States, and now they're bound and determined to git in on this war so they can be heroes too. Why, every cowboy with a horse and rifle is joinin' up with the Roughriders. Good strong men what oughta be home on their farms and ranches."

Mae knew that Sophie and her family were doing their best to stop Hank from signing up to fight the Spaniards.

Shade had darkened the river. Other children were wading out, some shivering, but Billy stood up to his knees glowering at the defectors—teeth clamped behind blue lips. Quietly Baby was packing the remains of the picnic. Mary Granlees came to get Georgie and Hilda.

Mae shook out the old blanket and smiled at Billy. "Time to go home now." She held the blanket like a bullfighter's cape. Hugging himself, Billy reluctantly emerged from the water, and Mae turned him around and around in the blanket. From the corner of her eye she saw John smile as he watched with almost as much glee as Billy. She held the tail of the blanket like a leash—Billy double-timing in mincing steps toward the horses and rigs. John swooped in with a teaser's gleam and captured Billy, ripping the leash out of Mae's hand and giving Billy a little toss in the air. Billy's happy squeals led the way to the surrey as John tossed Billy again and again. Mae and Baby hurried behind, Mae laughing.

"Oh John!" She exclaimed when they came through the trees and he opened an arm to the showy surrey. "It takes my breath away." Black angora chaps, a new high hat, and now a fancy surrey. She was impressed.

John handed the giggling mummy up to her in the comfortable black leather seat. Baby silently climbed into a back seat and set the hamper on the other one.

John's new team walked at a leisurely pace, Pal in tow, and Mae waited for the promised secret, but he said nothing. He looked steadily forward, presenting the profile of his straight nose and chin with a slight dimple. Not a bad-looking man.

Back at the cabin, with the chickens scratching all around, John pulled the team to a stop and looked at Mae. Billy and Baby raced to the door.

"Well," Mae asked, "what's going on under that big hat of yours?"

"Mr. Grimshaw signed a paper lettin' me start to buy a piece of ground."

"Oh, that's grand! But what does it mean? *Start* to buy ground. Don't people buy land in one fell swoop?"

"He signed with me on a bank loan. Any banker would accept Grimshaw credit. So now all I gotta do is pay the bank every month."

"Where is this ground?"

"I'd like to show you. You think they could watch Billy for a while?" He nodded toward the cabin. "Or bring him if you want," he quickly added. "It won't take long."

85

Mae climbed back into the surrey with Isabella's consent to watch Billy, and John turned the horses around.

"Don't b'lieve I told you before, but folks say you do a right smart business with them chickens. I sure do admire that in a lady."

She dismissed that with, "Oh, well, most farm wives raise chickens."

Reining right on jackson Road he made a click with his tongue while squeezing an eye shut in a don't-necessarily-agree-with-you gesture. "You're doin' it a sight bigger and better, I'd say."

They started crossing the bridge, Mae surprised how good it made her feel to hear praise for the business she'd worked so hard on and learned so much about.

"Thank you, John, I appreciate that."

The springs and sculpted black upholstery made an exceptionally soft ride, and the seat's backrest curved around their shoulders with perhaps too presumptive a coziness. John followed the trail behind Katy Irene's bungalow and along the fence line of the Warren pasture. He continued around the east side of the pasture and headed up the Michigan Bar river trail. Foot and horse traffic had been prevalent on it five years ago, when Mae walked to the Granlees place for the first time, but not since the High Hill Mining Company shut down. They had the old wagon trail to themselves.

"Right about here," John gestured around.

"The ground doesn't look very good to me," she said. That was an understatement. It was cracked clay like a dried-up lake or desert. Only a few thistles and locoweed stuck up here and there. Clearly, it had been distressed in some way.

"That's just the top layer," he explained. "Hydraulic operations brung down the slickens and spread it thick. Before that, there was the biggest flood of all time, back in sixty-two. Flooded ever'thing in California. That woulda brung down a lot of clay too, what with all them forty-niners diggin' upstream. But underneath, it's good ground. This hundred acres I'm buying is part of where that fella Jared Sheldon got hisself killed tryin' to get water to his crops. Right here. He knowed good ground when he seen it."

John hadn't put so many words together since she'd known him.

It wasn't as far upstream as she had imagined, only about a half mile up the river from the Warren's bungalow, but the real surprise was the condition of the land. Mae had grown up knowing good farmland, and this was about the sorriest she had ever seen. Yet he sat proudly at the reins, a man who knew farming.

"You think you're gonna grow crops on that?" she dangled lightly out to him.

"I'll rent a road-scraper to push the slickens off. This ground was a bargain, being like it is, but it's worth a good deal more than it cost. Even considerin' the work. Now that they stopped the hydraulickin', the overflow's a good thing, bringin' water to stand a while and soak in good. It'll help with the irrigating."

"That company might start up again."

He scowled ahead, walking the horses slowly. "I doubt it," he said. "There's been a big lawsuit about that kinda mining—takin' down mountains and puttin' 'em in the rivers. The farmers won."

"I remember hearing about that." Charlie had mentioned it. "But that lawsuit was ten-fifteen years ago. The company up on the American River was supposed to quit operations, but my brother was working for High Hill only five years ago, so I figured this company was doing it illegally and nobody cared, or the law is different up there than it is down here."

"It's a gamble, no doubt about that. But I've a hunch that company's done washing the guts outta the hills and spreading the goop all over the land."

"Isn't it a big gamble, to base on a hunch?" she said.

"Uh-huh." He straightened his shoulders and turned to her as the horses continued to amble up the faint tracks. "But I'll say this. If I gets the slickens off my land and my crops're growin' good and that there company sends down more slickens, I'll sue the bastards myself. I'll find a way. Fred Grimshaw told me if the law holds once, it'll hold again. His dad was a lawyer." He ticked the horses to walk a little faster.

She liked the way he said he'd sue the bastards. John didn't have much education but he was smart and determined.

"Where you going to build your house?"

"Back there," he said with a jerk of his head. "Close as I can put it to the Warren's place and still be on my land." His expression softened to a wry look. "My wife'll wanna be near the neighbors."

"What wife?'

He shrugged a tight smile. "Someday I'll get me one."

"How do you know ladies want to be near the neighbors?"

"It might surprise you, but I've known a few ladies in my time."

"You say that like an old man."

"I been older'n you for a number of years," he drawled.

The wagon tracks went to the right, around a steep decline, but John halted the horses on top and ground-tied the leader. He came around to help Mae step down. "I wanted you to see this place."

He slid down a steep little slope, turning to help her. Now they stood in a green and leafy place with the river running by it. This relieved the eye, after the clay-cracked ground above. With the cottonwood trees in full leaf and a couple of smooth boulders low and flat enough for people to sit on, the shade felt good.

John sat down beside her. "Doan know as I ever seen a spot purtier'n this, and it's mine." His dream of becoming a landowner had come true. *This* was his main chance. Of course he wouldn't run off to a foreign war.

The river moved at a sedate pace.

"It *is* nice." She liked the quiet seclusion of it. "Why don't you build your house here?"

"Well, for starters it'd be underwater after the first good rainstorm."

She chuckled at the laconic way he phrased things. "Guess that'd be a mite damp," she allowed.

"You see, this here's the little coulee where the river comes in, spreads out back over there. See?" He pointed along what had been a watercourse when the river ran high.

A darning-needle with dazzling transparent wings stopped midair to examine his nose and then hers. Mae waved it on its way. John was watching her, but then turned his head away like he'd been caught thinking something he oughtn't.

A few quiet seconds later he recovered his enthusiasm. "I'm gonna put a pipe through here to get water up to the land in the summer." Making a line with the side of his hand, he got up. "Right along there, between those boulders."

He squatted, elbows on splayed knees, hands hanging down, gazing at the water. Then he was moving the gravel with his fingers. He roughed it away from the sharp edge of rock running like a fault line where he planned to lay that pipe. He straightened his knees, scanning the place until he found a stick. He squatted again. Using the tool he wedged out something about three inches long. He rubbed the dirt off and handed it to Mae.

It was a length of porcelain outlined in white with the tiniest of white flowers sprinkled in a sky-blue color. "This is a Chinese spoon," she said, "with its bowl half broken off."

"Is that so. Prob'ly Chinamen mining here at one time."

"Too bad it's broken. Those are nice spoons."

Getting back to the other thing, she said, "John, I do believe you'll get the clay off that ground and turn a good profit on your farm." He was the responsible sort of man that would have inherited the farm in Iowa. Daddy's heart hadn't been in farming, she knew now, but John's was.

"I 'preciate that, a lot," he said looking straight at her. Enthusiasm elevated his tone half an octave. "I'll get me a band of sheep to work over fifty of those acres while I gets the other ready for crops. Wool's good again, with the gov'ment buying it fer all them uniforms."

"See, the war's good for something," she deadpanned.

He made a click in his cheek and sat down on the rock beside her. "It were a fine thing for Mr. Grimshaw to sign on that loan. I aim to keep workin' his place and mine too, 'til I pay off the loan."

The odd jobs he worked nights and Sundays would help. Doubtless, this man would be out of debt as fast as any mortal could be. As far as she could tell he rested only at picnics. Yet he was wasting time with her. She got up and brushed off her dress.

"Time we got back," she said.

"Uh, Mae," his voice cracked as he stood up, "now that I'm gettin' land, would you, that is, would you want to, ah… marry me?"

Marry crashed down upon her, being so unexpected. She liked John, but didn't feel the magic she'd felt with Billy. However this busy, thrifty man had dressed himself up and bought a surrey to woo her, she now realized. She felt the tenderness of that. But she wanted to feel an excitement beyond understanding with the man she would marry.

"Let me think about it, John. Is that all right?"

V
Condor
Dreaming

Condor's latest meal churns in his belly. He has eaten of the dead and lifted his heavy body to a branch of the cottonwood tree. And now he dreams the world as it is and ever will be.

We are quiet before him, for he represents the power of the universe, and we want his dreams to be good.

86

Mae tossed and turned on her bed as quietly as possible so as not to wake the others in the room. Out the open windows the owls reamed out the dark night with their hollow whoo-whoos, and her mind circled around the thought of marrying John. Indian Mary had taught her not to speak until she'd thought about it four times. She had thought only once about her lack of excitement for him, and told him she didn't know. But now a new path opened in the darkness, and she walked down it.

Maybe she was like Agnes, a woman waiting fifty years for a lost man. That made her squirm and throw off the soft old linen. Waiting for her man could have tied Agnes to Mrs. Miser and hampered her ability to cut the yarn of the story, their dream, which the widow Miser so enjoyed telling: The always-waiting Agnes in love. Maybe that story had inhibited Agnes from seeing a new love. Mae and Indian Mary had a similar arrangement—living together and helping each other while waiting for Billy. It gave comfort to two sad women and kept alive the dream of Billy's return. They hadn't talked about it after that first day, but Mae assumed that marrying John would hurt Mary's heart, and she recoiled from causing more grief to a woman who had seen her people slaughtered. Now Mae wondered if imagining Mary's hurt feelings dampened her ability to see a new love. Another thought emerged from the darkness. *I am selling her short, not respecting her strength.*

This was 1898, four and a half years without a word from Billy. First and foremost Mae was a mother, and she knew her boy should have a father. She remembered the smile in John's eyes as little Billy giggled in his mummy-wrap. She'd seen his gentle strength and care as he tossed Billy and caught him in his arms, and his pleasure in Billy's laughter. She knew that John would be a good father.

She pulled up the sheet and turned over again. *But I'd be the one marrying him.* She liked John, and there was excitement in him, in his exuberance over that land. She could well imagine being caught up in the challenge of helping him reclaim it. She liked a challenge. Any challenge involved risk, but John was no flimflammer. He was solid. Five years ago Fred Grimshaw had said, when John asked for a five-dollar loan to help the Duffys place a bet: *We'd trust John Dunaway with our lives.* Now Fred was co-signing on a big loan for him.

She could trust John. Next to that, his bad grammar faded to nothing. He could change that if he wanted, like she had done. But in her heart she didn't care. He was a farmer and that's how farmers talked. Actually, she felt a coziness in his diction.

But what about the animal excitement she'd felt with Billy? *Do I want to be under the covers with John?* She envisioned the somewhat high-strung man beneath that laconic manner, a man with drive and vitality. Would it feel good? Did she want the weight of him in bed every night? She let herself imagine it.

Yes.

She'd felt an attraction to John even when as a stupid girl she'd snubbed him. Jokingly she told Helen Rose she left the Cosumnes District for fear she'd marry him. He'd been dirt poor then, and they'd laughed over Helen's adage: Better to be a rich man's darling than a poor man's slave. However, John wasn't destined for poverty, and Mae felt certain that the only slave he'd drive would be himself. In the five years she'd known him he had come far despite the bad economic times. His dream of going up in the world was her dream too. John Dunaway could be her real, not imaginary, California Joe.

Four times yes.

～

Within five minutes of telling John she would marry him, Mae discovered that he possessed all the excitement she could handle, and she couldn't get enough of him.

He insisted on having a house of their own before they "tied the knot," so he rounded up all the boys and men he could find, including some that could be spared from the third corn harvest. Within two days they had the basement for a small house half-dug on the westerly boundary of his property near the river. The deep loam under the clay made the digging easy. John had been right about the prime soil.

Having more than enough to do as foreman on the Grimshaw ranch, he quit doing night and Sunday work at other ranches so he could work on his own place. The ranchers understood and wished him well. Some even offered personal assistance or the help of their hired men. It didn't surprise Mae that he had saved money for the building materials for a modest house.

"Mr. Grimshaw's a good fella," John announced a week later as they settled in for noon dinner in their pretty little spot by the water. "Said he'd gimme some slack this next couple of weeks."

He lay lengthwise in his work clothes, an elbow on the old picnic quilt. The brim of his hat was down so far she saw only the end of his elegantly compact nose. Behind him the river moved at a sedate pace, and the late September sky went on forever into dizzying blue heights.

"You're lucky to work for such a man," she said as she sat on the quilt digging into Mary's willow basket. She placed before him a thick slice of fresh buttered bread and a shank of venison that Mary had brought from a ranch house where the husband loved to hunt and the wife disliked the taste of game.

"The mud looks to be gone from the river," Mae noticed. "It's as blue as the sky. Why, you could tie a red neckerchief around that egret over there and it'd be a fitting Fourth of July decoration." The tall white bird stood knee-deep on the opposite shore, still as marble with its long neck stretched toward unsuspecting prey in the shallows.

He smiled and leaned toward her. "Here's the purtiest blue. Right there." He tapped a finger under one of her eyes and then the other. Back on his elbow, he continued to wolf down his meal. She chuckled, thinking how Uncle Ephraim would have terrorized him if John had been born into that family.

"What's so funny?" John tried to ask through the tough venison.

"Nothing. Just seeing how hungry you are."

Setting the sandwich down, John flipped himself over and around and was on her, nuzzling. "You got no idea how hungry I am." Now they were both down on the quilt.

Laughing, pushing at him, she looked up to see if any of the work crew was spying.

"They know I'll have their hide if they get within a hundred yards of this place."

She liked the playful tenderness of him.

"I can't wait to get married," she breathed between kisses. "We can shut the door and be legal."

"You mean that? You can't wait?" He had a spark in his eye. "'Cause I can't either."

He meant it. He was working on her buttons.

"Do we dare? Right here in the…"

He was all over her.

A tremulous boyish voice interrupted from above. "Mr. Dunaway, sorry to bother you, but—"

John exploded from the blanket and flew up the little hill spraying gravel off his boots. The tail end of him vanished over the ridge—after the hide of some poor boy likely sent by the wiser men of the crew. It was funny, because he wouldn't hurt the boy. He was just scaring him. John was a joker.

Mae moved sandwiches and Grimshaw plums to the flat boulder and got up to shake the dirt and gravel off the quilt. She floated it down, lining it up with the sharp little ridge of rock that she didn't want under them.

At that moment a breeze parted the cottonwood leaves above and a spike of sunshine struck the ground like lightning—a yellow gleam.

She kneeled down to look at what it was, now in the shade again. From the gravel she pulled out something resembling a small clinker, molten at one time. Heavy for its size. She rubbed it on her dress and walked it to the sunshine. Bright yellow.

John was already back.

"Look at this." She gave it to him.

It seemed smaller in the palm of his hand.

"Where'dya find it?"

"Right here, where you dug out that Chinese spoon handle." She pointed to the disturbed gravel.

He moved his hand up and down, feeling the weight, and then looked at her a long moment with his steady brown eyes. She could almost see his brain working. He extended the gold back to her, for surely that's what it was.

"No, you keep it, John. It came from your land."

"Soon to be your land too." He slipped it into the pocket of her skirt. "You'll need it to fix up the inside of the house."

Then he grabbed her and hugged her so hard he lifted her up. He swung her around, put her on her feet, and threw his hat in the air, yelling "Yahoo!"

The hat careened up through the branches and never came down. The tree had caught it, played a joke on him.

They stood laughing. Then they kissed, a long, thrilling, juicy kiss.

"Oh Mae, Mae, Mae, you've brought me luck," he said when they came up for air. "That nugget alone's worth near a hundred simoleons, and there could be more down along there." He looked where they'd been sitting.

"You think we've got a gold mine?"

"Won't know 'til we look. Mebbe the gold jes' got stuck behind that ridge of buried rock. I been told that's how most'a the gold came to be where it was found back in the Gold Rush." He looked at her in that steady way of his. "Or mebbe we do got us a gold vein. You recall that water pipe I'm gonna dig down through here?"

She nodded.

"Well, gittin' that dug has just moved to first place in my list. I'm goin' fer a shovel. Hold the fort."

She watched him surmount the cut bank and trot his horse to the building site, like he was in no hurry. This morning the men had finished the basement and already put the floor over it. Now they were nailing up the wall studs. She watched him lay a shovel across the saddle and ride back like he had all the time in the world.

"No need to raise suspicions," he said when he got there.

By then Mae had the picnic out of the way, and he dug into that gravelly ground like he dug into dinner—strong, persistent, enthusiastic, but measured. "Watch for anything yellow," he said as he took systematic bites out of the ground along that rim of black rock, starting on the inland side and moving toward the river.

"I think there's some more!" Mae pointed at a smaller piece of yellow metal dislodged by the shovel.

John dropped the shovel, squatted and picked it up. "Could be them Chinamen was onto something," he said as he stared at it. "Mebbe scared off by some'um."

⌒

A couple of nights later, John parked the surrey in a wide spot where the trail to Mary's cabin met Jackson Road. He spoke in spurts between bouts of nuzzling and kissing in the leather seat. "My guess is we got us a little vein of gold running up through that coulee and no tellin' how far into the field."

"I'd wager it runs under the river too," he added, "but that'd be tricky to get out."

High on emotion—the return of love and now the prospect of gold to help them build a paradise—Mae felt the sky was putting on a glittery show for the two of them. The stars looked like a barrel of diamonds spilled on black velvet.

"We'll be like the Cothrins," Mae said running her hand over John's back and arm. "They're ranchers up near Latrobe with a gold mine on their property."

"You told me. Where Billy was born."

"I didn't think you'd remember the name."

"Mmm," he said after another long kiss. "Everthin' you say is carved in my brain." The horses took another step and nibbled at the side of the road. "A lotta ranchers got little gold mines on their land. Just enough to keep 'em pickin' in their spare time. Some of 'em is poor on account of diggin' and hopin'."

"The Cothrins' vein runs into the ground. They have to dig at a steep angle and the deeper the hole, the more water seeps in. Mr. Cothrin's always pumping it out. So it's hard work, and there's acid in that water due to the minerals—"

He was at her again, making her want him so bad she wondered if snakes would be on the ground behind the trees. He seemed out of breath, forcing himself to back away for a while, his voice unnaturally rough.

"Our vein is mostly horizontal, if we got one. But mebbe years of overflow left the gold in a pattern. I'm no expert."

Her heart was beating so hard she'd almost forgotten what they'd been talking about, but loved hearing him call it *our* vein.

"It'd be a bear to dig under the river. Hafta make a partial dam to git to it, but that can wait. First we gotta git ourselves married." He ran a hand over her, and grabbed her again and squeezed her hard.

Mouth to mouth felt normal, everything else awkward and wrong, and she could tell it was the same with him. Apart the next time he said, "You brung me the luck 'o the Irish. Or is that brang?"

"Brought. But John, you're Irish too."

"Not normally this lucky." He was practically on top of her, planting little kisses all over her face.

"You still wanna get married in the new house?" she managed to get in.

"Umm. Maybe at the church."

He'd never mentioned church before. "You mean the little Catholic church?"

"Sure, right handy on Jackson Road." More kissing. "Folks say Protestants can have weddings there too." He kissed her lips too briefly. "If they give warnin'."

"Are you Protestant?"

"Methodist. My folks that is. I'm a lost cause." He was making up for lost time.

"There's a Methodist Church in Ione," she said quickly. "I'll write and see if the pastor'd come marry us here."

∼

Over the next week the little house materialized. Mae's sense of wonder couldn't have been greater if she'd flown to the moon and found heaven. In their entire lives Mom and Daddy never owned their own house, and now Mae was about to move into hers at the age of twenty-one. And with a possible gold vein to boot!

Somebody would have to take the gold to an assay house in Sacramento, but building the house took all John's free time. So Mae would be that somebody. She figured she'd buy furnishings for the house at the same time.

Some of the building materials were free. All over the hills on the north side of the river, huge chunks of slate stood on end. While there was still daylight, John took his surrey minus the back seats and, using a crowbar, removed slate from the hills behind the Gaffney place. Mae and Billy went with him one evening. The half-buried slate brought to mind a cemetery with the headstones all facing the same way. Constant exposure to the elements had separated many of the outcroppings into fairly uniform slabs, and sometimes a whole pile of blue-gray slate had fallen down into pieces of about the same thickness. Mae helped carry them to the surrey, a sturdy vehicle.

Besides that, all manner of boards and quarried stone and even iron lintels of doors and windows could be found in houses abandoned during the recent economic depression.

Their house had two bedrooms, a small parlor, a slate-floored kitchen, a slate-floored bathroom, a California porch wrapping around the south and west sides, and a cellar below. A hallway connected the parlor to the two bedrooms, and the peaked roof was insulated underneath by old newspapers and protected on top by metal sheeting to foil the woodpeckers. Shingles didn't last long near oak trees, with so many woodpeckers drilling holes and storing acorns. Some people assigned their boys to sit outside and shoot the birds, but the boys couldn't be there all the time.

One day a pair of men were installing the counter in the kitchen and two more just about had the window glass puttied in place. Mae took little Billy to see the house. He raced from room to room like a wild thing.

"This will be your room," she said.

He came to a standstill. "I gotta stay in here?"

"Just to sleep," she assured him.

His mouth and eyes widened in childish horror. "You mean I gotta sleep in here all by myself?"

"That's what big boys do."

His chin quivered. "But that man dint put no bed in here!" He pointed to the man installing the window. The man turned his head briefly and smiled.

"You and I are going to Sacramento on the stagecoach to buy beds and other things for this house," she told Billy. "Won't that be fun?"

His mouth made an upside-down U, like a vaudeville actor parodying tragedy. "A bed for me?" His lower lip trembled.

"That's right."

"You be sleepin' in it?"

"No."

He wailed, not in the high ringing tones amplified within the sinuses of the head, as Sister Delphine had explained, but the thicker tones of pure anguish that came from the chest, the heart. She realized that Mary's cabin where children slept with the adults was the only home he'd ever known.

As she squatted down and held her weeping boy, a thought struck. "I know!" She released him enough to look him in the eye, "We'll buy two beds for this room! One for you and one for Baby. Then she can sleep here if she wants, and if you want her to."

Some of the tragedy lifted as Billy considered that, his eyes silently overflowing.

"*She'll* sleep with me," he said as though Mae had betrayed him.

87

John asked Mae not to speak of the gold, not even to the Warrens, until he could get the place fenced off. He had learned that the price of gold had been stable for a good long time at $18.94 per ounce. That came to $227.28 if what they'd found was of the highest grade. That would buy champagne and refreshments for the reception, wedding clothing, and all the carpeting and curtains and furniture they needed. But they weren't rich by a long shot. They needed to pay someone to scrape the land free of slickens, or rent the equipment to do it themselves. Not to mention the need for work horses, a barn, tools, and sheep to graze the land until it was fit for crops.

The gold excitement died down a little as the wedding plans accelerated.

Old Mr. Driscoll, an elder and one of the builders of the little Catholic church, agreed to allow a Protestant service to be held in the building, and the minister in the Ione church agreed to ride over and perform the ceremony.

⟳

"I'm marrying John," Mae said while sitting at Mary's table.

"We know," said Isabella.

Indian Mary nodded.

I'm sorry, Mae told Mary mind-to-mind, hoping it transmitted.

Baby looked up with her coal-pit eyes. "Where's John gonna sleep?'

Isabella looked at her daughter, and then everyone looked at Mae.

"Over at the new house he built for me and little Billy," she told Baby. "I'd like you to see it. In a couple of days I'll take you over there. First I have to invite people to the wedding and go to Sacramento to buy furniture for the new house."

"Mommy's gonna buy you a bed so you can sleep with me," little Billy informed Baby.

"If you want to," Mae clarified to Baby. Then she turned to Mary. "I'll leave most of the chickens here, if you'd like."

Mary nodded. "Good. We like chicken, egg biness."

"I'll take six hens over there." Mae pointed with her head. "The rest are yours."

"I wanna see the house too," Mary said.

"Oh, of course. I'd like you to come see it. You're the expert on good houses. This is a good house here." She patted the table. "You told me so a long time ago, and you were right. I hope you think my new house is good, too."

Wise old Mary nodded. Next to her, innocent little Billy still looked worried. At the end of the table the new Isabella took it in like the clear-eyed businesswoman she had become. She had also established herself as a second Indian Mary, a respected midwife to the ranch wives with knowledge of the native medicinal herbs. The quietly intense and very adult Baby stared as though at something no one else could see. At twelve, she had bypassed childhood, and Mae thought it was time she had a real name.

"You remind me of Chloë," Mae said to Baby. "Daphnis and Chloë were children of nature in an ancient Greek story. They grew up without any schools or civilization." The Sisters in St. Mary's had intrigued Mae with the story.

Chloë meant "new green shoot" in Greek—in the process of becoming. It fit Baby. "Would you mind if I call you Chloë?"

Baby never answered questions right away, so Mae looked at Baby's mother and grandmother.

"That sounds nice," said Isabella.

Mary smiled kindly at Mae. "She gotta Inyan name too."

"Oh, you already named her!"

Old Mary gave Baby a special smile as she reached across the table and patted her hand, speaking a few words in her own tongue. Then in English she said, "Now she got two names." The Indian name wouldn't be used to address her, but the nickname Chloë could be used for all purposes.

～

The night had chill in it, and dawn brought one of those cloudless autumn days with golden leaves and a welcome sun. Mae packed a picnic and put Billy and Chloë in the front seat of the surrey with her. They drove around to invite friends to the wedding, which would be held on the second Sunday in October. First she went to the Sheldon place in Slough House. Mrs. Sheldon answered the door, expressed her joy for Mae, and said they'd be delighted to attend. Next she drove up Stone House Road and turned right on Latrobe Road. They were passing the house that had once looked so beautiful to her. Now it stood in ruins, the wall along the road completely gone as people removed the stones for their own use.

"Well, if everyone else is doing it, I want one too," Mae said, pulling the surrey up to the broken house. Chloë and Billy helped carry one of the big rectangular stones to the surrey. "We'll use this for a step-down from the porch," she explained.

Just up the road, Mrs. Long and her husband said they'd be at the wedding. At the Miser place, they were ushered into the parlor for cookies, milk and coffee. After Mae told them all about the wedding plans, Agnes and Mrs. Miser exchanged a long look.

Agnes went to a back room. Meanwhile Billy got up and ran outside to play with the Miser grandchildren. As they ran squealing around the house in a disorderly game of tag, Chloë, as usual, watched him with hawk eyes. Mae was seeing this through the front windows when Agnes returned with a shimmering white gown over her arm and shoulder.

"I made this afore I left my old home," Agnes said with quiet pride. She held it up by the shoulders for Mae to get a better look. "Nights on the wagon I sewed the seed pearls on. Ever night I put on more 'til my eyes'd give out." She ran a hand lightly over the bodice, shiny with the tiny pearls. The long sleeves had pearly streaks running partway down. "I'd be right proud if'n you wore this at your marryin.'"

Mae could barely speak for amazement and gratitude. "Oh, it's beautiful. I don't know if I should—"

"Laura got married in it," Mrs. Miser interjected. "I expect them little girls outside'll wear it in their time, too."

"Put it on," Agnes said, "so I can see how to alter it." She laid it carefully in Mae's arms.

"I expected to buy a gown in Sacramento," Mae said, "but I couldn't have found one this lovely. Thank you. It's a wedding gift I'll never forget."

○◡

The next morning Mae caught the stage from Bridge House and went shopping in Sacramento with little Billy.

In the assay office the nuggets brought the highest price, as hoped. Mae traded them for a pile of gold coins that lightened her purse. She and Billy rode the streetcar to 11th and K. At the new Weinstock & Lubin's she bought a ready-made suit for Billy, a pink ruffled gown for Chloë, a new dark blue gown with a full skirt for Indian Mary, and a turquoise gown of a modern style for Isabella. She also bought a suit and shirt for John. She had his measurements— inseams of leg and arm, waist, neck—but she decided to let Weinstocks ship the big box, also containing Billy's suit and shirt. The box for Mary, and the one for Isabella and Chloë, she wanted with her when she arrived home.

In the elevator Billy watched in awe through the open grill as they rose upward. The people and goods of the first floor grew small, the ceiling passed by under their feet, and a new floor of people and goods appeared. Stepping off on the second floor, Mae found herself surrounded by things she needed, including pull-down window shades in different patterns, hues, and borders.

A salesman came forward and asked what she was looking for. Mae told him about the new house, but soon learned that she should have measured the windows. She had, however, brought the dimensions for a parlor carpet. The man assured her the curtains could be shipped if she picked out the colors and fabrics now and mailed him the measurements later. Mae picked out lace curtains made in Ireland for the parlor, and heavy draperies to frame them. Meanwhile, Billy spied the toy department and tried to pull her in that direction. She made him wait until she purchased a carpet. She loved the colors and pattern in the best Brussels tapestry carpet, twenty-seven inches wide. It was a little dear, costing ninety-five cents per yard plus five cents per yard extra for having the lengths sewn together, but Mae loved the richness of it. The carpet would be shipped via Wells Fargo and delivered to Bridge House Store.

By now Billy had become a serious nuisance, and she let him run to the toy department. He squealed with joy to sit atop a velocipede, a cycle with a large front wheel and two smaller back wheels. It had bells on the handlebars and cost the princely sum of three dollars. His feet didn't quite reach the ped-als. He clamored down and over to what a sign called the improved tricycle. This one resembled a small trap with two very large wheels at either side of an upholstered velvet seat with an openwork brass backrest. From a tiny front wheel out in front, a metal T swooped up and stood before the throne-like seat for steering. Billy laughed like a crazy thing sitting on that seat, turning the little wheel back and forth. His feet reached the pedals, though he didn't know how to use them.

"I want it," he said.

She checked the tag. "Billy, it costs seven dollars. Twice as much as I paid for Pal. That's far too much for a toy."

"But I *want* it!" His cry turned the heads of several distant clerks.

"No, Billy. There's no place for you to ride it at home."

"Yes there *is*. I'll ride it outside!"

"Look, it has narrow wheels. It'll get stuck in the dirt and rocks."

"No! No!" he kicked and screamed as she lifted him off the seat. "I want it!"

Embarrassed to be the center of attention of a widening number of people, Mae gave Billy a swat on his behind, the first in his life. He screamed louder, wilting to the floor in an effort to escape her grasp. Every fiber of his being strained toward that seat.

"He's just tired," she told the male clerk who came to assist her.

"No! No! No!" Billy shouted as she tried to pull him from the toy depart-ment.

She picked him up off the floor, still kicking and yelling, and fought him as she struggled through the door of the elevator cage—the clerk trailing with the two dropped boxes. He bawled as they rode down to the first floor. With a box under each arm she carried him out the door of Weinstocks be-cause he wouldn't walk. He cried like his heart was broken, pointing back to where he wanted to be.

Fortunately Breuner's didn't sell toys. Mae laid him down, still weeping, on a display sofa. She leaned down to kiss his forehead, but he batted her away, his face red and wet with tears. Upset and bewildered at his behavior, she left him alone and walked around looking at the various sets of tables and chairs, sofas, and upholstered chairs. To her dismay nothing looked better than any-thing else, and she sat down some distance from Billy on a different display sofa and set her boxes beside her. The place had the quiet feeling of a church on Monday, with many places to sit but nobody in the store.

An older man dressed in a suit came smiling toward her, "Could I help you find something?"

"I'm getting married," she said, rising to her feet, embarrassed to be using his furniture. "We've built a house on our farm, and I came into town to buy the furniture. I've picked out curtains and a carpet at Weinstock and Lubin's, and wedding clothes. But you see, I have a little boy," she pointed to where he lay sadly sniffling, "and I'm having trouble deciding between all these things." She gestured around the very large place.

"Sit down and rest your feet," he said. "I'll bring you some catalogs."

Gladly she obeyed.

"I'm Mr. Breuner," he said as he returned, putting a hand out. They shook hands as he sat next to her, laying papers on a sundries table. Surveying her like a caring grandfather he said, "You don't have to buy everything today. You can always come back again."

That simple idea had not occurred to her. "Except there isn't a stick of furniture in the house," she remembered.

"If you walked in there right now, and the house had all its furniture, what's the first thing you would do?"

With a rueful smile she pointed at Billy. "Put him to bed, and go take a nap myself."

"Do you have beds?"

"No."

"Well then, let's go look at beds. Don't even think about the rest of it. Take these catalogs home. Study them while you're in the house where you can see what styles would look best. Then order them through the mail. We ship with Wells Fargo."

She followed him to the bed displays and within minutes selected a pair of identical beds for Billy's room, and a double bed for her and John. It took only minutes to pay Mr. Breuner and tell him where to ship the beds.

When she stepped on the streetcar with her exhausted little boy, Mae considered how simple life was in the country, where a child played with things that fell from the trees—sticks, acorns and feathers—and things brought by the river: rocks of all colors, shapes and sizes, and special things on occasion like the sole of a boot or the broken handle of a shovel. And always, the wet sand was for drawing pictures. Billy was also learning to swim and ride a full-sized horse. The city toys calling "Buy me! Buy me!" had frazzled his nerves. Mae's too.

They both slept most of the way home.

∽

Kindly, the driver let her off on the north side of the bridge. Billy stumbled sleepily as she walked him up the dark path, and he fell in bed like he'd never been awake.

Mae presented the boxes to Mary, and Isabella and Chloë. "These presents are from John," she said. It was true; the money to buy them came from his land. "Thank you for taking care of me and little Billy." This was the Indian way. Parents expected presents as part of the process of getting their children married, and Mary had been like a parent to Mae.

With smiles all around, the three generations of Indian women put on their new finery and paraded merrily around the cabin in a circuit through the big empty laundry room. Billy slept through it all.

While Isabella and Chloë were still admiring the way the other looked, Mary presented Mae with a stunning basket made from redbud. Perfectly round, it had a black zigzag pattern running on the bias. The zig-zag, Mae knew, symbolized power. It was tight enough to hold water. All along, Mary had known, and had been making a beautiful wedding gift.

"I still hope your Billy comes home," Mae said, unable to keep the hitch out of her voice or stop the tears of guilt and sorrow.

Mary pulled her to her big bosom and hugged her. Her face was wet with tears too. She understood, no apology needed.

"Now you rancher lady," Mary said, holding her at arm's length. "Mebbe you want Inyan lady clean house for you."

"I want you to come over often to visit, Chloë and Isabella too, but not as house cleaners. We are friends. If my house needs cleaning when you come, we'll clean it together."

ᕐᗅ

On her wedding day Mae stood at the door of the tiny church holding a bouquet of Katy Irene's white gladiolus. Chloë stood at her side in the pink gown holding a sprig of the same flowers. The wedding gown, expertly altered to fit, seemed heavy with all the dreams and hopes sewn into it fifty years ago.

Friends and a few relatives filled the backless pews. John in his new suit stood at the front with his father, who'd stepped off the train in Latrobe yesterday—all the way from Kentucky. Surprisingly, Laura Miser Russel was at an upright piano, although Mae had been assured the church had no piano and John had joked that he would whistle the *Wedding March*. Happy faces began turning to look at Mae and Chloë.

Laura's hands came down on the opening chords, and a rash of goose bumps tickled the backs of Mae's arms. "Now," she whispered to Chloë, who'd made it clear the day before that she would not go first.

Mae slow-stepped and Chloë followed up the side aisle, the benches being too long to accommodate a middle aisle. Everyone smiled as they watched, and Mae felt beautiful for John, in front of all these people.

Bob Warren and Katy Irene sat with Polly Sheldon—absent her lawyer husband from Sacramento, whom her father had pressured her to marry. Frail Mr. Driscoll sat with a string of his grandchildren. His daughter Mary Granlees and the new baby Arthur not there, feeling poorly. The gray heads of Mrs. Miser and Agnes bracketed another line of grandchildren. Ah Sen had ridden in the Sheldon wagon with Mrs. Sheldon, Jared, George, Jessie and little Tooty. The latter, now about ten years old, gazed at Mae with unabashed awe. Mae winked at her and felt pleased to see her brighten.

The Grimshaws were present, including Fred and his brothers and sisters, but not the pioneer matriarch, who had passed away last January. Young men Mae didn't know packed two of the pews, doubtless from various farms and ranches where John had worked. He had many friends, and that boded well.

Arriving at the front row Mae finally saw George, once presumed dead in the SP rail yards. Hank had located him in a Nevada mine. Now he stood with Hank and Sophie and their three tots. Yesterday he'd presented Mae with $300, which she took as a wedding gift though he called it a "payment for getting him out of jail." Farley's letter said he couldn't leave his work on the Sierra Railway. Seven days a week with his Fresno scraper he graded a rail bed from Oakdale to Chinese Camp—"The Gateway to Yosemite and Hetch Hetchy valleys."

Mae smiled at the bent beanpole of a farmer standing next to John. To-night he would stay in the Miller Hotel in Latrobe, and leave in the morning to return to the rest of the Dunaway family.

Indian Mary took Billy by the hand and brought him forward to stand be-tween Mae and Chloë, and then she stepped back to her place in the front row.

The sight of her sober little son in his suit and bow tie, hair plastered down with water, brought the first tears to Mae's eyes. These recent weeks had been hard on him, with his mother thinking about everything but him. She decided right then and there to mail-order the Improved Tricycle along with the remaining furniture. It would be her wedding present for him.

John closed the space between them. He stood about four inches taller than Mae in her two-inch heels. Brown hair neatly parted in the middle framed his clean-shaven face—tan except for the white forehead of a hardworking man.

The minister put a hand on the Holy Bible and began, "We are gathered here…"

88

We are alone, Rock Man, Mae, and I. Coyote left some time ago to trot his rounds.

Mae says, "Time flies when you're not telling lies and getting out of scrapes."

"What do you mean?" Rock Man's voice barely rises above the rush of the river.

"I can remember everything that happened to me before my marriage," Mae explains, "but after that my memory skips over the years like a stone on water. I told time by my babies. I would say: Alice was just walking, so that happened at the turn of the century. Or that was 1902, the year Johnny was born, or 1904, the year Emmett was born. In 1908 newborn Baby Emma died of whooping cough—the year Hiram Johnson won his graft case in San Francisco.

"Life wasn't always easy, especially when someone fell ill, but I had Mary's medicine and Chloë's help with the children. Your family was a part of ours, Howchia. John grew his amazing vegetable garden for them as much as for us, and we always gave them lamb and mutton. We helped each other."

"That's what families do," I remind her. "We are spirit sisters, you and I. My Indian family died out, but I am not alone. I feel the pleasant weight of other peoples in me—those of my father's people, the Cosumne, and your people from England and Ireland, and my Chinese descendents in Mexico."

Rock man says, "You are my descendant, Howchia, one of my family. A few of us begat the many of you."

I feel the strength of that, and the sadness of many becoming few again.

"The river spirit brought us all to this place," Rock Man says.

"And she brought the gold to Mae," I add.

We are seeing the river in a time of drought.

✳✳

Back from summer pasture, Mae was about four months pregnant. Ever since breakfast Johnny had been "walking" by means of pushing the old Improved Tricycle in the hallway, a precarious activity that often ended with the tricycle rolling out of his reach and crashing into a wall, leaving Johnny on his diapered bottom with tears of frustration. Mae did her best to keep him from injuring himself, but he wanted to do it all by himself and grew angrier by the minute, pushing her away. Mae was about to take the tricycle outside so she could get some rest, even though he'd put up a howl.

The back door banged open, John shouting , "Mae, Mae!"

Fear froze her. "What's wrong?" she called.

"Get my gun. I'm too muddy to come in."

An escapee from the Preston Boys School! Everyone around here kept guns handy to defend against desperate boys hiding in the bottomland as they made their way from Ione to this first populated area, hoping to steal a horse and gun. She rushed to the highboy and removed the pistol from the top drawer. John kept it loaded.

But as he took the gun, his mud-splattered face beamed with happy excitement. "We moved the big boulder and found a lock box… Come, you gotta see it! Bring Johnny."

Relieved not to be in a life and death emergency, Mae swept Johnny away from the tricycle and followed John down the Michigan Bar path— his high boots and every stitch of his clothing a uniform shade of pale brown mud. He'd been taking advantage of the drought to learn whether a gold vein ran across the river.

Every family rationed their pumping of water for daily use. Only a few mossy pools within the solid green of grass and cottonwood seedlings marked the former path of the river. Out where the current had been deep, a trench gaped open and a formerly upright boulder lay on its side. A trail of deep boot tracks connected that to the coulee where John had proposed. There, muddy shovels and crowbars littered the ground and Jeff Jaimeson squatted over a box wiping it with his shirt. His brother stood staring down.

Bending over Jeff, John exclaimed, "Would'ja look at that! Chinese writing!" Signaling them to stand back, he aimed his pistol at the lock and told Johnny to cover his ears.

Johnny jumped in Mae's arms and grabbed her neck at the gun's report, but didn't cry. John forced open the squeaky lid of the iron strongbox.

It was full of gold! Mostly little nuggets, and along one side of the box, wax-sealed vials. John pulled one out and lifted it. "Flour gold," he said in a tone of awe. He grasped handfuls of nuggets and let them leak through his fingers saying. "Somebody went to a lot of trouble to bury this."

"And they never come back," Jeff added in the same reverent tone.

∽

The house was quiet, the three children asleep across the hall. But the gold in the washroom kept Mae awake. John too, breathing quietly beside her.

"Musta been a lot of Chinamen workin' as a company," John said.

"I think we should talk to Ah Chung," Mae said. "He might know something about who buried that. Whether they're alive."

"I'll bet the Jaimesons already told 'im about it."

"I'm glad you gave some of it to them," She squeezed his hand.

"Couldn't'ov jimmied that bugger of a rock out without 'em. And they can use the money. Mebbe put some weatherproof siding on their cabins. But it's ours, Mae. The property line's the middle of the river. The box come from our side."

"Even if the ones who buried it are still living?"

"I doubt they're alive. Woulda come back or sent somebody for it. Go ahead and talk to Ah Chung. If they're alive, I'd think on givin' em part of it. But that's a long shot."

∽

After Billy and Alice left for school on Pal, riding double and bareback, Mae pulled on her mountain boots and took Johnny for a ride on the Improved Tricycle. Between the two large wheels she pushed on the brasswork of the seat. The road around to Jackson Road was bumpy and slow, and the highway thick with dust. However, the tricycle glided fast over the planks of the bridge, and Johnny squealed happily as his moccasined feet dangled above the churning pedals.

"Gid-up!," Johnny called when Mae returned to the dusty road with ridges and potholes. His little fists gripped the handles of the upswept steering post, which controlled the small wheel out in front.

"I can't go any faster," she said, huffing and puffing up the hill toward the Pratt house.

Joe Pratt was on the porch in his rocking chair. After his morning chores he always watched for rigs or horsemen to pass by. His gray hair hung down to his shoulders from a battered straw hat, and gray whiskers bushed out all over his face and down the bib of his overalls.

"Howdy Joe," Mae said, stopping before the house to catch her breath.

"Howdy," Joe replied. Up close, his overalls looked as unwashed and frayed as the sad earth waiting for rain. Katy Irene had said that when old Marie Pratt moved away in her last days, she arranged for Mary Granlees to acquire the property and look in on her simple son once in a while, allowing Joe to live out his life here. Katy wondered if that compact between the two women constituted the entire sale of this hundred and twenty-acre ground with river and road frontage. So Mary Granlees owned the Pratt place now, her elderly father no longer able to handle business.

"Is Ah Chung here today?" Mae asked.

"Yup." Pointing, Joe kept on rocking.

Apparently Ah Chung and the Jaimeson brothers also had the right to continue living where they had worked all their lives.

Eyeing the rutted and rocky ground between the house and the sheep camp Mae asked, "Joe, would it be alright if I left the tricycle here? Would you watch it for me?"

"Okay," Joe said.

Mae whisked Johnny off the seat and and walked away quickly, before he got a notion to fuss about leaving his favorite thing.

Ah Chung sat whittling on the chair before the sheepcamp. He looked up and smiled a big hello as Mae put Johnny down on the old floor where he wouldn't crawl under the corral fence to all the messy cow pies. Instead he crawled toward the three narrow iron steps leading up into the tiny covered wagon.

"I came to talk to you about— Is it all right if he goes in there?" She pointed at her son pulling himself up the steps.

The old man grinned. "He okay. No plobrem."

Mae looked into the compact dwelling with the table hooked up on the wall, the knives and forks out of sight, and decided nothing in there would harm him.

"Did Jeff and Andy tell you about the gold we found in the river?"

"Uh-huh," he nodded. "Them boys go cat house in Jackson. Hava big time."

"Did you ever hear of some Chinese men burying that gold in the river?"

He shook his head. *No.* "China man find gold, doan tell nobody."

Inside the sheep camp Johnny was on his feet against the drawers beneath the elevated bed, his head turned all the way around grinning at her.

"Mebbe China men put gold unda rock in sixty-one. No wata in riva. Nex day lotta rain comee. Big frud. No can find hidee prace."

"Were you here at that time?"

"No. Workee in high mountain, road work."

"Did someone tell you that's what happened?"

Shaking his head Ah Chung went back to his whittling. "Everbody know 'bout long dry time and big frud nex yeaw, in sixty-two."

"Would you mind coming over to read the Chinese words on the box?"

He smiled down in at his whittling in an embarrassed way. "No can read."

That night Mae told John she too thought the gold must have been buried in the drought just before the big flood of sixty-two.

"I heard of that flood," John said. "The Grimshaws said it were the biggest flood their people ever seen. One of their relations, John Rhoads I think the name was, died and they couldn't move his body from the upstairs of his house for three weeks, 'count'a that flood. The whole big valley was underwater. Every bridge washed out. People got around in boats for a long time. That boulder woulda been underwater. If it was the marker, they couldn't'ov found it."

After a while he said, "I'm glad you talked to Ah Chung." He put an arm over her. "I'm gonna build us a fine house with that gold. Big enough for all the youngin's we might have. So I want you to dream what kinda house you want. Look at the magazines. We'll hire an architect this time."

❀❀

MAE REMEMBERS IN HER PIERCE-ARROW.

"Several years later John found parts of a boat in the middle of the field. An anchor rock still had rope tied around it. We figured it belonged to those miners and they drowned trying to dig out the box."

"I remember that flood," I say. "Our storytellers told of a bigger flood in the time of the Ancients, but the one you're talking about was the worst I ever saw. The trees and other landmarks were all washed away. The river spirit liked you. She saved the gold for you."

"Maybe I did something for the river in return. Kept it running free. That might be the one thing I did that left a mark on the earth. Most people have forgotten about it, and even when it was happening, not many people knew of it."

Coyote trots up to us, bright-eyed and bushy-tailed, to hear the last of the story.

"It started with a conversation I had with Charlie Rogue," Mae says. "Emmett was still in diapers, so it must have been about 1906. Yes, that's right. The Great Earthquake hadn't happened yet. So it would have been March of that year."

89

The secretary to the Speaker Pro Tem escorted Mae down the corridor in the Capitol Building, their four heels tapping a syncopated rhythm on the marble floor. He stopped before the door, opening a hand to the gold-leaf lettering: CHARLES M. ROGUE, CHIEF OF STAFF, and then pivoted and departed in straight two-four time.

"Mae," Charlie said with a smile, standing up behind his wide desk as she entered his carpeted office. His vest and suit looked too respectable for his jaunty prizefighter face—the nose off to one side, flatter than it had once been and lumpy with red scars. More of those scars emphasized his right eye socket. His mangy mustache didn't quite hide the old wounds on his upper lip, and his lower lip had two vertical fault lines despite the extensive stitching.

"You're looking svelte," he said, pointing to a curvy mahogany chair across the desk from him.

Seating herself, she made a mental note to look up that word.

"Do you know what that means?" That same slightly mocking tone! Like a parent catching a young child in a fib.

"I assumed it was a compliment," she threw at him. *One minute into this meeting and you've already belittled me. Thank God I didn't marry you.*

"It means slender."

"Well, this might be hard for you to believe," she gave back, "but once in a great while I'm not heavy with child." Since her wedding she'd seen Charlie twice, once when she was eight months along with Alice and once when she'd been six months with Johnny—having taken Alice to the hospital with pneumonia. That was just after John bought into the SP hospital plan.

"A dramatic hat too," Charlie continued to notice. "An Oscar Wilde sweep. Gives you a look of—hmm, let's see—maybe authority is the word."

"When you're the mother of four you get used to ordering people around." Shifting the conversation to him she said, "I can see you've been promoted. Got a bigger office, and no other men in it. And somebody cleans it for you."

Nodding, Charlie folded his hands on the desk. "How is Billy?" Over the years, whenever those photographers came through, she'd ordered postal cards of Billy and mailed one to Charlie.

"Growing like a weed and smart as a whip."

"Chip off the old block."

The same joke he'd made last time. She couldn't smile, worried about Charlie's motive for asking her to come to his office—maybe angling to get Billy to Sacramento sooner. Twelve years old in a couple of months, Billy looked forward to the seventh and eighth grades in Stone House School. He had blossomed as a student under Anne King's teaching. Mae had agreed to let him live with Charlie during his high school years, except for summers, but she wouldn't abide any further reduction of her time with her son.

"I wanted you to know," Charlie was saying, "I started a bank account for him, to be used for his college."

"Thank you. That's generous of you."

"He's my only child." His eye twinkled as he added, "…that I know of."

Ignoring that tired joke, she started to head him off with, "He's got a good life with us on the farm and—"

"Of course he has. Farm life was a good start for me, and it's good for him too."

Perhaps her defensiveness was misplaced.

"Remember that work I was doing for Mr. Tevis? Getting options on water and property along the Cosumnes and American Rivers?"

"Yes."

"Well, I'm back at it."

"I figured that idea was put to rest long ago."

"It's happening now. And Mae, it's a magnificent, far-reaching project that will transform the entire San Francisco region and allow the development of millions of acres."

"If it's so magnificent, why has it taken so long?"

"Too many landowners, shifting titles, economy gone bust and staying flat. Then just when it was coming together again, somebody with an important piece would die or change his mind. But now all we need is one more impoundment. Twelve reservoirs in the mountains are a sure thing, all the way up to Carson Pass, but the entire—"

"Charlie," she interrupted, "you're saying *we*, like you're part of that, uh, what was that company?"

"Bay Cities Water Company."

"The one owned by the men who've got California dancing like a puppet on the strings of their fingers?"

Obviously not seeing the humor in that, Charlie seemed to be pushing an invisible particle around a little circle on his desk. "You asked me once if I could become a partner of James Fair, back when I was hoping to work for him. Or maybe it was William Tevis we were talking about. Anyway I probably said no, but one can never rule out such a thing with a project of this magnitude." He looked up at her with unblinking eyes.

"You see, I'm doing some important parts of this work, and I have my price." He pointed at the door. "Those words over there: Chief of Staff. They're not the words of a man's main chance. This big water project could put me on a different footing. A higher plane. The way it's planned now, I'd have a share in the ownership, and that kind of leverage leads—"

"Why are you telling me this?" With irritation she recalled her intense interest in Charlie's business prospects thirteen years ago.

"Well, we were just saying that Billy is my only offspring. I assume he still goes by the name Rogue?"

"Yes, John never adopted him formally." She caught his meaning. "He'll be your heir."

"Yes. I want him well educated and starting life a leg up from other boys."

"So you're saying that if this water project works out, you'll be one of the wealthy capitalists of San Francisco."

"Yes." The joking twinkle briefly returned to his eye, but then he resumed to pushing his invisible particle. "Here's the thing. We're looking at the whole Cosumnes River, in your area, where all the forks have come together and the river still has a little elevation. There'd be a hydroelectric power plant."

"Oh, I see. I'm one of your landowner targets?"

"Uh-huh."

"And you got me to come to you, instead of going to the hinterlands to talk to me." It was a friendly jab, but he wasn't playing.

"It'd be a bonanza for you. And your husband and family, including Billy."

"Exactly what would it do to our property?"

"We're not entirely sure of the details yet, not until an engineering study has been done, but your property would be needed one way or the other, either a high dike along the river or maybe inundation, depending on where the southern side of the basin would be."

"Inundation?"

"Flooding. Deep water if the impoundment goes to the ridge to the south of you, the bank of the ancient river. In exchange for…" He came to a stop.

"An incentive," she provided. "A big pot of money."

Elbows on desk, he steepled his fingers under his chin. "The sale of your land and water rights."

"How much money?"

"If you don't mind, could we discuss this out in the arboretum?"

Another ten-dollar word. He was already at the coat rack plucking his bowler from a hook. "The garden of trees around the Capitol," he clarified.

"Sure," she said.

The weather was cool, but she'd worn her black leather coat dress sewn in pleats down the front, a hat close to the side of her head, and black leather gloves. They strolled down a pathway through cut grass and blooming camellias, the pink petals beaded from the morning rain. Overhead, long shreds of gray cloud moved under the sun and scuttled onward in the fresh breeze.

"As I was saying," Charlie said, bending down as they walked so he could speak softly, "You could get a windfall."

"And I was asking how much?"

"That depends on several things, including the results of the engineering study. And how many landowners along the river are getting a share."

"Can't you make a guess?"

"This is just a wild hair, not to take to the bank. For your hundred acres along the south side of the river, maybe forty to fifty thousand dollars."

A gray squirrel dashed across the lawn as Mae tried to fit that number into her head—more than the cache of gold had brought!

"And I need to tell you, we're also looking to another solution."

"What's that?"

"The possibility that the water project could be developed by creating a legal instrument here in the Legislature. A means by which cities or counties could take water from distant rivers, and the needed lands involved, if it's found to be in the public interest."

Two men in black suits came toward them and Charlie doffed his hat. After they passed, he resumed, "The Legislature would define the public interest. And, keep in mind, the men behind this are, shall we say, very influential."

Mae felt a stirring of alarm as she thought about the rich farmland John had worked so hard to reclaim. "You're saying, 'take the land?' as opposed to buying it?"

He nodded perceptibly.

"And we could be flooded without getting paid for it? So that bunch of men can make San Francisco into the new Roman Empire, and they are drawing up a, uh, uh...."

"Law," he finished. "Or rather I am writing it for them. It would create a new governmental entity to handle such situations."

"Situations where land owners won't sell?"

"Uh-huh. Oh, it's possible you'd get paid eventually. I would certainly favor that. It's just that you wouldn't have any control over it. But, Mae, that's why I asked you here today, to think about signing a contract with the Bay Cities Water Company. That would make the governmental entity unnecessary—a far better solution. And I'm sure you'd be very pleased with what you'd get for your land."

She was about to say she couldn't agree to anything without time for her and John to think it over, but he was adding:

"There's one more factor in figuring the amount. If your husband could get a group of affected landowners together and be the leader and spokesman, and move it along before this bill is introduced in the Legislature, you'd get some additional payment, and perhaps an ownership piece."

All her instincts sensed danger. Do what he asks and you get paid. Don't do it and you get flooded property or a giant concrete dike covering your farm, and maybe get something in return. But with the threat in place, couldn't the payment shrink to a pittance? There would need to be an ironclad contract up front.

By now they'd arrived at the back wall of the Agricultural Pavilion where crimson tulips dancing in the breeze reminded her of the crimson dress she'd worn while escaping from that building with Oberon on her heels. The path split two ways, and Charlie guided her onto the one that circled back toward the Capitol Building, where new trees were being planted. She wanted to be very clear about his proposal.

"Why doesn't the water company go forward with the rights they already have, and pipe that water to San Francisco?"

"For a time they planned to propose just that. To make a long story too short, the benefits of a massive amount of water for Greater San Francisco are stupendous. The place would grow by leaps and bounds, so they want a really big project to out-bid our competitor. This legal instrument we're considering grew out of the long delay and the difficulty of getting so many owners to jump at the same time. But keep in mind"—again he glanced round them—"only a handful of men are aware that the alternative is being drafted. And I'm telling you a lot of support will be there in the Legislature and the Governor's office for this project."

"Bribes?"

"I wouldn't use that word."

He moved his lips around. "Mae, what I'm trying to say is, one way or the other, this time the water deal will succeed. And you would benefit greatly by signing on with it, particularly if you do it before the next session starts. You might recall that the Legislature meets on odd-numbered years, and session starts the first Monday of January. That's next January."

She couldn't think about calendar dates while her head resonated with: *One way or the other this time the water deal will succeed.*

Back among the older trees Charlie stopped before a park bench beneath a tall tree with sweeping branches. The English name on the plaque was DEODAR CEDAR. "Wouldn't you like to sit here a minute?" he gestured.

The bench felt good after the long stroll in stiff new shoes.

Charlie said, "Seems like yesterday these were saplings."

"I remember them being a lot smaller too." It had been fifteen years since she'd come to the Capitol hoping to become a type writer. "I guess they ought to have grown some," she said. "After all, that was a century ago."

His smile approved her joke. "The ground here is rich with centuries of river overflow."

"Our farm's like that now, and for the same reason. The other side of the river is higher and rocky."

Charlie's chest inflated and enthusiasm surged in his voice. "That's what we've been looking at. To make a forebay we'd need only to fill in some areas on the north side, and a dike along your side. The bigger dam would be up east of Michigan Bar, where the walls of the canyon are strong and steep on both sides. Ideal for a hydroelectrical facility."

She tried to picture all that concrete.

"As far as the alternative, the farm groups might fight the precedent and draw it out. So it's best to agree quickly to the Bay Cities Plan."

"I'll talk to John and the neighbors. Before January, right?"

"Actually I need to know long before that, before I start work on this public interest thing." His bright eyes looked into hers. "Bay Cities will be more appreciative of your decision if we get it by, say, July or August at the very latest. I can't promise an ownership share, but it's quite possible."

Mae stood up to leave. "I understand," she said. She and John and Billy could be very rich.

"I'll be waiting to hear from you," Charlie said.

90

Back from her meeting with Charlie, Mae stood on the porch of her Queen Anne home listening through the closed door to the delicate runs of Debussy's "First Arabesque." It played through her like trickles of water in a Moorish courtyard. Chloë had a natural ability to play with extraordinary feeling—a miracle of a girl playing a miracle of a composition. Adding to the sense of a mythic garden, the camellias and azaleas were outdoing each other in hues of rose and pomegranate, and the honey locust trees along the south side of the house, now in their tender leaves, admitted veils of sparkling sunshine between the rain squalls.

Bear bounded up the two stairs with his tail wagging his hairy hind end. As usual, he needed a bath and a good brushing, but his heart was pure. As she petted his ears back, he smiled as though enjoying the music with her. Keeping watch over home and grounds, the big mutt lived for love. She knew he would fight to protect her, as was his job, even though the original purpose for him had been garroted to death in the streets of Sacramento. She'd read about it right here on the porch last spring after the headline: POLICE INSPECTOR KILLED, MANHUNT ON seized her attention. The first sentence named Oberon Jones as the victim. An unbidden cry had come from her lips.

She would never forget that morning. Baby Emmett was down for his morning nap. Alice and Billy were back from the store with the newspaper and the egg money. Johnny looked worried, so she whisked him off his feet and whirled him around in a joyful little dance, hugging him to her.

He fingered the tear under her eye. "Mommy cwying."

"Mommy's just happy," she'd said.

Oberon's killer had never been found.

Now, in the thrall of the rippling Arabesque, she noticed John out in the green, unplowed field pointing as he walked with Mr. Hirata and Mr.

Yoshida, showing them where he wanted to expand the bean field. Japanese workers had taken up the slack after the strict Exclusion Laws had stopped the immigration of Chinese laborers—those still in California were old and dying.

She looked the other way, down the covered porch where white spindles framed the budding oaks along the river. Debussy's music perfectly expressed her feelings about her home near the flowing water. The theme rebraided itself in sidereal runs that gave her goose bumps. It sang in her veins like the river baby spirit of the Miwok or the Greek water nymphs, naïads—changing with the seasons and the time of day. Now in the late afternoon the oaks glowed maroon inside the accidental white frame, until another cloud drifted over the sun and the color shifted to lavender. The piano-water rested a little, and then the streams lifted in twining transparencies up and up in an otherworldly web, higher and higher, crystal bells tinkling in atmospheric heights until, like the celestial trick of the cloud admitting sun at that very instant, the last baby pearls sprinkled into space—an ending that made her laugh and weep at the same time.

Suddenly the heavy front door opened and Johnny called, "Mommy's home!" Two-year-old Emmett came squealing to the screen door. Let out by Johnny, he ran on his fat bare feet and gleefully squeezed Mae's legs through the pleated leather. She picked him up and pressed a kiss on his smooth round cheek. Johnny still liked to be kissed, so she put Emmett down and gave her older son a hug and kiss too.

"Were you good boys while Mommy was away?"

Johnny stood, obviously reviewing the day with some doubt while Emmett watched his big brother for clues on how to handle such a question. Mae flicked her watch open. Billy and Alice should be here at any time now. The golden wands pointed to 3:40 over the Grecian girls—perhaps water nymphs, it occurred to her.

Holding the screen for the boys she stepped into the vestibule and into the parlor just as Chloë set the fire screen—a brass peacock with spread tail—back in place.

"Thanks for keeping the fire going," Mae said. "I hope the boys weren't any trouble."

"Good boys," Chloë said.

"I loved hearing you play the piano just now. You play beautifully. Better than I ever will. You should be playing on a stage."

Chloë looked down and shook her head, embarrassed. For her to perform for a crowd would be like asking Bear to fly. Yet she had cared for every one of Mae's children just as she'd cared for little Billy, and Indian Mary had confided to Mae that the artistry in Chloë's baskets, with old and new patterns coiled together, equaled the best of the old-time weavers. Mary attributed the change in her granddaughter to a powerful spirit that had fought against the murderous spirits that howl after people who are very open to the unseen, as eighteen-year-old Chloë still was.

Mae handed her a half dollar. "Sure you won't change your mind and have supper with us?"

Chloë shook her head and walked, barefoot as usual, toward the front door, a slight girl wearing the same kind of homemade black blouse and skirt that her grandmother wore. She never changed the style of her straight black hair hanging blunt around her shoulders and across her brow.

"Say good-bye to Auntie," Mae told Johnny and Emmett.

They ran to the door yelling "Bye-bye, Auntie Chloë!"

Mae looked around the parlor she loved so well. The fine upright piano, first used in their marriage ceremony, had been John's surprise wedding present. Mae had given many piano lessons on it, but Chloë was her star pupil. The girl absorbed the meaning of the musical notations like she read bird tracks in the bottomland of the river. Chloë was an important part of this place, and would be as long as the place existed.

Everywhere Mae looked she saw her good life. One of their peacocks glided by the window followed by Bear barking on its tail. The big birds stole Bear's food and he tried his best to catch them, but they always escaped at the last moment, screaming into flight. Some people thought peacocks made too much noise to be keepers, but their loud calls were a small price to pay for the eradication of black widow spiders. They hunted the spiders with sharp eyes and long necks for poking into woodpiles and behind things. They fluttered up and picked them off their stringy webs, thus helping to keep the family safe. And every molted pinfeather was a find to be shouted through the house and brought to Mommy by the youngest child, each in his or her turn. A bouquet of feathers stood in a vase on the piano giving exotic iridescence to the Victorian room.

This home filled with perfect children was everything Mae had ever wanted. After a bad start, she now seemed to be doing everything right, but the decision she and John must make could change all their lives. And she feared making a mistake.

As she walked down the hall, Emmett's bare feet thumped double-time behind her. In her bedroom he pressed his nose against the window to better see the chickens in their fenced yard, and the turkeys in the adjoining yard. He looked like a fat little old woman in his floor-length baby gown. Mae put her hat in its box and changed into a housedress. She still raised chickens and about ten turkeys, not nearly as many as her good friend Polly, just across the bridge in the old Pratt place. Friends, Mae realized, played a big part in making this place perfect. They tethered the place to her heart.

Polly had annulled her marriage to the Sacramento lawyer and, to her father's consternation, married Jack Granlees, an Irish Catholic seven years younger —one of the boys Mae had looked after as a hired girl. So she had two friends within easy walking distance, Katy Irene across the front pasture and

Polly just over the bridge. The three enjoyed musical afternoons during the winter, and in the spring and fall the families attended community picnics at Dixon's Grove together, the older children keeping an eye on the younger ones. They were a happy little tribe. That would all end if Charlie's project succeeded and the families lived apart.

This was also the last remnant of Indian Mary's former life. And now that big Billy was gone, Mary, Isabella and Chloë were the last native people in their original home place. They believed the place was eternal and the river would always run wild.

In the kitchen peeling potatoes for supper, Mae heard horse hooves. Out the window, good old Pal plodded toward the stable with Billy and seven-year-old Alice on his back. Two minutes later Billy threw open the kitchen door.

"Mom, Miss King's gonna marry Bert Granlees!"

Brought up short, she stood looking at him. "I can't believe it."

"Miss King said so before the bell rang, didn't she Alice?" Red hair curving inward at her ears, Alice came inside. She nodded at Billy, and he continued, "Bert's face were red as paint. Ricky and me asked if it was true an' he said it was."

"Bert's face *was* as red as paint, and Ricky and *I* asked. But—"

Instinctively disapproving of a teacher marrying her eighth-grade pupil, Mae tried to figure how much older Anne King must be, but quickly gave up. Like many eighth-grade boys, Bert, a good-looking six-foot-two, was older due to having missed so much school. In winter, when there wasn't much farm work he went back to school. A year or so earlier his father had left home. According to Katy Irene, Bert had seen his father strike his mother, again. This time Bert socked his father and knocked him down. When Mr. Granlees got up, he went to live in Sacramento. So Bert and Jack worked on the place full time.

"Well," Mae said to Billy and Alice, who awaited her judgment, "I hope we can find a teacher as good as Miss King. I had so wanted her to teach Johnny and Emmett. And you, Alice. You've got your whole grade-school ahead of you."

Alice's pretty gray eyes widened with astonishment. "You mean she's gonna quit teaching?"

"Well, usually married ladies are not allowed to teach," Mae told them.

Alice cried, "They won't let her be our teacher no more?"

"*Any* more. I'm afraid that's right."

Billy grumbled, "I don't see why they have to get married."

"What marry mean?" little Emmett demanded with a stamp of his bare foot.

"Your daddy and I are married," Mae said, picking him up. "That's why you're here." She poked her finger into his soft belly. "Our love made you. When people get married they have babies."

Billy looked at her with an expression she'd been seeing more often of late. It said: I will evaluate what you're saying and decide the truth for myself.

Caught in a half-lie, Mae told him the truth, "Love is a powerful force." It didn't respect the conventions of age, race, or marital status.

This had been a day of surprises—Charlie's of much greater consequence.

⌒

John came in and washed up for supper, but the busy table was no place to talk about Charlie's plan. After the dishes were done, Alice on her way upstairs to read in her room, Mae went to the parlor. Billy held Johnny and Emmett under his arms reading to them. John had his head back on his leather chair, resting his eyes. Understandably tired.

In February after the lambing, he'd bought the Rudnicki place up near the Old Sacramento Road, sixty acres with a small house and a windmill pump. Mae had helped drive the sheep up there, where Jeff Jaimeson now lived and cared for them. Busier than ever, John rode back and forth between the two places—this morning he'd got Jeff started on a bigger wool bin.

Mae sat opposite him. "I've got something to tell you," she said in a quiet voice, just over the drone of Billy's reading.

He opened his eyes. "You're pregnant again."

She shook her head. "Not that I know of." When she told him what Charlie wanted, John sat up straighter with every word.

He whistled softly. "Forty to fifty thousand dollars! And a chance for an ownership piece of a thing that big!" He looked at the dark window, and back again. "How long we got before that new law steals our property?"

"He's working on it now, and it can't be passed by the Legislature until next spring. But the sooner he hears from us the happier he'll be, that is if we decide to let Bay Cities Water Company buy us out. He wants to know by July or August at the latest."

"We'll be up in the mountains."

"Yes," she said. "We'll have to make up our minds before we leave." Usually that meant by the first week of June.

⌒

DATELINE: APRIL 18, 1906

EARTHQUAKE DESTROYS SAN FRANCISCO! Massive Destruction to California's Largest City. Death Toll Mounts. Greatest Calamity in Modern Times. Survivors Flee Burning City. Huge Encampments of Homeless on Presidio Hill and Twin Peaks. Gas Mains Explode, No Water to Quench Fires.

These were only a few of the headlines coming from San Francisco and the local papers on Friday, Saturday, and Sunday. The first stories told too little. Four San Francisco papers temporarily set aside their enmity and pooled their work in a single newspaper printed on equipment loaned to them by *The Oakland Tribune*.

The earthquake happened just after five in the morning, before Mae woke up, and she felt cheated not to have felt it. John had been milking a cow, and saw the milk slosh in the bucket. Jeff Jaimeson, out pumping water at the Rudnicki place, saw waves of water move up and down the long sheep trough. Katy Irene had been feeding her youngest when she felt the house move. "At first I thought it was the ague coming on, a kind of dizziness," she said.

Everyone had a story of what they saw or felt, unless they'd been asleep. A few days later Mae noticed a thread-line crack in the parlor wall. The house had shifted a little.

Every day the local newspapers covered the continuing disaster in The City. The fire Friday night burned so brightly that reporters atop *The Sacramento Bee* building could see the red glow ninety miles away. Two miles away the people on Presidio Hill claimed they read the newspaper at night by the intense light of the downtown fire.

Men had different opinions about why there was inadequate water. One city worker was quoted as saying, "The quake severed the water main at Crystal Lake," the source of most of the City's water. William Tevis blamed the city government for the destruction because of their delay in adopting the American-Cosumnes Project put forward by his Bay Cities Water Company. Others blamed the same officials for not adopting the competing Tuolumne River project, or Hetch Hetchy as some called it.

That was interesting.

Before the earthquake she and John had made it a point to chat with the neighbors when they saw them, to get a feel for which of them would sell out to Bay Cities. But now all anyone talked about was the destruction of The City and the relief effort. The local papers were full of that. The Woman's Council of Sacramento coordinated the local effort to help earthquake victims. They located temporary housing in local private homes, at Sutter's Fort, and at the State Agricultural Pavilion on the grounds of the Capitol. They created a register of refugees so that relatives could find one another. On April 21 alone, the Woman's Council supervised the making of 15,000 sandwiches that were sent by train to Oakland, to be ferried to San Francisco. The Women's Federation of Amador County was doing similar work.

A few newspaper articles mentioned plans to rebuild. City Manager Abe Ruef was quoted as saying San Francisco would be rebuilt in just a few months. "Some of what crumbled and burned," another official said, "was an act of God, cleaning out what needed cleansing." Mae recalled that Bonanza King James Fair, who died some time back, had owned sixty acres of the downtown and allowed them to deteriorate.

"I don't see how they can get the loans to re-build," John kept coming back to. "People just don't believe in San Francisco the way they did before."

A woman stepped off the stage at Bridge House to buy a pickle and told Bob Warren that God had destroyed San Francisco for the same reason he destroyed Sodom and Gomorrah. She said The City had been her home but she would never return, even if it were to be rebuilt, for surely God would destroy it again.

That was hardly the kind of thing to inspire investors.

91

The children were out of school and it was time to pack for the mountains, and yet Mae and John had not looked each other in the eye and said: Let's sell out to Bay Cities. Nor had either of them heard anything like that from the neighboring farmers.

"It's hard to believe Bay Cities'll go though with the thing," John would say at night. "Well, morning gets here too quick. Gotta get some sleep."

Besides working on the Rudnicki place, he was enlarging the garden and planting tomatoes, melons and vegetables of all kinds. He had a way of walking fast and getting a lot done. Everything he touched thrived.

At noon dinner one day he said, "Even Fred Grimshaw don't know if he's still for it." *It* meant only one thing.

"When did you talk to him last?"

"About a week ago. After dippin' the sheep."

"Sheepie cry!" Emmett exclaimed. He and Johnny had seen some of the dipping when Mae let them ride in the surrey with supplies needed at the Rudnicki place.

"I should probably go talk to Charlie again," Mae said, "and find out if he thinks the City Supervisors will stick by the American-Cosumnes Plan."

John was buttering a slice of her bread. "For a while there I was leanin' hard toward the dam. Saw it as our chance to become owners of some'um big. A way to grow old and keep the money comin' in." He took a big bite.

"And now?"

"Dunno if those men can be trusted," he mumbled through the bread.

"You don't think Charlie's telling the truth?"

She saw Billy's ears prick up to hear that said about his "other" father.

John gave her a serious look from under gathered brows. "I'm not sayin' he's a liar, just a hoper. Laid his bet down on a horse and wants us to sweeten the pot so if he wins he'll win bigger. In the middle of the night mebbe he wakes up in a sweat 'cause he knows the horse is too hurt to run, but then mornin' comes an' he's not about to pour tongue oil on nuthin' else but that hope." He added, "What's *he* got in this thing? I mean of his own?"

Mae shrugged. "His time and work is my guess."

"No sweat and back misery."

"Maybe we should call a meeting at Slough House and see what the others want to do before I talk to Charlie," Mae suggested.

"Good idea," John said. "But you do the talkin'. You're better at it, and I can't waste any daylight hours before we head up the mountains."

"But I'd need you there."

"Why?" John ladled out a second helping of mutton stew.

Because men don't listen to women when it comes to money. "So we can show we're of a like mind, in case they ask."

"What like mind you talkin' about? I don't recall we got one one, you and me."

Mae closed her eyes and took a deep breath. "All right. I'll just try to get the sense of the rest of them."

John was working on a mouthful of mutton.

"You know," it occurred to her, "maybe I should go talk to Charlie again *before* that meeting, in case he's learned something that changes the deal."

John kept his head down, but she saw that flat look in his eye like when he was listening to someone he didn't like. She had never been that someone. She'd always felt herself in a tight circle of one with John.

He pursed his lips to one side and made a bump in his cheek as though digging something out. "He like seein' you? Time and again?"

That knocked the wind out of her. She should have known he'd be sensitive to her seeing Charlie. She saw his unease at having revealed his feelings—a man not given to pettiness. "The only time he asked to see me," she gently reminded him, "was to pry land and water rights out of us. But John," she realized, "there's no reason to see him in person. I'll write a letter and ask him what we all need to know. Then we'll have an answer in writing for the meeting."

John nodded, wiped his sleeve over his mouth, and got up from the table.

That night, as he stared at the ceiling in the dark, Mae stroked his chest under his nightshirt and tried to explain how she felt about him. "I love you, John, because you have good judgment; you're a hard worker and a good father. You make me feel appreciated, in how I raise the children." That sounded bland. There was more to it, hard to put into words, but she tried.

"You married me when I had another man's child. That's just the way you are. You don't look back and blame me for my old mistakes. You don't have a snobbish bone in your body. And I love that, the way you are. I love the way you feel to the touch too, soft skin with hard muscle underneath, and the way you smell," she chuckled, "when you're cleaned up." Then she snuggled in close to him and said, "It's just because you're you, nobody else, because you're my wonderful man and I need you to love me."

That brought him around.

ᔐ

Bob Warren waved a letter at Mae when she delivered eggs two days later. She tore it open. The letter was typed, the return address printed.

CALIFORNIA STATE CAPITOL BUILDING
OFFICE OF THE PRESIDENT PRO TEM OF THE SENATE

May 25, 1906

Dear Mae,

I understand your doubts about San Francisco, being that
you are so far away and do not meet face to face with the men
from the city, as I do. I herewith respond with the utmost
sincerity to those doubts as follows:

San Francisco is being rebuilt sooner than anyone here-
tofore thought possible. In fact some banks are already
open again. City government meets often to approve franchises and permits and all manner of new business. There
is a can-do attitude. Friends and relatives of people left
homeless have sent millions of dollars of gold coin to help,
and a new shopping district has been built the likes of
which could not have been imagined two months ago. Very
soon the city will outshine its former self.

The disaster proved the need for a better water source,
and Mr. T. is acting on it daily, as are the Mayor and other of-
cials. They are bully about the Bay Cities project. Greater
San Francisco needs the water from your river, and you and
your neighbors will reap the rewards of jumping on this
bandwagon. Get them to sign pledges for options. Send me
a map with their locations and names. Upon receipt, I will
drive out there forthwith to visit each of them about the
particulars of their properties. I will answer their questions and give them copies of the option agreement.

Eagerly awaiting your reply,
Charles M. Rogue
Chief of Staff, Senate Pro Tem

In from hoeing weeds in the bean field, John washed up at the sink inside the kitchen door and came to the table with his sleeves rolled up. Mae
handed him the letter. He sat down reading.

She was frying bread dough in deep fat. The big "scones" browned quickly
on one side, rising as they cooked. She turned the one in the deep fryer and in

a minute laid it to drain on a towel. While the next one puffed up, she shoved the spatula under the previous scone and delivered it to Alice, who had a gob of butter at the ready on her knife. How the children loved bread day! Busy with knives and forks, Billy and Johnny devoured their scones. John slowly read the letter as he cut one up for Emmett. The worn old high chair had stood next to John's chair for many years. He'd fed all the babies, each in her or his turn—mashed the food and spooned it in their mouths, then cut it until they could do it themselves. Mae always stood at the stove serving up seconds and eating afterwards, as Mom had done in Iowa.

John handed her the letter, and she laid it on the end of the counter.

"I'd say it's about time for that meeting at the Slough House Inn," he said as she slid a scone onto his plate.

∽

As always, these impromptu community meetings started at seven in the evening. Mae and Polly rode in the back seat of the Warren buggy. In the front, Bob Warren and Jack Granlees had their hats down over their eyes as the horses trotted straight into the sun. Katy Irene had stayed home to feed the children of the three families, and John was out irrigating the fields.

"Well," Polly said, "here we go again. Off to decide our fates."

"Like the gods on Mount Olympus," Mae joked in the same vein.

"It's interesting, isn't it," Polly said, "how once in a while the independent cusses that live around here will put aside their feuds and differences and work out problems."

Mae chuckled, and then blew out air. "Yes, but a levee break or a road washout is easy. Somebody reads a list of things to be done, hands go up, and everyone goes out to work. This is more complicated, and I wish I weren't leading the charge."

"I thought you were only collecting information."

"Well, I'm delivering it too. I've been over this so many times I feel like I'm going crazy."

She knew that Jack and his mother supported the dam, but it was Polly's nature to love the river and worry about the wild animals down there. However, Polly seemed resigned to whatever Jack wanted.

"It'll work out all right," Polly said. "You know, I'm proud meetings like this are held in my family's place of business. And I'm proud that people listen to each other." She laughed. "Tryin' to get out of there quick, I guess."

"I don't want it to drag on tonight. But this isn't simple." Charlie would have wanted to explain it to the people, but Mae didn't want him on John's territory, in public, and she didn't want his superior rhetoric unduly influencing people. So she hadn't written him about the meeting.

"Most times these meetings aren't simple," Polly disagreed. "Like the school thing last month. None of us liked the Stone House School shutting down next year, but we worked it out." She threw her head back and hawed. "The next day the backbiting started up again."

Just ahead on the road, Polly's mother-in-law drove her little white-top, a wagon with a short bed and canvas over the buckboard, and Mae knew that Polly considered Mary Granlees to be the most independent of all the cusses around here. The two had lived in the same house and stepped on each other's toes for years, until Jack and Polly moved into the Pratt place. Mary had insisted on driving alone to last month's meeting too. Her son's marriage to the teacher had triggered the school's closure, but Mary's focus had been on her youngest son, Art, who could have walked to second grade next year if the school stayed open, so she'd argued that the County Office of Education had no business advising the school closure and the Stone House District should ignore the Office and hire their own teacher, or let Anne continue to teach. But the majority didn't want to fight the county, since their taxes paid for teacher certification and oversight. Instead, they talked about which of the Stone House children would transfer to Hill Top School in Michigan Bar and which ones would go to Wilson or Rhoads School.

School enrollment had declined in the entire area. No progress had come. No railroad. No electricity. No telephone. The area had become even more of a backwater, and Mae knew that a big dam project might well reverse that. For starters, a rail line would be built along Jackson Road to deliver workmen, steel and concrete—but also passengers and harvested crops.

Bob Warren pulled up at the big Slough House barn, where aging graduates of the three local schools were arriving in all manner of vehicles, and on horseback. Also driving up were those too new to have attended local schools, like the Schneiders, who had recently bought ground from Bill Dixon and started to build a two-story house on it.

Crossing the road from the barn, Mae recalled the sad story of a stage driver back in the Gold Rush. It made her skittishness tonight seem foolish. One of the passengers had been successful in the mines, and he wanted to continue to Sacramento and not stay at the Slough House Inn for fear his purse would be stolen while he slept. But the driver insisted on staying the night—all stage drivers looked forward to the whisky and fun to be had at the famous Inn. So before he lay down alongside his fellow travelers on the upstairs floor, the man from New York hid his wallet in the barn. The next morning it was gone. He brought charges against the coach driver, who was convicted of grand larceny and sentenced to fifteen years in San Quentin. He served his entire term. Years later, in 1891, as the new barn was being rebuilt after a fire, a workman found the purse. Its owner had buried it in the hay where he thought no thief could find it; however, a pack rat had pulled it down a tunnel beneath the floor where it stayed dry for forty years. The lost bank notes were returned to their owner at his New York address, but no one seemed to know whether the hapless ex-convict ever learned of it.

Inside, the inn was dark and smoky as always. Bar regulars slumped on stools and chairs, but no band played tonight. Shoes and boots drummed on the perceptibly downward slope of the floor, heading past the wooden Indian to the back room. Mae had known it would be cool in the building on account of the high ceiling and the dearth of windows. She'd worn her leather jacket with fringe on the sleeves, belted over her leather skirt. All eyes were on her, and she felt ready to be in charge.

Two kerosene lamps hung over the meeting table, and Mae took a seat beneath one of them. As the seats filled at the table and around the walls of the room, the innkeeper asked if anyone wanted pie and coffee. Most ordered coffee, and about half ordered pie. "Bring in a fifth of whisky," a man said.

Not wanting food or drink, Mae stood up while people were being served. "Neighbors and friends," she asked, "has anyone *not* heard about the plan to dam the Cosumnes River?"

No hand went up.

She continued: "Mr. Charles Rogue would like us to sell our land and water rights to the Bay Cities Water Company in exchange for money and possibly an ownership piece in the company. The water is to supply San Francisco and surrounding areas. That was the plan before the earthquake. Earlier this week I wrote Mr. Rogue asking if the disaster had caused the backers to change their minds about the project."

Heads of all colors bobbed expectantly.

"This is his response." She unfolded the letter. "Keep in mind that the American-Cosumnes Water Project, known as Plan A, has already been approved in concept by San Francisco supervisors. Mr. T. is William Tevis, son of Lloyd Tevis, long time president of Wells Fargo Bank and Transportation Company. He's the main force behind the project."

The profound quiet as she read the letter allowed the muffled sounds from the kitchen to be heard. The end of it she read slowly:

> Upon receipt, I will drive out there forthwith to visit each of them about the particulars of their properties. I will answer their questions and give them copies of the option agreement.
>
>   Eagerly awaiting your reply,
>   Charles M. Rogue

Mae put the letter down and picked up a sheet of paper on which she'd made two columns: one for names, the other for location. Holding it up, she asked, "Are you ready to put your names down?"

An explosion of voices came from every part of the room. Hands went up. Mae called on Mary Granlees, sitting across the table from her.

Mary said, "I'm all for the dam. My family's been waiting two generations for something like this. Most of your parents came to California for gold, like my father. Bless his soul." She crossed herself, reminding Mae of the old man's death a couple of months ago. "They came for riches. Well folks, this is it, at long last." She looked at Mae. "How much do I get for selling them my land? I'm not putting my name on any piece of paper 'til I get that answered."

Mae replied to all: "Mr. Rogue explained to me that the amount will differ depending on the particulars of the properties, and that's the kind of question he will answer when he comes to talk to you. If you want to talk to him, put your name down. A pledge doesn't mean anything, except you'd like to do it if the particulars look good."

Peter Gaffney, sitting between his aging mother and spinster aunt, had his hand up—the Gaffneys whose barn dance Mae had forgotten about long ago. The family had come from Ireland for gold, but stayed to farm along the river where Indian Mary's old village once stood. Mae had gone there a couple of times with Mary and Chloë, and saw the contours of the missing roundhouse. Peter and brothers James and John worked the farm, none of the three married.

Mae nodded at Peter and he stood up, his head on his gaunt six-foot-six frame rising well above the height of the lanterns.

"You all know we're just upriver from the Granlees. We agree with everything Mary said. We're farmers and this is a hard life. If it's not one thing breakin' down or goin' bad, it's another. In a good year we barely make enough to keep going. As they say, we scratch with the chickens. I just wish my dad'd lived to hear this. He woulda gone for it big. I talked it over with my mother"—he gestured at old Mary Gaffney—"and my Aunt Ann, and my brothers. If the rich men in San Francisco wanna pay us for our land so we can have a good life without killing ourselves, let's get on with it. We'll sign that paper."

Mae took them the paper, pen, and ink bottle.

She let everyone with riverfront property talk first.

Charlie Ruman, from Michigan Bar, the owner of the hotel where the Duffy family had stayed their first few days in California, stood up at one end of the table. An elderly but erect man, he had come from Germany as a young man. Mae could still hear in his speech the precision of one who had learned English as an adult and had the bent of mind to attend a Business School in Sacramento.

"Thank you, Mae, for reading that letter. I also wondered if the quake and fire had stopped this dam. I'm glad to hear it's going again." He looked down the table and at the people in chairs along the wall. "Of all the landowners here, I certainly would be in the middle of this project. You Granlees and Gaffneys, and you, Mae, would be in the so-called forebay, from what I understand, with that smaller dam where the bridge is on the Allen property"—

he pointed at old Mrs. Allen, owner of the bungalow and store that Bob and Katy Irene Warren managed—"if Bay Cities builds a forebay. But whether they do or not, the main dam will back the water up behind my bridge in Michigan Bar and fill that rock canyon to the east. These men behind this project are not fools. You heard the name Tevis. I'm sure you downstream farmers can negotiate good water rights. Folks, this entire area will reap many benefits from the millions of cubic feet of water that now runs away, wasted, into the Pacific Ocean. Something intelligent is finally happening on the Cosumnes River. Of course I need the details before I sign a contract. This is just to get things started, so pass me that paper." He was reaching.

Mae walked to the end of the table and gave it to him. He signed his name with a flourish, wrote Michigan Bar beside it, and handed it back.

W. C. Sheldon was there with his son Jared. Mae called on the father, aware that her long-ago assessment was correct—Jared would be under the thumb of his father all his life. W. C. stood up and squared his shoulders. The waxed hooks of his mustache looking grand in the lamplight.

"Friends and relatives," he intoned, "I fear that this project will result in a shortage of water for the Sheldon Land Grant, and we farmers would be injured for the benefit of strangers in the San Francisco Bay region. Many others with the same worries are present. I appreciate what Charlie Ruman has said, but I want to assure all present that I will use my contacts in Sacramento to fight this project every way I can, and will continue to do so unless and until I have assurance on paper, in writing, examined and notarized by a knowledgeable lawyer to be assigned by the Governor of this state, that the downstream flow and the farms and ranches along it will not in any way be harmed by the proposed project."

A chorus of male voices rang out with, "He's right!" "Bully for W. C.!"

"Stand up and provide your names to the lady, please," Mr. Sheldon said.

Mae recorded all the names in opposition, including Mr. Sheldon's mother.

Next she called on Grandmother Catherine Sheldon Mahone Dalton, who had her hand up in spite of the fact that her son had just spoken.

"I have been authorized to speak for someone who couldn't come tonight," the lady began. "As you all know, the Wilder property is downstream in the Delta. I drove down there to explain what's happening to Elitha, my lifelong friend, and I'm speaking on her behalf and for her neighbors too, including the Desmonds and the Morses. They couldn't come either. You will recall that Elitha's husband Ben passed away in ninety-nine after a long active life in farming. Then the tragedy of her son George hit her hard just over three years ago—tried, convicted, and for all intents given a death sentence by *The Sacramento Bee*. If that atrocity of injustice had not occurred, George would be here speaking instead of me."

Mae recalled dancing with George Wilder at the magnificent Steffens' house. The article in *The Bee* after he hung himself in his barn insinuated that he was guilty of nailing the doors and windows shut and burning his wife and three children to death in their house. It hinted that he'd killed himself because he knew his story wouldn't hold up in court. Mae thought he could as well have hung himself in a melancholy after losing his wife and children, and he'd been sleeping in the barn fully clothed after a small argument with his wife. People were still talking about that tragedy. Poor Elitha, losing her son and three grandchildren, and then enduring that journalistic horror after she'd suffered so as a member of the Donner Party!

Mrs. Dalton was saying: "Elitha's remaining children and grandchildren will inherit the land that her husband and son worked so hard on, and she wants that land to have value. I want my land to have value. The river we all depend on must not be diverted while we dry up.

"Here's a cautionary tale." The tough old pioneer lady turned her blazing eyes around the room. "Just last year the farmers along the Owens River, south of us, were sweet-talked into a project like this to supply water to Los Angeles. They were promised benefits from the dam, assurance of a good water supply in the summer; but my son Ed just found out that the fat cats are buying up land in the San Fernando Valley, because that's where the water will go so thousands of houses can be built, and the farmers were hoodwinked into signing on to a project that will surely dry up their river within a few years and make farming impossible. Their land will have no value."

That story stunned Mae. The lady's son, Ed Dalton, was an investor himself. He knew what the captains of finance were up to.

Fred Grimshaw, normally a friend of progress, did not raise his hand to speak. Henry Schneider, another landowner with river frontage, listened and did not speak.

Lastly, she called on those who did not own riverfront property, including Mr. Long, the landlord of the house where Mae had briefly lived. He and the others were all for progress. They looked forward to a lake, resort hotels, better roads, and electricity from the hydroelectric plant. But the cautionary tale had put a pall over their words, and they spoke quickly.

Mae thanked everyone for coming, and invited people to sign their names on the way out.

"I didn't see the Dunaway name on top of that list," a man called. "You buying in?"

She hadn't spoken for herself. Nor had she invited the woman whose stake in the river went back thousands of years.

"Mr. Rogue already knows we're interested," she told the people waiting to hear her reply. "We'll make our final decision up at summer pasture. Meantime, I'll send Mr. Rogue this list in the morning mail." She waved the paper. "I imagine he'll contact you stockmen before you leave for the mountains."

92

Summer in the mountains was the highlight of everyone's year. The Indians felt the same way, having a tradition of leaving the hot valley to enjoy the cooler heights.

The gray carpet of sheep with a dull red D on every back moved through the tall pines following the tinkling bells of the lead sheep. The constant baa-baa of four hundred sheep and over a hundred lambs was a murmur so familiar as to be unheard, and somewhere beneath all those cloven hooves was a narrow, dusty road. Mae kept her neckerchief over nose and mouth against the dust, though the worst of it was behind them. She and John rode the two flanks to keep the flock from spreading out. Billy rode point—out in front showing the lead sheep where to go.

Mae galloped to the front, past Billy, to check on the little boys in the aging surrey, now with wooden sides to hold the tents, bedding, clothing, pots and pans, tinware, dry goods, guns, ammunition and fishing poles. The milch cow plodded behind on a tether. The little boys, she saw, were not missing her. They screamed with laughter as they scrambled back and forth from the baggage to the front seat. Emmett ducked into Indian Mary's lap and then into Chloë's, safe from the monster Johnny was pretending to be. Then he burst out and made another scramble over the boxes in the back.

Assured that the boys were all right, Mae turned Pal and trotted back to her position at the mid-right flank, waving to Alice, who sat next to Anne, the teacher she loved. Alice, Anne and Bert Granless fit tightly on the buckboard of the white-top that Bert had borrowed from his mother. He drove behind the flock giving whistle signals to the dogs. Alice waved back at Mae. All the children were happy.

Tom Jaimeson walked alongside the white-top helping to keep the tired ewes and exhausted lambs moving. Neither he nor his three brothers had ever married. Mae understood better than most people the difficulties faced by Indian men in the matter of women, but they weren't the only brothers showing no signs of courting women—Sheldons, Gaffneys, Huots, three brothers per family, appeared to be headed for bachelorhood. Thirteen men in a small community seemed a high percentage.

Seven days in the dust had given the sheep red eye. They wanted to browse the slender clumps of tall grass, different from the home kind. The lambs bleated and kept trying to lie down. As the mountain steepened before them, Mae worked ever harder to keep the big flock moving. This was the last and most difficult part of the drive.

Yesterday afternoon, six miles back, they had pitched their tents in the big trees at Silver Lake, near Caminetti's Resort, a small inn with a dining room, stage stop, post office, and store owned by a famous congressman, now an older man said to be availing himself of the invigorating atmosphere in his declining years. The sheep had lined the shore to drink from the pure lake water, and then man and beast alike had lain down in the pine-scented air. Fishermen always camped in that area, and it had been pleasant seeing their rowboats bob on the water—a lake destined to become part of the Bay Cities water project, along with Twin Lakes up beyond Kirkwood's resort.

The Caminettis had good news: The Kirkwoods had opened the road, which meant they'd driven their big herd of cattle through the snowbank that was slow to melt on the cold north side of Carson Spur. Ah Chung had been one of the Chinese workers who chipped those dangerous curves out of solid rock back in sixty-two. Now he was taking care of the home ranch in Mae and John's absence.

The Spur would be open to sheep unless an avalanche blocked the road again, as could happen in June. Dangerous as that section of road was, it cut off about a thousand vertical feet from the old Emigrant Road that went up through Plasse's Resort, along the ridge east of Silver Lake, past Round Top at about 10–11,000 feet of elevation, and over to Carson Pass.

This was June 22. They had left on June 15—late due to a cool spell.

Sheared in late February when the price of wool went up, the Dunaway sheep had enough new wool to keep them warm during a normal mountain summer. The timing was always tricky. The price of wool dictated the shearing schedule, but care had to be taken so that a cold spell in the mountains wouldn't decimate the flock. Some years ago, a famous freeze had killed off the entire flocks of Mr. Miller and Mr. Cothrin up in their Emerald Bay pasture at Lake Tahoe. Not one sheep survived, and the feet of one of their Indian herders had frozen so badly that the tendons shrank and his toes stuck straight up for the rest of his life. Mrs. Cothrin had told Mae about that—he was the husband of the Indian midwife who had birthed Billy.

John signaled Mae to pull back. She'd been watching for that. It meant he could see the Spur ahead, with its straight drop into depths so far below as not to be seen. Everyone knew the story about a man being bucked off his horse there. Horse and rider went over the edge and their remains had never been found. John and Mae turned their horses around, to join Bert and Ann.

The nearly vertical wall of rock on the right side of the road and the sheer drop on the left would keep the sheep funneled, Mae hoped—unless a rockslide or avalanche from above frightened them over the precipice. So far that hadn't happened to any sheep since John and Mae went into the stock business. She waited while the elongated flock made its way around the tight curves. By now Isabella would be driving the surrey into Zachariah Kirkwood's valley.

☙

Even the tired ewes in the back of the flock put their heads up and moved faster as they approached their green summer home. And when Mae rounded the curve where the pines opened to the horseshoe-shaped meadow beneath snow-capped mountains, she felt a thrill and a deep satisfaction.

The sheep bucked and kicked their heels in joy as they entered Mr. Kirk-wood's lush meadow. Mae dismounted and knelt beside the cold stream to wash her face. She dunked the gritty neckerchief and smiled to see John with his legs splayed wide, throwing water over his head. The noonday was warm, the air thin and dry, the sunshine welcome—not the torture it became every summer in the foothills and Sacramento Valley.

Mae walked into the meadow until the angle was right and she could see the surrey stopped in front of the Kirkwoods' saloon—a log cabin attached to a two-story frame inn. The log barn stood a short distance up the road, the milk house on the meadow side of the road—all rustic and welcoming. The air alone would be enough reason to summer here, but by some mysterious alchemy, grazing sheep in the mountain meadows increased the wool clip by a pound and half per head—six-hundred pounds of extra wool—and as a bonus the higher rate of twinning brought a substantial annual increase in the size of the flock.

Cattle put on more weight and gave more milk too. Each summer the Gaffneys drove dairy cows and hogs to a meadow near the Rubicon River, and camped beside a low-roofed icehouse made of logs—filled with blocks of ice the previous February. Their cows produced large quantities of milk, which the Gaffneys churned into butter and stored in the icehouse. The hogs lapped up the buttermilk, and the family returned home in the fall with an enhanced supply of butter to sell in Sacramento.

John came up from behind and put an arm around Mae. They gazed at the mountain peaks, white against the blue sky. Pal and Mack, still saddled, were tearing into the lush grass. They let them graze for a while before rid-ing them over to the saloon.

∽

"Mommy! Mommy!" Emmett and Johnny cried, running toward her from the surrey as she and John dismounted and tied the horses.

"You boys act like you haven't seen me all day," Mae teased. "Do you re-member this place, Emmett?" Of course he wouldn't.

He slowly raised his chin up and down, fibbing.

Waving thanks to the three generations of Indian women—their big baskets already removed from the surrey—Mae smiled as she led the little boys into the dark, low-ceiling saloon. A rock fireplace on the left wall heated the room on cold nights. At a table by the fireplace, several children and a man were playing cards with Elva Kirkwood, the owner's daughter. On the right side of the room a couple of drovers stood tossing back whisky at the bar—boots ragged, shirts grimy, faces creased with smiles. John and Mae joined them.

Zachariah Kirkwood, the rugged pioneer who had proved up on this resort, in addition to his ranch in Jackson, came through the door from the kitchen lean-to along the back side of the saloon.

"John, Mae!" he said with obvious delight, slapping John's shoulder. "How was the drive up?"

"No excitement at all," John said.

"Good!" Zack slapped him again. "Wanna red-eye?"

"Just water now. We gotta get settled and unpack somewhere. Our sheep are in the meadow across the road, temporary. If you're not askin' too much we'd like to lease it for the summer. I didn't see 'em, but I know you got your cattle on that grass. Got room for our woollies over there too?"

"How many?" The older man went to the front window to look.

"Not countin' the spring lambs, four hundred thirty-four."

"Well, let's see, that's prime over there. It'd cost you nine dollars a month. But nobody's camped in the place you had last year. As you know the Forest Service owns it, so it won't cost you nothin'. They still don't bother about four hundred sheep. It's the flocks of five, six thousand they're trying to keep movin' through."

"Thanks Zack. Thought I might as well ask. We'll go where we were last year."

"The inn's fillin' up, case you was plannin' to stay there," Zack added.

"Thanks, but we like our tents."

⟿

Darkness fell quickly in the mountains and wolves howled not too far away. The drovers down in the saloon mimicked their long cries. Inside the square canvas tent with crates along the walls, Mae slipped into her nightshirt. The food boxes, rigged for pulleys, hung in the high pines about forty yards from the tents. That protected the camp from bears and wolves. The smell of bacon lured such predators, so she also hoisted her skillet up a tree, wiped clean of grease.

The bacon-fried trout that they'd had for supper would be their fare twice a day for the next two months, and they never tired of it. Nor did Billy, Bert, John and Johnny tire of flicking their hooks into the cold stream and hauling out fish. It had taken the four of them only a half hour to catch grasshoppers for bait and come back with full creels.

"Listen to them wolves," John said as he lay down on their feather mattresses, three pushed together. "I'm glad Jeff's a good shot with a rifle. That Indian has the patience of Job. Sits like a rock 'til he's got a perfect shot."

John always worried about the sheep. Mae snuggled against him and pulled up the covers. On her other side Emmett slept. Not a sound came from the adjacent tent where Billy, Alice, and Johnny had their featherbeds. Mary, Isabella, and Chloë were camped with the Washoe Indians near the ice caves. Over the years they'd made friends with the Washoe, mostly women and children, who came up to the high mountains from around Woodfords and Markleeville. Chloë wanted to observe their basket weaving again this summer. They used the small red willows that grew along the streams of the high meadows.

For privacy, Bert and Anne had pitched their tent a little distance from the Dunaways. Bert was handy with a gun, too, and would spell Jeff in the night. Mae had somewhat expected that they'd go with the Granlees clan to their Union Valley meadow where that family had a cabin. Polly and Jack were there, having Joe Pratt to watch over the home place and feed Polly's turkeys. Polly once told Mae that the only time she and Mary Granlees got along was in the mountains. Mae had heard similar things from other families. The mysterious alchemy that benefited the stock soothed the human nervous system.

"Well John," she said with a comfortable sigh, "we're here, all in one piece."

"Yup." He slid an arm under her head. "Feels good, don't it?"

"Sure does." After a friendly silence she said, "This might sound strange to you, but I like the drive up. I really do. I like being one of the drovers."

"Once we git goin', it feels good to me too. Nuthin' to do but keep on movin'. I'm a son-of-a-bitch getting us ready," John admitted, "what with the shearin', dippin', plantin', all the figgerin' an' packin'. But Mae, I gotta say thanks for your part in it. After a long day I see you cookin'. You're like two men on the drive, cook and drover. I couldn't ask for better help."

"You ever read the Bible, after Jacob tricks his father and gets the blessing meant for Esau?" She'd been amusing herself thinking about it.

"Can't say as I recall that, but my grandma used to read aloud from the Bible when we was a passel of small-fry."

"Well, you see, Jacob goes on some big drives and it reminds me of us. He drives his herds a long way to the place of a rich man who promises his daughter's hand in marriage, if Jacob works for him for seven years. The man tricks him and Jacob has to stay and work fourteen years, because he has to marry the older daughter first before he can get the hand of the younger one. Well it sounds like they both have babies and so do the maid-servants. The herds and flocks get bigger too. But then Jacob wants to go home to his father, so he moves his tents. That means he packs up all his gear, folds his tents, and takes his many sons and daughters and—near as I can recall these are the Bible's words—he takes his man-servants and maid-servants, his herds and flocks, his he-camels and his she-camels, and his he-goats and she-goats, and he takes his he-asses and she-asses." Struggling to suppress giggles, she could scarcely get the last out.

John snickered too, both of them trying not to wake Emmett.

"Who are our he-asses?" he asked.

"Well, hmm." She loved it that he got her humor. "We don't have any asses, hes or shes. Otherwise I wouldn't like the drive. Our children like the drive too—even Alice, now that Anne King is with us. Mary and Chlöe love it too. I'm so glad Isabella came this year. I think she's finally getting over the rough stretches in her past."

John never talked about that.

The moon through the long-needled pine branches made a pretty sight on the canvas.

"John," Mae said, enjoying the feel of him, "you work too hard most of the year. Especially this year, what with getting the new corrals made at the Rudnicki place, but I love seeing you relax up here." She smiled into the filtered moonlight. "It was nice watching you heading out to fish with the boys scampering behind with their poles."

A wolf hit a high C and held it a long time before the slow glissando downward. That seemed to prompt the drovers down at the saloon to start a new song: "Oh give me a home, where the buffalo roam..." Their voices sounded strong and good in the distance, men harmonizing and taking pride in their singing.

John spoke quietly. "I been thinkin' on what Mrs. Dalton said at your meetin'. We oughta listen to Ed Dalton. He's a smart man, and he's been buyin' properties all over the place 'an talkin' to them that knows about things like this. He must'ov looked into the deals of those farmers along the Owens River and seen they wasn't protected. Them tycoons pro'bly laughed at the hillbillies when they got back to their offices. They figger farmers doan know sic 'em."

On the seven nights camping on the road Mae and John had talked about it off an on, starting back at Wait's Station; but they talked carefully, neither wanting to influence the other unduly until their minds were made up. Now Mae sensed that he was ready to talk, and she needed to tell him what had been on her mind.

"I haven't said this to you, John, but ever since I first heard of it, I've been realizing at every turn what a good life we have. I never imagined I'd ever be so happy. And just look at us up here, looking forward to the summer. The children so happy."

John turned toward her and put his other arm around her. "Do you mean it, Mae? You're really happy with me and the way we live?"

"Yes, very much so. Are you?"

"It's all I ever wanted," he said, "you and the kids and the place. As my granddad used to say, I'm purrin' like a blind cat in a creamery. 'Cause, you see, I kinda wondered if you was wishin' you'd married that Rogue fella."

"Oh no!" She gave him a full-length hug, snuggling into him. "You're the man I want. I'm very lucky to have you."

He took a deep breath and after a quiet minute said, "A man hadn't oughta gamble with some'um he can't afford to lose."

"You mean our place?"

"Yup."

"It is a gamble, isn't it?"

"Sure is."

"I was thinking about that too," Mae said. "We don't know what we'd get paid for it, and even if we got plenty we don't know if we could buy another place with ground as good as ours is now. We'd have to find a place along some river or year-round stream. Maybe too far from a stage road. Maybe we couldn't build another house as good as the one we've got, without a lot of extra work. And I doubt we'd find a community with a school, a store, a dance hall, stage-stop, good friends for the children, and picnics. And Mary, Chloë and Isabella! I think it'd about kill them to see their ancient place go under water. Maybe they'd come with us, but I doubt it. I need them, John, and I couldn't stand to see old Mary made homeless at this stage of her life. And look at us up here! Billy having the time of his life. The fun and companionship. It's like we've got two perfect places on both ends of a long dusty string. You're right. I don't want to gamble with it either."

His warm breath came through her hair. "I'm glad we agree."

"The only thing I worry about," she said in his embrace, "is you working too hard. You can't keep that up forever. Do you think you might be sorry some day for passing up a chance to retire with money when you're older?"

He spoke quietly in the moonlit tent. "Mae, I got a lotta time ahead of me. And good men to help with the farm. Got the Rudnicki place purtineer free. We'll pick up other ground that people can't afford. Some day I'll have enough for all our sons to work their own land, and when I get freed up a little I'll dig south of the river where that gold vein could be. That's how I see myself gettin' old. Jes' workin' as long as I can, with the boys takin' over more as time goes by. And when I die, mebbe one of 'em'll keep the place going. It just don't set right to clean up good ground like we done, and then turn around and put it under water and concrete."

"You really do love farming, don't you?"

"I never knew nuthin' else. There's a feelin' of working with nature, shiftin' when nature shifts. Understanding the soil. A farmer figgers things out. Nobody tells us what to do. Mebbe someday we'll change to cattle, if the price of beef keeps goin' up. That'd be some'um new." He chuckled a little in his throat and continued, winding down like the long day. "Ever year we're savin' more money, so if we don't got a real vein of gold but just little bits of it sprinkled around from the floods, that's all right. We'll do good with our crops and stock. I jes' wanna keep doin' what I'm doin'. If that's how you want it."

"It is. And I believe you when you say you'll keep saving money. You have a gift for growing things—crops, vegetables, herd animals, and children. We started out lucky, with that gold cache and all, and we've got the best house anywhere around." She chuckled. "It'll last longer than we will. What I mean to say is, I'll love growing old with you the way you paint it. The only question is, how would it be for us if we get forced out by that law Charlie's workin' on?"

"I been thinkin' on that too. I gotta a hunch that law could be stopped. Can you imagine how the farmers of this state would yell to hear of government takin' on the right to steal people's land and water? Why the hatred'ed come burnin' right out through their buttonholes and those lawmakers'd need to get under cover real quick. I'd march to Sacramento and do my part. Americans won't put up with that."

"So you're willing to say no thanks to the money from the tycoons and take a risk on the other?"

"Yup."

"So am I, John." She released a sigh to have the decision made. "Now we are of a like mind."

It was so quiet Mae could hear the creek's lively babble beyond the children's tent. She also heard a smile in John's whisper as he leaned over her. "Are we of a like mind?"

Wanting him, she moved his way, leaving Emmett fast asleep on his own narrow mattress.

93

The next morning Jeff Jaimeson milked the cow and brought the bucket of warm milk to the circle of tents. Mae stirred up hotcake batter and opened a jar of plum preserves while John and Bert and the boys caught trout. After breakfast John and the children rode the horses to a meadow of grass and wildflowers where the sheep were. They planned to spend the day there with Bert. Mae hoisted the skillet into the tree, and then sat down at the little table in the tent and wrote:

Mr. Charles Rogue
Capitol Building
Sacramento, California
Office of the Speaker Pro Tem

Dear Charlie,
John and I will not be participating in the Bay Cities project. We are happy on our land and doing well. We do not want to gamble with that.
Sincerely,
Mae Dunaway
c/o Kirkwood Inn
Round Top Station on Amador-Nevada Road

Sealing the envelope, Mae walked by Anne and Bert's tent before heading down to the Inn to post the letter. Anne was hanging a blanket over a tent rope. The small woman turned around as Mae approached, her dark hair pinned up.

"Wanna walk down to the Inn with me?" Mae asked, looking forward to getting to know this Stanford graduate better.

"I'd like that. I'll get my hat."

Together they swung down the fairly steep hill, Mae in her culottes, as Polly called them. They both wore boots, Mae's soft from years of wear, Ann's being broken in. She'd been limping on the drive.

Mae hoped Anne wouldn't be upset by the news. "John and I decided not to sell out to the Bay Cities Company. I'm telling Mr. Rogue in this letter."

"Bert will be disappointed." Anne said, dropping behind as the path narrowed.

Bert had been angling to acquire the twelve-acre ground owned by Vyries Brown, an elderly man on the opposite side of the river from the John and Mae. Bert was the cowboy of the Granlees family, a likeable sort with a gambling streak—good at breaking horses and enthusiastic about the idea of buying cheap land and selling it dear.

"I know he'll think we're stick-in-the-muds," Mae said, "but we have to be true to ourselves. We cleaned up that land, and we want the place to be there for our boys." Mae considered mentioning the possibility of losing it to Charlie's law, but thought it better to let that sleeping dog lie for now. If it came to that, John was right. The whole countryside would stand up and fight together.

The snowy mountains flashed in and out of the pines, and Mae watched her footing as she stepped over rocks and roots, and on dry pine needles that made the downhill path slippery. After a while Anne spoke.

"I'm not one to argue against people being true to themselves."

As far a Mae could tell, Bert loved Anne deeply, as only a teenaged man with a somewhat reckless heart could love. But Mae had heard an occasional discouraging word, as the popular song called it, from the Granlees' tent on the drive up the mountains. In addition, she'd heard retching, especially this morning while the trout were frying. Pregnancy could cause marital discord, Mae knew. Bert would have preferred to ride horseback on the way up, but for his bride's sake borrowed the white-top. It was now coming into sight, parked alongside the log barn.

"Feet feeling any better?" Mae asked.

"Nope. Walking downhill sure hits the sore spots."

As they passed by the barn, Mae kept her eyes averted from a man coming out the door picking hay from his hair, obviously a drover just waking up. The singing had gone on a long time last night. Tonight, when she and John wouldn't be so tired, Mae looked forward to joining them. People brought guitars and mouth organs, and last year she'd loved sitting with John on the porch of the saloon singing the old songs to the moon. Social barriers broke down in the mountains—ranchers, their wives and daughters, drovers, hired girls, people of all ages, and the Kirkwoods were like one big family.

Mae and Anne angled into the saloon. Dimly lit as usual, the log walls were steeped in the smell of tobacco smoke. Zachariah was cleaning up from last night.

"Got a letter to post," Mae told him. "Did I miss the Sacramento stage?"

"No, it leaves Woodfords at eight and won't be here 'til noon. Just put it there on that whatnot table by the door. I'll stamp it in."

"Thanks."

Elva Kirkwood was wiping down the far end of the bar. Anne went down there and sat on a barstool. The two began talking. Mae opened the heavy door to the bright morning and sat on one of the porch chairs watching the horses graze in the meadow across the road, a pretty sight under the high mountains and Red Cliffs on the left—not as high but straight up and interesting in their own way.

"Can I bring you a cup of coffee?" Zack stuck his head out the door to ask, releasing the sudden smell of bacon.

"Yes, thank you." The hired girl was starting a second round of breakfast.

Along the covered porch came a man looking too clean for a drover. His fine boots looked almost new. He glanced at her as he opened the saloon door and entered—dark skin, straight black hair cut short, perhaps Mexican.

A bit later Mr. Kirkwood came outside with Mae's coffee, and as he opened the door to go back inside, the dark-skinned man came out and sat in the next chair.

"You Mae Dunaway?" he asked without a trace of Mexican accent.

"Yes." People up here tended to know everyone else, so that didn't surprise her. But she couldn't place him. "Do you come up here often?"

"Most summers. I'm Raul Martinez. I do trick ridin' and such."

"Oh yes. Now I remember. I didn't meet you last summer, but my son Billy couldn't stop talking about you." She laughed at the memory. "For a while I was afraid he wouldn't go to school when we got home. All he wanted to do was learn to ride like you and practice your rope tricks."

"If he wants, I'll teach him."

"Oh, Mr. Martinez, thank you! He'll be in heaven. You stayin' at the inn?"

"Came in late yesterday with a herd, and wanted to sleep like a civilized man for a change." He laughed a little. "I'll be scoutin' out a campsite today."

"Well then, where can Billy find you?"

"Isabella will know."

Isabella! "You mean Isabella from near my place?"

"Yes. That nice lady with a daughter." Raul appeared to be about Isabella's age, both of them verging on being old. People in the last years of their full strength.

"This is her first year up here," Mae said. "When did you meet her?"

"Last night. I went to the Washoe camp lookin' for a friend, and met her instead. We got to talkin' and I found out she's his sister."

Mae almost dropped her coffee. Her hand shook and the cup rattled as she put it on the saucer in her lap. Raul was looking at her, suddenly appearing to be pure California Indian. His clothes and boots had fooled her, but his soft brown features gave him away.

"Do you know where big Billy is?"

His black eyes did a half-turn and came back to her with new knowledge.

She shouldn't have said *big Billy*. He would assume Billy was her son's father. Or maybe he already knew everything.

"I think he's in Mexico," Raul said.

Just where Mae thought he'd go.

"Got himself a Chinese wife down there," Raul said.

Chinese! She couldn't have guessed. She was questioning him closely and that felt rude with a stranger, particularly an Indian, but she couldn't stop. "How do you happen to know him?"

"Well, let's see. Mebbe ten, twelve years ago. He was looking for work in Railroad Flat. I was campin' on the road and he stayed the night with me. I told him there was good work driving cattle. He sounded interested. I thought I'd see him after that, but he never came up 'til last summer."

"I was up here last summer and didn't see him."

"He was a drover for a rancher with summer pasture around Ebbett's Pass. He found an Indian to take his place on the drive back to Stockton, and he came north through here before heading down the mountains. Had half his pay and no horse. The Indians up near Ebbett's must'a told him his mother was here. He was sorry to miss her. You left about a week before he got here."

Raul searched Mae's expression.

"He didn't follow us," she said, knowing it would have been easy for Billy to catch up to the flock, even without a horse. But maybe he'd gone around them and waited in his mother's cabin.

Politely, Raul didn't ask about Mae's interest in Billy.

She took a deep breath. "Is he happy?"

"Seems like it."

"Does he have children?"

"One or two." He stood up to leave.

"But why would he come all this way from Mexico to drive a man's cattle to the mountains?"

"Dunno. Mebbe already up here for some reason and needed money for the trip back. Sorry, gotta go now."

"Why did you think he'd be up here this year?" Now this really *was* rude.

"Jes' had a loco idea he might be."

"Sorry to be asking so many questions."

He shrugged, cocked a hand good-bye, and returned to the saloon, perhaps for breakfast.

Most Central Valley cattlemen started the drive to summer pasture in late May or early June. Billy could have been in Sacramento in May last year, when Oberon was killed. But surely he wouldn't risk coming all the way up from Mexico to kill Oberon. That would be foolhardy and dangerous. It'd be a risk for his family. And he wasn't that kind of man. At least she didn't think he was. But she admitted to herself that she wanted to think he'd done the deed.

Mae made an excuse to Ann, who by then was playing cards with Elva. Then she walked swiftly past the barn toward the Indian camp. She made her way uphill to the hodgepodge of windbreaks formed by blankets tied to poles and anchored on the tough little bushes on the ground. A couple of dogs slept in the sun. Chloë was there with a heavyset woman who wore a scarf tied around her head and a black dress similar to Indian Mary's. Basket-making materials were laid out before them.

As Mae approached, a dog got up and growled. The older woman looked up with a flat expression, her fleshy brown cheeks almost hiding her nose.

"I'm sorry to disturb you," Mae said, not taking another step. "Chloë, do you know where your grandmother is?"

"With Mother, over there." Chloë pointed up the trail leading to Twin Lakes. "They wanna see if the marsh grass is good now."

Mae hurried up the path, which led across the road. When she'd gone a ways along the base of the steep mountain—the other side of Red Cliffs—she saw two women up to their knees in the marshy edge of the nearest lake. With skirts folded up and tucked into the waistbands of their skirts, they were bent over the grasses around them. The big woman put some grass in the gathering basket on her back, the strap over her forehead. Indian Mary.

Mae walked as far as she could before she removed her boots, folded her culottes up, and belted the hems around her waist. She waded out to them with cold mud squishing through her toes. They turned and watched her slog through the sea of grass toward them.

"The boys okay?" Isabella asked in a worried way when Mae arrived.

"Yes, everyone's fine." She paused before saying, "I just talked to Raul."

Isabella looked down, and Mary gazed toward the distant end of the lake.

"He said Billy was here last summer."

They know. He must have been at the cabin when John drove them home. Almost a year had gone by and they hadn't said a thing. She tried not to feel hurt, reminding herself that Indians were good at keeping secrets.

They stood in a circle of three amidst a thousand spikes of reddish green grass. A breeze had kicked up a little, ruffling the water that had been glassy, and smears of white cloud marred the blue sky between the mountains.

"Why didn't you tell me?"

"Billy didn't want us to," Isabella said. After a silence, she added, "He was happy you have a good house and a good man, and mebbe he didn't want you feelin', uh, bad to know about him."

"Did you tell him he's not a murderer?"

They stood looking at her shoulder, her bunched-up culottes, and the hand shading her eyes, but they didn't answer.

Maybe it was no longer true.

"He has a wife and children in Mexico," Mae said to change the subject.

"Ho!" Mary said, Isabella nodding energetically.

"That's good," Mae said. "I'm glad he's happy." She was starting to shiver. "Do you mind if we get out of this water? I'm getting cold all over and I have something else we need to talk about." Now was as good a time as any to tell them about the dam.

Stepping carefully out of the marsh, Indian Mary led the way along the lake path at the base of the pine-covered mountain. Soon they came to a group of large granite boulders at the lake's edge. Several of them had nearly flat surfaces which the sun had made warm to the touch. They untied their skirts. Mae stretched out on a boulder and let the breeze skim over her as the stored up heat in the stone infused her with warmth. Old Mary lay down on a boulder, too, and Isabella sat on another one facing the sun.

Mae drew a deep breath and said, "Powerful men in San Francisco want to dam our river. Our farm and Mary Granlees' place and the Gaffney's place would be under water. And your people's old home place."

"Dam river?" Mary asked.

"Yes. Stop up the river with rock and dirt and concrete so it can't run."

It was strange talking about this with her eyes closed against the sun and a straw hat over her face. She lifted her hat and saw that neither of them had moved.

"The place is yours," Isabella broke the silence to say. "You and John can say no. You doan want your house underwater, do you?"

"No, but I'm afraid they can do it even if we say no. They have a lot of money."

There was a longer silence followed by low talk in the Indian language. Then Mary's voice. "Why those men wanna stop river?"

"They wanna pipe the water to the San Francisco area."

After another silence, Mary and Isabella spoke back and forth. Then Mary's voice came low and sorrowful. "Them people in San Francisco, they got no water? No water for drink and cookin'?"

"There's water in San Francisco now. The broken pipes are fixed, but the men who want to build the dam want millions more people to go and live around there. They would need plenty of water."

"My house be under water?" Indian Mary asked.

"I think the dam would be where the bridge is now."

Each thing Mae said was followed by silence.

"Ah, mebbe no water bym house."

"Some of the time water would come through a hole in the dam, but maybe not as much as before. The men will control the water. Turn off the flow, or let it run, whatever they want."

There was a rustling. Mae lifted her hat to see Mary, who had to be about seventy-five years old, rolling to her side and taking her time pushing into a sitting position. She scooted over and nested her behind in a scooped-out side of her boulder. There she faced the grass and water, and her callused toes hung three feet above the lapping water.

"My people live bym water," she said. "Your people live bym water. All peoples live bym water." She continued softly as though to herself: "River spirit good to my people long time. Sometime she big. People go way. Sometime she little. People dig holes for water come in. People talk nice to river. Be good to river. River be good to people. Tell white man…"

She spoke to Isabella, and the two talked for some time.

The warmth-giving boulder didn't feel hard on Mae's back. It relaxed her, and if it were not for this tense discussion, she would have taken a nap.

Isabella's voice: "Ma says, white men and China men cut the hills down and put the dirt in the river. The water was bad to drink. No fish lived in it no more. Sticky mud on banks and no animals lived there. No deer to hunt. Our people starved to death and many, many died. For long time the water had lots'a dirt in it. Then the men stopped washing the hills away and now the river's not so muddy. When the rains come it washes itself out. Every year more dirt goes to the ocean. Lots'a water runnin' in the river is good. The river spirit's more happy now. Mebbe salmon'll come back bymbye. If those men dam up the river, the spirit will get mad. She wants to be free. Mud will pile up behind the dam, and water will rise up and spill over. If white men don't stop hurting the river, it will kill them. Kill everybody."

Mae sat up and looked at Isabella, her slender frame and lack of flesh causing her face to be more wrinkled than her mother's. It was hard to tell if she believed in the river spirit.

"Tell those white men," Isabella finished, "people oughta go live where the water is already there."

It did seem ridiculously simple.

But Mae didn't want them to think white men were complete idiots. She tried to explain more carefully. "They want to make a lake to save water for when the new people build their houses. Then all those thousands and millions of new people will pay those men for the water. They will pay for maybe hundreds of years."

After the usual silence, soft chuckles came from old Mary as she gazed over the marsh. "That way white man get rich. Tricky like Old Man Coyote," she said.

"That's right." Mae added, "and the richer they get, the trickier they are."

"This rock," Mary said patting the granite beneath her, "someday he be sand."

That odd comment brought to mind a poem that Mae had been required to memorize in school. It was about a traveler in Egypt finding a sculpture of a colossal pair of legs in a vast and level desert of sand. Nearby, half buried in sand, was a shattered face with the sneer of command still intact. On the pedestal the mocking words:

> 'My name is Ozymandias, king of kings:
> Look on my works, ye Mighty, and despair!'

Mary meant that the dam would crumble someday.

94

Coyote has a wolfish human look. "You say rich men are tricky. Poor fellas can be tricky too, and have more need to be. Don't forget where Man got his cunning."

"I know," Mae says. "From you, The Trickster. But don't you think people could be trained to be kind and thoughtful towards each other?"

Suddenly, He-lé-jah and Mother Grizzly, his first wife, come walking down the path toward us. The cat's eyes shine like suns and his tail sways with his precise gait. At his side, the luxurious fur of the strongest fighter on earth ripples with each step, bespeaking her good health and underlying fat.

"Where are you going?" I ask, delighted to see her again.

"Seeing my old haunts," O-se-mai-ti says. "It was a long walk from Montana."

Lagging behind where the Gaffney house once stood, two bear cubs bat at the bees buzzing the pink roses that twine up the mulberry tree. Hearing their mother's huff, they romp after her like furry bouncing balls.

From a branch of a live oak Raccoon watches her husband and his first wife approach. Several pairs of shiny eyes peer out on all sides of her.

O-se-mai-ti sniffs a tire of the motorcar and then, at a respectful distance, Mae.

Coyote stays low, witnessing the fact that Mother Grizzly is not extinct as he claimed she was. In her day she was the hy-apo of the Animal People, and Coyote behaved well around her.

I introduce Bear to Mae, and I see that Mae is honored to meet her.

"We were talking about human nature," I explain to the newcomers, "and I think Mae was about to say something."

"Go ahead and finish," says O-se-mai-ti. "We are always interested in people."

Wistfully Mae says, "We used to talk about changing the world for the better. We believed in that. People thought they could create societies without evil, where people would be fair and truthful. And there would be no more war."

Coyote yodels in derision.

Mother Grizzly states, "People will always fight to protect their young."

Raccoon agrees. She is also a brave fighter.

"I mean war where thousands of men fight against each other," Mae clarifies.

"Like when Howchia's son fought the Españoles," O-se-mai-ti recalls. "Indios fled the missions by the hundreds to a good hiding place, knowing the soldiers would follow and try to force them back. Two thousand men with bows defeated that enemy. After that, the soldiers left the People alone in their villages. Others attacked them, but not government troops."

Mae sighs. "I supposed most soldiers believe they are fighting to protect their families. Like in that trumped-up European 'war to end all wars'." Her voice drops so low I can scarcely hear it. "My son Billy was killed over there."

We let the silence swallow that. Then Coyote asks, "Do you really believe it's possible to end war?"

"I'm sorry to say I don't believe that any more. Those were good people, though, the ones who used to think that way."

"First get smart, then life is good," The Trickster says.

Now I am curious. "Mae," I ask, "do you still believe we're on a thin crust of earth with fires below? Limbo, I think you call it."

"You're mixing that up with hell," she says. "This is limbo, where I am now—a waiting place, a vestibule of hell. You see, God hasn't judged me yet. The sinners in hell have been judged and they're down there being punished in the everlasting fires. I've seen pictures of hundreds of them boiling in big pots, trying to climb out while the devil pokes them back in with his pitchfork."

One of Coyote's eyebrows peaks. "How many devils are down there?"

"One," Mae says, "but he's supposed to be very powerful, maybe with helpers."

"The bad people wouldn't stay there," Coyote says. "Most of them are clever schemers, and if they've been collecting down there since the beginning of Man there'd be a big swarm of them by now. Quite a bunch from this place alone. They'd put their heads together and figure a way to ambush that devil and throw him in his own pot to stew. Stick him with his own pitchfork."

His merry warble echoes through the oak-strewn hills.

"That is a strange story," I am thinking aloud, "like a tale invented by a grandmother to make children behave. Earth is strong and good, Mae, not a hollow cavity full of bad people and devils. My taproot goes straight down, farther than my height above ground ever was. My roots sip cold water down there, and Earth holds me firmly. That water is never warm even when the surface scorches in the sun. Earth mother gives us power. But when we die we should leave our mother and let our spirit fly to the land of dancing deer, or the ocean to glide in a whale, or up in the clouds. My people had different stories, but those places were all restful. Now, borers and beetles have made too many tunnels in me, so soon I will die again. This time I will not look back."

"Don't you believe evil people ought to be punished?" Mae asks.

"They're punished, but I don't care where or when. And I doubt that anyone, or any spirit, could judge all the dying people and separate the good ones from the bad. We all have good and bad stretches in our lives. Isabella for instance. And Chloë needed more time than most for her spirit helper to find her. I don't think they should burn in fire for all time."

"I don't either," Mae says.

Raccoon breaks in, "Are good people the ones that are nice to animals?"

Coyote barks a loud Hah! "If that's the distinction, all people should go to hell. Just look what they've done to coyotes!"

I ask Mae, "Do you still believe you could go to hell?"

I see a smile pushing at her shut lips. "Well," she finally says, "maybe God won't open that trap door under me, but I sure hope he did it to Oberon!"

We all laugh, and it shakes out the memory of my son in Mission San Jose. "Indian people were interested in your devil," I tell Mae. "Many of them went to the missions to learn more about him."

For some reason Mae thinks that's funny. When she stops chuckling I say to her, "We will dance with the deer, you and I. We will go to the campfires of the spirit people and see our old friends again."

"Yes," Mae says. "And when we're too tired to dance any more, we'll lie down and rest where we fall—like your people used to do, but on soft clouds."

Coyote whines, "I came back to hear about the tricky men and the river."

"Mae kept our river free and wild," I explain to the newcomers.

Approvingly O-se-mai-ti nods her head in Mae's direction. "I used to roll in the shallows of that river," she says. "It's time I did it again."

She lumbers over there, and I love watching her in the water once more with her big feet in the air and her cubs splashing around. After her bath she shakes a spray of sunstruck water and returns to my shade—for a moment eyeing the shiny little man crouched with his bow and arrow on the hood of Mae's motorcar—then she settles on my mound with her sister-wife. The big cat leaps to my limb, and we all see Mae as she looked at that blue mountain lake, in the fullness of her beauty and strength.

❋❋

A t Caminetti's racetrack, twelve-year-old Billy sat astride Mack at the starting line. Most of the adult competitors had been practically born in the saddle, and they measured their worth by the speed of their horses. John and Mae had come in the surrey to watch, leaving Alice back in camp with Anne, and the little boys with Chloë in the Washoe camp where they loved to play with boys their age.

The half-mile track along the north shore of Silver Lake went up to a prominent boulder and back. Raul had done some rope tricks to entertain the waiting crowd, and now he sat against a big pine with Isabella to watch the race. They had become good friends, and no doubt Raul knew about Mae and big Billy.

She knew some things about him too. A full-blooded Indian originally from up around Oroville, he'd spent his youth on a cattle ranch in the San Joaquin Valley, where Mexican vaqueros taught him his trade. Posing as Mexican, he made good money doing exhibitions at private parties and the bigger rodeos in northern California. Isabella said his horse would likely have won today's race, but he enjoyed watching others run. He worked as a drover about half of the summers because he loved the mountains and because, as head vaquero and teacher of the younger hands, he made plenty of money doing what he would do for nothing. Everyone stood in awe of Raul's stunning palomino, which now nibbled tufts of grass while tied to a branch near his owner.

Mr. Caminetti, elderly and too slender, held the gun high. The crowd went silent—Billy hunched over Mack and ready with the switch. But the quiet was broken by the hoofbeats of many horses.

Mr. Caminetti lowered the gun as he turned to look. Mae looked too, and saw a stagecoach clattering down the road toward the station. To the obvious consternation of the racers, he waited until a six-horse team pulled into his yard and his wife went out to lead the stage to the side of building.

Then he pulled the trigger to start the race.

Mae watched from the crackled leather seat where John had kissed her so passionately eight years ago. "Go Billy!" she yelled.

The churning mass of horses and riders bunched up as they circled the boulder, briefly disappearing. Then the leader rode alone for a few seconds on the backstretch, rapidly growing bigger, hooves seeming not to touch the ground.

A crowd screamed them on, having laid their bets and drunk considerably from the Caminetti liquor supply. The Dunaways hadn't put any money on the race. They were here to see how Mack would do against the horses whose owners continually bragged that their horse was the best. "A race is the only way to stop the arguments," Billy had told his parents with swagger borrowed from the drovers.

Billy stayed in the knot of horses behind the two leaders, clearly not going to win. The leaders came in a nose apart. Cheers went up here and there, the gamblers and frontrunners wasting no time collecting from the losers. John had parked in a good place to see the finish.

When Billy dismounted, Mae was surprised to see a man walk up to him—a very tall man in a red-checkered shirt, suspenders, and a farmer's hat. She saw only the back of him, but knew he hadn't been there before. He had come in the stagecoach.

"That's Charlie Rogue!" She pointed. Dressed like a man of the West, he must have recognized Billy from her latest postal card.

"That don't surprise me," John said. "He hopes to change our minds."

Charlie walked over with Billy and, after Mae introduced him to John, invited the three of them to supper in the dining room.

"I realize it's a little early," he said with a glance at the fairly high sun, "but I've been bouncing in that stage all day after not much of a noon dinner at Ham's Station, and I recall being hungry all the time when I was your age." With a grin on his prize-fighter face, he looked down at Billy and slapped him on the back. "Whatdaya say, buckeroo?"

"Sure," Billy said uneasily.

Mae and John looked at each other, Mae waiting for John to lead.

"We'd be glad to accept," John said, "but just so you know, we're not changing our minds."

Isabella rode back to the Indian camp on Raul's palomino, having come on the surrey. John, Mae, Billy, and Charlie headed to the dining room, where they learned that the lasagna wouldn't be ready for at least half an hour. Meanwhile the three males who had changed Mae's life, each in different ways, munched antipasto, that strange mix of pickled things that Sophie and Hank always had before dinner.

The kerosene lamps didn't provide much light, and the front window didn't let in enough natural light—with the kitchen in the back and the walls of adjoining buildings up against both sides of the room. A round of beer was served to the adults, and a glass of milk to Billy. Then Charlie launched into his speech. It was nothing new.

After an awkward moment John said, "We been told the farmers in the Owens River valley got a poor deal. Some men we know looked at the paperwork and saw that the land could dry up and be just about worthless after the water's piped out'a there."

"That's idle talk," Charlie put down.

"Mebbeso, but just the same we'd be foolish to bite at this before we have a chance to see how that other turns out," John said.

"Unfortunately, we don't have time to wait that long," Charlie countered. "They can't push the first dirt on that project 'til ought seven. That's why, if we hurry on our project, we can beat 'em to the punch, and San Francisco will stay the biggest and fastest-growing city in California. You'd get a good share of that bonanza."

He gave John and Mae lead-pipe-cinch wink, and then turned to Billy with a wide-eyed smile for a young child. "What'da ya say, Skeeziks? Wanna get rich?"

Billy looked nonplussed to hear himself called Skeeziks, and Mae believed he would have traded future riches to win the race today in front of Raul Martinez.

"Here's the thing," she said, "John and I have a plan for the rest of our lives. Our land and our river are part of that and we don't want it ruined."

"Ruined!" Charlie looked hurt and puzzled. "You'd get big money. And you'd be helping millions of people grow a metropolis of the importance of New York City. If you refuse, you're standing in the way of progress."

"We don't think it's our duty to help other people grow a city." Mae knew that John, having announced his position, wasn't disposed to do it again. So she carried on. "People should move to where the water already exists," she said "Or get it from somebody else's river, like that Hetch Hetchy project."

Charlie showed his exasperation by chewing on his cheek. "You know very well that's our opponent's project. Look, I came today to offer you fifty thousand dollars up front plus a chance to be one of the minority owners in the forebay part of the project. I had to push the principals on that, and it's generous compensation. You could reinvest the fifty thousand and buy into the project."

"We got a gold vein," Billy said. "It would be flooded."

"Gold?" Charlie looked like he'd never heard the word before.

Mae didn't know whether to laugh or cry. Laugh at Charlie's astonishment, or cry over the spilt milk of Bay Cities being all the more eager for their land. The fathers of those tycoons had come to California for gold; they'd have no intention of flooding a ready source of income.

"Well," Charlie all but demanded, staring straight at John, "If you've got a gold mine, then why in the hell are you driving sheep up the mountains?"

Apparently not upset at Billy for letting that cat out of the bag, though he and Alice had been sternly warned against doing so, John calmly resplied, "We don't know for sure if it's a vein. The only important thing here is that we've thought about this carefully and made up our minds. We're not selling our land and water to your company. I'm sorry you came all this way to hear that."

His grammar was flawless, Mae noticed.

"There's gold in the wool, too," Mae added, "and in these mountains. And in the way we live. It's good for the children. It's the kind of gold I've seen advertised by the Railroad and the colonizing companies. Fair Oaks and Orangevale. It harks back to the good life, and freedom, and to the way the first American farmers felt about their land, the very thing your mother told me she and your dad love about the farm in... ah... near... ah—"

"Visalia!" Charlie's prize-fighter face tightened with exasperation. "I left that farm the first chance I got. I thought you wanted to get on a higher level, Mae. A chance for the brass ring. A life of travel and ease, meeting interesting people. Music and theater. Maybe I misjudged you. I came here to assure you that it's possible with this project. I sure as hell didn't expect this."

His head went down and he looked defeated. He didn't raise it as he added, "If it's the gold, I'll send an expert to assay the value and we'll add that to the up-front payment. That's only fair. We'd get it back anyway."

Mae and John exchanged a glance, John briefly rolling his eyes upward. He wasn't about to argue any more.

"Our minds really are made up," Mae said.

Charlie took a deep breath, shifted on his chair and addressed them in his calmly-in-control tone, which he used when on the verge of being out of control. "Have you considered that just maybe you'll be shoved out of that golden life when it becomes clear that a greater public interest, involving maybe four to five million people, would be far better served if your one single family moved out and let progress happen? And Billy here would still do well because his father will benefit from that?"

At that moment a hired girl came to the table with silverware on a stack of plates.

John showed her the flats of his hands, and as she backed away and left, he stood up, his face taking on the same stubborn expression as when a horse started to act up.

"Mr. Rogue," he said, "I'd like to point out that this is America. The land of the free. Where the king's men don't come in and take your land. Some of the men along our river didn't take a stand on the Bay Cities project, like Fred Grimshaw. He's downstream of it and always for progress, active in the Farm Bureau and a bunch of other groups. But if you try to take my land with that gimmick you're talking about, he would fight you with everything he's got. So would his cousin W. C. Sheldon and all his friends in high places. Every farmer and stockman down to the smallest operator would hear of it and raise a howl in Sacramento so loud it'd be in the history books. That's if you try'n make it legal to take other people's ground because rich men say it's in the public interest, when everyone knows it's in the interest of their pocketbooks. There's a hell of a lot more of us farmers and ranchers than your kind in this state. You'd find out what Americans believe in." He stood there looking totally in the right.

"Please," Charlie said in a low tone, eyes on Congressman Caminetti, who was walking toward the kitchen, "please sit down. I know that measure would be hard to sell in the farming districts. I said as much to Mae last March, didn't I?" He looked at her. She gave a little nod. "If I got a little impatient there, I'm sorry." He reached over and jiggled John's chair back. "Please, let's get the food over here and some good Italian wine, and we'll talk about what that investment opportunity means."

"I'm hungry, Dad," Billy said looking at John, and then uneasily at Charlie.

"Ma'am," Charlie said in a loud voice, raising an arm to the hired girl who had tried to bring dishes, "We're ready now."

While Charlie was looking at the girl, Mae winked at John telling him he'd done well. John sat down.

Later, after Billy had told Charlie all about Raul Martinez and his palomino, and everyone was well into the lasagna, Charlie dallied another argument.

"I'm curious. Seeing as how all your neighbors favor the project," he put a forkful into his mouth, chewed a few times, "are you concerned that the golden glow of your life might lose a little luster when they hear you've stood in the way of the project?" He hastened to add, "I've talked to them. They're all bully to move on to a better life."

Mae had been thinking about that for some time, and her answer came ready-made. "Polly Sheldon, Granlees now, is a good friend of mine. She said once, in a proud way, that the independent cusses that live around us always get together and work out problems even though they have their differences. We help each other in disasters. So yes, I think Mary Granlees will be peeved at us, and possibly her sons. And I suppose old Mrs. Allen would rather have a pot of money to give to her children before she dies, and no doubt the Gaffney boys will be upset, but they'll get over it. In a small farming community like ours there are only two kinds of people: friends and temporary enemies.

"And we've got good neighbors who do not own land," she continued. "Some of them think it's wrong to send our river's water to dry areas so people can build houses there, rather than building houses where the water already exists. So we're not alone."

John nodded in agreement. "And there's some'um else I'd like to get off my chest. That dam up at Michigan Bar better not short us of water. You need to talk to W. C. Sheldon. He's got a list of things your company needs to watch out for, to protect the downstream farms and ranches. We're one of 'em now. And I'd like to meet with you and W. C. before anything is set in concrete."

Charlie looked at Billy, and then at John. He let out a long breath of air. "It can be arranged. I'm always open to working things out."

❧

In the soft light of evening Mae and John reviewed the supper that had so disappointed Charlie. Billy rode in the front seat of the surrey with them, Mack tied behind on a lead rope. Charlie had stayed at Caminetti's and would take the 1 o'clock stage back to Sacramento.

As the horses pulled slowly up and over what seemed the top of the world, Carson Spur, Mae said with a tease, "Your grammar was as good as his. You been holdin' that back from me."

"A man can git a right good education living with you." John shot her a look—part smirk and part lover with more surprises in store. "But doan 'spect me to lay it out before them buckaroos in Kirkwood's saloon."

Mae laughed at that, and then said, "I'd like to sing with the drovers tonight. That all right with you?"

"I could use a red-eye myself."

He reached over and pulled her across the seat until he had her snug in his arm. "You been talkin' about goin' to Carmel-by-the-Sea," he said. "What say we go there in January? I heard tell the weather's downright warm there at that time of the year."

❧❧

Mae Tells Us The Rest of the Story

A light breeze ruffles He-lé-jah's fur, and his four legs dangle as he straddles my branch. The raccoon kits are making forays toward the cubs, wanting to play but unsure whether they'll be accepted. Watching this, O-se-mai-ti sits with her back against my trunk. Discernment is one of her strengths, and she is thinking about Mae's story.

"I didn't save the river," Mae confesses. "The river runs free because clever men trapped Mr. Tevis, and that's the truth of it. I've been fooling myself."

Raccoon says earnestly, "I don't know how to fool myself."

Being a human spirit I understand. "Mae," I tell her, "you delayed that project, and that must have helped to stop it."

After a considerable silence Mae says, "Maybe the delay kept Mr. Tevis out of jail, and Charlie, but that's all it did."

Coyote sits up and smiles. "What kind of trap did those men set?"

"It was complicated. Charlie knew nothing of it when we had supper with him, but the trap was being laid then. When we returned from summer pasture I saw the first reports about federal prosecutors being appointed by the district attorney to investigate graft in San Francisco. And City officials trying to kick out the District Attorney—a flurry of actions, back and forth. A judge ruling for the prosecutors. Then more back and forth about dismissing the Grand Jury and appointing a new one, with Boss Ruef trying to save his old jury. Next, newspapers told of huge crowds of people in the streets favoring the investigation. A lot of excitement."

A breeze from the ocean comes up through the Delta and whips through my upper leaves, and it feels good. The spirits around me appear perplexed, and I speak for all of us, "I don't understand, Mae. Many of your words mean nothing to us."

"How-ow-ow-ow did it happen?" Coyote barks.

"Well," Mae says with a slanted smile while pulling her close hat more securely on her head, "they were being bad and they got caught. See, people have a lot of rules, but in those days the rules weren't being enforced. Until this happened. Most people knew that the City leaders were taking money from houses of prostitution and gambling outfits to let them stay in business, though they weren't supposed to do that. The police were loyal to the leaders, so it didn't seem possible to stop the graft, or bribery, as it's called. But a group of former leaders met secretly. One of them visited President Teddy Roosevelt, the most powerful man in the country. Roosevelt lent them two of his top men, a prosecutor and an investigator—a team that had put a U.S. Senator from Oregon in jail for graft."

"They sent in the big dogs," Coyote says, sniffing the fresher air.

"That's right. Quietly, those men planned a way to catch the little dogs in the city leadership, the supervisors, and get them to tell on "Boss Abe Ruef.""

They were collecting evidence when the earthquake tore the City to pieces. That increased the graft and bribery, as wealthy businessmen wanted to rebuild, improve, and monopolize the broken services—streetcars, gas and electric, telephones, water."

"What are bribes?" Rock Man asks in his strained voice.

I was wondering the same thing.

Mae speaks carefully. "Well, those businessmen knew they could make a lot of money if their projects were approved, so they paid Boss Ruef to make sure the supervisors voted yes. That is bribery. The newspapers said Tevis offered Ruef the biggest bribe of all in exchange for the City agreeing to buy his Bay Cities water project. Ruef admitted that in a bargain to get softer punishment.

"When I met with Charlie in his office, in March, the supervisors had already taken steps toward buying Tevis' water system for nine and a half million dollars. That's why Charlie said the Bay Cities water project would succeed—it was secretly approved by Boss Ruef for a promise of a million dollars for his pocket and the pockets of Mayor Schmitz and the supervisors."

Coyote has been fidgeting and making faces. Now he blurts out, "Of course Tevis would pay a million dollars to get nine and a half million back. He's not stupid."

"You might think that's normal, but most people think our leaders shouldn't take bribes. People agreed upon rules against it, laws. Even though it happened in every city—"

Coyote hoots.

"I guess that's why the big newspapers printed the story of the graft trials. People everywhere wanted to see if powerful men could be punished for breaking the law, as they were in Oregon. And they were punished. Ruef and Schmitz were tried, found guilty, and sent to prison. The eighteen supervisors would have gone to prison too, if they hadn't helped to rat out Boss Ruef."

"What do you mean, they were tried?" Rock Man calls out.

"A group of people meet to decide if an accused person is guilty. If so, a punishment is ordered. That's a trial."

"My people had trials," says the man who died spearing a woolly mammoth. "Bad people were banished, never to come back. It was the same as being killed."

"We had trials too," I add, recalling a number of banishments. "Was Mr. Tevis judged guilty?"

"No," Mae says. "No money had changed hands yet. Tevis was waiting for the final approval of his project. That's the delay that saved him from jail."

Mae too is sniffing the fresher air. "I just realized, she says, "that Mr. Tevis was banished in a way, not by any law, but his water project was shunned after that."

"Well then," Coyote says reasonably, "he could have sold his project to the next batch of city leaders, or to some other city."

"Not after the newspapers printed the details of the bribery deal. No one else would have touched that project. It was dead as a doornail."

"What is a doornail?" He-lé-jah wants to know.

"I don't know." Mae smiles at him. "That's an expression from a bye-gone time."

"Did Charlie get into trouble?" I have been wondering.

"No. He was lucky the water project fell apart when it did. He could have been caught too. And as for our neighbors, they read the newspapers. They knew why Charlie never signed their deals, and why the new supervisors approved the Tuolumne–Hetch Hetchy plan instead." Mae's dark curls whipping around her face, escaping from her hat look pretty and lively. "The graft trials changed California," she says in a light manner, trying to find music on the radio of her automobile.

"What do you mean?" I ask.

"Reform. Making powerful men obey the law. Hiram Johnson was elected governor on a reform platform. It was exciting. John and I and most of our neighbors voted for him every time he ran for office. That was most of my life. He was California's U.S. Senator. He got his start as the hero of the graft trials, and it launched him into the governor's office. He promised to kick the Southern Pacific Railroad out of California government. And he did, too."

She sighs audibly. "It was exciting. John and I danced under the dome of the Capitol at the Johnson's Inaugural Ball. That was 1911, the year California women got the right to vote. I looked around for Charlie at the Ball but didn't see him. Maybe he wasn't welcome in the reform administration, or as staff to the Senate."

"But things don't always turn out the way we expect, do they?"

Coyote warbles a happy chuckle. "Are you saying that the clever schemers are still breaking the law to get rich, even after the reforms?"

"Yes," Mae says. "I believe they find ways around any law, if enough money is involved."

A piercing whistle comes up from a hole. "There's a piece of me in Man too," Ground Squirrel pops up to say.

Her people tunnel long distances through hard clay and impacted rock to reach something good to eat.

O-se-mai-ti is sitting up like a human person, legs apart, picking delicately at a scab on her foot with one shiny black claw. Coyote trots to the river to drink and returns with dripping chin hairs. He sits down on his haunches beside her.

"You and John should have taken the $50,000 when you had the chance," he says.

"I doubt they'd have paid us until the project was approved, but with the graft, it never was."

Mae looks straight at Coyote as she says, "Not one of the bribe givers were found guilty, though people said they were the root cause of graft. Even when evidence proved they had paid bribes, they wiggled free, each in his own way."

"The big fish get away," Raccoon says, getting up to check on her kits to see what of interest they have found in a cavity of an old pine. Mother Grizzly looks up and says after her, "Maybe they get away from *you*."

Mae ignores that. "The rich men had clever lawyers and toughs working for them. Bad things happened to witnesses at the trials—a house blown up, people kidnapped, the chief prosecutor shot in the head. That's why Johnson was appointed chief prosecutor and became a famous reformer."

Coyote laughs long and happily.

Another fresh wind sweeps through my leaves and across the old home place, lifting a cloud of dust from the flat area where the houses of the People once stood.

"What happened to Charlie?" I ask after the howl and the wind quiet down.

"When Billy lived with him during his high school years," Mae says. "Charlie owned a big house on T Street, so I guess he did all right. I saw him in a newspaper, described as a developer, but I lost track of him after Billy died in the so-called Great War."

He-lé-jah's claws tickle me as he balances on my branch, turns around, and then lies down facing Mae's sleek motorcar. The Animal People are quiet, hearing about Billy. Though I've known about him since Mae began visiting here, remembering his death gives me a pinch in the core of my trunk.

Mae muses, "So often our dreams don't turn out the way we expect You're right about that, Coyote. John and I dreamed of growing old in our pretty house while at least one of our boys farmed the land. But after Billy was gone, and John died of the flu. Then Johnny and Emmett left to become professional men, and I lost my interest in the land."

Coyote looks pensive with his chin on crossed paws, perhaps recalling his many plans that went awry.

"A lot of people," Mae says, "thought Hetch Hetchy Valley was more valuable than our land, but it got flooded instead. So both places were ruined.

"How did you ruin your land?" Mother Grizzly asks.

Mae speaks in short bursts.

"I was alone. One by one, my friends left. Old Mary passed on. We burned the cabin with her in it, the way she wanted. Made it look like an accident. Chloë moved in with me. She had the upstairs. Later we learned Isabella died in Santa Cruz. Raul didn't know how to write, so he came on a bus to tell us.

"More years went by. My savings drew clear down, but I didn't want to go live with Alice and have her boss me around.

Mae pauses in her remembering, and we wait in silence for her to continue.

"Then one day Mr. Humphrey knocked on the door. He said if I'd let him dredge for gold on my property he'd give me fifteen percent of the take. I knew that overflows had scattered bits of gold in the fields, likely for thousands of years."

"How would you know if he cheated you," Coyote says peaking his brows at her.

"He showed me his bank receipts. So I signed on. Other landowners did too, and that's how the land south of the river was turned upside down and the old community of Live Oak disappeared. The Doodlebug, as it was called, sort of floated on shallow water. It scooped up mud and gravel in giant buckets attached to a conveyer chain rigged like a Ferris wheel. The buckets tipped at the top and poured mud and gravel down through the filters of the boat's housing. A man in the bottom melted the amalgamated gold and made bricks of it. And every minute of the day and night, the Doodlebug buried the good loam under gravel and rock. Mounds of rock were left behind the 'boat' in wavy parallel lines, like the castings of a monster caterpillar."

"Did Mr. Humphrey have helpers to run that machine?" He-lé-jah asks."

"Oh my yes. Let's see. About twenty. He paid their train fare from Montana. They had worked for him in hard rock mine up there. When the gold played out he didn't want to leave them stranded without work in the depression of the 1930s, so he brought them with him—wives and youngsters too. He was a good man."

"Did they ever go back to Montana?" Mother Grizzly asks.

Racoon, having returned, interjects, "Are you going back to Montana?"

Bear peers over Coyote, shrugs at Racoon, and looks expectantly at Mae.

"I think they went to Florida and most of them stayed there. Anyway, it was interesting. Mr. Humphrey purchased the building supplies and his men hammered together a string of little houses arranged on a U-shaped road that joined Jackson Road in two places. That's how the Dredger Colony came to be. There were enough youngsters in those houses for the Stone House School to re-open. By then Art Granlees daughter Hilda went to school there with the Augustine and Jauch and Waloupe children."

I can't help but break in, "By then, Indians like the Waloupes were allowed to go to school with white children."

Mae groans, "Chloë passed away. I had her buried in the old church graveyard. She didn't want a marker, just a wooden box, so she's back in the earth like she wanted.

"Then I was entirely alone. I couldn't bear the constant noise. Or that Cyclops of a spotlight as the Doodlebug ate its way around my house at night. I got no rest. I didn't like my house anymore, so I sold it and the land to Mr.

Humphrey. They tore the house down and kept on dredging. I found an apartment in Sacramento."

"Did Mr. Humphrey pay you a lot?" Raccoon asks.

"The money bought everything I needed. This Pierce-Arrow was my one big splurge. I loved driving it—the car of kings and tycoons. A time or two, I drove some old-lady friends out here to see the dredging. Then the government did something that lowered the price of gold and the Humphrey Gold Dredge Mining Company moved to Florida. The whole kit and kaboodle. They must have torn down the houses and sold the lumber, because the land was dredged underneath."

Mae looks around at the Animal People. "That's how I ruined our good land."

Mother Grizzly tilts her head across the river. "Looks to me like about a thousand houses over there, all with grass and trees. I'll bet those people don't think it's ruined."

"They don't know the difference. They're city people."

"What is the difference?" Bear asks in her discerning way.

"None at all!" Mae grabs the wheel with both hands and throws her head back, abandoning herself to laughter, the way I love to see her. All of us laugh. We can't help it. Still chuckling, she says, "At least they moved to where the water was."

"Those are good dens over there," Bear says. "Good sleeping places for many people. Tight enough to keep rattlesnakes out and big enough to store plenty of food."

❋❊

Across the river, Molok awakens in the tall cottonwood. We watch him spread his wings, his ruby eye flashing in the light from the low sun. For a moment he is a magnificent statue, and then he jumps into the west-wind, corrects his glide, and lands on my mound between Mae's Pierce-Arrow and Mother Bear. He stands straight and tall, his head at the level of a man's waist, his inflated gullet-bag glowing reddish-pink.

"I had a dream," he says in a deeply resonating voice.

This shakes me to my taproot. Never in my two lives have I heard Molok speak.

"Rock Man, your people are gone," Condor says. "The animals you hunted are gone. Howchia, of the large animals your men hunted only the deer remain in this place. Mae, your people scatter many poisons. All the golden eagles and most of the coyotes died or went away after the ground squirrels were poisoned, and they continue to be poisoned if any move back. Lead bullets in deer carcasses have poisoned most of my kind. Only a few condors remain alive. Soon I will be gone too."

The silence crackles as that sinks in.

He continues. "Today I dreamed the world without people. Grass and tree roots widened the fissures in the roads, and the big pipes beneath rusted and collapsed. The roads become new streambeds. Houses shifted and cracked. So did the buildings in the cities. Windows fell out. Owls roosted in the top floors. Rat dung mixed with composting leaves on the aging carpets to become soil for windblown seeds. Later all the remaining buildings and dams and bridges buckled and fell. Trees and bushes sprouted in the rubble, and animals with the mixed blood of dog and coyote hunted rat-like animals. There were no condors."

"Was I free of this rock?" Rock Man calls in his distant voice.

"You were still in your rock, but it was beginning to flake." The giant bird flaps into the sky, wings whumping as he disappears through the trees.

We have listened with awful understanding.

Something stirs in my core. My leaves tremble and I feel vertigo all the way down my taproot.

Mae switches on the radio of her motorcar, and we hear Chloë, my great-great-granddaughter, playing the piano. He-lé-jah leaps down from my branch. The Animal People are on their feet. We start swaying. We can't help it with such music swelling up around us.

The bears are the first on their hind legs. Mother Grizzly holds hands with her cubs as they dance in a circle, lifting one leg and then the other. Coyote lets out a joyful howl skipping around on his skinny hind legs and kicking out at odd times. He-lé-jah's tail whips in time with the beat, and I see the upward curve in his normally sober lips. The raccoon kits jump up and down trying to dance. Their mother goes to their father. She is becoming tall and beautiful as she takes the soft paws of her mate and nudges him to his hind legs. They dance together. All of them have taken on a shadowy and more vertical look, their faces half hidden but somehow different, and I realize that I am seeing them as they looked before Man, before they became purely animal. On the hill the bird people are dancing too, their wings or shoulders or capes high around their ears.

Mae is floating out of her motorcar! She has a gauzy aura about her as her feet skim the ground and her skirt swirls in the pleasant west-wind. The strange sensations within me intensify and I feel myself pushing out of the bark with the slight thrust of a seed slipping from its pod.

I am floating. I am free! I am dancing!

We all dance in celebration of Earth and Spirit and the lives we have been fortunate enough to live in this peaceful oak woodland beside the flowing river.

Endnotes[1]

ENTIRELY FICTIONAL CHARACTERS

Lizzyanne
Mae Duffy and all her family
John Dunaway
Mrs. Cook in the Michigan Bar eating house
Mrs. Smith and her brood, including Shadrack
Oberon Jones and other personnel in the Sacramento police station
Baby, later Chloë
Isabella and Cowboy
Charlie Rogue, his mother and landlord
Senator Percival Unstead
Doctor Rudi and his nurse
The Chinese herbalist in Marysville
Ah Chin Chow in the Sacramento underground
Raul Martinez, the Indian vaquero
Mary Donahue, the seamstress in Sacramento and her husband Rob
Conductors on trains and workers at the Southern Pacific shops
Mr. Tesla, manager in the Southern Pacific foundry
ALL personnel working in the Big Canyon Mine

HISTORICAL CHARACTERS approximately in order of appearance

Billy McCoon—the first historical mention of Billy is when Wm. Perry McCoon, Billy's father, presented his infant son of the same name (and his Indian wife) to John Sutter to be recorded in Sutter's journal in 1845. All of Sutter's journals burned in the 1865 fire on his *Hoch* Farm,[2] however many incidents were recorded by Heinrich Lienhard or other men at the Fort (Sacramento Archives and Museum Collection and History Room of the California State Library).

---

1   For the full citations of books referenced here, see "Readings the Author Found Useful" at the end of these notes.

2   In German, hoch = high, upper, and north on a map. In German script, *h* bears a resemblance to the American *k*, hence the readers of Sutter's letters saw: "Hock Farm," and that awkward non sequitur has persisted ever since. Regarding Sutter's New Helvetia Journal: A document by that name was published and serialized in the 1870s, however it was a selective narrative penned by Sutter decades after the events, intended to convince the U.S. government to reimburse him for his losses. John Bidwell and other men helped Sutter keep the real New Helvetia journal, and one of their copies survived to be printed in the 1930s, but it begins in late 1845, six years after the founding of New Helvetia, too late for Billy's introduction. However, Heinrich Lienhard's "gossipy" vignettes are the source of much early information.

Perhaps because Lienhard was amused by Indian Mary's rejection of Sutter's advances, the incident of Perry McCoon presenting her as his wife, with baby, was remembered and written.[3] The next historical mention occurs in the fall of 1847. Orphaned Eliza P. Donner, 4¼, is taken to McCoon's cattle ranch to visit and possibly live with her older sister, Elitha C., 14. (Elitha married McCoon in June, 1847). Eliza recalls that visit in her memoir, *The Expedition of the Donner Party*, pp. 156. 157). Perry and Elitha were gone for a long time and Eliza felt lonely in the cabin with a young couple whose newborn baby absorbed all their attention. Out walking, she meets a "sprightly little Indian lad" with "a squaw" who came to get clabbered milk from the pans atop the ash hopper. "His face was almost as white as my own." Younger than Eliza, he wore a blue shirt and had "several strings of Indian beads around his neck and a small bow and arrow in his hand." She asks, "What's your name?" To her delight he answers: "Name Billy." After that, she watches for him, and he returns daily. Eliza learns some of his Indian words and she helps him climb up the hopper. He teaches her to make a spoon of her three fingers to eat the clabbered milk from the pans. One day, "chore man" takes Eliza for a walk and shows her the *rancheria* (Indian village) where the Indian herders live with others of their tribe. Among them he points out Billy's mother. He explains that "the nice little fellow" learned a few English words from his white papa, who had "gone away." "Mr. Choreman" tells Eiza that she is "too nice a little girl" to eat as Billy does or "to dip out of the same pan. I was ashamed and promised not to do so again, or to climb up there with him again." This was likely Billy's first brush with racial discrimination. Eliza does not stay at the ranch. In 1910, 63 years later as she penned that memoir, she would not have embarrassed Elitha by disclosing that Perry had an Indian wife and child—common at that time. The U.S. Census records Wm. McCoon in 1850 (est. age 7), and also in 1860, 1870, and 1880. He is a farm worker in the Cosumne area, has an Indian mother, white father, and is a dairyman for **Haskin C. Swain** in 1870 and 1880. An internet query erroneously brought up a 1874 deed recorded to Wm. McCoon from H.C. Swain, but county records show that Swain deeded to a different receiver and did so in the 1850s. Despite genealogical searches within the local Indian community and in Salt Lake databases, Billy McCoon vanishes from history in 1880. He is shown here in the 1860s–1890s facing discrimination, as would have been typical of any California native person, but with an extra twist in the case of young men.

---

3   "Race mixture in the Sacramento Area: 1839–1850" by Jack D. Forbes, professor emeritus University of California, Davis, author of *American Discovery of Europe* (University of Illinois Press, 2007). Forbes cites Lienhard as the source of the story of Sutter presenting Mary with rich gifts, but she still rejects him.

Indian Mary—Heinrich Lienhard[4] mentions Perry McCoon's "mistress," a "beautiful Indian girl named Mary," whose people herded cattle for McCoon on his Rancho Sacayak. Lienhard also writes that she "bamboozled" John Sutter" out of $2000 of gold when he was camped with his Indian and Kanaka miners in his "pine woods"[5] (now Sutter Creek). Thirty years later, the 1880 Census puts "Mary Lambut," Indian, housekeeper, in the Long household, within old Rancho Sacayak. Sketchy memories of "Indian Mary," also known as Mary Long, were passed down to Hilda Granlees, whose family acquired some of the Long property. "Mary Long," was about 70 when she helped birth Art Granlees (father of Hilda) in 1898. Hilda said she was not married, and she had a daughter with reddish hair, also called Indian Mary. Census takers frequently assigned the household name to Indian housekeepers and farm laborers. In the Mother Lode mining areas, native people considered "Mary" to be a respectful term for a white woman (See *Black Sun of the Miwok* and also "Charlie" for a white man). Traditionally, California native people did not speak their own names aloud, so when asked to do so, women probably answered: Mary. This could explain the many instances of "Indian Mary" recorded up and down the Gold Country. All five pioneer women on or around old Rancho Sacayak were named Mary.

Charles Ruman of Michigan Bar—an immigrant from Germany who built the bridge and adjacent hotel in Michigan Bar in the mid 19th century. Charles' wife collected bridge toll. The town declined with the end of gold mining, but the Ruman family remained to raise stock. The town further declined when Jackson Road became the main thoroughfare to the hard rock mines in Amador County. Additionally, with the advent of automobiles, Latrobe became less important as a railroad terminal. Eventually all commerce shut down in Michigan Bar. **Heath's**

---

4   Heirich Lienhard, a Swiss German journeyed to New Helvetia and wrote a great many notes and vignettes about life in Sutter's Fort. His descriptions and humor bring the Fort to life. Based on those notes, he wrote a memoir in German 20 years later. In 1941, Marguerite Eyer Wilbur translated Lienhard's book for the Califia Society of Los Angeles. At that time, John Sutter was viewed as an unassailably heroic figure, and Ms Wilbur's work was not well received because she included incidents that showed Sutter in a bad light. Edwin Gudde writes in the *Pacific Historical Review* (Vol. II, No. 2, June 1942), pp 233–34, that Ms Wilbur's book is "not a very valuable source for California history" because Lienhard had a hatred for Sutter. Gudde cites as an example the death of a little Indian girl after an "immoral attack" and the fact that Lienhard implicated Sutter as the man who raped her. Gudde sarcastically lists Leinhard's sources for that implication: an "influential squaw" told her sister, who told it to her Kanaka husband, who told it to Charley Burch, who told it to "the sensitive and gossipy Lienhard." Gudde's review seems to have swayed two generations of historians against Leinhard. Eight years later Ms Wilbur wrote, *John Sutter: Rascal and Adventurer* (Liveright: 1949).

5   This is a major incident in *River of Red Gold*.

Mercantile was moved to Jackson Road near the entrance of Van Vleck Road— sycamore trees mark the place. Today, grandson Edward Ruman and other family members continue to operate a cattle ranch on both sides of the river. He and his wife live in a modern house on a hill overlooking the former town. They use the old hotel as housing for their family ranch workers, and two of the old main street structures for their barn and shop. All other structures are gone. Among the historic photographs that the author provided to the Rancho Murieta Country Club Clubhouse (hereafter "Clubhouse"), is a view of Michigan Bar's main street with early automobiles and shoppers.

Isabella Miser—(1826–1904), a pioneer who expanded her holdings and nurtured 8 children as a single mother after the untimely death of her husband, a freighter whose loaded wagon shifted off its rocks while he was underneath repairing an axle. In the wrought-iron fence of the Miser cemetery, now in a cow pasture just outside the Rancho Murieta boundary, Isabella lies under the same headstone as Solomon (1823–1876). Nearby is a tall sandstone obelisk engraved **AGNES**—no other inscription. In about 2003, the author interviewed Isabella Miser's granddaughter, Wilma Anna Menke Welden (b. 1915) and learned the reason: Agnes never told the Miser family her last name despite being a helpmate for 40–50 years, because she was waiting to take the name of her lost forty-niner fiancé. Wilma Welden described the details of her grandmother's now-gone house and furnishings. The foundation stones now harbor rattlesnake dens. In visualizing Isabella Miser for this novel, the author borrowed the appearance, delightful energy, and obvious love of life from granddaughter Wilma. Wilma's maiden name comes from the big hops grower on Folsom Boulevard— the name in this book stenciled on wagonloads of Menke Hops heading for Sacramento while the train carried Mae and her family towards Folsom. The Miser daughters, Laura and Lilian, lived at home and in Walsh Station with their husbands, as shown in this book. Son Joe Miser lived on property shown on the 1895 map. Mrs. Miser ultimately had about 1000 acres of grazing land. She also conducted the first local school in her house. Vandals recently broke Agnes's monument, probably with a sledgehammer. The top half fell face down and can no longer be read.

John D. Driscoll—(1825–1906) an Irish pioneer who came for gold, built a dugout dwelling in 1853 that still stands despite stone pilfering, and stayed to farm. He wed Mary Driscoll, built the redwood house next to the dugout, and for the next 45 years raised sheep, cattle, and alfalfa. During this time he acquired the neighboring lands, either abandoned or sold to him. At his death he owned much of what would become Rancho Murieta, a distant suburb of Sacramento bisected by the Cosumnes River. His descendants do not know where he is buried. No stone for him exists in the local historic cemeteries, though he was a Catholic and likely helped build the little St. Joseph's mission church around which that graveyard lies (church gone now). A photograph of John Driscoll as an older man hangs in the Clubhouse. At his death, his property passed to his only child, Mary Granlees.

Mary Driscoll Granlees—(1859–1940) a tough little woman who continued to acquire properties on both sides of the Cosumnes River after her father's death. With a keen business sense, she kept the property intact during the Great Depression and added to it. The large property under a single ownership made it a desirable purchase for the developers of Rancho Murieta in the late 1960s. Mary had a short leg and a shoe built up with wood, with which she spanked misbehaving children. Granddaughter Hilda Granlees said Mary mixed chicken broth and mashed potatoes to keep her babies alive the first year, having insufficient milk to nurse them. She brought up six children after her first child died soon after birth. All the babies had "allergic colic" and barely survived their first year. As the children acquired spouses and offspring, Mary kept them in her small house until they had homes of their own. The one remnant of the redwood house her father built and she called home is the concrete sidewalk to the doorstep (seen from the parking lot of the RMA Building within the gates of Rancho Murieta). Mary's grandchildren tell various stories of Mary's stormy marriage to Robert Granlees. Relocating to Sacramento, he had a tobacco shop on J Street for many years and died in 1919. When Mary's youngest child, Art, built a house of his own on the newly acquired, adjacent Brown property, he included a room for Mary and extra wide doors for her wheelchair. Now Mary and Robert Granlees lie peacefully together in the Granlees plot in old Live Oak cemetery, dedicated to St. Vincent de Paul. The only extant photograph of Mary hangs in the Clubhouse display.

John D. "Jack" Granlees—(1882–1965) eldest child of Mary and Robert Granlees, married Polly Sheldon of Slough House. For nine years they lived in Mary Granlees' house, and then moved into "the Pratt place," where they remained until Jack's death. He grew alfalfa with his brothers, raised sheep, and then cattle. Polly raised turkeys. Jack was an active member and leader of several stockmen's associations. Jack's son Johnny said that his father worked hard all his life and never got out of debt, and that's the reason Johnny didn't want to be a farmer. Polly and Jack's daughter Anita joked that the only time the adults in her family got along was in the mountains. The Granlees family owned the Union Valley meadow, where they had a cabin. They herded stock there for summer pasture (now under the waters of Union Valley Reservoir, a Sacramento Municipal Utility District "SMUD" lake).

Robert "Bert" Granlees—(1883–1979) the second son of Mary and Robert Granlees, did in fact marry his 8th grade teacher, Anne King, a Stanford graduate. Bert's nephew Johnny Granlees said Bert was between 15–17 years old when they married, and he was older than most 8th graders because of missing school while working on the ranch. Described by his grandchildren as a tall, dark and handsome "cowboy with a "great sense of humor," Bert is mentioned in the annals of the Amador-El Dorado Stockman's Association. Besides working on the family ranch, he took outside work, bought and sold bulls, saved his money, invested it all in a ranch of his own in San Joaquin County, but lost his investment and assets during the Great Depression. He also lost his wife, though they never divorced. She taught school in other areas, and Bert negotiated with his younger brother Art for a life estate on Art's place, the 12½ acres of Granlees property now owned by the author and her husband. For the rest of his life Bert lived in the "ditch tender's cabin," trained horses to the saddle and harness, grew exceptionally sweet melons, whittled walking sticks, and delighted children with his stories. The cabin is now used for storage. A photo of Bert at 14, a lanky young man in black angora chaps and cowboy hat, hangs in the Clubhouse.

George Granlees—(1887–1956) third son of Mary Granlees, the only son who did not inherit land, and the "Georgie" of this story. His military headstone is in the Granlees plot in St Vincent de Paul Cemetery. Various relations describe him as having been emotionally disturbed. He served in World War I and likely left the Army-issue WWI gas mask in an old shed on the ranch where this author found it.

Agnes Hilda Granlees—(1893–1929) the newborn baby girl early in this novel, attended high school in Sacramento and "read all the time," according to her namesake and niece, Hilda Granlees Bloomstine, daughter of Arthur Granlees.

Arthur Granlees—(1898–1962) the youngest child of Mary Granlees, attended Cal Poly. He returned home, married Josephine Walker, and they lived in his mother's house until the family acquired the Brown property—12½ acres on which the 90-year old Mr. Brown had lived since at least the 1850 census. On that land Art built the comfortable two-story house where the author and her husband now live. Art originally raised sheep and dairy cows, and then he raised alfalfa and beef cattle, but he shifted to turkeys during WWII, becoming a premier turkey breeder and egg seller. Turkey men from all over the U.S. wrote their names, dates, and hometowns on the walls of Art's office in the turkey hatchery (now a book warehouse). Art was a leader of many agricultural associations and community boards, including the California State Fair. He was born near the end of this book. Photographs of Art and Josephine, their home, and their Scottish imported sheepdogs (trained to herd turkeys) are on display in the Clubhouse.

Elitha Cumi Donner Wilder—(1832–1923) a major character in *River of Red Gold*, married Perry McCoon in 1847, a few weeks after her rescue from the mountains after being snowbound with the Donner Party. They lived on "his" ranch (title not legal). Perry died 5 years later. In 1854, Elitha married Benjamin W. Wilder.

In 1855, Elitha and Ben traveled to Sonoma where Elitha's younger sisters lived on a dairy farm with the aging Mr. and Mrs. Brunner. Elitha determined to gather her orphaned sisters to live with her under one roof. "Grandma Brunner" had blocked correspondence. That time, the younger girls left stealthily (see Eliza's memoir, *The expedition of the Donner Party*). Elitha and Ben cared for the sisters until they married, seeing to it that they went to school. The Wilder ranch is in the Galt area, near the lower Cosumnes River (some of it now part of the Cosumnes River Preserve). The Wilders had six children. County histories describe Ben as an imposing and successful farmer, and pillar of the local Republican Party. He died in 1898. On August 10, 1902, a second huge tragedy befell Elitha when the wife and three children of her son, George Donner Wilder, died on the family ranch in a house fire. A coroner's report noted that George had been in the barn at the time, in the middle of the night. The *Sacramento Bee* implied that he had nailed the doors and windows shut and set fire to the house, and his guilt explained why he hung himself in the barn. The *Galt Herald* printed George's version, that his wife took the 3 little children (the youngest 4 months) to her bed and set the fire herself. After that, Elitha's son James Wilder, father of several children, worked on the family ranch until he was thrown from a horse and died of a skull fraction in 1919. Elitha has many descendants in the Sacramento-Stockton area. She died before her 91st birthday, and her grave in Elk Grove is a State Landmark. A photograph of her hangs in the Clubhouse display.

Ah Chung—the man living in a "sheep camp." Just after the 2007 interment of Anita Granlees Macklin, 96, in the Granlees plot in the historic St. Vincent De Paul cemetery, family members walked across the open ground to view the site of the house where Anita had lived as a child (Jack and Polly Granlees' house, originally called the Pratt place). The author lagged behind with Anita's cousin Jessie Grimshaw Saner, 95 at the time, and asked about a landmark that had puzzled her—a disturbed rectangle of stones between the site of the Driscoll-Granlees homestead and Jack Granlees's house. Ms Saner said it had been a wall-less floor when she was young, and on that floor Ah Chung lived in a sheep camp (a tiny horse-drawn covered wagon, see photos on Google). When Ms Saner was a child, Ah Chung had been an old man, a ranch caretaker when the Granlees went to summer pasture. Doubtless, many old Chinese men who could not afford to have their bodies shipped to China lived out their days in similar circumstances. His story is lost, but the author imagined that Ah Chung might have been on the crew that improved the pioneer wagon road—the "Amador and Nevada road" (now Hwy 88) in 1862–63.

Catherine Rhoads Sheldon Mahone Dalton—(1832–1905) emigrated from Illinois in the same year as the Donner Party. At 14, she married Jared Dixon Sheldon, ranchero and partner of William Daylor. Sheldon died as told in this book. Catherine was the mother of W. C. Sheldon and 3 other children by Sheldon. She also had children by John Mahone, her second husband, and a son by Dennis Dalton, her third husband. The latter was indeed 17 years her junior. Note that she died a year before she speaks at a meeting in this book.

William Chauncey "WC" Sheldon and Anna Cook Sheldon—"WC" was the only son of Jared Sheldon, pioneer settler of Rancho Omochumne (Omuchumne as he spelled it), the Mexican land grant bounded on the west by Grant Line Road in Sacramento County. After 3 years of college in Benicia, in 1871 WC went to Utah to visit his father's relatives. He came home with wife Ann Cook, a hard-working LDS girl. In 1888, when his six children were growing up, WC built a beautiful 3-story Queen Anne style house that stood as a Sloughhouse landmark until it burned in the 1970s. Active in the Masons and other groups, he imported pheasants from China and entertained bankers and senators by inviting them to hunt in his Thicket, which was off limits to people outside his family. Besides growing hops, fruit and alfalfa, he crossed corn and received a U.S. patent for his Dent variety. He kept the family letters and documents, which dovetailed closely with California history. The stuttering of his three sons must have been a great disappointment. According to some of his grandchildren, WC sternly corrected his sons in attempts to get them to speak clearly, however there is no evidence that he did so in public, as he did in this book. One of his grandchildren fondly remembers WC driving his Cadillac. "He liked to be out and about," she said. He picked her up at Wilson school and drove her home—in a time when children watched the road for automobiles and were excited to see one.

The Sheldon boys—Jared Sheldon (1873–1938) the eldest, played the violin, sang, and stuttered all his life. After his parents passed on, he farmed the ranch alone or with his brothers or, ultimately, his brother-in-law Amon Cothrin. Unlike his father, he did not go to college. Jared married for the first time when he was 65 years old, a few months before his death. George Sheldon, an accomplished trumpeter, stuttered more than his brothers. His father sent him to a special school in hopes of alleviating the speech handicap. It seemed of temporary help, but when he returned home the problem continued. Never married, George was a skilled pen-and-ink mechanical draftsman, particularly in the rendering of ships. In the 1990s, a member of a neighboring family told the author that he was proud to have a book of George Sheldon's beautiful drawings. Lauren, the youngest son, when he was six, stuck his right hand into an early corn-shucking machine and lost three fingers. Lauren never married. After his father's death, he helped his brother Jared farm the property. None of the three sons of WC Sheldon had children, hence the family name died out with that branch of the family.

The Sheldon girls—Polly, Jessie, and Kittie all married local men and bore children. Polly is remembered, often with moist eyes, as a remarkably sweet and talented woman whom everyone loved. A naturalist who could track birds and animals and who cared for orphaned wild animals, she also played the piano very well. Polly and her husband J. D. Granlees "Jack" lived just north of the yellow truss bridge on what had been the ranch of Emanuel Pratt since Gold Rush times. In real life they lived and raised their children there, starting about 10 years later than shown in this book. Kittie Sheldon Cothrin, the youngest daughter, carried on her father's work of preserving documents and correcting media stories about the history of the Sheldon family, and indeed much of Sacramento County. Kittie lined out errors in the print media, penned the true facts in the margins, and mailed them back to the publishers for retraction. She gifted the California state museum at Sutter's Fort with several artifacts related to the pre–Gold Rush Sheldon gristmill, a State Landmark. At her death, her daughter Ellen Cothrin Rosa assumed guardianship of the family papers and, like her mother, added to them and corrected the inaccurate stories. Ellen is a friend, an invaluable source of local history. She was born in the same room, along the same wall of the still lived-in house where the fictional Mae of this book gave birth to her son Billy. The current occupants of the house kindly allowed us to visit inside Mrs. Rosa's first home, still painted "railroad" yellow. Mrs. Rosa is making arrangements to give the voluminous Sheldon papers to a public library.

Catherine "Katy Irene" Warren—one of the "heirs of Cotton" shown on the 1895 property map, was a young child when her mother, Catherine Sheldon Cotton died in childbirth, and 7 when her father, Joseph Cotton, committed suicide while working in the toll station at the Meiss Bridge in Slough House. Katy's maternal grandmother took her in and raised her, but Katy also spent a great deal of her childhood in the nearby home of her aunt Anna and uncle W.C. Sheldon, as shown in this book. She married Robert Warren, manager of the Bridge House toll station-store-saloon-dancehall. A photo of the bungalow that came with that job hangs in the Clubhouse. In this book, Katy Irene makes some assertions about her grandmother, Catherine, with regard to why she divorced her third husband, which might not be true but which some people believed. Whether Katy Irene believed that in real life is unknown.

The Gaffney family—Mary and John Gaffney came from Ireland and settled on land adjacent to the Driscoll-Granlees property. They farmed there for many years, as did their three sons, Peter, James, and John. The boys never married, but the daughters did. The Gaffney's pig-and-dairy strategy described in this book is from Mignon Grimshaw Rothrock, daughter of **Rhoads Grimshaw**, a dashing racer of early automobiles and a pilot of early airplanes. In this novel he is the young man who gives Mae the once over at the Fourth of July picnic. His mother was one of the Gaffney daughters. Sometime after 1932 the Gaffneys sold their property to Mary Granlees. The house, corrals and outbuildings are gone, but the pink roses still bloom in June where Mary Gaffney planted them—now twining high up in the branches of the mulberry trees that once shaded the house.

Sarah Rhoads Daylor Grimshaw—the Grimshaw matriarch of this novel, married William Robinson Grimshaw after her first husband, Wm. Daylor, died of cholera in 1850. She inherited the land shown as "Upper Daylor" on the 1895 map as well as the store on Jackson Road—originally Daylor's Store, then Cosumne Store, which did lucrative business on the road to the "southern mines" and continued to serve the farming community. An educated teenaged man, Grimshaw had come to California on a commercial ship to learn the nautical business. He stayed as a much needed clerk in Daylor's store. After he married Sarah, he studied law in Sacramento but continued to farm and also served as justice of the Peace. Sarah had no children by her first husband, but with Wm. Grimshaw gave birth to seven living children in addition to five who died under the age of four. Six of the seven children were boys, the next to last of them being Fred Grimshaw of this story.

Frederick " Fred" Grimshaw—(1866–1950) foreman of the Sacramento County Grand Jury in the 1930s, and a leader in a number of organizations, Fred Grimshaw developed techniques for processing and marketing French prunes. He and other farmers organized the fruit storage co-op in a warehouse next to the Northern Electric Railroad line (now Sheldon Feed in Wilton), which transported the fruit to Chico, Stockton, and Sacramento in the 1920s. Fred's energy, efficiency, and can-do attitude was the model for the fictional John Dunaway in this novel. Fred's brother Walter signed on a loan for an energetic young man who worked for him— Avelino Signorotti who at 16 came from Switzerland and became a grower in the Cosumne area. That too was a model for the fictional Dunaway getting his start as a farm owner.

Collis P. Huntington—Information and physical description (photo) from *Sunset Limited: The Southern Pacific Railroad and the Development of the American West.*

Abbie Jane Hunter—owner of Ladies Real Estate Investment Company of Carmel, which in 1892 acquired 164 acres of the city tract. The first woman developer/builder in the area, she coined the moniker Carmel-by-the-Sea in her advertising. Hunter's Point in San Francisco, originally an upscale residential area, was named for her family. Abbie Jane sold about 300 lots to teachers, professors and writers, but her efforts to promote Carmel as a haven of rest could not overcome the nation-wide depression shown in this book. She had to sell her interests in 1898. The author attended Carmel High School with a collateral descendant of Ms Hunter, Yvonne Houghtelling Chapelle. For a photo of Abbie Jane Hunter see *Carmel: A History in Architecture*, by Kent Seavey (Arcadia Books, Images of America, 2007), p. 32.

Frank S. Isaminger—the independent freighter who overcame a childhood accident that burned off the fingers of both hands. Information about his childhood accident, his reputation with alcohol and women, his work as a whisky-barrel driver in the vicinity of this book, and the methods he used to control the horses and apply for jobs, are from "Pioneer Family Memories: Part I" by Don Uelmen in *Tailings*, a monthly newsletter of the El Dorado County Historical Society, February, 2005, pp 5–6. Isaminger also had a reputation as a tough fighter, and needed to be one to ward off jealous husbands. His technique involved using his legs to kick out an opponent's feet. The author received this publication from Margaret Rose, granddaughter of Jack and Polly Granlees of Bridge House. Margaret is married to Ellsworth Rose, whose father was raised by his uncle, Frank Isaminger.

Lily—the badly deformed Native American woman shown in this book crawling in the ditch along the road was based on a similarly deformed Miwok woman in the Gold Country town of Murphys, mentioned in *Black Sun of the Miwok* by Jack Burrows, (University of New Mexico Press, 2000). Burrows spent much of his childhood living with his rancher grandparents in Murphys. In the 1930s and 40s, he witnessed some of which he writes, and he interviewed old timers to learn about things that happened earlier. In his Preface he briefly mentions Lucy, "whose horribly mutilated legs were swathed in dirty rags. She was unable to walk, a grotesque and pathetic little figure, kicking along through the dust or mud at the side of the road or down in a ditch. One day (and as recently as 1895) a mile below Murphys, a group of white boys happened to see Lucy crawling towards home. They rocked [stoned] her to death." In their defense "they declared it was to put her out of her misery." Burrows includes a photograph of Lucy on, p. 96 of his book.

The James Miller family of Latrobe, Eliza, Harriett and Frankie—James Miller was an early settler in Latrobe, builder of the Miller Hotel, booster of the town, and a force in getting the SP railroad to extend its rails to Latrobe, and then to Placerville. He and W.S. Cothrin owned sheep grazing land at Emerald Bay on the shore of Lake Tahoe. Mr. Miller moved his family to Oakland, for the reason mentioned in this novel, and moved to the address given. Mr. Miller died in a fire in the living room of his house, just as the train conductor in this book relates. (Information from Ellen Cothrin Rosa).

Casus or Jesús Oliver—historic headman and Miwok elder in Jackson Valley Rancheria. Descendant Rhonda Morningstar Pope and her family are currently considering building a small casino near the site of her great-grandfather's roundhouse.

Robert LeRoy Parker (also George Parker, better known as Butch Cassidy)—one of the most famous outlaws of all time. The period just after his release from the Wyoming State Penitentiary has not been thoroughly documented. *The Californians: Magazine of California History*, a now-defunct monthly journal in which articles were checked by experts for factual accuracy, puts Parker briefly in Round Valley, Humboldt County, California, during some of that time. Assuming he traveled by train, he would have passed through Sacramento to get there. The author of this book imagined he would have stayed a while in Sacramento. However, in real life Parker was released from the Wyoming prison in 1895, after an 18-month stay. That was two years later than shown in this book. (Vol 1, No.2, March-April 1983, edition of *The Californians* in "The Saga of Round Valley," page 16.) Frank Asbill writes of a "young man who came to the little town of Harris (in northern California) in the fall of 1895. Mrs. Cox, needing help on the ranch, hired him. LeRoy Parker became very friendly with young Asbill, teaching him to shoot with a rifle and a six-shooter. LeRoy, it seemed, was expert with both. The next spring, Mrs. Cox heard that the law was after Parker for having stolen the horse he was riding. Mrs. Cox liked the young man very much and did not want to have him caught, so she warned him and suggested that he ride on.

A.J. Pommer—proprietor of music store in Sacramento. Taken from his advertisement in the 1893 *Sacramento City Directory*. His appearance was fiction.

Helen (also Grace or Beulah) Mrose (also Rose or Berry)—(1872–1904) originally Helen Eugenia Williams, married Steven Jennings and had three children by him. Two of her children died. She deserted her husband, taking little Eugenia with her. In Phoenix she married Martin Mrose, a well-to-do cattle rustler. He was arrested. While he was in prison she became the girlfriend of his attorney, John Wesley Hardin—the most feared gunslinger in Texas. The two gutted Mrose's bank account and traveled together with Eugenia. By Hardin's own account he murdered 27 men, and is reputed to have killed 30–40 more. Hardin's story is variously told. Helen disappeared, using aliases, pursued by Jennings, Mrose, and perhaps friends of Hardin. She put Eugenia on a horse and fled to Fresno, California. Later, they rode up the big valley to Sacramento, where newspapers reported her frequent arrests for prostitution, larceny, public drunkenness, and disturbing the peace. Helen used her looks and her disregard of social conventions to mesmerize men of all social stations. See "The Vagrant's Grave" by Dennis McCown in *Western Outlaw-Lawman History Association Journal*, summer 2003, pp. 24–31. And "The Death of Helen Beulah" in *True West Magazine*, May, 1999. McCown is currently writing a book-length biography. He writes that the Sacramento police treated Helen with "peculiar leniency," almost as a celebrity. Found dying on a mattress at the location Mae finds her in this novel (now across the street from Macy's Department Store), she died September 12, 1904, still telling lies. At that time, she was calling herself Helena Grace Rose or Grace Berry. Several years earlier she had given up her daughter to a Catholic school in San Francisco. A wealthy family in San Francisco adopted the girl, but Mr. Jennings, her father, found and returned her to Texas at the age of 12. Helen was buried in a pauper's grave in New Helvetia Cemetery near Sutter's Fort. In the 1950s that cemetery was removed to make room for Sutter Middle School. Hundreds of remains, including Helen's, were relocated to a common grave in East Lawn Cemetery, in

Sacramento. The author first learned of Helen from a presentation delivered by Dennis McCown at *Western Outlaw-Lawmen History Association (WOLA)* conference in Sacramento July 25, 2002. In a recent letter, McCown wrote that he became interested in Helen when his wife looked up a long-lost elderly aunt. She visited 96-year-old Eugenia. Over a tiny glass of sherry that weekend, Eugenia confided that this was the first alcohol she'd had in ninety years. She said that as a little girl she drank beer in saloons with her mother. She then told the story of her young life.

Hiram W. Johnson—(1866–1945) was born in the house on 7th and H Street in Sacramento as described herein. His mother's appearance, personality and opinions are inventions of this author. As a child, he played on the grounds of the Capitol Building while it was being built, and as a man occupied the Governor's Suite 1911-1917. After two years at the University of California, he read law with his father, Grove Johnson, a frequent candidate and holder of public office in the state legislature and Congress. Hiram was his father's campaign manager. Steeped in Republican politics, he was closely associated with the capitalists and lobbyists of the day. He well understood the influence of business upon government. After his 1893 speech, partly quoted in this book, his father never spoke to him again. Hiram left his father's firm and later set up practice in San Francisco, where he developed a reputation for winning cases before the bar. When Frances Heany, a federal prosecutor, was shot in court at the start of a nationally covered graft trials, Hiram Johnson was appointed to take his place. He made short work of the defendant and was credited with sending "Boss Ruef" to San Quentin for taking bribes. That launched him into the governor's office, where he famously made good his promise to regulate the railroad and "kick the Southern Pacific Railroad out of politics." The GOP put up candidates against him, causing Johnson to run as a Progressive, but he did not abandon the Party. He called himself an "insurgent Republican" and a reformer. Ultimately the Party took him back. Johnson remained "incorruptible" (his biographer's word) throughout his political career. In his 2nd term as governor, he was elected to the U.S. Senate, and was re-elected for many years, garnering 80–90 percent of the vote from both political parties. For years on the national stage, he was considered the second most popular politician in the United States, just under Theodore Roosevelt, with whom he worked. A steadfast isolationist, Johnson died in office soon after casting the only vote against ratification of the United Nations. See biography by Lower, *A Bloc of One)*. It was Memorial Day, 1893, not in September as shown here, that Johnson delivered the public address quoted in the *Sacramento Union*, May 31, 1893 and included in this book (Lower, p. 10–11).

James Fair, the Bonanza King—(1831–1894) one of the wealthiest men in the Gilded Age. His appearance, achievements and wealth were taken from books and the newspapers of that time. As he grew older he shuffled and wheezed as he walked, but was always a hard and crafty trader who gave no quarter nor expected any.

Divorced, with ex-wife and daughters enjoying New York society, he lived in the Lick Hotel in San Francisco a short walk from his office, which "bulged with papers." The newspapers said he ate and drank to excess, sometimes consuming huge amounts of brandy for a month while locked in his rooms and refusing to talk to anyone (but the hotel maid talked). Among the myriad of Fair's investments, he developed a rail line on Telegraph Avenue, from Oakland to the then College of California in Berkeley, and installed a full sized coal-fired steam locomotive puffing smoke, to the consternation of the owners of the beautiful houses along that avenue. The affected people organized such fierce opposition that Fair was forced to remove the locomotive. A smaller scale streetcar replaced the train. Fair died in December, 1894, 11 months after the fictional Charlie Rogue of this book dealt with him. Fair's house on Nob Hill was replaced by the famous Fairmont Hotel.

William Tevis—son of Lloyd Tevis, President of Wells Fargo for twenty years. As shown in this book, Wm. Tevis lived in Burlingame with his wife **Maybella Ramona**, the daughter of the first Californio governor after California became a state of he U.S. One of the wealthiest men in the country, young Tevis did indeed lead the Bay Cities Water Company in its effort to sell its project to the City and County of San Francisco for a cost of 10½ million dollars, a million of which was, according to City Manager Abe Ruef, earmarked for himself, Mayor Schmitz and the S.F. supervisors. The source of that water would have been all forks of the American River. Tevis's project failed due to the scandal and publicity of the graft trials. Ironically, beautiful Hetch Hetchy Valley in Yosemite National Park was flooded when the Tuolumne River was tapped instead, to provide water for the development of the burgeoning region later to be called the Bay Area. For a fascinating read about the San Francisco graft trials, see Walter Bean, *Boss Ruef's San Francisco*. The appearance of William and Maybella, their personalities, the reference to the Burlingame property being passed down though her family, and the description of that property are pure invention.

Steffens, J. P. and wife Louisa—lived in the beautiful house, later acquired by the state of California to be the Governor's Mansion, described in this book. Public tours are regularly conducted by State Department of Parks and Recreation. Governor Ronald Reagan and his wife Nancy were the first first-family who refused to live there, fearing that it was a "fire trap." The Steffens daughters, Lottie, Lulu, and Laura were as shown in this book, their gowns described in the *Sacramento Bee* social page for a different social event. This author imagines that J. P. and Louisa entertained state officials in their house, as shown herein.

Lincoln Steffens—(1866–1936) son of the above, Sacramento raised, nationally famous New York journalist in the early 20th century, called a "muckraker" by his friend President Theodore Roosevelt. Steffens's *Autobiography* is a delightful description of Sacramento and its people in the 1870s and 80s. Part 2 is a thoughtful analysis of the problems of a democracy in a capitalistic system (all chapters previously published in magazines and big-city newspapers). His book *Shame of the Cities* (1904), the first of that genre, was widely read in America. His personality comes through his writings and cartoons of him, his appearance from photos.

Two boys on H Street—Lincoln Steffens and Hiram Johnson were born in 1866. They grew up half a block from each other, walked to the same grade school, attended the same university, and both of them became renowned in their efforts to end the control of big business over government. Steffens traveled from New York to cover the San Francisco graft trials for the big newspapers. He wrote detailed columns about many players (See *Autobiography,* Part 2). This is the entirety of his writing about his old neighbor: "Hiram Johnson, an attorney in the graft prosecution, took the case, and it was he, with his fire and force, who won the great final victory and so came to head the Progressive movement in California and become governor and U.S. senator." In Part 1, Steffens names boyhood pals, but pens not a word about Hiram. The author finds this intriguing.

Ah Sen—In 1910, a woman 70 years old who had been in the U.S. at least since 1860 (the earliest date of agricultural records) owned a farm business in Sloughhouse, where she raised chickens. Ah Sen was the sole Chinese female agricultural business owner in all of California. (Information from 50 county archives, meticulously researched and analyzed in *This Bittersweet Soil,* by SuCheng Chan. Footnote p. 394–395). Nothing more is known about Ah Sen. The syllable "Ah" preceding Chinese names in early California was a language convention akin to the appended "san" on Japanese names, not a part of the actual name. At the time of this novel, Chinese people were prohibited from owning property in California; hence this author assumed that Ah Sen lived on Sheldon land, the land set aside for Chinese workers between Deer Creek and the Cosumnes River in Sloughhouse. The granddaughters of WC Sheldon described the location and appearance of the small houses used by the Sheldon's Chinese farm workers. They recall a photograph of one such house, partly on stilts, perched on the side of the river levee to keep it above the floods—the house of this novel. Mrs. Putt, a Miwok neighbor, told the author that as a child she walked around that area and found strange little melons growing wild on that levee. During and after the Gold Rush, perhaps 2-300,000 single Chinese men came for gold and other employment. In 1882, the Exclusion Law barred further Chinese immigration, excepting female prostitutes and male laborers under certain conditions. Thus, Chinese women in California were rare at the turn of the century. The author imagined that Ah Sen's story was the same as many others—sold by destitute parents in China and forced to work in San Francisco brothels. It was also assumed that she was the wife of **Soon Shin Sin** (b. 1833 in China – d. 1898 Sloughhouse). No marker is extant today, though he is listed among the interred in the Pioneer Cemetery. See *Historic and Cosumnes and the Sloughhouse Pioneer Cemetery*, by Norma Baldwin Ricketts 2nd printing 1992 (National Society of Utah Pioneers). Traditionally, Chinese men had their bodies shipped to China for burial. For more about that practice, see *Bury My Bones in California: the Saga of a Chinese Family*, by Lani Ah Tye (her family kept "Ah" in their American name). The author imagined that Soon Shin Sin opted to be buried in Slough House so that his wife or long-time companion, Ah Sen, could be buried beside him. It is not known where she is buried.

W. S. Cothrin of "Cothrin's Corner" or "Cothrin's Station"—like many men of early California he was an energetic opportunist. He raised large numbers of sheep (until the freeze that killed them all in their Tahoe-Emerald Bay summer pasture, as mentioned in this book). He and **Mrs. Cothrin** also built a store on the road (later the railroad station) and also had a thriving wood business on their considerable property, cutting/shipping wood to a wood yard in Sacramento. After the sheep died, W.S. became a dairyman, and all his life he worked his little gold mine not far from his front door. He also worked as a guard in Folsom Prison. The SP provided a building package for their station managers—all the materials including the yellow paint—for a two-story house. The Cothrin's house was new in 1894, when shown in this book. Also standard for railroad workers, the Cothrins had lifelong rail passes. The three children, **Carrie, Harry,** and **Roy** rode their horses to school in Latrobe as shown here. When the SP RR first extended the tracks to Cothrin's Station, the company built an oak floor amidst a forest of huge old-growth oaks, so that rail customers could dance in that romantic place under summer moons. A fire destroyed the oak forest, but the floor remained, no longer used for dances. The Cothrins relocated that floor to their dairy's milk house, where it is today (now used for storage by tenants). Cothrin Road, now paved, winds up the hill to a small subdivision, no longer to the enclave of Nisenan people who once helped on the ranch.

Mrs. Craig—the Native American midwife at the Cothrin Ranch, who lived up the road with her people in a little gulch. Nancy, one of her daughters, married Jeff Jaimeson of this book. Her husband's feet were disfigured by the freeze in Tahoe as described herein.

Dr. Thomas W. Huntington—the first physician in the United States to have an antiseptic operating room. He practiced during the 1890s at the Southern Pacific Hospital located at C and 13th street in Sacramento.

The Jaimeson brothers—Jeff, Andy George, and Allen are remembered as Indians working around the Cosumne and Slough House area. They lived in small cabins on various local properties. This author guesses that they were of the Cosumne tribe that settled at Old Sheep Corral with their people, but unlike the others, did not migrate to Auburn. Ellen Rosa's documents show that the Jaimeson brothers specified that when they died, they wanted to be buried in Auburn. They are buried there with the above spelling.

Zachariah Kirkwood and his daughter—settled on a ranch in Jackson, Amador County, and also received title to the beautiful meadow of his book (now part of Kirkwood Ski Resort). He built the log cabin saloon, and soon afterward attached the two-story little Inn to the saloon. Old timers recalled his daughter **Elva** as a devoted card player. Gone are the log barn, milk house, and butcher house, but the atmospheric old saloon and Inn are still in business, remarkably the same as in the 1860s. Three counties come together within the walls: Alpine, Amador, and El Dorado. The joke was that if you needed to elude the law, you could go up in the rafters (sleeping quarters at one time) and "get out of the county." The "kitchen leanto" in the back of the saloon is now restaurant seating, and the downstairs of the attached Inn is the kitchen. Other than that, it is the same dark and cozy place where you can almost hear the midnight howls of drovers into their cups in a far different time. A visitor in the saloon will still find cowboys who drive cattle to summer pasture, but they haul them in trucks. The biggest difference is that visitors stopping for lunch or dinner vastly out number the cattlemen.

Congressman Anthony Caminetti—(1854–1923), son of a successful gold seeker from Italy who settled in Jackson, Amador County, Anthony attended California State University (now U. C. Berkeley), and then studied law. He practiced law in Jackson, married, and had three children. Elected to the state legislature, and later to Congress, he continued to serve the interests of his state. His lasting fame is as author of the federal Caminetti Mining Act of 1893, which allowed hydraulic mining to return to the state (9 years earlier it had been stopped by the courts due to damage to agriculture). After 1893, the debris and mud or "slickens" had to be captured in prescribed dams. According to *Amador County History* (Ladies Club Publication), Caminetti "secured the highway during his congressmanship"— now State Hwy 88 over Carson Pass to Nevada. Always a lover of the Sierra, he bought property at Silver Lake where a large hotel had burned down, and built Caminetti's Resort approximately where Kay's Resort is at this writing (slated for demolition).The race track at the NW end of the lake was long remembered as "the center of many lively events" according to "One Hundred Years at Silver Lake," a report to the College of the Pacific, cited in Summerville's *Legend of a Road*. Due to the raised level of the natural lake (a PG&E impoundment now), the racetrack is likely under water. Drew Caminetti, the Congressman's son, operated the resort. Weakening in his last years, the old lawmaker spent a great deal of time there in the invigorating air.

MORE ABOUT HISTORICAL HAPPENINGS
Part I

The 1895 Property Map—Note that the top of the map is west, to fit the dimensions of this book. The fictional Duffy family appears on the scene at the start of the Panic of '93. By 1895, some of the properties had changed hands, and continued to do so as the depression lingered through the decade. Fictional John Dunaway would have purchased the property of Benjamin Bailey and James Gallogly. Author's apologies to the real people who lived on that land. Unlike the Slough House area, no descendants remain today, because the land was thoroughly dredged. Even the "**dredger colony**" of 1936–1944, with its horseshoe of little houses (see end of Part V) has been forgotten except by a few people who had childhood friends in the "colony", including Mary Augustine Kassis and Hilda Granlees. Rancho Murieta developers created a golf course on the dredge tailings, and a large subdivision called Rancho Murieta South has been built around it.

Toll roads and bridges—In California all roads and bridges were originally built as private enterprises. Toll stations often served as stage stops, saloons, restaurants and stores. In the setting of this book, three toll bridges crossed the Cosumnes River: Michigan Bar, Bridge House, and Meiss Bridge in Slough House. Additionally, Latrobe Road and parts of the Amador-Nevada Road (now State Hwy 88) were originally toll roads, and no doubt others were too. In February 1929, the California Highway Commission reported to the Legislature: "The further construction of all privately owned toll bridges should be prohibited." This 200-page report concluded that private bridge tolls were found to be excessive (on average about 88% higher than necessary) compared with what state-built and serviced bridges were estimated to cost. It was recommended that the state and counties "finance or build bridges by the issuance of bonds payable out of the income of such structures." The report found that private interests often built bridges where the traffic didn't warrant, but which opened areas where the bridge investors had financial interests. During the 1930s the state and counties of California assumed responsibility for building and maintaining all bridges and roads.

The Cosumne people—Archeological investigation of the original Cosumne mound, or midden, in the California Delta indicates continuous occupation since "about A.D. 1200" until abandonment during the "plague" of 1833, according to James A. Bennyhoff (1926–1993), professor of anthropology, who devoted much his career to righting the previous anthropological reports on the California native people. He notes that errors had occurred due to social dislocation after the Great Illness killed an estimated one-half or more of the Indian population up and down California. Further dislocation occurred due to missionization and its resultant warfare, the "pacification" efforts of John Sutter including military attacks, and the "coastal slave trade" in which women and children were stolen, and then the genocide and starvation of the Gold Rush—all within a 20-year period. The survivors consolidated to some extent, which added confusion, as did the traditional silence about deceased loved ones. The saga of the Cosumne people includes the battles of 1828–29 against Mexican government forces, their dramatic departure from Mission San Jose, about 10 years as a principal labor force in John Sutter's fort, perhaps 30 years at Old Sheep Corral on or near the Daylor ranch (later Grimshaw) working for some of the people in this novel, and finally to Auburn. This author has found a couple of missing puzzle pieces and plans to write in more detail about the Cosumne, who left their mark on every phase of early California history. They also gave their name to a river, a political district, a school, a town, and a once thriving store—the two latter entities now forgotten. In the Miwok language Cos = salmon. Umne (um-nee) = the people of.

Dixon's Grove, William Tecumseh Sherman's land—Thought to be the only prominent American named for an Indian chief, Sherman resigned his captaincy in the U.S. Army in 1853 to become a banker in San Francisco. Later in life he wrote, "I can handle a hundred thousand men in battle, and take the City of the Sun, but am afraid to manage a lot in the swamp of San Francisco." (*Memoirs* by William Tecumseh Sherman, Charles Royster, 1990, Literary Collections), pp. 133–134.) This author wonders if the swamp he jokingly referred to was located in Slough House (slough = swamp)—perhaps deemed by most of his readers to be the same general vicinity as San Francisco. Sherman's bank failed in the financial Panic of 1857, and he found himself in receivership, owning title to an agricultural property adjacent to the south bank of the Cosumnes River, Post Office: Slough House. He left California never to return. **William Dixon** leased the Sherman property, and at some point acquired title to it. He also acquired several other large properties nearby, and he makes a brief appearance in this book. Dixon's Grove, with its community picnics and carousel, was fondly remembered by the Sheldon family and others in the area. Horses from the carousel "rotted in somebody's barn," according to Ellen Rosa. In 1859, Sherman accepted an offer to administer the Louisiana State Seminary of Learning & Military Academy in Pineville, Louisiana, where he was a popular leader—until he advised his colleagues not to support the secessionists. He maintained that the South's secession was a folly doomed to fail. In 1861, at the outbreak of war, he resigned his position and returned to the North, where he rejoined the U.S. Army as a Colonel and became one of the most renowned generals in the Civil War.

Indians riding the rails to find farm work—this information is from an interview with Dwight Dutschke, Miwok elder and staff to the Office of Historical Preservation at the California Department of Parks and Recreation. Dutschke also provided details about the difficulty of Indians finding paid work in the late 19th an early 20th centuries. His father and uncle, as 10 and 11-year-old boys, shoveled ore into railcars for fifty cents per carload, helping their family survive.

Ione Methodist Church—Methodist Episcopal historic church. The cornerstone was laid in 1862 and the locally fired red brick church was completed in 1866. Dedicated as the Ione City Centenary Church and later popularly known as the Cathedral of the Mother Lode, this church was the first to serve the people in Ione and surrounding areas. The church is registered as California Historical Landmark #506 and is listed on the National Register of Historic Places (NPS-77000287). Services are still held there every Sunday, followed by potluck luncheons in the church basement.

Gold extraction techniques—An arrastra uses a stone boat for crushing gold-bearing quartz, pulled in circles by a horse or mule tied to a post. *Arrastrar* means "to drag" in Spanish. The stone leavings of an arrastra can be seen on a little hill near the Miser family cemetery. **Mercury**, historically called quicksilver, amalgamates fine gold and greatly facilitates its recovery from sand in pans and sluice boxes. Although miners tried to recover their mercury after use, much of it slipped away into streams, where it affects the health of those streams to this day. Most placer miners in the 19th and early 20th centuries purchased 5- and 10-gallon canisters of mercury several times a year; it was available in every Mother Lode mercantile. The hard rock mines bought the 25-gallon size. (From conversations in 1997 with Raymond G. Simpson, 95 at the time, who had just read *River of Red Gold*. He telephoned from a group home in Las Vegas and told of his life's work in gold. Starting as a young teenager, he supported himself as a solo placer miner in Lotus (near Coloma) and many other areas. Later he learned to detect quicksilver and mined that too. He provided simple instructions on how to build a crude mercury distillery. He never had a partner. He exchanged most of his gold for money, but in the 1930s pounded much of it into gold leaf at night and applied it to the windows of banks and other businesses by day. His tools were simple: a stencil for varnishing the letters onto glass to make them sticky, an oversized book for transporting the fragile gold leaves between the pages, and a boar-bristle hairbrush made magnetic by brushing his hair to pick up the fragile gold leaf from the pages and apply it to the sticky letters. He trimmed the gold with a razor and covered the letters with several coats of clear varnish. In the Great Depression of the 1930s, banks wanted the appearance of prosperity conveyed by gold lettering. When neon lights became popular in the 1940s, Mr. Simpson, still a placer miner, supplied gold to a neon factory in Los Angeles. In a shaky hand he wrote the author a letter and enclosed a generous packet of gold leaf inside a cardboard jacket. The need for a hairbrush to handle it was immediately obvious.

Proto-Indians—Just outside the boundary of Rancho Murieta, anthropologists doing a surface-survey in the 1990s found an ancient village site with a large number of greenstone chunks that had been quarried by people 10,000 to 14,000 years ago. Knapping debris on the surface indicated that the rock had been removed from a nearby ancient quarry—currently at the bottom of Lake Calero and subject of a full investigation by Peak Associates for an Environmental Impact Report before Rancho Murieta developers impounded the water in the 1970s. That dig pushed back the estimated time of arrival of the first people in California by about 5000 years. Apparently, the ancient quarrymen took blocks of stone to their village, where the knappers made large stone points used to hunt woolly mammoths, giant buffalo and other extinct mammals of the Ice Age. The surface survey in the 1990s also described the cellar of a Gold Rush–era cabin dug into the mound, or midden, of that earliest race of people. The author of this book has watched the site change over a 30-year period. Currently, cattle hooves are gradually leveling the cellar, which 30 years ago appeared to have been lined in part by chunks of the quarried greenstone. A full anthropological investigation of this Proto-Indian village and Gold Rush dwelling was never conducted because the large proposed "Deer Creek" development that prompted the surface survey failed to be approved by the County of Sacramento, and because developers, not public institutions, now fund nearly all anthropological digs as mitigation for environmental damage. As a result, anthropological findings in California are often found in private collections and corporate offices rather than on library shelves.

Miser Property—The Sacramento Valley Conservancy conducts public tours of the former Isabella Miser property, which is still grazing land as it was in the 19th century—cattle now instead of sheep. The Conservancy does not own the grazing land where the Miser cemetery and the apparent Proto-Indian village site are located, and therefore those places are not featured on the tour. The Conservancy is sensitive to providing information that could lead to more vandalism. For dates and times of walking and equestrian tours, star-gazing, birding, and other public Conservancy events see: *www.sacramentovalleyconservancy.org.*

The Sheldon house—Three stories, built in 1888 in the Queen Anne style by W. C. Sheldon, this house was a Slough House landmark for nearly a century. After WC's son Jared died, the house was sold, the land no longer capable of sustaining a farm family. The old home became housing for farm workers. In 1979, the brick chimney apparently shifted, and on a cold winter night a blaze left in the fireplace ignited the joists upstairs and the house burned to the ground. No one was killed. No building stands there now.

The Sheldon property—The original Mexican Land Grant, five leagues of land (17 miles long and 3 miles wide) along the Cosumnes River, estimated at 18,661 square acres is defined by its western boundary, Grant Line Road in Sacramento County, and its eastern boundary—the middle of the Cosumnes River. The river flows south along that stretch. The shape of the land grant makes an obvious footprint on the county map. In 1844, Mexican Governor Michaeltorena granted the land to pioneer Jared Dixon Sheldon, who immediately gave the northern half to his partner William Daylor, who died of cholera in 1850. His childless 18-year-old widow, Sarah Rhoads Daylor, inherited that half of the land and married William Robinson Grimshaw. Their property was divided or sold among the descendants.

The Sheldon portion of the Grant went to Jared Dixon Sheldon's 18-year-old widow Catherine Sheldon after he died in the shootout described in this book. Catherine remarried twice and had children by both husbands in addition to three children by her first husband. Her first son, W.C. Sheldon of this story, inherited and acquired a total of 1,000 acres. At his death in 1927, his land was divided among his six children.

Slough House Inn—the source of Catherine Sheldon Mahone's livelihood after her marriage to John Mahone. He had built the Inn into a major roadhouse, and for many years it served as a saloon, dancehall, and stage stop on the road to the "southern mines." Catherine tended bar after Mahone's death, and continued to do so after her marriage to Dennis Dalton. That marriage soon ended in divorce. Descendants tell of Catherine keeping her sleeping infant, Ed Dalton, in a crate under the bar while she worked. At this writing the Slough House Inn is shut down for the first time since the Gold Rush, and is for sale by a group of descendants and others. Current owners hope that a combination of public and private interests will buy the Inn and continue to operate it, perhaps partly as a museum and a restaurant-bar franchise, keeping its historic qualities intact.

Yellow Sandstone—sandstone with red splotches and veins, was skillfully quarried from the same area as the greenstone in Proto-Indian times—the quarry now under Lake Calero in Rancho Murieta. The sandstone lining the one-room dugout of John Driscoll (currently being pilfered from the unprotected site) came from that source. A second dwelling using those stones was the house after which some old timers believe Stone House Road was named, the one near the corner of Stone House Road and Latrobe Road. After it was abandoned every stone was removed. It is also possible that the school at the corner of Jackson and Stone House was built of that quarried sandstone, and when it shut down in 1872 the stones were pilfered; and when the school was reopened, the fathers of the students rebuilt it of wood. Elizabeth Pinkerton interviewed June Hogaboom, the last teacher in the Stone House school, regarding the school's name. Pinkerton summarizes Ms Hogaboom's response in her book, *History Happened Here. Book I, p. 1:* "Old timers say there were many Chinese who lived in the area. They came there after they finished building the railroad that linked the West to the rest of the nation... They perfected the craft of stone construction, and today, Stone House Road is a reminder of those days." A much larger house made from the same beautifully cut stones stood abandoned for at least fifty years. On June 4, 1986, *The Elk Grove Citizen* printed a photo of it in conjunction with Ms Pinkerton's column, *History*

Happened Here, soliciting information from any who might know its history. The 2-story, high-ceiling house stood near the Cosumnes River in a back field of the old Jauch ranch south of Hwy 16. On private property and not visible from the road, it wasn't pilfered as quickly, but the house is completely gone now. In the early 1940s, the parents of Lou and Mary Augustine sharecropped the Hanlon farm (now the equestrian facility). As children, they played around that eerie old house with missing doors and windows—a home for owls and bats. Later in life they wondered who had built it, but that story is lost.

Part II

Sacramento Electric, Gas & Railway Company—generated coal-powered electricity in the early 1890s. In 1895, the 25-mile transmission line from the Folsom Dam powerhouse, then the longest electric transmission line in the world, ended at the 6th and I Street facility in Sacramento, replacing coal generators. For a full description of the excitement that caused, see *Golden Notes: Carnival of Lights* (Sacramento County Historical Society, 75th Anniversary Edition, July 1970). In 1896, San Francisco–based Pacific Gas & Electric Company (PG&E) purchased the Sacramento company. Native son Hiram Johnson, who was governor 1911–1917, was a progressive supporter of customer-owned utility districts. In 1923, Sacramento County voted to found the customer-owned Sacramento Municipal Utility District (SMUD). PG&E investors quickly filed a lawsuit. The case was litigated for nearly a quarter century. Ultimately the courts sided with SMUD, which started providing power in 1946. PG&E continues to file lawsuits aimed at preventing communities near Sacramento from annexing to SMUD. They failed in the 1980s (Folsom City) and succeeded in 2006 (Yolo County).

The Pacific Water Cure and Health Institute—7th and L Street in Sacramento was established in 1870 by Mr. Marion F. Clayton, who came to California for gold but failed to find treasure. After his death in 1892, his accomplished widow, Sarah Babcock Clayton, a former teacher and Secretary of the Sanitary Commission in Ohio during the Civil War, continued her husband's Institute business. From the first, she involved herself in Sacramento health care issues, persuading the county supervisors to replace the run-down "pest house" (receiving hospital). At that time water treatments of various sorts were popular as curatives and preventatives of disease. While running the Institute, Mrs. Clayton also became known as "the orphan's friend." She served as director of the Sacramento Orphan Asylum, and ultimately founded the Sacramento Orphanage and Children's Home, which still operates today as the Sacramento Children's Home. Information from *Capital Women*, pp. 71–72. **Enemas and high colonics**—For an interesting analysis of the late 19th century and early 20th century fixation with flushing out the colon with water and caustic chemicals, see Sherwin B. Nuland in *The American Scholar*, summer 2002, pp. 131–134. After the discovery of microbes (seen through newly invented microscopes in 1867), the medical establishment endorsed the autointoxication theory of disease, which posited that feces in the colon, which could be seen teeming with microbes, were the source of most illnesses. At the time of this novel, many establishment doctors recommended "colonics" and "high colonics" (the flushing of the entire colon) as a regular part of a health regime to prevent the movement of microbes upward to the heart and lungs. In particular, this affected people with the time and money to visit water-cure establishments. Unfortunately, when done to excess, colon flushing caused weakness and death. The author assumed that the Water Institute would have been under the sway of that medical fad, though no evidence supports that. In the 21st century a resurgence of interest in water cures and colon flushing can be found on the web.

"Floaters" pushed downstream—the early police practice of pushing unrecognized corpses out into the mainstream of the Sacramento River in hopes they would become the problems of some other jurisdiction or float away through the Bay and into the ocean. (From a presentation by James E. Henley at a Corral of Westerners monthly meeting in 2001.) Henley has long been Sacramento's pre-eminent historian, serving for many years as staff to the Sacramento County History and Science Commission. View his entertaining videos about early Sacramento on YouTube.

Part III

Tubbs Hotel and Resort in Oakland—The largest structure in Oakland, when built by Hiram Tubbs in 1879. This destination resort cost $200,000 to build and covered a three-block area between 4th and 5th Avenue and East 12th to 14th Streets—originally amid old growth oaks. Tubbs also developed the surrounding area into fine Victorian housing. A second Tubbs Hotel was built by Hiram's brother in the hot springs area of Sonoma. The Tubbs brothers had profited from their rope manufacturing business during the Gold Rush boom. For about 10 years the Oakland resort operated is own streetcar (The Tubbs Line) to carry customers from the central city, across a trestle over Lake Merritt, to the hotel and back. Originally using horsepower, Mr. Tubbs later installed coal-powered generators in the hotel to supply electricity to the streetcars and a then fabulous number of incandescent lights in the structure. The streetcar line was renamed the San Leandro and Haywards Electric at about the time of this novel, and presumably it was sold to those developers. A large courtyard of lawns and gardens was used for games such as croquet and badminton. Spiritualists held séances, and famous speakers and entertainers appeared in the hotel's auditorium. Long-term hotel residents included Oakland's "Water King" Anthony Chabot (See *The Water King*, p. 124, for a photo of the hotel) and other wealthy men, who enjoyed the large dining doom and the gentleman's saloon. After his wife died in 1888, Daniel Stein, a financier and executive of an eastern railroad, whose investments in streetcar lines and real estate had made the family wealthy, moved into the hotel with his daughter Gertrude (of subsequent literary fame) for about a year. Daniel Stein died in 1891, not in January 1894, as shown in this book. On August 19, 1893, the entire hotel burned down in a huge conflagration preserved in photos. This occurred 4½ months before the fictional characters in this book supposedly stayed there.

The Strike at the Southern Pacific Rail yard—shown in his book as it happened in Sacramento, in tandem with the Pullman Strike in Illinois. The dates are accurate, as are the news reports about it, though most of those are cut or summarized. Homeless workers did indeed camp in the bottomland of the American River alongside a large number of people made homeless by the economic depression. The two Sacramento papers and the local militia did indeed side with the strikers. Sacramento was very much a railroad town. But as the strike continued, and national publicity recounted the deliberate crashing of the train and the death of federal troops, local support weakened as shown herein.

Part IV

Historic cemetery on Jackson Road—The acre of land for a Catholic church was donated by Señora María Teresa de la Guerra y Noriega Hartnell, wife of William Hartnell, after whom a California college is named. The seafaring Englishman, Mr. Hartnell, settled in Monterey before the U.S. acquired California under terms of the U.S.–Mexican War treaty. He and María Teresa had 19 children. During that time Mr. Hartnell worked for the Mexican governor and was often paid in land, including a large land grant along the south bank of the Cosumnes River. After he died, his widow traveled to view her inherited properties. By that time the Gold Rush was booming in the Sierra foothills, and land values were high along the Cosumnes. She felt sorry that so many of the miners had no place to worship. The pious widow sold her acreage south of the Bridge House bridge with the stipulation that an acre be set aside for a church. The mostly Irish miners built a small frame church and dedicated it to St John. Northern California Diocese archivist Father William Breault explained to the author that in 1850, the diocese was stretched too thin to handle hundreds of Gold Rush communities as well as coastal churches, so the tiny church, not being officially dedicated, was one of many so-called "mission churches." The doors were unlocked every other Sunday when an itinerant priest rode in on horseback from Amador County to perform Mass. As was the tradition, Catholics buried their dead in the sacred ground of the churchyard. In 1919, a new St Joseph's Church was dedicated in Elk Grove, and local church members demolished the then-hazardous old structure, leaving only the surrounding gravestones. In 2007 the Catholic Church reclaimed the historic cemetery and dedicated it to St. Vincent de Paul.

The Big Canyon mining camp—About 3 miles from old Shingle Springs, this area is now fenced off due to hazards from the old mine. Big Canyon Creek has flooded an area that appears to be a mine cave-in, and a number of years ago someone drowned there. The head-frame is gone, but the ruins of the brick powder magazine can be seen, as well as the foundations of the mine-house, the stamp mill, and the concrete chutes where trams angled down into the depths of the mine. The author used that layout for this book. Old exploratory tunnels dug into the hills remind the visitor of the days of individual efforts to find gold—also mentioned herein. Hard rock mining on the site had two phases, the first barely remembered. That older layout might have been more correct for 1894, had the details been known. The author is grateful to Wm. Scheiber, owner of the property, for showing her around.

Yellow Snake Peak—an old story about a giant snake in mythological times is associated with the little peak in Rancho Murieta. Somewhere in the 15 years of talking to people and reading Indian lore, or maybe dreaming it, the author learned that a giant yellow snake had made the peak by coiling up and squeezing the earth. Native people also told of a giant white snake in Clear Lake (See *Mabel McKay: Weaving the Dream* by Greg Saris, p. 9). People feared the poison made from it, and feared that certain people had possession of it. The author named the peak "Yellow Snake" in the early draft of this book, but a couple of years later read Brian Bibby's book *Deeper than Gold: A Guide to Indian Life in the Sierra Foothills* (Heyday Books, 2005). On pages 80–81 he tells a story told to him by Betty Castro of Auburn, which she heard as a child when she and her family lived in a labor camp harvesting hops in Cosumne and Sloughhouse circa 1915. She said that kiiki, a giant snake, once lived nearby, and people feared it because it could swallow a human being whole. One day it went to the level plain and coiled up, causing the earth to mound up and up, until its head was atop the mound. From there it spoke to the people, predicting a devastating future when most people would die. Then the snake went away and they never saw it again. The snake's color was not mentioned. The author searched her notes and looked in all the books, but could not find the source of the *yellow* snake story. She kept the color yellow, and invites anyone who knows more about it to contact her for a correction in the next printing. Today, although the point of the peak is bulldozed flat for a gazebo and a water tank, and Hwy 16 cuts across its northern side, the "coils" can still be seen. Rancho Murieta residents cap the peak with a tree of colored lights every Christmas and attend dawn services there on Easter mornings.

Historical Medicine—Dr. Irma West, retired physician involved in the preservation of medical artifacts and literature, when asked whether a man with the injuries of Charlie Rogue could have survived under the medical care of Dr. Huntington in 1894, consulted two other physicians. She reported back to the author that Charlie's chances of survival would have been about 5%. Irma West volunteers in the fascinating Museum of Medical History, where strange and frightening-looking machines are on display. Located at 5380 Elvas Avenue in Sacramento, telephone 916-452-267. Free to the public. Weekdays 9 A.M. to 4 P.M., except holidays. The unfolding medical examination table used by Dr. Rudi of this novel is in that museum and was displayed at the State Fair.

Part V

Farm Labor—Native Americans were the first farm workers in California, starting with the missions and early Spanish-Mexican ranches. As shown in this book, the Sheldon family employed the Jackson Valley Rancheria Miwok people to harvest their corn, and the workers made corn-stalk "teepees" as temporary shelters (From Ellen Cothrin Rosa). When growers needed more labor at harvest time, Native Americans rode the rails to obtain work. As placer mining declined, thousands of Chinese men left the streams and rivers. Many of them became the predominant farm labor force (1850s–1890s), and also the popular "China Garden" growers and vendors. The Alien Exclusion Laws of 1882 and beyond, designed to choke off Chinese immigration, almost succeeded. As Chinese laborers aged, died or returned to China, and those without the means became old and infirm, Japanese labor filled the void and quickly predominated in hops, grapes, berries, and in all Delta crops. However, WC Sheldon, like many specialty fruit growers in the state, continued to employ Chinese labor to work in his peach and plum orchards. Chinese labor contractors were allowed to import specialty workers from the Pearl Delta steeped in centuries of knowledge about fruit growing in a climate like California's. See Vaught, *Cultivating California* and Suchen Chan, *This Bittersweet Soil*. After the U.S. acquired the Philippine Islands as a result of the war against Spain at the turn of the century, Filipinos migrated to California, replacing other ethnic groups on many fields and ranches. Meanwhile, Mexican workers, always close at hand, gradually overwhelmed other ethnic and white workers. However in the Sloughhouse area, old-time ranchers report that it wasn't until the "Bracero" guest-worker program, after WWII, that Mexican workers were seen in local fields. The Japanese names mentioned in this book, Yoshida and Hirata, were taken from Stone House School records in the mid-1920s; it is possible those families were present as early as 1906. The Mori family is remembered in Sloughhouse. Perhaps the Hirata and Yoshida families, like the Moris, were relocated to internments camps during WWII and never returned. See *Dandelion Through The Crack*, by Kiyo Sato (Willow Press, 2008), reissued as *Kiyo's Story* in 2009, for a stunning and poetic memoir of a Japanese family in Sacramento losing everything in the relocation and starting over again as farm laborers, ultimately reaching their goal of citizenship and equality.

Interior of St. Joseph's pioneer church and religious tolerance—Information from author interviews in 1994 with men who attended church there as children: Tony Riella, then age 88, a worker on the Schneider ranch who married into the Schneider family, said that Art Granlees supervised the demolition of the old church in 1919, when a new St Joseph's church was dedicated in Elk Grove. George Signorotti, life-long resident and hops and asparagus grower in Cosumne, now deceased, described the spare interior of the tiny church. Cecil Brown of Placerville, then age 91, who in his youth lived in Live Oak, also described the church interior as depicted in this book and said that his family held a funeral there for his Protestant grandmother. They buried her in the tiny, unnamed non-Catholic cemetery, now between the 8th and 14th fairways on the Rancho Murieta South golf course. Jake Schneider, then 78, now deceased, said his Protestant parents sent him to Sunday school at St Joseph's Church because it was the only one around and they wanted him to be familiar with Christianity.

California's Great Flood—"Beginning on December 24, 1861, it rained constantly for almost four weeks, causing the largest flood in California's recorded history. All of the state's many rivers ran over their banks, and the entire Sacramento-San Joaquin Valley was inundated for an extent of 300 miles, averaging 20 miles in breadth. The rain created an inland sea in Orange County lasting about three weeks with water standing 4 feet deep up to four miles from the river" (Wikipedia). Average rainfall Dec-Jan-Feb in San Francisco = 12". In 1861–62, total rainfall during those months was 43". In the 2nd worst flood in California history (1997–98) 12" of rain fell in January in San Francisco. In January 1862, the rainfall was nearly 25". A quarter of all property in the state was destroyed. (From: "The Great California Flood of 1862" by Taylor and Taylor, The Fortnightly Club, Redlands, 2006). The catastrophe prompted Sacramento to raise the city as shown in this book. One of the worst droughts in California history 1862–65, followed that flood. This author altered the weather pattern to fit her story, and made the drought precede the flood.

The American-Cosumnes Water Project—Starting in the 1890s, San Franciscans interested in developing "Greater San Francisco" started looking for a bigger water supply from the Sierra. Doubtless the depression of the 1890s slowed them down. However in 1906, Bay Cities Water Company, with William Tevis at the helm, presented a project with 13 reservoirs. The San Francisco Supervisors, with the strong urging of "Boss Abe Ruef," took steps toward approving the Bay Cities project, including abandoning rights along the Tuolumne River. The Bay Cities project never included a dam at Michigan Bar or a forebay in the Rancho Murieta area, as in this novel. That part is pure fiction, but the cost of the project was real—$10½ million dollars, a million of it earmarked for the city officials. Also true is how that favored project was discredited due to public exposure of the bribe. Tevis tried to sue a newspaper for defamation of his character, but that backfired when the venue was cleverly shifted out of Kern County, where he filed it— a county in which the Tevis family owned much of the land and was said to run the government and courts like a medieval fief-dom (From *Boss Ruef's San Francisco*). An identical case was filed by a friend of the newspaper in San Francisco, and at the trial, two supervisors testified that Ruef had told them the money for a yes vote on this project would be larger than any they had as yet seen. The libel case was dismissed. One of the first acts of the next city administration was to approve Plan B. Hetch Hetchy Valley in Yosemite was flooded, triggering the environmental movement in California and the birth of the Sierra Club.

The San Francisco Graft trials—in some ways ended California's Old West. The two-years of trials fascinated readers nationwide, just as the story of the earthquake and fire had done. Many details omitted from this book included 1) The procedures used by the prosecutorial team to allow the trials to go forward in a city controlled by politically powerful defendants, 2) The counter punching by the city administration to suppress the trials, 3) The procedures to safeguard the high profile defendants from being released by a loyal police force, 4) The crimes of violence and intrigue aimed at prejudicing the trials and the witness-es. Capping off the latter, the chief prosecutor, Frances J. Heney was shot in the head during a court recess on the first day of Abe Ruef's trial. The gunman was seized by city police and put in a city jail cell for questioning, after being care-fully searched for weapons by police and the prosecution's investigator. Before the latter got any coherent motive for the shooting or a possible connection with Abe Ruef or other defendants, he left the cell on a short break. When he returned he found the accused man dead. The policeman guarding him said he'd com-mitted suicide by shooting himself in the head with a derringer while lying on a cot—in full view of the policeman on guard. No arrests or inquiries were made in the City loyal to Ruef. Prosecutor Heney, who would have died but for a mil-limeter of difference in the bullet's angle, had told his team a week before the trial began that he thought they were all in danger of being killed. The city was in a state of uproar. Hiram Johnson was appointed chief prosecutor in Heney's stead. In the courtroom filled with reporters, he gave the people of San Fran-cisco and indeed the United States, a sharp taste of progressive leadership and the heady belief that corrupt, business controlled government could be defeated. (See Steffens' concise summation at the end of "Two Boys from H Street" under Lincoln Steffens, above.)

The Cosumnes River—the only "unregulated" river draining into the San Joaquin-Sacramento Valley. Staff of the Cosumnes River Preserve prefer the word "un-regulated" in lieu of "undammed" because of a small stock dam built by the

Granlees family near the author's house—a dam so small that during the flood of 1997 the water flowed over it without a ripple. Downstream, the Preserve is conducting a long-term experiment, and has succeeded in showing how setting the levees back to allow the natural spread of the river can control flooding and restore the native ecosystem. For maps of the various PG&E and SMUD reservoirs along the American and Cosumnes rivers, many of them originally proposed for the Bay Cities Water project, as well as the complete history of various efforts to control the Cosumnes River, See "The River that Got Away." The ditches in the Sierra that became part of the SMUD and PG&E systems had crude origins in the Gold Rush. For a detailed evolution of those ditches see Stearns, *Wealth from Gold Rush Waters.*

Sheep vs cattle—Hollywood made much of the troubles between sheepmen and cattlemen. In reality many western stockmen started with sheep in the 19th century when the price of wool was high, and then changed to cattle when wool fell in price and beef rose. The disdain for sheep by cowboys is partly a Hollywood legacy but also a legacy of the Spanish/Mexican *vaquero*, (cowman in Spanish) a figure greatly admired in early California. This author's grandfather was a tough old cattleman in Montana, one whose personal horses had to be trained by Indians. He kept a small flock of sheep on his ranch—not saying much about it, but those sheep were living memorials of his younger days. The bugaboo about sheep killing grass by cropping it too closely could be said of overgrazing in general, whether sheep, cattle or horses.

The Pratt place—Emanuel Pratt (also Pratte) was a friend of Jared Dixon Sheldon, who died in the 1851 shootout on the Cosumnes. Pratt administered Sheldon's estate, as Sheldon wished him to. Emanuel and Marie owned the land on both sides of the river (see Part I map) and built their home and barn on the north side near the bridge. In 1895, widow Marie (Maria or Mary) owned the property. By 1915, Mary Granlees owned the Driscoll property, her father having died, and she acquired the 120 Pratt acres and buildings from the elderly Marie, with the stipulation that the Granlees would allow Marie's simple son, Joe, to live out his life where he was born. Several old timers recalled Joe Pratt helping the Granlees family with various chores. As mentioned above, the author of this book telescoped time for literary purposes and had the Granlees family acquire the Pratt place earlier than they did in history. In the American West, a farm or ranch typically retained the name of its first owner, sometimes for generations despite the legal ownership. This was a way to quickly describe a location on a big ranch and to remember history. Among Granlees descendents, the bygone homestead is still "the Pratt place." Now it includes the Clubhouse on the north side of the road and the shopping center, and more, on the south side.

California Condors—a rare variety of vulture with a wingspan up to 10 feet. Once prevalent in California and in the Southwest, it is the descendant of a vulture twice as large, seen in the fossil record. The first Euro-American settlers noted that the native people almost never killed a condor, and were in awe of them. Heinrich Lienhard writes that a rare condor-skin ceremonial robe was somehow acquired on behalf of John Sutter (a theme in *River of Red Gold*). While it lay in a room at the Fort, before Sutter gifted it to a Russian collector, the native people "ran screaming" from the room when they recognized the feathers—not having been purified against the bad luck of looking at them. The Russian traveler presented the robe to his czar, who displayed it in his palace museum. It stayed there until the last czar of Russia and his entire family were assassinated. Communist government officials took the displays to the People's Anthropological Museum, including a second raven-and-condor feather robe of a different make, possibly from the Delta, and the best collection of Miwok baskets in existence. When the USSR fell, those items were relocated to the St Petersburg Museum of Anthropology. *http://bss.SFSU.edu/Cherny/Peterburg.htm*. At least one filmmaker and reader of this author's books wants to film hoped-for negotiations with the Russians regarding the return of the robe(s) back to California.

Gliding up to 300 miles per day, the once widespread and prevalent condor feeds on carrion, which too often is contaminated by lead bullets. By 1982 their numbers had plunged to near extinction with only 22 individuals remaining. The condor has been listed as an endangered species under federal and state law since the inception of those laws 40 years ago. Biologists attempting to save the species raise condors in captivity, tag and release them back into the wild. All too often they find the birds dead or dying, x-rays showing a bullet in the bird's belly, ingested along with a carcass. Because copper bullets are more expensive, gun associations opposed the ban on lead bullets in condor habitat, which went into effect in July 2009. Since that law was enacted, more condors have been found sick with lead poisoning, in one case shot directly with lead from a shotgun.

Twin Lakes—one of the names of the natural meadow lakes (also formerly called Summit Lake) on Hwy 88, not far from Carson Pass. PG&E dammed the outflow of the two marshy lakes shown in this book, consolidating them into one deep lake named for James Caples. Note the name James Caples on the 1895 property map in Part I. In 1849 he passed the pretty meadow lakes on his way to California's gold counrty. After a brief stay in Old Hangtown (Placerville), Dr. Caples remembered the lakes and returned there with his family. He acquired the property and built a way station that served travelers for 30 years. A monument stands near the lake. In 1999, PG&E sold Caples Lake, a long-time fishing resort, to the El Dorado Irrigation District.

Readings the Author Found Useful:

Amador County History: Golden Anniversary Reproduction (Fun-times Publishing Co, 1985)

Beth Bagwell, *Oakland, The Story of a City* (Presidio Press, 1982)

Walton Bean, *Boss Ruef's San Francisco: The Story of The Union Labor Party, Big Business, and The Graft Prosecution* (University of California Press, 1967, reprinted from 1952 by Regents of the University of California)

Karen Louise Bennett, "The River that Got Away: An investigation into the proposed development projects, the players, and the political climate that helped shape the fate of the Cosumnes River" M.A. Thesis, California State University: Sacramento, Spring 1997

James A Bennyhoff, "Ethnography of the Plains Miwok," Center for Archeological Research at Davis, Publication No. 5, 1977, Library of Congress Card Number: 72-619583

Gray Brechin, *Imperial San Francisco: Urban Power, Earthly Ruin* (University of California Press (First Paperback Printing 2001)

Sherwood D. Burgess, *The Water King Anthony Chabot: His Life & Times* (Panorama West Publishing, 1992)

Jack Burrows, *Black Sun of the Miwok* (University of New Mexico Press, 2000)

Larry Cenotto, *Logan's Alley* (Cenotto Publications, 1988) Vols I.

Sucheng Chan, *This Bittersweet Soil: The Chinese in California Agriculture 1860–1910* (University of California Press, 1986).

Elaine Connolly and Dian Self, *Capital Women: An Interpretive History of Women in Sacramento, 1850–1920* (The Capital Women's History Project, 1995)

Arthur E. Hertzler, *The Horse and Buggy Doctor* (Harper & Brothers, 1938)

Eliza P. Donner Houghton, *The Expedition of the Donner Party and Its Tragic Fate*, (A.C. McClurg & Co, November, 1911)

Myrtle Shaw Lord, *A Sacramento Saga: The Living History of California's Capital City* (Sacramento Chamber of Commerce, 1946)

Richard Coke Lower, *A Bloc of One: The Political Career of Hiram W. Johnson* (Stanford University Press, 1993)

Dennis McCown, "The Vagrant's Grave", Western Outlaw-Lawman History Association Journal, summer 2003, pp. 24–31. And "The Death of Helen Beulah" by Dennis McCown in True West Magazine, May, 1999

C. Hart Merriam, *The Dawn of the World: Myths and Tales of the Miwok Indians of California* (University of Nebraska Press, 1993, 10th Bison Book Printing)

Richard J. Orsi, *Sunset Limited: The Southern Pacific Railroad and the Development of the American West 1850–1930* (University of California Press, 2005)

Elizabeth Pinkerton, *History Happened Here: Book 1, River, Oaks, Gold* (Laguna Publishers, 2000)

June Somerville, *Legend of a Road: A Witness to the Exploration and Emigration on the Road Above Silver Lake and Beyond* (June Wood Somerville, 2008)

Jean E. Starns, *Wealth from Gold Rush Waters* (Jean E. Starns with Word Dancer Press, 2004)

Lincoln Steffens, *The Autobiography of Lincoln Steffens: Complete in One Vol* (The Chautauqua Press, 1931)

Vanishing Victorians: A Guide to the Historic Homes of Sacramento (Sacramento Branch of the AAUW, 1973)

David Vaught, *Cultivating California: Growers, Specialty Crops, and Labor 1875–1920* (Johns Hopkins University Press, 1999)

Poems And Songs

Joe Arizonia, *The Preacher and The Bear* (Jos. Morris, 1904.)

Harry Dacre, *Daisy Bell (Bicycle Built for Two)* (1892)

Emily Dickinson, poem. *Autumn*

Stephen Foster, *I Dream of Jeanie With The Light Brown Hair* (1854)

Charles K. Harris, *After the Ball* (Oliver Ditson Company, 1893)

Thomas Hood, poem. *I remember, I remember the house where I was born*

Lillian Bos Ross wrote the lyrics of *South Coast*. This is the only song in this novel not contemporary with the 1890s. It's lyricist lived in Big Sur (south in Spanish) most of her very long life, and this poetry captures the wild spirit and loneliness of that stunning coastline. In the 1950s a recording of *South Coast* arranged by The Kingston Trio was released. For the full text of the original lyrics see *Recipes for Living in Big Sur* (Big Sur Historical Society, pp. 148–150)

Percy Shelley, poem. *Ozymandias*

Sketch of Cosumnes Store on Part IV by Ted Baggelmann printed August 25, 1968 in The *Sacramento Union*, a newspaper no longer in existence.

About The Author

Naida West was born Idaho. In her early years she lived in small towns and farms and ranches mostly in Idaho and Montana. She attended many schools, including a one-room schoolhouse. Graduating from high school in Carmel, California, she worked in Germany, never speaking English until she returned. Glad to be in her own country, she received degrees from California universities in Sacramento and Berkeley, and a Ph.D. from the University of California, Davis. She taught sociology, worked as a lobbyist in Sacramento, and served on various boards and commissions, including two terms on the Sacramento County History and Science Commission.

A life-long writer of poetry and non-fiction, in 1990, Naida quit all other work to become a full time novelist, writing about the little ranch on the Cosumnes River where she lives with her husband, two horses, and a very large, tawny Siamese cat that deigns to relax with them when not on his rounds of the nearby oaks, horse pasture, and the ever changing wilderness of the river bottomland.

The research and writing of *Rest for the Wicked* has stirred thoughts of 2-3 future books.

More Books By Naida West

Eye of the Bear: a History Novel of Early California (Book 1)
River of Red Gold: A History novel (Book 2, published first)
Murder on the Middle Fork (with her Uncle Don Smith)

She also helped her Uncle Don with: *Symon's Daughter: A Memoir of Elizabeth Symon Smith*. Mrs. Smith, Naida West's grandmother, was an important inspiration to her granddaughter in life and literature.